Praise for Peter Robinson

'If you haven't encountered Chief Inspector Alan Banks before, prepare for a crash course in taut, clean writing and subtle psychology.'
Ian Rankin

'[Peter Robinson deserves a place] near, perhaps even at the top of, the British crime writers' league' *The Times*

'Robinson also has a way of undercutting the genre's familiarity. With a deceptively unspectacular language, he sets about the process of unsettling the reader.' *Independent*

'Gut-wrenching plotting, alongside heart-wrenching portraits of the characters who populate his world.' Jeffery Deaver

'Banks is one of the most fully drawn figures in this genre of fiction' *New York Times*

'Most admirers of Robinson will find themselves utterly involved in this haunting, textured mystery . . . If Robinson is to turn out one-off novels as assured as this perhaps we wouldn't mind too much if Alan Banks was to retire and take up beekeeping in Sussex.'
Barry Forshaw, *Daily Express* on *Before the Poison*

'With adept professionalism, Robinson brings to the reader a story that is tantalisingly unravelled like a poisoned present . . . a haunting, moving tale that will get you thinking days after the last word has been read.'
www.crimesquad.com on *Before the Poison*

'Robinson writes with gusto . . . his tale cracks along at a satisfying lick, with splashes of dark humour along the way' *Metro* on *Bad Boy*

'Robinson writes solid, tense, police procedurals that depend on good plots, accuracy and the genuine likeability of the central character, Alan Banks. I would highly recommend *Bad Boy*.' *www.eurocrime.co.uk*

PETER ROBINSON

Watching the Dark

HODDER

First published in Great Britain in 2012 by Hodder & Stoughton
An Hachette UK company

This paperback edition published 2013

3

A CIP catalogue record for this title is available from the British Library

A format paperback ISBN 978 1 444 70490 7
B format paperback ISBN 978 1 444 70489 1

Typeset by Hewer Text UK Ltd, Edinburgh
Printed and bound by Clays Ltd, St Ives plc

Hodder & Stoughton policy is to use papers that are natural, renewable
and recyclable products and made from wood grown in sustainable forests.
The logging and manufacturing processes are expected to conform
to the environmental regulations of the country of origin.

Hodder & Stoughton Ltd
338 Euston Road
London NW1 3BH

www.hodder.co.uk

To Sheila

I

On nights when the pain kept her awake, Lorraine Jenson would get up around dawn and go outside to sit on one of the wicker chairs before anyone else in the centre was stirring. With a tartan blanket wrapped around her shoulders to keep out the early morning chill, she would listen to the birds sing as she enjoyed a cup of Earl Grey, the aromatic steam curling from its surface, its light, delicious scent filling her nostrils. She would smoke her first cigarette of the day, always the best one.

Some mornings, the small artificial lake below the sloping lawn was covered in mist, which shrouded the trees on the other side. Other times, the water was a still, dark mirror that reflected the detail of every branch and leaf perfectly. On this fine April morning, the lake was clear, though the water's surface was ruffled by a cool breeze, and the reflections wavered.

Lorraine felt her pain slough off like a layer of dead skin as the painkillers kicked in, and the tea and cigarette soothed her frayed nerves. She placed her mug on the low wrought-iron table beside her chair and adjusted the blanket around her shoulders. She was facing south, and the sun was creeping over the hill through the trees on her left. Soon the spell would be broken. She would hear the sounds of people getting up in the building behind her, voices calling, doors opening, showers running, toilets flushing, and another day to be got through would begin.

As the light grew stronger, she thought she could see something, like a bundle of clothes, on the ground at the edge of the woods on the far side of the lake. That was unusual, as Barry, the head groundsman and general estate manager, was proud of his artificial lake and his natural woodlands, so much so that some people complained he spent far more time down there than he did keeping the rest of the extensive grounds neat and tidy.

Lorraine squinted, but she couldn't bring the object into clearer focus. Her vision was still not quite what it had been. Gripping the arms of her chair, she pushed herself to her feet, gritting her teeth at the red-hot pokers of pain that seared through her left leg, despite the OxyContin, then she took hold of her crutch and made her way down the slope. The grass was still wet with dew, and she felt it fresh and cool on her bare ankles as she walked.

When she got to the water's edge, she took the cinder path that skirted the lake and soon arrived on the other side, at the edge of the woods, which began only a few feet away from the water. Even before then, she had recognised what it was that lay huddled there. Though she had seen dead bodies before, she had never actually stumbled across one. She was alone with the dead now, for the first time since she had stood by her father's coffin in the funeral home.

Lorraine held her breath. Silence. She thought she heard a rustling deep in the woods, and a shiver of fear rippled through her. If the body were a victim of murder, then the killer might still be out there, watching her. She remained completely still for about a minute, until she was certain there was nobody in the woods. She heard the rustling again and saw a fox making its way through the undergrowth.

Now that she was at the scene, Lorraine's training kicked in. She was wary of disturbing anything, so she kept her distance. Much as she wanted to move in closer and examine the body, see if it was someone she knew, she restrained herself. There was nothing she could do, she told herself; the way he – for it was definitely a man – was kneeling with his body bent forward, head touching the ground like a parody of a Muslim at prayer, there was no way he was still alive.

The best thing she could do was stay here and protect the scene. Murder or not, it was definitely a suspicious death, and whatever she did, she must not screw up now. Cursing the pain that rippled through her leg whenever she moved, Lorraine fumbled for her mobile in her jeans pocket and phoned Eastvale police station.

There was something about Bach that suited the early morning perfectly, DCI Alan Banks thought, as he drove out of Gratly towards the St Peter's Police Convalescence and Treatment Centre, four miles north of Eastvale, shortly after dawn that morning. He needed something to wake him up and keep his attention engaged, get the old grey cells buzzing, but nothing too loud, nothing too jarring or emotionally taxing. Alina Ibragimova's CD of Bach's sonatas and partitas for violin was just right. Bach both soothed and stimulated the mind at once.

Banks knew St Peter's. He had visited Annie Cabbot there several times during her recent convalescence. Just a few short months ago he had seen her in tears trying to walk on crutches, and now she was due back at work on Monday. He was looking forward to that; life had been dull for the past while without her.

He took the first exit from the roundabout and drove alongside the wall for about a hundred yards before arriving at the arched entrance and turning left on the tarmac drive. There was no gate or gatehouse, but the first officers to arrive on the scene had quite rightly taped off the area. A young PC waved Banks down to check his ID and note his name and time of entry on a clipboard before lifting the tape and letting him through.

Driving up to the car park was like arriving at a luxury spa hotel, Banks had always thought when he visited Annie. It was no different today. St Peter's presented a broad south-facing facade at the top of the rise that led down to the lake and surrounding woods. Designed by a firm of Leeds architects, with Vanbrugh in mind, and built of local stone in the late nineteenth century, it was three stories high, had a flagged portico, complete with simple Doric columns at the front, and two wings, east and west. Though not so extensive as some other local examples, the grounds were landscaped very much in the style and spirit of Capability Brown, with the lake and woods and rolling lawns. There was even a folly. To the west, beyond the trees and lawns, the outlines of Swainsdale's hills and fells could be seen, forming a backdrop of what the Japanese called borrowed scenery, which merged nature with art.

The forensic team had got there before Banks, which seemed odd until he remembered that a detective inspector had made the initial call. Kitted out in disposable white coveralls, they were already going about their business. The crime-scene photographer, Peter Darby, was at work with his battered old Nikon SLR and his ultra-modern digital video recorder. Most SOCOs – or CSIs, as they now liked to be called – also took their own digital photos and videos when they searched a scene, but though Peter Darby accepted the use of video, he shunned digital photography as being far too susceptible to tampering and error. It made him a bit of a dinosaur, and one or two of the younger techies cracked jokes behind his back. He could counter by boasting that he had never had any problems with his evidence in court, and he had never lost an image because of computer problems.

DI Lorraine Jenson stood with two other people about five or six yards away from the body, a lone, hunched figure resting her weight on a crutch by the water's edge and jotting in her notebook. Banks knew her slightly from a case he had worked a few months ago that crossed the border into Humberside, where she worked. Not long ago, he had heard, she had a run in with a couple of drug-dealers in a tower block, which ended with her falling from a second-floor balcony. She had sustained multiple fractures of her left leg, but after surgery, the cast and physio, she would be back at work soon enough.

'What a turn up,' she said. 'Me finding a body.'

Banks gestured towards the CSIs. 'I see you've already called in the lads.'

'Judgement call. I thought it best not to waste any time. The Divisional Duty Inspector made all the decisions.' She turned to introduce the others. 'By the way, this is Barry Sadler, estate manager, and Mandy Pemberton, the night nurse.'

Banks greeted them then asked them if they would mind returning to the main building, where they would be asked for statements. Still in shock, they headed up the slope.

'Who's the Crime Scene Manager?' Banks asked Lorraine.

'Stefan Nowak.'

'Excellent.' Stefan Nowak was one of the best. He would protect his scene to the death, if necessary, but he was still a delight to work with, Banks found, a charming, witty and intelligent man. Bank glanced towards the body, slumped forward by the treeline. 'Know who he is?'

'Not yet,' said Lorraine. 'But I might when I see his face. If he's from here, that is.'

It was too early for Dr Glendenning, the Home Office pathologist, who lived in Saltburn, so the police surgeon, Dr Burns, knelt over the body making notes in his little black book. Banks squatted beside him and watched, hands on his knees.

'Ah, Alan,' said Burns. 'I'd like to get him turned over, if I may?'

'Peter Darby finished with his camera?'

'Yes.'

Banks studied the body for a few moments and, finding nothing particularly interesting or unusual about it except for its odd position, helped Dr Burns. Carefully, they turned the body over on its back. As soon as they had done so, they exchanged puzzled glances. Banks stood up. He heard Lorraine Jenson, hovering over them, give a faint gasp.

Something was sticking out of the man's chest. On first appearances, it resembled the kind of wooden stake that Van Helsing wielded to kill vampires in the old Hammer films, though it had feathers on the end, like an arrow. But it was too deeply embedded to be an ordinary arrow. 'Looks like a crossbow bolt,' said Banks.

'I think you're right,' Dr Burns agreed.

'We don't get many of those around these parts.' In fact, Banks couldn't remember ever investigating a crossbow murder before.

'I can hardly say it's my area of expertise, either,' said Dr Burns. 'I'm sure Dr Glendenning will be able to tell you more, once he gets him on the table.' Dr Burns stood up. His knees cracked. 'From the position and angle, I'd say it almost certainly pierced his heart. He would have died almost instantaneously. Of course, he might have been poisoned first, but there are no apparent signs of strangulation, bruising or other physical trauma.'

'Do you reckon he was killed here, or was he moved after death?'

Dr Burns unbuttoned the man's shirt and examined the shoulders and chest area. 'These are lividity marks, hypostasis, which means he's been in this position for some time, and the blood has pooled here. But I can't say for certain. Not until Dr Glendenning does the PM. It certainly seems as if he dropped to his knees, then keeled over and fell forward, so that his head rested on the ground. You can see there are traces of blood on the grass there, approximately where his heart would have been directly above it. That's consistent with his injuries. There isn't much blood. Most of the bleeding will have been internal.' Dr Burns pointed towards the woods. 'The shot probably came from where those CSIs are working around that tree, say fifty, sixty feet away. Hard to miss at that range, but it means your shooter could also stay hidden by the trees, in case anyone from the centre happened to be watching out of a window.'

Banks glanced at Lorraine Jenson, who was still staring, horrified, at the crossbow bolt in the man's chest. 'He seems vaguely familiar to me,' said Banks, 'but I've met a lot of coppers in my time. Do you recognise him now, Lorraine?'

Lorraine nodded slowly, a little pale. 'It's Bill,' she said. 'DI Bill Quinn. He was a patient here, too.'

'Bloody hell,' said Banks. 'Bill Quinn. I thought I recognised him.'

'You knew him, too?'

'Only in passing. He worked out of Millgarth, in Leeds with DI Ken Blackstone.' Banks paused and turned back to Dr Burns, who was busy with his thermometer. 'Time of death?'

'As usual, I can't be really precise. You've seen the lividity. Rigor's started, but it isn't complete yet. Judging by the temperature, I'd say he's been dead about seven or eight hours. I'd guess that he was killed no later than one in the morning, say, and no earlier than eleven last night. Of course, that's only an estimate. You might do better pinning down his movements, such as when he was last seen. It shouldn't be too difficult in a place like this.'

'Just hoping you might be able to save us some time.'

'Sorry. Perhaps—'

'Actually, you have,' said Banks. 'Two hours is a pretty good window to work with. Wouldn't it have been too dark for the killer to shoot?'

'As I said, the killer was probably pretty close,' Dr Burns answered. 'Maybe even closer than I estimated. It was a clear night, and there was a bright three-quarters moon, very few clouds. The victim would have made an easy enough target against the backdrop of the building, especially if the killer knew his way around a crossbow. I don't think it would have been too difficult at all.'

Banks squatted again and went through the dead man's pockets. He found nothing and decided that that, in itself, was odd. When he mentioned it, Dr Burns said, 'Maybe he left his stuff in his room? You don't usually need your wallet and mobile if you're just nipping out for a quick walk before bedtime.'

'If that's what he was doing. And people these days tend to be glued to their mobiles. They're like a lifeline, or something. Then there are the keys.'

'What about them?'

'There aren't any.'

'Maybe he didn't need them.'

'Maybe not. Or maybe someone took them. We'll find out.'

A black Toyota swung through the arch, and the officers on the gate let it through after their usual checks. DS Winsome Jackman jumped out, all six feet something of her.

'Not like you to be late, Winsome,' said Banks, glancing at his watch. 'Wild night last night, was it?'

Winsome looked aghast, then smiled. 'No, sir. I never have wild nights. You should know that.'

'Of course not,' said Banks. He explained the situation. 'Will you go up to the house and get the practicalities organised?' he asked. 'A murder room in the main building, phone lines, civilian personnel, the usual.'

'Yes, sir,' Winsome said.

'You'd also better organise a thorough search of the build-ings and grounds as quickly as possible, before everyone gets wind of what's going on down here. We're after the murder weapon, a crossbow. Can't be that easy to hide.'

'Including the patients' rooms?'

'Especially the patients' rooms. They won't like it. They're cops, like us. But it has to be done. They ought to understand that much, at least. This is one of our own that's been killed. It could be an inside job, and if this place is as wide open as it appears, then anybody could come and go as they please. Set up interviews, too. You can start with the two who were just here. Barry . . .?' Banks glanced at Lorraine Jenson.

'Barry Sadler and Mandy Pemberton.'

Winsome headed off. Lorraine fell in beside her. She moved well, he noticed, despite the crutch. She made some comment, and Banks spotted Winsome glance over her shoulder and laugh.

Banks gazed down at the body again. Though they had only met once, at a retirement do with DI Ken Blackstone, he remembered lanky Bill Quinn, prematurely grey-haired, with his stained and crooked teeth, smiling quietly in his seat through the ribald speeches, a small whisky in his hand. 'Bill Quinn,' he muttered to himself. 'What have you been up to?' He looked around at the lake, the trees and the big house on the hill, sniffed the air, then set off after Winsome and Lorraine, up to the main building.

'You'll be treating me as a suspect, then, as well as searching my room?' Lorraine said, as she put her crutch aside and settled down in her armchair. Her bedsit resembled a pleasant hotel room, Banks thought, with a single bed in one corner, en suite bathroom and toilet, a writing desk, and three armchairs arranged around an oval table. There were also tea- and coffee-making facilities on the top of the chest of drawers, a spacious wardrobe, and a flat-screen television fixed to the wall. A combination radio, CD player and iPod dock completed the set-up.

'Don't be silly,' Banks said. 'Why would you think that?'

'I discovered the body. It's always the person who discovers the body.'

'Or the nearest and dearest,' added Banks. 'What have you been doing here, reading too much Agatha Christie?'

'It just stands to reason.'

'*Did* you do it?'

'No, of course not.'

'Well, we've got that out of the way, haven't we?'

'You should suspect me. I would if I were you. We're all suspects. All of us here.'

Banks gazed at her with narrowed eyes. Early forties, looking older and more frail since her injury, once-plump body wasted by the recovery process, pale skin sagging, shrewd eyes with bags underneath, a ragged fringe of dark hair. 'We'll talk about that later,' he said. 'For now, you're just a witness. We'll want a full written statement later, of course, but all I want now is a few basics, your immediate impressions, what you knew of the victim. That sort of thing. I saw you making notes, so it's probably still fresh in your mind. Let's start with what you were doing outside so early, and what made you walk down to the lake.'

'I'm not sleeping very well because of the pain,' Lorraine said, after a brief hesitation. 'Most days I get up early, when it starts to get light, and I feel claustrophobic. I need to get out. It's peaceful sitting there before the place comes to life. And I can enjoy a cigarette.'

'What drew you to the lake?'

'I saw something down there, at the edge of the woods. That's all. A bundle. It seemed unusual. Out of place. The grounds are usually immaculate.'

'And when you saw what it was?'

'I kept my distance and phoned it in.'

'You didn't touch anything?'

'No.'

'Did you notice anything else?'

'Like what?'

'Anything odd, apart from the bundle itself.'

'No, not really. I stood and listened. I saw a fox. The sound startled me. I thought the killer might still be in the woods, but it was only a fox.'

'You couldn't see the crossbow bolt at this point, could you?'

'No. He was practically face down on the ground. You saw for yourself.'

'But you just said "killer". What made you assume he'd been killed, rather than just, say, dropped dead of a heart attack or something?'

'I don't know. It was just the way he was lying, kneeling. It looked suspicious. It was instinct, a hunch. I can't really think of any logical explanation.'

Banks knew how easily witnesses got confused, and how easy it was for the questioner to take advantage of that, to make them even more nervous and defensive. Question anyone for a few minutes, and pretty soon they all sounded as if they were lying. Cops were apparently no different. 'I just wondered whether there was anything in particular that made you feel that way, that's all,' Banks said. 'You didn't see or hear anyone running away, a car starting out on the road, or anything like that?'

'No. Just the fox. And birds, of course. The birds were already singing. Why are you asking? When do you think he was killed? He must have been there for a while. Surely he can't have been killed just before I found him?'

'Did you know Bill Quinn well?'

'No, not really. I'd talked to him, chatted briefly in the

lounge over a nightcap, that sort of thing, but I wouldn't say I *knew* him. We're both smokers, so we'd meet up outside occasionally by chance and pass the time of day. We're all pretty civil here, but we don't really socialise all that much.'

'You weren't involved in any sort of relationship?'

'Good God, no.' She held up her left hand. 'The only people I'm in a relationship with are my husband and my two children.'

'Did you ever witness DI Quinn arguing with any of the other patients, or hear anyone making threats towards him?'

'No. It's a pretty peaceful place here, as you might have noticed. He was quiet most of the time, abstracted. I didn't see much of him. I didn't witness any arguments at all.'

'Noticed anyone hanging around? Anyone who shouldn't be here?'

'No.'

'When did you last see Bill Quinn alive?'

'At dinner last night.'

'When was that? What's the routine?'

'Dinner's usually at half past six, then three nights a week there's quiz night at eight. After that, about half past nine, people either meet for a drink or two in the library bar or head off to their rooms to watch TV.'

'And when there's not a quiz night?'

'There's a film sometimes, usually a quite recent one, in the gym, or people just amuse themselves, play cards, read, whatever.'

'No karaoke?'

Lorraine laughed. 'Hardly. Though I think sometimes it might liven things up a bit.'

'How did Bill Quinn appear at dinner last night? Did he seem agitated, distracted, edgy?'

Lorraine frowned with the effort of memory. 'Maybe a little. I'm not sure. He didn't say much, but then he rarely did.

He was always a bit distracted and edgy. Not agitated, mind you, just in another world, as if he was carrying a burden. It's far too easy to read things into a situation with hindsight.'

'What would you read into his behaviour last night?'

'That he seemed maybe a bit more anxious than usual, that's all, as if he had something on his mind. He didn't stick around to chat over coffee, for example, and he didn't go to the library bar for an after-dinner drink.'

'Did he usually stay for a chat and go for a drink?'

'Yes. A small malt. Just the one, as a rule. He also missed quiz night, which was not like him at all. He enjoyed quiz nights.' Lorraine paused. 'He wasn't easy to know. Hard to get a handle on.'

'Any idea who might have killed him?'

'I doubt if it was anyone here,' Lorraine said. 'We've all been thrown together by chance and circumstance, and there hasn't been really much of an opportunity to form grievances and vendettas so far.' She gestured towards her crutch. 'Besides, most of us are incapable.'

'Even so,' Banks said. 'An old grudge suddenly confronted?'

'Bit of a coincidence, though, wouldn't you say? I reckon you'd be better off checking out the villains he brought down, rather than cops he was spending a couple of weeks' rest and recuperation with.'

'Fair enough.' Banks glanced around the room. 'Nice digs,' he said. '*And* you can get a decent single malt here, too?'

'It's not a health spa, you know, or a fitness centre.'

St Peter's, Annie Cabbot had explained to Banks, was a charity-run convalescence centre for injured police officers, those recuperating from operations, or suffering from stress and anxiety, job-related or otherwise. It offered a range of treatments, from physiotherapy to reiki, including massage, sauna, hydrotherapy and psychological counselling. The general length of stay was two weeks, but that was flexible in some cases; Annie had stayed for three weeks and still returned regularly, as an outpatient, for physio and massage therapy.

'Did you hear anything during the night?' Banks asked. 'You said you don't sleep well.'

'I usually take a pill when I go to bed. That knocks me out for a few hours, then I can't get back to sleep again, so I get up early. But from ten o'clock, when I usually go to bed, until about three or four, I'm dead to the world.'

'So you didn't hear anything after you woke up early?'

'No. Only the birds.'

'Where did Bill Quinn go instead of staying for a drink and participating in quiz night?'

'I've no idea. I wasn't keeping tabs on him. To his room, I suppose. Or out for a late smoke. All I know is I didn't see him again.'

'And you didn't hear him leave the building after you went to bed?'

'No. As you can see, my room's right at the back, on the first floor, and he's on the second floor at the front. The ground floor is all offices and treatment rooms, along with the dining room and library bar. Then there's a basement, with the gym and swimming pool. I wouldn't even have heard Bill Quinn if he'd had a wild orgy in his room. I wouldn't necessarily hear anyone leaving through the front door. He could have gone out during quiz night for all I know. As I said, I didn't see him at all after dinner.'

'You were at quiz night?'

'Yes.'

'OK. We'll ask the others. Someone might have seen something. What's the security like here? Is access easy?'

Lorraine snorted. 'Security? There isn't any, really. I mean, it's not a prison, or even a hospital. More like a posh hotel. Maybe there are a few expensive bits of gym gear or medical equipment around, but they don't keep drugs or cash on the premises. As you know already, there's a big wall, but no gate, so I suppose anyone can walk or drive in and out whenever they want. We can. It would be easy enough for someone to slip into the woods by the gate without being seen and just wait there. The nearest village is a mile and a half away, and sometimes some of the people here nip out for a jar or two in the pub. There's no sentry post, no porter's lodge, no curfew, no book to sign. There's the night nurse on duty, you met Mandy, and she might have noticed something, but even she was probably fast asleep by then. We come and go as we please.'

'Was Bill Quinn in the habit of going down to the woods at night?'

'Not that I know of, no. Whenever I saw him outside, he'd be having a smoke by the front door.'

'Is there CCTV?'

'I don't think so. You'd better ask one of the staff. I mean, why would there be? We're all honest coppers here, right?'

'Hmm.' Banks stood up. 'I'll be off, then. Thanks for your time, Lorraine. I might be back.'

As he left, two uniformed WPCs entered Lorraine's room. 'Damn,' he heard her say. 'If you must go through my knicker drawer, try not to make too much of a mess.'

Banks walked down the broad wooden staircase to the reception area, letting his hand slide along the dark polished banister. A stair lift had been fitted on one side for those patients who had difficulty climbing the stairs. Annie had used it, he remembered. The whole place was crawling with police now. Banks spotted DC Doug Wilson and asked him if Winsome was still upstairs searching Bill Quinn's room.

'As far as I know she is, sir,' said Wilson. 'It's 22B, west wing. I'm just getting the guest interviews organised. It'll take us a while. We're using one of the staff meeting lounges as the murder room. It's being set up now.'

'Excellent. How many patients in all?'

'Only twelve, sir. Then there's the staff, mostly part-time. We'll use the library bar and the ground-floor offices and treatment rooms for the interviews. That way we can conduct more than one at a time and get finished sooner.'

'Fine,' said Banks. 'Got enough help?'

'I've got Gerry, sir. I mean DC Masterson.'

DC Geraldine Masterson had just finished her probationary period and was shaping up very well. She was young and still had a lot to learn, but that wasn't such a bad thing. More important, she was bight and keen, and showed above average aptitude for grasping things. She also had a degree in IT.

'I'll see if I can manage to draft in some help,' Banks said. 'Until then, just do the best you can.'

'Yes, sir.'

'And get a couple of officers asking around the general neighbourhood, the village, find out if anyone was seen hanging around here lately, last night in particular. A car, anything suspicious.'

'It's pretty isolated, sir.'

'That's why someone might have noticed something. You can get the word out to the media, too. No information about DI Quinn's murder, especially about method of death, but we want to talk to anybody who passed by St Peter's between, say, ten o'clock last night and two in the morning. The press will be here soon, so make sure you warn the men on the gate to keep them at bay. Did DS Jackman mention anything about searching the grounds and rooms?'

'Yes, sir. We're trying to get it done as quickly and discreetly as possible.'

'Carry on, Doug,' said Banks.

'OK, sir.' Doug Wilson strode off.

'Sir? Excuse me. Just a minute, sir. Are you in charge of all this?'

Banks turned towards the new voice. The woman behind the reception desk was calling out to him. The area reminded him of a hotel reception, with the rows of pigeonholes on the wall behind her for keys and messages, a laptop computer on a pullout shelf, filing drawers, printer, fax and photocopy machine. The woman was perhaps a little older than Banks, grey-haired, matronly, and her name badge read 'Mary'.

'I'm DCI Banks,' he said, offering his hand. 'Sorry for all this upheaval, Mary. What can I do for you?'

'Well, I was just wondering, you know, about the regular schedules. The patients. I mean physio, massage and suchlike. We do have our routines and timetables.'

'A police officer has been murdered,' said Banks. 'I'd say normal operations are pretty much suspended for the moment, wouldn't you? I'll let you know when they can be resumed.'

Mary reddened. 'I'm sorry. But what should I tell people? I mean, one of our physiotherapists drives all the way over from Skipton, and her first appointment isn't till two this afternoon. Should I phone and cancel?'

'I'm afraid not,' said Banks. 'We'll want to talk to everyone connected with the place as soon as we possibly can, including the staff. That means we'll need the names and addresses of any personnel who won't be coming in today. Were you here all night?'

'No, sir,' said Mary. 'I live in Eastvale. The desk isn't staffed twenty-four hours a day. No need. I'm usually gone by six or seven at the latest, depending on how much catching up I have to do. I start at eight, as a rule. In fact, I just arrived. I can't really believe what's going on.'

'Are you a police officer, Mary?'

'No, sir. Registered nurse. Retired.'

'No need to call me sir, then.'

'Oh. Yes. Of course.'

'I'm sure it's a shock,' Banks said. 'Apart from the patients and the nurse, is there anyone else who stops here for the whole night?'

'There's Barry.'

'Barry Sadler?'

'Yes. Head groundsman, porter, jack of all trades. He lives in the flat over the old stables, but he's here to help if there's ever a need for heavy lifting or anything, and he does most of the odd jobs himself. Of course, he has a small staff to call in, as and when he needs them. Cleaners, gardeners, a lawn-trimmer and topiarist and so on. But they don't live here.'

'I'll need a list of their names, too,' said Banks. 'Do you have a security system?'

Mary paused. 'Well, yes, sort of. I mean . . .'

'Yes?'

'The rule is that the front door's locked at midnight, and the burglar alarm is activated.'

'But?'

Mary gave Banks a lopsided grin. 'You know what it's like. It's a pretty laissez-faire sort of place. If someone wants to go out for a smoke, or stops out late at the pub, you don't want to be turning the burglar alarm on and off, do you?'

'Right,' said Banks, who used to smoke back in the days when it was possible to light up almost anywhere. He could hardly imagine the hassle these days, standing out in the cold in winter. Another reason to be grateful he had stopped. 'So what you're saying is that there isn't much in the way of security?'

'I suppose that's true.'

'And no CCTV?'

'Afraid not. St Peter's is a charity-run establishment, and the board decided that CCTV was too expensive to be worth it. Also, people don't like being spied on. Especially police officers.'

Banks smiled and thanked her for her time. Mary blushed. As he walked away, Banks figured he'd made a conquest there. His charm seemed to work especially well on the over-sixties these days.

Banks turned right at the top of the second flight of stairs, following the sign on the wall to rooms 20 to 30B. The door to Bill Quinn's room was open, and Winsome was still systematically searching through the drawers and cupboards.

Banks stood in the doorway. 'Anything for us?'

'Nothing yet,' said Winsome. She dangled a ring of house keys. 'Just these. They were on the desk. A few clothes in the wardrobe. Toiletries. No mobile. No wallet. No room key.'

The room was a mirror image of Lorraine Jenson's. Banks noticed a fishing rod and tackle in one corner and a stack of *Angling Times, Trout & Salmon, Gardeners' World* and *Garden News* magazines on the coffee table. An outdoorsman, then, Bill Quinn. Banks hadn't known that. Still, he hadn't known much about the man at all, a situation that would have to be rectified as quickly as possible. The solution to the crime, he had come to believe over the years, more often than not lies in the victim's character. 'I think we'd better send a couple of officers over to search his house. Where does he live?'

'It's already taken care of, guv,' said Winsome. 'He lives alone in a semi in Rawdon, Leeds, up near the airport.'

'Alone? For some reason, I thought he was married with kids.'

'He was. His wife's dead, and the kids have flown the coop. They're both at university, one in Hull, the other at Keele. The local police are trying to track them down. His parents, too. They live in Featherstone.'

'I didn't know that,' Banks said. 'About his wife, I mean.'

'I found out from his boss, sir. It was very recent. Only a month. Massive stroke.'

'Is that what he was in here for? Depression? Grief counselling?'

'No. Neck problems. Physio and massage therapy.'

'OK, carry on,' said Banks. He stood in the doorway watching Winsome work her way through Bill Quinn's room.

When she had finished, neither of them was any the wiser.

'There doesn't seem to be anything of a personal nature here,' said Winsome. 'No diary, journal, notebook. Nothing.'

'And no note signed by the killer saying, "Meet me by the lake at eleven o'clock tonight"?'

Winsome sighed. 'I wish.'

'Did it seem disturbed at all when you first came in? I suppose if someone could get into the woods to kill him and take his key, they could also get in his room.'

'No signs of it,' said Winsome. 'Anyway, it might be a bit riskier, actually entering the building.'

'Not according to what I've just heard from Mary,' said Banks. 'There's about as much security here as a kid's piggy bank. Do we know if he had a mobile?'

'I'd be surprised if he didn't,' said Winsome. 'I mean, these days . . .'

'Well, he doesn't appear to have one now,' said Banks. 'And that's very peculiar, wouldn't you say?'

'Yes, I would. I always take mine with me when I go out.'

'Better make sure we ask his fellow patients, or guests, or whatever they are, and the staff. Someone should remember if he had one. Same with a laptop or a notepad.' Banks slipped on the protective gloves he always carried with him to crime scenes and picked up a heavy book Winsome had found in a drawer. *Practical Homicide Investigation*. Bill Quinn's name was written in the flyleaf. 'And this is his only reading material, apart from the fishing and gardening magazines?' Banks flipped through the book. 'It hardly looks like the sort of reading you'd want to do if you were here recuperating for a couple of weeks, does it? Some of these pictures are enough to turn your stomach.'

'Well, he *was* a detective, sir,' Winsome said. 'Maybe he was doing a bit of studying?'

'I suppose we can check if he was doing any courses.'

Banks flipped through the rest of the book, but nothing fell out. He examined it more closely to see if anything was sellotaped inside, or rolled up and shoved down the spine, but there was nothing. Nor were the pages cut to hold a package of some sort, the way he had cut out *The Way to Keep Fit* to hide his cigarettes when he was fourteen. It hadn't worked, of course. His mother had noticed what an unusual title it was, mixed in with James Bond, The Saint, The Toff, The Baron and Sherlock Holmes. There was no denying from which side of the family Banks had inherited his detective abilities. He had fared about as well with his copies of *Mayfair*, *Swank* and *Oui*, too, hidden under a false bottom in the wardrobe. God only knew what had tipped her off to that one.

But Bill Quinn's secret wasn't hidden in a hollowed out book, or under the false bottom of a wardrobe; it was between the hard book cover and a loosened endpaper, which had only been very superficially smoothed and pasted back down.

Banks peeled back the edge of the flap and managed to prise out a small, thin buff envelope with the tips of his gloved fingers. He sat down by the coffee table, took the envelope, which was closed but not sealed, and shook out its contents on to the table's surface. Photographs. He turned them all the right way up and set them out in a row. Three colour 4 x 6 prints, run off an inkjet printer on cheap paper. There were no times or dates printed on them, and nothing written on the backs. But they were of good enough quality to show what was happening.

The first one showed Bill Quinn sitting in a bar enjoying an intimate drink with a very beautiful, and very young, woman.

She hardly looked old enough to get served, Banks thought. Quinn was leaning in close towards her, and their fingertips were touching on the table. Both had champagne flutes in front of them. The figures in the background were blurred, as were the details of the room, and it was impossible to make out any faces or decor to identify where it had been taken.

In the second photograph, the couple seemed to have moved on to a restaurant. They were sitting in a booth, and the decor seemed darker and more plush, brass, wood and red velour. On the table in front of them, on a white linen table-cloth, were two plates of pasta and two half-full glasses of white wine beside a bottle placed upside down in a metal ice bucket. Their faces were close, as if in intimate conversation, and Quinn's hand rested on top of the woman's thigh.

The third photograph was taken slightly from above and showed Quinn on his back with the young girl, naked now, straddling him, her small breasts jutting forward, nipples hard, dark hair hanging over her shoulders. Quinn's hands rested on her thighs. The girl had an expression of ecstasy on her face, but it was impossible to tell whether it was genuine. Probably not, Banks thought, because the odds were that Bill Quinn had passed out, or had been drugged, by this time. He couldn't be certain, of course, but there was something about the pose, the way Quinn's head rested slackly on the pillow, his body slumped, and his hands lying passively on her thighs. Maybe he should have been squeezing her breasts, rearing up and sucking them, kissing them, doing *something*, at any rate. The surroundings were in darkness except for an oblong of pale light that must have been a window, and one or two pieces of furniture in the shadows. A hotel room, Banks guessed.

'What do you think?' he asked Winsome, who was perching on the arm of the chair, beside him peering at the photos.

'Escort,' she said, without missing a beat.

'Perhaps it was more than just a sexual transaction?' Banks suggested. 'She's not dressed like a hooker. Those are more like student clothes, not slutty or expensively stylish at all. Could she have been a lover, maybe? He seems a bit out of it in the room, doesn't he? What do you think?'

'She could be a high-priced escort,' Winsome said. 'I imagine you can order them dressed any way you wish. Maybe he had a thing about student chic. And you're right, guv. There's definitely something odd about that picture in the hotel room. His position. He's sort of inert, when you wouldn't expect him to be.'

Banks raised his eyebrows. 'Winsome, you surprise me. What should he be doing, do you think?'

'He just seems too passive, that's all,' she said. 'I'd say that if a man his age was lucky enough to be in bed with a girl her age, a girl as beautiful as her, then he should probably be enjoying himself.'

Banks laughed. 'Good point, Winsome. Thanks for sharing that.' He stood up. 'Lots of questions that need answers. Whichever way you look at it, it seems as if our DI Quinn has been a naughty boy. Bit of a dark horse. OK, let's get these photos over to Photographic Services and have some copies made before they get to work on them. It would be interesting to find out when they were taken and who the girl is. Perhaps we can isolate her face so we can show it around without giving away what Quinn was up to. Will you seal off this room, Winsome, and make sure no one enters? I especially don't want any of the media getting a scent of this. They're bound to find out eventually – they always do – but let's keep it under wraps for as long as we can.'

'Yes, guv.' Banks glanced at his watch. 'I'd better be getting back to the station. I'm sure the boss will be chomping at the bit, wanting to know what's going on, and I need a few favours from her.'

2

Since the reorganisation, which meant more meetings, recently promoted Area Commander Catherine Gervaise had added a low round table and four tubular chairs to her office. There was plenty of room for them, and they allowed for a more informal meeting space than the boardroom, where the full team briefings were carried out.

Banks felt the tubes holding up his chair give gently as he sat and leaned back, carefully placing his coffee mug on a rose-patterned coaster on the glass table. The coffee was from Gervaise's personal filter machine, and it was good and strong. There was no doubt that Gervaise had brought a feminine touch to what used to be Superintendent Gristhorpe's very masculine office, though she would never thank anyone for telling her so.

Photographs of her husband and children adorned her desk and the top of the filing cabinet; the walls were painted in muted pastel shades of blue, complemented by a couple of well-framed water lily prints. The whole place seemed somehow more airy and light, with everything neat and in its place.

Most of the books were legal or forensic texts, rather than the rows of leather-bound literary classics Gristhorpe had kept on the shelves, though there was the tell-tale Stella Rimington autobiography that Gervaise had clearly forgotten to hide. The books were in neat groups, separated by the occasional cup or plaque for archery, dressage or fencing, which had been Gervaise's passions when she had had more time to indulge in such pursuits.

The window was open about three inches, and Banks could hear sounds from Eastvale's cobbled market square – delivery vans, children's squeals, shouted greetings – and the smell of fresh-baked bread from Bob's Bakery made his mouth water. It was going on for nine o'clock. He had been up since just after five, and he hadn't eaten anything yet. Maybe he'd grab a pasty or a sausage roll from Greggs after the meeting.

AC Gervaise was as fresh and business-like as ever in her navy blue suit and crisp white linen blouse, a little red, blue and yellow needlework around the collar adding a touch of colour to its strict lines.

'Is everything in hand?' she asked, sitting opposite Banks and smoothing her skirt.

'It is,' said Banks.

The mechanics of a murder investigation could be quite overwhelming, and it was as well to get everything set up and running, make sure everyone knew what his or her job was, before information started arriving in the form of forensics reports, witness statements, alibis and the like. Computer systems such as HOLMES and SOCRATES needed to be set up, and that job would probably fall to DC Gerry Masterson these days, with her IT background, but there was still so much reliance on actual paper in police investigations that plenty of good strong cardboard boxes and large filing cabinets would also be needed. And even though officers used their mobiles most of the time, dedicated land lines had to be set up, and the public needed to be made aware of numbers to call if they had information.

'Did you know DI Quinn personally?' Gervaise asked.

'I met him once,' said Banks. 'Seemed like a nice enough bloke. But I can't say I knew him. You?'

'Same thing. He was awarded a medal for bravery about three years ago. I was at the presentation.'

'I didn't know that.'

'Distinguished service record. I don't get this at all, Alan. From everything I've heard so far, it certainly doesn't seem like a random act of violence, or even an old enemy lashing out in anger.'

'No,' Banks agreed. 'The choice of weapon. It all seems very deliberate, as if it were planned. And then there are the photos.'

Gervaise's eyes widened. 'The what?'

Banks explained about the photographs he'd found in Quinn's forensic textbook. 'They should be with Photographic Services by now, though I don't imagine there'll be a lot they can tell us.'

'You'd be surprised. Quinn with a young woman, you say?'

'Very young.'

'What do you make of it? Blackmail?'

'That seems most likely.' Banks paused. 'Winsome told me his wife died just a month ago,' he went on, 'which makes me think that if the photos had been used for blackmail before then, there's a good chance they'd be quite useless after.'

'What about his children?'

'It's not the same, is it? Besides, they're grown up. At university.'

'Doesn't matter. I know that I wouldn't want my kids to know ... you know ...' Gervaise reddened. 'If I'd done anything like that.'

'I suppose you're right.' Banks imagined what Tracy or Brian would say if they knew about some of the things he'd done over the years. Not that infidelity had been a habit, but once was enough. There were other things he'd done, things he wasn't proud of, down in London when he was undercover and living on the edge, or over it sometimes. 'But the black-mail still loses a lot of its sting, doesn't it? I mean, your kids can hardly haul you through the divorce courts and take everything you've got, can they?'

Gervaise gave him a look that would freeze a volcano. 'You mean take what they're entitled to, surely, Alan?'

'Sorry, ma'am. Yes. Of course.'

Gervaise inclined her head regally. 'I should think so. And less of the ma'am. It does nothing to excuse your sexist attitudes.' She paused. 'All I'm saying is that the threat of blackmail might have still been there, if not as strong. Kids. Parents. Even bosses, work colleagues. And it's hardly a good thing for a police officer's career to admit that he left himself open to blackmail. There's been rumours lately, too. A rotten apple. Just rumours, mind, but even so . . .'

'So I heard,' said Banks. 'You think it was Quinn?'

'All I'm saying is that we need to keep an open mind. Back to the girl. You say she's young?'

'Yes.'

'Underage?'

'Just young.'

'But if it even *appeared* that way, he could have lost his job,' Gervaise pointed out.

'I still think that for Quinn the biggest fear would have been his wife finding out. Anything else he could have brushed off, or dealt with. There's no proof the girl's underage. And she's certainly a very attractive woman. Any man would be proud to be seen with her. Christ, some of his mates at work might even have envied him.'

Gervaise rolled her eyes.

'What?'

'Never mind. Why do you think he kept the photos with him?'

'I don't know. In my experience, people hang on to the strangest things for the strangest of reasons. Can't complain. It makes our job easier in the long run. Maybe he was proud of himself for pulling her, and they were some sort of trophy? Maybe he was in love with her, and they were all he had left?

Maybe he'd just got hòld of them? Maybe he was going to
pass them on to someone? Quinn obviously didn't expect that
he would never return to his room at St Peter's last night, and
that someone else would find them, unless . . .'

'Yes?'

'Unless that was why he left them there. As some form of
insurance against something happening to him.'

'You mean he was *expecting* to be killed?'

'No, not that. Expecting trouble, maybe, if he'd agreed to
meet someone he was wary of, to pay off the blackmailer,
say. But I doubt very much that he expected to be hurt or
killed. He may have left the pictures in his room as a form
of insurance, in case something went wrong. They weren't
very well hidden. Quinn was one of us. He knew we'd find
them on the first pass. Which means they may be important
now that something *has* happened to him. Not just insurance, but evidence. *She* may be important. We need to find
her.'

'It's not much to go on, though, is it? A handful of
photographs?'

'I don't know,' said Banks. 'I suppose we can get someone
to trawl through the escort agency file photos, check the online
dating services, see if she turns up on one of them?'

'So you think he was meeting someone he knew out there
last night, maybe about something connected with the girl
and the photos?'

'I don't know. Perhaps he even thought he was meeting the
girl herself? That would cause him to be less on guard.'

'Maybe he did meet her,' suggested Gervaise. 'Maybe she
killed him.'

'It's possible,' Banks agreed. 'But it's far too early to speculate. One way or another, I think the pictures are connected
with his murder, which is what makes me think of blackmail,
that they must have been taken while his wife was still alive to

be of any use to anyone.' Banks paused. 'Any chance of a few extra bodies?'

'You know what it's like these days, Alan. But I'll ask ACC McLaughlin, see what I can do. And I'll take care of the media. I should bring our Press Officer in on this. One of our own. A high-profile case. I'll set up a conference.'

'Appreciated. Winsome and the others are already working on the staff and patient interviews at St Peter's, but we also need to go over Bill Quinn's old cases, talk to his colleagues, see if anyone had a grudge against him big enough to kill him, any hard men recently released from jail, that sort of thing. I'll start by paying DI Ken Blackstone a visit in Leeds before I head out to Rawdon to check out Quinn's house. Ken knew Bill Quinn fairly well, so he should be able to tell me a bit more about what sort of copper he was. We also need his mobile phone records. Credit card and bank statements, too.' Banks glanced over at the trophies on the bookcase. 'Er . . . by the way, I noticed a few archery awards there. You don't happen to know anything about crossbows, do you?'

'Afraid not,' said Gervaise. 'I'm strictly a longbow person. And I think you'll find that most serious archers disdain crossbows. They're hunters' weapons, mostly, not for sporting competitions.'

'Well, they're pretty easy to get hold of,' Banks said. 'No questions asked, as long as you're over eighteen. They're quiet, and just as deadly as a bullet from the right distance. We need to canvass the shops and Internet sites where people buy these things.'

Gervaise scribbled something on her pad. 'What else does the choice of weapon tell you?' she asked.

'Well, I don't know much about the mechanics of crossbows, but I assume they could be used just as easily by a man or a woman. They're efficient, anonymous and cold. And quiet. I don't know about the range, but it was a moonlit night, and the killer was obviously able to get close enough and stay hidden in the trees. The bolt had buried itself deep in the chest, pierced the heart, according to Tom Burns. He thinks it was shot from about fifty or sixty feet away. If the killer was hiding behind a tree and wearing dark clothing, the odds are that Quinn wouldn't have known he was there. Or she. Dr Glendenning will be able to tell us more.'

'It sounds to me suspiciously like a hit.'

'That's one possibility,' said Banks. 'Which is why we need to find out if anyone had a reason for making a hit on Bill Quinn. We all make enemies on this job, but it's rare that any of them follow through with their threats, especially in such a cold-blooded way.'

'Maybe there was another reason?' Gervaise suggested. 'Maybe DI Quinn had got himself into deep trouble. Maybe he'd been sleeping with the enemy. It happens. The grey area. Money. Corruption. Gambling debts. Drugs. Or a woman. The girl in the photograph, for example? She must be some-body's daughter, if not someone's wife or girlfriend. A jealous husband or lover, perhaps? Maybe Quinn thought he was in love with her, and that's why he kept the photos? As you say, a trophy, or memento. All he had left of her. A mid-life crisis? Perhaps he was hoping to rekindle the romance after his wife had died and he was suddenly free. Maybe we're dealing with a love triangle?' She put her pad down and rubbed her eyes. 'Too many questions, too many possibilities. How's DI Cabbot doing, by the way?'

'Fine,' said Banks. 'She's in Cornwall staying with her father.'

'She's due back Monday, right. Clean bill of health?'

'Far as I know,' Banks said. Annie Cabbot had been recu-perating from a serious operation to remove bullet fragments from an area close to her spine. The wait for surgery had been a long one – she had first had to regain strength from a previous injury to her right lung before the operation on her back could be carried out – but it had been a success in that the fragments had been removed and Annie still had the use of all her limbs. Her recovery had been very slow, however, and involved far more excruciating pain than the surgeons had expected, followed by a great deal of physical therapy, some of it at St Peter's. The spinal cord was intact, but there had been some disc, muscle and vertebrae problems they hadn't foreseen. Annie had coped well with the pain and uncertainty, Banks thought, getting stronger every day, but he knew that the shooting had also left her with internal demons she would have to deal with eventually. She would be unlikely to go to a psychologist or psychiatrist because of the stigma involved. Rightly or wrongly, seeking professional help for mental problems was viewed as a weakness in the force. Many coppers still maintained that it was bad for the career, and perhaps it was.

'I was thinking of putting her on desk duties for a while, until she gets her sea legs back again. What do you think?'

'For what it's worth, I think Annie should be given a chance to dive right in. It will do her confidence no end of good to start working on a real case again. Even the doctor says her main hurdles now are psychological. She's been through a lot. First she gets shot, then she thinks she's never going to walk again, then she suffers from chronic post-op pain.'

'I'm simply pointing out that there are a lot of reasons why DI Cabbot, when she comes back next Monday, should keep a low profile on light duties for a little while and catch her breath before attempting to dash off and solve murders.'

'She can be useful. We need her. Annie's bright, she's—'

'I know all about DI Cabbot's qualities as a detective, thank you very much.' Gervaise ran a hand across her brow. 'Let me think on it,' she said. 'I know you need more officers on the case. I'll have a word with ACC McLaughlin when I talk to him about the personnel issue. I'll see what he says about DI Cabbot's future here. It's the best I can do.'

Banks held her steady gaze. 'OK,' he said finally. 'Thanks.'

'Anything else you'd like, while you're at it?'

'Well, a twenty per cent pay raise would be nice. And a bigger office.'

'Out!' Gervaise picked up a heavy paperweight and threatened to toss it at Banks. 'Out, before I throw you out.'

Smiling to himself, Banks left the office.

Banks munched on his Greggs sausage roll as he guided the Porsche towards the A1, the fourth movement of Mahler's 'Resurrection' symphony playing loudly on the powerful stereo system. It helped that this was a vocal movement. He had always liked Mahler's lieder, and he had only recently been getting to like the symphonies a lot, having spurned them as boring and bombastic in the past. Was this something that happened when you got older? Failing eyesight, mysterious aches and pains, enjoying Mahler? Would Wagner be next?

The last time Banks had been to Leeds, he remembered, it was to help his daughter Tracy move a few months ago. She had shared a house in Headingley with two other girls, but it hadn't worked out. Tracy had suffered a number of traumatic events around the time Annie had been shot, and after a brief period of depression and withdrawal, she had decided to change her life.

That first meant moving from Leeds to Newcastle, which was a little further from Eastvale, but not so much as to make a big difference. It also meant leaving a dead-end job and getting back on to a career track again. She had got a part-time administrative position at the university and enrolled in the master's programme in History, with a view to moving into teaching once she felt a bit more secure in her qualifications.

It was also time to live alone, too, she had told Banks, so she had rented a tiny bedsit close to the converted riverside area, and both Banks and his ex-wife Sandra were helping her with the rent until she got on her feet. Her brother Brian, whose band The Blue Lamps seemed to be going from strength to strength, had also been most generous. In an odd way, Banks thought, they were starting to act like a family again, though he knew that the gap between him and Sandra was unbridgeable. He had visited Tracy once already in Newcastle and had taken her across the river to The Sage to see The Unthanks in concert, then for a drink after. They had had a good time, and he was looking forward to doing it again.

The A1 was a nightmare. Mile after mile of roadworks, down to one lane each way from Leeming to Wetherby, and a 50mph limit, which everyone obeyed because the cameras averaged out your speed over the whole distance. As a result, it took well over an hour and a half before Banks approached the eastern outskirts of Leeds. The Porsche didn't like it at all; it had never been happy at 50mph. He had been thinking of selling the car ever since he had inherited it from his brother, but for one reason or another he had never got around to it. Now it was getting a bit shabby and starting to feel comfortable, like a favourite old jacket, jeans or a pair of gloves, and the sound system was a corker, so he reckoned he would probably keep it until it bit the dust.

Millgarth was an ugly, redbrick fortress-style building at the bottom of Eastgate in Leeds city centre. DI Ken Blackstone wanted to hang around his tiny, cluttered office no more than Banks did, so they headed out into the spring sunshine, walked up the Headrow as far as Primark, then turned left down Briggate, a pedestrian precinct crowded with shoppers. There used to be a Borders near the intersection, Banks remembered fondly, but it was gone now, and he lamented its passing. There was a Pizza Hut in its place.

Blackstone was a snappy dresser, and today he wore a light wool suit, button-down Oxford shirt and a rather flamboyant tie. With the tufts of hair over his ears, and his wire-rimmed glasses, Blackstone had always reminded Banks more of an academic than a copper. In fact, the older he got, the more he came to resemble some of the photos Banks had seen of the poet Philip Larkin.

Banks and Blackstone decided against the posh Harvey Nichols cafe in the Victoria Quarter and plumped for Whitelocks, an eighteenth-century pub in an alley off Briggate, near Marks & Spencer. The alley was narrow and high, with the pub stretching down one side, much longer than it was deep, and a row of benches down the other side, against the wall, with a few tables and stools where space permitted. Not much light got in at any time of the day, but it was always a popular spot with the city centre workers and the student crowd. It was lunchtime, so they were lucky to get space on the bench next to a group of office girls discussing a wedding one of them had just attended in Cyprus.

'You hang on to the seats, Alan,' said Blackstone. 'I'll get us a couple of pints in and something to eat.'

'Make mine a shandy,' said Banks. 'I've got to drive. And steak and kidney pie and chips.'

He reached for his wallet, but Blackstone brushed the gesture aside and headed into the pub. He had to stoop to get through the old, low door. People were much shorter in the eighteenth century. Banks remembered that the food was served canteen-style behind an area of the counter beside the bar, so when Blackstone came back he carried the drinks first, then went back for the plates of steaming pie and chips.

'And Josie got so drunk we had to take her to hospital,' one

of the office girls said. 'She nearly died of alcohol poisoning.'
The others laughed.

'It's terrible news,' said Blackstone, pushing his glasses up
the bridge of his nose. 'First Sonia, then Bill. I can hardly
bloody believe it. Not only one of us, but Bill.'

'Sonia was his wife, right?'

'Twenty-five years. I was at their silver wedding anniversary do last December.'

'How old was Bill, exactly?'

'Just turned forty-nine.'

'How did he take her death?'

'How do you think? He was devoted to her. He was devastated, naturally. This neck business that got him into St Peter's
was a bit of an excuse, if you ask me. Not that he hadn't been
having problems on and off for years. But I'd have said he was
on the verge of a breakdown. Depressed, too. Couldn't sleep.'

'Winsome said it was a massive stroke.'

'Sonia was always a bit frail. Heart problems. I think that
was why Bill was especially protective of her. Some people
said he was too much under her thumb, but it wasn't really
like that. He adored her. It was sudden, a stroke, yes.'

They both paused for a moment. Banks didn't know about
Ken, but he often felt a brief stab of worry about his own
mortality these days. He contemplated his steak and kidney
pie. He'd already eaten a sausage roll for breakfast. Not one
vegetable all day, unless you counted the chips. Hardly the
healthy diet he'd been promising himself since his last visit to
the doctor. Still, he had stopped smoking years ago, had cut
down on his drinking a bit recently, and he hardly ever put on
any weight. Surely that had to be a good thing?

'Poor sod,' said Banks.

Blackstone raised his glass. 'I'll drink to that. And to life.'

They clinked glasses. One of the office girls smiled at Banks.
'Birthday?'

'Something like that,' he said. The girls moved on to boasting about drunken exploits in Sharm-el-Sheikh, paying no further attention to Banks and Blackstone, who spoke quietly anyway. A gust of warm wind blew along the alley and carried just a hint of the summer to come.

'There are a couple of things I'd like to know,' said Banks, glancing around. 'First off, it looked very much like a professional hit.' Banks described what they had deduced so far about the crime scene.

Blackstone thought for a moment. 'Well, if access was as easy as you say, anyone could have done it, though it would have had to have been someone who knew Bill was there, I suppose, someone who knew his habits and the lie of the land, or somehow managed to lure him down to the edge of the woods. And what professional hit man uses a crossbow? Have you considered an inside job, or helper, at any rate?'

'Naturally,' said Banks. 'We're open to just about anything at the moment, and we'll be checking everyone out. But there are a few problems with that theory. How would someone on the inside get rid of the murder weapon, for example? As far as I'm concerned, the most likely scenario is that it was someone Quinn put away, a criminal with a grudge and a taste for revenge.'

One of the office girls lowered her voice, but not quite enough. 'And the last night we were there Cathy pissed herself right in the main street. It was simply dripping down her legs. Like something out of *Bridesmaids*. Talk about embarrassed! Laugh? I nearly died. Jenny said we should find a Boots and buy her some adult nappies.'

'Why do it at St Peter's?' Blackstone asked. 'Have you thought about that? If someone wanted Bill out of the way, there must have been better opportunities, surely?'

'Not necessarily, especially if timing was an issue. My guess is that it was easier. He was a sitting duck at St Peter's. It might have been a bit harder to isolate him in the city. More chance of witnesses there, too. And I wouldn't be surprised if there was an element of bravado. It probably appealed to the killer's warped sense of humour to kill a cop in a place full of cops, even though they were disabled, or geriatric, for the most part.' Banks paused. 'But that begs a few questions.'

'Like what?'

'Like how did the killer find out Bill Quinn was at St Peter's in the first place?'

'It wasn't a secret. I mean, anyone could have known, not only people on the inside with him, but others, friends, family, even his coll—' Blackstone stopped, and his eyes hardened. 'Wait a minute, Alan. Are you saying what I think you're saying?'

'We have to consider it, Ken. The possibility of a mole in Quinn's team, someone in the department. There have been rumours, you know.'

'You think it's Bill? So what's going to happen now? The works? Suspend operations, seize all the files? Send in Professional Standards or the Independent Police Complaints Commission?'

'I hope it won't come to that,' said Banks. 'We're not sure about anything yet. All I'm saying is that it's an angle we have to consider along with all the others until we can rule it out. Someone knew where to find him.'

'Any trace evidence? Forensics?'

'None yet. His pockets had been emptied, and his mobile is missing. We're tracking down the provider, then at least we'll have a list of calls to and from. The CSIs are working on the usual – footprints, fabrics, DNA, fingerprints. The area near the tree where they think the killer stood looks promising.'

'So what do you want from me?'

'Area Commander Gervaise will be asking for full details of Bill Quinn's cases from the brass, and for a list of villains he's put away, along with their release dates, but I thought I'd just pick your brains in the meantime, get a head start.'

Blackstone rubbed his cheeks. 'Another drink first?'

'Not for me, thanks, Ken.'

Blackstone studied the remains of his pint. 'No. I suppose I can make do with what I've got left, too. Where to begin?'

'Wherever you want.'

'Well, Bill's been around for a while. You'll have quite a job on your hands going through the minutiae of his career.'

'Let's start at the top, then. Any counter-terrorism investigations?'

'We try to leave that sort of thing to Special Branch. Of course, West Yorkshire can't avoid getting in on the peripheries at times, especially in Bradford or Dewsbury and some parts of Leeds, but nothing comes immediately to mind. Surely you don't believe this was some kind of a fatwa, do you?'

'Just casting flies on the water.'

'Aye. One thing I can tell you, though. It was Bill helped put away Harry Lake nearly twenty years ago. He was a young DS then, and it didn't do his career any harm, I can tell you.'

Banks whistled between his teeth. Harry Lake was famous enough to have had books written about him. He had abducted, tortured and killed four women in the Bradford area in the early nineties, cut them up and boiled the parts. Like the even more infamous Dennis Nilsen, he was only caught when the body pieces he'd flushed down the toilet blocked the drains, and a human hand surfaced in one of his neighbour's toilet bowls.

'He can't be out yet, surely?' said Banks.

'I don't think he'll ever get out. He's in Broadmoor. But it's worth checking. He always swore revenge, and maybe he persuaded some sick follower to do his dirty work for him? You know what it's like. People like him get marriage proposals, offers of continuing his work for him. According to the prison governor, he gets plenty of those.'

Banks made a note. 'There must be more?'

'I suppose his other most famous case was his biggest failure. Well, not *his* really.'

'Oh?'

'The Rachel Hewitt business.'

'Rachel Hewitt? Isn't she that girl whose parents keep cropping up in the news, the girl who disappeared in Latvia, or wherever?'

'Estonia, actually. Tallinn. Six years ago. Yes. And they were in the news again not too long ago. That phone-hacking inquiry. You might have heard. They've been complaining about being hounded by the media, phones tapped, private papers and diaries stolen and published. The sister went off the rails, apparently, and the press had a feeding frenzy.'

'Bill Quinn worked that case?'

'Bill worked this end, such as it was. Family and friends. Rachel's background. The Tallinn police worked the actual disappearance. But Bill spent about a week out there liaising quite early in the investigation. Rachel was a West Yorkshire girl, from Drighlington, part of City & Holbeck Division, and he drew the short straw, depending on how you look at it. But with the local police running the investigation, and in a foreign country with different ways of doing things, he didn't stand much of a chance. It was more of a show of strength and solidarity, really, and a bit of a PR exercise, if truth be told. Otherwise they'd have sent in a team.'

'They didn't?'

'No. The British Embassy was involved, of course, but they don't carry out criminal investigations in foreign countries. It was strictly Tallinn's case. Nobody expected Bill to solve it where the locals had failed. That was back in the summer of 2006. As expected, he got precisely nowhere, but he did get his photo in the papers quite often, and he did a few press conferences with the parents of the missing girl.'

'The Hewitts have had to use the media to keep their daughter's name in the public eye, haven't they?'

'It's a two-edged sword. You don't get owt for nowt from those bastards.'

'And what role did Bill play?'

'As I said, he was just a glorified consultant, really.'

'He's not been implicated in the hacking business?'

'Bill? Good lord, no. Though some days it seems we've all been tarred with same brush.'

'So it's unlikely to be connected with his murder?'

'I can't see how it could be. Nothing's changed. Rachel still hasn't been found. Her parents insist she's being kept alive somewhere, but we're all pretty certain she's dead. Thing is, it haunted Bill. I don't think he ever quite got over not solving it, not finding her. He was convinced she was already dead, of course, but I think he wanted to provide the parents with some sort of explanation, proof, some positive outcome. A body, for example.'

'Anything else I should be looking at?'

'Just the usual. Dozens of petty villains, domestic killings. What you'd expect from a long career in detective work. He's put away burglars, murderers, muggers, embezzlers, gangsters and hard men. None of them stand out much except for Harry Lake, and maybe Steve Lambert, that big property developer, the one who paid someone to murder his wife about three years ago.'

'I remember that one,' said Banks. 'Didn't he claim someone broke in, and she was stabbed while interrupting a robbery?'

'That's right. Appeared to have a watertight alibi, too. The usual citizens above suspicion. But Bill stuck at it, followed the money trail, found the bloke he'd hired, along with a strong forensic connection to the scene. It was a solid case in the end, and Lambert went down swearing revenge.'

'But he's still inside, isn't he?'

'If he hired someone to kill his wife . . .'

'Long tentacles?'

'Possibly.'

'I'll bear it in mind. Mostly what we should look at first, though, is anyone he put away who's actually come out recently, and anyone he's pissed off who's still wandering free.'

'There'll be a few. I'll see if I can narrow things down a bit for you.'

'Appreciate it, Ken.'

'All this . . . Sorry. Bill was a mate, that's all. It's getting to me.'

'I know, and I'm sorry, too. What about more recently? What was he working on when he died?'

Blackstone finished off his drink and stared at the empty glass. 'Well, as you know, he was off duty for a couple of weeks with his neck problems before he went into St Peter's, and before that he had a couple of weeks leave after Sonia . . . you know. Before that he was working with a specially formed city-wide team of detectives on a long-term surveillance and intelligence-gathering mission.'

'What was it?'

'Just the tip of the iceberg. It started with a gang of loan sharks. They operate around the poorest estates in the city, mostly targeting new immigrants, as often as not illegals, asylum seekers or unregistered migrants who still owe a bloody fortune for their staff agency fees, transport, lodgings and food. And, in some cases, for the risk of smuggling them in. Some of them live in dormitories in converted barns, or what have you, outside the city, but a lot of them have managed somehow or other to get hold of council houses, illegal sublets from fellow countrymen, mostly. Of course, the jobs they were promised and had to pay so much for didn't materialise, or they ended up cleaning out pig sties or public conveniences for ten quid a week. Unless they're attractive girls, of course, and then . . .'

'I get the picture,' said Banks. He thought once more of Quinn's photographs, the young girl, and how she reminded him of a young girl some years ago, involved in the case during which his brother had been murdered. That girl had been trafficked from Eastern Europe, along with many others. It still went on.

It was going to be tricky, broaching the subject of Quinn's infidelity and susceptibility to blackmail to Ken, but it had to be done, gently or otherwise. Sometimes, Banks felt, it was best to jump right in and dodge the retaliation, if it came. 'We found some photos of Bill Quinn with a young girl – and I mean young, Ken – hidden in his room.'

'Sexual?'

'Well, they weren't taken at a vicar's tea party.'

'And what do you make of this?'

'I'm not sure, but blackmail comes to mind.'

Blackstone thrust his head forward. 'Are you suggesting that Bill was in someone's pocket?'

'No. I'm asking you if you think it possible that he was being blackmailed. I assume that he wouldn't have wanted his wife to know, and I doubt that he'd have said anything to his friends.'

'Sonia? She'd have kill— No, he wouldn't have wanted her to know. Sonia was a naive, trusting soul. Bill was always very protective towards her. He genuinely loved her. Something like that . . . well, it would have devastated her. And if you're asking does it surprise me that he had a bit on the side, yes it does. Very much.'

'Nobody's judging him, Ken.'

'But they will. You're starting already.'

'Ken, I'm investigating his *murder*. I need to know. Surely you, of all people, can understand that?'

Blackstone ran his hand over his sparse hair. 'Shit. OK. I know. It just . . .'

'Did he play away from home?'

'No. I was only away from home with him once. A conference in Lyon, France. Interpol. Christ, he was only human. He'd look, like the rest of us. Married, but not dead. He'd watch them walk by, sitting at a cafe or somewhere, look a bit wistful. We both did. For crying out loud, there are lots of pretty girls in Lyon.'

'But he didn't get up to anything?'

'Not that I know of.'

'Would you have known?'

'I wasn't his keeper, if that's what you mean. We didn't share a room. We weren't together twenty-four hours a day. But no, I don't think he did. I think I would have known. When were they taken, these pictures?'

'We don't know. Has he been anywhere since his wife died? Any conferences, holidays?'

'Are you bloody joking, Alan? It was only a month ago. The man was shattered. A wreck. There's no way anything like what you're talking about happened between Sonia's death and now.'

'OK. Appreciate it, Ken. Was he working undercover on this loan-sharking case?'

'No, it was all quite open and above board. The chief villain's a bloke called Warren Corrigan. Small-time crook, really, or at least he started that way. Has his office in the back room of a pub called the Black Bull in Seacroft. Fancies himself as a sort of latter-day Kray. You know, man of the people, pillar of the community, tray of tea from Mum. We've got him down for a few assaults, demanding money with threats and so on, but nobody will talk. Everyone's too scared. We've got two bodies already that we're not entirely sure he didn't have something to do with, but we can't prove anything.'

'Bodies?'

'Yes. Suicides. They finally cracked under the pressure of their debts, according to friends and family. But more than that, nobody will say. The most recent was a trafficked Romanian girl with needle marks up and down both arms. Fifteen years old. The girl. She couldn't turn enough tricks to pay the interest. We've been trying to contact her parents.'

'Shit,' said Banks. He thought of the girl in the photographs again. At least from what he had been able to make out, she seemed healthy enough, and most likely older than fifteen, though sometimes it was hard to tell. No visible needle tracks, but then the quality of the photo wasn't that sharp. 'Does this Corrigan have any connection with the people-trafficking, the drugs?'

'Not that we can prove,' said Blackstone. 'But it seems more than likely. It's one of the things Quinn and the team were checking out.'

'Would he have had a good reason for wanting Quinn dead?'

'I can't see it. Killing a cop seems a bit extreme.'

'Did Corrigan know the team was on to him?'

'He knew. At this stage, it was all a bit of a cat and mouse game to him.'

'Are you working this case, too?'

'No. Bill and I chatted about it once in a while over a pint. Shop talk.'

'Who's on his team?'

'Nick Gwillam's probably the one you want to talk to,' said Blackstone. 'Trading Standards, Illegal Money Lending Unit. There's a bloke from SOCA and a couple of DCs, too, but Gwillam's your best bet. He worked closest with Bill on it.'

'Can you fix up a chat? Just informal at this stage.'

'He's off until Monday, but I'm sure I'll be able to arrange something. I'll let you know.'

'Thanks, Ken. I know this is tough for you. Has Corrigan uttered any threats against Quinn specifically, or against any members of the team?'

'Not that I know of. He's too smart for that. At least, Bill never mentioned it. We've had him in for questioning a couple of times, so he knows he's on our radar, and I helped out on one of the interviews. Played the good cop. It didn't work. Slippery bastard. Cocky as hell. I wouldn't put anything past him. But he may be a bit . . . I don't know . . . too overconfident to feel the need to eliminate Bill. I would imagine Corrigan always believes he'll come out on top without having to do anything but intimidate his powerless victims on the estates. Or get someone else to do it. He's not exactly a hard man, himself. And if he did do it, you can be sure he's got a solid alibi. Probably having dinner with the mayor or someone.'

Banks had come across villains like Corrigan before. They were bottom-feeders, parasites who exploited the poorest, most vulnerable members of society. His victims were unskilled labourers or jobless workers far from home, often from very poor communities, with no means of returning and nowhere else to go; they were frightened people who didn't even speak the language or understand the terms of interest being offered, living constantly under the threat of violence to themselves or their families. And people like Corrigan always seemed to get away with it.

'Can you put together a preliminary file on this Corrigan for me?' Banks asked. 'Links to Quinn, to any informants, undercover officers, members of the trafficking chain, that sort of thing. If you think it's just the tip of the iceberg, it could be a big operation, and there could be enough at stake to drive someone to murder a copper.'

'I'll see what I can do.'

'Thanks, Ken. Is there any way this Corrigan could have known Quinn would be at St Peter's for two weeks?'

'Not unless somebody told him. For all I know, Bill might have told him, himself. Or one of the team members.'

'Why would anyone do that?'

'Like I said, it was all a bit of a game to Corrigan, and Bill played along sometimes in the hopes of getting some titbit out of him. You know, how's the family, how's that bad neck of yours coming along. All very pally, the veneer of civilised conversation.' Blackstone snorted. 'Sometimes I think we should have just gone in with the rubber hosepipes.'

'Maybe,' said Banks. 'But one way or another we'll get to the truth.'

'And if anyone on Bill's team *was* responsible for tipping off Corrigan as to his whereabouts,' Blackstone went on, 'I'll have his balls, civilised conversation or not. Have you considered that it might have been the girl herself? The one in the photographs you told me about? As I remember, there was a girl with a crossbow in a James Bond movie once. Not that I use those things as my yardstick for real life, you understand, but it's a weapon that could be as easily used by a woman as a man.'

'We're keeping an open mind. *For Your Eyes Only.* That was the movie.'

'I can never remember titles. You'll keep me posted on developments?'

'Will do.'

Blackstone glanced at his watch. 'I'd better get back.' He touched Banks's shoulder briefly. 'Take care.'

Banks's conversation with Blackstone had depressed and exhausted him. It was a sudden and unwelcome reminder of the filth and sewage he had so often had to wade through in his job. The depth of man's inhumanity to his fellow man never ceased to amaze and appall him. It had been a quiet winter, and since the escapade with Tracy and Annie, life and work had generally been ticking along at a manageable, if rather dull, rate. Now this: a potentially compromised cop murdered, a thug running riot with the law. Still, this was what he had signed up for, not sitting at a desk making budget cuts or fudging crime statistics.

He finished his drink and realised that he had better call in at Bill Quinn's home in Rawdon before heading back to Eastvale. Before he went, though, he felt he needed a treat, the way his mother always used to buy him a toy soldier or a Dinky car after a visit to the dentist's. He had no one to buy it for him – his mother was in Peterborough, unless she and his father had taken off on another cruise – but he could do it himself. He bought a lot of stuff online these days, given that he lived in such a remote place, but it was always a treat to go into a real record shop or bookshop and browse around the piles of special offers and racks of new releases. This time, after half an hour in HMV, he came out with Kate Royal's *A Lesson in Love*, Martin Carthy's *Essential* two CD set, and a DVD box set of the first season of *Treme* on sale for fifteen quid.

Banks pulled up outside Bill Quinn's home in Rawdon early that afternoon. There was quite a mix of houses in the area, he had noticed, trying to find his way after the satnav had given up. Bungalows rubbed shoulders with brick terraces, and they, in turn, stood alongside detached and semi-detached houses with lower halves of exposed stone and upper halves fake Tudor, dark beams and white stucco. Quinn's semi must have cost a bob or two, Banks thought, but it probably wasn't out of his price range if he had bought at the right time, and if his wife had also worked. Two kids at university wouldn't help, though, especially these days. Still, it was too soon for theories about Quinn's financial situation; they should have his bank account details as well as his mobile phone log before too long. For now, they were interested in anything that seemed out of place.

The search team was already at work, and Banks recognised DS Keith Palmer, the officer in charge, who was standing in the doorway. 'Anything yet?' Banks asked.

Palmer led Banks into the house, where officers were busy searching through the sideboard drawers in the front hall. 'Not yet,' Palmer said, leading him to the kitchen at the back. 'But you might find this interesting.'

One of the small glass panels on the door had been broken, and the door itself was an inch or so ajar. It had to be connected with Quinn's murder, Banks thought, otherwise it would be too much of a coincidence. Banks glanced at the floor and saw the glass fragments scattered over the fake wood finish. 'There's no mess, except in Quinn's study,' Palmer went on, 'and even that is pretty orderly. Whoever did this probably knew what he was looking for. Want the guided tour?'

'Sure.' Banks glanced around the kitchen. Washed dishes were piled neatly in the metal rack on the draining board, small sandwich plates, cups and glasses. The rubbish bin was full of discarded takeaway containers, and the green box by the door held mostly empty Bell's bottles. Banks followed Palmer.

The living room was neat and tidy, as Palmer had indicated, though there was a thin layer of dust on the mantelpiece, and Banks guessed that while Quinn had kept things more or less in order, he hadn't taken much of an interest in housework since his wife's death. There was a small bookcase in the hall which held a number of angling, football, gardening and cooking DVDs, a few movies that had been given away in the Sunday papers over the past year or so, and several books, mostly on Quinn's hobbies, but mixed in with book club novels with titles like *Twiddling my Fingers in Timbuktu*, *Dwarf Throwing in Darwin*, or *Blowing Eggs in Uzbekistan*, nestling beside a couple of well-thumbed Mills and Boons.

Upstairs were four bedrooms, the smallest of them set up as a study. The cabinets and drawers stood open, covered with fingerprint powder. A cheap inkjet printer sat on the desk. Banks glanced down at the power socket bar and saw one charger plugged in that wasn't connected to anything. 'Laptop?' he asked Palmer.

'Looks that way. If so, it's gone.'

'Any signs of a desktop?'

'No. That was it.'

'Bugger. No files, no emails, nothing.'

'We could access the server. There could be emails stored there. But someone's been thorough. If there were any portable storage devices, flash drives and the like, they've also been taken.'

'Any prints?'

'Only Quinn's.'

'I'll have a closer look here later. Let's move on.'

Two of the bedrooms were obviously the children's, and had been for a number of years. Now that they were both grown up, they probably just stayed there when they came back from university for the holidays. One was a light airy space containing a storage unit stuffed with old dolls and a bookcase full of classics. Banks pulled out a copy of *Middlemarch* and saw the inscription, 'To Jessica with love from Auntie Jennifer on your 15th birthday.' Banks whistled between his teeth. Reading *Middlemarch* at fifteen was pretty good going; reading *Middlemarch* at any age was pretty good going. Like most people, Banks had watched it on TV.

The second room, which bore a plaque marking it as 'Robbie's Room', was much darker in colour scheme and had little sign of childhood memorabilia other than a collection of model boats, but there were a few festival and concert posters on the walls: Green Man Festival 2010, Glastonbury 2009, Elbow, Kaiser Chiefs, Paolo Nutini. Banks noticed the electric guitar resting against a small amp in one corner. It reminded him of his own son Brian. No doubt Quinn's son owned at least one other guitar, probably acoustic; he wouldn't go off to university for weeks on end without one. There was also a compact CD player, but very few CDs. He probably downloaded most of his music. As for books, there were a few science-fiction and fantasy titles, old copies of *MOJO*, and that was it.

The third bedroom, the largest, clearly belonged to Quinn and his wife. Like the living room, it was tidy, the bed made, no discarded clothing on the floor, but there was more dust on the windowsill. The wardrobe held a hamper full of dirty laundry. Banks wondered what would happen to it now that its owner was dead. Would it ever be washed? Maybe one of Quinn's children would wash it and give it to Oxfam.

'Better go through that lot, too,' Banks said to DS Palmer. 'You never know what people leave in their pockets and put in the wash.'

'Don't worry,' said Palmer. 'We have. Not even so much as a used tissue or bus ticket. And there are no signs of disturbance in any of the bedrooms.'

Banks and Palmer returned to the study. Set aside at the edge of the desk was a small heap of file folders. 'We picked those up off the floor,' Palmer said. 'It's mostly just a lot of general correspondence, day-to-day stuff, bills and so on. We'll take it all in and go through it in detail, but these may be of more immediate interest.'

Banks doubted it. Not if someone had already been through the place first. He picked up the first folder. Harry Lake. Like most good detectives, Quinn supplemented his official notes and reports with his own observations. These often consisted of intuitions, gut feelings and imaginative ramblings that wouldn't make it past his SIO's scrutiny. They might be worth taking back to the station and studying, but Banks wouldn't give them a high priority. If there had been anything of interest to him in Quinn's study, it would be gone now. He flipped through the stack. There was nothing on Warren Corrigan or Stephen Lambert, he noticed, but also very little on Rachel Hewitt, the failure that had apparently haunted him. If Quinn had been in the habit of keeping personal files on all his cases, or at least his major cases, then what was missing would probably reveal far more than what was present, even though a clever villain would know to take a few irrelevant files along with the important one, just to muddy the waters.

Banks picked up some more folders and flipped quickly through them. He found a mix of handwritten notes and printed pages, yellow stickies and file cards, along with the occasional photocopy – a parking ticket, train ticket, passport photo, the usual odds and ends of an investigation. As a matter of routine, he checked the undersides of the drawers and backs of the filing cabinets to see if anything had been taped to them, but found nothing.

One thing he did find, in a folder stuffed with old Visa bills, was a photograph. Either the burglar had seen it and decided it was of no interest to him, or he had missed it. Curious, Banks pulled it out. It was of a young girl, aged about eighteen or nineteen, cropped from a group shot. Her arms were stretched out sideways, as if wrapped around the people on either side of her, both of whom were represented only by their shoulders.

At first Banks felt a tremor of excitement because he thought it might have been the girl in Quinn's photos, but it clearly wasn't her, even allowing for the possibility of disguise. This girl had fine golden-blonde hair down to her shoulders. It looked as if it had been braided then left free to tumble. She had a small nose in the centre of an oval face, an appealing overbite and light blue eyes, set in the most delicate porcelain complexion. The girl in the photo with Quinn was darker-skinned, more exotic, with fuller lips and dark eyes. This one was an English rose. So who was it? She seemed familiar, a face he had seen, perhaps more than once, and he guessed that she was Rachel Hewitt. Keith Palmer couldn't help him. Just in case Banks was completely out on a limb he took the photo downstairs and checked it against the framed family shots he had noticed on the sideboard. It certainly wasn't Quinn's daughter. She had coarser brown hair, was carrying far more weight, and could by no means be said to have a porcelain complexion.

And when he looked up from the family photo, he got the shock of his life to see the same face, this time in the living, breathing flesh, standing right in front of him, a red-faced PC behind her, saying, 'I'm sorry, sir, I couldn't stop her. She says she's Jessica Quinn, DI Quinn's daughter. She lives here.'

'I came as soon as I could,' said Jessica, brushing past Banks into the living room, 'What's going on? What are all those people doing here? Have they been searching the house? Have they been in *my* room?'

Her voice was rising to a hysterical pitch. Banks put his arm on her shoulder, but she shook him off. 'Jessica—'

'You can't do this. You just can't do this. It's an invasion of privacy. My father will . . . my father . . .'

And suddenly she crumpled and fell in tears on the sofa. Banks sat down opposite her in an armchair. It was best to let her cry, he thought, as the great chest-racking sobs came from her, even though she buried her face in a cushion. He gestured for DS Palmer to leave the room and carry on with the search. Jessica was still a little overweight, as she was in the family photo, and the baggy jumper and shapeless peasant skirt she wore didn't flatter her. Her face, when Banks saw it again, was pretty enough, but dotted with teenage acne as well as streaked with tears. Her tangled hair hadn't been washed or brushed for a few days. She seemed to be what his old politically incorrect colleague DS Jim Hatchley would have described as 'a hairy-legged eco-feminist,' though Banks could vouch for neither the legs nor the eco-feminism.

'Jessica,' he said, when she had been quiet for a while, 'I'm sorry. I'm sorry you had to walk in on this. But it has to be done, and quickly.'

Jessica reached into her shoulder-bag for a tissue and rubbed her eyes and nose. 'I know. I'm sorry, too,' she said. 'It was just driving up here all by myself, knowing about Dad . . . it got to me. I just got into a terrible state. I couldn't stop thinking about it. I was lucky I didn't have an accident.'

'One of our cars would have brought you.'

'No, I wanted to drive myself. Really. I needed . . . just to be alone. The last place I wanted to be was in the back of a police car. I used to think it was exciting when I was young, when Dad . . .' She started crying again, more softly this time, and took out another tissue. 'You must think I'm a terrible softie.'

'Not at all,' said Banks. 'Where's your brother?'

'Robbie's on his way. We talked on the mobile. He was just leaving when I got to my turn-off. You know Keele. It's in the middle of bloody nowhere, and he doesn't have a car. I just had to drive along the M62.' Her eyes filled with tears again. 'I can't believe this. How could it happen? First Mum, and now Dad. My God, we're orphans now.' She cried again.

'I know it's a terrible shock,' said Banks, 'but I do need to ask you some questions. How about a cup of tea before we start? It's a bit of a cliché, but I could really do with one myself.'

Banks followed Jessica into the kitchen. He offered to make the tea, but she told him to sit down, she knew where everything was. Banks sat at the solid pine table while Jessica set about boiling the kettle and putting two tea bags into a white teapot with red hearts all over it. The kettle didn't take long.

As she poured the boiling water, Jessica looked at the sink and rubbed her sleeve across her eyes. 'Typical Dad. He just lets things pile up like that. All neat and tidy and clean, of course, but honestly, I mean, who else would just leave a dish rack full of dishes if he knew he was going away for two weeks? And I'll bet he didn't think to empty out the fridge. I don't even dare open it.'

'It's not too bad,' said Banks. 'There's a bit of green stuff here and there, but at least it doesn't smell. The milk's off.' His own fridge went like that occasionally, too, with things changing colour and starting to smell a bit, but he saw no point in admitting that to Jessica.

'*Men.* Just sugar do, then?'

'Please. Two teaspoons.'

The tea ready, Jessica poured, set the two mugs down on the table and slumped in a chair, resting her chin in her hands. 'I just can't get my head around this.' She gave Banks a sudden sharp glance. 'What happened? Will I have to identify the body?'

'Somebody will,' said Banks. 'You or your brother. Don't worry. The family liaison officer will deal with all that. She should be here soon. Didn't they tell you what happened?'

'Only that he was dead.'

'He was murdered, Jessica. That's why we're here. That's why there are men searching the house.'

'Murdered? Dad? But he wasn't even at work. He was . . .'

'I know. He was killed in the grounds of St Peter's. It was quick. He wouldn't have suffered.'

Her eyes brimmed with tears again. 'They always say that. How do you know? I'll bet you suffer a lot if you know you'll be dead in even a split second.'

There was no reply to that. Banks sipped the hot, sweet tea. Just what he needed.

'There's been a break in here,' he said. 'We think it's connected. They've been through your dad's study. Maybe you can help us determine what's missing.'

'I'm only here in the holidays. I wouldn't know what's supposed to be where, especially in Dad's study. None of us were allowed in there.'

'Do you know whether your father owned a laptop?'

'Yes, he did.'

Well, that was one question answered, but it begged another. 'Did he use it much? I'm wondering why he didn't take it with him to St Peter's. I mean, laptops are small and light enough to carry around. That's what they're for. As far as I know, they had Wi-Fi available up there.'

Jessica gave him a sad, indulgent smile. 'Dad was such a Luddite when it came to things like that. Oh, he had one – he could just about do email and stuff like that – but it was always me or Robbie had to sort it out for him whenever we came up. He was always messing it up, getting viruses, ignoring error messages. If something didn't work immediately, he just kept pressing the "enter" key or clicking the mouse. Honestly, he'd have about ten copies of Internet Explorer open at the same time, and he wondered why it was running so slowly. He was hopeless.'

'Did he use it for writing or anything else? Facebook?'

'Writing? Dad hated writing. Reports were the bane of his life. And Facebook ... well, I'd blush if I had to tell you what he thought about social networks. No, if anything, he probably used it a bit for surfing the Internet, you know fishing and gardening sites, that sort of thing. And he did manage to work out Skype so we could talk for free during term time. Half the time he couldn't get the video bit working, though, so it was voice only.'

'Games?'

'I doubt it. He wasn't much of a one for computer games. Now trivia, that's another thing. He probably used Wikipedia a lot.'

Banks smiled. He supposed, then, that there wasn't much, if anything, of value on Quinn's laptop, except, perhaps, for some emails. Whoever had taken it had probably done so as a safety measure, just in case there was something incriminating on it, or because he believed it contained information he wanted. In either case, he was probably out of luck. If Quinn wasn't a big computer fan, they had a far better hope of finding something interesting in his phone call logs than in his emails, Banks reckoned. 'Do you know of anyone who might have wanted to harm your father?' he asked.

'No. I mean, really. I suppose maybe some of those villains he caught. But he was well liked. He didn't have a lot of close friends outside of work. He was a bit of a loner, bit of an anorak, if truth be told. He liked being off by himself fishing and bird-watching. And working on his allotment. I used to go with him and help him sometimes when I was younger, especially on the allotment, but you know . . . you change . . . lose interest . . . grow apart. Robbie used to go to the tarn sailing model boats with him. He used to build them himself. Lovely, some of them, the detail. Now we just tease him about being an old anorak.' She put her hand to her face and stifled a sob. 'Sorry.'

Banks could feel sympathy. His own children had been the same, interested in whatever seven-day wonder he had been passionate about at the time until they were about thirteen, and then they didn't want to know; they just wanted to be off with their friends. He made a mental note to ask Keith Palmer's lads to check out Quinn's allotment. The odds were that he'd have at least a little gardening shed there. It might be just the sort of place to hide something, and the burglar would probably not have known about it.

Jessica's expression had become wistful, and Banks got the impression that she wished she hadn't lost interest in the things that bound her to her father, that she had continued to help him on the allotment and accompany him on fishing trips and bird-watching expeditions, that they hadn't grown apart. But it happens to everyone. There was nothing he could say to her to make her feel better. It was too late now.

His own father had been a keen cyclist in his younger days, Banks remembered, and many was the day Banks had accompanied him on rides beside the Nene, or across the Cambridgeshire flatlands, when he was eleven or twelve. But like his own children, and like Jessica, the older he had got, the less interested he had become in going with his father on bicycle rides. All he wanted to do was hang around with his mates listening to the latest Beatles, Bob Dylan or Animals record. There had been no room for adults and their boring interests in his world. He was lucky his father was still alive – at least they had been able to rebuild a few bridges in the past few years – but they wouldn't be going on any bicycle rides together again.

'It was most likely to do with his work,' Banks said. 'Do you know if he received any threatening letters or phone calls recently?'

'No. But I've been at university since Christmas, except I came home when Mum died, of course, and he didn't mention anything then. He never talked about that stuff at home. His job. Well, hardly ever. Sometimes he'd tell us funny stories about things that happened at the station, but I think he liked to protect us from the bad stuff.'

Exactly as Banks had done with Brian and Tracy. 'So you can't think of anyone who wanted to harm him? He didn't get any threats or anything?'

'Not that I know of.' Jessica cradled her mug in both hands and took a sip.

'I did find one thing you might be able to help me with,' Banks said, going back into the living room for the photo he had left there. He brought it through to the kitchen and turned it around on the table so that Jessica could get a good look. 'Is this Rachel Hewitt?'

'That's Rachel. She's so beautiful, isn't she?' Jessica bit her lower lip, the tears flowing over. 'He could never let it go, you know. Never let *her* go. It's like she was his only failure, and he had to beat himself up with it every time he got a bit down. It used to drive Mum crazy.'

'It wasn't his fault,' said Banks. 'They still haven't found her.'

'That's because she's dead,' said Jessica. 'She was dead right from the start. And if you don't mind my saying so, you're being terribly naive if you think saying it wasn't his fault ever did any good. As far as he was concerned, it *was* his fault. He wasn't entirely logical about it. We tried to tell him, time after time, but it didn't work. Why couldn't they all just believe that she was dead? Why couldn't *he* just believe it? Besides, can you imagine what her life would be like if she'd been abducted by some pervert and kept in a cellar as some sort of sex slave? Or forced into prostitution?'

'Even if he had believed that she was dead,' said Banks, 'it wouldn't have stopped him from doing his job, or from blaming himself. If he was a good copper, he would still have needed to know what happened to her, and why.'

She gave Banks a sharp glance. '*A good copper*. What's that supposed to mean? Anyway, why do you want to know about this? What does any of it have to do with Dad's death?'

'I've got no idea. Probably nothing. The photo was just sitting there in a folder full of Visa bills, with no identification or anything. The name came up before. She seemed familiar . . .'

'She should be. Her face has been plastered over the papers often enough these past six years or so. Still is every now and then, when her parents step up the campaign again.'

Banks could hardly imagine how he would feel if his own daughter disappeared completely without trace in a foreign country, but he had always felt a deep sympathy for the Hewitts and their ongoing grief. They had suffered at the hands of the media, too, and were now caught up as victims in the never-ending phone-hacking scandal, which must make it hurt all over again. Banks was suspicious of 'closure' and all it implied, thought it was some sort of modern psychobabble, but he knew that in their case there could be no rest, no peace, until their daughter's body was recovered and returned home.

'Did your father have much contact with Rachel's family?'

'None. Except when she first disappeared, I suppose.'

'He didn't stay in touch?'

'No. Why would he?'

'No reason. They didn't . . . you know . . . blame him, or anything?'

'He didn't need them to blame him. He managed that all by himself.'

Banks realised that Jessica was probably right. The Rachel Hewitt connection was interesting, but that was all it was, just another item to drop in the bulging file, along with Harry Lake, Stephen Lambert and Warren Corrigan. Soon they would have even more material from West Yorkshire, and a whole host of other names from Quinn's past to sift through. There was nothing more Banks could think of, so he stood up to leave. 'Where are you staying?' he asked Jessica at the door.

'Here. Why? It's not a crime scene, is it?'

'Well, it is, really . . . technically . . . the break-in . . . It's obviously connected with what happened to your father. But the CSIs have already gathered all the evidence they can, and they'll be taking the rest of his papers away. They should be finished here soon.'

'Well . . .?'

'I just thought ... I mean, are you sure you want to stay here? Is there someone I can call for you? A relative? Boyfriend?'

'Thank you for your concern, but I'll be fine. Really. Robbie will be here soon. We'll probably just get pissed.'

A very good idea, Banks thought, but he didn't say so.

3

Banks arrived in his office early on Friday morning after a quiet evening at home listening to Kate Royal, watching the first in the *Treme* series and sipping the best part of a bottle of Rioja. So much for cutting back.

He had phoned Stefan Nowak, the Crime Scene Manager, as the team was packing up at St Peter's around sunset the previous evening. They had finished their search of the woods and lake, and had found no sign of a weapon. They had, however, found a cigarette end close to the body, some synthetic fibres, and traces of what might have been blood from a scratch on the tree trunk where they thought the killer had leaned. There was also a fresh footprint that definitely wasn't Bill Quinn's. Their expert said that, at first glance, it was a common sort of trainer you could buy anywhere, but they might be able to get a bit more detail from it. There was often a correlation between shoe size and height, for example, and measurements could give them at least a working estimate of how tall the person who wore them was, and how much he or she weighed. Any distinguishing marks on one or both of the soles could be as individual as a fingerprint.

DS Keith Palmer and his team had finished searching Bill Quinn's house and allotment in Rawdon, including his garden shed. They had even dug up a good deal of the allotment, but had found nothing.

Banks linked his hands behind his neck, leaned back in his chair and listened to Ravel's 'Gaspard de la Nuit' on Radio

Three's *Breakfast*. As he glanced around his office, he realised that he had been in the same room for over twenty years, and that it had only been redecorated once, as far as he could remember. He didn't much care about the institutional green walls, as they were covered in framed prints and posters for concerts and exhibitions – Hockney's Yorkshire scenes, Miles Davis at Newport, Jimi Hendrix at Winterland, a Chagall poster for the Paris Opera – but he certainly needed a newer and bigger desk, one that didn't require a piece of wadded-up paper under one of its legs. He could do with another filing cabinet, too, he thought, as his gaze settled on the teetering pile of paper on top of the one he had already. A couple of shelves and an extra bookcase wouldn't go amiss, either, and perhaps a chair that was kinder to his back than the antique he was sitting in now. No wonder his neck was starting to play up after long days at the office, especially with all the extra paperwork he seemed to have these days. He'd be in St Peter's soon, himself, if he wasn't careful. At least the heater worked, and the tatty old Venetian blinds had been replaced.

But now was not the time to ask for such things, he knew. He should have made his demands a few years ago, when the police were getting almost everything they asked for. Those days were long gone. Like everywhere else, Eastvale had been recently plagued by twenty per cent cuts across the board and a drastic county reorganisation designed to implement some of those cuts. The three 'Areas' had been replaced by six 'Safer Neighbourhood Commands'. Changes at County HQ in Newby Wiske also meant that the Major Crimes Unit, or Homicide and Major Enquiry Team as it was now known, still operated out of Eastvale, but covered more ground.

The team came under Assistant Chief Constable (Crime) Ron McLaughlin, known as 'Red Ron' because of his leftist leanings, but it was run on a day-to-day basis by Area Commander Catherine Gervaise, and it was now responsible not just for the defunct Western Area, but for the whole county – with the same team strength, and no increase in civilian support staff.

It was time for the nine-thirty briefing, and the team gathered in the boardroom, which despite its modern glass writing board, along with the whiteboard and corkboard, still managed to retain some of its old-fashioned appearance, with the large oval table at its centre, high hard-backed chairs and the portraits of eighteenth- and nineteenth-century wool barons on its walls: red-faced, pop-eyed men with whiskers and tight collars.

Banks took his place nearest the writing boards as the others drifted in, most of them clutching mugs or styrofoam cups of coffee as well as files and notebooks. AC Gervaise had managed to borrow a couple of DCs, Haig and Lombard, from County HQ, but it wasn't a big team, Banks reflected, nowhere near big enough for a major investigation into the murder of a fellow police officer. It would have to be augmented if the scope of the investigation ballooned, as Banks expected it would, unless they caught an early break. He would be especially glad to see Annie Cabbot back, but DS Jim Hatchley, one of the officers Banks had known the longest in Eastvale, had retired as soon as he had done his thirty years, as Banks had always known he would. He missed the lumbering, obstinate sod.

First, he shared what he knew with the team, then asked if they had anything to add. The short answer was that they didn't. Scientific Support were still working on the footprints, Photographic Services had the photographs, and the DNA results from the cigarette end and blood didn't come back anywhere near as quickly as they did on *CSI*. All the specialist was able to tell him so far was that the brand of cigarette was Dunhill, which a few quick inquiries on Winsome's part ascertained was Bill Quinn's brand. There were no other cigarettes found in or near the woods. Obviously the groundsman did a good job.

There was nothing new on the murder weapon, or on the state of Bill Quinn's body, as Dr Glendenning, the Home Office pathologist, was not due to perform the post-mortem until later that afternoon. A list of possible enemies would be on its way up from West Yorkshire sometime later in the day, if they were lucky, and Quinn's bank statements, credit card details and home and mobile calls log should also be arriving before the day was out, again with luck. It was a Friday, so there was always a possibility of delays. Inquiries were being made in the village nearest to St Peter's, as well as at the nearest petrol stations and any other places where strangers were likely to have been spotted. Uniformed officers were canvassing the neighbourhood of Quinn's Rawdon home to find out if anyone had noticed an interloper recently. The interviews at St Peter's had been concluded and had revealed nothing of interest except that Quinn was in the habit of going outside for a smoke before bed each night.

'So it would seem,' Banks summed up after the team had digested all this information, or lack of it, 'that we need to get our fingers out. We're no closer than we were when DI Jenson found the body yesterday morning.'

'We do have the photos, sir,' Winsome pointed out. 'Photographic Services say they're digital, printed on a common or garden inkjet printer, so nothing new there. They're analysing the ink content and pixels for comparison with Quinn's own printer, but it's not an entirely accurate process.'

'Their thinking being?'

'That Quinn may have received the photos as JPEG images and printed them out himself. Which also means there might be more.'

'And we might be able to trace them to a sender?'

'If we had them,' said Winsome, 'then it's possible they could be traced to a specific computer.'

'But we don't.'

'No.'

'Well, that's one dead end,' Banks said. 'I don't think it really matters whether he printed them himself or someone sent them by post, unless we have the envelope, and it has a postmark and prints on it, which we don't.'

Winsome stood up and started handing out 8 x 10 prints. 'They also came up with this enhanced blow-up image of the girl from the restaurant photo,' she said. 'It was the best they could do. They're still working on the background to see if they can get any points of reference.'

'Any prints on the photos?'

'Only the victim's.'

Banks examined the blow-up. It was a little grainy, but Photographic Services had done a great job, and he believed that someone could recognise the girl from it. 'Excellent,' he said, then addressed the two young DCs on loan. 'Haig and Lombard, I want you to make it your priority to check the photo of this girl against escort agency files, Internet dating services, and whatever else you think is relevant. You can use the spare desks in the squad room. We've no idea when or where the pictures were taken, of course, but my thinking is sometime over the last two or three years.'

'It sounds like a long job, sir,' mumbled Haig, the bulky one.

'Better get on with it, then. You never know, you might even find you enjoy it. But be careful. If either one of you comes back with a smile on his face and a cigarette in his mouth, he'll be in deep trouble.'

Everyone laughed. Haig and Lombard exchanged dark glances, took two copies of the photo and left the room.

'Anything else?' Banks asked Winsome.

'We've just about finished interviewing the patients and staff at St Peter's,' she said. 'Nothing so far. Barry Sadler and Mandy Pemberton were the last up, but neither of them saw or heard anything.'

'Are they telling the truth?'

'I think so, sir. I interviewed Barry Sadler, and he's very cut up. He's an ex-copper. The nurse has a clean record and a spotless reputation. Of course, we can always have another go at them if something else turns up pointing in that direction, but I think it's doubtful.'

Banks took the photograph of Rachel Hewitt from his brief-case and stuck it on the glass alongside the blow-up of the unknown girl with Quinn. He still didn't understand why the Deputy Chief Commissioner had seen the necessity of spending close to £500 on a glass writing board when the white-board worked perfectly well. Basically, you could write and rub out and stick pictures on it, which was all you needed to do. He'd probably seen one on *Law & Order UK* or some such television programme and thought it was a necessity for the modern police force.

'This may mean nothing at all,' Banks said, 'but Bill Quinn worked on the Rachel Hewitt case for a short while in the summer of 2006, not long after she was reported missing, and he had this photograph in a file in his study. Quinn spent a week in Tallinn helping with the investigation there and carried out background checks into Rachel and her friends. Both DI Blackstone in Leeds and Quinn's daughter said the case haunted him.'

'Was it ever closed?' asked Winsome.

'No,' Banks said. 'Just inactive. Officially, Rachel Hewitt is still a missing person, but there haven't been any fresh leads for six years – there weren't any leads at all – so until new information comes in, there's nothing more can be done, and the investiga-tion has been mothballed. She'd be twenty-five now.'

'Surely she's dead?' said Doug Wilson.

'In all likelihood. But families don't give up that easily, Doug. Think of the McCanns. Little Madeleine's been gone for years now, but they won't let themselves believe that she's dead, even though, compared to the alternatives, some might say death would be a blessing. They can't. Rachel Hewitt's family is the same. They won't give up. They won't accept that their daughter is dead. Anyway, as I said, it's probably nothing, but at some point we'll have to talk to the parents and friends. In the meantime, I'd like one of you to put together a dossier on Rachel Hewitt. Clippings, photos, names, whatever you can find on the investigation. There should be plenty. Gerry, maybe you can get started on that?'

DC Geraldine Masterson scribbled something down on her pad. 'Yes, sir.'

Banks turned to Winsome. 'I think in the meantime you and I should get back to St Peter's and see if we can wrap up there,' he said. 'The rest of you all have your actions and TIEs to be getting on with. Doug, I want you here when the list of Bill Quinn's possible old enemies and his phone records arrive, and I want you to head the examination. Coordinate with DI Ken Blackstone at Millgarth. Ken mentioned a bloke called Corrigan. Warren Corrigan. He's got his finger in a few pies, all of them nasty, but basically he's a loan shark. Ask around. See if he has any sort of presence in these parts. We want to know who Quinn has been talking to lately, and who's been talking to him. Keep an open mind about the old cases. Something might leap out at you, but you can't rely on that. You can probably forget the junkies and alcoholic wife-beaters – they probably wouldn't even remember making threats, let alone have what it takes to stalk and kill someone with a crossbow – but give them all at least a passing glance. Anything that strikes you as odd, interesting, possible, make a note of it. Gerry here will give you a hand in her spare time. If she has any.'

'Yes, sir.' Doug glanced over at DC Masterson, who tapped the end of her pencil on her notepad.

'And we also need to find out if Bill Quinn had ever worked with or had any close connection with anyone staying at St Peter's. Or if anyone there had a connection with someone he put away, someone who threatened him, had a grudge. You might as well include the staff, too. I realise this all adds up to casting a very wide net indeed, but we've either got to rule all these things out, or find a link to Quinn's murder somewhere, if we're to narrow it down to a viable line of inquiry. I shouldn't have to remind you that Bill Quinn was one of our own and that we'll be under extreme scrutiny on this. Clear?'

Everyone nodded, glum expressions on their faces. They knew what it meant: say goodbye to the weekend, and all leave is cancelled.

'Sir?' said Winsome.

'Yes.'

'Well, I've just been thinking. The choice of weapon, the murder in the woods . . . Could we be looking for someone with hunting experience? Hunting and tracking? We know that Quinn himself was into outdoors stuff – angling and gardening, specifically – so he might have known people who were hunters, who belonged to the same clubs or societies he did.'

'That's a good point, Winsome,' said Banks. 'Doug and Gerry, you should keep an eye open for anything like that, too. Any hunters, flag them. Check on Quinn's friends outside the force, too, if he had any, and any organisations he belonged to. Also,' Banks went on, 'one of you will need to check sources for crossbows and bolts, including online. And I want someone to search for any similar crimes, anything involving a crossbow, in fact, over, say, the past five years. OK?'

'Yes, sir,' said DC Wilson.

Before the meeting broke up, the door opened and Area Commander Gervaise walked in with another woman behind her. Late thirties or early forties, Banks guessed, a tall attractive blonde, elegant suit, the skirt ending just above her knees, black tights – no Primark for her – a trim, lithe figure with gentle curves, a smattering of freckles across her small nose, intelligent green eyes, regal bearing. Her blonde tresses were piled and coiled on top, giving the impression of casual simplicity, though Banks guessed the haircut was expensive and the arrangement took a lot of time. She seemed a little nervous, he thought.

'If you'd all just hang on for a minute,' Gervaise said, avoiding Banks's gaze, 'I'd like to introduce Inspector Joanna Passero. Joanna is from Professional Standards, and she'll be working with you all very closely on this case.'

'The rat squad,' Banks muttered.

Gervaise raised an eyebrow. 'What was that?'

'Nothing,' said Banks. 'Welcome to the squad. Pleased to meet you, Inspector Passero.'

'Likewise,' said Inspector Passero. 'Call me Joanna.' Even in those few words, Banks thought he noticed a hint of a Scottish accent, which went quite against her Italian surname, as did her blonde good looks. Still, he thought, remembering Bill Forsyth's *Comfort and Joy*, with its Glasgow ice-cream wars, a lot of Italians had settled in Scotland over the years.

'In my office, Alan,' said Gervaise. 'The rest of you can get back to work.'

Banks gestured for Winsome to wait for him and followed Gervaise and Joanna Passero down the corridor.

The three of them made themselves comfortable around Gervaise's circular glass table and drank coffee made from Gervaise's machine. Banks felt lucky; it was his second cup in two days. On the other hand, when he realised why Inspector

Joanna Passero was present, he didn't feel so lucky after all. She crossed her long, black-stockinged legs and leaned back with the mug in her hand as if she were at her book club, or a Women's Institute coffee morning. A half smile played around her full pink lips. Perhaps she was enjoying Banks's obvious discomfort, he thought, or perhaps she had noticed his stolen glances at the swell of her breasts under the finely tailored jacket, or the shapely ankle of her crossed leg.

There was a Nordic aspect to her beauty, despite her Italian surname and Scottish accent. All that lovely blonde coolness, Banks thought. Alfred Hitchcock would have loved her. And tied twenty birds to her clothes with long nylon threads.

'You could have given me some warning,' Banks said to Gervaise. 'You made me look a right twat back there at the briefing.'

'That wasn't my intention,' said Gervaise. 'The decision's just been made. I've been at a breakfast meeting with ACC McLaughlin and the Chief Constable over at County HQ, and we are all agreed that, given the circumstances of DI Bill Quinn's murder, and what was discovered in his room, we need a representative from Professional Standards on board. ACC McLaughlin suggested Joanna, who is relatively new to the county, but comes along with an excellent pedigree from Thames Valley. I brought her back here with me. I'm sure she'll be a valuable addition to the team.'

'Valuable in what way, ma'am?' Banks asked.

'I've told you, less of the ma'am. We can be informal in here.'

'Valuable in what way?'

Gervaise deferred to Inspector Passero. 'Joanna?'

Joanna Passero held Banks's gaze as she leaned forward and set her coffee mug down on the table. There was a pink lipstick stain on the rim. Banks realised that he was being outflanked by two strong women, one above him in rank, and the other with a cool demeanour and any number of little feminine wiles up her sleeve. He also realised that there was probably nothing he could do about any of it. Once Gervaise's mind was made up, that was it, and she had the backing of ACC McLaughlin and the Chief Constable. This meeting was a mere formality, a courtesy, perhaps. Banks wasn't going to get Joanna Passero sent back to Newby Wiske or Thames Valley, no matter how much he might try. About the only thing he could hope to get out of this meeting was to escape with his dignity intact and maybe gain a few minor concessions. But he wasn't going to give up without a struggle. He listened as Joanna Passero spoke in her lilting Edinburgh accent.

'I'm sure you'll agree with me,' she began, 'that in the light of the compromising photographs you found in DI Quinn's possession, implicating him in the possible corruption of a minor, not to say grave dereliction of duty, this investigation goes somewhat beyond the norm.'

'There's no evidence that the girl was a minor.'

'Oh, for goodness' sake.' She gave an impatient twitch of her head. 'Look at her. Just look at her.'

'It's possible that DI Quinn was being blackmailed because of those pictures,' Banks said. 'It's also possible that he was set up.'

'In what way?'

'If you look at the way he's lying in that bedroom photo, you can see he seems quite out of it. Maybe he was drugged?'

'Or drunk.'

'Possibly. But—'

'He didn't appear drugged in the bar, or in the restaurant. In fact, he seemed to be very much enjoying himself.'

'And where's the law against having a drink or a meal with an attractive young woman? If he was drugged, have you considered that the restaurant or the bar may well have been where the drug was administered? In his drink or his food? She may even have been as much a victim as he was. We just don't know. This is all a bit premature, in my opinion.'

'There's no point you two arguing back and forth about this,' Gervaise said, glancing first at Banks. 'Alan, you have to admit that the whole business is extremely fishy. The photos, the murder method, everything. You said yourself that you think DI Quinn might have been blackmailed because of the girl.'

'But we're just starting out on our investigation,' Banks argued. 'We don't really know anything yet. These are just theories.'

'That's why I want Joanna in right at the beginning.'

'To do what?'

'My job,' said Joanna. 'What do you think? I'm happy to tag along and observe and ask what questions I think necessary. Believe me, DCI Banks, I have no intention of getting in the way of this investigation, or of slowing it down in any way. I want the same as you. A result. I also want to know if there is any hint of wrongdoing on the part of the police. Is that so unreasonable?'

'Not when you put it like that. But this is already a complex investigation, and I don't want to be in the position of having to describe or explain my every move and decision to someone else. I also don't want someone looking over my shoulder and judging my methods all the time.'

Banks didn't think he had anything to fear from Professional Standards. Whatever his methods, whatever corners he cut and instincts he followed, he stayed within the boundaries of the law. Usually. He noticed once again the intelligent pale green eyes, the expensive blonde hair, the freckles, straight nose, full lips lightly brushed with pink lipstick. She held his gaze without flinching. She would probably be formidable in an interview room, or at a poker table.

'I understand that,' said Joanna, picking up her coffee again, flicking him a Princess Di upwards glance, 'and I can only repeat that I have no intention of slowing things down, or of looking over your shoulder. I know all about your methods, DCI Banks. They're legendary at County HQ. But you're not my brief. DI William Quinn is.'

'But you *will* slow things down, whether you intend to or not. Your presence will affect my whole team.'

'I can only repeat: neither you nor your team is my brief.' She paused and shot him a cool glance. 'Why? What have you all got to hide?'

'Oh, come off it. You know perfectly well what I mean. When the taxman calls, you don't expect it's about a rebate, do you? We're working at cross purposes here. I'm after the person who murdered Bill Quinn. Period. You want the dirt on Quinn. You'll be trying to prove him corrupt or perverted, or both. I'm not saying you shouldn't be, or that his reputation doesn't deserve to be trashed if you find evidence he was bent. I have no more tolerance for bent coppers than you have. But as yet, there's no evidence that Bill Quinn was crooked, and plenty that he was murdered. We're not searching for the same thing at all.'

'I had hoped you would be more understanding, Alan,' Gervaise chipped in. 'Quite frankly, I'm disappointed in you. I realise that some of your arguments are not without merit, but no matter what you say, you will do this. There's no point in getting off on the wrong foot. This thing is going to happen. I say it's going to happen. ACC McLaughlin says it's going to happen. The Chief Constable says it's going to happen. The purpose of calling this little tête-a-tête right here and now was to see that it happens in the spirit of cooperation and amicability. Is that too much to ask? If Bill Quinn were alive, and you found what you found hidden in that book in his room, with all its implications, what do you think would happen then?'

'I presume there would be an investigation by Professional Standards, probably in the form of Inspector Passero here. But that's not the case. Bill Quinn was *murdered.* That changes things. Please excuse me if I sound dismissive, but that makes it a fully fledged murder investigation, not a hunt for a bent copper.'

'But it's both,' argued Joanna. 'And they may be connected. Can't you see that?'

'Right at the moment, all I can see is that the murder investigation takes precedence, and I want everyone on my team to have some expertise in that particular area. Have you ever been involved in a murder investigation before, Inspector Passero?'

'I don't see how that's relevant.' Joanna paused, licked her lips and inclined her head slowly. Her voice softened. 'Of course, I understand what you're saying,' she went on. 'Don't think for a moment that I don't know what you all think of Professional Standards. I've heard all the insults you could possibly imagine, and more. Aren't we the "rat squad", which you called me just a few minutes ago? It's not very nice or polite, but I can live with it. Like you, we have a job to do, and it's an important job, even if it is an unpopular one. In this case, we have a murdered detective who may or may not have been having sex with an underage girl, but who most certainly had in his possession proof that he was sexually involved with someone other than his wife. And that proof, as you have already pointed out yourself, suggests that he was subject to blackmail. Whether he paid this blackmailer in cash or in inside information, it makes no difference. We're talking about possible police corruption here, and what one man does taints us all.' She glanced at AC Gervaise, and Banks noticed Gervaise give an almost imperceptible nod. 'There's been rumours, as you probably know,' Joanna went on. 'Rumours of corruption, of a "bent copper", as you call it. Now this. No smoke without fire, I say.'

'So that's why you're here,' said Banks.

'It's one reason. All I'm saying is that his murder and the discovery of the photos makes that possibility more . . .'

'More possible?'

'I was going to say more realistic.'

Banks held his hands up. 'Fine,' he said. 'Fine. I agree. As I said, I'd no more turn a blind eye to police corruption than you would. But can't we give the poor sod the benefit of the doubt? He's not even in his grave yet, and we're already acting as if he were a criminal. What about his children?' He glanced towards Gervaise, who remained expressionless. 'If I find out anything that points towards Quinn being the one involved in corrupt or criminal activities, the first whiff of a scandal, you'll be the first to know. And Inspector Passero here. I promise. All right? Now can't you just leave us alone to get on with our murder investigation? It's complicated enough already.'

'There's no negotiating on this,' said Gervaise. 'I told you. Respect my honesty and directness in calling this meeting, and respond with a little generosity of your own. You know it's the right move.'

'What about Annie? DI Cabbot. Where does she fit in with all this?'

Gervaise sighed. 'DI Cabbot will be back at work on Monday, as I told you yesterday. According to all the reports I've read, she's fit for duty, so that's exactly what she'll be doing. Her normal duties.'

'Not deskbound?'

'ACC McLaughlin has met with her doctors, and they have assured him that she's ready for a full return to duty. Personally, I still think she should take it easy for a while and get some counselling, but that's only me.'

'She's been taking it easy for six months.'

Annie would be livid about Joanna Passero, Banks thought. She would be convinced that the Professional Standards officer was being set up as her replacement on the team, perhaps even that they were going to get rid of her after she'd almost sacrificed her life for the job. Not just for the job, but for Banks's daughter Tracy, who had also risked a great deal herself to save Annie's life.

For the moment, though, Annie wasn't the main issue; Joanna Passero was. Banks knew that he couldn't trust her, that he would have to be constantly on guard, but he also knew, as he had known going into the meeting, that he had no choice in the matter. It would never do to be too nice to Professional Standards, certainly not in public, and there may be one or two times ahead when he might want to hold his cards close to his chest, and he would do so. He wasn't going to make things easy for her. At least she was a great improvement on that old fat bastard Superintendent Chambers, who had retired due to ill health after Christmas, thank God. It was politic, he thought, to offer a tentative olive branch.

'OK,' he said. 'Let's assume that we work together.'

Joanna Passero's expression indicated that there was no 'let's assume' about it, but that she was willing to listen to what he had to say for the sake of politeness.

'How's it going to work?' Banks asked. 'I mean, I'm still Senior Investigating Officer on this case, right?' He glanced at Gervaise. 'What does that make Inspector Passero? Deputy?'

'No,' said Gervaise. 'DI Cabbot will be your DIO, as usual. As I said, Inspector Passero in on board to investigate Bill Quinn. She's attached to your team as an advisor and as an observer.'

'That certainly complicates things,' said Banks.

'No, it doesn't,' said Joanna. 'It means I won't get under your feet. Why don't we just see how it works out first before coming to any conclusions? If my participation causes problems that jeopardise your investigation, or interferes in any way with the swift progress or smooth running of the operation, then we'll re-evaluate and find some other way of uncovering the bad apple.'

Gervaise looked at Banks. 'Can't say fairer than that, can you, Alan?'

Banks sat for a moment, feeling neither defeated nor victorious, then he leaned forward, fully aware he was inviting the wolf into the fold, and offered Joanna his hand. 'Welcome to the team,' he said. 'You'd better come and meet the others, get up to speed.'

'You know,' Banks said, turning down the volume on Anna Calvi's 'Baby It's You' as they approached the roundabout before St Peter's, 'I've been thinking. Our killer obviously didn't walk here, and I very much doubt that he parked his car out front.'

'Which means,' Winsome said, 'that he must have found a nice, quiet out of the way spot to leave it not too far away.'

'Exactly. Preferably somewhere that couldn't be seen from the road. The centre's less than a hundred yards past this roundabout, which is an easy enough walk. There are no major roads feeding into it, they're all B roads, so let's go and see what we can find.'

'But what about Inspector Passero?' Banks was driving Winsome in his Porsche, and Joanna Passero was following in a red Peugeot.

'I'm sure she'll be able to keep up with us.'

Instead of taking the exit to St Peter's, which was the first one off the roundabout, Banks took the third, which headed in the opposite direction from the centre entirely. He saw Joanna's Peugeot in his rear-view mirror. She started to turn off at the St Peter's exit, then swerved when she saw what he'd

done, skidded, and did a 180-degree turn back to the roundabout to follow him, barely missing a white delivery van, which
was going too fast. Its horn blared.

The Peugeot seemed to stall in the roundabout for a few
moments, then it started up again and followed them.

There were no hiding places along the stretch of road Banks
had chosen, and after about a quarter of a mile, he used a
lay-by to do a U turn and headed back towards the roundabout. Joanna Passero whizzed by on the other side, and he saw
her slow down behind him, then pull into the lay-by and turn
around to follow. Winsome didn't seem very amused. 'What's
wrong?' Banks asked. 'Aren't you having fun?'

'If you want my opinion,' Winsome said, 'this is very silly,
dangerous, and childish. Sir.'

'Ouch. That puts me in my place.' Banks turned into the
roundabout and took the only other exit he hadn't explored,
again the third, which took him away at a right angle from the
road on which the centre was located, a continuation of the
road he had first come in on.

Winsome folded her arms. This time, less than twenty yards
along the road, on the opposite side, Banks saw a rough track
leading off at a sharp angle. There were high trees on both
sides, and the lane was so narrow that it would have been
impossible for two cars to pass without one backing up. There
was nothing coming on the road, so Banks turned into the
lane, blocking the entrance with the Porsche. He hadn't seen
Joanna behind him, and assumed that she either hadn't
reached the roundabout yet or had given up and gone on to
St Peter's by herself.

Banks didn't want to drive any further in, just in case this
was the right place and there were tyre tracks or other evidence.
He and Winsome got out of the car and walked carefully along
the edge of the rutted track, beside the hedgerow. There was
no drystone wall on either side. When they stopped a few

yards in, they couldn't see, or be seen from, the road at all, but they could see some tyre tracks. The uneven surface was just stones and dirt, no doubt intended for farm vehicles, though there was no farmhouse in sight. It would have made the perfect hiding place for the killer's car after dark. Farmers don't usually drive tractors around country lanes at that time of night. Banks wasn't even sure whether tractors had headlights.

'A hundred yards walk from the centre,' he said, 'hidden from the road by trees, very little traffic. I think we've found the spot, Winsome. It would have been very bad luck indeed if he'd been spotted here, and we can assume that he probably had a contingency plan. Professionals usually do. No prints. Car rented under an assumed name.'

Banks heard a car screech to a halt on the road behind his Porsche, then the sound of a car door slamming. Joanna Passero appeared in the entrance to the lane and started walking towards them. About the same time that Banks held up his hand and called to her to stay back, she went over on her ankle and cursed, then grabbed on to a roadside tree branch to keep her balance and cried out again. Thorns. Banks started to walk back towards the main road, still keeping close to the hedgerow. It wasn't long before he came up to a fuming Joanna Passero standing, or rather hopping, at the entrance to the track, one leg bent up behind her, like a stork's, grasping a shiny black shoe in one hand and wobbling dangerously. 'Banks, you bastard! You just made me break a bloody heel! Do you know how much these shoes cost? What the hell do you think you're playing at?'

'Just doing my job,' said Banks. He approached her gingerly and explained about the need for the killer to hide his car, and this being a likely spot.

As he talked, she visibly relaxed and leaned against his car, keeping her stockinged foot just above the rough surface. 'You could have bloody warned me,' she said. 'That road surface is lethal.'

'I'm sorry. I only thought of it when we got to the roundabout. It's like that in a real investigation sometimes. Anyway, I think we should get the CSIs down here. We found some tyre tracks, and there may be footprints. We'll stay here and protect the scene. Would you mind driving on to St Peter's and asking the lads to send someone over asap?' He glanced down at her foot. 'Sorry about the heel. I've got some old wellies in the boot, if that's any help, though they might be a bit big for you. How's your ankle? Not sprained or anything, I hope? Can I help you back to your car?'

Joanna glared, as if she wanted to throttle Banks. She turned and hopped back to her Peugeot with as much dignity as she could manage and drove off in a spray of roadside dirt and gravel.

'See what I mean?' said Winsome, standing behind him, arms folded. 'Childish.'

'Who?' said Banks, with a straight face. 'Me or her?'

The mortuary, along with Dr Glendenning's recently modernised post-mortem suite, was in the basement of the old Eastvale Infirmary. Banks thought it would be a good idea to take Inspector Passero along. She probably wouldn't learn anything of relevance to her case, but if she was working with Banks, it was time she got used to the late hours. And the blood and guts. It was after five on a Friday afternoon, and a Professional Standards officer would likely be well on her way home by now, if not sitting back with her feet up in front of the telly with a large gin and tonic. Or was Joanna more the cocktail party and theatre type? Probably.

She turned up in a new pair of flat-heeled pumps that she had clearly bought that afternoon at Stead and Simpson's in the market square. No fancy Italian shoe shops in Eastvale.

The new shoes didn't make as much noise as Banks's black slip-ons as the two of them walked down the high, gloomy corridor to their appointment. The walls were covered in old green tiles. DC Gerry Masterson had told Banks earlier that Robbie Quinn had been brought in to identify his father's body that morning, so the formalities were done with for the moment. Dr Glendenning had the coroner's permission to proceed with his post-mortem.

Banks gave a slight shudder, the way he always did in the Victorian infirmary, and it wasn't caused by the permanent chill that seemed to infuse the air as much as by the smell of formaldehyde and God only knew what else.

'Something wrong?' asked Joanna, her voice echoing from the tiles.

'No. This place always gives me the creeps, that's all. It's probably haunted. There never seems to be anyone else here. And I can just imagine all the patients back in Victorian times, the primitive instruments and lack of anaesthetic. It must have been butchery. A nightmare. Corridors of blood.'

'You've got imagination, I'll give you that,' Joanna said. 'But you must have been misinformed. They had anaesthetics in Victorian times. At least they used chloroform or ether from the 1850s on, and I think it said over the door this place wasn't built until 1869. I also think you'll find the instruments were perfectly adequate for their purposes back then.'

'University education?' Banks said.

'Something like that.'

'Well, it still gives me the creeps. Here we are.'

They donned the gowns and masks provided by one of Dr Glendenning's young assistants and joined the doctor, who was just about to begin.

'Tut tut, tardy again, Banks,' said Dr Glendenning. 'You know how I hate tardiness. And me working late on a Friday especially to accommodate you.'

'Sorry, doc. You know I'm eternally grateful.'

'Who's your date?'

Banks glanced towards Joanna. 'This is Inspector Joanna Passero. Professional Standards.'

'In trouble again, Banks?'

'She's here to observe.'

'Of course.' Dr Glendenning scrutinised Joanna, who blushed a little. 'Ever been to a post-mortem before, lassie?'

'No,' she said. 'I can't honestly say that I have.'

'Aye . . . well, at least you're a fellow Scot, by the sound of you.'

'Edinburgh.'

'Good. Excellent. Just try not to be sick on the floor.'

'Now you've got the Scottish mutual admiration society well and truly off the ground,' said Banks, 'do you think you could get started, doc? We've still got a murder to investigate.'

Dr Glendenning scowled at Banks. 'Sassenach.' Then he winked at Joanna, who smiled. He adjusted his microphone, called over his first assistant and took the scalpel she handed him. Quinn's clothes were already lying on a table by the wall. They would be searched and put into labelled paper bags – not plastic, which didn't breathe and caused mould to grow on moist fabrics – and sent over to Evidence, signed for at every stage of the way to ensure chain of custody.

Before beginning his incision to get at Quinn's insides, Glendenning studied the external details of the body, had his assistant take a number of photographs, then he leaned over and slowly pulled out the crossbow bolt, which had already been tested for prints, to no avail. There was no blood, of course, as Quinn's heart had stopped pumping some time ago, but the sucking sound it made when it finally came out made Banks feel queasy, nonetheless. He glanced at Joanna from the corner of his eye. She wasn't showing any reaction.

She must be pretty good at hiding her feelings, Banks thought, though maybe you didn't need feelings to work for Professional Standards.

Dr Glendenning laid the bolt down next to a ruler fixed to one of the lab tables. 'A twenty-inch Beman ICS LightningBolt,' he said. 'Carbon, not aluminium, in my opinion. That's fairly common, I should say.'

'How do you know the make?' Banks asked.

'It says so right there, down the shaft. Now, a lot depends on the power of the crossbow your man was using, but you're generally talking a hundred-and-fifty-pound draw, maybe even as much as two hundred pounds these days, so I think if I take the measurement of how deep it went into him and an average of the bow's pressure, then we might get an approximation of the distance it was fired from.'

'We think it was about fifty or sixty feet,' said Banks.

Dr Glendenning stared at him. 'Is that scientifically accurate or just pure guesswork, laddie?'

'Well,' said Banks, 'it's about the distance between where the evidence shows the shooter was standing and where the victim fell. He might also have nudged the bolt on the ground when he fell forward and pushed it in a bit further. That's why it always pays to attend the scene.'

Dr Glendenning narrowed his eyes. 'You can't miss at that range if you know what you're doing and have a decent weapon. Even in the dark. I'll let you know when the calculations are done.' He went back to the body, measured and took swabs from the wound, probed it and muttered his findings into his microphone.

A lot of what happened at post-mortems, Banks often found, was simply a matter of restating the obvious, but once in a while something knocked you for six, which was why it was a good idea for the SIO to attend. This time, however, everything was pretty much as he had expected it to be. Dr

Glendenning sorted through the stomach contents – chicken casserole, chips and peas, followed by apple pie and ice cream – and agreed with Dr Burns about time of death, placing it at between 11 p.m. Wednesday evening and 1 a.m. Thursday morning, on the basis of digestion. The internal organs were weighed and sectioned for tox screening. Apart from Quinn's tarry lungs, on which Glendenning could hardly comment, being a smoker himself, and his liver being a bit enlarged, on which Banks certainly wouldn't be so hypocritical as to pass judgement, everything was in tip top shape. Quinn was no athlete, but he was fit enough, and his heart had been in good working order until the crossbow bolt had pierced it. Both kidneys, and all the other various important bits and pieces Dr Glendenning had removed, had also been up to par. If he hadn't been murdered, Dr Glendenning ventured, he would probably have lived another thirty years or more if he'd stopped smoking. Every once in a while, Banks would sneak another glance at Joanna, but she seemed quite impassive, fascinated by the whole thing, if anything, and as icily cool as ever.

'So the cause of death is?' Banks asked as Dr Glendenning's assistant closed up.

'Oh, didn't I say? How remiss of me. Well, barring any surprises from toxicology, he died of a crossbow bolt through the heart. It pierced the aorta, to be exact, just above the pulmonic valve. Death would have been as instantaneous as it gets, the chest cavity filled with blood, breathing impossible, no blood flow. A matter of seconds. You'll have my report in a day or two. Tox should take about a week.'

'Thank you, doc,' said Banks.

'My pleasure. And charmed to meet you, ma'am,' the doctor said, giving a little bow to Joanna, who put her hand to her mouth to stifle a giggle, or perhaps a gagging reaction, Banks thought. She seemed anxious to get out of the post-mortem suite, at any rate.

'Fancy a drink?' Banks asked when they were back in the corridor. 'I must admit, I always do after a PM. Or is that an arrestable offence in Professional Standards?'

'Why not?' said Joanna, glancing at her watch. 'The sun's well over the yardarm. You obviously don't know me very well.'

The Unicorn was just across the road. It wasn't one of Banks's favourite pubs, but it would do, and luckily it was still too early for the noisy crowd that filled the place on a Friday and Saturday night. At least the landlord served a passable pint of Black Sheep, if Banks remembered correctly.

'What would you like?' he asked Joanna at the bar.

'I'll have a brandy please. No ice.'

Banks's eyes widened. He'd pegged her as a white wine spritzer kind of woman, and definitely not on duty, even if she turned a blind eye to him. Then he realised they weren't on duty. 'Soda?'

'Just as it comes, please.' She seemed amused by his surprise, but said nothing except, 'You bring the drinks and I'll take that table over there by the window, shall I?'

Banks paid for the drinks and carried them over.

'I see you got some new shoes,' he said, sitting down.

Joanna stretched out her legs. Banks admired them, as he thought he was intended to do. 'Had to, didn't I? It's such a hard job to dress for. You never know what sort of garden path you're going to be led up from one day to the next. Or country lane.'

'What do you mean?'

Joanna took a sip of brandy and leaned forward, her elbows on the table. 'Oh, come off it, DCI Banks. Don't play the innocent with me. You spin me around the roundabout, you make me break my heel, then you drag me off to a post-mortem thinking it'll make me sick all over the nice tiled floor. Isn't that true? Wasn't that the idea?'

'But you weren't sick, were you? You didn't even flinch.'

'Don't sound so disappointed.' She sipped some brandy and grinned. 'My mother's a cardiovascular surgeon – was, she's retired now – one of the best in the country. She often invited me to watch her operate when she thought I was old enough. I've seen more operations than you've put villains away.'

'But you said . . .'

'I said this was my first post-mortem. That's true. But I've seen plenty of by-passes, valve replacements, and even a couple of heart transplants. Beats telly. There was a time when I seriously thought of becoming a surgeon myself, but I don't have the hands for it.' She held them up, but Banks had no way of telling what was wrong with them. They didn't seem to be shaking or anything. He tried to stop his jaw dropping, then he started to laugh. He couldn't help it.

She let him laugh for a few moments, tolerant and slightly bemused, then, when he had finished, she said, 'Can we please just stop it now? Bury the hatchet. Whatever. It's been a crap day so far. Do you think you could just lighten up a bit and stop treating me as your enemy? We both want the truth behind DI Quinn's murder, right? If he was the rotten apple, I'm sure you want to know as much as I do. So why can't we work together? I honestly can't afford a new pair of shoes every day, for a start. And I'm not trying to replace Annie Cabbot. I'm sorry she got shot, but it wasn't my fault. At least she's still alive. I had a partner I grew to trust and like very much once, before I came to Professional Standards. Can you just give me the benefit of the doubt? If Quinn was bent, I'll need to report it. I won't lie about that. If he's innocent, then his memory remains unsullied, he has a hero's funeral, twenty-one gun salute, whatever, and his reputation has nothing to fear from me. How about it?'

'Your partner? What happened?'

Joanna paused and sipped some more brandy. 'He died,' she said finally. 'Was killed, actually. Shot by a bent cop trying to avoid being exposed. Ironic, really. It was someone Johnny trusted, someone he was trying to help.'

Banks remained silent and drank his beer. There wasn't much to say after that.

Joanna's mobile hiccupped. A text. She took it out of her bag and glanced at it, frowned briefly, then stuck it back in her handbag without replying.

'Anything important?' Banks asked. 'Bad news? Your husband?'

Joanna shook her head and finished her drink. 'What now?' she asked.

Banks looked at his watch. 'I don't know about you,' he said, 'but I'm going to call in at the station and see if there are any developments, then I'm heading home.'

She got to her feet. 'I'll come with you,' she said. Then paused. 'At least, as far as the station.'

Banks was sitting on a wicker chair in the conservatory, feet up on the low table, sipping a Malbec and listening to June Tabor sing 'Finisterre'. Only one shaded lamp was lit, and its dim orange-tinged light seemed to emphasise the vast darkness outside. A strong breeze had whipped up, and now it was lashing rain against the windows. April showers. Fortunately, the CSIs had finished their investigation of the St Peter's grounds and covered over the lane where Banks and Winsome had found the tyre tracks.

Banks thought about Joanna for a moment, how she had become more human to him when they had a drink together in The Unicorn and she told him about her mother the surgeon and her partner who got shot. Was it all just a ploy to gain his sympathy, to lull him into being careless and weak? He didn't know. There was something likeable about her.

Annie Cabbot, he remembered, had worked Professional
Standards for a while a few years ago, and it hadn't turned
her into a monster.

Banks tried to put Joanna Passero and the case out of his
mind for the time being. June Tabor was singing 'The Grey
Funnel Line', the dark warmth of her voice filling the room.
He sipped his wine and abandoned himself to the music. It
was easy enough to imagine that he was out at sea, here in the
semi-dark surrounded by glass, the wild night outside, the
wind howling and rain lashing.

He had just reached for the bottle to refill his glass when the
doorbell rang. It made him jump. He glanced at his watch.
Close to ten. Who on earth could be calling at this time?
Worried that it was probably not good news, Banks put his
bottle down and walked through the kitchen, hall and study to
the front door. When he opened it, he was surprised but
relieved to see Annie Cabbot standing there without an
umbrella.

'I was just thinking about you,' said Banks. 'When did you
get back?'

'Yesterday. Can I come in? It's pissing down out here.'

Banks stood aside as she stepped past him, and closed the
door on the chilly rain. Annie hung up her coat and shook her
hair like a wet dog. 'That's better. Any chance of a cuppa?'

'I've got wine.'

'Why doesn't that surprise me? But a simple cuppa would
work wonders right now.'

Banks walked through to the kitchen, Annie following. He
turned his head. 'Regular, green, chamomile, Earl Grey,
decaf?'

'Chamomile, please,' said Annie. 'My God, where did you
come up with all those choices?'

'California,' said Banks. 'They like their fancy tea in
California. I learned to appreciate green tea there, especially.

They have lots of different kinds, you know. Sencha, gyokuro, dragonwell.'

'I'd forgotten you'd been there. I've forgotten most things around that time. Ordinary chamomile will do fine for me.'

'How was St Ives?'

'Wonderful. Beautiful. I got back into sketching and painting. Did a lot of walking on the cliffs.'

'And Ray?'

'He's fine. Sends his regards. He's got another floozy. She can't be a day older than me.'

'Lucky Ray.' Banks had spent a lot of time with Annie's father during her illness and recovery, and they had got along remarkably well. Ray had even stopped over at the cottage a few times after they had opened that second bottle of wine, or hit the Laphroaig.

Banks put the kettle on. He decided to have some tea himself. He was trying to cut back on the wine intake, after all, and chamomile was particularly relaxing late at night. It might help him sleep. Annie leaned her hip against the counter. He was about to tell her she could go through to the conservatory and he'd bring the tea when it was ready, but he realised it would be tactless. He could even see it in her face under the toughness, a vulnerability, an uncertainty about whether she really should be facing the conservatory right now.

Several months ago, while Banks had been enjoying himself in sunny California, Annie had been shot in his conservatory. When he had first found out, he had wondered whether he would be able to go back in there again himself and enjoy it the way he had done before. But he hadn't been there when the shooting happened. The clean-up team had done a great job before he returned home, and Winsome had even had the sensitivity and good taste to refurnish the whole place for him. New carpet, new paint job, new chairs and table, new everything. And all sufficiently different in colour and style from the originals. It was like having a new room, and he had felt no ghosts, no residual sense of pain, fear or suffering. He had lost a table, chairs and a carpet but not, thank God, a dear friend.

He was apprehensive after what had happened to Annie there, though, worried that it might bring on a panic attack or something. It was her first visit since the shooting.

They chatted in the kitchen until the kettle boiled, then Banks put the teapot and cups on a tray. 'Want to go through?' he asked, gesturing towards the conservatory.

Annie followed him tentatively, as if unsure what effect the room would have on her.

'It looks different,' she said, sitting in one of the wicker chairs.

Banks set down the tea tray on the low table and took the chair beside her. He looked at her, trying to gauge her reaction. Annie was in her early forties now, and Banks thought she had never looked so good. During her convalescence, she had let the blonde highlights grow out and her hair had returned to its previous shoulder-length chestnut cascade. Banks decided he preferred it that way. 'If you want, we can sit in the entertainment room,' he said.

Annie shook her head. Toughing it out, then. 'No, it's fine. I was expecting . . . you know . . . but it's fine. It's really nice, and it's very cosy with that warm light and the wind and rain outside.' She hugged herself. 'Let's just stay here, shall we? What's that music?'

'June Tabor,' said Banks. 'This one's called "The Oggie Man". Want something else on?'

'No. I'm fine. Really.' That made a change; she was always complaining about his tastes in music. 'What's an oggie man?'

'A pasty seller,' said Banks. 'It's a song lamenting the disappearance of street pasty sellers in Cornwall in favour of hotdog stands. An oggie is a Cornish pasty. You ought to know that, being a good Cornish lass.'

'Never heard of it. Sounds like a very sad song for such a silly little thing.'

'Folk songs. You know. What can I say? I don't suppose it was silly or little to them at the time. It's about loss, the passing of a tradition.'

'You know,' Annie said suddenly, 'I *do* remember that night. I remember when everything was fading to black, and I was feeling so cold and tired. I thought this was the last place I would ever see in my life, and for a moment, that was what I wanted.' She glanced at Banks and smiled. 'Disappearing like the silly oggie man. Isn't that funny?'

'I don't know. I don't think so.'

'But I'm seeing the room again. That's the point. I know everything's different and all, but now it feel like . . . like being reborn. I didn't disappear. I didn't die. It wasn't the last thing I saw. It's the same room, but it's different. Not just the way it's been refurnished or decorated. Oh, I can't explain myself. I'm not good with words. I'm just saying it's a special place, that's all. For me. And the memories start now. I'm back, Alan. I want you to know that.'

Banks gave her hand a quick squeeze. 'I know you are, and I'm glad. But that's not why you came, is it?'

'No, it's not. I heard about DI Bill Quinn getting killed at St Peter's. I want you to bring me up to date so I can jump right in on Monday morning. I've got to be more than a hundred per cent on this one, or I'll be out.'

'Don't be daft,' said Banks.

'It's true. I'll bet you Madame Gervaise doesn't think I'll be fit enough, mentally or physically. I'll bet you she thinks I've lost my mojo. She'll be trying to drive me to resign.'

'I think that's going a bit too far, Annie.'

'Is it? Then what about that other woman in there with you? Your new partner. Miss Professional Standards. She's very attractive, isn't she? What's her name again? I've had a word with Winsome. She told me most of what's been going on, but I've forgotten the damn woman's name.'

'Inspector Passero. Joanna Passero. She's just tagging along to nail Quinn. Or his memory.'

'Are you being thick, or naive?'

'Aren't you being a little bit paranoid?'

'Just because you're paranoid, it doesn't mean they're not after you.'

'Fair enough. You worked Professional Standards for a while. You know what it's like. You didn't let the job swallow you up, or change your basic attitude.'

'It fucks you up, whether you fight it or not.'

'I'm sure it does. But you're all right now, aren't you? What do you know about Inspector Passero?'

'Not much, but I do have my sources at County HQ. She lived in Woodstock, worked for Thames Valley, got an Italian husband called Carlo. And she's an icy blonde. I don't trust icy blondes. You never know what they're thinking.'

'As opposed to feisty brunettes? All what you see is what you get? Jealous, Annie?'

Annie snorted. 'Something's going on. Mark my words. I'd watch my back if I were you. I hear the sound of knives being sharpened.'

'Don't worry about me. What are you going to do?' he asked.

'What do you mean?'

'You think Gervaise wants you out. What are you going to do about it?'

'I don't know. My options are a bit limited at the moment.'

'Going off half-cocked and trying to prove you're better than everyone else won't work.'

'Look who's talking.'

'I'm being serious, Annie.'

'So am I. I like my job. I'm good at it. And I want to keep it. Is that so strange?'

'Not at all,' said Banks. 'I want you to keep it, too.'

'So you'll help me?'

'How?'

'Any way you can. Trust me. Give me decent tasks. Don't sideline me.'

Banks paused. 'Of course. I'll help you all I can. You should know that.'

Annie leaned forward and rested her hands on her knees. 'Use me, Alan. Don't keep me in the dark. I know I might seem like a bit of a liability at first, that I might seem a bit wobbly, and it'll take me a while to get back to normal, but it doesn't mean I have to be left out in the cold. Keep me informed. Listen to what I have to say. If I have a good idea, make sure people know it's mine. I'm resilient, and I'm a quick learner. You already know that.'

'Across the Wide Ocean' ended, and with it the CD. Rain beat against the windows, and the wind howled through the trees. Annie sat back, shuddered and sipped some tea. 'I enjoyed that,' she said.

'I'm glad.'

'"The Oggie Man". I'll remember that. Poor oggie man. I wonder what happened to him. Did they kill him? Was he murdered? The rain softly falling and the oggie man's no more.' She shifted position and crossed her legs. 'Tell me about Bill Quinn.'

'Not much to say, really,' said Banks. 'According to everyone I've talked to, he was a devoted family man. Devastated by his wife's death. No trace of a reputation for womanising or anything like that.'

'But there are some pictures of him with a girl. I've seen them. I dropped by the squad room after a visit to Human Resources this morning, while you were out. The copies arrived while I was there. She looks like a very *young* girl.'

'She wasn't *that* young.'

'She was young enough. But that's not what I was thinking. Men are pigs. Fact. We all know that. They'll shag anything in a skirt. Quinn did it, and he got caught.'

'Or set up.'

'All right. Or set up. But why?'

'We don't know yet. Obviously blackmail of some kind.'

'He didn't have a lot of money, did he?'

'Not that we know of. We haven't got his banking information yet, but there's nothing extravagant about his lifestyle. Nice house, but his wife worked as an estate agent, and they bought it a long time ago. Mortgage paid off. Kids at university before the fee increases.'

'So he wasn't being blackmailed for his money.'

'Unlikely.'

'Then why?'

'To turn a blind eye to something, or to pass on information helpful to criminals,' said Banks. 'That's what Inspector Passero believes. She said there were rumours. But when Quinn's wife died, their hold over him was broken, all bets were off, and that caused a shift in the balance of power. Quinn became a loose cannon. All that has happened since resulted from that. At least, that's my theory.'

'I should imagine right now you're casting your net pretty wide?' said Annie.

'We have to. There are a lot of questions to answer. Quinn worked on a lot of cases. I must say, though, that unless we're missing something, or the girl herself killed him for some reason we don't know about yet, it seems professional, organised.'

'Cut to the chase. He wouldn't have kept those photos with him if there wasn't something important about them. Far too risky, even hidden as they were.'

'His house was broken into,' Banks said.

Annie shot him a glance. 'When?'

'Probably around the time he was killed, maybe even long enough after for it to be the same person. We're not sure. They took his laptop and some papers. And we've got some tyre tracks from a farm lane near St Peter's that might help identify the killer's car.'

'Why don't you bring me up to speed with the rest of it?'

Banks shared the last few drops of tea and told her what little he knew.

'One of the first things that came into my mind when I saw those photos,' said Annie, 'and what seems to be even more relevant now, after finding out that Quinn was supposedly a devoted family man, was what would make him do what he did with the girl?'

'Like you said, men are pigs.'

'They let the little head do the thinking, right? Given the right circumstances, they'll shag anyone. But they've still got oodles of the old self-preservation instinct. They don't only lie to their families; they lie to themselves, too.'

'Meaning?'

'Meaning that a man like Bill Quinn – devoted family man, as you say – was very unlikely to shit on his own doorstep, if you'll pardon my French. It's harder to lie to yourself about that if you smell it every day, to pursue the metaphor. Meaning you need to check out any conventions he went to, any holidays he took without his wife and kids – a trip to Vegas with the lads, for example, or a golfing holiday in St Andrews. The further away from home, the better. Something so far away that it made it easy for him to pretend that he was on another planet, and everything that happened there had nothing to do with his earthly life, nothing to do with everyday reality, nothing to do with the family he was devoted to.'

'Fishing. With Quinn it was more likely to be a fishing trip.'

'Right, then. Whatever. Any period when he was away from home, either alone or with other like-minded blokes, staying in a hotel. You can't tell much about the place from the photos, but you might get one of the digital experts in Photographic Services to see if he can blow up a few beer mats and bring a sign or two into focus.'

'We're working on it.'

'Good. Because that might tell you whether we're dealing with a trip abroad. In my limited experience of such things, the further away from his own nest a man gets, the freer and friskier he feels, and the more likely he is to stray. It's like the wedding ring becomes invisible. Some men take it off altogether for the duration. And the shackles, the inhibitions, they conveniently fall off with it.'

'You sound as if you're speaking from experience.'

'I did say it was limited experience. And don't ask.'

'But Quinn got set up.'

'Indeed. What is it? What are you thinking?'

Banks hadn't realised that his expression had so clearly indicated a sudden thought. 'Two things,' he said. 'A conference in France – Lyon – with Ken Blackstone, among others, and the Rachel Hewitt case.'

'The girl who disappeared from the hen weekend in Tallinn?'

'That's the one.'

'I've been to Tallinn once,' said Annie. 'Lovely city.'

'I didn't know that.'

'You don't know everything about me.'

'Obviously not. When was this?'

'A few years ago. After Rachel Hewitt disappeared.'

'Hen party?'

'Do I *look* like a hen?'

'What, then?'

'Dirty weekend.'

'The married man?'

'Mind your own business.'

'Anyway, there might be other trips Quinn made abroad, in addition to Lyon and Tallinn. We'll ask around. Thanks for the tip. That's a good line of enquiry, and I'll see it gets priority, and that your name is mentioned in dispatches.'

Annie put her mug down and stretched. 'All I wanted to hear. And now I'd better go.'

'You sure? No more tea? One for the road?'

'I'm tired. I really think I'd better get going. I've got a massage appointment at St Peter's tomorrow afternoon.' Annie stood up, took a long look around the conservatory, then headed for the front door. Banks helped her on with her coat. It was still raining outside, but not so fast now, and the wind had dropped. 'See you on Monday,' she said. 'Maybe I can help run down Bill Quinn's trips abroad?' Then she gave him a quick peck on the cheek. 'Remember, watch out for the blonde,' she said and dashed outside. He watched until her car disappeared down the drive, waved, and went back inside. She'd given him a lot to think about, he had to admit. In the initial flurry of questions, information and possibilities, he had neglected to zoom in on the important psychological details the way Annie had.

It was just after eleven o'clock on Friday night, and he didn't feel like going out. Helmthorpe would be closing down for the night, anyway, unless they had a lock-in at the Duck and Drake. But Banks didn't feel like company. Instead, he made a detour through the entertainment room and pressed PLAY again with *Ashore* still in the CD player. 'Finisterre' piped through the good quality speakers in the conservatory, where the rain was now no more than a pattering of mice's feet. The tea had been nice, but he poured himself another glass of Malbec and settled down to listen to the music and think about what Annie had said. He did his best thinking when he was listening to music and drinking wine.

4

'Are you sure this is the right place?' asked Banks.

'According to the phone company, yes.'

'But it's . . .'

'I know,' said Winsome. 'Apparently, it's won prizes, though.'

Banks gave her a quizzical glance. 'Prizes?'

'Yes. It's quite famous. A tourist attraction.'

Banks opened the door and glanced inside. 'Bloody hell, I can see what you mean.'

'That's why it's famous,' said Winsome, smiling.

The old red telephone box abutted the end wall of a terrace of cottages in the village of Ingleby, not far from Lyndgarth. The paintwork and the window panes were as clean as could be, not a scratch or a greasy fingerprint in sight. Inside, there was a carpet on the little square of floor, a vase of fresh-cut pink and purple flowers on the shelf by the directory, a box for donations, and an empty waste paper bin. Banks shook the donations box. It rattled with coins. The whole place smelled clean and lemony, and all the surfaces shone every bit as much as the outside, as if recently polished. There was even a functioning telephone, as shiny black as could be, and no doubt sanitised, too. In almost every other telephone box Banks had seen over the past few years, the cash box, if there was one, had been broken into and the phone ripped, or cut, from its connecting wire. The donations box wouldn't have lasted five minutes, either.

What was more, Bill Quinn had received two telephone calls on his mobile from this very box over the past ten days, the last one on Tuesday evening, the day before he had been killed. There were other calls, of course, including several to and from his son or daughter, and one from an untraceable mobile number on the morning of the day he died, but this one seemed really odd. The team was already checking to find out what other calls had been made from the telephone box in the past ten days, especially around the same time as the calls to Bill Quinn.

Ingleby was a beautiful village, slate roofs gleaming in the morning sunshine, still a little damp from last night's rain, limestone cottages scrubbed and rinsed clean by the wind and rain, the gardens neat and already colourful, though it was still only late April, ready to burst forth in spectacular fashion as soon as summer arrived. Smoke curled up from one or two of the chimneys, as there was still a slight nip in the air. Behind the village, the daleside rose steeply through green and sere slopes to the rocky outcrops that marked the beginnings of the moorland. A narrow track wound up the hill, then split and ran along the daleside in both directions, about halfway up. Cloud-shadows drifted slowly across the backdrop on the light breeze.

Banks felt as if he were in a place where nothing had changed for centuries, though the telephone box was clear evidence that they had. No signs of vandalism, neat gardens, obviously tended with pride. No wonder Ingleby had won the prettiest village award more than once. There were people in the cities who didn't know, or even believe, that such places existed. Everybody believed in the urban landscape, with its no-go areas, dodgy council estates, riots, looting, terrorist hot beds, street gangs, people who would mug you as soon as look at you, and people who would kick the shit out of you if you so much as glanced at them. But this was something else. This was Arcadia.

Banks remembered the stories in a book he had read recently about wartime evacuees sent from the cities to the country panicking when they saw a cow or an apple tree because they had never experienced such things in their natural environment before. They thought that cows were no bigger than dogs or cats, and that apples grew in wooden boxes. Of course, there were other people, mainly in America, who believed that all of England was like this. The fact was that, while such pastoral idylls did exist in many pockets of the country, even in places as picturesque as Ingleby appearances could be deceptive; even in the prettiest villages there were things under the surface that didn't bear close examination. As Sherlock Holmes had once observed about the countryside in general; there were stones you didn't want to turn over, cupboards you didn't want to open.

Banks took a deep breath of fresh air. 'We'd better get the CSIs to come and check out the telephone box,' he said. 'I doubt we'll find anything, the way it's been cleaned and polished, but it's worth a try.'

'I suppose we'd better start asking a few questions, too,' Winsome said. 'Shouldn't take long, a place this size. Should we ask her to help?' She nodded in the direction of Inspector Passero, who had insisted on accompanying them from Eastvale and was now standing back, checking her mobile for texts.

'I don't think so,' said Banks. 'Let's just keep her at a distance for now. She can tag along, but I don't want her taking any leads.' At least Joanna was wearing more appropriate clothing today, Banks had noticed, though even to someone as unversed as he was in matters of style and design, its quality and fashion cred were unmistakable. With her skintight designer jeans disappearing into tan leather boots a little below her knees, and the green roll-neck jumper under the light brown suede jacket, all she needed was a riding-cap and crop and she would be ready to set off on the morning gallops out Middleham way.

'Please yourself,' said Winsome with a shrug. 'You're the boss.'

There were several cottages clustered around the small square facing the telephone box, and Banks had noticed the net curtains twitching in one of them while they had been standing there. 'Let's start with that one,' he said. The cottage he pointed to had a gate of blackened iron railings and worn steps leading up to the arched stone porch around the door. Creeping vegetation covered almost the entire front of the building like something from a horror movie Banks remembered seeing many years ago.

A few seconds after Banks rang the bell, an elderly woman answered the door. She reminded him of Margaret Thatcher; at least her hair did. The rest of her was plump and matronly, like a cook from a television costume drama, and she was dressed for gardening, in baggy trousers and a shapeless jumper. Banks showed his warrant card and introduced Winsome. Joanna lingered at the bottom of the garden, inspecting the herbaceous borders, as if not quite sure what to do. Banks identified her for the woman anyway, just for the record.

'Gladys,' the woman said. 'Gladys Boscombe. Please, come in. I saw you looking at our telephone box, and you don't seem like the usual tourist types we get.' She had a hint of a Yorkshire accent, but it sounded to Banks as if she had worked at adding a veneer of sophistication to it over the years.

Banks and Winsome followed her first into the hall, then through to the living room. Joanna didn't seem at all sure what to do, so Banks gestured for her to accompany them. It was a small room, and it seemed crowded with the four of them in it, but they each found somewhere to sit, and Gladys Boscombe dashed off to make tea. Nobody had refused her offer. The front window was open a couple of inches, despite the chill, and the silence was punctuated only by birds singing. The room smelled of lavender. The velour sofa and armchairs were covered with lace antimacassars, and even the hard-backed chair Banks sat on had a covered seat cushion. Knick-knacks stood on every surface and filled every alcove: delicate porcelain figurines of piping shepherds or waiting princesses, whorled seashells and pebbles, silver-framed family photographs, a carved ivory and ebony chess set.

That gave him a sudden, sharp memory of Sophia, who had been his girlfriend until a few months ago. She liked to collect shiny pretty things, too, and he had been partly responsible for some of them being vandalised. She had never forgiven him for that; in a way, it had helped precipitate the end of their relationship. He still missed Sophia, despite everything, and sometimes he thought he should try to get in touch with her again, try to rekindle the spark, which he was certain was still there. Then he remembered how she had ignored his calls and emails before, and he didn't want to risk rejection again. Her 'dear John' email had been banal, chatty and brutal. He remembered how low it had made him feel, and how he had half-drunkenly responded with some gibberish he could hardly remember now. He wished he had acted in a more grown-up manner, been more accepting and kind. Clearly such happiness as he had known in those few brief weeks they had been together was not meant for him. Sometimes he felt dragged down by the recent past, and he wanted desperately to get beyond it, to be OK with Annie, with Tracy, with Sophia, even though he realised he would probably never see her again. Right now, there was nobody in his life except family and friends, and that was just fine for the moment. He had nothing to give anyone else.

Gladys Boscombe came back with the tea service on a silver tray, delicate little rose-patterned china cups rimmed with gold, matching saucers and teapot. She put the tray down on the low table in front of the fireplace and beamed at them.

'We'll just let it mash a few minutes, shall we? Giles will be sorry to miss you. That's my husband. He's always been interested in detective stories. Never missed a *Midsomer Murders*. The proper ones, you know, with John Nettles. But he's out walking the lads on the moor. Perhaps he'll be back soon.'

'Your children still live with you?' She looked far too old to have children young enough to take for a walk, but Banks thought it best to be polite.

Mrs Boscombe patted her hair. She ought to be careful or she'd cut herself, he thought. 'Oooh, don't be silly, young man. Both our children are long grown up and moved away. No, I mean the lads, Jewel and Warris, the Jack Russells.'

'Ah, of course.' Banks managed to suppress his laughter at the thought of two Jack Russells named after a pair of music hall comedians. Jimmy Jewel and Ben Warris; he hadn't thought or heard of them in years. Must be dead now, he supposed, along with their contemporaries Mike and Bernie Winters. 'Right. Thanks, Mrs Boscombe. We're here about the telephone box, as you might have gathered.'

Mrs Boscombe eased herself down on the sofa beside Winsome. 'Yes, I couldn't think for the life of me why you were all standing around it chatting, then examining it like some museum exhibit. I can't imagine why on earth you would be interested in that old thing,' she said, a note of distaste creeping into her tone. 'True, I suppose it is famous in its way, but it's still an eyesore. And some of the people it seems to attract . . .' She gave a mock shudder.

'Actually,' said Banks, 'that's what we're interested in. The people it attracts.'

'Tourists, mostly. A lot of foreigners. They leave their litter in the street and keep their car engines running, filling the air with that dreadful carbon monoxide. Some of them even stand and smoke cigarettes. I suppose we should think ourselves fortunate it doesn't draw the younger generation, or

it would soon be vandalised, no doubt, but even so . . .' Mrs
Boscombe poured the tea, offering milk and sugar to all who
wanted it. When Banks lifted the cup to take his first sip, he
felt that he ought to stick his little finger in the air. Joanna did
so, he noticed. She caught him glancing and blushed.

'Do the villagers use it often?'

Her eyes widened. 'Villagers? Why would we? We all have
proper telephones. Some of the newcomers even have mobiles.'

What year was it here? Banks wondered. And just how new
were the newcomers? He was surprised that mobiles even got
coverage in such a remote area, but there were towers all over
the place these days. Still, the fact remained that Bill Quinn
had received two telephone calls from the very box in question over the period he had been at St Peter's. That certainly
didn't smack of passing tourists; it indicated deliberation,
rather than chance. 'Perhaps for privacy, or a fault on the
home line?' Banks suggested. 'Have you noticed anyone you
know using that public telephone over the past week or two?'

'I haven't noticed anyone I know using it for the past *year*
or two,' Mrs Boscombe replied.

'Are any of the cottages rentals?'

Mrs Boscombe bristled. 'I should think not. We have strict
rules about that sort of thing in the village. Besides, who'd
want to rent a cottage here? There's no pub, no general store,
nothing. You'd have to go all the way to Lyndgarth for anything
like that.'

'Perhaps someone who likes the country air, a walker, bird
watcher, naturalist? Some people enjoy the solitary existence,
at least for a while.'

'Perhaps. But there are no rental cottages available in the
village.'

'Mrs Boscombe,' Banks said, hoping not to betray in his
tone the desperation and frustration he was feeling. 'It's very
important. We have information that someone we're

investigating received two telephone calls from that box within the past ten days. Now, does that sound like a tourist to you?'

Her face lit up. 'No, it certainly doesn't. The tourists rarely use the telephone, or if they do, they use it only once. Mostly they just take photographs of their husbands or wives pretending to use it. Is it a true mystery then? Has there been a *murder*? Oh, I do so wish Giles were here.' She checked her watch. 'Perhaps if you could just stay for another half hour or so? He's usually not so long. More tea? I have fresh scones.'

The prospect of spending any longer in the cramped living room surrounded by twee knick-knacks and a garrulous old woman had about as much appeal as a poke in the eye with a sharp stick. Winsome and Joanna were looking twitchy, too, Banks noticed. 'Can you think of anyone?' he asked. 'You have the perfect view of the place. If the locals don't use it, and the tourists don't use it, then who does?'

'Only the Gypsies, I suppose, if you care to count them.'

'Gypsies?'

She waved her hand in the air. 'Oh, you know. Gypsies, Travellers. Whatever they call themselves. They don't stop anywhere long enough to have proper telephones installed, do they, and I don't suppose they can afford mobiles, anyway. Not when they're all on the dole.'

'Who are these people?'

'I'm afraid I have no idea. I've just seen them in the village occasionally, a man and a woman, separately. It may be terribly superficial of me to jump to conclusions, but there it is. Greasy hair, dirty clothes, unshaven face. And you should see the man.'

It took Banks a moment, but he glanced at Mrs Boscombe and saw the glimmer of a smile on her face. She'd cracked a joke, knew it, and was proud of it. He laughed, and the others laughed with him. 'So did you see this Gypsy man or woman use the telephone recently?' he asked.

'Yes. A couple of times in the past week or two,' Mrs Boscombe said.

'But they weren't together?'

'No.'

Banks took out the photo of the girl with Bill Quinn. 'Is she anything like the woman you mentioned?' he asked.

She shook her head. 'I didn't get a good look at her, but I would say the one I saw was older, and she had a bit more flesh on her bones. No, it wasn't her.'

'OK,' said Banks, feeling disappointed. If the photo had been taken a few years ago, the woman might have changed, he thought. 'What about the man? What can you tell me about him?'

'I'm afraid I don't know anything about him, or about any of them.'

'Are there any others?'

'I don't know. I only saw the two of them use the phone, and it was always after dark. I could only see what I did because the box is well-lit, of course.'

'Do you remember what days?'

'Not really. I think the man was last here on Tuesday about nine, because I'd just finished watching *Holby City*, a little weakness of mine. The woman . . . it might have been Sunday. Or maybe Saturday. The weekend, I think, anyway.'

'Can you describe him?'

'I could only see him in the light from the telephone box. About your height, perhaps, wearing dirty jeans and a scruffy old donkey jacket, hair over his collar, hadn't been washed in a while, beginnings of a beard and moustache.'

'Fat or thin?'

'Maybe just a little more filled out than you. Certainly not fat, not by any stretch of the imagination.'

'The colour of his hair?'

'Dark. Black or brown, it would be impossible to say exactly.'

'Did he talk on the telephone for long?'

'I don't know. I didn't linger at the window to watch. All I know is by the time I'd finished what I was doing, he was gone again. Say maybe fifteen or twenty minutes.'

That didn't quite match the four-minute call that Quinn had received from the box last Tuesday, so perhaps the man had made more than one call. The records from the phone box would tell them what other numbers had been called. If he had phoned Bill Quinn at about nine o'clock on Tuesday, that would have been during quiz night, so perhaps Quinn had missed quiz night because he had been expecting the call. It was a possibility, at any rate. 'Is there anything else you can remember about this man?' Banks asked. 'How old would you say he was?'

'I have no idea. Quite young. Mid-thirties, perhaps? The beard may have made him look older, of course.'

'Would you recognise him again?'

'I don't know. I couldn't really make out any clear features, if you know what I mean. I'm quite good at remembering faces, though, even if I'm not very good at describing them. I might remember him.'

'Do you know where the camp is?'

'There isn't one, really. Not exactly a camp, as such.'

Banks's shoulders slumped. 'So you don't know where he was living?'

'I didn't say that. I said there isn't a Gypsy camp as such. Giles told me he heard it from a rambler that there's someone living up at the old Garskill Farm. It's about two miles away, on the moors. I can't imagine what the poor fellow was doing walking up near there, even if he is a rambler, as it's well off the beaten track and . . . well . . . it's not the sort of place one wants to be alone.'

'Why is that?'

'One hears stories. Old stories. It's a wild part of the moor.

Most people give it a wide berth. There's something eerie about the place.'

'You mean it's haunted?'

'That's what some folk believe.'

'And you?'

'I've no cause to go up there. It's wild moorland. You'd risk getting lost – sometimes those fogs creep up all of a sudden, like, and you can't see your hand in front of your face. And there are bogs, fens, mires, old lead mine workings, sinkholes. It's not safe.'

'Good enough reason not to go there, then,' said Banks, smiling. 'Even without the ghosts. What about kids? Is it somewhere the local kids might go to drink, take drugs or have sex?'

'No. There aren't really any local kids around here, and there are plenty of places nearer Lyndgarth or Helmthorpe for that sort of thing. Less remote, perhaps, but a lot more comfortable.'

'So you think this man and the woman you saw might be squatting up at Garskill Farm?'

'It's the most likely place.'

'Tell me about it.'

'Not much to tell, really. Someone must own it, but I can't tell you who. It's been abandoned as long as I can remember. Falling to rack and ruin. I'm not even certain it was ever a working farm. It's my guess it belonged to whoever owned the lead mines, and when the industry died years back, well, they moved on.'

Why on earth, Banks wondered, would someone walk two miles each way twice, eight miles in all, to talk to Bill Quinn on a public telephone if it wasn't important? Clearly whoever had done it didn't have access either to a closer land line, or to a mobile, or he feared that someone might be listening in to his conversations. But why? And what, if anything, did he have to do with Bill Quinn's murder?

They heard the sound of the gate opening and dogs barking. Mrs Boscombe got to her feet. 'Ah, here's Giles and the lads. He *will* be glad to see you. You can tell him about all about the murders you've solved. I'll just put the kettle on again.'

There was no easy way up and over the dale to Garskill Farm, Giles Boscombe had explained, before they managed to cut short his analysis of what should be done about the presence of Gypsies and Travellers. Neither Banks's Porsche nor Winsome's Toyota would make it up the winding track, let alone over the top and across the moorland. There were probably other ways in – from the north, perhaps, or even the east or west – but they would most likely involve long detours and, no doubt, getting lost. Even if mobiles worked, satnavs weren't always reliable in this desolate part of the world. People often mixed up the dales and the moors, but Brontë country was a few miles south-west of where they were, though the moorland landscape on the tops between the dales had many similarities with the moors the Brontës had walked.

There were no village bobbies any more; like the oggie man, they were a thing of the past. But Banks did happen to know that the Safe Community officer in Lyndgarth happened to drive a Range Rover, and when they raised him on the phone, he sounded only too willing to whizz over to Ingleby and do his best to get them as close to Garskill Farm as possible.

When Constable Vernon Jarrow arrived, they left their own cars by the telephone box and piled into his Range Rover, Banks in the front and Winsome and Joanna in the back. PC Jarrow was a pleasant, round-faced local fellow with the weather-beaten look of a countryman. He said he was used to driving off road. Banks got out and opened the gate to the winding lane up the daleside, closing it behind him. Jarrow drove slowly and carefully, but the Range Rover still bumped over the rocks sticking out of the dirt and the ruts made by tractors. Some of the bends were almost too tight, but he made them. Banks was reminded of a tour bus he had once taken with Sandra to an ancient site in Greece, hugging the edge of a steep precipice all the way.

'Do you know Garskill Farm?' he asked Jarrow over the noise of the engine.

'I know of it,' Jarrow answered. 'It's been like that for years. Abandoned.'

'Ever been up there?'

'No reason to.'

'Not even just to check on it?'

Jarrow gave Banks a bemused sideways glance. 'Check on what? There's nothing there.'

'Mrs Boscombe heard rumours there's been some Gypsies or Travellers staying up there recently.'

Jarrow grunted. 'They're welcome. Long as they don't cause any trouble in the community.'

'How do you know they haven't?'

'I'd have heard about it, wouldn't I?'

It seemed like unassailable logic. Banks didn't blame Jarrow for not checking out every square inch of his patch as frequently as possible, but that kind of complacency in assuming that he would know the minute anything was wrong was no excuse. Still, he let it go. After all, the man was driving them to a remote spot, and there was no sense in giving him a bollocking on the way.

When the track came to the east–west lane halfway up the daleside, PC Jarrow kept going straight on, up the daleside, where the road became even more rudimentary, so much so that it was hard to make out at all sometimes, forcing them back in their seats. Soon, they were weaving between outcrops of limestone, bouncing around even more than on the rutted track below. If Banks had contrived this whole business to irritate and upset Joanna Passero he couldn't have done a better job, he realised, as he caught a glimpse of her ashen face in the rear-view mirror, hand to her mouth. But he hadn't, and he found himself feeling sorry for her. He had no idea that she suffered from carsickness, and she hadn't said anything. Still, there was nothing he could do about it at this point; she would simply have to hold on.

Soon they were driving across the open moorland, and while it was still as bumpy, at least they were more or less on the flat. This had once been an area of about two or three thriving villages, Banks knew. There was an isolated old house known locally as the School House, which was exactly what it had been even as late as the First World War. After that, the moorland had fallen into decline and never recovered. The military had been making noises for years about taking it over for manoeuvres, but they already had plenty of land in the area, and they didn't seem to need Garskill Moor yet.

There were roads, tracks or laneways criss-crossing the rolling tracts of gorse and heather, and soon the bumpiness of the ride improved somewhat. Joanna took her hand away from her mouth, but she was still pale. Winsome didn't seem bothered by any of it. Jarrow drove slowly, straight ahead. It was an interesting landscape, Banks thought. People often assume the moorland that runs along the tops between dales is flat and barren, but this landscape was undulating, with surprising chasms appearing suddenly at one side or the other, unexpected becks lined with trees, clumps of bright wildflowers, and the ruined flues and furnaces of abandoned lead mines in the distance. Even in the pale April sunlight, it resembled an abandoned land, an asteroid once settled, then deserted.

'Does nobody live up here any more?' Banks asked.

'Not for miles. There used to be an old woman in the School

House. Everybody thought she was a witch. But she died a couple of years ago. Nobody's moved in since, so that's falling to rack and ruin, too.'

'Are we almost there?' Joanna asked from the back.

'Not far now, miss,' Jarrow assured her. 'You just hold on there. It's in a hollow, so you can't really see it until you come right up on it.'

They crossed over a tiny stone bridge and bumped along beside a fast-flowing beck for a while, then up the steep bank, along the top and, sure enough, as they turned a corner by a small copse, there, in the hollow, stood Garskill Farm; or rather, the ruins of Garskill Farm.

Actually, it didn't look as bad as Banks had been led to expect. The three solid limestone buildings, arranged around what might have once been a pleasant garden or courtyard, were for the most part structurally intact, though there were slates missing from roofs here and there, and all the windows were broken. Most of them had been boarded up. The two outlying buildings were smaller, and had probably been used for storage, while only the central, larger building was meant to house people. Even so, if anyone was squatting there, they must be desperate.

Jarrow pulled to a halt by the remains of a drystone wall, which had clearly marked the border of the property. They all got out of the Range Rover. Banks felt shaky, as if all his joints had worked a bit loose, and Joanna Passero immediately turned her back and walked a few yards away before resting her palms on her knees and bending to vomit quietly into the shrubbery. Everyone pretended to ignore her. Even Banks felt no desire to take the piss. Only Winsome had had the sense to bring bottled water, and she offered some to Joanna who immediately accepted and thanked her, apologising to everyone for her little display of weakness. The wind howled around them and seemed to use the buildings as musical instruments, whistling in the flues and rattling loose window boards like percussion. Mrs Boscombe had certainly been right about how eerie it was up there.

Banks stepped over some variously shaped stones that had once formed the drystone wall. A lot of skill had no doubt gone into building that wall, he thought, and now it had collapsed, brought down by stray cattle or sheep, or winter storms freezing the water in the cracks and expanding. Such drystone walls were built to withstand most things nature could throw their way, but they needed a little repair work now and then, a little tender loving care.

Finding himself standing in a garden completely overgrown by weeds, mostly nettles and thistles up to thigh height, Banks paused and turned to address the others. 'OK,' he said, stepping back. 'There doesn't seem to be any kind of an easy way in here, and if anyone was using the place you'd think they'd at least clear a way in and out.'

'Round the other side?' Winsome said.

'Exactly. So let's make our way around the perimeter and see if we can't find an easier access point. And be careful. There are bloody nettles and thistles everywhere. Winsome, will you take Inspector Passero and check out that first outbuilding, on the left there. PC Jarrow, you come with me, and we'll start with the centre building, then we'll all meet up in the one on the far right.'

'I've got a couple of torches in the Range Rover,' said Jarrow. 'We might need them in there.'

'Good idea,' said Banks.

They waited until Jarrow brought the torches and tested them, then Banks led the way around the remains of the garden wall, just as overgrown on the outside as on the inside, and along the end of the building to their left. They were at the back of the house now, and able to step into the yard over a ruined section of wall. When they arrived at the doorway of the first building, Winsome and Joanna pushed it open and disappeared inside. Banks and Jarrow continued across a stretch of high grass to the back of the house itself.

It was just as dilapidated as the outbuildings from the outside, though it might have been a grand house in its day. Banks stopped before they got to the door and pointed. Jarrow followed his gaze. The pathway worn through the undergrowth from the door to a driveway that crossed the back of the property was clear to see. Obviously, if one or more people had been squatting here, they needed to be able to get in and out, no matter how far they had to walk to the nearest shop or telephone. Ultimately, through a network of unfenced roads, tracks and laneways, if they had any means of transport they could connect with the A66, and from there to Carlisle, Darlington, the M1, A1, and pretty much anywhere else in the country. But the quickest way to Ingleby was the way Banks and the others had just come.

There were no signs of any cars around, except the burned-out chassis of an old Morris Minor in a backyard filled with rusty farm, gardening and mining equipment. Banks's father used to drive a Morris Minor years ago. He remembered family outings to the countryside as a child, his mother and father sitting proudly up front, him and his brother Roy fighting in the back. They were good memories: hot sweet tea from a Thermos, orange juice and sandwiches and buns in a field by the river, or even on a roadside lay-by, ice creams, swimming in the river shallows if it was a warm enough day.

The implements were nothing unusual. Banks had seen similar things in some of the Dales' museums. The closest anything came to transport was an old wooden cartwheel with most of the spokes missing. The silence beyond the wind was even more all-encompassing up here than in Ingleby. A curlew's sad call drifted from the distant moors, but that was all, apart from Jarrow's heavy breathing and the moaning of the wind in the flues, a loose board clattering somewhere. There was a heavy wooden door with peeling green paint wedged into the doorway at the back, halfway along the building. A simple push from Jarrow's shoulder opened it and they walked inside, switching on their torches. It seemed to be one long room, like the banquet hall of an old Viking dwelling or a school dormitory, and the torchlight picked out two rows of thin foam mattresses. There were ten on each side, all stained and damp. Here and there, two of the mattresses had been pulled close together, as if their occupants were trying to mimic a double bed or huddle close for warmth. There were no pillows. Whoever had been there, it looked as though they were gone. The walls were stone, and there was no ceiling, only bare rafters holding up the roof. In one or two places, the tiles and surfacing had disappeared, letting in the light from outside. Rain, too, no doubt, as the buckets carefully placed under each hole attested. Dirty blankets lay bunched up beside most of the mattresses.

The smell was almost overwhelming. A human smell, only magnified: dirty socks, urine, vomit, sweat. The smell of poverty and desperation. Gnawed bones, chicken legs most likely, and some empty takeaway food cartons and Costa Coffee cups littered the floor. McDonald's. Burger King. Kentucky Fried Chicken. The food must have been freezing before it got here, Banks thought, even though someone must have had a car. The nearest McDonald's was probably the one in Eastvale, at least fifteen miles away. Still, perhaps it was better than nothing. There appeared to be no cooking or food storage facilities here.

At the far end of the room was a trough of murky water with a long spoon on a hook, curved at the bottom so it could be used for drinking. Next to it, behind a ratty, moth-eaten curtain, was a bucket. Banks didn't need the torchlight to show him what was in it. He turned away in disgust. His eyes lighted on a tattered paperback lying beside one of the mattresses. He knelt down and picked it up carefully. It wasn't in English, and he couldn't guess what language it was from any of the words, though the sheer number of consonants, and the odd symbols crowning some of the letters, made him think of Polish. The paper was already faded, and some of the pages were torn. Banks put it back.

'What do you think?' Jarrow whispered.

'I don't know,' said Banks, still kneeling by the thin foam mattress. He stood up and brushed off his trousers. 'I can tell you one thing, though. I doubt very much we're dealing with Gypsies or Travellers. They don't usually live like this.'

'Squatters?'

'More like it. Let's go.'

Glad to be outside again, Banks and Jarrow took a few deep breaths of relatively fresh air and watched the women coming over to meet them. 'It's a rudimentary loo,' Winsome said, 'though there's no sewage system from what I can see.'

'There's a sort of basic shower, too,' Joanna added. 'It's hooked up to a cold water tank. There doesn't seem to be any hot.'

'There wouldn't be,' said Banks. 'Someone would have to pay for that. Maybe they fill a cold water tank from the beck, or just let the rain collect.' He told them what he and Jarrow had found in the larger building.

Winsome and Joanna poked their heads inside and came out quickly. 'My God,' said Winsome. 'What's been happening here?'

'I'm not sure,' said Banks. 'It looks like a squat, but do you remember that converted barn outside Richmond a few years back? It was in a bit better shape than this set-up, but not much. They found a whole bunch of unskilled migrant labourers living there in dreadful conditions. They were mostly Eastern European, and they'd been enticed over here by promises of work. For a fee, of course. Instead they found themselves basically bound in slavery to a gangmaster, owing so much money they could never pay their way out of it, and what they did have to pay left them nothing to live on – or to run away with.'

'The kind of people Warren Corrigan preys on,' said Winsome.

Banks gave her an appreciative glance. 'So you do listen to the briefings?'

Winsome smiled. 'Of course, sir. Sometimes.'

'The impression I got was that he operates mostly in the cities, but it's a good point. Keep it in mind. It looks very much as if Bill Quinn's team might have had a man on the inside. We'll have a little talk with pal Corrigan soon.' Banks glanced towards the final, and smallest, of the three buildings. The boards were still in the windows, and the back door was shut, though, again, it proved not to be locked, and it wasn't much of a barrier against Jarrow's firm shoulder.

At first, the two torch beams picked out nothing except a pile of dirty bedding, another trough of filthy water, a rickety old chair and a few damp ragged towels and lengths of rope. A broken broom handle leaned against the wall by the door, and Banks used it to poke among the tangle of sheets and blankets on the floor. The handle touched something firm but yielding. Already feeling that clenching in his gut that warned him what was coming, Banks used the stick to hook and pull away the rest of the sheets and blankets, and the four of them gazed down on a man's body. He was naked, and his skin gleamed with a strange greenish tinge in the artificial light. He was thin, he had longish, greasy dark hair and the beginnings of a beard, and beside him, among the heap of filthy bedding, was a worn donkey jacket and a pair of dirty jeans.

★   ★   ★

As the strong fingers worked on the muscles around her neck and shoulders, Annie finally gave herself up to Daniel Craig's magic touch. Her breath came sharply, and her whole body tingled with warmth and pleasure. His hands slid down the small of her back towards the base of her spine. She waited for the touch of his lips and that slight scrape of five o'clock shadow in the sweet spot between her neck and shoulder, then he would turn her over, his lips would continue slowly down her body, and his hands would—

'That's it for today, love.'

The gravelly voice shattered Annie's erotic reverie. Of course it wasn't Daniel Craig; it was just Old Nobby, the St Peter's masseur. Old Nobby was ex-navy and a bit long in the tooth, with anchor tattoos on both forearms and enough of the sea-dog about him that his other nickname around the place was Popeye. But he had magic fingers, was a damn fine masseur, and Annie found that if she closed her eyes and let herself drift, he could be anyone she wanted him to be for half an hour.

'Thanks, Nobby,' Annie said, pulling the bathrobe around her and securing the belt as she sat up. She might not mind letting Daniel Craig see her charms, but not Old Nobby. Not that he seemed interested. He had his back turned to her, and he was bent over the desk filling out forms. She liked Nobby. He was a bit of an amateur philosopher. He had an open and inquiring mind and often seemed happy to chat for ages about practically nothing at all after sessions. The conversations were almost as relaxing as the massages, though not quite as sexually stimulating. Her skin still tingled pleasantly. Whether he knew of the effect he had on her, she had no idea, and she was certainly not going to ask him.

Now that Annie was back in the real world, she could hear sounds from outside. Though St Peter's was trying to drag itself back to normal – the regular massage routine, for example – the place was still crawling with police and CSIs. It shouldn't take much longer now, though, she thought. All the guests and most of the part-time staff had been questioned, according to Winsome, some more than once, their back-grounds and alibis no doubt thoroughly checked, and it didn't seem as if anyone from the centre either knew anything or had anything to do with what had happened to Bill Quinn. There might still be some connection they hadn't unearthed yet, but Annie doubted it. Whatever fate had befallen Bill Quinn, she believed, had happened because of outside, and had come from outside. It had followed him here, or found him here, without any help from St Peter's itself. His presence here had been no secret; no tip-off from the inside would have been needed for anyone who wanted to locate him.

'You're doing a grand job, Nobby,' she said.

Nobby turned from his paperwork and sat on the only office chair. Annie remained perched on the edge of the massage table.

'Thanks, lass,' he said. 'Bad business, all this, eh?' He gestured towards the activity outside.

'It certainly is.'

'You knew him?'

'No. You?'

'Just professionally, like.'

'Did he talk much?'

'Sometimes. You know, I've always thought a good massage can work a bit like hypnosis. Take a person deep down to those long forgotten places, events and feelings. Sometimes that's where the answer lies.'

Sexual fantasies, too, Annie thought. She wondered if Bill Quinn had dreamed of the girl in the photo as Nobby's fingers worked their magic on him. Or was it different for a man, especially when it was another man touching him? 'What do you mean?' she asked.

Nobby shifted to make himself more comfortable. His chair creaked. 'Must get this bloody thing oiled. I suppose what I mean is that often the root of the problem isn't obviously physical. Even something as simple as neck pain or back pain.'

'You mean like when something's psychosomatic?' she said.

'A massage can work both ways, you know.' Nobby held his hands up. 'Lethal weapons,' he said, and laughed.

Annie laughed with him, but she guessed there was more than a grain of truth in what he said. After all, rumour had it that he had been seconded to the SAS at one time.

'You have to be careful not to exacerbate the problem,' he went on. 'As you can attest better than most, nerves are sensitive things.'

'I certainly can. What about Bill Quinn?'

'His neck? There wasn't a lot wrong with it, as far as I could tell. Certainly not the kind of physical problems you had when we first started our sessions.'

'Swinging the lead?'

Nobby paused before answering. 'No. I don't think so. We can resist getting better for any number of reasons we're not aware of.'

'Like what?' she asked.

'The usual. Fear. Despair. Indifference. Indecision. Lack of confidence. Guilt, even.'

'And in Bill's case?'

'He was troubled.'

'By what? Did he talk to you, Nobby? Did he tell you something?'

'No, not in the way you mean. Not anything you could put your finger on.' Nobby flashed her a crooked grin. 'Always the copper first, I suppose, eh?'

'Well, I am due to start working on the case officially on Monday. Thought I might get a head start.'

'Aye, well. To answer your question, yes, we talked sometimes.'

'And you didn't tell the police officer who questioned you?'

'You make it sound like there was something to tell. It was nothing but blethering, smoke in the wind. We had some conversations, as you do. As we're doing now. Our conversations were rambling, vague and philosophical.' He snorted. 'All the police officer asked me was where I was after dark on Thursday evening, if I knew how to use a crossbow, did I belong to any archery clubs? Had I known Bill Quinn on the force? I was never even on the force, for crying out loud. I was a navy medic, and now I'm a qualified masseur. They asked about practical things. Our conversations weren't practical.'

Banks would get along with Nobby very well, Annie thought. He placed as much value in the vague and philosophical as Nobby did. That was why he often went against the rules and spoke to witnesses, even suspects, by himself. He said most detectives didn't know the right questions to ask. 'Go on,' Annie said. 'What were they about, then?'

'Mostly my own thoughts and imaginings, I suppose,' said Nobby.

'Will you tell me?'

'No reason not to, I suppose. It's not as if it's under the seal of the confessional, or the Official Secrets Act, or anything. And I'm not his shrink. But only because I like you. There's nothing to tell, really, so don't get your hopes up. Like I said, I got the impression that Mr Quinn was a troubled man. He said he'd been having these neck pains for about five or six years, and he'd never had any problems before then. It didn't sound as if the cause was ergonomic. You know, too long at the computer keyboard – he hated computers – or even bad posture at the desk. Apparently he was like you, the kind of copper who liked to get out on the streets, and in his spare time he worked on his allotment, went fishing, spent time with his family. Even so, necks are funny things. The vertebrae deteriorate with age, but the

X-rays didn't show any serious deterioration in his case. Only moderate. What you'd expect.'

'So you're saying the causes were psychological?'

'I'm not a psychiatrist or a physiotherapist, so don't quote me on that. Can you see why it's not something you'd find easy to put into words? I don't even know why I'm telling you. I suppose it's because he's dead, and I've been thinking about him. Just days ago, he was alive as you or I.' He held up his hands. 'I could touch his skin, the muscle underneath, feel the give and the push, the knots. You know his wife died recently?'

'Yes.'

'Of course you do. He was devastated, grief-stricken, poor bloke. I think that was something that brought us together. I knew what he felt like. I lost my Denise five years ago, so I suppose you could say we had something in common. I'm not a grief counsellor, so I couldn't help him with it in any way, but it was something we could talk about.'

'So you talked about grief, the death of his wife?'

'Yes. Sometimes. And about grief in general. And guilt. Could he have done more? Did he let her down? Was he to blame?'

'He wasn't, was he?'

'Of course not,' Nobby said. 'That's just the way you think sometimes when you lose somebody you love. You blame yourself. He was out on surveillance, incommunicado, the night she died. He didn't find out until the next morning. The kids were away at university. She died alone. Guilt over things like that can gnaw away at you.'

'What did you tell him?'

'I told you. I'm not a counsellor. I couldn't do anything but sympathise with him, as I would with anyone in that position, and reassure him that all this was normal.'

'What did he want? I mean, why was he telling you all this?'

'Like I said, we had something in common. He seemed to want some kind of absolution, as if he was seeking atonement.'

'Atonement for what?'

'Dunno. He didn't say. But it was something that haunted him.'

'Something he'd done?'

'Or not done. It's far too easy to regret things you've done. He was drinking a bit too much. One of his kids had said something, and he'd read up on AA. He hadn't joined, hadn't thought he needed to yet, that there was still time to gain control over it. He saw the drink as temporary relief, a crutch, you know the sort of thing. Anyway, I've been there, too, in my long and chequered career, and we got talking a bit philosophically, as you do, about addiction and the whole twelve-step programme, and he seemed fascinated by the idea of being given the chance to change the things you can change and let the higher power deal with those you can't, and having the wisdom to know the difference.'

'I've heard it,' said Annie. 'It sounds heavy. And complicated.'

Nobby laughed. 'It's not so heavy,' he said. 'It's definitely not easy, though. He asked me if I thought that if a person knew a wrong had been done, and he thought he could put it right, should he try to do it, no matter what the cost to himself or others?'

'What did he mean?'

'I don't know. That's all he said about it.'

'What was your answer?'

'I didn't have one. Still don't.'

'Was he talking about himself?'

Nobby stood up. It was time for his next patient. 'That I don't know. Like I said, he was a haunted man.'

*　　*　　*

Fortunately, Jarrow had a police radio in his Range Rover, but even so, it took over three hours to get a CSI team, police surgeon and photographer up to Garskill Farm. In the end, ACC McLaughlin had to bite the bullet and pay for a helicopter to get Dr Burns and Peter Darby there, complaining all the while about how expensive the whole business was becoming, and hinting that this was somehow Banks's fault. The CSIs managed a bumpy journey up from Ingleby in their well-sprung van, which looked a bit the worse for wear when it pulled up by the garden wall. They were especially disgruntled as it was the weekend, and they weren't even Eastvale CSIs, who were still busy at St Peter's. They had come all the way from Harrogate. They also seemed to blame Banks for all their woes, especially the Crime Scene Manager, a particularly surly and obnoxious individual called Cyril Smedley, who did nothing but complain about contamination and bark orders at all and sundry. It made Banks long for Stefan Nowak, who went about his business in a quiet and dignified manner. But Stefan had St Peter's to deal with.

On the phone, Banks had warned everyone to avoid coming in from the north of the buildings, as there was a driveway leading to a lane, and that was the most likely area they would find tyre tracks, footprints and other trace evidence. It needed to be preserved, in case the rains hadn't washed every scrap of evidence away. On a brief reconnoitre, Banks had noticed a couple of sandwich wrappers and an empty paper coffee cup in the grass beside the worn path to the driveway, all of which might prove useful in providing DNA or fingerprint evidence if they had been sheltered well enough from the elements. Whatever these people were up to, they certainly weren't very tidy about it. Already several CSIs were taking casts and collecting whatever they could find on the path and driveway. Peter Darby was taking digital video of the whole show.

Darby had finished photographing the body, and Banks crouched beside Dr Burns as he examined it in situ under the bright arc lamps the CSIs had set up. The helicopter was waiting beyond the compound to take it to the mortuary when he was finished, but Dr Glendenning, the Home Office pathologist, was away for the weekend, and there would be no postmortem until Monday. Anything Dr Burns could tell them today might prove vital.

Banks had already been through the pockets of the discarded clothing and found nothing but fluff. It was the same as with Bill Quinn; everything had been removed from the victim's pockets. Now the various articles of clothing had been bagged and labelled by the CSIs along with the growing pile of exhibits. It was going to be a tough job to get everything out of here. The idea of establishing a mobile murder room at the site was out of the question, but officers would have to be left on guard day and night as long as it was still classified as a crime scene. The CSIs had already divided the area into zones, which the designated officers were searching thoroughly. Banks didn't envy them crawling around in the wet nettles and animal droppings.

'What do you think, doc?' Banks asked, returning his attention to the body.

'There are signs of violence,' Burns said. 'Bruising on the shoulders and upper arms, indications that the wrists were bound.' He pointed out the red chafing. 'But none of these seem to me to constitute cause of death.'

Banks pointed to the thighs and chest. 'What about those bloody marks?'

'Small animals. Rats, most likely.'

Banks gave a shudder. 'No crossbow bolt?'

'Not this time.'

'What do you think of his hands?'

Dr Burns examined them. 'They seem in pretty good condition. He bit his nails, but not excessively.'

'Are they the hands of an unskilled manual labourer?'

'Of course not. There are no callouses, no ground in grime. These hands haven't been used for anything more strenuous than carrying the shopping home.'

'I thought not,' said Banks. 'What about his general condition? He was living pretty rough.'

'Not bad, considering. I'd place him in his late thirties, early forties, generally quite fit, probably runs or works out in some way. The liver's not enlarged, at least not to the touch, so he's probably not a serious drinker. No sign of tobacco staining on the teeth or nicotine on the fingers, so he's probably not a smoker. I can't really say much more from a cursory external examination. I'm only really here to pronounce him dead, you know. And he is. Quite dead.'

'I know that,' said Banks. 'But I also need some indication of time and cause of death.

Dr Burns sighed. 'The same old story.'

'I'm afraid so.'

'All I can say is that rigor has been and gone, and taking the temperature up here into account, I'd guess three days, probably more. But as you know, there are so many variables. It's not been that cold outside, but it does get chilly at night.'

'He died before Bill Quinn?'

'Oh, yes. I'd say he definitely died before the last body I examined. You just have to look at the greenish tinge to see that, especially around the stomach area. That's caused by bacteria on the skin, and it doesn't usually start until about forty-eight hours after death. It spreads outwards and reaches the hands and feet last, and you can see it's there, too. The cool nights may have slowed it down a bit as well, but not much. I'd say between three and four days. Remind me. The first body was found when?'

'Thursday morning,' said Banks. 'But you said it's almost certain he was killed between eleven and one the night before, and Dr Glendenning's post-mortem confirmed it.' Banks glanced at his watch, surprised to see that it was already after four o'clock in the afternoon. 'That makes it about two and a half days from then until midday today. Definitely less than three days. Could this one have been dead even longer than you're suggesting?'

'Hard to say for certain, but I doubt it. After about four days the skin starts to get marble-like, and the veins come closer to surface, become more visible. That hasn't happened yet. There's also not much insect activity. Some signs of blue-bottles and blowflies, but they're always the first. Sometimes they come on the first day. The ants and beetles come later. I'd say Tuesday evening or Wednesday morning. That would be my preliminary guess, at any rate.'

'Much appreciated,' said Banks. If it was the same man who had phoned Bill Quinn around nine o'clock on Tuesday evening, it would have taken him probably about an hour to walk back to Garskill Farm from Ingleby, maybe a bit less, so he had to have been killed sometime after about ten o'clock on Tuesday evening and before, say, eleven on Wednesday evening.

Dr Burns turned the body slightly so that Banks could see the pooling, or hypostasis on his back and legs. 'All that tells us in terms of time is that he's been dead more than six hours,' said Dr Burns.

'But it also tells us that he more than likely died here and hasn't been moved from that position, am I right?'

'That's right. You're learning.'

'So what killed him?'

Dr Burns said nothing for a few moments as he examined the body again, touched the hair and looked up at the roof. Then he examined the front and back for signs of fatal injuries. 'There are no knife wounds or bullet entry points, as far as I can make out,' he said. 'Sometimes they're hard to spot, especially a thin blade or a small calibre bullet, but I've been as thorough as I can under the circumstances.'

'Blunt object trauma?'

'You can see for yourself there's nothing of that sort.'

'So what killed him? Was he poisoned? Did he die of natural causes?'

'He could have been poisoned, but that'll have to wait until the post-mortem. As for natural causes, again, it's possible, but given the bruising, the condition of his body, the rope marks, I'd say they rule it out somewhat.' Dr Burns paused. 'You're probably going to think I'm crazy, and I don't want you repeating this to anyone except your immediate team until the post-mortem has been conducted, but if it helps you at all, it's my opinion that he drowned.'

'Drowned?'

'Yes. He was naked. His hands were bound behind his back.' Dr Burns pressed the chest slightly. 'And if I do that, you can just about hear a slight gurgling sound and feel the presence of water in the lungs. If I pressed much harder it would probably come out of his nose and mouth, but I don't want to risk disturbing the body that much.' He gestured to the trough of water, the twisted towels, lengths of rope and overturned chair. 'In fact, if you ask me, this man died of drowning, probably in conjunction with waterboarding. Those towels by the trough are still wet.'

Banks stood up and took in everything Dr Burns had mentioned. He had never understood the term 'waterboarding'. It sounded so much like a pleasant activity, something you do at the lake on a lazy summer afternoon, something you do for fun. Along with the rest of the world, he'd had a rude awakening when it hit the news so often over the last few years, especially when George Bush said he approved of it. Now he knew that waterboarding meant putting a cloth or towel over someone's face and pouring water over it while they were lying on their back. It was said to be excruciatingly painful, and could cause death by dry drowning, a form of suffocation. 'He didn't die of the waterboarding, then?'

'He could have,' said Dr Burns. 'Depends on the water in his lungs. Dr Glendenning will be able to do a more thorough examination than I can. If he finds petechial haemorrhaging in the eyes, which I am unable to see, then you could be right. You would get that in dry drowning, but not in the case of drowning by water. Rarely, at any rate.'

'But you can't see any?'

'That doesn't mean they aren't there. Sometimes they're no larger than pinpricks. You'll have to wait for the post-mortem.' Dr Burns stood up. 'If he was drowned,' he went on, 'you should be able to find enough forensic information to prove it, to tie the water in his lungs to the water in the trough, for example. On the other hand, if he died of dry drowning as a result of waterboarding, you probably won't find any water. There's always a chance it was accidental. Torture isn't an exact science. But if he was drowned in the trough, then the odds are somebody would have had to hold his head under until he died. It's a natural human reaction to breathe, and we'll use every ounce of strength we have to keep on doing so.'

'How come you know so much about it?' Banks asked.

'I've been to some places nobody should ever have to go to,' said Burns, then he picked up his bag and walked outside. 'I'll tell the helicopter pilot we're ready for him,' he said over his shoulder. Banks could remember when Burns was still wet around the ears. Now he had been to places where he had regularly seen the sort of things they had seen here today. Sometimes Banks wondered whether there was any innocence left in the world, and he felt terribly old.

By ten o'clock on Saturday night Banks felt like getting out of the house. He had been home only an hour or so, just enough time to eat his Indian takeaway, and he was feeling restless, tormented by the images of the dead bodies of Bill Quinn and the unknown man at Garskill Farm. He couldn't concentrate on television, and even Bill Evans's *Sunday at the Village Vanguard* CD didn't help. He needed somewhere noisy, vibrant and full of life; he needed to be with people, surrounded by conversation and laughter. He realised that he had become a bit of a stop-at-home lately, cultivating a rather melancholy disposition, importing his solo entertainment via CDs and DVDs, but The Dog and Gun had folk night tonight, and Penny Cartwright was guest starring. There would still be time to catch a set.

Banks had met Penny on his second case in Eastvale, more than twenty years ago. She would be about fifty now, but back then she had been a young folk singer returning to her roots in Helmthorpe after forging some success in the big city, and her best friend had been killed. Over the years, her fame had grown, as much as a traditional folk singer's fame can be said to grow, and she had recently moved to a larger house close to the river, which always seemed to be full of guests and passing visitors when she was in residence, many of them well known in folk circles. The wine flowed freely, and the gatherings always ended in a jam session and a mass sing-along. Though Banks had treated her as a suspect on the first case, and it took her many years to forgive him, she seemed comfortable enough with him now and had invited him to her home on occasion. He had joined in with the singing, but very quietly. He had hated his singing voice ever since the music teacher at school made everyone in class sing solo and gave them a mark out of twenty immediately after they had finished. Banks had got nine. He would never forget the public humiliation.

The evening was breezy but mild enough for him to walk by Gratly Beck and cut through the graveyard, then down the snicket past the antiquarian bookshop into Helmthorpe's high street, where one or two groups of underdressed teenagers wandered noisily from one pub to another. They wouldn't go to The Dog and Gun. It would be too crowded already, for a start, and they didn't seem like the folk music type. There was a disco in the back room of The Bridge and cheap beer at The Hare and Hounds, which was now part of the Wetherspoons chain.

Banks arrived during a break between sets, and saw Penny standing at the bar surrounded by admirers, a pint in her hand. She looked radiant, tall, slim, her long black hair streaked with grey. She spotted Banks through the sea of faces in the semi-darkness, and he could have sworn her expression perked up, just a little. She waved him over and manouevred a bit of room for him beside her. They were pushed together by the crush of people trying to order drinks. It wasn't an unpleasant sensation as far as Banks was concerned.

'Hello, stranger,' she greeted him, leaning forward to give him a quick peck on the cheek. The young man beside her, in the midst of a rather tedious lecture about the 'folk revival', seemed a bit put out by Banks's appearance, but Penny seemed relieved at the interruption and focused her attention on the newcomer. Banks did likewise. When you were that close to her, looking into her eyes, it was difficult to do otherwise. They sparkled with an inner glow, full of mischief, sorrow and wisdom. The young man trailed off in mid-sentence and drifted away, crestfallen, back to his mates and more beer.

'He's too young for you, anyway,' said Banks.

'Oh, I don't know. I'm not averse to the occasional toyboy,' said Penny. 'Though I do admit to being more partial to a real man. So what have you been up to?'

Banks realised that he hadn't seen her since the nasty business with Tracy the previous autumn, having either been working or shutting himself away in his cottage for the winter. He told her briefly about his travels in Arizona and Southern

California. Penny, it seemed, had been doing quite a bit of travelling herself during the winter, mostly in Canada and the US on a promotional tour for her new CD. There was no mention of a man in her life, and Banks didn't ask.

'I see your son Brian's doing well,' Penny said.

'Yes,' said Banks. 'He's just got back from America himself. I think they had a good tour, then they did some recording in Los Angeles.'

'I saw a few posters while I was over there. Impressive. I'm sure The Blue Lamps sell a lot more than I do.'

They did, of course. Britpop with a tinge of psychedelia and a smattering of country-folk-blues did far better than traditional British folk music in the States. 'I'm hoping he'll be able to support me in my old age,' Banks said.

Penny laughed. 'I suppose that's one use for children. So what have you been doing since you got back? I heard someone was found dead up at Garskill Farm Is that true?'

'News travels fast,' said Banks. 'It's no secret. Someone told us there was a group of Gypsies or Travellers living up there, but I'm not so sure.'

'How perceptive of you,' said Penny. 'What an insult. I've got friends in those communities, and they wouldn't stay in a dump like Garskill. It's migrant workers.'

'How do you know?'

'I'm a folk singer. I have my finger on the pulse of the folk.'

Banks laughed. 'Seriously.'

'A friend told me. I still have my connections among the local historians and writers, you know.'

'But where do they work?'

'There are plenty of places where they're not fussy who they employ, as long as the labour comes cheap enough, and most of these people aren't in a position to complain. Varley's Yeast Products, just north of town, for example. They've been using slave labour for years. Then there's that slaughterhouse outside Darlington, a meat-packing factory out Carlisle way, the chemical-processing plant south of Middlesbrough. I'm surprised you don't know about all this.'

'It comes under Trading Standards or Immigration,' said Banks. 'At least it did. Now I'm not so sure. Anyway, you seem to know a lot about it. Do you know anything about the people who were living there?'

'Not about any of them specifically, or individually, no. Are you grilling me now?'

'It sounds like it, doesn't it? Actually, I came out to get away from thinking about it. I was up there today, and it's a bloody depressing place. Have you ever been there?'

'Years ago,' said Penny. 'It was pretty much in a state of disrepair back then. I can only imagine what it's like now.'

'Those places were built to last,' said Banks, 'but I don't envy the poor sods who were staying there.'

'It wouldn't have been their choice,' said Penny. 'They're lured over here by the promise of jobs. It costs them all their savings, then they're paid less than minimum wage for shit work, and they've got no recourse. Most of them don't even speak English. They start out in debt; they get deeper and deeper in debt. Can you believe there are even loan sharks who prey on them?'

Banks could. Once more the name Warren Corrigan came to mind. He would be paying Mr Corrigan a visit on Monday.

The musicians – acoustic guitar, accordion, stand-up bass and fiddle – assembled on stage again, picking up and tuning their instruments. 'I've got to go now,' said Penny, touching Banks's arm lightly. 'Will you be here later?'

'I don't know,' said Banks. 'It's been a long day. I'm dog tired.'

'Try to last out the set,' she said. 'Any requests?'

'"Finisterre",' Banks said, without thinking.

Penny blinked in surprise. '"Finisterre"? OK. It's been a long time, but I think I can manage that.'

And she did. Unaccompanied. Her low, husky voice seemed to have grown richer over the years, with the qualities of warm dark chocolate and a fine Amarone. It wasn't quite as deep in range as June Tabor's, but it wasn't far off. She went through 'Death and the Lady', 'She Moved Through the Fair', 'Flowers of Knaresborough Forest' and a number of other traditional songs. She didn't neglect contemporary works, either. Dylan was represented by the moving and mysterious 'Red River Shore', Roy Harper by 'I'll See You Again', and Richard Thompson by a version of 'For Shame of Doing Wrong' that brought tears to Banks's eyes, the way Penny's voice cracked in its heartbreaking chorus. She finished with what could, in someone else's hands, have been a mere novelty, a slow, folksy version of Pulp's 'Common People'. But it worked. Her version brought depth out of the anthem and gave its lyrics a weight that was often easy to miss. Everyone sang along with the chorus, and the applause at the end was deafening. What Jarvis Cocker would have made of it, Banks had no idea, but it didn't matter; he'd never been able to take Jarvis Cocker seriously, anyway, though he did like 'Common People' and 'Running the World'. Maybe it was just his name.

As the crowd settled back to drink up their last orders when the band had finished, Penny came over to the corner table, where Banks had managed to find a chair, and sat down. A couple of the band members joined her, and the young man from the interval lurked in the background looking sulky and swaying a little, pint in hand. Banks had met the band members before and said hello. The accordion player was actually a DS from Durham Constabulary moonlighting as a folkie. 'You made it,' Penny said, smiling. 'Didn't doze off, did you?'

'Not once. Thanks for singing my request.'

'Pleasure. It's a lovely song. I'd forgotten how lovely. Thanks for reminding me of it. So sad, though.'

'Well, there aren't an awful lot of happy folk songs, are there? It's all murders, demon lovers, vengeful spirits, things that have vanished, how fleeting life and pleasure are, love turned cool, died or lost.'

'Too true,' said Penny. 'Look, a few of us are going back to the house. Want to come along? No doom and gloom, I promise.'

'I'd really love to,' said Banks, 'but I fear I wouldn't last long.' In fact, he wanted to end the evening as he ended most evenings, at home in his dark conservatory looking at the moon and stars outside, with a nightcap and some quiet music. He felt he could face it now. He didn't feel like a party any more.

'OK,' she said. 'I understand. Murderers to catch, and all that.'

Banks nodded. 'Murderers to catch.' If only it were that easy. 'Goodnight.'

As Banks left, the eager young man with the theories about the folk revival took his seat, swaying and spilling a little beer as he moved. Penny said hello and smiled politely at him but immediately fell into conversation with her guitarist. Banks didn't think she would be inviting the young man back to her house. She looked in Banks's direction as he was leaving and smiled.

Outside, he noticed a hint of peat smoke in the cool night air, reminding him that it was still only April, no matter how pleasant the days were becoming. No music followed him into the night as he walked the half mile home, mostly along the Pennine Way, with a bright moon and a scattering of stars to light his way. The exercise and fresh air would do him good after a day hanging around in the mire of Garskill Farm.

As he walked along the path that clung to the hillside, which stepped down in a series of lynchets to Gratly Beck, he pictured the migrant worker's body again. Somehow, no matter how many times it happened, he never got quite used to it. He thought of Penny again and knew he shouldn't read anything into her friendly behaviour. It was just her way; she was a free spirit, a bit flirtatious, mischievous. Still, he couldn't help but hope. It seemed that nothing had cured him of that. Not Sandra. Not Annie. Not Sophia.

5

Banks got to the office early enough on Monday morning to listen to *Today* for a while as he went through his in tray. Before long, sick to death of hearing how bad the economy was and how violent things were in the Middle East, he switched over to catch the end of *Breakfast* on Radio 3, where a stately Haydn symphony was playing.

As expected, nothing much had happened on Sunday. Banks had called in at the station briefly, and he found Haig and Lombard working away at the escort agency websites. Doug Wilson and Gerry Masterson were out conducting interviews. He guessed that Joanna Passero would be at home, as would most of the CSIs and lab technicians they so needed to start producing results. Winsome had arranged for the Garskill Farm victim's photo to be on the evening news that night, and it would be shown again the following morning and evening. She had spent most of Sunday asking more questions in Ingleby. There hadn't been many calls made from the telephone box there, and the ones of interest to Banks, made around the time Mrs Boscombe had seen the man resembling the victim, had all been to mobiles. One was to Bill Quinn, another was a pay-as-you-go, impossible to trace, and the third was an Estonian number they were trying to track down.

Early on Monday morning, the upper floors of the police station were still mostly empty, and Banks enjoyed a little quiet time gazing down on the market square, the gold hands against the blue face of the church clock telling him it was a quarter past eight. He made some notes, answered a couple of emails and binned most of the official memos and circulars that had piled up. As Banks worked, he heard people arriving, footsteps on the stairs, office doors opening and closing along the corridor, good mornings, brief comments on the weekend's football and television. A normal Monday morning.

By nine o'clock he was ready for a gathering of the troops, but before he could round them up, there was a knock at his door and Stefan Nowak, Crime Scene Manager, walked in. The two had known one another for years. Stefan was unusual among CSIs for being a detective sergeant rather than a civilian. He was working towards his inspector's boards, and he already had a BSc and a number of forensics courses under his belt. He wasn't a specialist, but something of a jack of all trades, and his management skills made him perfect for the job. He still spoke with a slight Polish accent, though Banks understood that he had been in England for years. He never talked much about his past or his private life, so Banks was not certain what his story was. He sensed that Stefan liked to cultivate an aura of mystery. Perhaps he thought it made him more attractive to the opposite sex. He had a reputation for being a bit of a ladies' man, and dressed as stylishly as Ken Blackstone, though in a more casual, youthful way. He was a lot better-looking, too, with a full head of healthy, well-tended hair. 'I hope you've got something for me, Stefan,' Banks said. 'We could do with a break right now.'

Nowak sat down, pulling at his creases the way Ken Blackstone did. 'I don't think you'll be disappointed,' he said. 'I paid a visit to Garskill Farm yesterday and had a chat with the Crime Scene Manager Mr Smedley. I must say, he's a bit tense and prickly, isn't he?'

'That's one way of describing him.'

'Anyway, I wanted to compare some fibres and tyre tracks

as soon as possible, and it seemed the best way.'

'And were you able to?'

'Not until just now,' said Nowak. 'The team worked very hard and late up at that dreadful place. The report was in my tray when I got in a little over an hour ago. Someone must have dropped it off late last night.' Nowak spent most of his time in Scientific Support, next door, which had been taken over as an annexe when Eastvale was the headquarters of the Western Area. It would probably remain as it was, because it was damn useful, and it saved money in the long run. Like most county forces, Eastvale sent most of the evidence collected at crime scenes out to an accredited forensic laboratory for analysis, but there were one or two things they could handle in their own labs here, such as fingerprint and basic fibre analysis, photographic services and documents. Not DNA or blood, though. In the end, most trace evidence went to the official Forensic Science Service Laboratory at Wetherby, or to one of the specialist labs dealing with such matters as entomology or forensic archaeology. But having some services in-house saved time as well as money.

'Anything useful?'

'Depends what you mean. The book that someone left behind there was in Polish, by the way. A translation of *The Da Vinci Code.*'

'That's a promising start. Fancy a coffee?'

'Sure.'

Banks rang down for a pot of coffee. He still needed about three cups to kick-start him in a morning, and so far he had had only one at home to wash down the slice of toast and marmalade that passed for breakfast.

Nowak shuffled the files in front of him, picking out photographs of hairs and tyre tracks that didn't mean much to Banks. 'The long and the short of it is that we can place the same car at both scenes,' Nowak announced. 'The tracks at Garskill Farm were poor because of the rain, of course, but the ground was very hard to start with, and Smedley's lads managed to get some impressions. There's some very distinctive cross-hatching on one of the tyres.' He showed Banks two photographs; even he could see that the little scratches on both were the same.

'So hang on a minute,' said Banks. 'These are photographs from two different scenes, right? You're saying that the tracks from the farm lane near St Peter's match tracks found in the old driveway at Garskill Farm?'

'Yes.'

'Excellent,' said Banks. It was the forensic link he had been hoping for. It wouldn't offer an easy solution to the case, and perhaps it wouldn't stand up in court, but it would help them focus, give them a sense of direction and a fruitful line of inquiry. 'I don't suppose you can tell the make, year and colour? Licence plate, too, perhaps?'

Nowak laughed. 'Not the year. Not yet. It's not a rugged terrain vehicle, though, I can tell you that much. We've got the wheelbase measurement and identified the brand of the tyres, ContiSportContact 2. So now we have to see how many car manufacturers use them, but we should be able to come up with a bit more information soon. Going by the size and wheelbase dimensions, I'd say we're looking at something along the lines of a Ford Focus. All this is still preliminary, of course. Guesswork. We're working from photographs, and we won't be able to state with any more certainty until we get the Dentstone KD impressions done.'

Banks scribbled on his notepad. 'But you think that what you've told me is accurate so far?'

'Ninety per cent.'

'That's good enough for me right now.'

'Oh, I forgot to mention. It's dark green.'

'What is?'

'The car. It's dark green.'

'You're having me on.'

'Not at all. It brushed against a fencepost and got a little scratch. We're having the paint analysed as well as the tyre tracks. We can probably get you the make, model and year from the paint reference databases, wheelbase and tyre type, when we've got it all itemised, but I'm afraid even that won't be able to tell us the licence number. Still, taken in combination, it should all help us be a lot more accurate.'

'I'm impressed,' said Banks.

'You should be.'

The coffee arrived. They both took it black, so Banks poured from the metal pot into a couple of mugs and passed one to Nowak. 'There's more,' said Nowak, after he had taken his first sip. 'I've just been having a look through the comparison microscope at fibres from both crime scenes. We found quite a few strands of synthetic fibre, most likely from a cheap, mass-produced overcoat of some kind, stuck to the tree from which we think the killer fired his crossbow. Smedley's team found similar fibres at Garskill Farm, in the building where the body was found. Doorpost, chair.'

'So the same person was in both places?'

'So it would seem. Or the same overcoat. We still have a fair way to go to be certain – spectrographic analysis, dye comparisons and so on – but from what I can see at first glance, the fibres match. I wouldn't read too much into that as a scientist without all the other things I've mentioned. After all, it's pretty common. These overcoats are mass-produced, as I said, and anyone could buy one from Marks and Spencers or wherever. When we've got a better sense of the make-up of the fibre and the dyes used, we'll start searching the databases and talking to manufacturers and retailers. But all that will take time, and it's still very unlikely to give us a name. I thought you might want a few preliminary signposts as soon as possible. There are footprints, too. Rather too many to be especially valuable, but their expert thinks some of them match the ones you took from the woods at St Peter's. Same size and distinctive cut on the sole. He was there, in both places.'

'You're a wonder, Stefan.'

'None of this will stand up in court. I hope you don't—'

'Nothing's going to court. Not for a while. But it sheds a little more light on the cases if we can think of them as definitely connected in this way. Thanks. I'll need to do a bit of thinking about what all this means.'

'Smedley's team also found traces of another vehicle on the driveway at Garskill Farm. Seems it has a slight oil leak, so we've got a sample. We've also got tyre tracks. This is a larger vehicle altogether, bigger wheelbase and tyres. A good size transit van.'

'People mover? Big enough for twenty?'

'Maybe. It'd be a bit of a crush, but when you've seen where they were living, I doubt they'd have minded much.'

'I don't think they would have had much choice. Will Smedley's team be able to tell us much more about this other vehicle?'

'Sure. They'll do the measurements, the impressions and analysis. I just thought you might like to know that there was someone else there.'

'Now all we have to do is find him.'

'Give us time,' said Nowak, getting to his feet. 'Give us time. By the way, I've been meaning to ask you. Who is that good-looking blonde with the delightful figure I've seen about the place the past couple of days? Is she new? Visiting? Permanent? Why don't I know about her?'

Banks smiled. 'She's Professional Standards, Stefan. I'd stay well clear of her if I were you.'

'There's nothing wrong with my standards,' Nowak said.

'Professional or otherwise. Professional Standards, eh? Interesting. She's a foxy one.'

'She's married.'

'But is she happy, Alan? Is she happy?' He glanced at the coffee mug in his hand. 'Anyway, I must get back to work. Can I take this?'

'Of course,' said Banks. 'Be my guest.'

He shook his head slowly at Nowak's departing back.

Though Winsome, Banks and the rest of the team gave Annie a heroine's welcome when she arrived in the boardroom for the morning meeting, she nonetheless felt disassociated from the investigation, from the processes of police work as a whole. As she listened to Banks and Winsome, who did most of the talking, and watched them stick photographs and write names on the glass board, it all seemed very remote and distant from what her life had become, and she found herself drifting away, missing bits and pieces, unsure of the connections. Sometimes the voices sounded muffled, and she couldn't make out what they were saying; other times she would notice that two or three minutes had passed by and she hadn't heard a thing. She didn't even know what she'd been thinking. It was only to be expected, she told herself. She had been away a long time.

Area Commander Gervaise dropped in at the end of the meeting to welcome her, and to remind her to take things easy for the first few weeks, not go running around the county. If Annie felt tired, Gervaise told her, she only had to say so, and she would be allowed to go home. The most important thing was that she make a full recovery. *Bollocks*, thought Annie, making a rude sign at Gervaise's departing rear. The main thing was that she got back on the tracks again before it was too late, and she lost all her skills, not only her powers of listening and concentration. She didn't want to be treated like an invalid, like one of those wounded soldiers back from the war who nobody wants to know, or even acknowledge.

She had spent a pleasant weekend reacquainting herself with her tiny cottage in Harkside after over a month at the sprawling artists' colony near St Ives. The cottage in the heart of the maze, or so Banks had described it when he had first visited her there, years ago. She remembered those days well, the late mornings in bed, the warmth and humour, the love-making. Whatever their relationship, however it had ended, at the beginning it had felt like falling in love, full of promise, with that joyous sense of abandon, of falling without a net: feelings that she very much doubted she would let herself experience again, should she be fortunate enough to have the chance. None of those things was a part of her life now, and she had an idea that they weren't a part of Banks's life, either. Maybe she was romanticising their time together. Perhaps it hadn't been that way at all. Memory plays strange tricks on us, she thought. We often remember things the way we would have liked them to be. Besides, it's foolish to try to rekindle what has gone. She had ended her last day of sick leave with a long hot bath and a stack of gossip magazines.

In the large open-plan squad room she shared with the rest of the team, there were flowers on her desk from Banks, along with a box of chocolates from Winsome. The rest of the squad had had a whip round and bought her a fancy teapot, a little gizmo that made it easy to use loose leaves instead of tea bags, and a nice selection of exotic teas, from green to lapsang souchong. It was a nice gesture, and by half past eleven, as she sipped her late elevenses of Darjeeling, sampled a chocolate and looked at the flowers – roses, of course, what else would a man think to buy? – she thought things might not work out too badly after all.

Her main job on her first day was catching up on the Bill Quinn case. Banks had told her a fair bit on Friday night, and at the morning meeting she had learned about the other murder, at Garskill Farm, and its connection with Bill Quinn's murder. Now she had to fill in the gaps, read the witness statements, study the forensic and post-mortem reports.

Over in the corner at the spare desk sat two detectives she didn't know. They were on loan from County HQ, Winsome had said. Haig and Lombard. From what Annie could see, they were watching porn on their computers, and the most unattractive of the two, wispy-haired, shiny suit, skinny as a rake, with bad skin and a Uriah Heep look about him, kept giving her the eye. She couldn't remember from the briefing whether he was Haig or Lombard. All she knew was that they were supposed to be checking Internet sites for the girl in the photo with Quinn. They seemed to be enjoying themselves.

Annie returned to the growing pile of statements, reports and photographs. As she flipped through them, something caught her attention, a blow-up from one of the photos found in Quinn's room, and she went back to it. If anyone had mentioned it at the meeting, she had been drifting at the time. She put the end of her pencil to her lower lip and frowned as she thought through the implications.

Closing the folder, she stood up and walked over to Haig and Lombard. The one who had been ogling her averted his gaze like a guilty schoolboy caught smoking or masturbating in the toilets. They appeared furtive, pretending to concentrate on their respective screens. As they both showed images of big-breasted women in lingerie with knowing expressions on their faces, that didn't help the two detectives to appear any more innocent.

'Enjoying yourselves?' Annie asked, arms folded.

'We're working,' said the wispy-haired one.

'Who are you?'

'DC Lombard, ma'am.' Generally, Annie didn't like being

called ma'am, but these two young pups needed a lesson. She would put up with it.

'Getting anywhere?'

'No, ma'am.'

'Where are you looking?'

'Lyon,' said Haig. 'It's the only place we know DI Quinn has visited in France.'

'What makes you think the photos were taken in France?'

'Huh?'

'Huh, ma'am.'

'Right. Huh, ma'am?'

'I asked why France? I suggested to DCI Banks that it had probably happened in a foreign country, but it didn't have to be France.'

'It's the beer mat, ma'am,' explained Lombard, as if he were talking to a particularly backward child. 'You must have seen it. It says "A. Le Coq".' He pronounced the last word with the requisite manly gusto and bravado, a smirk on his face. 'That sounds French to me.'

Annie could see it took them all they had to stop bursting out sniggering. She held her ground. 'Did you look it up?'

'What do you mean?'

'The beer, the brewery. A. Le Coq. To find out where it is.'

'No need to, was there?' said Lombard. 'I mean, it's French, isn't it? Stands to reason. Or maybe Belgian.'

'But DI Quinn never went to Belgium, did he?' Haig said.

'I thought so,' sighed Annie. 'You pair of bloody idiots. You can stop that right now. You're miles off.'

'What are you talking about? Ma'am.'

Annie leaned over the nearest computer and typed the words 'A. Le Coq' into the Google search engine, then she brought up the first site on the list, moved back so the two DCs could both see the screen. '*That's* what I mean,' she said. 'See how simple it is? Ever heard of Google? And you couldn't be bloody bothered to check. That's sloppy police work.'

Annie walked away, leaving the two open-mouthed. Time to talk to Banks. She picked up the phone.

Banks found a parking spot on North Parkway and walked to the Black Bull. The road, not far from the big Ring Road roundabout, had a central grass strip dotted with trees, and two lanes of traffic on either side. The houses, set back behind pleasant gardens and walls or high privet hedges, were brick or prefab semis, with a smattering of bungalows and the occasional detached corner house. There weren't many small shops, but he passed a mini Sainsbury's and a Job Centre Plus, and saw a small church with a square tower across the street. The area had a pleasant open feel to it, with plenty of green in evidence. There was a council estate behind the opposite side, and two tower blocks poked their ugly upper stories into the quickly clouding sky like fingers raised in an insult.

Banks was feeling pleased with himself for getting rid of Joanna Passero for the day. Naturally, she had wanted to accompany him to Leeds, but Dr Glendenning was performing the post-mortem on the Garskill Farm victim, and seeing as she liked post-mortems so much, Banks had suggested she should go along with Winsome. The rest of the time she could do what she wanted; there was plenty to keep her occupied. She didn't like it, but in the end she reluctantly agreed. With her along, Banks knew he would have an even tougher time with Warren Corrigan, and he probably wouldn't get anything out of Nick Gwillam at all, even though he wasn't actually a copper himself, not with Miss Professional Standards sitting next to him. Still, it remained to be seen whether he got anything useful on his own.

Before Banks got to the Black Bull, his mobile rang. At first he thought he would just ignore it, but when he checked, he saw the call was from Annie, and he felt he owed her all the encouragement he could give her. He stopped and leaned against a bus shelter. 'Annie?'

'I've just been having a word with those two young lads from County HQ,' Annie said. 'Where on earth do they find them these days?'

'Needs must,' Banks said. 'Why? Surely they can't be doing any harm on a soft-porn search?'

'No harm, no, but they're wasting time.'

'What do you mean?'

'The beer mat.'

'What beer mat?'

'"A. Le Coq". A blow-up from one of Quinn's photos. It came in after you left. I don't think they bothered to check on the brewery's location. They're checking escort agencies in the Lyon area.'

'I don't follow. Look, Annie, I've got rather a lot on my plate and—'

'A. Le Coq is *not* a French brewery.'

'It's not? Sounds like it to me. Belgian, then?'

'Not Belgian, either.'

'OK, you've got my attention. I have no idea where it is. Never heard of it. Enlighten me.' A woman, not much more than a girl really, passed by with a two-tier pram in which her twins lay sleeping. She puffed on her cigarette and smiled shyly at Banks, who smiled back.

'If either of them had taken the trouble to find out,' Annie went on, 'they'd have discovered that A. Le Coq is an old established Estonian brewery.'

Banks paused to digest this, work out how it changed things. 'But . . .'

'As I mentioned the other night, I've been to Tallinn,' Annie went on. 'I've even tasted the stuff. It's not bad, actually. You do know what this means, don't you?'

'That the photos were most likely taken when Bill Quinn was in Tallinn six years ago on the Rachel Hewitt case.'

'Exactly. I'll start researching the case immediately. Where are you now?'

Banks explained.

'Will you keep me informed?' Annie said.

'I will. And you me. Thanks a lot, Annie.'

'No problem.'

'One more thing. Don't forget that one of the calls we think the Garskill Farm victim made from the telephone box in Ingleby was to an Estonian number. You might check if anyone's run it down yet. Or do it yourself. It shouldn't be too difficult.'

'Will do.'

Banks put his phone back in his jacket pocket and made his way towards the pub, which rather resembled a rambling old house, with a red pantile roof, a whitewashed facade and a small area of picnic benches in a stone-flagged yard out front, separated from the pavement by a strip of grass and a low wall. Banks made his way past the empty tables to the door and entered the cavern-like space. The ceiling was high, and the room seemed to swallow up the little groups of tables, even the bar itself, though it was long, and the tiers of bottles reflected in the mirror gave the illusion of depth. The place had clearly seen better days, but there was a certain warm welcome in the shabby velveteen, brass fixtures and framed watercolours of old Leeds scenes on the walls. It smelled of domestic cleaning fluid, but all the Domestos in the world couldn't get rid of the years of stale smoke. A few slot machines flashed and beeped here and there by a nicotine-stained pillar, but no one was playing them. Peter and Gordon were singing 'A World Without Love' on the jukebox. It was lunchtime, and there were a few family groups picking away at baskets of chicken and chips or bowls of lasagna, and the usual ensemble

of regulars stood at the far end of the bar chatting up a buxom
blonde barmaid. She looked like a retired stripper, Banks
thought. Or perhaps not even retired yet. He walked over to
the barman, who was studiously polishing a glass.

'What can I do for you, sir?' the barman asked.

'I'd like to see Mr Corrigan.'

The man's expression changed abruptly from welcoming
to hostile. 'And who may I say is asking for him?'

Banks showed his warrant card.

'Just a moment, sir.'

The barman disappeared. The blonde pulling pints at the
far end of the bar glanced over and cocked her hip. A few
moments later, the barman reappeared, and a giant material-
ised beside Banks.

'Curly here will take you to him,' said the barman, then he
turned away. Curly was as bald as one of the balls on the
snooker table at the far end of the room, and about as unsmil-
ing. Banks followed him through a maze of small lounges,
past another bar, through doors and down corridors by the
Gents and Ladies toilets towards the back of the pub, until
they came to a small private function room, perfect for the
office lunch. Curly gestured for Banks to enter, and he did.
The decor was much the same as the rest of the pub, with
plenty of brass and velvet in plush dark shades, with heavy
varnished tables, ornate iron legs. Banks had expected an
entourage, but one man sat alone at a table, a few papers
spread in front of him. He gathered them up and put them in
a folder, then smiled and stood up when Banks came in. Banks
was surprised at how slight and skinny he was. He had a sort
of ferret face, thinning ginger hair, no eyebrows and a high
forehead. Banks put his age at about forty. He was casually
dressed, wearing a navy sports jacket over his shirt. No tie. He
extended his hand in greeting. Banks thought it churlish to
refuse, so he shook.

'I know Kelly at the bar checked your ID, but you don't mind if I have a butcher's, myself, do you? One can't be too careful.'

'Not at all,' said Banks, showing his warrant card.

Corrigan examined it. 'Detective Chief Inspector Banks,' he read slowly. 'Impressive. It's a pleasure to meet you at last, Mr Banks. I've heard so much about you. Sit down, sit down. You're a long way from home. What brings you to these parts? But please excuse my manners. Can I offer you a drink?'

'I wouldn't mind a coffee,' said Banks.

'Coffee, it is.' He called Curly in. 'Get Mr Banks a coffee, Curly. How do you take it?'

'Black, no sugar,' said Banks.

'You might think this set-up a bit odd,' said Corrigan, gesturing around the room when Curly had gone for the coffee, 'but I find it far more congenial than some soulless office in a building full of soulless offices. This place has history, atmosphere. And I'm comfortable here. Don't you think it's comfortable?'

'Very,' said Banks.

'Of course, I travel quite a lot, too, but when I'm in town, I find it most pleasant to work here. It's also useful for entertaining, too, of course. The chef can put together a decent menu when the occasion demands it, and there's never any shortage of drink. Plus, I find it's a good way to stay in touch with the neighbourhood. It's a part of the community.'

'You've sold me on it,' said Banks. 'I'll ask my boss if I can relocate to the Queen's Arms as soon as I get back to Eastvale.'

Corrigan laughed, showing rather long, yellowish teeth. The coffee arrived. Corrigan didn't have anything except the bottle of sparkling water already in front of him. 'It's a lovely part of the country you come from, the Yorkshire Dales,' he said. 'You should be proud of its heritage. I'd live there like a shot if I was in a position to retire. Do you know Gratly?'

'I do.'

'One of my favourite spots. The view from the bridge, the old sawmill. Picnic by the falls on Gratly Beck on a warm summer's day. I like nothing better than to take the wife and kids there for a day out when I can manage it.' He paused. 'Still, I don't suppose you've come here to talk about the beauties of the Yorkshire Dales, have you?'

'Not exactly,' said Banks. He knew that Corrigan was trying to rile him, or scare him off, by showing that he knew where Banks lived, which he had no doubt checked up on after Bill Quinn's murder, but he was damned if he was going to rise to the bait. 'It's about DI Quinn. Bill Quinn.'

'Ah, yes.' Corrigan scratched the side of his nose. 'Poor Bill. Tragic. Tragic. I understand it happened in your neck of the woods. I should imagine that's why you're investigating the case and not the locals here?'

'Got it in one,' said Banks. 'But I shouldn't worry too much. DI Quinn might be dead, but he'll be replaced so quickly you won't even notice it's happened. I understand he was causing you a few problems?'

'Problems? Bill? Not at all. I enjoyed our conversations, though I must say he was a rather dour man. It was hard to get a laugh out of him. Still, an intelligent man. Well informed. Well rounded, too. I like a man who has an interest in outdoor pursuits like fishing and gardening, don't you, Mr Banks? I think it adds character, dimension.'

'Frankly,' said Banks, 'I couldn't give a toss. What I'd like to know is where you were last Wednesday evening between about eleven and one in the morning.'

'Me? I'm assuming this is to do with Bill's death, but I'm surprised you're asking where *I* was. Surely if I had anything to do with what happened – and I assure you, I did not – then I'd hardly do it myself, would I? Do I look like an assassin?'

'Assassins come in all shapes and sizes,' said Banks. 'And it's murder. Not just death. Bill Quinn was murdered. I think we'd be best calling a spade a spade.'

'As you will. Plain speaking. I'm all for that.'

'What kind of car do you drive?'

'A Beemer. Some think it's a bit flash for these parts, but I like the way it handles.'

'So where were you?'

'At home, I should think. Certainly nowhere near St Peter's.'

'But you knew where Bill Quinn was?'

'Everyone knew where Bill Quinn was.'

'Did you tell anyone?'

'Why would I do that?'

'You tell me.'

'No.'

Banks suspected he was lying. 'Where's home?' he went on.

'Selby.'

'Any witnesses?'

'My wife, Nancy. Lily and Benjamin, the kids, ten and twelve respectively. Quite a handful.'

'Anyone else?'

'Isn't that enough?'

'How about Curly out there?'

'We don't live together.'

'Where was he?'

'Curly!' Corrigan called.

Curly stuck his shiny head around the doorway. 'Boss?'

'Mr Banks here wants to know where you were last Wednesday night.' He glanced over at Banks, an amused expression on his thin pale face.

'At the infirmary,' Curly said.

'What happened?'

'Bumped into a lamppost. They kept me in overnight for observation.'

'We can check, you know.'

'Then check.' He lowered his head. 'You can still see the bump.'

Banks saw it. 'Ouch,' he said. 'Nasty one. Dissatisfied client?'

Curly grunted and walked away.

'So, as you can see, Mr Banks,' said Corrigan, showing his palms in a gesture of frankness, 'we have nothing to hide. Our consciences are clean.'

'I can't see how that could be,' said Banks, 'when you prey on the most vulnerable members of the community. You're nothing more than the school bully demanding cash with threats in the playground.'

'Unfortunately, there will always be the weak, and there will always be the strong,' said Corrigan, 'just as there will always be the poor and the rich. The poor are always with us. Didn't Jesus say that, or something very much like it? I know which I'd rather be in both cases. Do *you*, Mr Banks?'

'Misquoting the scriptures doesn't help your case,' said Banks. 'Besides, I think it's more a matter of the decent and the morally bankrupt, and I know which I'd like to be. But that's just me.'

'Oh, we have an outraged moralist here, do we? Yes, I remember I'd heard that about you. One of those religious coppers, are you? I provide a service. Do you think these poor vulnerable people, as you choose to see them, are any more decent than the rest of the rabble? Well, let me tell you, they are not. They think this country is the land of milk and honey. For a start, they're greedy. They have no money, no jobs, they're already in debt up to their eyeballs, but they want that new flat-screen television, they want the new car, their wives want to shop somewhere other than Primark for their clothes and their children's clothes. They are also lazy, but they still want to be able to go out to fancy restaurants for dinner, and the younger ones want to go clubbing. All that takes money, and I supply it. I'm doing them a service.'

'You make it sound very generous, Mr Corrigan, if it weren't for your rates of interest.'

'High risk, high interest. A businessman has to make a living.'

'And the occasional broken leg? What happens when they can't pay, and you come around asking for the money?'

'Now, what good would my clients be to me if they weren't healthy enough to work, should an opportunity and inclination present itself? Ask yourself that, Mr Banks. Yes, we have had to administer a gentle reminder on occasion, as an example, let's say, but is that so different from any other line of work? Examples must be made. The message soon gets around.'

Banks had dealt with criminals like Corrigan before. They don't really see themselves as criminals, or else they are so cynical about society and human nature that it doesn't matter to them what they are, as long as they have the power and the money. On the surface, everything is all very cosy and upper-middle class, ponies and piano lessons for the kiddies, cashmere sweaters, Hugo Boss suits, Beemers and Range Rovers, golf club membership, perhaps even a friend or two on the local council. Underneath, it's another matter. A trail of misery and woe, broken bodies and trampled souls going back as far as the eye can see. Someone has to pay for the Corrigans of this world to live in luxury, after all, whether they be junkies, gamblers or just poor sods who have fallen for the whole consumer society deal hook, line and sinker. But there was no point in saying it; there was no point arguing.

'Tell me what you know about migrant labour camps,' said Banks.

'Only what I read in the papers. People come over here seeking for jobs, unskilled workers, asylum seekers, illegals, and they don't always find one. Then they start whining about how badly done to they are. Well, that's a big bloody surprise isn't it, given that half our own people can't find a job either?'

'You mean that sometimes they start out in debt to someone like you, are made to work at jobs no one else wants to do, forced to live in squalid dormitories for exorbitant rents?'

'You've been reading the *Guardian*, haven't you? No wonder your heart's bleeding all over your sleeve. I told you, I know nothing about them except what's on the news, and I can't say I pay I much attention to that. If they come over here stealing our jobs, they get what they bloody deserve.'

'What about the people who bring them here? The agents? The gangmasters? The staffing companies? You must have some contacts with them?'

'Don't know what you mean.'

Banks sensed that he was lying again but moved on quickly, anyway. 'Ever heard of a place called Garskill Farm?' he asked.

'No,' said Corrigan. 'It sounds a bit Dales-ish, though. Is it somewhere near you?'

'Close,' said Banks. 'We just found a body there.' He slipped a picture of the victim out of his briefcase and put it on the table. 'Recognise this man?'

Corrigan examined it. 'No. Not looking very healthy, though, is he?'

Banks followed it with a blow-up of the girl Quinn was with in Tallinn. 'How about her?'

'Nope. Wish I did, though. She looks good enough to eat.' He ran his pink pointed tongue across his upper lip.

There was no evidence that Corrigan trafficked in young girls or acted as pimp, so Banks couldn't really push him on any of this. It had been a long shot, anyway. All of it. Corrigan was a villain, no doubt, legally and morally, and Quinn had been on to him. But had Corrigan murdered Quinn, or had him killed? Had Quinn been in Corrigan's power and tried to escape? And the man at Garskill Farm? What part had he played? There were still too many unanswered questions.

Leaving the rest of his coffee, Banks stood up. As soon as Curly heard the chair scraping against the stone floor he was in the doorway again. Corrigan gave him an almost imperceptible signal, and he stood aside.

'It's been a pleasure, Mr Banks,' said Corrigan. 'Next time you come, let's make an occasion of it. Have a real drink. They've got a very nice selection of single malts in the main bar. You should enjoy the ten-year-old cask strength Laphroaig especially.'

Banks smiled. 'Your information's a bit out of date, Corrigan,' he said. 'I'm more of a red wine man, these days.' Then he left.

Annie had experienced an extraordinary amount of satisfaction after bollocking Lombard and Haig for doing a half-arsed job on A. Le Coq, but now she was feeling guilty. It had been like shooting goldfish in a bowl. After all, they were just probationers, still wet around the ears, transferred in from elsewhere to help out. And they had done a lot of the shit work. For all the jokes made at their expense, it can't have been a lot of fun spending day after day trawling through sleazy Internet sites searching for a face.

On the other hand, if they didn't have what it took to carry out a simple Internet search, a no-brainer, then it was best they should find out now, rather than later, when they had more responsibility and could do more damage. They would get over it and move on. They might even make decent detectives one day. At least now they were checking the Estonian escort sites.

Though Annie had been to Tallinn for a dirty weekend with a DI from Newcastle four years ago, she knew very little about the place. They had done some sightseeing, but not much, sat at tables outside bars in an old part of the city drinking beer – A. Le Coq, as it happened – and eating pasta. The rest of the time they had spent in the hotel room having sweaty sex.

To Annie, that whole part of the world was tainted with the old Soviet curse, and she assumed that the Baltic states were an extension of Russia when it came to crime and Russian Mafia activity. Drugs, people-trafficking and illegal labour scams would be right up there. Perhaps Quinn got involved in something like that, and the Russians were behind it? Weren't they behind almost everything illegal these days? The girl herself could be Russian. There was no way of telling from the photographs, but she did have that certain sad and tragic aspect to her beauty that Annie had associated with Russian women ever since she saw *Doctor Zhivago* on late-night television. It was one of Banks's favourite movies, she knew, but that was because of Julie Christie.

Anyway, there was no point in speculating further. Whatever his motive, and whoever he was, Quinn's killer had been in the woods at St Peter's four days ago. They had a few solid leads to him now – the forensics on the tyre tracks and fibres, Quinn's involvement in the Rachel Hewitt case, and now the blown-up part of one of the blackmail photos showing an A. Le Coq beer mat. She had Haig and Lombard checking if it was sold in other Baltic countries, too, or anywhere else in such quantities as to justify handing out free beer mats to bars – she wasn't going to make the mistake of assuming too much at this point – but given that Rachel Hewitt had disappeared in Tallinn, and that Quinn had spent a week there working on the case there with the locals, she felt pretty certain about it.

There was very little about the Rachel Hewitt case in DC Gerry Masterston's research so far, or in Quinn's old files, which had arrived in the early afternoon. It was hardly surprising, really, Annie thought, as he had been only marginally connected with it. The real stuff would be in Tallinn. In

Estonian. Whether it would be possible to get hold of those files if she needed to, she had no idea. In the meantime, she could at least start digging a bit into the background of what happened on that night six years ago.

Rachel Hewitt was to be maid of honour to her best friend Pauline Boyars at her wedding at St Paul's Church in Drighlington on 5 August 2006. Before that, from 21 to 24 July they were going to Tallinn with four other close female friends for a hen weekend. The girls, all about nineteen years of age, were excited about the trip. They booked their cheap EasyJet flight early, and made sure they all got rooms at the Meriton Old Town Hotel, which someone told them was very comfortable and very close to lots of bars and clubs. To save money, the girls asked for twin beds and doubled up; Rachel shared with Pauline.

On the Friday they arrived, the girls met up in the hotel bar for a drink at six o'clock, then walked into town to find somewhere to eat. It was a hot evening, but they were early enough to get a table outside and enjoy some 'authentic' Estonian cuisine of pork in beer, and elk sausage. The idea was to have a relatively civilised and sedate Friday night out, which is exactly what they did, returning to the hotel around 11 p.m.

Saturday was for sightseeing and shopping, then came Saturday night, the big night itself, party time. They all got dolled up in their micro-skirts, spangly tops and fishnets, put on a bit of war paint and headed for the bars and clubs. At least they weren't wearing bunny ears and tails, or little whiskers painted on their cheeks, as far as Annie could gather from the reports. They started with a few drinks in the hotel bar, then hit the town. After stopping at a few other bars, they ate steak and frites and drank wine outside at a restaurant, and after that things started to get a bit hazy.

Annie realised that she would have to go through the individual statements made by each of the girls before she could build up a clear picture of the order of events, but according to the newspaper and Internet reports, the girls went on to a couple of dance clubs, getting rowdier as the evening wore on. They were seen talking and dancing with various groups of boys over the course of the evening. Pauline was sick in the street, but soon recovered enough to go on with her friends to another bar on the main square.

Naturally, the boys flocked around them, their predatory instincts sensing the lack of inhibitions that comes with drunkenness, expecting easy pickings. According to all the accounts, though, there was no trouble. At least all the girls agreed on that. They moved on to yet another bar with a group of German youngsters they had befriended earlier at a nightclub, and it was maybe twenty minutes or so after that when Pauline began to wonder where Rachel had got to.

They checked all the rooms and toilets of the bar they had just arrived at, but she was nowhere to be seen. One of the others thought she might have been in the toilet when they left the previous bar, and may have missed their leaving, but she was equally sure that they'd told her where they were going. Pauline argued that they can't have done, as they didn't decide where they were going until they got outside, and it was the Germans' idea, anyway.

Somehow, Rachel had become detached from her group.

Pauline asked one of the German boys to accompany her back to the previous bar, but in the winding streets of the Old Town they couldn't remember exactly where it was, so they eventually gave up. They tried Rachel's mobile, but all they got was her answering service. The police discovered later that Rachel had forgotten her mobile, left it in her hotel room.

At this point, Pauline said she assumed that Rachel would find her way back to the hotel, or get a taxi to take her there. They didn't know the city well, having been there only a day, but although it was winding and confusing, the Old Town wasn't very big, and Pauline thought that anyone wandering around for long enough was bound to return to the place they started from eventually. Besides, Rachel marched to the beat of her own drummer, and whatever she was up to, she would come back when she was ready.

Even so, Rachel's defection put a bit of a damper on the night, so they all returned to the hotel, disappointing the German boys. They expected to find Rachel slumped in the bar, or passed out in her room, but when Pauline went back to her room to lie down, she wasn't there. She said the room started spinning, and she was sick again. Then she fell asleep, or passed out, and when she awoke it was daylight. There was still no sign of Rachel. She felt awful; her head ached; her stomach churned, but despite the ravages of the hangover, concern for her friend gnawed away at her. It wasn't like her to stay away *all* night. Pauline started to think that Rachel must have got lost somewhere and maybe ended up at another hotel, or maybe got caught up in a group and gone to a party. At worst, she worried that her friend had hurt herself, got hit by a car or something, and was in hospital. She went down to the hotel reception and asked to speak to the manager. The young assistant manager who came out to talk to her was concerned enough to bring in the police, and thus the whole nightmare began. Of course, the girls had drunk so much and visited so many bars and clubs that it took the police close to two days to get any sense of where they had been and what they had done, and by then, anyone who might have been there on the night in question was long gone.

Rachel Hewitt was never seen again, and no clues to her whereabouts were ever discovered.

Annie put aside the clippings and rested her head in her hands. Christ, she thought, what do you do? As a police-woman, she had seen the worst in human nature, and she thought that if something like that had happened to a friend of hers, she would have been down to the cop shop like a shot screaming for some action. But would she?

There had been no real reason to assume that anything bad had happened to Rachel. She sounded like a bit of a character to start with, up for adventure. Annie remembered when her best mate from school, Ellen Innes, had disappeared on a night out in Newquay. It wasn't exactly a foreign country or anything, but there were some wild pubs, and things could get pretty crazy there on a Friday and Saturday night. Annie and her other two friends searched, but they couldn't find Ellen in any of their usual haunts, so they went home, assuming she would come back when she was ready. Annie went to bed without calling anyone.

In the morning, after a few frantic phone calls between the girls' parents, it transpired that Ellen had simply felt tired and decided to go to sleep on a quiet bench by the harbour. She was none the worse for wear, except for a bad hangover and a stiff back. Her parents gave her a strict curfew, and that was the end of the matter. But Annie thought of the things that could have happened, things that probably *had* happened to Rachel Hewitt. Of course, she realised that she had the benefit of hindsight and the experiences of twenty years as a police officer.

She didn't blame Rachel's friends. Anyone in their position, and their state of mind, would have done the same as they did. And the odds were that if Pauline had insisted on calling the police when she got back to the hotel that night, they would hardly have combed the city for the missing girl. At most, they might have done a sweep of some of the most popular bars, checked the hospitals for accident victims and scoured a few patches of open ground in case she'd nodded off somewhere, but they were hardly going to pull out all the stops for a nineteen-year-old foreign tourist missing a couple of hours at most. They would most likely have assumed that she went off with some boy and was happily screwing her brains out somewhere. In the morning she would be back. Police thinking could be very basic, Annie knew. Especially male police thinking.

Whether she was pregnant when she came back, had been infected with some STD or HIV, or whether she had tried to say no but had been too drunk to resist, was not their problem. Annie understood that much. The police couldn't be the moral touchstones or guardians of the world, and to be honest, nobody would want or expect them to be. It was pointless trying to assign blame, except to whoever it was who had taken and hurt Rachel, for Annie was sure that was what must have happened. As sure as she was that Rachel Hewitt was dead. She could only hope it had been quick and painless. Annie sighed. Time to check and see if there was any progress on the Estonian mobile number called from Ingleby.

She turned to see Joanna Passero standing behind her, all blonde hair and elegant curves. Why did her appearance always make Annie feel so dowdy and tomboyish?

'Is everything all right?' Joanna asked.

'Just fine and dandy.'

'Are you in pain? Ca—'

'I'm fine. Is there something you want to tell me?'

Joanna seemed taken aback. Annie was aware of the harshness of her tone, and blamed it mostly on the dark place her mind had been wandering in when she noticed her standing there. 'I'm sorry,' she said. 'I was just . . . the Rachel Hewitt case.'

Joanna glanced at the computer screen, which showed a photograph of a smiling Rachel under the heading 'West Yorkshire Girl Disappears in Estonian Hen Weekend Tragedy'.

'Oh,' she said. 'Did you once know someone who disappeared like that?'

'We've all worked on cases,' said Annie. 'It's nothing

personal. Just empathy. Anyway, I'm sorry I was rude just now. Did you have something to tell me?'

Joanna pulled up a chair and sat down. 'I've just got back from the post-mortem with DS Jackman,' she said. 'It was pretty straightforward, really. The man was definitely drowned, and Dr Glendenning is pretty certain he was drowned in the trough of water at the scene. They have to do various tests on the samples to be absolutely certain, of course.'

'*Was* drowned, rather than just drowned?'

'That's how it appears. There were bruises on the back of his neck, on his upper arms, and on his shoulders. There were also marks on his wrists, where they had been bound with some sort of cord. The lab's working on the fibres. Somebody held him under the water deliberately. He struggled. And Dr Burns was right, he was definitely waterboarded first.'

'Jesus Christ, the poor sod,' said Annie.

Before meeting Nick Gwillam, Banks ate lunch by himself at the Pizza Express behind the Corn Exchange and allowed himself a small glass of Sangiovese to wash down his Sloppy Giuseppe. He had considered giving Ken Blackstone a call to see if he was free for lunch, but decided that after his session with Corrigan he preferred his own company for a while. Talking to Corrigan, he thought, had probably been a waste of time, but as with so many similar conversations, he could only know that in retrospect. Just another in the long line of sad, tired, cocky, depressing villains that seemed to be Banks's daily round.

Corrigan was small-time, though there was a chance he had connections with some big players in the people-trafficking world, whose victims provided him with his victims, and whom he helped keep in bondage. Essentially, he was a parasite on the bigger organism, but many animals willingly went through life with millions of parasites living on their skin or inside their bodies. It became something of a symbiotic relationship. There was always room for a bit of give and take in the world of crime. Especially take.

But that didn't mean Corrigan had anything to do with Quinn's death. Curly's alibi would be easy to check out, so easy it had to be true, and Corrigan's would be impossible to break, even if it were a lie. No doubt he had other minions capable of doing the job for him, and they should be easy enough to round up, but so far his little gang had no history of crossbow use, or of murder. He certainly intimidated people who owed him money, resorted to threats and even to violence on occasion, but he had never, as far as they knew, killed anyone yet. A dead debtor might well be a lesson to the rest, as Corrigan had pointed out, but he was also a loss of income. Why start the killing with a cop and bring down the heat? He was surely under enough pressure already, with the citywide investigation into his operation, and the suicides that could possibly be linked to it. If Corrigan had had Bill Quinn in his pocket, was somehow tied in to the photos and the blackmail, then it now appeared that there was a definite Estonian connection, too. Curiouser and curiouser.

After Banks had finished his lunch, he wandered up to Call Lane, then down Kirkgate. Hands in pockets, walking slowly and taking in the colours, sounds and smells, he cut through the indoor market with its white-coated barkers and stalls piled with scaly fish, marbled red meat and bright shiny fruit and vegetables. No matter how fresh everything was, there was always a faint smell of decay underneath it all.

He came out by the back of the bus station to Millgarth, at the bottom of Eastgate. Though the day had clouded over, it was still warm, and was quickly getting more humid. There'd be more rain before nightfall, Banks was sure.

When he presented himself at Millgarth, Nick Gwillam came down to meet him and, not surprisingly, suggested that he'd like to get out of the office for a while, so why didn't they go for a coffee? Banks had had enough coffee for the day, but he was quite happy to enjoy an afternoon cup of tea. They ended up sitting outside the Pret A Manger on the corner of Lands Lane and Albion Place, opposite WHSmith.

'So, you want to talk to me about Bill?' said Gwillam, with a large latte and an egg salad sandwich in front of him.

'You worked with him closely, I understand?'

'Recently, yes. I suppose you know I'm only temporary up here? A civilian, really. Trading Standards.'

'Yes. But you worked on the Corrigan case with DI Quinn?'

'For my sins.'

'I just had a word with him, and he seemed to know a fair bit about me. Where I live. What I drink. I wonder how he could have found out all that?'

Gwillam leaned back in his metal chair and regarded Banks through narrowed eyes. He was tall and lean, with cropped dark hair already thinning and turning grey around the edges, like Banks's own. He wore a pinstripe suit, white shirt and an old club or university tie. Finally, he let out a chuckle. 'Oh, he played that little trick on you, did he?'

'What trick?'

'See, it's a thing of his. A little trick he likes to play. He rattles off bits and pieces he knows about you. Tries to shock you. I assume he knew you were on the case, Bill's murder, so he'd find out a bit about you.'

'Yes, but it's where he gets his information that interests me. He also knew that Bill Quinn was at St Peter's.'

'There was no secret about that. Everybody knew where Bill was. Everybody who had any sort of connection with him, at any rate. He probably told Corrigan himself.'

'Why would he do that?'

'No specific reason. Just in conversation.'

'Do you think he also happened to mention where I live and the name of my favourite tipple?'

'Everyone knows you're a single malt man.'

'I must say you're very nonchalant about this. But the questions remain. Where does Corrigan get his information, and what else does he do with it other than show it off to impress visiting coppers?'

'Are you suggesting that Corrigan gave away Bill's whereabouts to someone who wanted him dead?'

'It's possible, isn't it? He has to be connected to some pretty violent people in his line of work. If DI Quinn had found out too much, or crossed someone . . .? But it's just another theory. One of many, unfortunately.'

Gwillam sipped his latte. It left a faint white moustache on the top of his lip. 'Corrigan talks to a lot of people, mixes a lot,' he went on. 'People talk to him. Tell him things. He listens. He's a like a jackdaw going after silver paper, and he remembers, he absorbs information like a sponge. Sorry about the mixed metaphor, but I think you know what I mean.'

'Anyone could have told him?'

'Yes. Even Bill himself.'

'And Corrigan could then have passed on the information to anyone, himself?'

'Yes. For any reason, or none at all. If he did pass on Bill's whereabouts, it might not have necessarily seemed significant to him at the time. He might simply have done it in passing.'

'OK,' said Banks. That meant there were two strong contenders for telling the killer where Quinn was staying: the Garskill Farm victim, under torture, and Warren Corrigan, for any, or no, reason at all. Banks also realised with a shock that he had been as guilty as anyone else of giving Corrigan information. At the end of their conversation, he had intimated that he didn't drink Laphroaig any more, which was only partly true, but that he was more of a red wine drinker, which was wholly true. He had intended it as a put down of Corrigan's out-of-date source in information, but he realised that through his own showing off, through his need to get one up on Corrigan, he had actually fallen into the trap and told him something he didn't know: that Banks was a red wine drinker. It didn't matter, had no real significance, at least none that he could see, but it shed some light on the way Corrigan worked, and some of the snippets he picked up were clearly very useful indeed.

'What more can you tell me about Corrigan and his business?'

'My interest is mostly in the loan sharking, of course, but we also think he's in a bit deeper with the whole people-trafficking and migrant labour business. It's quite a wide-reaching racket. Has to be. There are agents and runners all over the place. Even Customs and Excise and Immigration officers have to be paid off to turn a blind eye. There are fake visas, passports, too. But it's a connection that's hard to prove. He's nothing if not cautious.'

'Drugs?'

'Not yet, at any rate.'

'Prostitution?'

'He's clearly got contacts among the pimps, but we don't think he's one, himself. Probably thinks it's beneath him.'

'And gouging the poorest of the poor isn't?'

'What can I say? Blokes like Corrigan have a skewed version of morality.'

'You're telling me. So how deep is he in it? How high up?'

'That's what we're not sure of. We've seen him once or twice with a bloke called Roderick Flinders. Flinders runs a staff agency. Rod's Staff Ltd. Get it?'

'"My rod and my staff"? Cute. What do they do?'

'They provide cheap labour to whoever wants it, no questions asked. They deal mostly in asylum seekers, illegals of various kinds, unskilled migrant workers. Place them in shit jobs for shit pay.'

This was the kind of thing Penny Cartwright had told Banks about on Saturday night, the factories where no questions were asked. 'Illegal work?'

'Sometimes. You could certainly argue that it's slave labour. Below minimum wage.'

'The same people Corrigan preys on himself?'

'The very same. It would be to his advantage, wouldn't it, to be sure of the supply, know what's heading his way? It makes sense. Helps him expand his markets. You scratch my back, I scratch yours. We suspect that Flinders also helps fix forged temporary work permits for asylum seekers. In some cases he's even got hold of faked passports, which is a bit more difficult, but not so much as you think. He's part of a chain that starts with the agents in the various countries involved and continues through drivers, gangmasters, employers, people who rent out the accommodation, and the rest of the hangers-on. Everyone takes a slice except the poor sod doing the work. It's a pretty big operation. That's why Trading Standards is involved.'

'Why hasn't this Flinders been arrested?'

'He's slippery. Got a smooth front, clever lawyers, and nobody's been able to come up with any hard evidence on the other stuff. Besides, the ones watching him are still excited about where he might lead them. Sometimes I wish we could just seize his phone records and bank accounts, but even I know these buggers are too clever. We've got no cause, for a start. And they use encryptions and untraceable mobiles and numbered bank accounts in countries that don't care where the money comes from.'

'He and Corrigan are mates?'

'That's right. Dinner. Drinks. Holidays in the sun.'

'And Bill?'

'Me and Bill were just keeping an eye on Corrigan, having the occasional chat, hoping to hook something a bit bigger.'

'How long has this been going on?'

'With Corrigan? About eight months.'

Banks mulled over what he had been hearing. If Corrigan had these links to organised crime, there was clearly a chance that he was, indirectly or otherwise, behind Quinn's killing, or at least that he knew more about it than he was willing to admit. Quinn could have been bent, as Joanna Passero seemed to think, and suddenly become a liability. But where did the Rachel Hewitt case fit in? What was the connection? And the girl in the photo? Or was all that simply a red herring? Surely it couldn't be? There was definitely a forensic link between Quinn's murder and the murder at Garskill Farm, and there was a link between the two victims; they had spoken twice on the telephone. There was also a possible connection between the Garskill Farm murder and Estonia.

'Just out of interest,' Banks asked, 'does Corrigan have any connections with Estonia?'

'Estonia? Not that I know of,' said Gwillam.

'Maybe through the migrant labour scam? Through Flinders?'

'I suppose it's possible, but I've never seen or heard anything.'

'I was just thinking about the Rachel Hewitt case. Bill Quinn worked on that. He even went to Tallinn in the early stages.'

'You think there's a connection?'

'I don't know. Right now, we're just looking more closely at the Hewitt case for various reasons, but as far as I know she was simply an innocent English girl who disappeared abroad. No body has ever been found. But that was six years ago. Where was Corrigan then?'

'No idea, but I don't think he was on anyone's radar that long ago. Maybe mugging old ladies and robbing sweet shops.'

'It might be worth checking.'

'Bit of a long shot.'

'I know.' Banks sighed. 'That's the way everything seems in this case. I'm just hoping one of them will hit the mark. Even if Corrigan wasn't involved, he might be doing business with people who were. Did Bill ever talk about Rachel?'

'Not much. It was long before my time, and way out of my areas of interest. It came up once or twice in conversation, but you soon got the sense that it wasn't a good idea to mention it. Bill didn't like to talk about it. He'd get all broody.'

'Why do you think that was?'

'He felt he'd failed the girl.'

'But he never really got a chance to succeed.'

'Doesn't matter. He was just that kind of copper. Took it personal, like.'

'But why?' Banks paused to collect his thoughts. 'This is something that puzzles me. Everybody I talk to tells me Bill Quinn was haunted by the Rachel Hewitt case, that he felt he failed, but in reality he didn't have very much to do with it. Why did Bill Quinn care so much? He spent a few days in Tallinn, that's all, surely more of a public relations exercise than anything else, by the sound of it, and when he comes back it's as if his life has been blighted by the whole thing. Why?' He wasn't going to tell Gwillam about the added complication of the mystery girl and the photos, clearly taken in Tallinn, too, which might go some way towards explaining Quinn's obsession.

'Like I said, he was that kind of copper,' said Gwillam, through tight lips. He pushed his cup aside. 'And I've worked with all types. Bill took everything seriously. And he happens to have a daughter about the same age as Rachel. He doted on Jessica. Now, if you don't mind . . .'

'Work to do?'

'Something like that.'

Gwillam got up and walked down Lands Lane, turning left on Bond Street, out of sight among the crowds of shoppers.

Banks swirled the remains of his tea and mulled over what he had just heard. He'd been searching for connections and finding too many, each of which seemed to cancel out or contradict the other. He remembered Annie telling him what she had heard at St Peter's about Quinn's overriding sense of guilt. He had been out on surveillance when his wife died, and that kind of thing could eat away at you. Every copper had missed something important in his family life because of the job – an anniversary party, kid's graduation, a birth, a wedding, even a funeral. Most learned to live with it, but it dragged some of the best men and women down.

Banks glanced at his watch. Time to head back to Eastvale so he could check on developments there before the end of the day.

6

On Tuesday morning, Banks was in his office early again, and this time the first to knock on his door was an excited Gerry Masterson brandishing a sheaf of papers, her wavy red hair cascading over her shoulders in all its pre-Raphaelite glory.

'It's not that there haven't been a few crimes involving the use of crossbows,' she began before even sitting down, 'but nearly all of them are domestic, or they involve some nutter going on a spree and either getting caught or killed.'

'And the ones that aren't?'

'That's what's interesting. I looked for a pattern.'

'And did you find one?'

'I found three unsolved murders overseas involving the use of a crossbow – same make of bolt used as in the Quinn killing, too, by the way – all in one way or another connected with the world of people-trafficking and illegal immigration.'

'Now that's interesting,' said Banks, taking another sip of coffee. Masterson had brought her own mug with her.

'I thought so. There was one in Vilnius, that's in Lithuania, one in Amsterdam, and one in Marseilles.'

'How hard is it to get a crossbow across European borders?'

'Not very,' said Masterson. 'You probably wouldn't want to carry one on a plane, but you could take it apart and put it in with your checked luggage. Or why not just buy a new one in each country, if you're paranoid about getting searched? It's not as if you need a permit or anything. However you look at it, it's a lot less trouble than a gun.'

'True enough,' said Banks. 'The victims?'

'Not known to us, sir, but with definite Interpol profiles. In all cases the conclusion was that the victims were either skimming the profits or about to blow the whistle on a lucrative people-trafficking route, usually connected with Eastern Europe.'

'I don't suppose any suspects' names cropped up, did they?'

'Afraid not, sir.'

'Pity. You said overseas. What about in this country?'

'I was just getting to that, sir. We've had two over the past three years: a gangmaster in South Shields, and a hoodie on a housing estate in Stockton-on-Tees. Both unsolved. The gangmaster was connected with illegals, and local intelligence suggests that the hoodie was attempting to break into the loan-sharking business on his own.'

'Interesting,' said Banks. 'So we've got some sort of enforcer for the people-trafficking and loan-sharking business?'

'It seems that way, sir.'

'Any links to Corrigan?'

'No, sir.'

'OK. Do we have any idea who this bowman works for?'

'No, sir. I suppose it could be just one person, some sort of crime kingpin who employs him when he's needed. Or he might be for hire. A freelance.'

'Hmm. Anything more on the car?'

'I checked with the local rental agencies. There was a Ford Focus with similar cross-hatching on the front left tyre, the same shade of green paint as the scraping we found, rented from Hertz in Leeds last Wednesday and returned on Friday.'

'Details?'

'Arnold Briggs, address in South London. UK driving licence. But it's all fake, sir. I checked. There's no such address.'

'I suppose if these people can forge passports and work

visas, they can forge driving licences, too. So whoever Arnold Briggs is, he's long gone?'

'Afraid so, sir.' Her expression brightened. 'But the car hasn't been rented out again. It's been cleaned, of course, but forensics might still find something, mightn't they?'

'Indeed they might,' said Banks. 'It's worth a try, at any rate. Get on to them and—'

'I've already talked to DS Nowak, sir.' DC Masterson flushed slightly as she spoke Nowak's name. 'I took the liberty. I hope you don't mind. He says he's on it. This does get us forward a little bit, doesn't it?'

Banks admired her enthusiasm, and he didn't want to dampen it. 'Yes, it certainly does,' he said. 'That's good work, Gerry. You showed initiative. Let's go through what we know, or suspect, point by point.' He counted off on his fingers. 'One: the same car was at both crime scenes. The methods of killing were different, so maybe there are two killers. Two: Quinn and the victim at the farm had spoken twice on the telephone shortly before their murders. Three: we think the victim at the farm was also a victim of some sort of migrant labour scam. Four: Quinn had in his possession a number of photographs of himself in a compromising position with a young woman, most likely taken six years ago in Tallinn. Five: Quinn was briefly involved in investigating the disappearance of Rachel Hewitt, also in Tallinn, at that time. Six: Warren Corrigan, on the surface a petty loan shark, is connected with Roderick Flinders, owner of Rod's Staff Ltd, a front for migrant and illegal labour scams. Seven: Bill Quinn was involved in the investigation of said Corrigan. Have I missed anything? I'm running out of fingers. Yes. Eight: There were rumours of a bent copper, possibly Quinn, and possibly through blackmail. It's all giving me a headache.'

'Arnold Briggs was the fake name of the person who rented the car,' said Masterson. 'It's not that easy to kill. I think it would be a bit unbelievable, not to mention too much of a coincidence, if there were two different killers, sir.'

'Good point. Now, what could Bill Quinn possibly have in common with the Garskill Farm victim, a migrant worker?'

'Unless he wasn't a migrant worker, sir,' said Masterson. 'You said yourself he didn't have the hands of a manual labourer. What if he was an informant, or even an undercover police officer?'

'Possible,' said Banks. 'But I'm certain Ken Blackstone or Nick Gwillam would have brought it up, if he was Quinn's informant. But it's an interesting thought. Perhaps our man *was* at the farm under false pretences. Either that or he got all the soft jobs.'

'Maybe West Yorkshire didn't know, sir? Not if he was an undercover officer from Poland or Estonia or somewhere.'

'Maybe you're right, at that,' Banks agreed. 'One of the numbers called from the telephone box in Ingleby was an Estonian mobile. Again, though, it's bloody untraceable. Annie's tried ringing it, but there's no answer.'

'Just the sort of phone an undercover officer might have, or his controller,' said DC Masterson. 'A throw-away?'

As Banks thought over what Masterson had just told him, there came another knock at his door. When Annie and Joanna Passero walked in, the office started to feel crowded.

'What is it?' Banks asked.

'I just got a call from a woman who says she knows the Garskill Farm victim,' said Annie. 'She recognised his photo in the paper this morning.'

'Why didn't she call before?' Banks said. 'It's been all over the papers and TV for the past two days.'

'Says she's been away on some sort of retreat.'

'Religious?'

'Dunno.'

'You think she's genuine?'

Annie rolled her eyes. 'We've had a few cranks. I think I can tell the difference. Yes, I think she's genuine.'

'Sorry.'

'Anyway,' Annie went on, 'she's in Manchester, but she says she's willing to drive over now and identify the body, tell us all she knows. She was upset, naturally, and I offered to arrange a car for her, but she said she could manage it by herself.'

'What's her name?'

'Merike. Merike Noormets. And according to her, the victim's name was Mihkel Lepikson. She said he was her boyfriend.'

'Dutch? German? Scandinavian?'

Annie grinned. 'Wrong, sir. Estonian. Both of them.'

'My, my,' said Banks, rubbing his hands together. 'This *is* starting to get interesting, isn't it?'

Before Merike Noormets arrived, Banks and Annie agreed that they would interview her together, preferably in a more congenial environment outside the police station, after she had identified Mihkel Lepikson's body down at the mortuary. But they hadn't reckoned with Joanna Passero, who claimed that she couldn't be excluded from this interview because it impacted directly on the Quinn case. She actually said 'impacted'. Banks cringed, but there was nothing he could do except let her come along under sufferance. She would only go crying to Superintendent Gervaise if he didn't. Having three people present, four including Merike Noormets herself, would be a bit of an overload, but Banks trusted that Annie knew when to keep quiet and take notes, and he stressed to Joanna that she was present only to observe. He would do most of the talking. She didn't like it, clearly didn't like any of it, but she grudgingly agreed. Annie seemed rather more sympathetic to Joanna's predicament than Banks, but then she had worked for Professional Standards herself.

Merike Noormets was an attractive woman in her early thirties, with hennaed hair and a couple of minor piercings, wearing jeans, and a light yellow cotton jacket over an embroidered Indian-style top of some kind. She also carried a stitched leather shoulder bag. She looked a bit hippy-ish to Banks. She had clearly been crying when Annie and Joanna brought her up from the basement of Eastvale General Infirmary.

Banks had waited for them outside in his car, feeling that he had no need to see the man's body again. The rain that had threatened yesterday afternoon had started during the night and was still falling. With it, a cold front had moved in, and the temperature had dropped considerably.

The identification was positive, Annie told him, and now they could get in touch with the parents back home in Tallinn and arrange for them to come over. As soon as the three women had piled into the Porsche, Banks headed out of town. It was a Tuesday lunchtime in late April, so a lot of country pubs and restaurants would probably be closed, but he knew he could depend on the Blue Lion in East Witton.

It was very much a silent journey from the Eastvale mortuary. Banks concentrated on his driving and listened to the lovely strains of 'The Lark Ascending' and 'Fantasia on a Theme by Thomas Tallis'. He thought the music might help sooth Merike Noormets and relax her enough to make her open up.

All the parking spots in front of the pub were taken, so Banks parked opposite the long village green, and they walked back over the road to the rambling old building. Merike smoked a cigarette on the way and got through about a third of it before they went inside and found a table in the bar. The menu was chalked on a blackboard over the enormous fireplace. Rain dotted the windows. A few logs burned in the hearth and threw out more than enough heat to compensate for the weather outside. The starters were written on another blackboard over the bar, and to read all that was on offer would have taken all day. Merike said she would like a glass of white wine, and Banks was unable to resist a pint of Black Sheep, but the other two stuck to diet bitter lemon. Annie because of her medication, Banks supposed, and Joanna Passero just to show him up. He bet she was making a note, too: 'DCI Banks drinking on duty, during interview of important witness.' Well, screw her. Banks knew how to interview an important witness, and it wasn't in a dingy interview room smelling of stale sweat and fear with a styrofoam cup of canteen coffee in front of you. Especially a witness who had just come from identifying her boyfriend's body.

Merike pushed her hair out of her eyes, pale green flecked with amber, Banks noticed. For some reason he thought of the Jimi Hendrix song 'Gypsy Eyes', though she was hardly a Gypsy, and they were hardly gypsy eyes. There had to be some connection somewhere in his mind, but, as so often these days, he couldn't grasp it. Maybe there was a hint of wildness about her that chimed with the music, he thought; perhaps she had a gypsy soul, whatever that was.

When the landlord came around to take their orders, Merike said she wasn't hungry. The other three ordered. Banks went for his favourite, smoked haddock with a poached egg, leeks, mushrooms and Gruyère cheese.

'I suppose you want me to tell you everything I know?' said Merike, with a hint of irony. Her husky voice was only slightly accented. If she was in her early thirties, Banks calculated, she would have been in her teens when Estonia won its independence from the Soviet Bloc. Old enough to remember life under the old regime. He found himself wondering what her childhood had been like.

'Not everything,' he said. 'Just what you can. First, I'd like to thank you for coming forward and getting in touch.'

Merike seemed surprised. 'Why shouldn't I?'

'Not everyone does. That's all. Sometimes people just don't want to get involved.'

Merike shrugged. 'It was such a shock, seeing Mihkel's photograph in the newspaper like that.'

'What was your relationship with him?'

'I suppose he was my boyfriend. My partner. My lover. I don't know. With Mihkel it was always difficult.'

'Why?'

'He is the kind of person who comes and goes in your life. Sometimes he disappears for weeks, or months. At first, it used to drive me crazy, because he would tell me nothing, but now he tells – he told me – a little more, and we talk on the telephone.'

'When did you last talk?'

'On Tuesday. Tuesday evening, at about nine o'clock.'

Banks searched for a sheet of paper in his brief case and showed it to Merike, pointing to a number. 'Is this yours?'

'Yes, it's my mobile number. It's a pay-as-you-go I use when I'm over here. Cheap phone, occasional top-ups.'

'Did you and Mihkel live together?'

'No. I travel also, for my job, and we are never in the same place together for long enough. It would be too complicated.'

'How long have you been seeing each other?'

'Three years now.'

'What are you doing in Manchester?'

'I work as a translator. I'm on a two-week course at the university there. Almost finished.' She glanced at Annie. 'I just returned from a weekend retreat in the Lakes, and I haven't seen any newspapers or television from Friday until this morning. Part of the course. It was beautiful. Much more grand than our Estonian lakes. But it rained a lot.'

'It always does in the Lake District,' said Banks. 'Your English is excellent, by the way.'

'Thank you. I lived in London for many years, in my twenties.'

'Do you speak any other languages?'

'German,' Merike said, 'Finnish, Russian, French and a little Spanish. I'm learning Italian. When you grow up in a small country like Estonia, you soon realise that nobody from anywhere else is going to understand you unless you speak their language. Who learns Estonian except Estonians?'

Who, indeed? Banks thought. He hadn't even known Estonia had a language of its own. He had assumed they spoke Russian there, or perhaps some version of Polish. But languages were not Banks's strong point. 'Was Mihkel a translator, too?'

'Mihkel? Oh, no. His English was very good, but he was no linguist. It seems so strange to be talking about him in the past tense. I must get used to it.'

'I'm sorry,' said Banks.

'Mihkel knew the risks.'

'What risks? What was he doing at Garskill Farm?'

'Is that where he was when it happened? I don't know it. I had no idea where he was, except that he was somewhere in England. It seemed so strange to be in the same country and not be able to meet. I couldn't even telephone him. I had to wait for him to ring me.'

'Mihkel phoned you from a public telephone box in Ingleby,' said Banks. 'It's the nearest village to where he was found. It was about two miles away from where he was staying.'

Merike smiled sadly. 'Mihkel walked four miles just to talk to me? I would never have thought it of him.'

Annie gave Banks a sharp sideways glance. He knew that she was hoping he wouldn't spoil Merike's illusion by telling her that she wasn't the only reason Mihkel had walked all that way to the telephone. 'Do you know what he was doing there?' he asked.

'He was on an assignment. Mihkel was a journalist. He specialised in investigative reporting. He was freelance, but he worked mostly for a weekly newspaper called *Eesti Telegraaf*. They specialise in the sort of articles he liked to write.'

'What were they?'

'In depth, usually about crime. He also contributed sometimes to a weekly column called "*Pimeduse varjus*". In English it means "in the shadow of darkness". Very sinister. The idea is looking into the darkness. Watching. It's also about crime.'

'*Watching the dark*,' said Banks.

Merike flashed him a brief smile. 'Ah, so you like Richard Thompson?'

'Yes, I do. Very much.'

'I like that,' she said. 'A policeman who admires Richard Thompson.'

'His father was a Scotland Yard detective,' Banks said. 'And a lot of his songs are about murders.'

'I didn't know that. About his father, I mean.'

'My own son's a musician,' Banks went on, unable to stop himself, now he felt he was bringing her out of herself a bit, and enjoying the way the gypsy eyes were seeing him in a new light, not just as some faceless authority figure. 'He's in a group called The Blue Lamps.'

'But I know them!' said Merike. 'Their new CD is wonderful. The best they have ever done.'

'Brian will be pleased to hear that.' Banks felt proud, but he could tell from the waves of impatience emanating from Joanna Passero that she wanted him to get the interview back on track. It was one reason he hadn't wanted her around. She didn't understand how important it was to find some common ground with the interviewee, to forge a bond. She was used to interviewing dirty cops, where there was never any possibility of her creating a link because it was an adverse situation from the outset. Annie had been more impatient and aggressive in her interview techniques at first, when she had come from

Professional Standards, despite the courses she had taken, but she had learned over the years since then. She knew how Banks operated.

Their food arrived. As they were getting it sorted out, Merike excused herself and went outside for another cigarette. When she came back, they were eating, and her henna hair was damp with drizzle.

Merike sipped some wine and made an apologetic shrug in Banks's direction. 'Can't smoke anywhere these days, even in Estonia.'

'So what assignment was Mihkel working on at Garskill Farm?' he asked.

'I don't know any details, except that he told me before he left it was something to do with migrant labour, and he wasn't sure how long he would be away. That was typical Mihkel. He didn't even dare to take his mobile phone for fear of what would happen if they found it. Not so long ago, a Lithuanian journalist disappeared while he was working on a similar story, all because they found a mobile with a built-in camera among his belongings.'

'How did Mihkel deliver his story to the newspaper?'

'I assume he gave it in short pieces to his editor over the telephone. So I am sure he didn't walk four miles only to talk to me, however gallant it sounds. Though I would like to believe he did. He might have risked writing some things down if he had a good hiding place, in the lining of his clothes or somewhere like that.'

Banks glanced at Annie, who shook her head. They would have taken his clothes apart already, and had clearly found nothing. If Mihkel had hidden any notes, then his torturers had found them first.

'Why was it so secret?'

'The people who run these things are all connected with very powerful and dangerous criminals. It's not a one-man operation. Everything must be in place. Every step of the way must be planned. It takes capital, organisation, enforcement, and the ones in the best position to do that are organised gangs. There is much at stake.'

'Russian Mafia?'

'Like everyone in the West, you think the Russian Mafia is behind everything. They may be involved, yes, of course, if there is money to be made, but it is not the only one.'

'Baltic Mafia?' said Banks.

'Something along those lines. When people speak of the Baltic Mafia, they usually refer to Latvia, Lithuania and Poland, but we are not without our own bad men in Estonia. We don't have to import them all from Russia or Latvia, you know.'

'I'm sorry,' said Banks. 'I don't know much about your country.'

'Don't worry. Nobody does. It is very small and has a troubled history. May I have another glass of wine?' She held out her glass.

Banks gestured to Joanna Passero, who glowered, but took it to the bar for a refill. 'Is there anything you can tell us about the people Mihkel was investigating?' Banks asked.

'All he told me was that he was posing as an unskilled labourer. He started out at an agency in Tallinn, where you go to seek for work overseas, and this place you mentioned . . .'

'Garskill Farm.'

'Yes. That is where he ended up. I assume he was with others in the same position, and they would be taken out to their places of work at the start of the day in a van, and delivered back to the dormitory at the end.'

Dormitory was a rather grand word for Garskill Farm, Banks thought. 'We think so,' he said. 'About twenty of them altogether. Unfortunately, they've all disappeared.'

'I'm sorry, I can't help you.'

Joanna returned with the wine and handed it to Merike, who thanked her.

'What did Mihkel say to you during your conversations?'

'They were very brief. He would just tell me he couldn't talk long, that he might be missed. He told me that he was all right. He told me . . .' she paused and lowered her head down shyly. 'He told me that he loved me, that he missed me.'

When she looked up again, Banks saw there were tears in her eyes. 'I'm sorry if this is difficult,' he said. 'But we need to find out everything we can if we are to find the person who killed Mihkel.'

'I understand,' said Merike. 'But I have told you all I know.'

'Are you certain? Think. Was there nothing else he said to you?'

Merike bit her lip. 'He did say something a bit mysterious the last time we talked.'

'Last Tuesday evening?'

'Yes.'

'What was it?'

'He said he thought he was on the verge of finding a big story to work on. There was something about some photos, too.'

Banks's ears pricked up. 'A big story? Photos? Was it connected to the story he was already working on? Did he give you any idea what it was?'

'No. He was very guarded. He said I would know soon enough if he was right. Only that it was big, and that it could mean trouble for some very important people. He could say no more about it.'

According to the logs from the telephone company, Mihkel Lepikson had rung Merike *after* he had talked to Bill Quinn on Tuesday evening. Within a short while, both Mihkel and Bill were dead. Did their conversation, and their murders, have something to do with this big story he was talking about? It would be too much of a coincidence, Banks thought, if they didn't. Perhaps Quinn was going to pass on the photos to Mihkel, but he never got the chance. But there was also a third number Mihkel had called. 'Can you give me the names of Mihkel's contacts in Tallinn, at the newspaper or elsewhere?'

'Of course. He always worked with the same editor. Erik Aarma. It was a close relationship. They were good friends. Erik is a good man. Mihkel wouldn't work with anyone else, and his reputation was big enough that he could make his own rules like that. Erik will be broken-hearted. It was like, how do you say, a spy and his handler. Like in Mr le Carré's books.'

Banks smiled. He was a le Carré fan, too. 'I understand,' he said. Then he referred to his notes again and showed Merike the Estonian number. 'Do you know if this is Erik's number?'

She shook her head. 'I have no idea. He would probably use an untraceable mobile. Secrecy was very important, and the work was dangerous, as I have said. Erik might be able to help you with some other names and contacts, people in the organisation. Mihkel would have spoken to Erik and only Erik on the telephone. He would also have discussed his ideas for the story first with Erik. In his line of work, you learn not to trust many people, and he trusted Erik.'

Banks bet that other number dialled from the telephone box in Ingleby was Erik's dedicated line to Mihkel. 'Will Erik reveal his sources?'

'I don't know. I am sure that Erik will help you all he can without compromising himself.'

'Will he come over here?'

'Perhaps, if you pay his fare and reserve a room for him at the Dorchester.'

Banks laughed. 'Not much chance of that, I'm afraid.'

'Has Mihkel worked on this kind of assignment before?' Annie asked. 'Crime. Migrant labour. That sort of thing. You said he contributed to a weekly column about crime.'

'"*Pimeduse varjus*". Yes. But not all the assignments are dangerous. It is true that Mihkel always did like living on the edge a bit too much. He got beaten up once when he wrote about the sex trade in Tallinn. Mostly he keeps his head down. He was very good at blending in with the scenery, which is strange when you think how handsome he was. People would notice when he walked into a room, but he could lose himself in a role, be an uneducated, unskilled migrant labourer and nobody would look twice at him. He could be invisible when he wanted. It was very useful in his work.'

Except he couldn't hide his hands, Banks thought. And that might have been his undoing.

'So he habitually sought out dangerous situations?' Annie said.

'Good stories,' Merike corrected her. 'There was sometimes danger involved, and Mihkel didn't shy away from the risks. I said he lived on the edge, but he wasn't a fool. He didn't put himself in harm's way without good reason. He wasn't a thrill-seeker. Perhaps more of an adventurer, the way he liked to travel to exotic, dangerous places like Somalia, Syria or Haiti. He was very fond of the writings of Graham Greene.'

'How do you think the people who did this to him found out who he really was?'

'I don't know. He must have made a mistake. That isn't like him, but it must be what happened. They could have seen something he wrote. Or perhaps they had a spy in their dormitory? An informer in Tallinn? Or somewhere along the route. Maybe somebody followed him to the telephone box that night? There are many ways it could have happened.'

'Have you ever heard of a policeman called Bill Quinn?' Banks cut in. 'Detective Inspector Bill Quinn?'

'Bill? But of course. He was a good friend of Mihkel's.'

The three police officers looked at one another. 'A good friend?' Banks repeated. 'Close?'

'Well, they knew each other, talked on the telephone some-times, met on occasion when Mihkel was in England. But not very close. Mihkel was not very close to anyone, except perhaps to Erik.'

'Did you know Bill? Had you met him?'

'No. But Mihkel talked about him sometimes.'

'So it wouldn't surprise you that Mihkel also called Bill Quinn the same night he phoned you?'

'No. Not really. Why shouldn't he?'

'No reason. I'm just trying to get all this clear. You see, we didn't know of any connection between Bill and Mihkel.'

'It was before we met,' Merike said. 'There was a big case in Tallinn. An English girl disappeared, and Bill came over to help the investigation. Mihkel was covering the story. They kept in touch. Mihkel also came to England to talk to the girl's parents and friends.'

At last it became clear to Banks. He hadn't seen the Rachel Hewitt files yet, only got the bare bones from Annie's research, and he hadn't known who Mihkel Lepikson was, or what he did for a living, until just now, so no one had made the connec-tion. Now it made sense. 'Was it just the Rachel Hewitt disap-pearance, or did they have other things in common?' Banks asked.

'Mihkel was mad about fishing,' Merike said, smiling at the memory. 'I used to tease him about it. That he'd rather be sitting by a river with a hook in the water than be in bed with me. I think they went fishing together once or twice, him and Bill. In Scotland. And there was Rachel Hewitt, of course. Bill kept Mihkel abreast of all the developments over here. The Rachel Foundation. What her friends and her family were doing.'

That made sense. A hobby in common. And Rachel Hewitt. But what did it all mean? For one thing, it meant that the Rachel Hewitt case was coming up with such alarming regularity that it was now number one priority. But they still had to find a link to Corrigan, Flinders and the migrant labour racket. There were too many pieces missing.

Banks reached for the envelope in his briefcase and tipped out the photographs of Quinn with the girl. 'Could these be the photos Mihkel was referring to? Bill Quinn had them in his possession. Do you recognise the girl?' he asked.

Merike studied the photos. 'I don't know if these are what he meant,' she said, 'but I don't know her.'

'They would probably have been taken about six years ago,' Banks added.

'No. I would remember her.'

He pushed the blow-up of the beer mat towards her. 'I assume that's familiar to you?'

'Yes. Though I prefer Saku, myself. Can I see that one again?' She pointed at the photograph of Quinn and the girl having a drink in the bar. After studying it for a moment, she said, 'I think that's the bar in the Hotel Metropol.'

'You know it?'

'Yes. I've been there many times for my work, and with Mihkel and Erik.'

'Pardon my being a little indelicate here,' Banks said, 'but is it the kind of hotel where . . . certain women might be found?'

Her eyes widened. 'You think I would go to a hotel like that.'

'No, of course not,' Banks blustered on. He could tell that Annie and Joanna were enjoying his discomfort tremendously, and he was desperately thinking of a way to get out of this without putting his foot any further down his throat. 'No. I mean, we think, you know, that . . .'

'This girl?' said Merike. 'The one in the photograph?'

'Well, yes. Possibly.' He hadn't shown her the bedroom shot, so she wasn't to know the context of the business.

'But she does not look like that sort of girl. Is that how you say it? That sort of girl?'

'I suppose so. Yes. You don't think so?'

Merike examined the photo more closely. 'No. Just because she is young and beautiful?'

'And with a much older man.'

'Many women prefer older men. I'm not saying it isn't possible. Perhaps you know something I don't. But the Metropol is definitely not that kind of hotel. It doesn't mean you can't have a drink with an attractive woman there, though.'

'Thank you, Merike,' Banks said. 'That's a great help.'

The question was: where next? There was one thing Banks was certain of, and that was that if he wanted answers, before very long he would have to pay a visit to Tallinn himself, whether Madame Gervaise liked the idea or not.

It was after seven o'clock when Banks walked through his front door that evening. He picked up the post, gave it a casual glance and tossed it on the computer desk behind the door, along with his briefcase. It had been his habit lately on arriving home from work to put on some music, make a cup of tea, and relax in the conservatory with a book before microwaving the remains of yesterday's takeaway, or throwing together a sandwich from whatever he happened to have in his fridge. Today was no exception. He put the kettle on, dug out his old CD of Arvo Pärt's *Fratres*, put it in the CD player and, when the tea was ready, took it and the book he had bought earlier to the conservatory. He wasn't even hungry. The smoked haddock he had enjoyed at the Blue Lion was enough to last him a while, and if he did get hungry later on, he had some Seriously Strong cheddar in the fridge. He could grill himself a sandwich. If that wasn't enough, there was always the leftover Indian takeaway from Saturday.

Banks sipped the green tea and let Pärt's slow repeating piano chords and flurry of strings drift over him; the strings reminded him of Philip Glass. He was due to fly out of Manchester the following morning at 10.25 for Tallinn, changing in Helsinki. Area Commander Gervaise hadn't liked the idea of the trip at all, as he had expected, but after complaining for ten minutes about budget cuts and constraints, she saw that it was the only logical next step in the investigation and approved his travel application, with limited expenses.

The only drawback was that Joanna Passero was to accompany him. Gervaise was quite firm on this. Annie Cabbot had been livid. Having been cooped up in hospital or in St Peter's for so long, she complained, a nice trip abroad would have done her the world of good. Gervaise argued that someone had to handle the investigation back in Yorkshire, and the budget wouldn't run to three detectives going abroad. Besides, hadn't she just got back from Cornwall? As it appeared that Tallinn was where Bill Quinn had committed his unforgivable sin of adultery and got his photo taken in the act, then Inspector Passero had to be there.

Despite the company, Banks felt excited about the journey. Estonia was a country he had never visited before, and he loved new places, especially cities he could explore on foot. He had picked up the Eyewitness *Top 10 Tallinn* guide from Waterstones before coming home, and he glanced through it as he listened to the music. 'Fratres' gave way to the solemn, tolling bell and eerie strings of 'Cantus In Memoriam Benjamin Britten', slowly building in volume.

The visit would be mostly taken up with work, Banks knew, talking to the police who had investigated the Rachel Hewitt case, and to Erik Aarma, Mihkel Lepikson's friend and editor, but there would always be a free hour or two now and then to take a walk. They had booked in at the Metropol, and he soon discovered from his guidebook that the Meriton, where Rachel Hewitt and the hen party had stayed, wasn't very far away.

Banks had the names of the Investigator and the Prosecutor on the case. The Investigator had now retired, but he had said that he was sorry to hear about Bill Quinn's death, and he would be happy to talk to Banks at a place to be agreed upon later. Someone would contact him at the hotel.

Merike Noormets had also told Banks that she was returning to Tallinn the following day and would be happy to help out as a translator, or to drive them around if they needed her. She said most Estonians spoke English, but difficulties may occur with some words or concepts. Banks had her telephone number in his mobile, and he thought he would get in touch. She would be grieving over Mihkel for some time, and perhaps something interesting to do would help take her mind off her loss.

After his talk with Merike, Banks had gone back to his office and looked over the Rachel Hewitt files. As Annie had already told him, there wasn't much in them because it had been essentially an Estonian case, starting as a local investigation by the Tallinn Central Prefecture, then quickly becoming a case for the National Criminal Police Department when the seriousness of the matter, and the involvement of a foreign national, became apparent.

The investigation itself had gone on for about two months, but the case was still officially open, as Rachel Hewitt was still a missing person, not a murder victim, though most people outside the family believed that she was dead. Banks could glean very little from Bill Quinn's reports, and it seemed to him very much as if the whole thing had been a matter of national niceties and ticking the boxes. Still, Quinn had been there for a week shortly after Rachel disappeared, and he had worked closely with the Investigator from the Criminal Police Department, whose name was Toomas Rätsepp, and with the Prosecutor, Ursula Mardna.

Annie and Winsome would be questioning Rachel Hewitt's parents and friends from the hen party while he was away.

Banks also asked Annie to slip in a few questions about the night of the disappearance to Rachel's friends, to fill in some of the gaps and details, if possible. From what he had read so far, it all sounded very vague and haphazard.

The haunting 'Spiegel Im Spiegel' was playing when Banks put the book aside and took another contemplative sip of tea. He felt the stirrings of excitement in his chest, not only at the prospect of a trip abroad, but at the possibility of making some sense out of this irritating, puzzling and complicated case that had been gnawing at his brain for six days now.

Maybe, with a bit of luck, a bit of help, and the right questions, he might just find out what the hell was going on. There was one idea he couldn't get out of his mind now, and that was that Bill Quinn may well have been killed because he found out what happened to Rachel Hewitt. And finding out who killed him might depend on finding out what happened to her.

7

Banks and Joanna were barely talking when they got to the hotel. Banks had spent the long flight from Manchester to Helsinki listening to Arvo Pärt's piano music and reading the only Estonian novel he had been able to find in Waterstones: *Purge*, by Sofi Oksanen. It was heavy-going at times, but absorbing nonetheless. Sometimes the engine noise drowned out Ralph van Raat's delicate piano playing, but the noise-cancelling headphones Banks had bought at Manchester helped. Joanna had sat beside him with her laptop on the tray in front of her, to all intents and purposes working on a report. During the stopover at Helsinki, she went off to do some duty-free shopping, and Banks sat by the gate drinking a latte and reading his book, occasionally glancing out at the planes through the large plate glass window.

At the Metropol, there was a message waiting for them at reception. It read simply: 'Lunch at Clazz tomorrow 1230. Tourists pay.' The name was Toomas Rätsepp.

'Cheeky bastard,' said Banks. 'Fancy a bite to eat now? Discuss strategy?'

Joanna shrugged. 'Fine with me. Let's just dump our stuff and get freshened up first.'

Half an hour later, map in hand, Banks led the way across a broad, busy avenue, where traffic swarmed and trams rattled by. They brought back childhood memories. There had been no trams in Peterborough, of course, and he was too young to remember the ones in London, but he was sure he had visited one or two cities with his parents and ridden on them. Leeds or Manchester, perhaps, where they had relatives.

The weather was absolutely gorgeous, bright sun low in a clear blue sky, with a faint half moon in the south. Banks hardly even needed his jacket, which he carried slung over his shoulder because he did need its pockets for his carefully stowed wallet, book, iPod, mobile, pen, notebook and various other bits and pieces. It was all right for women, he thought, glancing at Joanna; they had handbags. Bottomless pits, most of them. Some Frenchmen carried little leather bags with straps, too, but that trend had never caught on in Yorkshire. Banks just used his pockets.

Though it was still light, the evening shadows were lengthening in the cobbled streets of the Old Town, which were lined with three- or four-storey buildings with pastel facades of lemon, white, orange, pink or pale green, many of them cafes with tables outside. Some had ornate gables and dormers. Even narrower alleys led off to the left and right, some with signs above doorways indicating cafes or bars, others bare, perhaps with hidden cellar clubs, the kind you had to get text messages to know about. Most of the streets were free of traffic, though the occasional delivery van or utilities vehicle edged its way along, bouncing on the cobbles.

They reached a broad crossroads, almost a square in itself. There seemed to be a few cars and taxis around this area, though they all came to a halt and turned back about where Banks and Joanna were standing, by a large bookshop. Banks guessed that traffic wasn't allowed beyond that point and, indeed, most of the streets were not wide enough for cars anyway.

On their left was the bookshop, and beyond that Banks could see the sign for Fish & Wine, which was recommended in his guidebook. Over the road was a grassy area sloping up to an ancient church. According to his guidebook, the church

was called Niguliste and was famous for the medieval painting, *Danse Macabre*. By the sloping lawn in front of Niguliste,
young people lounged around, smoking and talking, enjoying
the early taste of summer, young girls in short shorts and
skimpy tops, tanned tapered legs, henna or bottle-blonde hair.

The church stood in all its majesty, drawing the soft evening
light to itself, the top of the white square tower pale orange in
the glow.

Joanna stopped for a moment. 'It's beautiful,' she said.

'You religious?' Banks asked.

She gave him a funny look. 'No.'

'Me, neither.'

All the outside seating at Fish & Wine was full, according to
the waitress, but they managed to get a table at the end of a
bench inside that was right next to the open doors of the side
patio. It was a good spot, and they could see the edge of
Niguliste and all the people walking by.

They made themselves comfortable and read the English
language menu. Like most places in Tallinn, the restaurant
had free Wi-Fi, and Joanna checked her email and text
messages before slipping the phone back into her handbag
without comment. Banks was curious as to what she was
expecting, the way she seemed obsessed with constantly
checking her phone. Was it something to do with the job?
Coded messages from Professional Standards headquarters?
Reports on his behaviour? If she wanted to tell him, he
assumed that she would do so in her own time. They both
ordered the turbot, along with a bottle of Pinot Grigio. Banks
poured the wine. Joanna was wearing an off-the-shoulder
frock with a gathered waist. During the flight, she had worn
her hair tied back, but now she wore it piled up on top in
elegant blonde tresses, the way it had been when he first saw
her, showing off her long graceful neck to best advantage. She
also wore some dangling silver earrings and a locket around

her neck. She smelled of the hotel's body lotion and shampoo. She must have checked the Tallinn weather forecast before setting off that morning to know what to pack, Banks thought. It had been raining in Manchester.

'Travelled much?' Banks asked, to break the tension that seemed to stretch between them like a taut elastic band.

'I've never really been anywhere before. Well, I tell a lie. I did go to Barcelona once, and I've been to Italy, of course. But that was family, so it doesn't really count.'

'Your husband?'

Joanna nodded and twisted her wedding ring.

Sensing that she didn't want to linger on the topic, Banks moved quickly on. 'I'd suggest you do a bit of sightseeing, enjoy yourself. Did you bring your camera?'

'No.'

'You should have. You can probably buy a cheap one in any tourist shop.'

'I'll be too busy working. What are you trying to tell me?'

'I just don't think you'll have a lot to do, that's all. I've got two murders to investigate now, three if you include Rachel Hewitt, and I work better alone, without interference. I don't need someone watching my every move, looking over my shoulder. Also, no foreign cop or prosecutor is going to talk to you. I'll be lucky if they talk to me with you present.'

'I—'

'You're Professional Standards. You do what you do.'

'Can we clear the air a bit?' Joanna said. 'Why are you being so nasty to me? You don't have a reputation as a particularly mean person, so why pick on me? I'm not here to investigate you. Is your ego so big you can't get over that? I've been trying to work with you for six days, and if you're not actively against me, you avoid me, you shut me out. You play silly practical jokes, and now you expect me to go off sightseeing while you do the real man's work. You didn't want me with you yesterday to interview Merike Noormets. You didn't want me to come with you today to Tallinn. You ignored me throughout the entire journey here. You were surly all the way from the airport. What is it with you?' She paused and gave him a level gaze.

'It's just that I can't imagine what there is for you to do here, that's all. Say we find the girl, say she admits she drugged Quinn and put him in a position to be blackmailed. So what? What does that prove? It certainly doesn't prove he was bent, working for Corrigan or anyone else. To find out about that you'd need to be back in England. There's nothing for you here is what I'm saying. I'm sorry.'

'No, you're not. You like to humiliate me and make me feel small. Fine. Go ahead if it makes you feel good. If it helps you to think I've got no feelings, that I'm just some sort of robotic persecutor of good honest cops. As a matter of fact, I do have feelings. If you prick me, I bleed. All right?'

'All right,' said Banks. 'I mean it. I'm sorry. All I'm really saying is that I work better alone.'

The food arrived, and they paused to take a few bites before continuing their conversation. The turbot was good, Banks thought.

'Well, I'm sorry, too,' said Joanna eventually, 'but you're not alone on this one. The point is that I do the job I do, but it doesn't define me. I am not my job. And I'm not made of stone. I meant it. You can be very hurtful, you know. Very cruel. That's not in your file.'

'Yet.'

'See what I mean? The sarcasm. It's nasty. Mean.'

It was what Winsome had said and, if truth be told, what Banks himself had felt. He didn't know why he did it, but couldn't seem to stop himself. He felt guilty and foolish now, but he saw Joanna in a new light. She was nobody's fool. She said her job didn't define her, and she was right. This was a living breathing person, with feelings, as she had made abundantly clear. But he still couldn't forget that she was Professional Standards and, as such, represented a stumbling block to any success he might hope to have.

Joanna glanced around the restaurant, almost as if to check that no one was listening. Nobody was paying them any attention now, as far as Banks could tell. 'I'll let you in on a little secret,' she said.

Annie and Winsome were skirting the southern edges of Leeds on the M62 towards the Drighlington exit. The Hewitts had agreed to see them that afternoon, intrigued by what little Annie had told them on the phone. 'Poor people,' Winsome had said. 'I didn't intend for them to get their hopes up. But they'll grasp at any straw they think might help them find their daughter alive.' And it was true. Pathetic, really, the little tremor of excitement in Maureen Hewitt's voice the moment Annie mentioned she was from the police and wanted to talk about Rachel. If she were in Mrs Hewitt's shoes, would she accept that her missing daughter was dead after six years? Would she *hope* that she was? Probably not, she realised. When you give up hope, what do you have left? At least if someone found Rachel's body, her parents would *know*, would be able to bury her and move on with their lives, however painfully and slowly. Closure.

'We're almost there,' said Annie, checking the signs. 'Next exit. Get in the lane.'

Winsome edged the Toyota into the exit lane and turned off the motorway towards a large roundabout.

'Not far now,' Annie said.

She had read up as much as she could on Rachel Hewitt that morning. Nobody had done a psychological profile of the victim, but Bill Quinn had put together a thumbnail character sketch that described her as an intelligent girl, but given to occasional wild flights of fancy and impulsive behaviour, a social drinker, a loyal friend, a person who cared for other people and wanted to make the world a better place. Reading that last bit had made Annie feel like putting her finger down her throat and gagging. It sounded like one of those speeches candidates for Miss World or whatever beauty pageant contestants spout in their skimpy swimming costumes. World peace, save the children, the seals and the whales, feed the hungry and all that. But there was a hint of a dark side. Rachel was also a dreamer and something of a material girl. She harboured a fantasy of meeting her Prince Charming one day, but he would have to be rich. It was a common, and possibly dangerous, blend of naïveté and avarice.

Naturally, Quinn had been thorough in his investigation of Rachel's friends and contacts. She could have been targeted for trafficking. Though she didn't seem to fit the usual victim profile, it was a possibility no good copper would fail to check out. A foreign boyfriend woos her, swears undying love, and arranges to meet up with her in Tallinn, where they live blissfully together until he reveals his true self and tells her what she has to do to help repay his debts. What she *will* do, if she really loves him. Then the beatings, the rapes, the mental and physical abuse begin, the brainwashing. It happened all too often. But not, apparently, to Rachel. There were no foreign boyfriends in her life, no suspicious characters, no one who didn't check out cleanly. It seemed she had lived an exemplary life with exemplary friends before Tallinn swallowed her up.

They found the house, a compact redbrick semi in a street of compact redbrick semis. There was nothing about it to distinguish it from the rest, no poster of Rachel in the front window or sign in the garden, only a beat-up old Astra in the drive, and a lawn that needed a bit of loving care. It was tragic in its ordinariness.

Annie rang the bell and the door was answered almost immediately by a woman she took to be Maureen Hewitt. She was about fifty, Annie guessed, rather on the tall, gaunt side, with a long face and fair hair tied back in a ponytail. She wore no make-up, but her complexion was good, though pale, as if she didn't go outdoors very much. There was an unnatural, brittle brightness in her pale blue eyes that Annie found disconcerting. Someone who lived for hope, no matter what reality presented her with.

She led them to the front room, where her husband was sitting in an armchair.

'It's the detectives who rang earlier,' she said.

Mr Hewitt got up and shook hands with Winsome and Annie. 'Very pleased to meet you,' he said. 'Perhaps . . . some tea before we begin?'

For some reason Annie couldn't quite work out, Mr Hewitt reminded her of a vicar – not quite grounded, but with a certain aura of authority, weight of sorrow and sense of purpose. He went and made the tea, and when it was done, Mrs Hewitt suggested they go into the 'office' as they were dealing with 'official Rachel business'.

The office was in the spare bedroom, and this large room was the real heart and nerve centre of the operation, Annie felt as soon as she walked in, the mug of tea warm in her hand. In an odd way, the Hewitts seemed somehow more relaxed in the office than they had in their living room. Two of the walls were taken up by desks and office equipment. There were two computers, a fax machine, a photocopier, a couple of laser printers, two telephones, filing cabinets, and even a television tuned to a twenty-four-hour BBC world news channel that was on mute. Though the room was generally clean and tidy, there were piles of papers around, many of them flyers with Rachel's picture and a plea for help, in various languages. Framed photos of Rachel lined the walls, from one of her in her mother's arms shortly after she'd been born, to the slightly glamorous studio shot in her teens. She had a half smile on her face, lips slightly parted, and the diffuse, fuzzy lighting you get on glamour shots highlighted her spun-gold hair and her blemishless porcelain skin. Her features were delicate, finely chiselled, but not sharp or pinched, and her cheekbones were high. She looked a bit Nordic, Annie thought, and also a bit like a doll. Fragile, too. But there was more, beyond all that. The intelligent eyes, the serious girl behind the smile. The girl who cared, who wanted to do some good in the world, who wanted to be rich.

'This is our operations centre,' said Mr Hewitt, who asked them to call him Luke and his wife Maureen. 'Please, sit down.'

In addition to the office-style chairs in front of the desks, there were a couple of small armchairs in the centre of the room, no doubt kept for interviewers and visitors just like Annie and Winsome.

'You said on the phone you had some news,' said Maureen Hewitt, hovering over them keenly.

'Well, it's not really news,' said Annie. 'But we do have a few questions for you. First of all, have you heard about Bill Quinn?'

'Inspector Quinn,' said Maureen. 'Oh, yes. Isn't it terrible? And he was so good to us.'

'You knew him well?'

'I wouldn't say well, would you, Luke? But we knew him.'

'Even after the investigation?'

'We sent him bulletins, let him know what we were doing to keep Rachel's name in the public eye. That's all.'

'When did you last see him?'

'Let me think. It was shortly after his wife died, wasn't it, Luke?'

Luke agreed. 'About a month ago,' he said. 'Late March.'

'What did he come to see you about?'

'Nothing in particular,' said Luke. 'It was a bit of a puzzle really. Why he came. We hadn't actually *seen* him for years. Not since he got back from Tallinn six years ago, in fact. He told us what had happened to his wife, of course, and we offered him our condolences, naturally. He was very upset. He said he envied us our strength and belief.'

'What did you say?'

'Well, I told him it hadn't been easy. My wife and I are regular churchgoers, and we've had a lot of support from the parish, of course, but sometimes even faith . . .' He shook his head. 'There've been times when . . . Anyway, you don't want to know about that. You know, a lot of people think we're just keeping up a front, putting on some sort of a show, that we should long ago have let go and moved on.'

'What do you think?' Annie asked.

'As long as there's a chance that our darling Rachel is still alive, then we'll carry on trying to find her,' said Maureen. She picked up one of the flyers and handed it to Annie. 'Look at this. Latvian. We had a sighting near Riga just last week.'

'There must be a lot of sightings.'

'You'd be surprised,' said Maureen.

'Fewer and fewer as time goes by,' said Luke. 'The hardest thing is to get anyone to take them seriously and follow up. That's why it's so important to keep her face out there, keep her name on peoples' lips. We have to keep up the pressure, make sure nobody forgets. No offence, but we can't depend on the police. You have other cases, other things to occupy your time. Rachel is all we have. It's up to us to try to keep the investigation going at some level. People think we're publicity seekers. Well, we are. But the publicity is for Rachel, not for us.'

'We try to stay on good terms with the media,' said Maureen, 'but it's difficult sometimes. They can be very intrusive, as you know, if you've been reading the papers and watching TV lately. They're your best friend and helper one minute, then they turn on you the next. We've tried being as polite and informative as we can, but then they turned on us for being too cool and unemotional, not being passionate and anguished enough, for not crying all the time. Honestly, sometimes you just can't win.'

Annie had read the stories in the papers about their recent testimony in the hacking inquiry, about how an unscrupulous reporter had hacked into their private telephones and hounded their remaining daughter, Heather, stealing her diary. At one point, this same reporter had even 'borrowed' Maureen's journal and reproduced sections of it in the newspaper, her deepest fears about her missing daughter, a breakdown of communication with her other daughter, her feelings of despair and thoughts of suicide. It had been headline news – MOTHER OF MISSING GIRL ON SUICIDE WATCH – but then so had their evidence against the reporter and his editor later, at the official inquiry.

Heather Hewitt, Annie knew, had gone off the rails at some point during the six years her sister had been missing. Excerpts from her diary showed a troubled teen upset and worried about her big sister, but feeling increasingly neglected, side-lined and unloved because all her parents' energy went into the Rachel Foundation, and all their time into finding Rachel. It seemed to her that they didn't care that they had a living, breathing, troubled daughter right there who needed them. Heather felt that they wished she had been abducted instead of Rachel, and in her worse moments, she even believed she had heard them saying that, whispering it at night when she was lying in bed trying to get to sleep. She had turned to drugs, become publicly addicted to heroin. From what Annie knew of heroin, it was hardly a surprising choice. Heroin offers a deluxe escape, takes away all your problems, all your worries, all your fears, and wraps you in a warm cocoon of well-being until it's time for the next fix. Hallucinatory drugs throw all your perceptions into disorder and all your fears and worries back at you in the form of nightmares and rising paranoia, and amphetamines and Ecstasy keep you on the move, keep you running, dancing, sweating, feeling good. But only heroin takes all the pain away. The closest Annie had come to truly understanding that feeling was with some of the morphine-derived painkillers they had given her in hospital when she was at her worst.

'How is Heather?' she asked.

Maureen's face clouded. 'She's progressing,' she said. 'I know people said we were being cold and cruel having her put away like that, especially after they leaked her diary in the papers, but the institution was a good idea, for a while at least.'

'Until she's ready to face the world again,' added Luke.

'Yes,' agreed his wife, nodding. 'Do you know, she's just the age Rachel was when she went missing.'

Annie let the silence stretch for a respectful moment, then she took a photograph of Mihkel from her briefcase. 'Have you ever seen this man?' she asked the Hewitts.

They both studied the photo closely, then Luke said, 'I think so. Can you tell us his name?'

'Mihkel,' said Annie. 'Mihkel Lepikson.'

'Yes, of course.' Luke glanced at his wife. 'Don't you remember, love? He's that nice Estonian journalist who came to see us with Inspector Quinn six years ago.'

'That's right,' Maureen said. 'He was writing about the case back in Tallinn. We've kept him up to date, too, over the years. He's written updates on the story, tried to help as best he can. They're not all rotten. Reporters.'

'He was nice, you say?'

'Yes,' said Luke. 'Not like the others. At least he was straight with us, and he didn't write about our private grief, or apparent lack of it. It was the case that interested him, the search for Rachel, what might have become of her.'

'Did he have any ideas?'

'None that helped,' said Maureen.

'Have you ever seen him again recently?'

'Not for years. But we've had emails and telephone conversations. He's been helping us to keep Rachel's name out there, and he usually sends us a clipping if he's written anything about her in his paper. It's in Estonian, of course, but you can still see it where he mentions her name, and he writes out a nice translation for us. It's very difficult when you're so far away. People forget so easily. We've been meaning to get in touch with him.'

'I'm afraid there'd be no point,' said Annie. 'He's dead.'

The Hewitts looked at one another in shock. 'Dead? But . . . how?'

'He was also murdered. Shortly before Inspector Quinn, we think.'

'But why? He seemed such a nice young man.'

'Well, his business is a dangerous one. He worked on exposing crimes and criminals, and they don't like it when someone does that. There were probably a lot of people had it in for him because of the things he wrote.'

'About Rachel?'

'That's a possibility we have to consider. Do you have these clippings? Could we take them with us and have a look at them? We'll make sure you get them back.'

'Yes, of course.' Maureen opened one of the filing cabinets and pulled out a red folder. 'They should all be in here. Translations, as well. So you do think Mihkel Lepikson's death had something to do with Inspector Quinn's?'

Annie could have kicked herself. She had gone too far. She didn't want to lie to the Hewitts, but she couldn't tell them the whole truth, either. A good investigation depended on holding back information from the public. 'It's possible,' she said. 'We just don't know. That's why we're asking all these questions. I know it must seem a bit strange to you.'

'But don't you see?' Maureen went on. 'If the two are linked, they might both have something to do with Rachel. It could all be connected. This could be the sort of lead we've been waiting for. They might have known where she is.'

'I wouldn't get your hopes up,' Annie said.

'Hopes? What else could I have except despair? Do you know, there isn't a day goes by when I don't imagine the terrible things that could have happened to Rachel over the last six years. That could be happening to her somewhere, even now. Her fear. Her pain. Her desperation. People doing terrible things to her. My little girl alone in the dark with monsters, abandoned. Believe me, I don't sleep much any more. The nightmares are too frightening.'

Her husband touched her shoulder and said, 'Or that she's lost her memory somehow, and has forgotten about us, but is living her life happily somewhere. That's what I try to think about, anyway.'

Maureen moved towards the doorway. 'Come with me. Let me show you something.'

Annie raised her eyebrows and glanced at Winsome.

'I mean it. Just follow me,' Maureen said. Annie and Winsome did as they were asked.

Maureen took them across the landing and into another, smaller bedroom. 'This is Rachel's room,' she said, in slightly hushed tones. 'It's ready for when she comes back. It's always ready. I wash the sheets every week, and her clothes, even though she hasn't worn them for a long time. It's important to keep things clean. *That's* hope. And when our daughter comes home at last, it will all have been worthwhile. I suppose you think I'm insane now, but I don't care. It's one of the things that keeps me *sane*. The hope.'

Annie took in the room. It was quite ordinary, not pink or black or anything you might expect from a teenager, thank God, but a neutral tone of blue, with a small writing desk and chair, television and CD player, a few CDs and books in an antique glass-covered bookcase. Posters of Coldplay and Franz Ferdinand adorned the walls. There was also a glossy picture of a sleek BMW standing outside an ugly art deco mansion. Someone, presumably Rachel, had written a thought bubble with the words 'MINE ONE DAY!!' in a Sharpie at the top. Annie smiled. Just under window was a collection of stuffed and fluffy animals, clearly going all the way back to Rachel's childhood. Very girly, she thought.

'She loves fluffy animals,' said Maureen, catching Annie's expression. 'Collected them. That's Paddy.'

Annie glanced at the bed. A one-eyed teddy bear missing a fair bit of stuffing sat propped up against the pillow staring at them. It gave her the creeps.

'Paddy was her first ever animal, when she was a baby. She took him everywhere with her. He was with her in Tallinn. In her hotel room. Inspector Quinn very kindly got him back for us. Paddy's waiting for her, too. He was her good-luck charm.'

'I see she liked cars, too,' said Annie.

'Oh, that. That was just a bit of silliness. I can't understand what it was with her and fancy cars. That's more a boy thing, isn't it?'

'Did Rachel still live at home when she . . .?'

'When she disappeared. It's all right, love, you can say the word. Yes, she did.'

'Did she have a boyfriend?'

'Not for a while. She'd been seeing Tony Leach for a couple of years, but they split up about a month before she went away.'

Annie remembered the name from Bill Quinn's reports. 'Was she upset about it?'

'Of course. Two years is a long time. But she soon got over him. You do when you're young, don't you, though it seems like the end of the world at the time. She shut herself away in her room and cried for two days, then she put him behind her and got on with her life again.'

Maureen led them back into the office, but they remained standing. There wasn't really an awful lot more to say. Annie got the names and addresses of Tony Leach and the five female friends who had been with Rachel on that fateful hen weekend, thinking one of the girls might know something and might have kept quiet for reasons of her own. At the door, she turned and asked the Hewitts if there was anything more they could tell her about Bill Quinn's last visit to the house.

'Like what?' asked Maureen.

'What sort of mood was he in?'

'Well, he was very sad, of course. The poor man had just lost his wife. And he seemed distracted.'

'Did he say anything odd or surprising? That sort of thing.'

It was Luke who answered. 'He said one thing that struck me as odd when I thought about it later. We were talking about his wife's death, and one of the comments he made was that it "changes things". I'm sure one thinks many things about the death of a spouse, but "it changes things" seems an odd one to me. I mean, it's sort of self-evident, isn't it, so why say it? Probably nothing, but there you are. And he told us not to give up hope.'

'Thank you,' said Annie. She knew what Bill Quinn had meant.

'You will keep in touch, won't you?' said Maureen. 'If there's anything . . .'

'Yes, of course.'

*   *   *

'What little secret would that be?' Banks asked.

'Nobody wants to stay in Professional Standards for ever. Annie Cabbot didn't; I don't. As you know, it's not possible, anyway. There's a strict time limit on the job.'

'Don't tell me you want to work Major Crimes,' said Banks.

'Well, I'd like something a bit more juicy than PS, yes, and something that earns me a bit more respect from my fellow officers.'

'And this is a way of getting some on the job experience? In the back door, so to speak.'

'Something like that. Believe or not, I *asked* for this job. I wanted the opportunity to work with you.'

'You were out to get me from the start?'

'No, you idiot. Stop it. I'm not out to get you, I'm out to learn from you. You might not be aware of it, but you have a reputation, whether you know it or not. Yes, you're a bit of a maverick and all the rest, and as I've just found out, you have a cruel and selfish streak, too, but you're generally thought of around the county as a pretty damn good detective. Just don't let it go to your head.'

'I should have known. Gervaise is grooming you. She's—'

Joanna waved him aside. 'She is doing no such thing. She gave me an opportunity to work with you, said if I was lucky I might pick up a few pointers on how a homicide investigation is conducted. That's all.'

'But she does know about your ambitions, and she was willing to encourage them?'

'Area Commander Gervaise is an enlightened woman. We could do with more like her around the place.'

Banks liked and respected Catherine Gervaise, but he had never quite thought of her in that way. He sat in silence for a moment, digesting what he'd just heard, joining the dots. Why hadn't he figured this out before, right from the start, at that meeting in Gervaise's office? It gave him choices he hadn't considered before. He could either continue being an arsehole and leave Joanna out in the cold, or he could make use of her, work her hard, test her skills, treat her as a member of the murder team and try to forget the Professional Standards angle, see if she had the makings of a good homicide detective.

But could she forget the Professional Standards angle? Banks doubted it. He didn't care if she found out that Quinn was bent. If he was corrupt, then his corruption deserved to be exposed, especially if it had spread to others close to him and allowed a toerag like Corrigan to thrive. Besides, Quinn was dead. What could they do to him now except cloud his reputation? And what was a dead copper's reputation worth to start with? The ones who found out would soon forget; the rest would neither know nor care. The ones who would be hurt most would be his two children, and they were grown-up enough, resilient enough, to deal with it in time. He already knew that Quinn had probably committed adultery with a woman young enough to be his daughter, and they would no doubt find out about that, too, one way or another. The point was, that he now had Joanna Passero to help him rather than hinder him, if he chose to include her. On the other hand, he was in a foreign land lumbered with an amateur wannabe, if he cared to think of it that way. But these days, he was more of a cup half-full sort of bloke. She had to have some skills he could use. And maybe she could learn.

The waitress came and asked them if they wanted any dessert. Neither did. Banks said they would just stick with the wine, and she smiled and went away.

'So what you're saying is that you want to work on all aspects of the investigation, not just the bent copper angle?' he said.

'Yes.'

'So you'll do what I say, follow my lead?'

'Depends what you say, what the lead is. I won't break any laws, and I won't turn away from any law- or rule-breaking on DI Quinn's part. I'll still do my job.'

'Fair enough,' said Banks. 'I can't really explain why, but I can't get the idea out of my mind that Bill Quinn may well have been killed not because of the photos or Corrigan, but because he found out what happened to Rachel Hewitt. And that finding out who killed him might depend on finding out what happened to her. Can you work with that hypothesis?'

'If you think there's a definite connection between the time Quinn spent here on that case and what happened subsequently,' said Joanna, 'then I'm with you. Let's find out what it is. But we're not here to solve the Rachel Hewitt case.'

'It might not be so easy,' said Banks. 'I have a feeling that nobody around here is going to want to open up to us about it. Too much wound licking and mud slinging under the bridge, I'll bet. We'll see what we can get from this Toomas Rätsepp tomorrow. If he's like most cops, it won't be very much. Then we'll have a chat with Mihkel's editor, Erik, see if we can get him to talk a bit. Journalists are pretty simple souls really. They can be very closed mouthed, in my experience, but if they think you can do something for them – i.e., give them an exclusive – then they'll bend over backwards to help you.'

'What exactly are you after?' Joanna asked.

'Well, ideally I'd like to find Rachel Hewitt alive and well, take her home to her parents, bring her abductor to justice, solve Bill Quinn's and Mihkel Lepikson's murders and have their killer put away for life, then world peace would be a nice bonus. But in reality? First I'd settle for finding out who the girl in the photo is and having a good talk with her, see if I can find out who put her up to it. If she did set Quinn up, I very much doubt that it was her own idea. After that, we'll see where that leads us.'

'Do you think anyone knows?'

'I think there's a good chance that someone does, yes,' said Banks. 'It's more a matter of whether we can get anyone to tell us. If Quinn and Mihkel stayed in touch over the years after they first bonded over Rachel – you know, went fishing together and so on – then I think there's a chance that Quinn was going to meet Mihkel by the lake and tell him the truth about what happened here, and why. He may have been going to hand the photos over to him.'

'But Quinn didn't have the photos on him when he was killed.'

'That bothered me at first. But remember the mysterious phone call from the pay-as-you-go mobile?'

'Yes.'

'What if Mihkel was forced to make that call, to change the time of the meeting or something, or even to arrange it, and what if the different number or something in Mihkel's voice set off alarm bells, made Quinn suspicious?'

'But he still went.'

'Yes. It doesn't mean he wasn't on guard, though, cautious. But he clearly wasn't expecting a crossbow bolt through the heart. He may have left the pictures back in the room until he was sure Mihkel was coming.'

'That's possible, I suppose,' said Joanna. 'Do you think this Toomas Rätsepp knows?'

'Why would Rätsepp know? Quinn certainly wouldn't tell him, and I doubt that anyone else would, either. He might be able to give us some general details about the direction of the investigation, but I wouldn't expect much more from him. I still think Erik is our best bet, if he's willing to help.'

'What makes you think you can solve this after so long, when everyone else has failed?'

'Because I'm better than them,' Banks said, smiling. 'Watch and learn. Seriously, though. A lot's happened since then. Are you with me?'

Joanna rolled her eyes and laughed. Then she raised her glass and they clinked. 'I'm with you. Seriously, though,' she said, leaning forward. 'I really don't want us to be working at cross purposes here. I know what you think of me and my job, but we're both concerned with catching Quinn's killer, too, right? Are we OK on all this?'

'We're OK.'

8

Thursday turned out to be another warm day, and by lunchtime Banks and Joanna were ready for a cold drink and some food. They had spent the morning getting the feel of the city in which Rachel Hewitt had disappeared and discussing their strategy for the forthcoming interview. They had been all the way up to Toompea and seen the onion domes of the Russian Orthodox Nevsky Cathedral, walked around the Dome Church, admired the views of the city in various directions from the different viewing points, and wandered the quiet cobbled streets. There were very few shops and cafes up there, and it seemed remote, even from the rest of the Old Town, quiet and peaceful. Not the sort of area for a hen party.

They found Clazz, back down in the Old Town, opposite a large restaurant Banks had seen mentioned in his guidebook called Old Hansa, a cream-fronted building with lots of wooden benches on its covered patio, which seemed to contain almost as much shrubbery as it did customers. The waitresses were dressed in medieval-themed costumes, and Banks could imagine evening sing-alongs with everyone waving tankards of foaming ale in the air.

But Clazz was much less ostentatious. A man sitting at one of the outside tables waved them over and introduced himself.

'How did you know it was us?' Banks asked, when they had sat down.

'Two foreigners looking lost? It does not take much detective skill to work that out, Hr Banks.'

'Please, call me Alan. This is Inspector Joanna Passero.'

Joanna smiled and shook Rätsepp's hand. 'Joanna,' she said.

Banks noticed that he held on to it for a few seconds longer than necessary. Joanna clearly noticed it, too, but she said nothing.

'And I am Toomas. Do you enjoy our lovely weather?' Rätsepp went on. 'We often have good weather at this time of year. You are very lucky you come now.' His English wasn't quite as good as Merike's, but then he wasn't a translator. It was far better than Banks's non-existent Estonian.

'It makes a pleasant change,' said Banks.

Rätsepp was in his late fifties, overweight, with a head of thinning grey hair, wary, hooded eyes and bushy grey eyebrows, rather like a pair of horns above his eyes. Banks decided he must cultivate them that way deliberately, thinking they were sexy or something, because he couldn't fail to see them every time he looked in a mirror. He reminded Banks of the actor who had called Michael Caine 'Eenglish' with a sneer in his voice in *Funeral in Berlin*. Oscar Homolka. He was wearing a white shirt, open at the neck, with the sleeves rolled up, showing hairy forearms and throat. A grey sports jacket hung over the back of his chair. There were sweat stains under his arms, and the buttons were tight around his middle.

The waiter wandered over and handed out menus.

'I would recommend the steak,' Rätsepp said, 'but of course, it is entirely up to you. Perhaps you are vegetarian, yes?'

They ordered steak and A. Le Coq beer for Banks and Rätsepp, and a Diet Coke for Joanna. She had told Banks she felt a little the worse for wear this morning, so he guessed she was laying off the wine for a while.

'I understand you retired recently,' Banks said as they waited for their drinks. 'How is that working out?'

'Excellent, excellent,' said Rätsepp. 'It is something I wish I have done many years ago.'

'Why didn't you?'

He rubbed the thumb and fingers of one hand together. 'I must work to earn money.'

Their drinks arrived, and Rätsepp proposed an Estonian toast. '*Teie terviseks!*'

They sipped their drinks and chatted about police work and for a while, then when their lunch arrived, Rätsepp indicated he was ready to talk.

'It is terrible shame about Hr Quinn,' he said after his first mouthful of very rare steak. A drop of blood hung at the side of his fleshy mouth like a teardrop. Fortunately, he used his serviette a lot while he ate. 'He was good man. Very good man. What happen?'

'That's what we're hoping to find out.' Banks didn't want to get on to the subject of Quinn's transgressions so early in the conversation, though he hoped that at some point Rätsepp might be able to help him with the photographs, if he felt he could trust him enough to show him them. If, on the other hand, he got the impression that Rätsepp was in any way involved with what had happened to Quinn or Mihkel Lepikson, he certainly didn't want to give too much away. But he would reserve judgement for the moment. He was half-surprised, and very pleased, that Joanna didn't jump in with some comment about Quinn's murder. She must be learning; she must have listened to him after their set-to the previous evening. 'I'm afraid we're all still a bit at sea about it all.'

'At sea?'

'Sorry. Confused.'

'Ah. I do not really see how an old case will help you, or what it has to do with Hr Quinn's death,' Rätsepp said. 'It was long time ago, and Hr Quinn had only minor role.'

'I understand he was over here for about a week?'

'That is correct.'

'How soon after Rachel Hewitt's disappearance?'

'Perhaps two days.'

'That's very quick, isn't it?'

'There is no real measure for such things.' Rätsepp paused
and ate more steak. 'I think the girl's parents demand he come,'
he went on. 'They call local police in England and ask them to
do something. I think the parents are, how do you say, very
pushy? It is quite understandable, of course. We do our best,
but what can I say? This is beautiful nineteen-year-old girl,
young woman, and she is missing forty-eight hours. I know it
is very confusing and upsetting for her parents, to be so far
away, in foreign country. They do not understand our country.
They want someone to communicate what is happening before
they come here themselves. Difficult time for everyone.'

'What did DI Quinn actually do in the investigations?'

'Nothing very much. What can he do? He is not involved
here. He is not Estonian. He attends meetings, of course, so
he can go back and tell his bosses what we are doing. But that
is all.'

'He didn't do any searching, any questioning, any investigating?'

'No. Observing only.'

Banks wasn't sure he believed Rätsepp, but he moved on,
nonetheless. What reason could he have to lie? 'Were there
any leads at all?'

'Sadly, no. We check the hospitals, airport, railway station,
buses, ferries. We check other hotels. We speak with staff at
Meriton to ask if she go back there and go out again. We visit
many bars and clubs popular with young tourists. Ask everywhere. Nothing. It is like the girl disappear into air.'

'What about since then? Any nibbles? Any traces?'

'For two months we investigate. More. Sometimes now we
send out her description again. Nothing. I am sure you also
get many mistaken sights, which is all that we have had. From
St Petersburg to Prague, and in the south, Odessa and Tirana.

Her parents encourage many of these mistakes. We have also work with an artist on what Rachel look like now. It is not so very big change in six years, perhaps, but it helps.'

'What about CCTV?'

'What is that?'

'Closed-circuit television. Cameras. In the streets, in bars. We have them all over England.'

'Ah. Yes. We have here, too. But then not so many, of course. We examine all we can find, but nothing show us where Rachel is gone.' He paused. 'As I am sure you know, many camera images are not so good.'

'True enough,' said Banks. 'Most CCTV's crap, no arguing with that.' He gazed around at the other diners. Many were obviously tourists, given away by their cameras or bulging dayglo bags. He heard some people speaking German, and some Italian. There were also quite a few of young professionals, and he took most of them for locals, who perhaps worked in the Old Town or had come in from the suburbs to have lunch with friends during the spell of fine weather. 'This is very good steak,' he said.

'I am glad you approve. And the charming lady?'

Joanna, the 'charming lady', smiled sweetly at him and said, in her best Morningside accent. 'Absolutely delicious, Toomas. One of the tastiest I have ever eaten.'

Rätsepp beamed at her. 'In what capacity exactly are you here?' he asked, his forehead wrinkling into a slight and, so Banks thought, definitely choreographed frown.

'I'm sorry,' said Joanna. 'I don't understand the question.'

'I apologise for my bad English. You work for Professional Standards, am I not right?' he went on. 'But Inspector Quinn's murder is matter for Homicide, no?'

'I can see there are no flies on you, Toomas,' Joanna said, waving her fork at him and smiling to take the sting out of her tone.

He checked his arms. 'Flies? I do not understand.'

'She means you're very quick to grasp a situation,' Banks said. 'It's just a saying.'

'Ah, another of your charming English idioms. I see. It is one I do not know. I will remember. She is here to keep an eye on you, Alan, you lucky man? Have you been naughty boy?'

'It's nothing like that,' said Banks. 'Inspector Passero is training for her transfer to Homicide and Major Crimes. Her boss thought working on this case with me would help.'

'So you are her teacher?'

'Something like that.'

'You must be very good to be trusted with such lovely pupil.' His eyes narrowed. 'I hear things about you.'

'All good, I hope?' said Banks.

'But of course.'

Banks wasn't sure he liked being such common knowledge. First Corrigan, now Rätsepp. True, one of them was a cop, and it would be only natural for him to find out something about a visiting officer from another country. Even so, it was disconcerting, and he felt it put him at a disadvantage. He wondered exactly how much Rätsepp knew about him, and what.

Rätsepp turned back to Joanna again, still smiling. 'But I am not so certain that you tell me complete truth.'

Joanna smiled at him again. 'Toomas! Would you doubt a lady's word?'

'But of course not.' Rätsepp took her hand again for a moment. 'It is merely that I understand there is some . . . shall we say . . . confusion over Hr Quinn's circumstances, some possibility that he was involved in affair of the heart, or perhaps a business transaction of some kind, and you think it happens here.' He let go of Joanna's hand and gave it a light pat.

'Well,' said Banks, 'you've certainly done your homework, haven't you, Toomas? But that's really a non-issue. We're here because we've managed to make a connection between Bill Quinn and an Estonian journalist called Mihkel Lepikson. Have you ever heard of him?'

Rätsepp seemed taken aback at the name, Banks noted, and he got the impression that he was quickly trying to think how to respond. Rätsepp already seemed like a tricky person to pin down, and Banks hadn't expected smooth and easy sailing. How had he known about Quinn and the girl, for a start? There could be a leak in Yorkshire. Or was Rätsepp in touch with the villains themselves? Was he feigning surprise at the mention of Lepikson? He was hard to read. It was entirely possible that he had something to hide, but even if he didn't, the habits of a lifetime die hard. Given his age, Rätsepp must have been a cop during the Soviet era. He would be used to keeping his own counsel. Or lying. Policing must have been a whole different business under the Russian rulers, who would no doubt have brought in their own security organisations. Banks had heard and read many things about the Stasi in East Germany, for example, and he wondered if things had been at all similar here. If so, Rätsepp might be a very skilled dissembler, and he would also make it a point to know everything about everyone. He obviously already knew something about the Quinn case, and the girl, but Banks didn't know exactly how much. Did he know about the photographs, the possible blackmail, the crossbow?

'Lepikson . . . Lepikson . . .' Rätsepp muttered. 'The name sounds familiar, you know. A journalist?'

'The *Eesti Telegraaf*. He wrote about Rachel at the time she disappeared, then on and off over the years. Mihkel Lepikson was found dead under very mysterious circumstances in North Yorkshire, not far from where Bill Quinn was killed, a few days ago. Your government has been advised, and his parents have been located. I believe they have already left for the UK.'

'Ah, yes. I can know only what I read in the newspapers, of course,' said Rätsepp. 'Now I am retired, just private citizen like everyone else, I am out of the loop, as I believe you British say.'

'Of course. And I'm sure you can understand that I can't tell you any more, even as one police officer to another, with this being an ongoing investigation.'

'Naturally,' said Rätsepp. He sounded disappointed, and gave Banks the kind of look that seemed to beg for ten minutes alone with him in a soundproof interrogation cell. 'I understand completely.'

Banks could tell the Estonian was reevaluating him; he could almost hear the cogs turning, new gears engaging. Rätsepp had no doubt expected someone he could get information from easily, but now that was proving not to be the case, he was having to rethink his strategy. Banks tried to work out exactly where the Estonian stood in this whole business, but he had too little to go on. Was Rätsepp involved with Corrigan, with the crossbow killer, with Rachel Hewitt's disappearance? It was all possible, especially as he seemed to know so much, but there was no evidence to believe so yet. It was more than likely that he had made mistakes in the Rachel Hewitt investigation and was simply covering his arse.

The waiter came around again and asked if they wanted anything else. Banks and Rätsepp both ordered a second A. Le Coq, and Joanna asked for a cappuccino. She pronounced the word deliberately, with what Banks took to be a perfect Italian accent, not the way most Scots or Yorkshire folk would say it.

'I am sorry,' said Rätsepp, 'but there is really nothing more I can tell you about Hr Quinn, or why he was killed.'

'Can you think of anyone here who might have wanted him dead?'

'Here? But why?'

'A connection with the Rachel Hewitt case, perhaps?'

'What possible evidence is there?'

'No evidence, Toomas. Just a gut feeling. Don't you ever have gut feelings?'

'Of course. But not about this.'

'Mihkel Lepikson wrote about the case, and Bill Quinn investigated it. That seems like a connection to me. Were there many of you working on it?'

Rätsepp sipped some beer before replying. 'I have support investigators, as usual. And I report to Prosecutor.'

'That would be Ursula Mardna?'

'That is correct. Very senior and very competent Prosecutor, of blameless character.'

'We'll be talking to her later,' Banks said. 'I understand that DI Quinn mostly coordinated the investigation back in Yorkshire?'

'Yes. He talk with Rachel's parents and friends. Make some interviews. Communicate with us relevant information.'

'Such as?'

'Times, places, minor details.'

'Do you have such a thing as a map of the girls' movements that night?'

'Impossible. We try to make one, of course, but it is too difficult. Their memories . . . unreliable. The girls so drunk. The next day also.' He made a gesture of disgust. 'These girls. They come here and act so indecent and noisy. They must expect . . .'

'What? To be abducted?'

'No, of course not. That is not what I am saying. But they must learn to be more careful and more respectful.'

'They were just having a good time, Toomas,' said Joanna. 'They weren't doing any harm.'

'They ruin the peace of our Old Town.'

'You should try Nottingham on a Saturday night,' Joanna said.

Banks glanced at her, impressed. She was baiting Rätsepp, and doing it with great charm.

'My dear Joanna,' he said. 'It is not the same. They are visitors. Guests in our country. They should not behave that way.'

'Well, it's a bit late for Rachel Hewitt, isn't it?'

Rätsepp looked as if he'd been slapped. His face reddened. 'We do our best. We cannot do more. Now you come here and . . .' He waved his hand in the air disgustedly.

Their beers arrived, along with Joanna's cappuccino. Time to put the bridges back together again, Banks thought. He could play good cop when required. 'I'm sure you all did your best, Toomas,' he said. 'But these girls . . . well, as Inspector Passero says, they're young and wild and out for a good time. They don't think about public order and upsetting people. Yes, it's selfish, but you must have been a young lad once. Surely you sowed a few wild oats?'

Rätsepp gave Banks a knowing man-to-man smile. 'Certainly I did. But those were very different times. Russian times. You must very careful what you do and who see you. Much more careful. I do understand it is important, your case, but I do not see connection to Mihkel Lepikson and Rachel Hewitt. I do remember the journalist. He write about case back then. But why do you think the murders were connected to this?'

'It's just too much of a coincidence,' said Banks. 'Quinn befriended Lepikson while he was over here consulting on the case, *your* case. And both were murdered within about ten miles and ten hours of one another just after they'd been in touch again, just after a telephone conversation in which Bill Quinn told Mihkel that he might have a very big story for him.'

Rätsepp frowned. 'Big story, you say? What big story?'

'We don't know,' said Banks. 'I'm just saying it's too much of a coincidence. We also have forensic evidence to indicate that the same man and car were present at both scenes. Most likely the killer. We don't know who he is yet, but we're getting close.' Banks realised that he was probably telling Rätsepp too much, but he felt that if he didn't give at least something up, he would get nothing in return. If Rätsepp thought he was getting the best side of the bargain, if he believed that he had succeeded in tricking Banks into giving up too much, it might make his own tongue a bit looser. It was just a matter of exactly what Banks did give away and how valuable it was.

Rätsepp nodded. His chins wobbled. 'I still do not understand how I can help you. Our case records are in Estonian, of course, but you are most welcome to see them. Everything is in correct order. We can get translator, though it will take long time. We have nothing to hide. But I assure there is nothing about Hr Quinn.'

'I'm sure you're right, Toomas. And I don't want to read your case files. All I really want is a general picture of what happened while he was here. And the girls, of course. I know some of the details of the night in question, the drinking, clubbing, no doubt boys following them around. But where did they go, for example? You say you don't have a map, but you must have some idea.'

'This was six years ago,' said Rätsepp. 'So many bars, clubs and restaurants open and close since then that it is impossible to say. And the staff are all new. People have moved on. Even at the time it is very difficult to get an idea of their movements. Yes, we do have list of bars and nightclubs I am happy to give you, but we do not know the times and order of visiting. There are many Irish pubs with names like Molly Malone's and O'Malley's, for example. And many others in Old Town. Nimeta Baar – that is Pub With No Name now. Club Havana. Venus Club. Stereo Lounge. Club Hollywood. The girls go to many of these.'

'But not beyond the Old Town?'

'We do not think so.'

'Where did they lose Rachel?' Banks asked.

'In Irish pub on Vana-Posti, near south edge of Old Town. St Patrick's. Nobody see Rachel after there.'

'Except her killer.'

'Yes,' said Rätsepp with a sigh. 'The other girls go to bar on Raekoja Plats, main square, with some German boys they meet at Club Hollywood. They notice Rachel is not with them perhaps twenty minutes, half an hour, after they get there. Then it is too late, of course. They cannot find her. They cannot remember where they were before. It is only later that we can put some pieces together.'

'And then you went to these places and asked about Rachel?'

'Of course. But we find out nothing.'

Annie had already told Banks as much, but he wanted to find out if Rätsepp knew any more. 'Rachel didn't know where her friends were going, did she? They had no destination in mind, just picked somewhere at random. She could have just wandered around trying to find them for hours in the Old Town, couldn't she?'

'It is possible,' admitted Rätsepp. 'But I do not think so. Nobody report seeing her, except a waiter in St Patrick's, who say he think she go wrong way, other way from her friends. But he not so certain. As you see for yourself, it is not a very large area. It is very busy that night. We can find nobody who see her. That is because it is two days later before girls can tell us where they go. Tourists go home. German boys gone. Everybody gone.' He shook his head in frustration.

'Did no one report seeing her at all after she left St Patrick's?'

'Nobody. And we do not hear about her disappearance until the following morning. It take us two days to get information from her friends about where they go and what they do. They were so drunk they cannot remember. By then everyone who is there on that night is gone. Nobody knows anything. She is gone. Pouff.'

'And that's the last of Rachel,' said Banks. 'No body. No nothing.' He felt a wave of sadness ripple through him as he imagined what fear and pain Rachel must have gone through, whatever had happened to her. His daughter Tracy had gone through a terrible ordeal not too long ago, and thoughts about what might have happened to her still gave him nightmares. He could hardly begin to imagine the horrors Rachel's parents must have visualised over and over in their minds, the loop tapes of porn and snuff films. He took a hefty slug of beer.

He remembered the time he had been lost in a foreign city, and how frightening that had been. He was fourteen years old, on a school exchange with a French family in Lille. They had all gone to see *Gone With the Wind* in the town centre. Banks thought it was boring enough in English, so it would be even worse in French. He found a horror film showing around the corner, one of the old Dr Mabuse films, and said he would go there and meet them afterwards. Naturally, his film was much shorter than *Gone With the Wind*. Finding himself with plenty of time to kill, he bought some Gauloises at the nearest tabac and then went and sat in a bar, ordered a beer and waited. When it was time to meet up, he took a wrong turn and couldn't find the cinema. He wandered and wandered, deeper into the backstreets, rows of brick houses, little corner churches, washing hanging across the street, the locals giving him strange looks. He knew enough French to ask directions but not enough to understand the answers. The feeling of utter helplessness came over him, verging on panic. In the end, Banks had got to a main street he recognised and boarded a tram back to where he was staying. But Rachel . . . where did she end up?

Rätsepp held his hands open in a gesture of openness. 'What more can I say?'

'What do you think happened to Rachel, Toomas?' asked Joanna, cappuccino in her hand. 'Just out of interest.'

Banks was glad that Joanna had asked the question, feeling he was pushing a bit too hard himself. It was perfect coming from her. Rätsepp seemed to have forgotten her earlier insensitivity, because he favoured her with a condescending smile and patted her knee. 'My dear,' he said, 'you must know as well as I do that it cannot be good news. The most obvious theory is that someone take her, some stranger or someone the girls had meet earlier in some in nightclub or bar. Perhaps it is someone who has stalked them, or someone she has *arranged* to meet. We have no evidence of this, of course, and it poses many questions and many problems, but it is the best explanation.'

'She must have been taken by car,' Banks said. 'Cars can get into certain streets of the Old Town, can't they? I've seen them.'

'Of course,' Rätsepp agreed. 'Certain streets, certain areas, mostly near the edges. There are many cars around Niguliste, for example, which is not far from the pub where she was last seen. Yes, you are right. It is likely that this person persuade her to get in car. Perhaps she know him from earlier and trust him. We do not know.'

Banks remembered the big bookshop, the grass slope and the church, the restaurant where he had eaten dinner with Joanna last night. They were just around the corner from there right now. Somehow, the area was taking on a greater significance in his imagination of what might have happened to Rachel. It was true that a lot of cars and taxis seemed to drop people off there and turn around. It was also quite likely that nobody would notice a girl getting into a car or a taxi. Even if someone was pushing her, it might easily appear he was helping her. 'Did you talk to the taxi companies?'

'Of course. We talk to all drivers who work that night.
Nothing.'

'Could one of them be lying?'

'It is always possible. But we do our best.'

'I'm sure you did, Toomas. I'm not being critical, believe
me.'

'Is all right. I believe she meet someone from earlier. Maybe
from Club Hollywood, where they dance and drink before. Is
near St Patrick's. Perhaps he invite her to party or say he drive
her back to hotel. She go with him. Then . . .'

'Possibly,' said Banks. He remembered Annie telling him
that Rachel could be impulsive, and he knew only too well the
bad misjudgements that can be made when drunk. 'So,
however it happened, you think it happened quickly. Someone
got her out of there, abducted her, took her away from the Old
Town and then . . .?'

'Otherwise we would surely find body.'

Banks gestured around to the three- and four-storey buildings. 'Some of these places must be like rabbit warrens inside,'
he said. 'There must be old cellars, crypts, attics, places where
nobody goes, places nobody's been for centuries. You can't
have searched every nook and cranny of an area like this.
Could she have been taken inside one of them?'

'Is possible,' said Rätsepp. 'And there may be such places as
you say. We cannot search every room in the Old Town with
no information, but we make thorough search.'

'Somebody must have seen something,' Joanna said.

'No, my dear. Do you think your people in Nottingham on
Saturday night see something? A girl get in a car? Is that so
unusual there people notice? No. I do not think so. It is not so
strange. Do you not agree, Alan?'

'The general public can be remarkably unobservant,' Banks
agreed. 'Even when they're sober.' But especially, he thought,
a milling, drunken crowd, as had probably been out on the

streets of the Old Town at the time of Rachel's disappearance. Rätsepp was right. You could probably commit a murder on the street on a night like that, and everyone would just assume it was part of the fun. Maybe that was what had happened. 'Any other theories?'

'We try to consider everything. Perhaps her friends somehow kill her accidentally? Perhaps she fall down some steps, or somehow poison herself through alcohol? They panic, get rid of body and lie. Or they have a fight and she is accidentally killed.'

Banks had a sudden flash of the office girls outside at Whitelocks talking of their exploits in Cyprus, laughing about a friend being taken to hospital for alcohol poisoning, joking about another girl who was so drunk she pissed herself in public. Was it only a week ago? Less, even. 'And got rid of the body where?' he asked. 'You checked all the hospitals and searched all the waste ground and possible hiding places, didn't you?'

'Yes. That is problem with all theories, of course,' Rätsepp said. 'No evidence. No body. And girls do not have car. We even talk to car rent companies. Nothing.'

'Any other theories?'

'Well,' said Rätsepp, scratching his head, 'it is not a popular line of inquiry, but we think perhaps Rachel get involved in crime. In drugs, for example. Young girls do such things, for some boy they like, perhaps. They become mules, couriers.'

'Did you find any evidence of that?'

'None. But, of course, nobody wishes to think ill of Rachel, and it is not something people talk about. We have cases of foreign girls killed by drug-trafficking gangs they have become involved with, for stealing or for threatening to talk.'

'So you still think there might be something in this?'

'Is possible, yes.'

'I was just thinking that drug-traffickers might also be the kind of criminals who would consider a hit on Quinn, if he was getting too close to the truth.'

'It is professional job, Hr Quinn?'

'We think so,' said Banks. 'Both killings.'

'Then you can perhaps believe that some big drug-trafficker did not want to be named. That is another area you must investigate. I understand drugs are big problem in England.'

'But why after so long?'

'That I do not know. There could be many reasons. It take Hr Quinn so long to find him, perhaps? This could be "big story" for journalist.'

'In all these possibilities you're talking about,' said Joanna, 'Rachel Hewitt is dead. What if she's alive? Is there anything that could explain what happened to her if she's still alive and well?'

'That is, of course, what her parents wish to believe,' said Rätsepp solemnly, 'and I do not want to rob them of all hope. But what is the explanation? She hit her head and lose her memory and wander off somewhere? Poland? Russia? She is working in flower shop in Minsk and married with two beautiful little children? Or she do not like her parents and run away from home? This the parents do not wish to accept. They must continue to believe their daughter loves them.'

'What if she was abducted and forced into prostitution, trafficked?' said Banks.

'Again, is possible,' Rätsepp admitted. 'But we are not Albania or Romania. Estonia is not destination for such victims, and is not usually a source. Is a station on the way. Traffic passes through here to England and Finland and Sweden, from the east, from the south. Drugs. People. Girls. Illegal immigrants. So it is possible. But her parents and many others search over the years, send out pictures, and find no trace of her.'

Banks thought of Haig and Lombard trolling the Internet sites for the girl in the photographs with Quinn. He had decided not to bring her up with Rätsepp, after all; he didn't trust the man enough. He would save her for Erik, Mihkel Lepikson's friend and contact at the *Eesti Telegraaf*. He could think of no more questions.

Rätsepp seemed to sense they had got to the end of their discussion and glanced at his watch. 'I must be leaving now,' he said. 'I have appointment.' He took out his wallet and left a card on the table. 'If you need to get in touch. Anything.' He started to pull out some bills, but Banks held his hand up. 'No, Toomas,' he said. 'Remember, tourists pay.'

Rätsepp laughed. 'Ah, yes. Thank you very much. I hope to repay the favour in England one day.' He stood up, bent gallantly to kiss Joanna Passero's hand, gave Banks a quick salute, grabbed his jacket and disappeared into the crowds around the corner on Viru.

Pauline Boyars lived in a flat above a fish and chip shop on the Wetherby Road. She was at home when Annie and Winsome pressed her doorbell at half past two on Thursday afternoon, and she buzzed them up. The fish and chip shop was closed, so there was no smell of deep-frying, Annie thought gratefully. It was probably a good thing. Fish and chips was one of her weaknesses, and had played havoc with her fading dream of vegetarianism. At least most places didn't use lard for deep-frying any longer.

Whether Pauline overindulged in the services downstairs, Annie had no idea, but she was certainly on the large size, and her complexion was pasty and spotty, as if she ate too much fatty food. Her hair was lank and uncared for, and her nails bitten to the quicks. More signs, Annie thought, that Pauline Boyars had very much let herself go. She was only twenty-five or -six, but she looked over thirty.

The flat was untidy, with clothes lying on the floor, piles of gossip magazines and unwashed dishes, but it didn't have that all-pervasive smell of fish and chips Annie had expected. Several windows were open, and she could hear kids playing football in the small park at the back. Didn't anyone go to school any more?

Pauline cleared some newspapers from a couple of chairs, and they sat down. She didn't apologise for the mess, the way many people would have done, but lit a cigarette and sat on the sofa, leaning forward, elbows resting on her knees. 'What's it about?' she asked.

'It's about Detective Inspector Bill Quinn,' Winsome said.

'Sounds familiar. Refresh my memory.'

'The detective from Leeds who worked on Rachel's case?'

'Oh, yes. I remember him. Worse than useless, like the rest of them.'

'He's been murdered,' said Winsome.

'It didn't do anybody any bloody good, though, did it?' Pauline went on, as if she hadn't heard. Her right foot was tapping the whole time they were talking. 'It didn't bring Rachel back, did it? If you're going to be asking me about all that stuff, I need a drink. I won't offer you any because you're on duty, and because I don't have much left.' She got up and poured a hefty shot of vodka into a tea mug.

'Pauline, we're hoping you can help us here,' said Winsome, in her most soothing voice. 'Getting drunk won't help.'

'Are you crazy?' She held out the mug. 'You think this would get me drunk? If only. What do you want to know?'

'You might have read in the papers that Bill Quinn was killed a few days ago, and his death was suspicious. We've been assigned to investigate.'

'Well, bully for you. It was probably some vicious tattooed drug-dealing Hells Angel he put away years ago.'

'That's one possibility,' said Winsome. 'But another is that his death was somehow connected with what happened to Rachel.'

'Nobody knows what happened to Rachel. That's the bloody point. She might as well have been abducted by aliens.'

Annie saw that Winsome was struggling with Pauline's hostility, so she gave a quick signal and cut in. 'You were there that night, Pauline? What do you think happened?'

Pauline stopped tapping her foot and gazed at Annie. Then she stubbed out her cigarette and gulped some vodka. The foot started tapping again. 'What good would it do to go over it all again? Don't you think I've been over it a million times with the bloody Estonian police, and with your mate Quinn?'

'I'm sure you must have,' said Annie. 'But that was a long time ago, wasn't it? Maybe over the years you've remembered things you didn't say then?'

'Remembered? Some hope. Forgotten, more like. I didn't remember much in the first place. That was the problem.'

'It's not surprising,' Annie said. 'You were out celebrating. Having a good time. You couldn't have had any idea what was going to happen.'

Pauline stared at Annie again and sipped more vodka, then stared into the depths of her mug.

'I'm not judging you, Pauline,' she went on. 'I've been in this job long enough to know that the best will in the world can't stop a criminal getting his way. And I've been pissed often enough to have done more than a few things I'm ashamed of.'

'So why do you do it? The job, I mean.'

'Now there's a question. I wish I knew the answer.'

Pauline managed a brief smile, which changed the whole structure of her face and showed a flash of the beauty that might still lurk under the ravaged surface. She lit another cigarette.

'Come on, Pauline,' Annie said. 'Tell us about it.'

'They didn't believe us, you know.'

'Who didn't?' Winsome asked, picking up the questioning again.

'The Estonian police. Can you believe it? They thought we'd done it and hidden her body somewhere. They kept going on about it, asking us where we'd put her.'

'That was probably one of the many theories they developed,' said Winsome. 'They have to cover all the angles, no matter how unbelievable some of them seem.'

'But they never found anyone, did they? They never found Rachel. I think they decided it was us but couldn't prove it, and they didn't bother to look any further.'

'This policeman I'm talking about, Bill Quinn,' Winsome went on. 'He was haunted by the failure to find her. We think he might still have been trying to find out what happened right up until the end, when he was killed last week.'

Pauline stared down at her fingernails and nicotine-stained fingers. 'I don't get many visitors,' she said. 'You must forgive me. I seem to have dropped my social skills down the toilet.'

'That's all right,' said Winsome. 'Where's your husband? Is he not around?'

It could have gone either way, and Annie was mentally ready to give Winsome a bollocking later if it blew up in their faces, but Pauline actually softened. Her eyes dampened.

'We never did get married,' she said. 'Isn't that a joke, after everything that happened?'

'Whose idea was that?'

'Both of ours, really. But I suppose I started it. I stayed on in Tallinn. It seemed . . . I don't know . . . disrespectful to leave before the police discovered anything. I couldn't just leave Rachel like that, could I? But in the end I had to, or I'd still be there, wouldn't I?'

'So you postponed the wedding?'

'At first, yes. It seemed the best idea.'

'So what happened?'

'We just postponed and postponed for so long that in the end the whole idea lost its appeal. I was preoccupied with Rachel. I neglected Trevor. He found someone else. They got married two years ago. The old, old story. When I look back, we were way too young in the first place. Young love. What a joke.'

'I'm sorry,' said Winsome.

Pauline straightened up. 'Don't be,' she said. 'I'm not. Good riddance. That's what I say.' She ran the back of her hand over her eyes and glanced from one to the other, then clapped her hands together, showering ash and spilling vodka on the already stained and threadbare carpet. 'So, enough of this maudlin rubbish. What is it you want to know?'

'First off,' said Winsome, 'about Detective Inspector Quinn. Do you have any idea why he would remain interested in the case, and why it might get him killed six years later?'

'Absolutely none at all. I hardly saw him. I mean, I only talked to him once or twice. I know he saw a bit of Maureen and Luke, too. That's Rachel's parents.'

'Yes, we've talked to them,' said Winsome.

'Well, we keep in touch, like, occasionally. I'm afraid there's not much more I can add. But why do you think it was that? Rachel? Couldn't there be many other explanations for why he was killed?'

'We have our reasons,' said Winsome. 'Did you like Bill Quinn?'

'Like? I never really thought about it. I must admit, I was a bit of a mess back then, and he was kind enough, his manner, you know . . . nicer than some of those Estonian cops. There was a bloke called Rätsepp. "Rat's arse", we called him. He was the one who kept going on about us doing it and dumping her body.'

'They were probably all very frustrated,' Winsome said.

'I'm sure they were. Sexually, most like, the way some of them were giving us the eye.'

'You don't have to go to Estonia to find sexist cops,' said Annie. 'Come to Eastvale with me now, and I'll show you a few.'

'No thanks,' she said. 'But I appreciate the offer.' The kids started shouting down on the playing field, and Pauline went over to shut the back window. When she returned, she poured herself another shot of vodka to replace what she had spilled, and lit another cigarette from the stub of the old one. 'Noisy little buggers,' she said.

'Whose idea was it to go to Tallinn?' Annie asked.

'Mine. I was the bride-to-be, after all.'

So much for the idea that Rachel had arranged the hen weekend so she could meet up with a foreign boyfriend in Tallinn. She could have met someone between the decision to go there and the trip, but that seemed too much of a coincidence.

'What was Rachel like as a friend?' Winsome asked.

Pauline paused. 'Like? She was full of life, loved to help people, bright, beautiful, funny, stubborn, a bit wild sometimes, spontaneous. Christ, she was just nineteen, you know. What are nineteen-year-olds like? I don't remember. Do you?'

'Did you take drugs?'

Pauline paused and looked at Winsome through narrowed eyes. 'We might have done E once or twice, you know, at a club.'

'In Tallinn?'

'No way. Far too dodgy getting drugs off some stranger in a foreign city.'

'Rachel?'

'No.'

'In your opinion, was she likely to go off with a stranger in a car?'

'Maybe, if it was a nice car and she liked the look of him.'

'So what do you think happened to her?'

'I think she got lost. Wandered off the beaten track. Some sick bastard abducted her, raped her, then killed her and buried her, or chucked her body in the sea, and it floated all the way to Sweden or somewhere.'

'You don't believe she's alive? That she lost her memory, or decided to start a new life?'

'No. That's not Rachel. She loved her family and her friends. And her bloody budgie. If she was alive she'd have been in touch. She would have gone home. And this amnesia business is just a load of bollocks. I don't blame Maureen and Luke for clinging on to hope, you know, but sometimes I find them a bit hard to take.'

'And why haven't the police found Rachel, or the person who abducted her?'

'Because they're useless.'

'But you weren't able to give them much help,' Winsome went on. 'From what I've been able to make out, it wasn't until the following morning that you reported her missing, and then it took the police nearly two days to get any sort of coherent story out of you about where you'd been, who you'd talked to.'

Annie had to give it to Winsome, she was coming along nicely, developing a tough edge. Many others would have shied away from asking an obviously disturbed person like Pauline those sorts of questions.

To her credit, Pauline just shook her head sadly. 'Do you know,' she said, 'since I came back from Tallinn, there isn't a day gone by when I haven't tortured myself with the same thoughts. If only we hadn't forgotten her in St Patrick's. If only we'd told her where we were going. If only she hadn't forgotten her mobile. If only I had insisted right from the start that we call the police. If only I hadn't passed out in my room. If only I hadn't been so drunk and then so hung over I couldn't remember a single useful snippet of information. If only. If only. If bloody only. And there isn't a day gone by when I haven't imagined what she went through, played the movie in my brain of what he must have done to Rachel, and how much pain and fear she must have suffered before she was killed. It varies a little each time, the details, but it's basically the same movie.'

'Any chance you would have recognised who did it in your movie?' Annie cut in.

Pauline looked at her in surprise. 'That's a bloody clever question,' she said. 'Nobody asked me that before. But I'm afraid not. No. He's always just a vague shadow. It's only Rachel I see clearly. One of the cops suggested it could have been someone we met during the course of the evening, but we danced with a lot of lads, and nobody stands out as particularly weird. Still, they wouldn't have to, would they? Don't they always say it's the boy-next-door type you have to watch out for?'

'It was worth a try,' said Annie. 'I just thought it might have been someone you'd seen in the course of the evening, even just from the corner of your eye, and for some unconscious reason, you cast him in that role.'

'No. I'm sorry. No.'

'Were you aware of anybody following you, or paying undue attention during the evening?' Winsome asked.

'I've racked my brains to dredge up something time and time again, but I just can't do it,' said Pauline. 'It makes me want to tear my hair out. We talked to a lot of lads that night. Just for fun, nothing serious. We danced, chatted, had a good time. I mean, I was getting married, so I wasn't interested in other blokes. Rachel had just split up with shit-for-brains dickhead Tony Leach. The others, I don't know ... I don't even know if I would have noticed if someone *had* been stalking us.'

'Do you still see the others?' Winsome asked.

'No. Funny that, isn't it? People used to say we were inseparable. Course, Janine topped herself. Took an overdose. That'd be three, four years ago now.'

'Because of what happened?'

'Boyfriend troubles, but that covers a multitude of sins, doesn't it? She was always the sensitive one. Gillian's all right. She got married last year, and she plans on turning herself into a baby factory. First one's out already. She even sent me a wedding invitation and a Christmas letter. I think they're living in Canada. Helen's an alcoholic. I don't know where she lives. On the streets in London, I think. And Brenda's a social worker. She finally got it together after treatment. She's discovered she's really gay, so she's shacked up with some African woman. Our Brenda. Sweet little naïve Brenda. Would you believe it? What a turn up.'

Five young lives destroyed, Annie thought. Except maybe for Gillian and Brenda, who seemed desperately trying to put their lives back together, even if the paths they had chosen were difficult ones.

'How bad was Rachel, really, that night?' Winsome asked.

'Well, she wasn't totally legless. She was a bit wobbly, like, but she could have got back to the hotel on her own, or at least managed a taxi. She had some money. Other than that, it's hard to say. Her judgement was probably a bit fucked up, but I think if someone had grabbed her, she'd have known what was happening. She was streetwise enough. She wouldn't just have gone along with it.'

'She would have struggled?'

'And screamed. I think so. Yes. But if it was someone strong, with an open car door, or maybe even two people, there wouldn't have been much she could do, would there? All he'd have to do was put his hand over her mouth and push her in.'

'Is that how you think it happened?'

'More or less.'

'What happened in St Patrick's?' Winsome asked.

'We were just talking to the German lads. They all spoke good English, and they had a great sense of humour. You don't think that about Germans, do you, but they did. It was busy, but not as crowded or hot as that dance place we'd been to. Club Hollywood. I think we even had something to eat.'

'A bit of an oasis, then?'

'Something like that. A breather. Then we went off to another bar, and we were thinking of leaving there and going dancing again when I missed Rachel.'

'It was you who noticed she was missing?'

'Yes.'

'What did you do?'

'First we searched through the place we were in, then we went back to try to find her.' Tears welled up in Pauline's eyes. 'Me and one of the German boys. But we couldn't remember where we'd been, could we? We were too pissed. Neither of us knew the city, and we couldn't find it again. We didn't remember St Patrick's until later. Too late.'

'So what happened there?' Winsome asked.

'It's all very vague, but I remember someone asked us to leave. Quietly, like. It was one of the places where they didn't like English stag parties, or hens. They had a bit of a reputation for hell-raising by then.'

'And did you leave?'

'Yes. We might have given a bit of lip, I don't really remember, but we left. That's why we left. And Rachel had been flirting with the barman. Good-looking bloke. Australian. Can't remember his name. Steve, or something.'

'They'd been talking?'

'Flirting. On and off. I mean, he was really busy, so he couldn't just stand there and chat, but I remember myself thinking, I'll bet she's back here again tomorrow.'

'Did you tell the Estonian police this?'

'Yes, of course. When I remembered. But it was too late by then. When I asked them about it, they said the barman was gone. They didn't know where. Back to Australia, I suppose. Anyway, they couldn't trace him, so that was that. Dead end.'

'Do you think he had anything to do with it?'

'I doubt it,' said Pauline. 'I mean, he was working, wasn't he? He couldn't just disappear. And the police said he didn't have a car. It was just that he might have known where she'd gone, that's all. Rachel might have said something to him.'

'Maybe she arranged to meet him later,' said Winsome, and she and Annie looked at one another. The three of them sat silently for a moment, thinking over the implications. Winsome seemed to have covered just about everything, Annie thought. She couldn't think of anything else to ask. Pauline's company was becoming depressing, and the messy flat oppressive.

'We should be off now, then,' Winsome said. 'Thanks for your time, Pauline. I'm sure you've got work or something.'

'Work? Huh. That went the same way as marriage.'

'You packed it in?'

'Sort of. Though I think they made the final decision for me. I'd got my A levels, but I wanted to start work – like Rachel – and I got a job with Debenhams. In management, not shop floor. Anyway, it was a start. Sort of a management trainee. I got transferred here after things started to go off a bit in Bradford, then . . . I don't know. Couldn't keep up my concentration. Still can't. It was rude of me, I know, but I didn't even offer you a cup of tea. Sure you won't stay and have one?'

Annie could see the desperation in her eyes, but she didn't feel she could stand another fifteen or twenty minutes in this mausoleum of guilt and shame. Luckily, Winsome must have agreed, because she was the one who refused the offer of tea, gently, and led the way out.

Erik Aarma had agreed to meet Banks and Joanna in the hotel lobby at five o'clock, and they spent the time in between talking to Rätsepp and meeting Erik going over their notes and clarifying theories. Both agreed that Rätsepp hadn't been much use and had told them nothing Annie hadn't already gleaned from reading over Quinn's files.

It had taken a long time to set the investigation in motion, Banks thought, but that was more than likely for the reasons Rätsepp had given: the memory of the girls, or lack of it, being paramount. For a start, the police didn't hear about the disappearance until the following day, and the girls were unable to give an accurate account of where they went, what they did and who they talked to, even on Monday morning. Thus, Rachel had been missing for close to thirty-six hours before anything approaching an investigation stumbled into motion. By then, of course, the rest of that night's revellers were long gone.

Perhaps if one of the girls had pushed a little harder a little sooner and reported Rachel missing to the police the night she had got lost, rather than the following morning, something more might have been done. But that was a long shot. Rachel was nineteen, hardly a minor, and there was no guarantee that the police would start an immediate all-out search for her. Most likely they wouldn't, unless they had good reason to think something had happened to her. It was natural enough to think that she may have simply wandered off, or met some young man, and would turn up by morning. It is all very well to apportion blame in retrospect, but at the time, nobody thought for a moment that they were never going to see Rachel again, that she was about to disappear from the face of the earth. You don't plan for these things; nobody is ever prepared.

Erik Aarma was a big bearded bear of a man with piercing blue eyes and straggly, ill-cut hair, wearing a baggy checked work shirt and jeans. He was carrying a scuffed leather satchel of the kind Banks used to carry back and forth to school every day, in the days before rucksacks became de rigeur. He wished he had kept his now; it looked cool.

Erik lowered his bulk into the semicircular Naugahyde chair and apologised for being late. He gave no reason, and Banks suspected he was a person who was rarely on time. They ordered coffees and quickly got down to business. Joanna had agreed to make notes, so she took out her notebook and pen. Erik's English was excellent, and it turned out he had worked in London on the *Independent* for a few years. Banks was wondering if he would ever run into an Estonian who needed a translator. That reminded him to get in touch with Merike soon.

As a rule, Banks didn't trust journalists; in the past they had screwed up so many of his cases in the name of people's right to know. But he felt he had no choice as far as Mihkel and Erik were concerned. They were his only allies, and Mihkel was dead. Bill Quinn had clearly trusted Mihkel enough to become friends with him. This from a man who, according to his own daughter, didn't have many friends outside work, followed solo pursuits, preferred his own company. Now Banks was in a position of wanting to trust Erik a lot more than he had trusted Toomas Rätsepp. He hoped his faith would be justified.

Erik's handshake was firm, and his anger and sadness over the loss of his friend and colleague clearly genuine. 'I do not know how I can help,' he said, glancing from Banks to Joanna and back, 'but I promise I will do what I can.'

'Thank you,' Banks said.

'Poor Merike. She must be heartbroken.'

'She was very upset, yes,' said Banks. 'Perhaps you'd like to call her?'

'Yes. Yes, I will.'

'How long have you worked with Mihkel?'

'Fifteen years. Ever since he began to work at the paper.'

'Was that before "*Pimeduse varjus*"?'

'Yes. He worked on general duties at first, then he later came to specialise in crime stories. He started the column in 2001. Sometimes others contribute, but it was his idea in the beginning. Can you give me any idea what happened to him? The stories we heard were very vague.'

Banks quickly weighed his options before answering and decided that, given the information he wanted from Erik, it would be best to tell him as much as realistically possible. 'He was found dead at an abandoned farm called Garskill in remote North Yorkshire last Saturday morning. We think he had been dead since the Wednesday before. The place looked as if it had been home to a group of about twenty bonded or migrant workers, possibly illegal, most likely Eastern European. We found a paperback book on one of the mattresses, and it turned out to be in Polish. When we found Mihkel, everyone else was gone, and we suspect that they left for work on Wednesday morning and were later directed to new quarters. We haven't been able to discover where they are yet.'

'But how did he die? How did you come to find him there?'

Banks paused. 'He was drowned,' he said. 'In a water trough. We know it wasn't accidental because there were bruises to indicate he had been held under. I'm sorry if this is distressing, but you asked, and I'm telling you as much as I can.'

'I'm all right. Please go on.'

'There isn't much more to tell,' Banks said.

'I talked to Mihkel on Tuesday evening,' Erik said. 'He told me he was calling from a telephone box. He had to be very careful. The men in charge were suspicious because someone had smuggled a mobile phone into another group and used it to take photographs and make calls to a Lithuanian magazine.'

'What did you talk about?' Banks asked.

'Conditions there. He said they were terrible. It was cold. There were holes in the roof. They did not get much food, and what they did get was bad. The pay was low.'

'Where were they working?'

'Different places. A chicken hatchery. A frozen-food factory. A chemical-packing plant.'

'Can I get the full details from you later?' Banks asked. 'We'll need to track these places down. That's not my immediate concern, but it will have to be done.'

'Of course.'

'So he was writing a story for you about this?'

'Yes. We have known about these illegal labour schemes for a long time, but Mihkel thought it would be useful to go undercover, to follow one from the beginning to the end and write an in-depth article. He could not know what that end would be, of course. That it would be his own.'

'Did he mention someone called Quinn at all? Bill Quinn?'

'Bill? But yes, of course. They had talked.'

'That was all he said, that they had talked?'

'He spoke about another story, a possibly big story, but that was all he could say.'

'And this was connected with Bill Quinn?'

'I think so.'

'Do you have any idea what it was?'

'No. Not unless Bill Quinn had found out what happened to Rachel Hewitt.'

'Or had always known,' Banks said to himself.

'What?'

'Sorry. Nothing. So you know about that, about Rachel?'

'Of course. That was how they met, Bill and Mihkel. The

Rachel Hewitt case. Mihkel wrote much about it, and he and Bill became friends. They kept in touch over the years.'

'The thing is,' Banks said, 'Bill Quinn was killed, too, around the same time and, we believe, by the same person.'

Erik's mouth opened and flapped like a landed fish. He rubbed his forehead. 'I . . . I don't . . .'

'I know. It's very confusing,' Banks said. 'We don't pretend to know what's going on, but there are some very far-reaching connections here. One of them is the Rachel Hewitt case, and another is the migrant labour scheme you mentioned, the one Mihkel was writing about and Bill Quinn was investigating. Have you ever heard of a man called Corrigan? Warren Corrigan?'

Erik thought for a moment, then said, 'No. I'm sorry.'

'No matter,' Banks went on. 'Can you tell me how Mihkel ended up in North Yorkshire?'

'His story?'

'Yes.'

'I suppose so,' said Erik. 'It's not as if he can tell it himself now, is it?'

'It might help us catch his killer.'

Erik thought for a moment, then a brief smile flickered through his beard. 'I am sorry. It is difficult for me, as a journalist, to give information to police. Old habits die hard.'

'If it's any consolation,' Banks said. 'It's very difficult for me even to be in the same room as a journalist.'

Erik stared at him for a moment, then burst out laughing. Joanna joined in. 'I have no problem with most journalists,' she said. 'We'd very much appreciate it if you could give us a few details.'

'Of course. As I said, it was Mihkel's idea. Well, mostly.'

'Pardon me for interrupting so early,' said Banks, 'but was that usually the case with his stories, or was he given assignments?'

'It varied. Sometimes, if a subject was hot at the moment, he would be given an assignment like any other reporter. But something like this, something that would take him under-cover for some time, and perhaps expose him to danger, that would have to be his own idea.'

'I see. Carry on.'

'Like most of us, Mihkel had heard about unskilled workers heading for what they thought was a paradise in the UK and other countries, and finding quite the opposite. He wanted to follow the whole process through every stage, find out who the main players were and how it was done. It was actually Bill who told him about this.'

'Bill Quinn sent Mihkel in there?'

'No. No. He simply told Mihkel about how the business operated and gave him the name of the agency in Tallinn. It was Mihkel who had the idea to start at the beginning and follow the trail. He was always . . . what would you say?'

'Adventurous? Impetuous?'

'Both,' said Erik, smiling sadly.

'Did he send you written reports?'

'No. Not this time. It was too risky. No phones, no cameras, no paper and pencil. We talked on the telephone, and I made notes. He was allowed out, of course, when he wasn't working. They weren't prisoners. At least not prisoners in solid prisons. You understand?'

'I think so,' said Banks. 'He was living in a very remote place. It was a two-mile walk to the telephone. Did you write up the reports in Estonian?'

'Of course.'

'OK. Go on. Can you give me the gist?'

'It's a simple enough story. He first approached an agency here in Tallinn, where they charged him two hundred euros, gave him a telephone number and told him there was a job waiting for him in Leeds.'

'Did they say what kind of job?'

'No. But he knew it would be casual labour of some sort, perhaps in a factory, or on a battery farm. About fifty hours a week at minimum wage. I think that is about seven euros an hour, perhaps a little more. That's three hundred and thirty euros a week, anyway. He travelled by train and was met at St Pancras by another agent of the company, who asked for another two hundred euros. So already this job had cost Mihkel four hundred euros and his travel expenses. For all this he had no receipt. The man told him he could get a train to Leeds at King's Cross, just across the road, and he disappeared with the money. Mihkel never saw him again.'

'These people, the agents, do you know their names?'

'Yes. The man in London was a Latvian, but he worked with the same agency as the one in Tallinn.'

'If it came to it, would you turn these names over to the police or the immigration authorities?'

Erik hesitated. 'I don't know,' he said. 'It would be ... perhaps unethical. Even though Mihkel is dead. I would have to think.'

'OK,' said Banks. 'No pressure.' Not yet, he thought.

'Mihkel went to Leeds and contacted the number he had been given. It was a staffing agency.'

'It wouldn't happen to be called Rod's Staff Ltd, would it?'

Erik's eyes widened. 'How did you know that?'

'Run by a Mr Roderick Flinders?'

'Yes. The agency said they had never heard of Mihkel, that there must have been some mistake, there was no job waiting for him in Leeds, but they might be able to help him. They gave him a bed in a room shared by ten people in a converted barn outside Otley and told him to wait for further instructions. Four days later he was told he was moving to another area right away. They took him to that farm you mentioned, where he was killed three weeks later.'

'What happened during those three weeks?'

'The conditions were terrible, Mihkel told me, and he was sharing with about twenty people. They had only one toilet, a shower that mostly did not function. Filthy drinking water.'

'I've seen it,' said Banks. 'I know.'

'Then you will understand. Did you also know that not all the workers were men? There were three young women also, and two couples, all together in the same damp, cold dormitory. Sometimes some of the men tried to touch the women. There were fights. Mihkel said he tried to help. He spoke to a girl from Poland and another from Lithuania. The third girl never talked to anybody. Mihkel didn't know where she was from, but her skin was darker. He thought Kazakhstan, or Georgia, perhaps. For the privilege of living there, they had to pay Rod's Staff Ltd. Sixty euros each week in rent. This was deducted from their pay.'

'Where did they work?'

'All over the north, from Carlisle to Teesside. Darlington. Middlesbrough. Stockton.'

'What sort of work?'

'The worst. Slaughterhouses, chemical packaging plants, fertiliser factories. You name it. The work was hard and the hours long. Mihkel's first job was at a mushroom farm, picking mushrooms, but that was only for one shift. He never saw any money from that. Then he was sent to a frozen-food factory on day shifts, twelve hours a day, seven days a week, picking any bad beans or peas from the conveyor belt after they had been frozen and before they were packaged.'

'A lot more than fifty hours,' Banks said.

'Yes. After two weeks he had worked a hundred and sixty-eight hours and he received his first payslip. It was for sixty-five euros.'

'How did they explain that?'

'There were many discrepancies. He was not paid minimum wage to start with, but only five euros for each hour.
Would this be easier in pounds?'

'No, it's OK,' said Banks. 'I can keep track. Besides, there's
not a hell of a lot of difference these days.'

'Too true,' Erik agreed. 'Perhaps we should have kept the
kroon. Anyway, Mihkel was also told that Rod's Staff Ltd
withhold two weeks' wages and pay . . . what is the word?'

'In arrears?' Banks suggested.

'Yes. Two weeks in arrears. Of course, one hundred and
twenty euros for two weeks' rent had also been deducted, but
had not been included in the deductions on his payslip. By
then, he also owed money to people, and when he had paid
them back, he had almost nothing left. This was when someone from Rod's Staff Ltd, perhaps even Mr Flinders himself,
approached him and told him he knew someone who lent
money to people in Mihkel's situation and asked if he was
interested. Mihkel said yes, he was, as he had no money left
for cigarettes or food. Anyway, this was the stage of the investigation he had reached when he was killed. It was on Tuesday
evening he told me about the payslip and the errors on it.'

'How did he get to work and back?'

'Someone with a van picked them up in the morning and
dropped them off at night. They got weak coffee and stale
bread for breakfast. If they were lucky and had enough money,
they could just make a dash to the nearest fast-food outlet
before the van arrived to take them back, and buy a burger or
fried chicken.'

'Are you sure he never mentioned someone called Corrigan?'

'No. I will check my notes, but I would remember. I have a
very good memory.'

It was too much of a coincidence, Banks thought, for someone else to be in the same business in the same general area.
Corrigan must have used his minions to reach out to

operations like Flinders', while he remained at the business centre in Leeds. The two men knew each other, had drinks together, so it seemed obvious to Banks that they were in cahoots over this. Flinders created and supplied the victims, not only on city housing estates, but also in remote dormitories like Garskill Farm, which cost him nothing and netted him about a grand a week in rents. To say nothing of the kick-backs he was getting from the employers.

On Wednesday morning, more than likely, the killer had arrived at Garskill Farm and Mihkel had been kept back from work that day. He was tortured, at which time he had proba-bly agreed to the mobile call to Quinn to set him up, arrange to meet in the woods later that night, which had set off the detective's alarm bells, though they had not rung loudly enough to keep him away from the rendezvous completely and save his life. Quinn had, however, kept the photographs in his room, and perhaps had planned, if all turned out to be above board, to go back and get them for Mihkel. But it wasn't Mihkel who turned up in the woods at St Peter's that night.

'Who knew of Bill Quinn's friendship with Mihkel?' he asked Erik.

'I don't know. It was not something they hid. Anyone could know. Sometimes Mihkel wrote updates on the Rachel Hewitt case, and he often mentioned his connection with the English policeman.'

'In the newspaper?'

'Yes.'

'So anyone at all could know?'

'It would surely not be of much interest to anyone. What are you thinking?'

'I'm not sure,' said Banks. 'But someone wanted Bill Quinn out of the way, and that same person also wanted Mihkel out of the way. Can you think of anyone who would want that?'

'No.'

'I'm missing something,' Banks went on. 'There has to be some connection between Rachel Hewitt and the illegal worker scam.'

'Why? How?'

'Because we believe someone sent the same killer to get rid of both Bill Quinn and Mihkel.'

'But why bring up Rachel Hewitt? You have already said that Bill Quinn was also involved in investigating the workers.'

'That's true. Maybe he was working both sides.'

'And perhaps with Mihkel's help he was about to become a danger to them, and they knew that? Perhaps they were both killed for the same reason. The Rachel Hewitt case was simply what brought them together in the first place, not the reason for either of the murders.'

Banks had always been aware of that possibility, that he could be wandering way off target by taking Rachel Hewitt into consideration. But there was something about her disappearance that bothered him, and something had obviously been gnawing away at Bill Quinn ever since his trip to Tallinn six years ago. There were the photographs with the unknown girl, too. Banks knew, however, that he had to try to keep an open mind on this, that he was in danger of allowing one set of facts to obscure or distort another. Maybe the two events weren't connected, but that didn't mean Banks shouldn't try to find out what had happened to Rachel as well as solve Quinn's and Mihkel's murders. He didn't think he could go through the rest of his days not knowing what happened, the way Bill Quinn had. Look what it had done to him. And her parents deserved better.

Banks took out copies of Bill Quinn's photographs, including the blow-ups and the cropped version showing only the girl. He laid them before Erik on the table. 'We believe that these photographs were taken here in July 2006, when Bill

Quinn was over at the start of the Rachel Hewitt case. This is the only real *evidence* that convinces me that what happened to Bill Quinn was connected with Rachel's disappearance, otherwise I'd accept that he and Mihkel were both killed because of the migrant worker scam. The rest is simply copper's instinct. But the photographs are important. Trust me on that. We believe that someone set him up with this girl. It's possible that she drugged him or got him so drunk he didn't know what he was doing, then got him up to his hotel room so these photographs could be taken. Are you with me so far?'

Erik looked puzzled, but he said, 'Yes.'

'We don't know why, but one good guess is that he had somehow or other got close to whoever it was abducted Rachel. Everyone said he was haunted by the case right up until his death. I wonder. One thing that would explain it is that he found out what happened to Rachel and was unable to do anything about it, that he was blackmailed into silence. Bill Quinn was devoted to his wife, but he stumbled this once, and it came back on him in a very big way. When his wife died a month ago, that silence was no longer so important. What he had to do was find a way of making his knowledge public without revealing that he had hidden the truth for six years.'

'And to that end, he enlisted Mihkel's help?'

'Yes,' said Banks. 'I think so. I know it's only conjecture at this point, but it's the only thing that makes sense. The killer knew that Mihkel and Quinn were in touch, knew that Quinn was free now that he was no longer troubled by anyone showing the pictures to his wife. That Mihkel was in England at the time was irrelevant to the killer, really. He could have been anywhere. It simply made things more convenient for the killer, or whoever sent him. Two birds with one stone, so to speak.'

'How did the killer know Mihkel was at this farm?'

'I don't know,' said Banks. 'But it would be my guess that Mihkel slipped up somehow, despite taking such care. I would imagine that all these migrant gangs have spies planted to keep an eye out for infiltrators like Mihkel. They've been stung too often before, as you yourself mentioned earlier. Then someone was sent to tidy up.'

'But surely if Bill had discovered anything about Rachel Hewitt, the Tallinn police would know? There was no way he could simply go about and make the investigation by himself.'

'That is a problem, I agree. Unless it was something he uncovered on his own, either here or back in England.'

'But if it happened here, he would have told someone, surely? The Investigator. The Prosecutor?'

'Yes, he probably would, wouldn't he?'

Erik stared at Banks in disbelief. 'Are you saying the police here were corrupt? The Office of the Prosecutor?'

'I don't know,' said Banks. 'It wouldn't be the first time. But again, it's mere speculation. So much police work is. I'd like you to do me a couple of favours. First, I'd like you to see if you can find out who this girl is. She's probably local, or was in 2006, and may well have been connected with the sex trade or perhaps worked in one of the nightclubs. She might also have been trafficked from somewhere, forced into prostitution. You must have extensive files at your newspaper. You've got the resources, and I don't. Can you do it? Will you help us?'

Erik examined the photos and nodded slowly. 'I can try,' he said. 'If it helps to uncover who killed Mihkel. You mentioned two favours.'

'Yes,' said Banks. 'There's a retired cop called Toomas Rätsepp and a Prosecutor called Ursula Mardna. I'd like you to find out all you can about them, too.'

After dinner at a Thai restaurant not far from the hotel, at which they discussed their conversations with Toomas

Rätsepp and Erik Aarma, Joanna begged off early for the night, pleading the jetlag and the change of scene were catching up with her. Two hours wasn't much of a time difference, Banks thought, but travel itself certainly was tiring. He didn't know why, as all you had to do was sit there and be delivered to your destination, but it was.

It was only half past nine. Banks felt restless, and he knew it would be no use heading up to his room so early. Besides, having got at least some sense from Toomas Rätsepp of the places the hen party had visited, he wanted to wander the Old Town after dark and get a better feel for the streets, where the cars were, the nightclubs, the bars. It was just around sunset, so he decided now was as good a time as any to set off. Of course, it would have stayed light much later in July, but Banks guessed that the girls would also have been up a lot later than nine fifteen, and that it would have been quite dark when they left St Patrick's. Some clubs didn't even open until midnight or after, like the ones in cities at home that opened when the pubs closed. He imagined that Tallinn was the sort of place where you could get a drink at any time of the day or night.

It was Thursday, close to the weekend, and the Old Town was much livelier than it had been the previous evening. Walking past the front of Old Hansa, Banks saw a line of young men shuffling along wearing chain-gang uniforms. A stag party, no doubt. One of them raised a bottle of Saku, smiled and said, 'All right, mate?' Banks recognised the northern accent.

Once again he found himself by the large bookshop on the corner of Harju and Niguliste, opposite the church at the top of its grassy slope. He walked along the front of the bookshop, recognising a few of the English titles he saw displayed in the window, past Fish & Wine, where he turned left, past the corner where he and Joanna Passero had been sitting last night, and continued on, down Vana-Posti.

It was one of the narrower streets in the Old Town, but there were a few cafes and bars, including St Patrick's, and further down, on his right, an elegant four-storey hotel with dormer windows on top and a white facade stood on a corner. It formed a little triangle with benches and fountains, and on another side stood the concave front of a building with SOPRUS written across the top in large letters. It looked like an old cinema, with its steps and massive pillars along the front. There were a couple of large movie posters on the wall, one for *Submarine* and another for a series of classics by master directors. To the left of the second poster was a sign for 'Hollywood', where the girls had been dancing and met the German boys in July 2006. Banks was tempted to go in, just to check out the place, but he realised there would be no point. It would simply be a hot, noisy, jam-packed club, which would stifle his breath and hurt his ears. There were some things worth suffering for the job, but not that.

Instead, he started to walk back up Vana-Posti to St Patrick's, went inside, stood at the bar and ordered a beer. The place probably hadn't changed much since 2006, he reckoned. Their food was supposed to be pretty good and it wasn't one of the major stag-party haunts. There were no guys in chain-gang uniforms in evidence, at any rate. It was busy, though, and most of the tables and all the chairs around him were taken. There was quite a mix of age groups and accents, from what Banks could make out, and he reckoned it was the kind of place you might kick off an evening, or somewhere you might end up to mellow out for a while. It didn't seem like the sort of establishment that would tolerate rowdy behaviour.

There was music playing, but Banks had no idea what it was. It wasn't obtrusive, at any rate. He finished his beer and left, turning right, the way the girls had turned. He turned right again at Fish & Wine, the way he had come, and followed the street straight across Niguliste. In no time he was at the

Raekoja Plats, the main square. It had taken him no more than
five minutes from St Patrick's, but the girls and their German
friends had probably taken a bit longer. There were plenty of
lively bars and restaurants opposite the town hall on the large
cobbled square, all with tables outside under awnings, nicely
lit by candlelight and dim table lamps: Molly Malone's,
Kaerajaan, Fellini, Karl Friedrich. The girls would probably
have stayed outside drinking wherever they went in the square,
and at some point, they realised they had lost Rachel.

Banks walked back to St Patrick's, but this time he didn't go
inside. He continued past the pub, in the other direction.
Rätsepp had mentioned that a bartender thought he saw
Rachel go the wrong way when she left St Patrick's. Maybe he
was right. Banks wanted to know what was around there other
than Club Hollywood and the My City Hotel. Then he saw,
just to his left shortly after passing the pub, one of those long,
narrow lanes curving into the distance, mixed facades of four-
storey buildings on each side, narrow strips of pavement, and
a cobbled road perhaps wide enough for a car.

Banks turned left and started walking along the street. In
places some of the plaster had fallen away from the fronts of
the buildings, revealing the stone and brickwork underneath,
like the skeleton without flesh, bared teeth and jawbone where
the cheek has been ripped away. There were flags hanging
above some of the doorways, and Banks guessed most were
residences, or perhaps business offices with flats above.

Then he noticed a small illuminated sign above one of the
doorways about thirty feet along. It had nothing written on it,
only a stylised cartoon of a man in a top hat and tails, who
seemed to be helping a voluptuous woman into a carriage.
Banks paused and looked at the door. There were no prices or
opening times posted – he supposed it was a place you just
had to know about – and all he could make out was a vague
sort of reception desk and perhaps cloakroom area lit by a

reddish glow behind the heavy glass doors. It was elegant, with polished brass and dark wood, certainly not like some of the seedier sex clubs he had seen in Soho, if that was what it was. And it was open.

Would anything have been likely to draw Rachel down here, Banks wondered, assuming she actually had turned the wrong way, unless she perhaps recognised the street, thought it was a short cut to the hotel or the main road and the possibility of a taxi? Vana-Posti would lead eventually to Pärnu, a broad boulevard with a constant flow of traffic and trams running along the southern edge of the Old Town. But that was not in the same direction as the Meriton Hotel. Still, if Rachel might have known she could get a taxi on or near Pärnu. It was a very busy road, beyond the confusing and possibly by now claustrophobic and frightening maze of the Old Town, and she could soon get herself reoriented there. Might something have drawn her down this street, caught her attention? The illuminated sign? Something else? Someone? Had the toilets at St Patrick's been too busy, and did she still need to go? Perhaps she was looking for a quiet, sheltered doorway to pee in. Or perhaps she had spotted a taxi with its light on down the road and dashed to try and catch it. Then what?

Banks sensed, rather than saw, a shadow entering the street behind him. He had been wary of being followed most of the time he had been in Tallinn, but it had been impossible to tell in the busy streets and bright sunshine. If someone wanted to find out where he had been and who he had been talking to, it wouldn't have been too difficult. This was the first time he had been in the Old Town after dark by himself. It could just be someone taking a short cut, of course, or someone who lived on the street, but it was still enough to make Banks nervous. More likely than not, Rätsepp had sent a man to follow him and he was in no danger, but he didn't need to make the man's job too easy.

He tried the doors of the mysterious club and found himself in the small reception and coat check area. The woman standing behind the front desk wore a black bustière that left little to the imagination. Her breasts looked augmented to Banks's unskilled eye. She had a beauty spot painted to the right of her mouth, bright red lipstick and tumbling black waves of hair. Beside her stood two bruisers. Well-dressed, in Armani suits, relaxed, at ease, both giving Banks pleasant nods of welcome, but bruisers nonetheless, with no necks and cauliflower ears.

'Do you speak English?' Banks asked the woman.

'Of course, sir. What is it you require?'

'Can I go in?'

'Are you a member, sir?'

'No. I didn't realise that . . .'

'If you would just like a drink in the bar, then a one-time membership is available for twenty euros.'

'That's just to go in?'

'Yes, sir. Into the lounge.'

'There's more?'

She gave an enigmatic smile. 'There are many rooms, sir.'

'Is there any entertainment?'

'Here, we make our own entertainment, sir.'

Already feeling as if he had fallen down the rabbit hole, Banks forked over twenty euros, for which he got a stamped pass, and the woman directed him to a pair of swing doors. 'Just through there, sir.'

It was a dimly lit lounge bar with leather chairs around low round tables, definitely not built for bottles and litre glasses. Each table bore a shaded lamp with a low wattage bulb. There was no music and no windows. Waitresses in tastefully scanty clothing with a vaguely S & M theme drifted between the tables, carrying silver trays. Banks had no sooner sat down when one appeared at his side. 'What is your pleasure, sir?'

English, it seemed, was the language of choice here, and her accent was impeccable. 'Perhaps a glass of red wine,' Banks said.

'We have a very good Merlot, sir, a Rioja or Chianti Classico by the glass. We also have an extensive wine list.'

'I'll have a glass of Rioja, please,' said Banks.

'Very well.'

What the hell am I doing here? Banks wondered as he waited for his drink. The conversations around him were hushed, most of the customers in business suits, men from their thirties to sixties. There were no women other than the waitresses. Occasionally, the door at the far end would open and someone would leave or enter.

'What happens in there?' Banks asked the waitress when she brought his drink. Her breasts were not augmented, he decided, as she bent to place the wine on a white coaster. She said nothing. 'Can I talk to the manager?' he asked.

'Police?'

'How did you know?'

'They're the same the whole world over, sweetie.' She held her tray in one hand and pointed to a man standing by the cash register beside the bar. 'He's over there. Good luck.'

Banks picked up his wine and walked over. He had no idea whether the manager spoke English but was now used to the idea that everyone in Tallinn did. It was a skill, he thought, that the manager of a club like this ought to have. And he did. In fact, he spoke as if he had just got off a plane from London.

'Can I help you, sir?'

Though he knew it was no use here, Banks flashed his warrant card. Humour twinkled in the manager's eyes. 'You can buy those in the shops over here, you know, mate.'

'I'm sure,' said Banks, 'but I figured that seeing as I'm not here to cause you any trouble, merely just to ask a couple of questions for curiosity's sake, it wouldn't do any harm.'

'There's certainly no harm trying,' said the manager. 'I'm Larry, by the way. Larry Helmsley.'

Banks shook hands. 'Pleased to meet you. How did you end up in a place like this?'

'I started working the clubs over in London years back, but I wanted to travel, see new places. Mostly, I see the inside of a dark club and sleep all day.'

'What kind of club is this?'

'Private. Gentlemen's. Members only.'

'OK. I get it. What I'm interested in happened six years ago.'

'Then I'm not your man. I was in Brussels then. Or was it Barcelona?'

'Was this place here?'

'I assume so. It's been through a lot of changes over the years.'

'Who owns it?'

'A consortium of interested parties.'

'And that's who you work for?'

'I'm more of a freelance, but they're my employers at the moment.'

'How long have they owned the place?'

'About two years. What is it exactly that you're after, mate? What is it that happened six years ago?'

'An English girl disappeared near here. She was leaving a pub around the corner—'

'St Patrick's?'

'Yes. And she may have taken the wrong direction from her friends and got lost. Maybe she came in here.'

'Why?'

'I don't know. Looking for a phone, maybe. She'd forgotten her mobile. To use the toilet. Or trying to find her friends.'

'Was she drunk?'

'It was a hen party.'

'If it's anything like it is now, she wouldn't have got past the front door. Just a minute. I think I remember the case you're talking about. Her parents have been in the news. Rachel something-or-other, isn't it?'

'Yes. Rachel Hewitt. She was never found.'

'Tragic. I didn't know she was near here when she vanished. But I can't help you, mate. Like I said, I wasn't here then, and the present owners have only been around a couple of years.'

'It was a long shot, anyway,' said Banks.

'I appreciate a man who goes for a long shot. Nothing like it when one pays off. Sorry.'

'That's all right,' said Banks. He finished his drink, left the glass on the bar and made for the front doors. He passed the waitress on the way, and she touched his arm. 'You did quite well with him. You two seemed to hit it off.'

'Two strangers united by a common language,' he said. 'Tell me, is anyone here from Estonia?'

Her accent slipped. 'I wouldn't know, sweetie. I'm from Wigan, meself.'

Smiling to himself, Banks walked outside, careful to scan both directions of the street. His shadow could easily be hiding in a doorway, like Orson Welles in *The Third Man*, but there was no obvious sign of him. Come to think of it, the whole place had a look of *The Third Man* about it. Banks put his hands in his pockets and strolled watchfully down the curving narrow street until it ended at a square full of packed and well-lit cafes. There, he decided to sit and have a final glass of wine before heading off to bed, and to see if his shadow turned up. The Rioja he had paid ten euros for at the club had not been very good, and it had left a nasty taste at the back of his throat.

The person whom Banks thought had been following him was still there, though it was sometimes hard to make him out through the crowds passing back and forth. He was of medium height, about the same as Banks himself, in his late thirties or early forties, already showing signs of thinning on top, casually dressed in jeans and a dark shirt underneath some sort of zip-up jacket. He sat down at the cafe across the square. Good. They could sit and stare at one another.

Banks ordered a glass of Shiraz, sipped and watched the people go by. A group of girls in red micro dresses, carrying heart-shaped red balloons on strings, snaked by in a conga line, giggling and chanting, hips bumping this way, then that, some almost tripping in their impossibly high heels on the cobblestones. When they had passed by, he glanced across the square again, only to find that his shadow had disappeared. He jotted a few notes in his notebook, finished his drink and decided to call it a day. It was two hours earlier in Eastvale, so he could probably still call Annie and get up to date when he got back to the hotel. On his way back, he noticed the man once again, about a hundred yards behind him walking down Viru. It didn't matter, Banks decided. He was going to his room for the night. The streets would be well lit and full of people all the way. He would make sure the door to his room was secure. Tomorrow, he would keep his eyes open and his wits about him.

9

Tony Leach lived in an old terrace house off the Skipton Road on the outskirts of Ilkley, where the streets eventually ran into fields, woods and open country. The bay window in the high-ceilinged living room had a fine view of the Cow & Calf, though the rocky outcrops were partly shrouded by mist and low-lying cloud that morning.

Annie and Winsome had driven down from Eastvale, avoiding the A1 this time, to find out what Rachel Hewitt's ex-boyfriend had to add to the picture they were building up. Annie had had a long chat with Banks the previous evening, and he had told her of his talks with Toomas Rätsepp and Erik Aarma, and of being followed in Tallinn. It had been a lot to digest, but Annie was glad to be up to date and pleased that things were moving along. She told him to be careful, and meant it. She had shared the information with Winsome on their way to Ilkley. The only other welcome piece of news that morning had been the analysis of DNA from the trace amounts of blood on the tree the CSIs thought the killer used for balance when he shot Bill Quinn. There was no match on any of the databases, but at least if they found him they would be able take a sample and compare them. It probably wouldn't convict him in itself, but it might help. The way this case was shooting off in all directions, Annie thought, it was as well to remember that this was the man they were after: the killer of Bill Quinn and Mihkel Lepikson.

Tony worked at a car dealership in the town centre, but that day, his boss had told them on the phone, he was at home with his wife, who was in the final stages of her second pregnancy. The fruits of the first, little Freddie, toddled around in a play-pen filled with safe soft toys in the corner of the living room. They looked as if you could eat them, hit yourself on the head with them and jump up and down on them, and neither you nor they would be harmed in any way. Luckily, he was a quiet toddler.

Melanie Leach was lying down on the sofa listening to *Woman's Hour*. When she asked for a cup of tea, Annie suggested that she and Winsome accompany Tony to the kitchen to chat while he made some. Annie hoped they might get a cup of tea out of it themselves, too, but most of all she didn't want to talk to Tony about his ex-girlfriend while his pregnant wife was in the same room.

Tony was reluctant to leave Melanie alone, at first, but Annie reassured him that he wouldn't be far away, and that he had two able-bodied police officers in the house. Why that should comfort him, she had no idea – though they were able enough in many ways, neither Annie or Winsome had any experience in delivering babies or attending to pregnant women – but it did. The only thing Annie knew was to shout for plenty of boiling water. She supposed, if anything happened, they could manage to call for an ambulance with-out panicking too much, and maybe even persuade it to arrive a bit quicker than it normally would, but she wasn't even sure about that.

'She'll be fine,' Tony said nervously, filling the kettle. 'She's just a bit jittery because it was a difficult birth last time, with our Freddie.

'I'm sure,' Annie agreed. She studied the view from the window, a small back garden full of bright plastic toys, includ-ing a blue and yellow tricycle, orange skittles and a purple ball. There was also a swing, which reminded Annie of the swing her parents had put up for her in the artists' commune where she grew up. She had loved that swing. She had very strong memories of her mother pushing her up higher and higher in it when she was very little. At the end of the garden was a brick wall and a privet hedge. 'It's just a quick word we wanted, really,' Annie went on. 'I can see you've got a lot on your plate.'

'Oh, don't worry. She'll be all right. Doctor says there's nothing to worry about.'

Tony was a handsome lad in his mid-twenties, fair hair combed back, a lock slipping over his right eye, tall, footballer fit, a nice smile. He pulled two teabags from a Will & Kate Wedding tin and dropped them into a large teapot, warming it first with hot water from the tap. The teapot was easily big enough for four cups, Annie thought. She might be in luck. The kettle soon came to a boil and Tony filled the teapot.

'Why did you and Rachel split up?' Annie asked. She had taken a chair at the kitchen table, and Tony was leaning against the draining board by the window.

'Why does anybody split up?' he said. 'We stopped getting along. Fell out of love.'

'But you were in love once?' Winsome said.

Tony paused before answering. 'I thought so,' he said. 'We'd been going out for two years, after all.'

'Was there someone else? Another boy?'

'Not as far as I know.'

'Did Rachel go out with other people?'

'Sometimes, in the early days. We both did. We weren't exclusive.'

'But you got more serious?'

'I'd like to think so.'

'You never got engaged, though?'

'No. It never got that far.'

'Sex?' Annie asked.

'None of your business.'

'Fair enough. Milk and two sugars for me, please.'

Tony brought some mugs down from the cupboard, asked Winsome how she wanted hers and poured them both some tea. Then he put what seemed like half a pint of milk and three tablespoons of sugar into one mug and took it through to Melanie. Annie heard their voices, but not what they said. He came back and poured himself a mug of black tea, builder's strength. 'I get the impression that you'd rather continue the discussion in here,' he said, sitting down opposite Annie. Winsome joined them at the table. 'Not that I have any secrets from Melanie.'

'All we want from you,' said Winsome, 'is some insight into Rachel, what she was like. It might help us understand what happened to her.'

'But I went over all this years ago with the other detective. Why drag it all back up now?'

'It never went away,' Winsome said. 'Rachel was never found. Now her name's come up again in connection with another case we're working on, and we have to pursue the line of inquiry.'

'What line of inquiry?'

'The "other detective" you mentioned was murdered a week ago. You might have heard.'

'DI Quinn?'

'That's right.'

'Bloody hell. I'm sorry. I hadn't heard, actually. He was the one who talked to me back when it happened.'

'That's right.'

'He was a decent enough bloke.'

'So they say. What happened to Rachel might have some bearing on what happened to Bill Quinn. That's why we're going through all this. I can't really tell you any more than that.'

'That's all right. I understand.'

'Only you can tell us certain things. Her parents have one view – it was their darling daughter – but you might be able to provide a different perspective.'

'I don't know about that,' said Tony. He glanced at Annie. 'I'm sorry. You asked about sex. It was fine. No problems there.'

'She enjoyed it?'

'As far as I could tell. Rachel wasn't promiscuous or kinky or anything. I'd say she was pretty normal in that department.'

'Did you argue much?' Winsome asked.

'Every couple argues, don't they?'

'What sort of things did you argue about?'

'I don't remember, really. Nothing important. Holidays. She liked beaches, and I preferred cities. Money. We never seemed to have enough to go to all the fancy clubs and shops she liked. That sort of thing.'

Annie gestured around the kitchen and garden. 'You seem to be doing all right now financially.'

'All this came later. I've got nothing to complain about. Melanie and Freddie are happy here. It's even big enough to accommodate Chloe, when she comes along.'

'So you already know the gender?'

Tony beamed. 'Yes. Ultrasound. We couldn't resist.'

'A girl,' said Winsome. 'One of each. That's nice.'

'So you're doing all right?' Annie pushed on. 'Can afford a decent house and two kids to bring up. That's pretty good in these tough times.'

'Well, I wouldn't mind a raise and a promotion, but yes, I think I'm damn lucky to have a job I like, and I'm good at. The thing is, this would hardly have made it as "all right" for Rachel.'

'What do you mean?' Annie asked.

'It was probably the one thing we argued about most. She liked money and the things it bought. Maybe a bit too much for my liking.'

'She was greedy?'

'Not greedy or grasping or anything like that. It was just . . . like the magazines she read, with pictures of fancy cars and houses and yachts and stuff.'

'But that's just fantasy, surely?'

'Not to her it wasn't. It was her dream. She was serious about it. The worst thing I could do was criticise her dream.'

Annie remembered the photograph of the BMW outside the art deco mansion on Rachel's bedroom wall. 'MINE ONE DAY!!'

'How did it manifest itself?' Annie asked.

'She had a lot of rows with her parents. They wanted her to go to university and get a good education – she was certainly bright enough, and they were willing to pay – but she wanted to get right out there and start making money. She said she could learn any job she wanted and make her way up the ladder quickly, as she went along. She could, too. She got a job in a bank. Not as a teller, but at head office, in the investments department. She was doing pretty well. She was smart, quick, ambitious. I know she would have gone far.'

'And by then she would have left you behind?'

'That was always a fear. Yes. Or she would have found someone richer.'

'It sounds a bit mercenary. Was that why you split up?'

'Mostly. I just wasn't doing well enough for her, not progressing fast enough. And it didn't exactly sound glamorous – a car salesman. At best you could say I wasn't a *used* car salesman, I suppose. It's true I'm not very ambitious, but is that such a terrible thing? Does everyone have to be pushy and grabbing? I'm happy as I am. She saw me stuck in a dead end job – I was in a showroom in Drighlington then – and never getting any further, wasting away her life in some dull suburb. It wasn't what she wanted. I told her surely family came first. We could get a mortgage, buy a home, make it our own. But it wasn't a home she wanted. It was one of those bloody mansions she goggled at in the celebrity lifestyle magazines and that other rubbish she read.'

'Surely a girl can dream,' said Annie. 'Was there someone else on the scene? Someone who promised her all this?'

'Not that I know of,' said Tony. 'No, we didn't split up over someone else. After Rachel, I'll admit I went wild for a bit. I don't know. I just didn't care. Love them and leave them. Not very nice, but there it was. Then I met Melanie, and she turned everything around. It was like I'd finally found what I wanted in life.'

'And Rachel, after you split up?'

'Her ambition made her restless. I don't think she'd found anyone else. She wasn't going to settle for a loser like me next time, that's for sure, and as it turned out, she didn't have to, did she?'

'But as far as you know, there was no one else in the offing, no one she might have invited to meet her in Tallinn, for example?'

'No. Besides, that was a hen weekend. Strictly no boyfriends.'

They all paused and sipped tea, then Annie said, 'This might be a rather indelicate question, but we think it's important. You say that Rachel was ambitious, liked money and its trappings, that she rowed with her parents about getting a job instead of going to university, right?'

'Right.'

'Do you think that might have led her to do anything illegal?'

'What do you mean?'

'Drugs, for example.'

'Not that I know of.'

'I mean selling, smuggling. Not necessarily taking them.'

'Dealing? Rachel?' He started shaking his head. 'No way. Rachel wouldn't get involved in anything like that. Rachel really did want to do good and help people, you know. If she'd realised her dreams and got hold of oodles of money, she'd probably have ended up like Warren Buffett or Bill Gates or someone, as long as she could have her Disney mansion and her magic carpet. No, you're on the wrong track entirely.'

'Believe it or not,' said Winsome. 'We're perfectly happy to know that. It would have made our job a lot more complicated if it were true. But we have to check on these things.'

'Leave no stone unturned, right?'

'Something like that. We're just trying to find reasons for what might have happened to Rachel in Tallinn, and falling foul of international drug-smugglers was one scenario. They can be very ruthless.'

'When did you find out what happened?' Annie asked.

'I suppose it was about three or four days after she'd disappeared. A policeman came around. Uniformed. Wanted to know if I knew anything about where she was. Apparently DI Quinn was over in Tallinn then. He interviewed me in more detail when he got back a few days later, but I couldn't help him.'

'How did you react when you heard what had happened?'

'I was gutted. Naturally. God, it was a terrible time. I went to see her parents, you know, just out of support and friendship, like, but they weren't interested. I was yesterday's news.'

'How had you got along with them before?'

'Well enough, I suppose. Or as well as anybody who wanted to steal away their precious little girl.'

'What do you mean?'

'It was weird. Sometimes it was like they didn't want her to grow up, and she didn't want to. She was very childlike in some ways. If ever she was away, she had to phone her mother every day. They were always lovey-dovey, you know, with pet names and lots of hugs and kisses. You must have seen those awful stuffed animals if you've been to the house. And there was a stupid budgie she doted on. She'd spend hours talking to the bloody thing. I never thought I'd be jealous of a budgie, but if I'd had the chance I'd have opened the front door and the cage.' He smiled. 'But it was just a facet of her, that's all. The little girl who doesn't want to grow up, but who wants to be rich, a Disney princess. But she was bright and ambitious, good at her job, and she could be ruthless if she needed to be. At the same time, she couldn't cut herself loose from her mother's apron strings. It sometimes seemed like a tug of war between me and them, with her in middle. In the end none of us won.'

It sounded like a nightmare to Annie, who had enjoyed a relatively liberal childhood in the commune. Admittedly, she had lost her mother at an early age, but there had been surrogates, even if there was no replacement. And her father Ray always did his best, even if he was a bit forgetful when he was 'in' a painting, as he used to say.

'Did the two of you ever go away together?' she asked.

'Once,' said Tony. 'The year before . . . you know. We went on holiday together. Well, not just the two of us, a group, like.'

'How did her parents react?'

'They weren't too keen at first, but Rachel was good at getting her own way. She probably had to promise not to sleep with me.'

'Did she?' asked Annie.

Tony gave a wistful smile. 'It was one of the best times of my life,' he said.

'I'll take it she did, then. Where did you go?'

'An all-inclusive on Varadero Beach, Cuba. We'd been saving up for it. It was expensive, but worth it.'

'Cuba hardly sounds like the sort of environment for a girl like Rachel,' said Winsome.

'You're right about that. She hadn't much to say for the political system or the cleanliness of Havana. But she did love the beach and her Danielle Steele. And she phoned her mother every day.'

'Dutiful daughter,' Annie commented.

'Look, I know some of this is coming out all wrong,' said Tony. 'But Rachel was a good person, despite it all, the ambition, the love of money. She had the biggest heart of anyone I've known. She'd do anything for you. She wasn't greedy, and she wasn't selfish. In the end, I suppose we just weren't meant to be together.'

'Did she make any friends over in Cuba, at the hotel, on the beach?'

'Like who?'

'Europeans, perhaps? Especially Eastern Europeans. Russians or Estonians, for example?'

'Not that I know of. We pretty much stuck together the whole time.' A sound came from the front room. 'Is that Melanie calling?'

Annie heard the voice, too. 'Sounds like it,' she said. 'I think it's time for us to go now.' She was certain that when Tony took in the tea they had prearranged some signal to bring the interview to an end, and this was probably it. Annie looked at Winsome, who just shrugged, and they followed Tony through to the front door, wished him and Melanie well, and left.

'I am not at all sure how I can help you,' said Ursula Mardna. The Office of the Prosecutor General was in a neo-classical style two-storey house on Wismari, a peaceful, treelined street, not far from the Parliament building and the British Embassy. The place was an old private house, and Ursula Mardna's office had probably been the master bedroom. It was a large space, with all the trappings of an important and powerful government official. Banks had been watchful on their walk over there, and he didn't think they had been followed. If his theory were correct, and Rätsepp had put someone on his tail to keep track of the progress of his investigation, then he probably already knew that Banks would be visiting Ursula Mardna this morning.

You couldn't really compare the function of the Prosecutor here that closely to the Crown Prosecution Service back home, Banks thought. From what he had read, the relationship was a lot more complicated and political, rather than just a matter of decisions being made on whether there was enough evidence, and whether the evidence was good enough to merit a prosecution. The Prosecutor guided an investigation in a very hands-on way, including the collection of evidence and use of surveillance. In some ways, he imagined, the Prosecutor was more like the American District Attorney, but perhaps even more complicated. Prosecutors would also turn up at crime scenes. Of course, the disappearance of a young English girl in Tallinn was a high-profile case, especially when she hadn't been found after several days, or years.

'We're just trying to cover all the angles we can,' said Banks, 'and you were instrumental in the Rachel Hewitt investigation.'

Ursula Mardna waved down Banks's comment. 'Please. It was not a most glorious success. I wake up still and think about that poor girl some nights.' She had a strong accent but her English was clear, and for the most part correct. Banks placed her at about forty, or just over. That would have made her in her mid-thirties when she worked the Rachel Hewitt case. Quite young. It could have been a career-making case, if it had been solved. As it was, she didn't seem to be doing too badly. She was stylishly dressed and attractive, with an oval face, lively brown eyes and reddish-blonde hair cut short and ragged around the edges, in a rather punkish, pixie style. She had no piercings that Banks could see, but wore some rather chunky rings and a heavy silver bracelet.

'You don't believe she might still be alive somewhere?' he asked.

She gave Banks a pitying glance. 'No more than you believe it, Hr Banks. Or you, Pr Passero.'

'It would, indeed, be a miracle,' Joanna said, and turned a page in her notebook.

'We got most of the details from Hr Rätsepp,' Banks went on, 'but we were just wondering if you have a different view of things? Perhaps there were things he didn't tell us?'

'Toomas Rätsepp was a fine investigator,' said Ursula Mardna. 'One of our best. If he could not solve the case, nobody could.'

'What about his team?'

'Fine officers.'

'So in your opinion, everything that could possibly be done was done?'

'Yes. We were most thorough.'

Banks wondered about that. Rätsepp had said the same thing. He also had to keep reminding himself not to expect too much, that he was talking to a lawyer, basically, however high-ranking and however close her role was to that of the investigator. What was she going to say, that Rätsepp was a sloppy copper and the investigation was a shambles? No. She was going to defend her team, especially to an unwelcome foreign detective. 'Do you remember DI Quinn?' he asked. 'That's really who I'm here about.'

She tilted her head to one side. 'Of course I do.'

'What exactly was his role?'

'His role?'

'Yes. The part he played, his function in the investigation.'

'Ah, I see. I think he was ambassador from the British police, no?'

'But he must have got involved somehow?'

'He was here for only one week.'

'But quite soon after Rachel's disappearance, I under-stand?'

'Then you will also understand that there were many obsta-cles in beginning of the investigation. The girls, themselves, they could not remember.'

'I understand that,' said Banks. 'Hr Rätsepp said the same thing. But DI Quinn was in at the start?'

'You could say that. He was allowed to accompany a junior investigator to get some feel of the city, to observe the investi-gations we were starting to make.'

That was the first Banks had heard of it. Another thing Rätsepp had neglected to mention. In fact, he had told Banks and Joanna that Quinn had played no active role in the inves-tigation, had merely attended meetings. 'Who was this investigator?'

'I cannot remember his name. It is so long ago.'

'Would it be in your files?'

Ursula Mardna gave him an impatient glance and picked up the telephone. 'It would.'

A short scattershot phone conversation in Estonian followed, and several moments later a young pink-faced man in a pinstripe suit knocked and walked in with a file folder under his arm. Ursula Mardna thanked him and opened the folder. 'His name is Aivar Kukk. According to this file, he left the police force five years ago.'

'A year after the Rachel Hewitt case. Why?'

'To pursue other interests.' She pushed the folder away. 'It happens, Hr Banks. People are sometimes lucky enough to find out that they have made a wrong choice in life early enough to correct it.'

'Do you have his address?'

'I am afraid we do not keep up-to-date information on ex-police officers. Even if we did, there would be much red tape involved in giving it to you.'

'Of course.'

She favoured him with an indulgent smile. 'We have come a long way since the Soviet era, but red tape is still red tape.'

'Never mind,' said Banks. 'I'm sure we'll be able to find him if we need to.'

Ursula Mardna gave him an assessing glance, as if trying to work out whether he would be able to, or perhaps whether it mattered.

'What were your impressions of DI Quinn, Ms Mardna?' asked Joanna.

'He seemed a good man. Very serious. Dedicated.'

'Did he change at all during the course of the week he was here?'

'Change?'

'Yes. His attitude, his feelings about the case, his commitment, his mood. Anything.'

'I did not see much of him after the first two days,' she said, 'but I did get the impression that he placed himself more in the background. Is that how you say it?'

'He stood back?' Joanna said.

'Yes. When he started, he was so full of energy that he did not want to sleep. He just wanted to walk the streets looking for the girl. I suppose he became tired, and perhaps depressed when he realised there was so little he could do here. I think he perhaps lost hope.'

Or he gave up when someone showed him the compromising photos, Banks thought.

'I suppose so,' said Joanna. 'It must also have been intimidating, a foreign city, different customs, different language.'

'As you can see, the language is not much of a problem here, but the other things . . . yes. I think he came to feel, how you say, out of his depth? That things were best left to us. The locals.'

'That would explain it,' said Joanna, making a note.

Ursula Mardna seemed a little alarmed. 'Explain what?'

'The change in him.'

'Oh, yes.'

Banks showed her a photograph of the girl who had been with Quinn. He hadn't shown her image to Rätsepp because he hadn't trusted him. While he thought Ursula Mardna might well be erring on the side of caution and self-protection in all her responses, he took that as the reaction of a canny lawyer, not a bent copper. But he still didn't want her to see Quinn and the girl together. There was something rather too final and damning about that. 'Do you recognise this girl?' he asked.

She studied the photograph closely then shook her head and passed it back. 'No,' she said. 'I have never seen her. Who is she?'

'That's something we would very much like to find out,' said Joanna.

'I am sorry I cannot help.'

'Was there any possibility that Rachel Hewitt's disappearance was connected with drugs?' Banks asked.

'Naturally, it was a direction we explored. We found no evidence of such a connection, but that does not mean there was none. Perhaps back in England. I do not know . . . Why do you ask?'

'I suppose you kept, still keep, pretty close tabs on the drug-trafficking business around here?'

'Tabs?'

'Keep an eye on. Watch.'

'Yes, of course.'

'And there was no link between Rachel or her friends and drug smuggling?'

'We did not reveal any such link.'

'Could it be possible that any . . . er . . . uncovering of such a link might have been, shall we say, diverted, suppressed, avoided altogether?'

'What are you saying?'

Banks leaned forward and rested his arms on the table. 'Ms Mardna,' he said. 'I've worked as a police officer for more years than I care to remember, most of that time as a detective. I have worked undercover, vice, drugs, just about anything you would care to name, and if there is one thing I have learned, it is that there is *always* the possibility of corruption and intimidation, especially when drugs are involved, mostly because of their connection with organised crime. Now, can you honestly sit there and tell me there has never been a whiff of corruption in the Tallinn police?'

Her face reddened. 'I cannot tell you that, Hr Banks,' she said. 'But I can tell you that in this case, the possibility of drugs was thoroughly investigated by Investigator Rätsepp and his team, and reviewed by myself. The girl had no connections with any of the known drug-traffickers at that time, and as far as I know, investigations back in Britain found no hints of any such a connection there either. All of which led us to believe,' she went on, 'even in the absence of a body, witnesses or forensic evidence, that we were dealing with a sex crime.'

'Stands to reason,' said Banks. 'Attractive young girl, alone in a strange city. Odds are someone might take advantage of her. But why kill her?'

'We worked on the assumption that whoever abducted her – or whoever she arranged to meet during the evening – also killed her to avoid identification and disposed of the body somehow.'

'Why should somebody she arranged to meet do that?'

'I can only speculate. Perhaps things went too far? Something went wrong? The girl became nervous, tried to back out? Protested, struggled. I do not know. There could be many explanations.'

'And the body?'

'Estonia is a small country, but there are many places to get rid of a dead body. Permanently. And before you ask, we did search as many of them as we could.'

Banks scratched the scar by his right eye. 'It seems the most convincing scenario,' he said. 'In which case we're probably wasting our time here.' He gestured to Joanna and they both stood up.

Ursula Mardna stood up with them, leaning over the desk to shake hands. 'You would never waste your time in Tallinn, Hr Banks. Especially as we have such wonderful weather this week. Goodbye. Enjoy yourselves.'

That, Banks thought, was what Rätsepp had wanted them to do, too. Have a holiday, don't bother chasing ghosts. But it only made Banks all the more suspicious.

'Since when have we been arresting people for begging in the street?' Annie asked PC Geordie Lyttleton, who had just nipped into the Major Crimes office to report an incident.

'Well we don't usually,' said Lyttleton, 'but she was getting quite aggressive, ma'am. She scared the living daylights out of one old lady, following her down the street shouting some sort of gibberish after her.'

'And what sort of gibberish did it turn out to be?'

'Polish gibberish, ma'am. She can't speak English. Jan from Traffic speaks a bit of Polish, though. His mum's family's from Warsaw. Anyway, he got it out of her that she has hardly eaten since last Wednesday. She lost her home and left her job. She was in a bit of a state. What she actually meant was that she was squatting up at some ruined farm and—'

'Garskill Farm?'

'She didn't know what it was called. I just thought, with the murder and all . . . well, there might be a link of some sort.'

'Excellent thinking, PC Lyttleton. Good work. We'll make a detective of you yet. Where is she now?'

'Well, ma'am,' said Lyttleton, scratching his head. 'She was bit, erm, aromatic, if you catch my drift, rather ripe, so I took her down to the custody suite and got WPC Bosworth to show her to the showers and fix her up with one of those disposable Elvis suits.'

Annie smiled. He meant the coveralls they gave to prisoners while their clothes were being examined for trace evidence. A bit of embroidery in the right places and they might look a bit like the jumpsuits Elvis Presley wore in his Las Vegas shows. The basement had been modernised recently, and there were decent shower facilities for the use of anyone being held there. Letting the girl use them was stretching it a bit, but if Lyttleton was right, it beat sitting in a small warm room with her as she was. 'Did you arrest her? Charge her?'

'No. Not yet. I thought I—'

'Well done, lad.' She thought of the starving girl, set the vestiges of her vegetarianism aside, put some money on the table and said, 'Go and get her a Big Mac, large fries and a Coke, will you, and get someone to send DS Stefan Nowak over from next door, if he's not too busy. I know he speaks Polish.'

'Yes, ma'am. What shall I—'

'When she's finished with the shower, take her up to interview room two and let her eat there. Try to put her at ease. Tell her she's nothing to be frightened of.'

'She doesn't understand English, ma'am.'

'Do your best, Constable. A kind smile and gentle tone go a long way.'

'Yes, ma'am.'

Interview room two was no different from any of the others, except that it had a viewing room beside it, with a one-way mirror. Annie wanted to see what sort of shape the girl was in before Stefan arrived, so she installed herself in the tiny room and waited there.

The girl was shown into the interview room. A lost, pathetic figure in the overlarge jumpsuit, small and frail, skinny as a rail, clearly scared, wide-eyed, starving and exhausted, damp brown hair clinging to her cheeks and neck, she seemed no older than fourteen, though Annie estimated she was probably eighteen or more. When the door closed and the girl thought she was alone, she flicked her eyes around the room as if checking for monsters in the corners, and then just sat there and started to cry. It made Annie want to cry herself, it was so bloody heartbreaking. Just a frightened, hungry kid, and there was no one here to comfort her, to hold her and tell her that she was loved and everything would be all right. You didn't have to be a *Guardian* reader to raise a tear or two for that predicament.

Lyttleton entered the interview room and handed over a McDonald's package. Before Annie even had the chance to feel guilty and wish she'd sent her a salad sandwich or a tofu burger instead, the girl fell on it and ripped off the wrapping paper. Annie had never seen anything quite like it, but it reminded her of one of those nature shows on BBC with David Attenborough. In a matter of moments, burger, fries and Coke were gone. Lyttleton had been decent enough to leave her alone to eat – he must have suspected it would not be a pretty sight – and Annie now felt guilty that she had been riveted to the spot by such a personal degradation as someone eating like there's no tomorrow. She felt like a voyeur, or a participant in a sick reality TV show.

When the girl had finished, she carefully picked up all the scattered wrapping paper and put it in the wastepaper basket, then she used one of the serviettes to wipe the table where it was stained with grease or ketchup. Christ, Annie thought.

A few moments later, DS Stefan Nowak arrived in the viewing room. Annie explained the situation. 'Can you help?' she asked him.

Nowak looked through the one-way mirror at the girl. 'I can speak the language, if that's what you mean. I'm not a translator, though. It's a special skill I don't have.'

'This isn't official,' Annie said. 'We'll get a statement and all the rest the correct way later. Right now, I need information.'

'Does AC Gervaise know?'

'I'm sure she would agree if she were here.'

Stefan grinned and held up his hands. 'OK, OK. Only asking. Come on, then. Let's have at it.'

The room still smelled of McDonald's, and it made Annie feel slightly queasy. Fish and chicken she could handle, but she always avoided red meat. The girl jumped up when they entered, but she stopped short of running away and curling up in the corner. Instead, she regarded them sullenly and fearfully and sat down again slowly. She had a sulky, downturned mouth, lips quivering on the verge of tears and dark chocolate eyes. Her fingernails were badly bitten down, some showing traces of blood around the edges. All in all, she was probably a very pretty girl under normal circumstances, Annie thought, whenever she was lucky enough to experience them.

'Could you ask her name, please, Stefan?' Annie said.

A brief conversation followed. 'She says it's Krystyna,' Nowak said. 'After her grandmother. She wants to know when you are going to let her go and what she is accused of doing.'

'Tell her she's got nothing to be afraid of,' Annie said. 'I just want to ask her a few questions, and then we'll see what we can do to help her.'

Nowak translated. Lyttleton came in with a pot of hot coffee and three styrofoam cups, powdered milk and artificial sweetener. Annie guessed the girl might crave real sugar, but then she'd just had a large Coke. It was a wonder she wasn't bouncing off the walls.

'Ask her how old she is,' Annie said.

Stefan talked with Krystyna and said, 'Nineteen in July.'

She's of age, then, Annie thought. Though of age for what, she didn't know. For the life she had been leading? 'Where does she come from?'

Nowak spoke to Krystyna, and the answer came slowly, hesitantly.

'She from a small town in Silesia,' he said. 'Pyskowice. Industrial. Coal mining.' He paused. 'She ... I mean, she doesn't speak very good ... Her Polish is very ... provincial. She's not well educated.'

'Spare us the Polish class distinctions, Stefan. Just do the best you can, OK?'

Nowak's eyes narrowed. 'OK.'

Annie had always thought Stefan could be a bit of a stuck-up elitist prick at times. He was well educated and probably descended from some Polish royal family. Maybe he was a prince. She'd heard there were a lot of Polish princes about. Maybe it was a good line for getting laid. Stefan did all right in that department, she'd heard. She wondered if a line like that would have worked on Rachel, with her dreams of wealth and opulence. Then she got back to the matter at hand. 'Ask her why she came here.'

Annie watched Stefan translate. Krystyna's expression turned from puzzlement to surprise.

'For a better life,' was the answer Stefan translated. There was no irony in Krystyna's voice or her expression. 'Why do they all think we owe them a better life?' Stefan added.

Annie ignored him and paused for a moment, then asked, 'Where was the farm she lived on?'

'In a wild place,' came the answer. 'There was nothing to do. No shops. No movies. No television.'

'What was it like?'

'Cold. The roof leaked. The garden was all overgrown with weeds and nettles. There was no proper place to wash and no real toilet.'

'It sounds like Garskill to me,' Annie said. 'Can you ask her when and why she left?'

'Wednesday morning,' the answer came. 'They were all told to pack up their belongings – not that they had any, apparently – and that they wouldn't be coming back there after work.'

'Where was she working?'

Nowak and Krystyna conferred for a while, then he said, 'A yeast factory. There was a sign outside that said "Varley's" she said. I think I know the place. They make yeast products for animal feed and for prisoners, diet supplement pills and suchlike.'

'A yeast factory? Sounds bloody awful,' said Annie. 'How did she end up living at Garskill Farm and working there?'

This time the conversation in Polish was longer, with a clearly frustrated Nowak asking for more repetitions and clarifications. Finally he turned to Annie and straightened his tie. 'She went to Katowice, the nearest large town, but there were no agencies there, so she went to Krakow and found someone who took her money and gave her an address in Bradford. I think she said Bradford. It was all phony, of course. These people are so gullible. Anyway, she ended up at the farm with about twenty other hopefuls doing a variety of rubbish jobs until they found somewhere to place her permanently, or so they said. And they kept most of her earnings back for bed and board and to pay off her debt to the agency.'

It was a familiar story. Annie looked sympathetically towards Krystyna. 'Where is this yeast factory?' she asked Nowak.

'Northern edge of Eastvale. That old industrial estate.'

'Ask her why they had to leave.' She thought she knew the answer, but she wanted to hear Krystyna's version, nonetheless.

'A man came to the farm in the morning,' Nowak said a while later. 'Different man. She hadn't seen him before. He came in a dark green car. A shiny car, I think she said. It looked new. The other two men, the regular ones who drove them to their jobs and back in the white van, seemed frightened of him. He told everyone to pack up, that they wouldn't be coming back tonight. That was it. She didn't mind so much because she didn't like living there. Apart from everything else, men kept trying to mess with her. That's what she said.'

'What language did this man speak?'

'English,' Stefan translated. 'At least, she thinks it was English. She actually does know a few words. And then someone translated for the workers who couldn't understand.'

'Did he have an accent of any kind?'

Annie saw Krystyna shake her head before answering. 'She doesn't know. She couldn't understand much. She'd hardly be likely to know if he had a Scottish accent or something.'

'Can you describe this man?' Annie asked Krystyna. Nowak translated.

Krystyna nodded.

'Excellent. We'll see if we can rustle up a sketch artist after our little talk. If the worst comes to the worst, I can always have a go at it myself.'

'Do you want me to translate that?'

'No. Don't bother,' Annie said. 'Ask her what happened next.'

Nowak asked Krystyna and translated her reply. 'They all piled into the van as usual. All except for Mihkel. They held him back. He had told her his name was Mihkel. He was from Estonia. She liked him. He was nice to her, and he didn't . . . you know . . . want anything.' Stefan cleared his throat. 'Some of the men tried to touch her at night. They were very crude. Apparently, there were two couples at the farm, and everyone could hear them when they made love, however quiet they tried to be. These men imitated them, made funny animal sounds and laughed. Mihkel protected her and her friend

Ewa. She would like to see her friend Ewa again. She is sorry
for leaving her, but she was scared.'

'That's probably how Mihkel gave himself away, the poor
bastard,' Annie said. 'Being nice to people and asking too
many questions. At least one of the men in the work gang was
probably a plant for the other side. Don't translate that. Did
she ever see Mihkel again?'

'No,' said Nowak after another brief exchange. 'They were
taken to work, as usual. She was to be picked up outside the
factory at six o'clock, but she says she got out early and ran away.'

'Why?'

Krystyna seemed confused when Stefan translated the
question. She muttered a few words. 'She doesn't really know,'
he said. 'She was unhappy at the farm. She thought she would
not see Mihkel again, and the new place would be worse.'

'Was there anything else?' Annie pressed.

After a while, Krystyna cried and told Stefan that the regular van driver had been pressing her to sleep with him, and that
he wanted her to go on the streets to make more money. He
said she could earn money very well that way and pay off her
debts in no time, but she didn't want to do it. She ran away.

Annie found some tissues in her bag and handed them to
Krystyna, who thanked her politely in Polish. Even though
she had nothing, Annie thought, Krystyna had chosen to flee
the work gang rather than stay there and suffer their mauling
and end up deeper and deeper in debt, trawling the streets for
prospective clients. What had she thought would happen to
her, on the run, alone in a strange country? She had been
desperate enough not to care. 'Do you know where they are
now, the others?' she asked.

When she understood Stefan's translation, Krystyna shook
her head. Then she spoke again.

'She doesn't know where they were taken,' Nowak explained.
'She's been in Eastvale ever since. She walked from the factory.

She has no food or money. Since then she's been living on the streets, sleeping in shop doorways and alleys.'

Krystyna spoke again. A question, this time.

'She wants to know if she can have a cigarette,' Nowak said.

'Afraid not,' Annie replied. 'But tell her I'll buy her a whole packet when we've finished in here.'

Krystyna merely nodded at that.

'She says Mihkel asked her about herself,' Annie went on. 'Did they talk much? How did they communicate?'

'They couldn't speak the same language,' Nowak said, after listening to Krystyna for a while. 'But Mihkel knew a little Polish, so they managed a few basic exchanges. His accent was funny.'

'What did he ask her about?'

Annie could tell by Krystyna's gestures and facial expressions that she wasn't going to get much of answer.

'Just her life in general,' said Nowak finally. 'She said mostly he asked about her, like you. How did she get there? Where was she from? Why did she come? He wanted to know her story. She asks if he was a policeman, too.'

'No,' said Annie.

'She also asks where has he gone.'

Annie sighed. *Bugger it.* This just wasn't fair. Should she tell Krystyna the truth? That they suspected the man in the dark green Ford Focus had tortured and drowned Mihkel? If she did, she risked scaring the girl so much that she might balk at giving a description of the man. If she didn't tell her, she was being dishonest. She topped up everyone's coffee and moved on. 'Can you ask her if she ever saw anyone else around the place who wasn't part of the normal furniture and fittings?'

Krystyna seemed surprised at the lack of an answer to her question, and the change in direction, but she listened to Stefan's translation as she sipped her coffee.

'A man came once who seemed to be in charge,' Stefan translated. 'He was dressed better than the driver and his friend, who brought them stale bread and weak coffee in the morning before work. He was wearing a hat and an overcoat with a fur collar. He was English, she thought. Probably half the people there were Polish, and some of them spoke English, so word got around that he wanted them all to know that if they needed money, there was a way. A friend of his would lend them money, and they could pay him back when they got more pay for their jobs, after they had paid off the agency.'

No mention of interest, of course, Annie guessed. She bet the boss man was Roderick Flinders, himself, or one of his men, and that Corrigan was involved somewhere down the line. She excused herself for a moment, reassured Krystyna that she would be back soon and went to her office. She had photographs of both Corrigan and Flinders, which she took back with her and set in front of Krystyna. 'Do you recognise either of these men?' she asked.

Krystyna studied the photographs and pointed to Flinders. 'This one,' Nowak translated. 'He was the one who came and told them he could get them money. She hasn't seen the other man.'

It figured, Annie thought. Corrigan wasn't likely to venture out into the trenches when he had others to do that for him.

'Excellent,' she said. 'I'm going to see if I can rustle up a sketch artist. We can use Menzies, from the art college, if he's available. He doesn't live far away. I'll send a car. I know it's upsetting for her, but I don't want her to leave here until we've got sketches we can use. This is the first time we've got anywhere close to a description of our man, and I don't want to lose it. Do you think you can entertain Krystyna for a few minutes while I'm gone? I promise I won't be long.'

'Sure,' said Stefan. 'We'll have a laugh a minute.'

Annie gave him a cold look as she stood up. *Some people,*

she thought. Krystyna's eyes followed her, as if she wanted to go with her, too, but Stefan's voice was soothing enough when he started to speak Polish, and Annie turned at the door, smiled and gave Krystyna a thumbs up sign.

Erik Aarma said he would be happy to have dinner with Banks and Joanna that evening, and that he would like to bring his wife Helen along. Nobody had any objection to that, so it was arranged for half past seven. In deference to the tourists and the fine weather, Erik said, they would eat in the Old Town, something he rarely did, and a nice treat for Helen, too. She loved pasta, and they didn't have it very often. They had an apartment in Kristiine and usually ate locally, or at home. Perhaps an evening out would dispel some of the gloom they had been feeling over Mihkel's death.

It was a Friday night, and getting quite busy, as they took their table at a small Italian restaurant on Raekoja, quite near the main square, and just around the corner from Clazz, shortly after half past seven. The revellers weren't out in full force yet, but the chain gang was back, and a group of girls dressed as Playboy bunnies tottered by on their high heels, attracting many wolf whistles, searching for a bar in very loud Glasgow accents. Whenever Banks saw groups of girls such as that now, he thought of Rachel. In a way, he felt that since he had been in Tallinn, he had drifted away from his starting point, the murder of Bill Quinn, then the discovery of Mihkel Lepikson's body at Garskill Farm, and his case had turned into a quest for the truth about what had happened to Rachel. Not that he believed she was still alive, but her body had to be somewhere, even after all this time. Annie was doing the real work, back in Yorkshire, he thought, getting closer to identifying Quinn's killer with every moment. It would be a great success for her to have on her first case after the injury. A real confidence booster. Banks had not entirely lost sight of Bill

Quinn, or of Mihkel Lepikson, but it was Rachel he sought in the winding cobbled alleys and long evening shadows of Tallinn's Old Town.

Erik seemed pleased with himself, so Banks was hoping for good news. Joanna was chatting happily away with Helen, only pausing to glance at her mobile every now and then. Helen was almost as large as her husband, but minus the facial hair, and quick to laugh. A fresh breeze had picked up during the day, and Erik said it might mark the end of the warm spell. It was still pleasant enough to sit outside, but they definitely needed to wear jackets. Joanna had a wool shawl wrapped around her shoulders. Where did she get these things? Banks wondered. She had the perfect item to wear for all occasions. Every once in a while, Banks caught a whiff of burning tobacco as a smoker passed by.

'I am not going to beat about the bush, as you say,' said Erik as they clinked glasses and toasted absent friends. 'I will not keep you in the suspense. I have found your girl.'

Banks almost dropped his glass. He looked at Joanna, whose eyebrows shot up so far they were almost lost under her blonde fringe. 'Are you sure?' he asked.

'I am sure.'

'But . . . how?'

Erik tapped the side of his nose. 'Ah, but we have our resources. People say sometimes we have more files than the Stasi did.'

'Seriously?' said Banks.

'Do you want to know who she is?'

'Of course we do.'

'Her name is Larisa Petrenko.'

'Like the conductor?'

'Vasily Petrenko? You know of him? Yes, like that.'

'She's Russian, then?'

'It is a Russian name. But that should not be a surprise to

you. Forty per cent of Tallinn is made up of Russian-speaking citizens. Helen is Russian-speaking, but we speak Estonian. The most popular last name in the whole country is Ivanov.'

'I thought people were changing their names to Estonian to have a better chance of getting on here?'

'You should not believe all you read in the newspapers, my friend. The next thing you know they will have us dragging Russian-speaking Estonians away at midnight and locking them up in Patarei.'

'You don't do that already?'

Erik laughed. 'Not for some time.'

It was clearly a touchy subject, though, Banks sensed. The whole Russian–Estonian thing was beyond his comprehension, though he knew the basic facts, the history of the relationship. He felt it was something you had to live through, grow up with. 'You don't happen to know where she lives, do you, this Larisa Petrenko?'

'Of course. She lives in Haapsalu. She has a restaurant there with her husband.'

'I can't believe this,' Banks said shaking his head slowly. 'Where is Haapsalu?'

'On the west coast. About one and a half hours to drive. We will not be able to join you, I am afraid. Family matters. But Merike is back. I have spoken with her. She will pick you up at your hotel after breakfast tomorrow. Is ten o'clock too early?'

It was all moving so fast. Banks glanced at Joanna, who shook her head. 'Not at all.'

'Merike is very sorry she could not join us tonight also,' said Erik, 'but there you are. You will see her tomorrow.'

'I'm still rather taken aback by this,' Banks said. 'What you're telling me is that you found the girl in the photo with Bill Quinn, and she lives an hour and a half away, and runs a cafe with her husband, right?'

Erik beamed. 'That is correct. You pay attention. A restaurant. Haapsalu is a tourist town. Nice. You will like it.'

'So she's not a hooker in Budapest, or a stripper in Belfast?'

'Not at all. She is a most respectable young woman, which makes me think she might not enjoy to talk about her past.'

'We'll manage it somehow,' said Banks. 'I have to know how you found her, Erik. Come on, you can't just leave us guessing like this.'

Erik tilted his head to one side. 'I could,' he said. 'You only asked me for the information. Not how I found it. Should I give up my trade secrets so easily?'

'I'm not asking—'

Erik waved his large hairy hand in the air. 'It is all right, my friend. I am only kidding. Is that what you say? Kidding?' He winked at Joanna.

'Damn right, it is,' said Banks.

A pretty dark-haired waitress appeared to take their orders. She wore a nametag that identified her as 'Irena'. Nobody had had a chance to study the menu, as they had all been too busy talking, so they took an extra minute to scan the list, then Irena came back and they all ordered pasta and a bottle of Chianti. It was starting to get dark now, the shadows long and deep in the narrow cobbled streets of the Old Town. Someone was singing in the distance. A glass smashed a little closer. Banks fancied he could hear a zither playing somewhere.

'We have some very good facial-recognition software,' Erik said. 'Perhaps you do not know this, but Estonia is very famous in high technology. We invented Skype.'

'I had heard that,' said Banks. 'So that's how you did it?'

'Not exactly.' Erik pointed to his head. 'I also have a fantastic memory.'

Helen laughed. 'He does,' she said. 'It is true. He has memory like steel hat.'

'I think that's "steel trap", Helen,' Joanna corrected her.

'Yes. That is right. Like steel trap.'

'So how did you do it?' Banks asked.

Erik paused for dramatic effect, then he said, 'I'm a news-paper man. It is in my blood. The ink. The hot lead. Which we do not use any more, of course. When I first saw the photo-graph, I knew the face was familiar, but the context was not. I do not know any escort girls or prostitutes. Only through news stories, and that was not where I had seen her. No, it was something else. Two years ago there was a big celebrity wedding in Haapsalu, which is unusual in itself. This beautiful Russian girl, who had just graduated from university in Tartu, married one of Estonia's most famous artists, Alexei Petrenko. Very handsome. He had a reputation for being a ladies' man but he seemed to have settled down at last. We reported on the wedding, with photographs. Not me, of course. And not Mihkel. But a reporter who writes such celebrity stories. But I am editor for many different reporters.' He tapped the side of his head. 'And that is how I remember.'

He seemed exhausted by his long speech in English, took a long swig of wine and leaned back in his chair.

'You are certain?' Banks asked.

'Yes. As soon as I stopped thinking she was an escort or a hooker, I started to remember and looked through file photo-graphs.' He pulled a photo out of his inside pocket and slid it over the table to Banks. 'This is her, is it not?'

Banks studied the picture. There was just enough light at the table to make it out. The happy couple. It was definitely *her*, all right. There was no mistaking those cheekbones, those eyes, even though her hair was shorter and styled differently. Banks felt a frisson of excitement. He showed the photo to Joanna then made to pass it back, but Erik waved it away. 'Keep it,' he said. 'I made a copy for you. I don't need it.'

'That picture was in the newspaper?' Banks asked.

'But of course. All the newspapers. It was big news.'

If anyone had been searching for the woman, Banks thought, the photo would have been a giveaway. But if anyone had been after her, he told himself, she would have known not to invite public scrutiny that way. Which meant that she probably had no idea what she had done, or why. The problem was that things had changed over the last month, since Quinn's wife's death, and that might include her situation, too. There was no reason why she should become a liability if she knew nothing – if all she had done was play a seduction game six years ago with a man she didn't know while someone took photographs – but she could be a loose end, and it seemed as if someone had been tidying up loose ends. Banks felt no reason for undue alarm, but the fact that two people had been killed already, and that he had been followed around Tallinn, made him a little nervous. Ten o'clock the following morning hardly seemed soon enough. Still, if she had survived unharmed up until now, there was no reason to fear that tonight she would meet her doom. Banks quelled his concerns and thanked Erik profusely for the information.

'My pleasure,' said Erik. 'Especially if it helps to catch whoever killed Mihkel.'

'It could help,' said Banks. Their food arrived, and there was a short break in conversation while everyone got settled with serviettes, side dishes and knives and forks. Irena smiled at Banks and refilled their wine glasses.

'I think she fancies you,' joked Joanna.

'Get away with you,' said Banks. 'My charm only works on the over sixties.'

'I don't know. She may have visions of an English husband, an English passport, an English country house.' She turned to Erik. 'Irena? Is that a Russian name?'

'Probably,' Erik said. 'Could be Polish, too. Or Slovakian. Many names are common to more than one country.'

'There you are,' she said to Banks. 'An exotic Eastern European bride.'

Banks twirled up a forkful of spaghetti and smiled at her. 'Rather like an exotic Italian husband.'

Joanna seemed to freeze for a moment, then she blushed. 'Not at all,' she said. 'Not at all like that.'

'Anything on Toomas Rätsepp and Ursula Mardna?' Banks asked.

'The prosecutor's clean as a whistle. High-flyer. Tipped for even bigger things. The Rachel case set her back a bit, but she's more than made up for it since then. Feared and respected.'

'She seems so young.'

'It is a young woman's job.'

There were plenty of young women around the CPS offices, too, Banks realised, but he had never really thought about it that way. 'What about Rätsepp?'

'Nothing definite. No dirt that sticks, so to speak. There are those who think he mixes too closely with the wrong elements. Not real gangsters and criminals, you understand, but businessmen, rich and powerful people who might need occasional favours, who sometimes move very close to the edge.'

'"Businessman" is a word that covers a multitude of sins, I've always thought,' said Banks.

'He has a very nice apartment in Kadriorg, which is most unusual for a retired police officer. It is an expensive area.'

'Wouldn't he be more careful if he had something to hide?'

'Of course. That is why there is no dirt that sticks. He would not dare to be so open, as you say, if he could not explain the money.'

'How does he explain it?'

'Inheritance. It is true that his father was quite wealthy. He began with one small shop and ended up running a chain of electronics stores. He died around the time Rätsepp retired.

Rätsepp didn't get everything, of course – he had brothers and sisters – but he ended up with a decent share.'

'And that explains the flat, the money?'

'To the satisfaction of most people,' said Erik. 'You must draw your own conclusions.'

'Was Rätsepp involved with anyone who might be responsible for what happened to Rachel Hewitt, for Bill Quinn and Mihkel?'

'"In the right circumstances don't you think, everyone is capable of anything."'

'*Chinatown*,' said Banks. 'Or close enough. Is there any way of finding out more?'

'Not without ruffling too many feathers. The wrong feathers to ruffle. We have a free press, but with freedom comes responsibility.'

'That's a lesson we're still learning back home,' said Banks.

'Yes. I know.'

'Thanks for all you've done.'

'You are welcome. As I said, it is for my friend Mihkel. And now to other things. Vasily Petrenko. Is he still with the Liverpool Philharmonic?'

Joanna pulled a face, and Helen started questioning her about her job, investigating bad cops. 'Yes,' Banks said to Erik. Yes, he is.' And as he went on to talk about the young conductor's successful career, he noticed a familiar figure sitting outside across the small square. It was the man who had been following him the previous night.

Banks returned to his conversation, and when he looked again a few minutes later, the man was gone. But Banks knew he was around somewhere, watching, watching the dark.

It was getting on towards the end of Friday afternoon, and the working week for most people would soon be over. It wouldn't be much of a weekend for Annie – she would still have plenty of tasks to keep her busy – but things slowed down when the people you relied on weren't around. It was hard to get any lab work done, for a start, let alone a rush job. Thankfully, they had Stefan Nowak and Vic Manson and the team next door, but they weren't equipped to do everything, and they liked to keep as normal hours as possible if they could.

The question of what to do with Krystyna remained paramount in Annie's mind. They had got Rick Menzies, their sketch artist from the art college, and between them, Rick, Krystyna and Stefan had come up with a good description, which Annie thought translated into a more than usually clear sketch, from the five o'clock shadow to the cropped hair and crescent scar by the hairline, the bulbous nose and ears slightly sticking out, to what Annie could only describe as a cruel mouth.

Annie glanced briefly at the notes and message she had received throughout the afternoon. The most interesting item was that Vic Manson had managed to get a couple of fingerprints from the inside of the glove compartment of the Ford Focus they thought the killer had hired under the name of Arnold Briggs. Of course, there could be no guarantees they were his at this point. Like the DNA, the fingerprint was not on any of their databases.

AC Gervaise poked her head around the door. 'Got a minute, Annie?'

'Of course,' said Annie, following her out into the corridor. She was surprised when Gervaise led her towards the staircase down to the ground floor and the exit, rather than up to her office. She was even more surprised when they crossed to the corner of Market Street, heading straight for the Queen's Arms.

'I guessed you might feel like a break,' said Gervaise. 'It's been a long week.'

'Yes, ma'am.'

'And you can stop that. I enjoy it about as much as you do.'

Annie grinned and followed her through the door. The place was busy, a popular destination for the post work crowd on a Friday, but a lot of people liked to stand at the bar and relax, so they found a quiet round, copper-topped table by the window looking out on the market square, which was in that in-between twilight period, after work, so few shoppers were around, but before play, so the young revellers hadn't arrived yet. The chairs and tables were outside, on the wooden stand, but nobody was sitting there at the moment. A brisk wind was blowing, and if Annie wasn't mistaken she could see a drop or two of rain on the windows.

'My shout,' said Gervaise. 'What's it to be?'

'Am I off duty?'

'As far as I'm concerned you are.'

'Right, then. I'll have a pint of Cock-a-Hoop, please.'

'Excellent.'

Gervaise came back a few minutes later with two pints. Judging by the colour, Annie guessed them both to be Cock-a-Hoop. The name made her think of A. Le Coq, and of Banks and Joanna Passero, no doubt enjoying another nice open-air dinner in Tallinn.

'Where's DS Jackman?' Gervaise asked.

'She's talking to some of the other girls who were at the hen weekend, to see if they remember anything Pauline Boyars didn't.'

'I'm not sure about this sudden concentration on Rachel Hewitt. I hope you remember we're looking for the man who killed DI Quinn and this Estonian journalist.'

'Of course. And we're getting close. But they're connected.'

'Hmm. We'll see, no doubt. Anyway, how was your first week back at work?'

'Fine,' said Annie. 'Busy, of course, but it's great to be back.'

'I did advise you to take it easy.'

'With all due respect, I've been taking it easy for long enough already. It's time to get back in the saddle.'

Gervaise sipped some beer. 'You've got a point. How did you get on with the Polish girl?'

'Krystyna? We got an excellent sketch of the suspect,' Annie said. 'I've sent it off to everyone I can think of. NCS, Trading Standards, Force Intelligence Unit, SOCA, the Human Trafficking Centre and Interpol. Not to mention the county forces nationwide. Wanted: handy with a crossbow, interested in waterboarding.'

'That should do it,' said Gervaise.

'I'm not too sure,' said Annie. 'I mean, there's definitely foreign involvement in this. Estonian and Polish for starters. If our man was sent to kill Quinn and Lepikson, there's every chance he doesn't live in the UK, and if that's the case, the odds are that he's left the country. Who'd hang around after a double hit? He could be anywhere.'

'Interpol's got pretty good data these days. They'll pull something up on him if there's anything there.'

'Let's hope so. They drew a blank on the DNA. Anyway, I'm not expecting a lot until after the weekend, but I'm trying to stay hopeful.'

'What have you done with Krystyna?'

'That's the problem,' said Annie, leaning forward and resting on her elbows. 'She's down in the cells right now. She's not under arrest or anything – she hasn't really done anything wrong except yell at an old woman in Polish – but I want to keep her around until we find our man, then see if she can make a positive identification. Besides, she's got nowhere to go, poor thing. She's got no fixed abode, and if immigration get their hands on her, they'll whisk her away from us.'

'I see your problem. We might be able to stretch to a B & B for a couple of days.'

'I'm not sure she'd stay. She's scared. It took me and Stefan a while to put her at ease and convince her she wasn't going to be locked up. She's got no clean clothes to wear, either. I mean, you can only get so far in an Elvis suit.'

'A wha—' Gervaise said, then stopped herself. 'Oh, I see. That's what you call them. Well, no. You're right about that. You could take her to Oxfam or Sue Ryder and buy her a few things.' She checked her watch. 'Though you'd probably have a job at this time.'

'And then what?'

'Well, short of taking her home yourself, lending her some of your cast offs, I don't really know.'

'Don't think I haven't thought of that. She doesn't speak any English.'

'People get by. I had a Spanish roommate once, when I was at police college. She didn't speak a word of English, and I know no Spanish, but we managed all right. I'm not saying you should do it, if the idea bothers you, though. I suppose we can accommodate her in the cells for a few days at the taxpayers' expense, though let's hope it doesn't get leaked to the local press, or we'll have swarms of homeless heading up from the cities.'

Annie laughed at the image. 'Think what the press would say if a female police officer took a young girl home with her. Not that I care.'

Gervaise paused. 'Do we know for certain she's illegal?'

'We know nothing except that she's Polish, and Poland is a member of the EU. I don't know if she has the right documents or filled in the right forms. She has no identification now, no passport, no money, nothing. God knows where they are. I'm thinking of ordering a raid on Roderick Flinders' business offices and home. Krystyna identified him from a photograph as someone who came around with offers to lend money, so that clearly links him with Corrigan's nasty little business. He'd probably be too canny to keep anything incriminating there, but I might just do it anyway, just to put the jitters up the bastard. And for my own pleasure, of course.'

Gervaise finished her pint and glanced at Annie's glass, still about a quarter full. 'Another?'

'No, I shouldn't. I'd better—'

'Oh, come on with you. How often do we get a chance to take a break from the station and have a good old natter?'

'Well, seeing as you put it like that.' Annie drained her glass and handed it over. 'I'll have the same again, please.'

As Annie sat waiting for Gervaise to come back with the drinks, she thought of poor Krystyna shut in the cells. Though an inner voice warned her about getting involved, perhaps, she thought, it wouldn't be a bad idea to take Krystyna home. Just until the dust settled and she could get her life sorted out. They could communicate through sign language. She could sort out some clothes for her. Nothing would fit her well, of course, as she was so thin, but there were ways of making do, a little nip here and a tuck there. Anything was better than the oversized Elvis suit. Best of all, Krystyna would be in a clean and comfortable house, not a cell. Annie would order a pizza. They would watch television. Krystyna could sleep in the spare room. Annie saw Gervaise talking into her mobile at the bar. When she came back her hands were empty, and her face was serious.

'I'm afraid that second pint will have to wait,' she said. 'I've just received notice from West Yorkshire. Warren Corrigan's been shot.'

IO

Saturday morning was a little cooler than it had been earlier in the week, with a fresh wind off the Baltic bringing in a few ponderous clouds. Merike was wearing a patterned jumper that reminded Banks of Sarah Lund's sweater from *The Killing*.

'Haapsalu is a spa town, right?' she was saying, as they drove through the outskirts of Tallinn on a major road, all apartment blocks and shopping centres. 'Like Harrogate and Bath.'

'I understand,' said Banks, sitting next to her in the front of the messy yellow VW Bug. He was keeping an eye on the rear-view mirror. It was perhaps too early tell, but he didn't think they were being followed.

'It has an old castle, the Episcopal Castle, some beautiful old wooden houses and a nice waterfront. Peter the Great used to go there. And Tchaikovsky. There's a bench dedicated to Tchaikovsky.'

'I'd like to see that,' Banks said. 'But this isn't exactly a day at the seaside.'

'I know,' said Merike, casting him a sideways glance. 'I am hoping we are successful, too.'

The plan, such as it was, was for Merike to first talk to Larisa, try to set her at ease, assure her there would be no comebacks or consequences, and then for Banks to question her, with Merike's help as a translator, if necessary, about her past. If her husband didn't know, and if he was there, they would get her away from him for a while. Joanna Passero, who had a special interest in this part of the investigation, would be taking notes and asking questions whenever she felt it necessary. Banks could hardly sideline her on this. They had not telephoned in advance. There were many reasons why Larisa Petrenko might want to forget her past, and they didn't want to scare her away before they got there.

The suburbs of Tallinn gave way to fields and woods. Here and there, a narrow unpaved lane led between rows of hedges to a distant village. The road they were travelling on wasn't very busy, though it was obviously a main east–west route, with bus service and all, so they made generally good progress. Merike had the radio tuned quietly to some inoffensive pop programme. In deference to her passengers, she refrained from smoking, though Banks assured her she was welcome to do so in her own car, which was pretty thick with the smell of tobacco anyway. Joanna sat in the back gazing out at the scenery. She didn't seem ill, the way she had on the way to Garskill Farm, but then the road here was much smoother. Banks was thinking about the phone call he had received from Annie late last night. Warren Corrigan had been shot. She said she would call when she had more news. He wondered whether that triggered bad memories, or whether she could disassociate from what had happened to her.

Soon they were entering a town – Haapsalu itself, Merike announced – with a few modern buildings dotted around grassy areas, all very low-rise, then streets of old wooden houses as they drove slowly down the main street. Merike found a place to park and pulled to a halt. She pointed out of the window to a restaurant. 'There,' she said. She glanced at her watch. 'They should be open for lunch. It is very popular because the restaurant is above Alexander Petrenko's gallery, where he has some paintings for sale.'

'It seems a good business idea,' said Banks. 'Have a stroll around the gallery, see something you like, head upstairs for a nice meal and a couple of drinks to think it over.'

'He does very well, I think, but he is so rarely there, of course. His studio is elsewhere in town.'

Banks could sense, if not smell, the fresh sea air when he got out of the car. He took a deep breath to rid himself of the tobacco smell that lingered in the upholstery. The first thing Merike did when she got into the street was light a cigarette. 'You want me to go in alone first, right?'

'Yes, please. I don't think we should all go traipsing in there at once and scare the living daylights out of her,' Banks said. 'You go have a word with her, tell her what we have in mind. See if she can get someone to cover for her for a while, and we'll all go for a walk on the seafront. Sound OK?'

'OK,' said Merike, stamping out her cigarette. 'I feel like a cop.'

Banks smiled. 'There's no need to take it that far. Just be yourself.'

'Who else could I be?' said Merike, then she checked for traffic and wandered across the street. Banks and Joanna hung back by the VW. There were a few tourists walking about, checking antique and gift shops. 'It's famous for shawls, Haapsalu,' said Joanna. 'Beautiful shawls of knitted lace.'

'Maybe later,' said Banks, thinking something like that might make a nice present for Annie, though on second thoughts, she didn't seem much like a lace shawl kind of girl. Still, there were plenty of gift shops in the Old Town. Some amber jewellery, perhaps, or ceramics.

Joanna wandered a few yards down the street to look in a shop window while Banks kept his eye on the door of the restaurant. It was about ten minutes before Merike came out. At first Banks thought she was alone, then he saw the woman behind her. Larisa Petrenko. She was a slighter figure than he had imagined – for some reason he had thought her a tall, leggy, exotic beauty. The closer they came, the more he could see that she was definitely a beauty, though in a very natural way. She now she wore her hair tied back in a ponytail. Her jeans were not the kind you had to put on with a shoehorn, but they certainly showed off the curves of her hips, rear end and legs. She had put on some weight since the photograph with Quinn had been taken, but not much. She was still slim and petite, and very young-looking. And she was nervous. Banks gave Merike a quizzical glance.

'This is Larisa,' Merike said. 'She is willing to talk to you. Her husband is not here today. He is at his studio working. She does not believe she can tell you very much, but she will help if she can.'

Banks smiled at Larisa and offered his hand. She shook it. Her grip was firm, her skin soft. 'I cannot be gone for long,' she said, in clear but accented English. 'Kaida is by herself, and we should be busy soon.'

'Can we walk?'

Larisa led them down some quiet streets of wooden houses, and they soon came out at the sea. There was a large white wedding-cake style building on the water in front of them with a covered walkway all around it, like the covered porches in the Southern USA. To the right was something resembling a white bandstand sticking out from the shore. They walked along the waterfront path. Larisa had already told them on the way about her simple life in Haapsalu with her husband and her cafe, about how she had gone to university to study modern languages, and wanted to teach, but changed her mind. Now she made pottery and ceramics and ran a success-ful restaurant in a tourist spa.

'I take it that's a long way from your old life?' Banks said.

'Yes.'

'Do you want to tell me what happened?' Banks had already showed her the photographs, which had embarrassed her.

Banks saw a polar bear in the water near the shore, then he realised it was just a statue of a polar bear. Haapsalu's version of The Little Mermaid, he guessed. They came to a stone bench that was inscribed 'P.I. Tsaikovski 1840–1893' under a circular etching of the man himself. 'Let's sit here,' said Larisa. 'I like to sit here when I walk by the sea.'

'Do you like Tchaikovsky's music?' Banks asked.

'Not particularly. But I like the idea that he was here. I like to think of him enjoying the same view and hearing great music in his mind.'

Banks liked that idea, too, and he also liked Tchaikovsky's string quartets and symphonies very much. The four of them sat in a row, Banks half-turned towards Larisa. 'Do you remember that night when the photographs were taken?'

Larisa gazed out to sea, screwing her eyes up against the glare from the water. 'Pieces of it,' she said. 'I met him in the hotel bar. I was pretending to get change for the telephone, and I caught his eye, as was planned.'

'So you didn't approach him directly?' Joanna asked, from beside Banks.

'I smiled at him. He came up to the bar and asked if he could help. He gave me some change. A few minutes later I came back in to thank him, and he offered to buy me a drink. After that, it was easy.'

'But at no time did you proposition him?' Joanna asked.

'What kind of girl do you think I am? Of course I did not proposition him. We talked. He was nice. He was lonely. He had nobody to meet, nobody to talk to.'

'What did you talk about?' Banks asked.

Larisa frowned. 'I do not remember. Wait. We talked about fishing at some time. He did. I remember how intense and alive he became when he talked about fishing. The rest is gone. Small talk. How he liked Tallinn. The sights. That sort of thing.'

'Did he talk about his job?'

'I do not know what his job was. Perhaps he did.'

'He was a police detective.'

'I would have remembered,' Larisa said. 'And I would have left. In those days I avoided the police.'

Banks let that one go by. 'So you talked,' he said. 'Then what?'

'Dinner. I said I was hungry, and he took me to dinner. And we drank some wine. And we talked some more.'

'When did the subject of going to his room come up?'

'Towards the end of dinner. We were perhaps both a little drunk. He said it would be nice to continue the conversation up in his room. I agreed.'

'You did this all of your own free will?' Joanna asked. 'Not for money?'

'Yes, of course for money,' said Larisa. 'But not from him. I am not a prostitute. Not even then.'

'So someone paid you?' Banks said.

'Two thousand kroon. It was a lot of money.'

'Do you know who paid you?'

'Of course I do. It was the same man who gave me the powder to put in his wine.'

There had been no point heading down to Leeds on Friday evening, as it was West Yorkshire's crime scene, and they would only be in the way, so Annie had given in to her softer nature and taken Krystyna home to her little cottage in Harkside. They had spent the evening in companionable silence watching American cop shows on Channel Five while sharing an Indian takeaway and a bottle of chilled Sauvignon Blanc. Annie's clothes hung on Krystyna, but she seemed to appreciate just having something clean to wear. She had spent over an hour in the bath and used most of the scented salts that Banks had bought Annie for Christmas. She never touched the stuff herself. He was crap at presents, Banks, but at least he tried.

Annie had got Stefan Nowak on the phone that morning and had him explain to Krystyna where she was going and that she was coming back soon, where the food was, and so on. She could tell by the coolness and distance in his voice that he didn't approve of her taking Krystyna home with her, but Annie didn't care. Stefan said he expected to be in the lab all morning, barring another murder scene, so Annie left his number for Krystyna in case there were any problems. She promised to be back by late afternoon. When she thought about it, she realised that she actually expected Krystyna would still be there, and that she would be disappointed and sad if she weren't. Then she shook that feeling off and got into Winsome's car, come to pick her up for another drive to Leeds.

The way Annie managed to piece it all together later, this was what happened: Late on Friday afternoon, Corrigan was in his 'office' in the Black Bull with Curly, finishing up for the day, and counting the take brought in by several of their debt collectors that afternoon. It had been a lucrative day, and Corrigan was in a festive mood, ready to take his wife to Anthony's in central Leeds. Curly was about ready to head off to his local in Wortley with his mates for a Friday night darts match. They were both enjoying an end-of-the-week drink, as was their habit, a pint of bitter for Curly, and a double Glenmorangie for Corrigan.

A man walked into the Black Bull at about 5.45 p.m. Of medium height and build, with a short dark beard, he was wearing a navy blue overcoat and a woolly hat. None of the staff had ever seen him before. He bought a half pint of Guinness and a packet of pork scratchings and sat down at a table by the far side of the public bar. He didn't remove his overcoat, though it was warm in the pub. Nobody paid much attention to him. The Black Bull wasn't very busy at that time. Apart from one or two punters dropping by for a stiff one on their way home from work, it was too early for the two-for-the-price-of-one dinner crowd and the karaoke night regulars.

Somebody noticed the man get up and go to the toilet shortly after he had arrived. He was gone for about five minutes. The theory was that he had spent that time checking out the lie of the land. At 6.05 p.m., he went back to the bar and bought another half pint of Guinness and a packet of salt and vinegar crisps, with a new ten-pound note, fresh from the cashpoint. Getting up his nerve, so the theory went. The barmaid who served him noticed that he had a foreign accent, but that wasn't so rare around those parts. His hands were also shaking slightly, and he spilled a little beer when he picked up his glass.

It was about 6.15 p.m. when he went to the toilet a second time, or so the woman at the next table, who was the only one who noticed, assumed.

According to a barmaid who was walking past the office on her way from the staff room to the main bar, the man negotiated the maze of corridors and bars in the back of the pub and approached Corrigan's office. Both Corrigan and Curly were sitting on the banquette sipping their drinks. Hence, there was no one to prevent the man from walking straight into the office.

Curly got immediately to his feet and moved forward to stop the man coming any closer. 'Hey, you!' he said. 'Private office. Nobody's allowed back here.' Startled by his loud voice, the barmaid paused to see what was happening and glanced into the room.

Before Curly could get any further, the man pulled a gun from the pocket of his overcoat and shot him. Curly fell to the floor, clutching his side. The man then turned his attention to

Corrigan, who was now cowering on the banquette, pleading for his life, trying to shield his body with his briefcase. The waitress was terrified, but she said she was rooted to spot; it was like watching a road accident in slow motion. Corrigan picked up a handful of money and held it out, telling the man to take what he wanted and leave. The man fired again, and Corrigan jerked up off the banquette, holding his arm out, trying to make a dash for the door. The man shot him again, this time in the stomach. Corrigan fell to the floor and groaned, trying to hold in his oozing insides. The man stood for a few moments and surveyed the scene, perhaps enjoying the sight of Corrigan suffering before he died, then he raised the gun again and emptied it into the prostrate body. Corrigan jerked with each shot, but not another sigh or groan escaped his lips, only a final bubble of blood that slid down his chin and hung there.

By this time, the waitress had snapped out of her trance and made a run for the back exit, which proved no problem. Nobody tried to stop her. The shooter wasn't interested. It would appear that once he had completed the deed he set out to do, he sat down on the bench where Corrigan had been sitting and simply waited for the police to come.

It didn't take long. The manager had heard the shots and phoned 999. The customers had all dashed outside before anyone could stop them, and most of them had gone home by the time the police arrived, about ten minutes later.

When Annie and Winsome met Ken Blackstone there the following morning, the pub was still taped off as a crime scene, and the CSIs were still busy, but there was no sign of Corrigan. His body had been removed from the back-bar office, though his blood had spread in great stains across the floor like a map of the world, and the CSIs would have the time of their lives deciphering the spray patterns that had spurted over the nicotine-stained walls. Curly was in Leeds General Infirmary.

'It's Killingbeck's patch, of course,' explained Blackstone, 'but they know we have an interest, and of course, we know you have an interest. Besides, I'd say this counts as Homicide and Major Crimes, if anything does. Nice to see you again Annie, Winsome.'

'Yeah,' said Annie. 'We must stop meeting like this. People will talk.'

'Not Warren Corrigan, it seems.'

'The other bloke?'

'Curly? Aka Gareth Underwood. Last I heard, they had some hope for him.'

They stood and surveyed the scene of carnage for a while, before the CSIs shooed them away, after which they took a table in the main bar.

'Drink?' Blackstone offered. 'Manager says to help ourselves.'

'It's a bit early for me,' said Annie.

Winsome agreed.

'Suit yourself,' said Blackstone. 'The sun must be over the yardarm somewhere. I'll have a small brandy, Nick. Get one for yourself as well, then come and join us.'

The man did as Blackstone said. When he came back, he sat down opposite Annie.

'This is Nick Gwillam,' said Blackstone. 'Trading Standards, Illegal Money Lending Unit.'

'Where's your boss?' asked Gwillam.

'Tallinn,' said Annie.

'Lucky for some.'

'So what's the story?' Annie asked Blackstone.

'Not long ago, a young girl called Florica Belascu topped herself here in Leeds. She'd borrowed money from Corrigan, or one of his minions, and it had come time to collect. Naturally, she couldn't pay, and she had a small drug habit to support. Corrigan suggested she try going on the game, make a bit of money from kerb-crawlers. He wasn't into that line of business himself, he said, but he thought he could fix her up with someone who'd take good care of her. She refused. Seemed she hadn't sunk so low that she'd sell herself on the street. A couple of days later, the minion and one of his underlings came back and raped her, gave her a bit of a slapping around and left. Reliable witnesses bear that out. Next morning, she was found hanging from an old wall fixture in the bathroom. CSIs had little doubt she did it herself, despite the rape and beating. Either way, the finger points at Corrigan.'

'Who was the minion? Curly?'

'No. Curly's mostly for show. Like a guard dog. It was a scumbag called Ryan Currer. We've already got him banged up for an assault on another estate.'

'Who found the body? How did you find out about all this? Surely the girl didn't tell you?'

'Florica was too scared to talk, but her girlfriend wasn't. She had no debts, and she hated what Corrigan was doing. Florica was a lezzie, but she wasn't out of the closet. They lived together, but kept it low key. Tatyana, the girlfriend, was the smarter of the two. She'd managed to keep herself hidden during their visits. They didn't know about her. She'd tried to help Florica with the money, but she didn't earn enough herself, even though her employment was legitimate. She'd witnessed a lot of what had happened, though not the rapes and beating. She'd been at work then, cleaning offices in the city centre. We checked. She found Florica afterwards, which is how we know she was still alive when she went to bed that night. Florica didn't want the police involved, and she refused to go to hospital. Tatyana patched her up. In the morning, Tatyana found her hanging in the bathroom.'

'She talked to me, Tatyana did,' said Gwillam. 'Me and Bill.'

'Is this connected with Bill Quinn's death?'

'Don't think so. Can't be a hundred per cent certain, but I don't think so. This is a family matter. A matter of honour, of vengeance. The man who walked in here last night and did us all a favour is called Vasile Belascu. He's the girl's father. He said he shot Corrigan in revenge for his daughter's death. They believe in vendettas where he comes from, apparently.'

'How did he know what happened and where to find him?'

Gwillam winked. 'A little bird told him.'

'You're sailing a bit close to wind, aren't you?' Annie said. 'You, too, Ken.'

'We contacted the girl's father in Romania,' Blackstone said. 'We told him his daughter had committed suicide, and we wanted him to come and identify the body. We had no idea what he would do.'

'So who told him about Corrigan?'

'Same person told us, I should think,' said Gwillam. 'We didn't tell her not to tell anyone else. But we might never know. She's gone back to Odessa now, it seems.'

'Christ,' said Annie. 'This just gets better and better. I think I will have that drink, after all.'

'You'd better tell me who it was,' said Banks. 'Who told you to seduce Bill Quinn and drug his wine?'

'It does not matter,' said Larisa. 'The man who instructed me was not the man who wanted it done.'

'How do you know?'

'I heard him on the telephone.'

'Who was it, anyway?'

'The club manager at the time. I do not remember his name. Marko or something.'

'Where was this?'

'I was working in a nightclub. Not doing anything wrong, you know, just a waitress, coat check girl, sometimes hanging out and talking with the customers. Downstairs was a big noisy bar and a dance floor with spinning balls of light and strobe shows, but upstairs was just a quiet bar where people could relax and have a drink.'

'Where was this club? What was it called?'

'Here in Tallinn. On a small street off Vana-Posti. It had no—'

'With just a sign outside showing a man in a top hat and tails helping a lady into a coach?'

'That is right.' She seemed surprised. 'You have seen it? It is still there?'

'I've seen it,' said Banks. It was the place just around the corner from St Patrick's, where Rachel Hewitt had possibly been spotted going the wrong way by the Australian barman. 'It may have changed quite a bit since your day. It's a sort of exclusive sex club now, or at least that was the impression I got. What sort of club was it back then?'

'Just a nightclub, for dancing, parties. Mostly young people. It was very good class. More expensive, perhaps, than Hollywood and Venus, more popular with Estonians than with tourists. As I said, it has no name. We just called it The Club.'

'How does Bill Quinn come into this?'

'It was just fun, really. A joke. I was given his picture and the name of the hotel where he was staying, told to seduce him, to pretend we were making love. We never did. It just looks like it. But we never did have sex. He was asleep by then. It was all really very funny. Someone took photographs. I got two thousand kroons. That was that.'

'You didn't know who ordered it?' Joanna Passero asked.

'No.'

'You didn't know why you were doing it?'

'No.'

'Weren't you just a little bit curious?'

'Two thousand kroon was a lot of money.'

Joanna looked at Banks and shook her head as if to say a promising lead had turned to dust right in their grasp. Banks wasn't too sure.

'Were you taking drugs then?' he asked.

Larisa hung her head. 'Yes. My life was a mess. I was only eighteen. I had run away from home. I drink too much. But soon after, maybe one, two month, I left, left Tallinn, went home to Tartu, became sober. When I was well again, I enrolled in the university. After three years I met Alexei, and here we are. I left that life behind me, Hr Banks. Now I am only twenty-four, and I sometimes feel I have lived a whole lifetime. I am sorry if I cannot help you more. I have done nothing wrong.'

Except drug a man and set him up for blackmail, Banks thought. But he said nothing. He couldn't see any point in trying to ruin a young woman's life over a misguided act committed six years ago, no matter what its consequences had been. 'You said the man who actually instructed you and paid you was not the man who ordered it done, that you overheard a telephone conversation.'

'Yes.'

'Do you know who he was talking to?'

'No, but it was someone who was . . . I do not know how to say this. His boss? Someone who told him what to do?'

'Do you have any idea who that might be?'

'No. I only know the club manager who tell me. Perhaps other people employ him.'

'Why did you leave the club, Larisa?'

Larisa paused and picked at a fingernail, as if struggling to find an answer. 'I had a friend there, a friend called Juliya. She was from Belarus. She was a very beautiful girl, very funny, clever, and very nice. She was good to me. She made me laugh when I felt bad. She showed me how to live in that world. We shared a flat together.'

'Did something happen to her?' Banks asked.

'She ran away.'

Banks and Joanna looked at one another. Banks also noticed Merike's eyes open a little wider. 'Ran away?' Banks echoed.

'Yes. Just like that. One day she was there, then she was gone. All her clothes and belongings – not that she had much – gone. Not a word of goodbye, not a note to say where she has gone. Nothing.'

'But she took all her things?'

'Yes.'

'What did you think happened to her?'

'I think she went back to Belarus. She had a boyfriend who came to the club a lot. He was very rich and handsome. What do you call it, like a playboy? He always had good drugs, the best clothes, a fast car, and women were drawn to him. He was charming, but I think underneath he was dangerous. Young, rich and wild. For him there were no boundaries, no rules. There were many rumours about him. I do not know if they were all true. Juliya did not go into details. Wild orgies. Kinky sex. Every drug you can imagine. He had friends in St Petersburg, people said, criminal friends. Russian Mafia.'

'And this was Juliya's boyfriend?' Joanna said.

Larisa gave her a sad smile. 'We were living in a very strange world back then. Very unreal. It all feels like a dream, sometimes like a nightmare. At first he excited her, but soon I think she became frightened of him.'

'So you think Juliya left to get away from this boyfriend?' Banks asked.

'Perhaps. I just knew that was the end for me after she had gone. I was alone. I had to get away, too.'

'Why? Because of Juliya?'

'Because he was turning towards me. I always thought I was safe. He liked blondes. But I realised soon that he was not so particular as I thought. When he turned his attention to me at

The Club, asking me to go away with him for weekends in St Petersburg or Helsinki, that was the end. I disappeared quickly, too.'

'Just like Juliya?' Banks said.

'Yes. But I went first to Tartu,' Larisa said. 'I think Juliya went home to Minsk. I have never heard from her again until I got married. She must have seen something in the newspaper because she sent a postcard with congratulations to Alexei's studio. It was from Athens.'

'What about the man? Weren't you worried he'd try to find you?'

'No. A man like him has no attention span. Someone else would come along. A new toy. He would forget what I look like in a few days.'

'Do you remember his name?' asked Banks.

'Yes, of course. It is Joosep Rebane.'

'That's an Estonian name,' Merike said.

'Oh, yes,' said Larisa. 'He is Estonian. Not all the bad people here are Russian you know.'

'Do you know where he is now?' Banks asked.

'I have no idea. I turned my back on that life. He is not a man who seeks to have his picture in the newspapers, or his name, I think. Then he was just rich and spoiled, but now I suspect he is in the criminal underworld, trafficking drugs, girls, perhaps in St Petersburg. Maybe even in Tallinn. But he keeps out of sight. And perhaps he behaves differently from when he was younger.'

'Do you think he could have been the one who ordered the club manager to get you to set up Bill Quinn?'

'I do not know. Perhaps. But why?'

'I have a few ideas about that,' said Banks. 'When did all this happen?'

'It was six years ago. Summer.'

'Around the time the English girl disappeared?'

'I think so. I do not remember. I really . . . I did not hear much news.'

'You never linked the events in your mind? The English girl disappearing. You being asked to seduce an English detective?'

'I did not know he was a detective. This Quinn man. He did not talk about his work. And my brain did not make link.'

'OK,' said Banks. 'Can you remember whether Juliya disappeared before or after you went to the hotel to meet Bill Quinn?'

'I think it was just before. Can we go back now?' Larisa asked. 'I do not know any more. I cannot leave Kaida alone for too long.'

'Of course,' said Banks, standing up. 'We'll walk with you. It's a lovely town.'

Larisa smiled. 'Yes. Is very small, but in summer many tourists come. There is much business. Much to do.'

'Perhaps we can eat at your restaurant before we return to Tallinn?' Banks said.

Larisa looked alarmed.

'Don't worry,' he went on. 'I only say that because we're hungry. If I think of any more questions, I will be very discreet. We have no intention of spoiling the life you have made here.'

Larisa gazed at him seriously for a while, as if trying to decide whether he was telling the truth, then she said, 'Yes. Yes, that will be nice. I will cook for you myself.'

Annie and Winsome managed to fit in a quick sandwich at Pret with Blackstone and Gwillam before they got a call from Leeds General Infirmary saying that Gareth Underwood wanted to talk to them. It took a moment for the penny to drop: Gareth Underwood was Curly.

There was a police guard on the private room in which Curly was being kept for observation after a bullet had been removed from his left side the previous evening. As far as the doctor was concerned, it was nothing but a flesh wound, having missed all the important organs, though it had done some minor tissue damage, and one always had to keep an eye open for infection.

Curly was lying propped up on his pillows, connected to various machines that displayed his heart rate, blood pressure, oxygen levels and other bodily functions comprehensible only to doctors and nurses. Annie swallowed as she walked into the room, her mouth dry. It brought back too many memories, most of them bad. Curly was also hooked up to an MP3 player, with his eyes closed. He had a large glass of water with a bent straw on his bedside table.

Neither Curly's doctor nor Blackstone wanted to crowd the room, so only Annie and Ken Blackstone went in, leaving Gwillam and Winsome outside. Gwillam seemed put out by his exclusion, perhaps because he felt it was because he wasn't a real copper, being Trading Standards, but Winsome took it in her stride.

Curly seemed to sense someone in the room. He opened his eyes and took out the earbuds. 'Woz is a goner, isn't he?' he said, as they sat beside the bed in the hospital chairs.

'Woz?' said Blackstone.

'Mr Corrigan. Warren. It's what I called him. Woz.'

'Yes, Curly, he's a goner.'

'Would you mind calling me Gareth? I always hated Curly.'

'What do you want, Gareth? We're busy.'

'It's that copper who came to see Woz on Monday I want to talk to. Where is he?'

'DCI Banks?' said Annie.

'That's his name.'

'I'm afraid he's out of the country,' said Annie. 'I'm his partner. You can talk to me.' She checked with Blackstone, who nodded. Her dry mouth had turned into a tightening sensation in her chest when she entered the hospital room, and she wondered whether it meant the onset of another panic attack. They happened sometimes when she skirted too close to her recent experiences. Careful, slow breathing soon brought it under control. This was nothing like what happened to her, she told herself. Curly, or Gareth, seemed fine. He'd be back out in a day or two, right as rain, not spending months in and out of places like this, having operations, fearing for his legs. But she was past that now, she told herself. It was over; she was fine. And Gareth might well be spending the next few months and more in a place even less pleasant than a hospital room.

'First off,' said Gareth, 'before I tell you anything, I want to do a deal.'

'What sort of deal?' Blackstone asked.

'I want immunity. I know all about Woz's business. I even know where he keeps his books. I can name names. I know a lot, and I'm willing to tell it all, but I don't want to go to jail. And I want protection. A new identity.'

'I don't know about all that, Gareth,' said Blackstone. 'It's not up to me. We can put in a word for you.'

'You'll have to do better than that.'

'Gareth,' said Blackstone, 'you haven't been charged with anything yet. You're not even under arrest. No doubt you have done many bad things, but they're not our concern at the moment. Corrigan's shooting is.'

'It's not as if you don't know who did it, and why.'

'Tip of the iceberg, Curly, tip of the iceberg.'

'Gareth. And some of these bad things you think I've done might just become your concern if I start talking.' He rested back on the pillow and grimaced with pain. 'Bloody painkillers they give you around here are useless.'

Annie could certainly relate to that. There never seemed enough painkillers available when you were really in pain.

'Why don't you just tell us, Gareth?' Blackstone pressed on. 'You know it can only count in your favour. Otherwise, you'll be spending countless hours in detention, in smelly interview rooms. No painkillers there.'

'You can't fool me, Mr Blackstone. I know my rights, and medical attention is one of them. But I'll admit you've got a point. See, the thing is, I want to go straight. I've had enough of this.'

'Of what?'

'This life. Woz, and what he was doing. Robbing the poor to pay the rich. It's disgusting. He was scum. I've got a conscience, you know.'

'A bit late for that, isn't it?'

'It's never too late to repent.'

'Don't go all religious on us, Gareth.'

'Don't worry, I won't. I just think that every man should be given a second chance, that's all. I want to go straight. I want to go back to my old line of work.'

'What was that?'

'Club bouncer.'

'That's a step up in the world.'

'At least it's honest work.'

'That's debatable.' Blackstone leaned forward. 'Gareth, I appreciate your change of heart, I really do. But I'll appreciate it a lot more if you actually tell us something useful.'

'What did you want to talk to DCI Banks about?' Annie added.

Curly paused for a moment. The mental turmoil was clear for even Annie to see, as he debated whether to open up or not. 'I want a lawyer first,' he said. 'I'll make a deal, but I need some guarantees. On paper.'

'So what do you think of it all,' Joanna asked Banks that evening. They were dining alone this time, and as it had been a long day, and the weather had turned a little chilly, they had decided to eat at the hotel, but changed their minds when they heard the noise from the Karaoke Bar. Instead, they skipped over to the steakhouse at the bottom of Viru, near the gate, away from most of the parties and noisy groups. They found that wearing jackets or sweaters, and with the help of the well-placed heaters, they were fine outside, and plenty of others seemed to agree. The steaks were a bit more pricey than Clazz, but excellent quality.

'I liked her,' Banks said.

'I expect most men would agree with you.'

'Hey, now, wait a minute before you start getting all women's lib on me. I admire what she's done. She was on a downward slope – drugs, sex clubs, bad boys, the lot – and she pulled herself up by the boot strings. She's got guts, and a fair dollop of common sense. Not a bad-looking broad, either.'

Joanna nudged him playfully. 'Bastard,' she said.

Banks drank some more wine. 'You don't believe her story?'

'Most of it,' Joanna said. 'I'm inclined to think she abridged it, and censored it a little here and there for general consumption.'

'Oh, you're such cynics in Professional Standards. Don't you believe anybody?'

'I've always found it's a good starting point.'

'So what are you going to put in your report?'

'Which one?'

'What do you mean?'

'The one on Bill Quinn, or the one on you?'

'If you're planning a report on me, I can guarantee you'll have met with a mysterious accident before you get to the airport.'

Joanna laughed. 'Oh, you're not as bad as you like to make out. There'd be no point doing a report on you. Nothing to put in it. Boring.'

'I don't know what's worse,' Banks said, 'being a fit subject for you or not.'

'Oh, take my word for it, not is best. As for Bill Quinn . . . I don't know. He's dead. I think that whatever I have to say, I'll do my best to make sure it remains internal, depending on how far he went. Unless anyone else, anyone still alive, that is, turns out to be involved. There's still the possibility that someone was manipulating him, though, that he was a rotten apple.'

'Do you think that's the case?'

'I don't know. Tell me what you think. Instruct me, oh great homicide cop.'

Banks finished his glass and poured another. Joanna held her glass out, too. He emptied the bottle. They were both a little tipsy, partly with the success of the day, and partly with the wine. 'Larisa worked at that club I saw just around the corner from St Patrick's. A waiter in the pub said he thought he saw Rachel turn the wrong way when she went out after her friends, but later he said he wasn't certain.'

'She didn't even know where her friends were going.'

'Let's assume she went the wrong way. The others turned right. Rachel turned left.'

'OK. I'm with you so far. But after that?'

'After that, it gets a bit speculative, of course, but I think I'm assuming that Juliya's boyfriend was involved somehow, by the sound of him. Joosep. Perhaps Rachel wandered into the club, intrigued by the sign, the lack of a name, whatever, and she bumped into him. He liked blondes, remember.'

'He liked anything in a skirt, according to Larisa.'

'But blondes especially. Rachel was a very pale blonde. And very lovely. I think he turned on his charm, or he did the caveman routine, one or the other, and he got her away from there, back to his flat, or wherever. Maybe she felt she was in a new exciting city, so she should have an adventure. Everyone seemed to think she was an impulsive and spontaneous sort of girl. I don't know the details. But I think she soon realised what a big mistake she'd made, and perhaps she struggled. He didn't like to let her go. He liked his own way. I think he had it, and then he got rid of her.'

'How? Where?'

'I don't know the answers to that yet.'

'How does DI Quinn come into it?'

'I think Bill Quinn and Toomas Rätsepp came to the club asking questions. That's the link we've been missing. That's what Rätsepp lied to us about. They ruffled too many feathers somehow, got too close, and Joosep Rebane had to think what to do pretty fast. I think he bribed Rätsepp, but he couldn't do that with Bill Quinn. He was a foreign cop. Another kettle of fish entirely. So he made a few enquiries. No doubt friend Rätsepp would have helped, for a fee, and found out that Bill Quinn was a happy family man with a wife and two kids he adored. But Bill Quinn was also human, and you've seen Larisa. So Rebane got the club manager to pick the prettiest girl in the club to set a honeytrap for him. The rest is history. They showed him the photos, told them what they wanted of him, and that was that. He didn't like it, but what could he do? When Quinn's wife died, word got back that the hold was broken, and perhaps that Quinn had been haunted by guilt at not being able to do anything all those years. We know Joosep Rebane likely has connections with a rough crowd, gangsters, whether in St Petersburg or Tallinn, Russian or Estonian, and he sent one of them over to deal with Bill Quinn and Mihkel Lepikson, who was going to help Quinn get his story out without incriminating himself.'

'But how did this Joosep Rebane come to have so much power over a senior police investigator?'

'That I don't know,' said Banks. 'I don't know how the system works here, but I can guess there's just as much corruption as there is back home. Maybe you should get a job here?'

'No, thanks. Do you think the Prosecutor, Ursula Mardna, was involved?'

'Probably not. I don't think she would have told us about the young cop Bill Quinn went out investigating with if she was involved. Aivar Kukk. I'd like to talk to him. There must be something there. Rätsepp omitted to tell us about that. But there are obviously a lot of connections we don't get yet.'

'And what about Mihkel Lepikson?'

'Mihkel was the journalist on the original story, and he became friendly with Quinn. He's an investigative reporter and contributes to a column on crime in *Eesti Telegraaf* called "*Pimeduse varjus*". Watching the dark, or something along those lines. Joosep Rebane would have known this. He would also have kept an eye on him. Mihkel didn't know anything, not at the time. Quinn didn't confide in him about the photos and the blackmail. He didn't tell anyone. Joosep Rebane nipped the investigation in the bud when it had only got as far as Rätsepp and Bill Quinn. But when Rebane found out Lepikson was also in England, he got nervous and commanded a double act. No point only killing Bill Quinn, if Mihkel Lepikson was going to blast the true story on the front page of *Eesti Telegraaf.*'

'And the bonded labour scheme?'

'It wouldn't surprise me if Joosep Rebane doesn't have his finger in that little pie, too. I'll bet you he knows Corrigan and Flinders, at any rate. Drugs, people. It's all the same to some, as long as the profits are good. What do you think?'

'There's a lot of holes,' said Joanna. 'Like how Joosep Rebane knew Mihkel Lepikson was in Yorkshire, and in contact with Bill Quinn. But it's not bad, as theories go. From my point of view, Bill Quinn obstructed the full investigation of a disappearance, perhaps a murder, for six years. I'd hardly say he comes out of it smelling of roses, no matter what his reasons. God knows what else he did, too.'

'True,' said Banks. 'But you can't crucify a man who's already dead.'

'As I said before,' said Joanna. 'I'm not out to crucify anyone. It'll be an internal report, I hope, but there *will* be a report.' She paused and swirled some wine in her glass. 'There's still one big question we haven't answered yet,' she said.

'I know,' said Banks.

'What happened to Rachel Hewitt?'

'I wish I knew. I wish I could think of a way to find out. I'm pretty sure she's dead, but . . .?'

'Erik might be able to help.'

'How? We still need a starting point.'

'The nightclub,' Joanna said. 'You seem to know a bit about it.'

'I've been there,' said Banks.

'You've *what*?'

'I went there after dinner the second night we were here. I was wandering around, trying to follow what I imagined might have been Rachel's footsteps on the night she disappeared, and I just stumbled across it. Rachel might have done the same, too.'

'You didn't tell me you'd actually been *inside*.'

'You're starting to sound like my ex-wife. Do I have to tell you every time I go to a sex club?'

Joanna flushed, then saw Banks was teasing her, and smiled. 'What did you find out?'

'Nothing. That's why I didn't tell you. There was nothing to tell. I talked to the manager, Larry something-or-other, and a buxom waitress from Wigan. That's it. Oh, and I had kinky sex with a ladyboy from Bangkok, but that was nothing to write home about. The place has changed ownership God knows how many times in the last six years. There's no connection left to the old days, or none that I could find.'

'But there *is* a connection to Larisa and probably to Joosep Rebane.'

'And possibly to Rachel,' Banks said. 'I'm sure Erik will be only too happy to do a bit more digging, maybe even find out what happened to Aivar Kukk, if we ask him nicely.'

It took close to two hours, but Blackstone and Annie managed to rustle up a lawyer from the CPS and a duty solicitor, who thrashed out a deal for Curly between them. There was no way he was getting a new identity, but they found they could keep him out of jail if he told everything he knew, and if he was guilty of no major indictable offence. Curly thought about this for a while, no doubt going over in his mind exactly what he *was* guilty of, and agreed. When it came to it, he had probably done no more than intimidate a few people and administer a minor beating or two. When everything was signed, the lawyers took a back seat, and Blackstone and Annie pulled their chairs close to the bed. Annie had phoned Stefan and asked him to tell Krystyna she would be late, and she was worried because he had got no answer. She tried to tell herself that Krystyna had just gone to the shop for some food or cigarettes, but it gnawed away at her even as she listened to Curly's story.

'So give,' said Blackstone.

'I saw him,' he said.

'Saw who?' asked Annie.

'The bloke who killed Bill Quinn and that foreign reporter.'

'You know about Mihkel Lepikson?'

'Course. Woz knew he was up at Garskill Farm. Flinders had a bloke on the inside keeping an eye out for things like that. They've tried it before. The reporter was just too good to be true. Always asking questions. Making friends with the others. Always off to the telephone box. That's what they said. Flinders came down for a chat with Woz, who gets on the blower to Rebane. Flinders is another cunt, by the way. I can tell you things about him would make your hair curl.'

'Hang on a minute,' said Annie. 'Slow down. Are you telling me that Warren Corrigan gave the order for the deaths of Bill Quinn and Mihkel Lepikson?'

'Not him, no. Not directly. He was what you might call a station on the way, but it went through him, if you see what I mean. He supplied the crossbow, I can tell you that. Had me go and get it, actually. But he was doing it on orders.'

'Whose orders?'

'Bloke called Joosep Rebane, or something like that. Not sure how you pronounce it or spell it. Russian or something.'

Annie made a note of the name, though she was also far from sure about the spelling. 'And who's this Joosep Rebane when he's at home?'

'The boss. Kingpin. He says jump, Woz asks how high. Like I said, he's Russian Mafia or something, but he's behind all these migrant labour schemes, the phony agencies, bonding them with debt, all that stuff. It's also a front for drugs. That was going to be the next big thing. Woz was gearing up for it. Flinders and Woz both worked for Rebane, when it came right down to it. They didn't see him very often – he liked to keep a low profile and was paranoid about secrecy and security – but I can tell you, they were shit scared of him. He had a reputation as a bit of a wild man, which I think he liked to cultivate. You know, like in those Mafia movies. Horse's head under the bedclothes. Kind of bloke who'll be asking about your dear old mother one moment, and laying into you with an axe the next. I must say, he gave me the willies.'

'Did you meet him?' Annie asked.

'Only twice. At the pub. Back way, of course. Car waiting, dark windows.'

'Can you describe him?'

'Youngish bloke, about thirty, maybe a bit over. Tall, good-looking. I suppose the girls would find him attractive, if you know what I mean. Wears nice expensive suits, Armani, Hugo Boss, that sort of thing, hair always cut perfectly. Dark brown. Brown eyes. More like black. Charming on the surface, but there was something in his eyes that told you you wouldn't want to upset him.'

Annie took out the sketch of the man Krystyna had described, hoping to God that nothing had happened to her. 'Recognise him?' she asked.

'He's the one Woz gave the crossbow to. He's done a couple of jobs for him before.'

'What's his name?'

'Robert Tamm.'

'Nationality?'

'I don't know. He had one of those sort of Russian accents, too, but it might have been Bulgarian or Slovakian for all I know. I can't tell one of those buggers from another.'

'Do you know where he lives?'

'Aye. Glasgow. He came down on the train and picked up a rental car. But he's not Scottish. No way. I could spot a Jock accent a mile off.'

'Arnold Briggs,' said Annie. 'OK, let's get back to Mr Big. You say you met this Joosep Rebane on two occasions. When was the most recent?'

'About six months ago.'

'Do you know what the meeting was about?'

'No. Woz sent me out to the main bar.'

'But he was hardly a frequent visitor.'

'No. I should imagine this was one of the far-flung outposts of his empire. He communicated by phone and through the agents mostly. Untraceable mobiles, of course.'

'So what were these recent developments you want to tell us about, whatever resulted in death warrants for Bill Quinn and Mihkel Lepikson? I assume this Robert Tamm worked for Joosep Rebane?'

'That's right, far as I could tell. Enforcer. Hit man. What have you. Did his dirty work.'

'So you acquired the crossbow that Warren Corrigan gave Robert Tamm, on the orders of this Joosep Rebane, to kill Quinn? And the same man tortured and drowned Lepikson?'

Curly swallowed. 'Yes. But it sounds bad if you put it like that. I didn't know what he was going to use the crossbow for, did I?'

'A spot of grouse hunting, perhaps?' said Blackstone.

Curly looked towards the solicitors again, who both seemed fascinated by the discussion. 'See what I mean about me wanting some guarantees here?'

'You've got all the guarantees you're getting,' said Annie. 'Go on.'

Curly sighed. 'See, Joosep Rebane always let on that he had a cop in his pocket, had something on him. Bill Quinn. But when Bill Quinn's wife died, Rebane started to get worried. Woz got more phone calls from him. Rebane asked him to keep an eye on Quinn, then . . . well, you know what happened.'

'Did you know why he was worried?' Annie asked.

'Not at the time, no. We didn't know what Rebane had on DI Quinn.'

'And now?'

'Well, I've only really been able to work it out while I've been in here, but remember I mentioned that things started to go pear-shaped around the time Bill Quinn's wife died?'

'Yes.'

'Well, it must have meant that Rebane didn't have anything on him any more. Stands to reason. So I reckon it was probably a woman. That was the only thing that made sense, really. Why Rebane would get worried and all. If Quinn didn't have a wife, then he didn't have to worry about Rebane telling her he'd been playing away from home, did he? And he obviously had videos or photos or some sort of proof. Again, it stands to reason.'

'You're not as thick as you look, are you, Curly?' said Annie.

'Gareth. And no, I'm not.'

'Are you telling me that Bill Quinn was bent?' said Blackstone. 'Alan mentioned the possibility, but I ...' He shook his head.

'I'm telling you that I think Quinn was being blackmailed by this Joosep Rebane to go easy on Woz,' said Curly. 'I'm not saying Quinn liked it, but he had no choice. He was in a position to warn Woz about raids, and anything else that might act against his interests. But something put the heebie-jeebies up them all around the time Quinn's wife died. Not immediately, like, but over a couple of weeks. If you think about it, and if Quinn *was* being blackmailed, then he couldn't just suddenly go to his boss and say, guess what, guv, I've been passing information on to Woz Corrigan and doing my best to keep him out of jail this past while. Could he? Anyway, when they found out that this reporter had infiltrated the migrant group, and that Quinn knew him, it was double trouble. They figured Quinn had put the reporter on to the operation in the first place, to give him a good story like, but that the real story was going to be what Joosep had been up to. Apparently Quinn and the reporter had been buddies for years. Quinn was looking for a back door to spill the beans without getting any comeback, and the reporter was it. The way Woz explained it to me was that if Quinn could find a way to use the reporter to get his story out, then Rebane and Woz and Rod Flinders wouldn't be safe any more. So they both had to go.'

Annie rubbed her forehead and stood up. 'What a tangled web we weave,' she said. Her thoughts returned immediately to Krystyna. She wanted to get back to Harkside as soon as she could, but there was one more stop to make on the way, something Banks had asked her to do.

As Winsome drove, Annie phoned home again but still got no answer. She phoned Stefan and managed to get through to him at the lab, but he had heard nothing from Krystyna. Annie cursed and ended the call.

'What is it?' Winsome asked.

'Krystyna. She's gone.'

'I shouldn't worry too much. She's probably just gone for a walk or a drink.'

'She's been gone for hours. She's got no money.'

'We'll be home soon. Sure you want to make the stop?'

'We're almost there now. Might as well.'

Pauline Boyars was already well into a bottle of vodka, and the place was still a tip.

'It's just a little thing,' Annie said, without even bothering to sit down, 'but we were wondering if you remember a night-club in Tallinn that didn't have a name? All it had was a sign with a man in top hat and tails helping a woman into a coach.'

'I don't think we ever went to such a place,' said Pauline, 'but it does sound awfully familiar. Just give me a minute will you?'

She brought a tin down from one of the bookshelves and scattered its contents on the table. It was full of all kinds of rubbish, a keychain with a plastic Eiffel Tower on one end, an old cigarette lighter, a ticket for an exhibition at the Prada, a postcard from Rhodes. And there, amid the detritus of Pauline's travels and memories, was a small laminated card which bore an image of a man in top hat and tails helping – or pushing? – a woman into a carriage.

'I don't think we ever went there,' said Pauline. 'Though I can't be sure. I think someone was handing these out in one of the other clubs.'

Annie thanked her and they left, grateful as before to get out of the cloying atmosphere.

'What was all that about?' Winsome asked.

'Something Alan asked about. Apparently this club has come up in connection with Rachel's disappearance, and he wanted to know if any of the others knew about it.'

'Well, he's got his answer, hasn't he?'

'Yes,' said Annie. 'I'll phone him when I get home.'

When they arrived at Annie's cottage, Winsome got out of the car and went up to the door with her, and they both went inside. Everything looked normal, but there was no sign of Krystyna. Annie checked upstairs and Winsome checked the kitchen.

'You'd better see this,' she said, when Annie came down.

Annie went into the kitchen and saw the cocoa tin where she kept her petty cash. It was open, and there was nothing but a brief note in Polish inside.

'How much was in there?' Winsome asked.

'About thirty quid.'

'She won't get far on that.'

There was also a note in Polish stuck to the fridge with a magnet shaped like a buttercup. Winsome put the kettle on and Annie returned to living room, flopped on the sofa and started to cry.

11

On Sunday morning around eleven, Banks took the lift down to the Metropol lobby and went out to meet Erik and Joanna for coffee in Viru Keskus. Last night he had spoken for a long time with Annie on the phone. She had been worried and upset by the disappearance of a young Polish girl who had been staying at Garskill Farm with the migrant workers. She had run away on the day Mihkel Lepikson had been killed, and Annie was worried that someone might think she knew too much and try to harm her. He had reassured her as best he could, but he could tell it hadn't done much good. Annie had also told him about Curly's lengthy, and quite perceptive, deposition, and that Rachel's friend, Pauline, remembered the club with no name, that she even had a card bearing its sign. Rachel, too, might have been given such a card, Banks thought, and if the place looked familiar to her, that might well have tempted her to go inside. Perhaps she had thought it was where her friends had gone after St Patrick's. Bit by bit, he felt, he was getting closer to the truth of what happened.

Annie had also come up with some more names Banks could try on Erik, including the name of the killer Robert Tamm. Surely it could only be a matter of time now? Perhaps most importantly, Joosep Rebane's name had come up in her inquiries into Corrigan's business, as well as in Banks's inquiries about the nightclub. Larisa had named him as Juliya's boyfriend. Now they had a direct link between Rebane,

Corrigan, Flinders and the whole migrant racket. But he still had to find out if, or where, Rachel fitted in.

He made his way inside and up the escalators. The shops were open, and the shopping centre was busy, even though it was Sunday. After a few wrong turns, he finally found the cafe in the large bookshop, where Erik had arranged for them all to meet. Estonians must be great readers, Banks thought, with so many huge bookshops in the capital.

Erik was sitting at a table alone drinking Coke from a bottle and reading a newspaper. Banks went and bought himself a coffee and joined him. People bustled all around them, carrying bags, looking for tables, heading to the shops.

'Where's your charming colleague?' Erik asked.

Banks checked his watch. 'Shopping,' he said. 'She'll be here soon. I want to thank you once again for that information you got for us the other day.'

'It helped?'

'A lot.'

'I spoke briefly with Merike last night, and she said you seemed happy with your talk with Larisa.'

'Interesting woman,' Banks said. 'And she was able to give us— Ah, the wanderer returns.'

Joanna bent down and set her bags and packages on the ground around the third chair, like presents under the Christmas tree. Banks noticed designer names he didn't recognise: Marc Aurel, Ivo Nikkolo. There would be no carry-on only going back for Joanna, Banks could see. She might have to buy a new suitcase. Ever the gentleman, Erik offered to go and get her something to drink, but she insisted on going herself. They waited politely until she returned with a bottle of fruit juice.

'We've got a few more names for you to check out, if you will,' said Banks.

'It's getting to be like a hall of mirrors,' said Joanna. 'Every time we get one name, it leads to another, and so on.'

'It's always like that when you're getting close,' said Banks. 'The storm before the calm.'

'Don't you mean—'

'No. It always gets more and more confusing until it settles down, when you know. The storm before the calm.'

'A good story can be like that, too,' Erik said. 'Mihkel knew that. He always talked of so many balls in the air. Like a juggler. Give me the names. I will try tomorrow. I feel like I am working for the British police.'

Banks laughed. 'We'd snap you up like a shot. First of all,' he said, 'I'm curious about a bloke called Robert Tamm. He lives near Glasgow, but my source thinks he's Eastern European, perhaps Estonian.'

'It could be an Estonian name,' said Erik.

Joanna looked puzzled, and Banks realised that he hadn't had a chance to talk to her since Annie's phone call. She had been in her room sleeping, he assumed, when Banks took the call, and he hadn't seen her so far that morning. This time, it was simply circumstances; he wasn't deliberately keeping her out of the loop. He explained to her briefly what he had learned, including that Joosep Rebane claimed to have a DI Bill Quinn in his pocket.

'So we're pretty sure this Robert Tamm is the killer?' she said, when he'd finished and she had scribbled some notes.

'So it would appear.'

'That's the case over, then, isn't it? I mean, I know we have to get the Glasgow police to go—'

'Hang on,' said Banks. 'Wait a minute. Are you going to abandon Rachel Hewitt, just like that? Like everyone else?'

'That's not fair. She's not our case.'

'Dismissing her isn't fair, either. She deserves more than that. She became our case. You said you were with me on that.'

'Yes, but only if it helped lead us to Quinn's killer. It has done, so we're finished now.'

'You can do what you want, but I'm not leaving Tallinn until I find out what happened to Rachel.'

'Don't be so melodramatic.'

'I'm not being melodramatic. We owe her. You know what your problem is? You lack—'

'If you will excuse me for interrupting, children,' Erik said, holding up his hand. 'Perhaps you two can save the argument for later? I do have to go home soon. My mother-in-law is coming for dinner.'

'Sorry,' said Banks, giving Joanna a dirty look, which she returned with bells on. 'Robert Tamm, yes. Perhaps you can find out if he has any Estonian underworld connections. Also, there's a nightclub on an alley off Vana-Posti. It doesn't have a name, but there's a sign of—'

'A gentleman helping the lady into a coach?'

'That's right. You know it?'

'I've passed by. I just assumed it was some sort of exclusive sex club.'

'It is now. Well, not that exclusive. They let me in. And there's a waitress from Wigan.'

'Then what do you need to know?'

'Its history,' said Banks. 'Specifically what sort of place it was and who owned it, or ran it, six years ago, when Rachel disappeared.'

Erik made a note. 'OK. Now you mentioned another name.'

'Joosep Rebane,' said Banks. 'We think he's the one who hired Tamm to kill Mihkel and Bill Quinn. He said he had Quinn in his pocket but started to get nervous as soon as Quinn's wife died.' Banks paused and waited for Erik to catch up, but he put down his pen. 'Well, aren't you going to write it down?' Banks went on. 'Joosep Rebane. I think I've got it right.'

'Oh, you have got it right, my friend,' said Erik. 'I don't even need to go to my files for that one. Where do you want me to begin?'

Annie had slept badly on Saturday night. She had tried to phone Stefan to see if she could beg him to come over and translate the note for her – or she would even drive out to his place – but all she got was his answering machine. She even got hold of Jan from Traffic, but he explained politely that, whereas he could manage a few phrases in Polish, he certainly couldn't read and translate the language. Annie realised when she got up that she had been lying awake waiting most of the night, waiting for a knock on the door, for a phone call that she wouldn't be able to understand. She tried Stefan's number again. Still no reply. *Bastard*, she thought. He must have picked up some slut or other and was still at her place for a morning shag. She wished it wasn't a Sunday, then she might be able to gather a posse, get an official search or something going. On the other hand, Krystyna wasn't a criminal; she was a victim. Annie didn't want to frighten her, make her feel she was being hunted and chased. God only knew what she would do then. She might also be a witness, able to help against Flinders and Robert Tamm, when the Glasgow police found him. But mostly she was a victim. She had no papers, no passport, but she was a citizen of the EU. Annie could report her missing, she supposed, but Krystyna was over eighteen, and they wouldn't exactly pull out all the stops so quickly, unless perhaps she stressed that the girl might be in danger because of something she knew. That was what worried Annie most, that Krystyna didn't realise the danger she was in, that she might go back to these people. The inactivity was driving her crazy. She needed to do something.

Krystyna hadn't known where her colleagues were being taken after leaving Garskill Farm on Wednesday morning, but Annie remembered that she had spoken of another Polish girl,

Ewa, who had been her friend at the farm and, Annie assumed, had also worked with her at the yeast factory. It didn't prove very difficult to locate Varley's Yeast Products in the phone directory, and given the hours that Flinders' agency demanded of its workers, it also seemed likely the place would be operating seven days a week.

Before she left, Annie tried Stefan one more time. Nothing. She left a message for him to call her as soon as possible on her mobile, and took Krystyna's note with her in case she got a chance to meet up with Stefan before going home again.

It wasn't a long drive to the northern edge of Eastvale. The shops soon gave way to housing estates, several leafy enclaves of the wealthy and, finally, after a stretch of wasteland, the old industrial estate where the yeast factory was located. The weather had turned wet, and wind lashed the rain against her car windows. Those few brave souls who had ventured outdoors, most likely on their way to or from church, struggled with umbrellas, many of which had blown inside out.

Annie arrived at the factory gates shortly after eleven in the morning, and she was pleased to find them open. There was a little gatehouse where visitors were required to report and sign in. Annie wound her window down and flashed her warrant card at the man on duty. He barely glanced up from his newspaper before waving her through. As soon as she had opened her window, she could smell the yeast, and she wondered what it must be like to work there day in, day out. It must permeate everything. How could you even get the smell off your skin or your clothes when you got home? Even if you had a decent bathtub or a shower, which the workers at Garskill Farm didn't.

There were several buildings scattered about the compound, and the yard was filled mostly with pallets, some of them loaded down with containers, others waiting, all getting wet. She found a place to park outside what appeared to be the offices, which must be working on a skeleton staff on a Sunday. She noticed a couple of people standing outside one of the other buildings having a smoke and went over to introduce herself. One of them told her she needed to talk to one of the white hats. She wouldn't find one inside the building they were closest to, he added, as that was where the yeast grew in vats. The white hats would most likely be over in the main building, where the yeast was processed.

Annie entered through a door at the far end and soon found herself in an open area, where several giant rollers, like the front wheels of bulldozers, turned slowly as the yeast coated them, dried and was shaved off by a fixed razor-sharp blade into large boxes, and then no doubt fed into the other machines. The smell was even stronger inside.

She found a white hat, which happened to be a trilby. He was also wearing a white coat and carrying a clipboard. He seemed to be standing around doing nothing, so she went over and showed her identification.

'Can I have a word somewhere?' she asked over the noise of the factory.

He jerked his head in the direction of a row of small offices, and when he closed the door behind him, the volume level dropped considerably. It was a shabby office, furnished only with a cheap desk, chair and gunmetal filing cabinet. There was an ashtray on the desk with several cigarette stubs in it. The room felt uncomfortably small to Annie with the two of them in there. 'Len', as he was called, was a red-faced, paunchy man in his fifties who, to Annie's eye, was fast heading for a coronary, if he hadn't had one already. He rested one buttock on the desk, which creaked in complaint. Annie remained standing by the door.

'I've come about some migrant labourers you employed here recently.'

The man's eyes narrowed. 'They come and go. That's nothing to do with me.'

'Are they here now?'

'Not any more. They wouldn't be in here, anyway. Most of them usually work over in the extracting department.'

'In particular, I'm trying to find a Polish girl. I think her name is Ewa. She's friends with another Polish girl who worked here until a week last Wednesday.'

'I don't know anything,' Len said. 'Like I said, they come and go. I don't know their names. As long as they do their jobs, I don't give a fuck what they're called. You'll have to try Human Resources, and they don't work on a Sunday. It's not my department.'

'Said Werner von Braun.'

'What?'

'Never mind. Thanks for your help.' Annie left the office, muttering 'arsehole' under her breath. She stood for a moment in the doorway watching the people work. Most seemed absorbed in their tasks, such as they were, and they didn't return her gaze. Krystyna certainly wasn't there. Not that Annie had expected her to be.

Before leaving the factory altogether, she thought she might as well drop by the extraction department and see if she could find out any more there. As there was only one large building left, she assumed that was it, dashed across the yard, avoiding puddles as best she could, and headed inside.

The factory floor was quiet, no thrum of machines or banging of gears and metal drums. There was one man, sans white hat, walking around the equipment, checking things and jotting notes on his clipboard. Annie coughed loudly enough that he could hear her, and he turned, surprised to see her there.

'Yes?' he said.

'Police.' Annie came forward and showed him her warrant card.

He put his clipboard down. 'What can I do for you?' He was younger than Len, and a lot more trim, as if he played football in a local league on Saturdays maybe.

'I'm looking for someone who works here, or used to work here,' Annie said. 'Len over in the other building said I'd have a better chance here.'

The man, who introduced himself as Dennis, laughed. 'Len's very old school. There's nothing much he doesn't know about yeast.'

'How can you stand the smell?' Annie asked.

Dennis shrugged. 'You get used to it, like anything else.'

'Hmm. Anyway, I understand you employ a number of migrant labourers around here?'

'That's right, though I don't actually do the employing. That would be the personnel officer, or Human Resources as they call it now. I believe we have a contract with Rod's Staff Ltd, who supply most of the workers.'

'Do you know anything about them?'

'What do you mean?'

'The conditions they live in, the wages they're paid, that sort of thing.'

'No. I just make sure they do their jobs, and they're treated well enough on the shop floor, get their tea breaks and all. There's quite a turnover. As you can imagine, nobody wants to do this sort of work for very long.'

Annie took in the row of industrial washing machines and the racks of hanging canvas sheets, about twenty of them in a row, stretching from one side of the room to the other. 'What kind of work would that be?'

'As you can see, we're not in operation normally today. We have to do maintenance and equipment checks once in a while. That's me. As a rule, we make the yeast extract here.

Basically, you force the yeast through those canvas sheets and collect what gets through to the far end. It's concentrated and thick by then, sort of like Marmite.'

Annie felt her stomach churn. She hated Marmite, more because of its consistency than its taste. 'What do you do with the used canvas?' she asked.

'That's what the big washing machines are for. You flip them in there and wash them. It's a dirty job because by then they're covered in slime. It's sort of the consistency of—'

'I can guess, thanks,' said Annie. 'You don't have to spell it out.'

'They usually wear neck-to-toe leather aprons.'

'I'll bet they do. Do you remember a young Polish girl, very thin, short dark hair, pretty if she had a chance. She could hardly lift one of those canvases.'

'She sounds familiar, but as I said, they come and go. A lot of them are thin and seem none too healthy.'

'Haven't you ever wondered why?'

'Not really my business. I assumed it was because of where they come from. Poor national diet.'

'As opposed to the north of England, where we all eat so well?'

'No need to be sarcastic. I'm only saying.'

'Sorry.' Annie scratched her head, thinking a visit from Trading Standards might be in order. Or Immigration. 'Sorry. It's just a bit frustrating, that's all.'

'There was a girl hanging around the gates this morning about the time the shift started. She sort of fits your description. She might have worked here at some time.'

'Did anyone talk to her?'

'I don't think so. We get quite a few Eastern European girls here. Poles, Ukrainians, Lithuanians, Estonians and Latvians.'

'That'll be Rod's Staff connections.'

'I suppose so. If it's illegal immi—'

'No, no,' said Annie. 'I know we're one big happy family now they're all in the EU. They might not all have the correct or up-to-date permits and visas, but we won't worry about a little thing like that.'

'Then what is it?'

'Murder.'

Dennis swallowed. 'I knew something was up,' he said.

'What do you mean?'

'When they didn't turn up for their shift yesterday.'

'Who didn't?'

'The nine people we've been employing from Rod's Staff. The van usually drops them off at eight o'clock. Yesterday it didn't turn up.'

'Why not?'

'No idea. The boss was furious. They've always been relia-ble before. That's one reason we use Flinders. But the boss got no warning at all. He couldn't get in touch with the Rod's Staff office. Mind you, it is a weekend, and most offices are shut.'

'So none of the casual labour turned up for work yesterday, but this girl you think might have been Polish, and you might have seen working here, was standing at the gate this morning?'

'Yes.'

'Could she have been one of the Rod's Staff girls?'

'She could have been. Yes.'

'What happened to her?'

'A car came, and she got into it.'

'Whose car?'

'Roderick Flinders. I know because I've seen him here before.'

'What make of car?'

'A grey Clio.'

'What happened?'

'I don't know. I wasn't watching. I was just crossing the yard, coming here, as a matter of fact, when I saw her walk out of the gatehouse and get in the car.'

'Did she get in of her own free will?'

'I suppose so. I mean, I think I'd have noticed a struggle. I can't really say I paid a lot of attention. I had other things on my mind.'

'It's all right, Dennis,' said Annie. 'I've finished now. You can put it out of your mind again. For the moment.' Then she turned away and walked off.

When she got in her car, out of the rain, Annie thought things over and realised that Flinders would certainly have heard about what happened to Corrigan, and that would have shaken him up a bit. He wouldn't necessarily know *who* had shot Corrigan and Curly, that it was an angry parent of a girl their organisation had exploited, or why, so he might well have imagined that it was something to do with the murdered policeman and journalist, and that the whole enterprise was falling apart. Perhaps he thought that he himself was next for the chop. The sensible thing to do would be to abandon ship.

And no doubt Joosep Rebane back in Estonia, or wherever he lived, would have heard the news by now, too, and his most sensible course of action would be to extricate himself as completely as possible from the whole business. Three murders meant way too much pressure and scrutiny. Best to wash his hands and walk away.

But where, Annie wondered, did that leave Krystyna? And how had she got to the yeast factory? She probably knew the name of the place, Varley's, having seen it day after day, and she had enough money for a taxi. She thought she would find Ewa there, but she had found Roderick Flinders instead.

Annie stopped at the gatehouse on the way out. The man was still reading his paper.

'Got a minute?' she asked.

He acted as if it were a great hardship to tear himself away from the *Sunday Sport*.

'What is it?'

'There was a young girl here earlier this morning. She was seen coming out of your office and getting in a car, Roderick Flinders' car.'

'That's right.'

'Want to tell me why?'

'Because Mr Flinders asked me to get in touch with him if I saw any of them. They weren't supposed to be here, see. He'd placed them all somewhere else, but I suppose not all of them knew. She couldn't speak English, anyway.'

'You work for Flinders?'

'No. Varley's. But he treats me well, and I keep an eye on his crews. It's good for everyone.'

'What did she want?'

'I think she was looking for someone. She kept saying a name. Sounded like Eva. I told her to come in out of the rain and sit down for a minute and I'd try to find out for her.'

'And you phoned Flinders.'

'Yes.'

'What did he say?'

'To keep her there, and he'd be over as soon as he could. He only lives about fifteen minutes' drive away. I gave her a fag and a cup of tea. She seemed content enough. A bit nervous, maybe.'

'And Flinders took her away?'

'She went with him. He nodded when she said Eva, to let her know he knew what she meant and he could help her, like.'

'Where did he take her?'

'Now, how the hell should I know?'

'So, am I to understand that Joosep Rebane is something of a celebrity?' said Banks, lowering his voice. Joanna had stopped sulking and pricked up her ears now.

'Celebrity criminal, you might say,' Erik answered, scratching at his bushy beard. 'Nothing proven, of course.'

'Of course,' said Banks.

'It does not harm his reputation that he looks like a rock star and has the lifestyle to match,' Erik went on.

'But I'll bet he doesn't play an instrument.'

'He plays many. The gun. The knife. The baseball bat.'

'A veritable symphony,' muttered Joanna.

Banks sipped some coffee. It was cold but strong.

'Thirty-one years old, and for the past four of them, he's been the leading man in the drug-dealing and people-trafficking rackets and, clearly, also is involved in these migrant labour schemes that your friend and Mihkel have been investigating. Baltic Mafia. Estonia is not a destination, you understand, but it is a route. Rebane is a skilled fac— what is the word?'

'Factotum? Facilitator?' Banks suggested.

'Facilitator. Yes. He has connections with all the organised criminal groups in Eastern Europe, especially the Russians, but in some ways he stands very much alone and aloof. Very Estonian.'

'Have the cops ever got close to him?'

'It is possible,' Erik said. 'But I do not know. My guess would be that he always has someone powerful on the inside. He greases the palms. Is that how you say it?'

'That's how we say it.'

'We have corruption here, like everywhere. Police, local government, parliament, for all I know.'

'You say he's been in the business for about four years?'

'Yes. Before that he was just another wild, spoiled, rich kid who got away with far too much, and spent his time with the wrong sort of people. He came to prominence in his own right when a storage container full of illegal immigrants was found at Southampton docks. A container that was discovered to have shipped from Tallinn. You may remember the incident.

Two of the people inside were dead. Of course, there was no evidence to link him to the crime, but his name was whispered in many circles, and it soon became something to fear.'

'Was the newspaper involved?'

'We could not name him, but we came as close as we could without risking a libel suit. His father is Viktor Rebane, a very famous and powerful businessman. He was fortunate enough to be able to buy into utilities after the Soviets left and everything was privatised.'

'I wonder what he thinks of his son.'

'Viktor Rebane has never spoken publicly on the subject. He is a very well respected figure, himself, but he must be aware of his son's activities. Sources, however, say he becomes furious every time Joosep's name is linked to some crime or bad behaviour, but he can do nothing to stop him. Joosep is headstrong.'

'Did Mihkel write about Joosep?'

'Yes. In "*Pimeduse varjus*".'

'So there was no love lost between them?'

'Pardon?'

'I mean, they didn't like each other.'

'I do not know if they ever met. I do not think so. But no. Mihkel recognised Joosep Rebane for what he was, a thug come into power. And Mihkel could be merciless in his attack, so that everyone knew who he meant.'

'Does Joosep have a reputation with women, too?'

'There have been complaints. Rape. Violence. All withdrawn.'

'Any deaths?'

'None that could be directly linked to him.'

'His name comes up six years ago,' Banks explained, 'when Larisa worked at the club, and her friend Juliya was Joosep Rebane's girlfriend for a while. Juliya left town rather suddenly around the time Rachel disappeared. Larisa thinks she went back to Belarus. His name has also come up more recently in connection with Warren Corrigan, Roderick Flinders, and their migrant worker scheme. Rebane probably runs the agencies here, Flinders does the staffing and accommodation in northern England, and Corrigan puts them all in debt. Nice little scam. Robert Tamm is probably Rebane's enforcer, or one of them. Can you search around for any links?'

'I can try,' said Erik. 'But as I told you, he's low profile. He manages to keep his name out of the newspapers. Even ours.'

'Yes, but people know things. You, for a start. You know things you can't print. I'm not after evidence I can use in court, just something that might help me sort this whole mess out and find out what happened to Rachel. I'd also like to know where I can find Joosep Rebane.'

Erik laughed. 'That is very unlikely to happen,' he said. 'Rebane has the money and contacts to disappear, and if he has any sense that is exactly what he will do the way things are now.'

Joanna sighed. 'The case is over,' she said again. 'Or it will be when the Scottish police pick up Robert Tamm and deliver him to Eastvale. My priority, after what you just told me, is to get back home and interview this Gareth Underwood.'

'Fine, then,' said Banks. 'Why don't you go home? Be my guest. You'd have found out more if you'd stayed there in the first place, wouldn't you?'

'Maybe I will go back if you keep playing the tough guy, going off hunting hardened criminals. What is this, a pissing competition?'

'My job.'

'Well, don't expect me to scrape you up off the street.'

'Please,' said Erik. 'You must stop quarrelling. People will think you're in love. And while you're here, you should try some real Estonian food. It will help you make peace. There is a very good restaurant on Vana-Posti called Mekk. Have you tried it?'

They both said no.

'Go there tonight, eat some smoked eel and roast duck and bury the hammer.'

'It's hatchet,' said Joanna. 'And I don't like eels.'

'Whatever. Veal cheeks, then. I will make a reservation for you myself. Seven o'clock.' He wagged his finger. 'Do not be late. And be thinking of me having dinner with my mother-in-law.' He picked up his newspaper, put on his cap and waved goodbye. 'I will be in touch.'

Joanna gathered her shopping bags, and they followed Erik down the stairs and out of the Viru Keskus. They were just across the road from their hotel, but it was a wide road and the system of traffic lights was a little haphazard.

Banks stole a glance at Joanna as they waited for a light to change, a tram rumbling by. 'What do you think?' he asked.

'You know what I think.'

'I mean what Erik said. Mekk. Burying the hammer. Seven o'clock.'

'I suppose I've got to eat.'

'Once more with enthusiasm.'

They arrived at the hotel. Joanna favoured him with a small smile. 'I'll meet you in the bar here at half past six,' she said, and headed for the lift, manoeuvring her packages. Banks made for the bar, but before he got very far the receptionist called his name. 'Hr Banks?'

'Yes.'

'I have message for you.' She took a small envelope from under the desk and handed it to him.

'Did you see who delivered it?' he asked.

'No. Sorry. I just come on.'

'It doesn't matter. Thank you.' Banks tapped the envelope against his palm thoughtfully as he took a stool at the bar and ordered a beer. Who was it from? Rätsepp? Merike? Ursula Mardna? There was only one way to find out. He was thirsty from the day's walking and from the sticky, unpleasant taste of cold coffee. When he had taken a few sips of chilled beer, he turned the envelope over in his hand and opened it. There was no signature, just a short message in block capitals. 'MONDAY 1400 PATAREI. COME ALONE.'

Stefan Nowak lived in one of the new luxury apartments about half a mile outside town, down by the river. The building used to be an old monastery, but it had been gutted and converted into a number of apartments of all shapes and sizes. Stefan's was one of the smaller units, but he had a balcony and a fine view down to the riverbank and the woods beyond.

His answer to Annie's message had been brusque and clipped, but he had agreed to see her if she would drop by. This she did after she left the yeast factory. His flat was, as she expected, immaculate and tasteful, with framed prints of art exhibitions and classic movies on the wall, module or Ikea-style furniture, and not a speck of dust to be seen. She had to admit, whatever he had been doing last night and this morning, he didn't seem at all the worse for wear. Casually dressed in jeans and a black polo neck, he looked every bit as cool and elegant as ever. The room smelled vaguely of cinnamon, and Annie wondered if Stefan had given his date cinnamon buns for breakfast before kicking her out. Did he bake them himself? That would be too good to be true. The smell reminded her that she hadn't eaten anything since last night. She had been so worried about Krystyna.

Stefan frowned as he read over the notes. 'I'm afraid the grammar and spelling aren't very good,' he said. 'And her handwriting . . .'

Annie was sure her mouth flapped open. It felt as if it did. It was hard to get the words out. 'You bloody complain about the spelling in a language that as far as I can see has nothing but consonants with funny squiggles on them?'

'It matters,' Stefan said. 'And if you understood anything at all about the Polish language, you would know it's not as simple as that.' He waved the note. 'This girl is barely literate.'

'What do you expect?' Annie said. 'She's from a poor working-class area, and she ran away hoping for a better future here and ended up working in a bloody yeast factory. I've been there. Believe me, Stefan, you wouldn't want to set one Camper-shod foot in the place. Can you just please translate the fucking note.'

Stefan stared at her, perplexed and annoyed, but he started to translate, anyway, stumbling and correcting himself here and there to make his point. 'This first one's quite easy,' he said. 'It says "I owe you thirty-two pounds sixty. Sorry. I will pay back." In the other note she says she's very sorry and she thanks you for all you've done for her. Also the clothes and money that she promises to pay back. She stole money from you, Annie?'

'Borrowed. The poor creature couldn't even go to the shop and buy a chocolate bar or a packet of fags, for Christ's sake.' Krystyna must have seen Annie take some cash from an old cocoa tin in one of the kitchen cupboards to pay for the takeaway, and she had stolen the rest, but she wasn't going to admit that to Stefan. 'Carry on.'

'There's not much more,' Stefan went on. 'She wants to find out what has happened to her friends, to Ewa particularly, and she can't sleep until she knows they are all right. She was foolish to run away without saying goodbye. She will be in touch with you when she can. There's a heart and—'

'Yes, I could read that bit, thank you,' said Annie, snatching the note back.

Stefan shook his head. 'Annie, why are you getting so involved? It's not like you. Do you know what you're getting yourself into? You're letting this get to you, you know. It will only end badly.'

'What do you mean?'

'The girl. She's a user. Probably a junkie as well as a thief.'

'She's no junkie.'

'But she is a thief, isn't she? She stole that money from you, didn't she?'

'What makes you say that?'

'Her words. The way she says it in the note. I didn't translate exactly, but she says something about being sorry for money she *took*.'

'You bastard!' Annie felt her face burning. She had no answer for Stefan's questions. Had no idea why she was going out on a limb for this pathetic young girl, who had lied and stolen and taken advantage of her hospitality, and left without so much as a by your leave. Perhaps it was because she had watched the way she ate the Big Mac and fries in the interview room, and then cleaned up after herself with the serviette. Or the way she had watched the American cop shows intently while eating her takeaway, although she didn't understand a word. It was true that she was unsophisticated, but that didn't mean she had no manners or breeding. Or feelings. It was true she was a thief and liar, but those are habits that are easy to come by when you are exploited and have nothing of your own. Did Annie want to change her? Maybe. But all she had really wanted to do was offer the hand of friendship in a world that had so far proved unfriendly.

She grabbed her jacket, thanked Stefan grudgingly and went back down to the car. After she had sat down and taken a few deep breaths, gripping the wheel tight, she phoned Winsome who, as she had guessed, was at the station. 'You did say to call if I needed anything,' she said. 'Are you up for an adventure?'

'I know you don't approve of my direction on this,' Banks said, between tastes of delicious smoked eel, 'but I just feel that we've got so close to solving the mystery of Rachel Hewitt, it would be a disservice to her parents, for a start, if we just turned away now.'

'I'm not as heartless as you think I am,' said Joanna. 'I'm just not used to the ways of . . . the ways you . . . I mean, I haven't been involved in this kind of investigation before. When you explained it to me the other night, that finding out what happened to DI Quinn might depend on finding out what happened to Rachel Hewitt, I understood. It made sense. But we know who killed Bill Quinn now. It's just a matter of finding him and bringing him in. Rachel Hewitt isn't your case. Never was. We should go home. But you're all over the place. Usually things are a lot more focused and straightforward in my job.'

'True. But you're here to learn, aren't you? You do want to make a move out of Professional Standards. We do things differently here.'

'You're telling me.'

'What I was going to say back at the coffee shop was that you lack breadth of vision. That's the difference between your job and mine. And if you want to make a move, you're going to have to learn to think in a different way. Yes, you could argue that you've solved your case. Or Annie has. We know who killed Bill Quinn and Mihkel Lepikson, and he'll no doubt soon be in custody. There's probably enough forensic evidence to put him away even if he doesn't sign a confession. We also know that Quinn was bent, in thrall to Joosep Rebane, and through him to Warren Corrigan. For you, it stops there. That completes your chain of thought. But Rachel Hewitt hasn't been found, and we have several leads on what might have happened to her. Now, you might worry about expenses and justification, but I'd pay my own hotel bill and airfare to stay here and settle my curiosity about what happened to Rachel and, with any luck, give her parents a bit of peace. That's the difference between us.'

'What? You're a romantic, a knight in shining armour, a tilter at windmills?'

'I've been called worse.'

'I'll bet. But isn't it someone else's job now?'

'Probably. Technically. Officially. But I'm doing it. You can either come along with me, or go back to Eastvale and write your report.'

Banks ate some smoked eel. It was delicious. He had to admit that Erik had done them proud. Not only a reservation, but attentive service, a table for two in a quiet corner far from the kitchen and toilet doors. He must have told the maître d' that they were VIPs. The restaurant was a joy, with its modern decor, dark orange walls, muted lighting and unusual food. Banks's smoked eel came with potato cakes and a horseradish sauce, among other things. Joanna Passero's artichoke soup came with pork crisps and rye bread.

'What do you think about your precious DI Quinn, now you know a bit more about what happened?' Joanna asked.

'Bill Quinn let himself get compromised. He was a fool. He should have known to stay away from Larisa, that she was a honeytrap. It's not the first time that trick's been used. They caught him off his guard, just like Robert Tamm did at St Peter's. Do I feel sorry for him? Yes. Do I condone what he did? No. There were other ways out.'

'Like telling the truth?'

'That's one strategy. Not necessarily the best in his case.'

'But whatever strategy he used, it got him killed.'

'Yes. Like too many other people in this case. But we also have to think of the good ones left alive. Rachel's parents. Erik. Merike. Larisa. Even Curly, if what Annie tells me is true about him wanting to go straight.'

They finished their starters and sipped some more wine, then the mains came: duck fillet for Banks and baked cod for Joanna. Much as Banks spent far too much of his time microwaving Indian takeaways, eating fish and chips on the move and munching on Greggs pies, he loved a fine meal when he got the chance. Joanna made sounds of delight at her first mouthful, then stopped to check her mobile. Whatever it was she saw, it made her frown.

'What is it with that?' Banks asked.

'What do you mean?'

'Your mobile. I know people get obsessed with checking their email on the go, and all that – it makes them behave rudely at dinner parties – but you're never off it. It's as if you're waiting for the announcement of the end of the world or something. What is it that's so important?'

Joanna gave a sound halfway between a sniff and a snort. 'It's nothing,' she said, snapping the case and putting her mobile away. 'It's personal. Private.' She wouldn't meet his eyes. 'None of your bloody business.'

'Don't you think we know each other well enough by now, even if no one could call us the best of friends? And if we're working together, it is my business. It's a distraction.'

Joanna raised her eyes, and Banks saw a vulnerability and pain in them that he had never noticed before. She must have realised because she quickly reasserted her usual ice-maiden manner. 'It's nothing.'

'Come on, Joanna.'

'Why do you want to know?'

'My curious nature.'

'So you can laugh at me, make fun of me?'

'What? Why would I do that?'

'You've been doing it right from the start.'

'So what is it? Come on. Tell me. I promise I won't make fun of you.'

Joanna toyed with her food, obviously trying to decide whether to tell him or not. In the end, she averted her eyes and said. 'It's my husband. I think he's having an affair.'

'So who keeps texting you?'

'A colleague. I asked her if she'd keep an eye on him, see if anything unusual happened.'

'And has it?'

She nodded. 'The bastard.'

Banks could tell that she was welling up by the way she kept her eyes down on her food. He didn't say anything for a while, but when he sensed she was in control again he rested his hand on her arm and said, 'I'm sorry, Joanna. Really, I am.'

She looked at him then, and he thought she seemed surprised by his words and his tone. At least she didn't jerk her arm away. 'The thing is,' she said, 'I should have seen it coming. He's Italian. He's always maintained that it's perfectly OK for the husband to take a mistress. I feel such a fool. I always thought he was teasing, you know, but . . .'

'What are you going to do?'

'I've been trying to decide. I'll have to have it out with him when I get back, of course, then I'm leaving him. We don't have any children, so that's one less thing to stand in my way. I can't bear it. I can't bear living like this. Some people might be able to put up with such behaviour, but I can't do it. I've got a nice flat in Northallerton, I like it there, so I might as well just stay up north.' She smiled. 'I'd still like to work in some other unit. Maybe I'll chase after your job.'

'You're welcome,' said Banks. 'Do you still love him?'

'What kind of a question is that?' Joanna said nothing for a while, just stared down at the tablecloth. Then she spoke so softly that Banks could hardly hear her. 'Yes.'

They ate on in silence, Joanna quaffing her wine rather quickly now, and needing a refill well before Banks. 'So now you know everything about me,' she said, when she was able to manage a cavalier, fuck-it-all tone in her voice.

'I doubt that,' said Banks. 'But I am sorry to hear about your problems. I've been there. If you ever want—'

She waved her hand. 'No, it's fine, thanks. I don't need to talk about it. I don't suppose your wife was unfaithful to you, was she?'

'As a matter of fact, she was. Knocked me for a six.'

She looked at him as if seeing him for the first time. 'Well, well. Wonders never cease. And I'd have thought . . .'

'That I'd be the one at fault?'

'Yes.'

'I'm not saying I wasn't at fault.'

Joanna studied him for a moment. 'For some reason,' she said, 'I find myself unusually hungry after this conversation. Have you got room for pudding?'

'I think so,' said Banks. 'And I've got a little job I'd like you to help me with tomorrow.'

There was a grey Clio parked in front of the newish, detached house outside Eastvale, and the man who answered the door seemed very nervous indeed. When Annie and Winsome showed their identification, he kept the door on the chain while asking them what they wanted.

'Mr Flinders?' Annie asked. 'Roderick Flinders of Rod's Staff Ltd?'

'What if I am?'

'Mind if we come in for a moment?'

'As a matter of fact, I'm busy. It's not convenient.'

Annie gave him the scathing look she reserved for the most obvious liars, and after a thirty-second staring match, during which she could swear she saw sweat break out on his brow, Flinders shut the door, fiddled with the chain, and opened it to let them in, ushering them towards the living room at the front. The furniture was all slightly old-fashioned, as if it had been bought at auctions. The large plasma TV was probably worth a small fortune. Flinders himself was not quite what she had expected of the sleazy exploiter of unskilled labour, but an overweight, red-faced, balding man in his early fifties, wearing a chunky-knit cardigan, who looked as if he would be more at home behind a desk in an insurance office than shepherding poor migrant workers around from factory to factory. His skin was baby smooth and had the sheen of wet plastic. Still, Annie realised, he didn't do much of the shepherding himself; he had minions and gangmasters to work for him.

'What is it?' he said, turning to face them. 'As I said, I'm very busy.'

'With what?' Annie asked.

'Pardon?'

Annie glanced around the room. 'What are you so busy with?' she asked. 'I don't see anything in here to occupy your time.'

'A business matter. In my home office.'

'Ah, I see. Then we'll get straight to the point. Winsome?'

Winsome consulted her notebook. 'We're investigating a series of infringements of the law under the Asylum and Immigration Act, and the Anti-Slavery Act,' said Winsome. There was no Anti-Slavery Act, but it sounded more dramatic than Coroners and Justice Bill, under which such matters came.

'What are you talking about?' Flinders cried. 'I'm a legitimate businessmen. Everyone who goes through my company is closely vetted. We have no truck with asylum seekers or illegal immigrants.'

'They don't need to be illegal, sir,' Winsome went on. 'All we need to prove is that violence, intimidation or deception were used to bring a migrant worker into the country.'

'And, of course,' Annie added, 'moving people around the country without their consent is also a form of trafficking under the law, and is therefore prosecutable under the Act. Sentences can be rather excessive, as many judges take a dim view of these activities. In other words, mate, you could get banged up for a long time.'

'But I've done nothing wrong.'

'Do you know a man called Warren Corrigan?'

Flinders averted his eyes. 'I've met him.'

'Perhaps you've heard he was shot on Friday evening?'

'I . . . yes . . . I . . . on the news. It's terrible. Just terrible.'

'Indeed it is,' said Annie. 'A real tragedy. Do you know the circumstances under which he was shot?'

'No. I don't know who did it, either. I was here at home. It was nothing to do with me.'

'We know that, sir. But we understand that you met with Mr Corrigan on a number of occasions?'

'We did some business together, yes.'

'What sort of business would that be?'

'Business of a financial nature. Warren was a financier.'

'That's a nice name for it, isn't it?' said Annie. Winsome nodded.

'For what?' Flinders demanded.

'Loan shark.'

Flinders did his best to appear indignant, but succeeded only in looking more scared. 'I know nothing about that. As far as I was concerned, Warren Corrigan was a legitimate businessman, like myself.'

'"Like me",' corrected Annie. 'What about Mihkel Lepikson?'

'Who?'

'The Estonian journalist found murdered at Garskill Farm.'

'I know nothing about that.'

'But you know Garskill Farm, don't you?'

'Yes. The company used it as temporary accommodation for some of our workers.'

'The "company" being you?'

'Well, yes.'

'I'm glad to hear it was only temporary,' Annie said, 'though it turned out to be a bit more permanent for Mihkel Lepikson.'

'I told you, I don't know him.'

'Did you visit Garskill Farm the other Wednesday morning?'

'No, I didn't.'

'I'm not sure if I believe you,' said Annie. 'Still, we'll leave that for the moment. Mind if we have a look around?'

'Have you got a search warrant?'

'No, But I'd be happy to wait here with you while Winsome goes and gets one.' She glanced at her watch. 'I must remind you, though, it's Sunday, and magistrates can be awfully hard to find on a Sunday. It's unlikely we'd be able to get hold of one until tomorrow morning, at the earliest. In the meantime, we might as well take you to the station, and you can spend a night in the cells. Don't worry. It's not as terrible as it sounds. It might not be as comfortable as this place, but you get three square meals a day, there's a working toilet and the showers are hot.'

'All right. Get on with it then.'

'Like to give us the guided tour?'

Flinders led them around the house – his office, first, with the filing cabinets and computer, which would definitely be worth a search warrant in itself – then a large well-equipped kitchen complete with island and pots and pans hanging from a ceiling fixture, too spick and span to have been used recently, a cloakroom, plenty of cupboard space, dining room with heavy dark wood table and overstuffed chairs. Upstairs were four bedrooms, two of which were empty, and one of which was set up for guests.

'Do you live here all alone?' Annie asked.

'My wife and I have separated,' said Flinders. 'I've been thinking of selling the place and moving somewhere smaller, but the market is poor.'

'Oh. Sorry to hear that. About your wife, I mean.'

The final room was Flinders' bedroom. He seemed reluctant to open the door, but he clearly sensed that he wasn't in much of a position to refuse. Two suitcases lay open on the four-poster bed, half filled with clothes and toiletries.

Annie glanced at Winsome and raised her eyebrows. 'Going somewhere, Mr Flinders?'

'If you must know, I was planning on taking a short holiday. It's been a stressful time at work lately. My heart ... angina, you see.'

'Somewhere nice, I hope?'

'Acapulco.'

'Very nice. All alone?'

'Yes.'

'What about the business?'

'It can run itself for a little while. I have helpers. One needs to recharge one's batteries every now and then. Even a police detective should know that.'

Annie laughed. 'I've been recharging mine for the past few months. They're in pretty good shape by now. Right, Winsome?'

'Right,' said Winsome, smiling.

Flinders' chin started to wobble. 'You can't possibly read anything into this,' he said. 'It's a coincidence, that's all.'

'What's a coincidence?'

'Well, you know ...'

'No. Tell me.'

'You coming here just before I was about to leave. I know it might appear bad, but ...'

'And here's me thinking you meant us coming here after Warren Corrigan was shot, and after Mihkel Lepikson was murdered by a hired killer called Robert Tamm, in your presence.'

'I wasn't there, I tell you!'

'We think you were.' Annie actually doubted that Flinders had the bottle to watch Robert Tamm torture and drown Mihkel Lepikson, but she was aiming for maximum discomfort. People seemed to think the police fitted people up all the time, so why not let Flinders believe that he was going to get fitted up for conspiracy to murder.

Flinders licked his lips. 'I should go. I have to get to the airport. I have a flight to catch.'

'I don't think that's going to happen,' said Annie. 'You might as well relax and get used to the idea. I hope you took out some cancellation insurance.'

'But you can't . . . I mean, I have freedom of movement. I—'

'Like your workers?'

'I resent that.'

'Shut up, Mr Flinders I'm sick of your whining. Where's Krystyna?'

'Who?'

'Krystyna? The girl you picked up this morning at the yeast factory where some of your migrant crew used to work.'

'I don't know wh—'

'You were seen. Your car was seen. Your man in the gate-house told me everything. Didn't seem to think he'd done anything wrong. We know that nobody showed up for their shift yesterday morning, the morning after Corrigan was killed. We think you're running scared because you're worried that what happened to him might happen to you. You cut the crew loose, but the guard on the gate phoned you when he saw Krystyna hanging around the gates. She was looking for her friend Ewa. Krystyna had been gone for over a week, since the day Mihkel Lepikson was killed, in fact. You were worried she knew something. What have you done with her?'

Flinders was very red. He flopped into an armchair beside the bed and his head sank to his chest. His breathing sounded laboured. Annie glanced at Winsome, a little alarmed, worried that he'd had a heart attack or something. He fumbled in his pocket, brought out a little cylinder, then opened his mouth and sprayed lightly under his tongue. 'Nitro-glycerin,' he said, patting his chest.

Annie knelt so that her eyes were level with the top of Flinders' head and spoke softly. 'Take it easy. It's all over now, Roddy. Tell us where she is and things will go better for you.'

'I never wanted any of this,' Flinders said. 'Nobody was supposed to get killed. Nobody. Do you understand? That wasn't part of the plan. I abhor violence. Nobody was supposed to die. I had nothing to do with any killing.'

Annie felt a chill run through her. Was he referring only to Corrigan, Quinn and Lepikson, or did he mean that Krystyna was dead, too? 'That's what you get for playing with the big boys. You can't just pick up your toys and go home whenever you want. You're in, and you're in deep. Accessory to murder. It'll help if you tell us where Krystyna is.'

Flinders raised his mournful, tear-stained face to hers. 'I told you, I don't know. I haven't see her.'

'But you do know her?'

'If you say she's one of my workers, then I suppose I must do. I don't know them all by name. Can't even pronounce most of them.'

'Have you hurt her, Roddy?'

'I haven't hurt anyone.'

They went back downstairs. Annie looked towards the open kitchen. 'Is there a cellar here?'

'No.' Flinders answered just a little too quickly, and sounded just a little too desperate.

Annie pointed to a door beside the stainless steel fridge. 'Where does that door lead?'

'Nowhere. It's just a larder.'

'I'll go see,' Annie said to Winsome. 'Why don't you stay here and keep Mr Flinders company? He still seems a bit peaky to me. We don't want him having a coronary or something, do we?'

'You can't do this. It's private. It's—'

But Annie had already opened the door, and what she saw was a flight of stairs leading down to a basement. It probably wasn't a cellar in the old sense, coal cellars having been out of fashion for many years now, but a lot of modern houses had basement areas that could be used for storage, entertainment rooms, or even extra living space. Annie flicked the light switch, but nothing happened.

She turned to Flinders across the room. 'No lights?'

'I never go down there.'

'Got a torch?'

'No.'

Annie searched through the drawers and cupboards in the kitchen, and finally found a small torch, along with a box of candles and matches. She checked to make sure the battery worked and set off down the wooden steps. The basement floor was concrete, and the large area under the house was separated into a number of rooms or storage areas by wooden partitions. Annie could make out some lawn furniture, an old barbecue, a bicycle with flat tyres, an upturned wheelbarrow, some camping equipment, an ancient radiogram.

She stood still, shone her torch into the dark the corners and walls and called out, 'Krystyna!'

She thought she heard a sound. Hardly daring to breathe, she listened closely. It could be a mouse or something, though it sounded more like a muffled voice trying to speak. She couldn't be completely clear where it was coming from, so she began a systematic search in the general direction.

In the third partitioned area she entered, the torchlight picked out a small bundle curled on the floor in the foetal position. On examination, this turned out to be because Krystyna's feet and arms were tied in such a way that she could stretch neither without tightening the rope around her neck.

Annie dashed over and tore off the sticky tape that covered Krystyna's lips, then she pulled out the rag that had been shoved in her mouth. Krystyna gagged and coughed while Annie worked on the ropes, which she finally managed to untie. When Krystyna was free at last, she threw her arms around Annie's neck and buried her face in her shoulder, crying and muttering thanks or prayers in Polish. Annie got her to her feet, and together they made their way upstairs. When Annie appeared with Krystyna in the kitchen, Flinders held his head in his hands and wept.

'What were you going to do with her while you buggered off to Mexico, Rod? Leave her down there to starve or suffocate to death alone in the dark? She's half starved to start with. It wouldn't have taken long. Or had you been in touch with Robert Tamm? Was he going to come down and take care of her after you'd gone, do your dirty business for you? Like he killed Mihkel Lepikson and Bill Quinn?'

'That wasn't my idea,' said Flinders through his tears. 'None of it was my idea. I told you. Nobody was supposed to get killed. Nobody was supposed to get hurt.'

Annie stood up. For the first time in many a year she wanted to kick someone hard in the balls. But she suppressed the urge and tightened her arm around Krystyna. 'We'll sort out the blame later,' she said. 'First we'll get you to the station and see how sweetly you can sing.'

12

Stone walls do not a prison make | Nor iron bars a cage. The lines from the old poem came to Banks as he got out of the taxi in front of Patarei. Perhaps in some cases, that was true, he thought, but nobody had mentioned it to the builders of this prison. Beyond the rusted, graffiti-covered gates, a guard tower stood commanding a view over a prison yard overgrown with weeds and scattered with rubbish. The long grey brick building stretched alongside it.

Banks followed the signs to what he thought was the entrance, all the while keeping his eyes open for a tail. But he saw no one. Eventually he came to the entrance. Beside it stood a small ticket office in which an old woman sat alone. She took some euros from him, gave him a guidebook, then smiled, showing a relatively toothless mouth, and pointed the way in. Banks thought she was probably the first Estonian he had met who didn't seem to speak English. Perhaps she didn't speak at all.

Though it was warm and sunny outside, the interior of the old prison was dank and chilly. There were puddles on the floors and damp patches had discoloured the walls and ceilings. In places, the whitewash and plaster on the arched roof and the institutional green paint on the walls had peeled away to expose red brick underneath.

And the place smelled. Probably not as bad as when it was a functioning prison, but it smelled. Damp. Rot. Sweat. Fear.

Banks was alone, or so he thought until he walked into one of the cells to get a better look and saw a young couple already there, guidebook in hand. They might have been a honeymoon couple, handsome young man and pretty girl, and Banks wondered what the hell they were doing visiting such a place. They smiled, and he smiled back.

On the wall of the cell were head-and-shoulders shots of young girls, along with a few nude models. Further along the corridor, Banks passed what must have been an office. It was impossible to get in the doorway now, as it was piled almost to the top with rubbish, mostly old telephones, radio parts, bits of desks and chairs, papers, various broken circuit boards, and in front of it all, a rusty old mechanical typewriter. Banks crouched and saw that the keyboard was in Cyrillic script.

The next floor seemed to be have been devoted almost entirely to the prison hospital. The cells were larger, more like wards for ten or twelve people, with tubular-metal frame beds and thin stained mattresses. It reminded him of Garskill Farm. In the doctors' offices, medical forms, sheets of handwritten figures and old newspapers still littered the desks, next to old typewriters, again everything in Russian. One of the newspapers had a colour photograph of a beach and palm trees on the bottom corner, and Banks guessed it was probably an advert for vacations in the sun.

Worst of all were the operating theatres. Metal gurneys slatted like sinister beach recliners stretched under huge bug-eyed lamps beside old-fashioned machines with obscure dials and buttons, like something from a 1950s science-fiction movie. The glass-fronted cabinets still housed bottles of pills, phials, potions and boxes of ampoules and syringes. The tiles had come away from the walls in places to reveal damp stained plaster. The dentist's chair with the old foot-pedal drill just about did it for Banks. He moved along quickly, tasting bile.

He had been wandering for about fifteen minutes and was standing in an eerie room with splotchy brown and red walls when it happened. The sudden but surprisingly gentle voice came from behind him.

'They say it was used as a pre-trial holding facility, but have you ever seen an execution room in a pre-trial facility?'

Banks turned. The man behind him was youngish, mid-thirties perhaps, prematurely balding, with a goatee beard and moustache. He was slightly taller than Banks, and skinny, and he didn't seem in the least threatening. Banks recognised him immediately as the man who had been following him around Tallinn.

'You get my message, then?' he said, in heavily accented English.

'Who are you?' Banks asked.

'My name is Aivar Kukk. I was policeman many years ago.' Even though he spoke softly, his voice still echoed in the cavernous corridors of the decaying prison.

'Why have you been following me?'

'To make certain that you were not being followed by Hr Rätsepp or his men.'

'And am I?'

'Not that I have seen. Perhaps he does not see you as much of a threat.'

'To him? I'm not.'

'But you may be when we have finished talking. Even so, I do not think it is Hr Rätsepp you need to fear. Shall we be tourists? This is an interesting place. The execution room was used before it became a pre-trial holding facility, of course. It was first a sea fortress, but is most famous as Soviet-era prison. Many were executed and tortured here. Now art students work on projects, and there are exhibition openings and many other functions. People even get married here. It was to be an art college, but nobody can get rid of the damp.'

There seemed to be no one else around except the young couple about fifty yards down the corridor, Banks thought as he walked along with Aivar Kukk. He wondered if the young couple were thinking of getting married here. The arched corridors seemed to stretch on and on ahead for miles, and the chilly damp had seeped into his bones. Banks gave an involuntary shudder. 'I can believe it. So what's all the cloak-and-dagger stuff about?'

'I do not understand.'

'I mean why the note, and following me. And why meet here?'

'We will not be disturbed. You were not followed here. Patarei has just opened again for the tourist season. Nobody will come here at this time. Do you not think it is an interesting place?'

'All prisons give me the creeps.'

'This one certainly should.'

As they walked and talked, Banks wasn't paying quite as much attention to the crumbling decor and the claustrophobic cells, but in some places he noticed there was so much graffiti and paint splashed over the walls and floors, as if someone had let loose a bunch of drunken art students. 'How did you know I was here in Tallinn?' Banks asked.

'I read what happened to Bill Quinn in the English newspaper, and then Mihkel Lepikson. I knew it would be a matter of time. If nobody came soon, I would have sent a message. I still have friends in the department and at newspapers. We meet, drink beer, gossip, and they keep me informed. Tallinn is small city. Estonia is small country. Is not too difficult to know when a policeman comes from England, or what he is doing here.'

'And what *am* I doing here?'

'You are looking for killer of Bill Quinn and Mihkel Lepikson.'

'How do you know that?'

'Is not difficult. You have talked with Toomas Rätsepp, Ursula Mardna and Erik Aarma.'

'Anything else?'

'Yes. You are looking for Rachel Hewitt.'

'What makes you think that?'

'I saw you go in club, remember? Club with no name.'

Banks tried not to show how perplexed he was by all this. 'Seeing as you know so much of my business,' he said, 'perhaps you can tell me where Rachel is?'

'I am afraid I cannot. I do not know.'

'Then why are we here?'

'Please come here,' Aivar said, entering another open cell with rows of bunk beds in it. Banks followed him over to the window and saw through the bars the beautiful pale blue waters of the Baltic dancing with diamonds of sunlight, the undulating line of a distant shore across the bay. It made him think what the view must have been like from Alcatraz. He had looked out on the prison island from Fisherman's Wharf just last year, but he hadn't taken the boat out and seen the San Francisco skyline from the inside. He hated prisons, and he wouldn't have come here today if he hadn't been curious about the note.

'I think that must have been the greatest punishment of all,' said Aivar. 'To look on a view like that and to be locked in a cell.'

They remained silent, admiring the view that had represented unattainable freedom to so many. 'I can help you,' Aivar said finally. 'I was junior investigator. I work with Bill Quinn on original case.'

'I know,' said Banks. 'Ursula Mardna told me.'

'Ursula Mardna was good Prosecutor. Toomas Rätsepp was lead investigator. Boss. I was junior. But I work with Bill, all night we are asking questions, walking streets, just two, three days after girl disappear, as soon as we have some information where they had been drinking.'

'What really happened?'

'I have never told anyone.'

'Why not?'

'Fear. First for my job, then for my life. But now it is too late.'

'What do you mean?'

'I mean I no longer have anything to fear. Nothing anybody does can stop truth coming out now. Too many people know things. Too many people are asking questions. Murder was a desperate move.'

'We think Bill Quinn was killed because his wife died, and he got in touch with Mihkel about what really happened over here. There were photographs,' Banks said. 'A girl. Bill. Here in Tallinn. He was blackmailed. With his wife dead, they didn't matter.'

Aivar gazed out over the water, a sad, wistful look in his eyes. 'So that is what it was,' he said. 'I wonder how they get to him. They cannot use the same threats they use with me.'

'What do you mean?'

'Let's walk again.'

They left the cell. Banks just caught from the corner of his eye the figure of a blonde woman disappearing into a cell several yards away. Joanna Passero. Aivar clearly saw her, too. 'Your colleague?' he said, smiling.

'Inspector Passero.'

'A good idea. I approve. I do the same in your position. Perhaps she need to learn how to keep better hidden, but let her follow. Very beautiful woman, is she not?'

'What happened?'

Banks saw a small room off to the side that looked as if its walls had been splashed with blood from a bucket. Someone had drawn red hearts and written LOVE in big dripping red letters. In the old library, there were still books on the wooden shelves, piled haphazardly, all in Russian, or so it appeared from their covers. On one window ledge stood a big old reel-to-reel tape recorder, its innards partially exposed. And everywhere the damp and the smell.

Aivar leaned against a rickety wooden desk. 'We walk around Old Town, Bill and me, asking questions. Tuesday night. We know they are in St Patrick's bar because girls have remembered some things. That is last bar they are all together. Australian boy, bartender, he tell us he see Rachel leave after her friends and turn in the wrong direction. I think he likes her, so he quickly runs after her to warn her, and he sees her turn corner into side street. Not far along is nightclub with no name, where I see you.'

'What happened?'

'Outside is a car, very expensive car. Mercedes. Fill whole street.'

'What colour?'

'Silver grey. Barman, his name is Steve, he sees Rachel go in club. He thinks to go after her, then he thinks perhaps she meet someone, she is not so lost after all.'

'He was sure it was Rachel?'

'She wears short yellow dress. Blonde hair. He can see.'

'Jesus,' said Banks, glancing towards the window. 'I knew there was something about that place.'

'You have hunch, yes?'

'Something like that. So what happened?'

They left the library and walked back down the arched brick corridor. There was no sign of Joanna, but Banks knew she was not far away. Not that it mattered now; he didn't feel he was in any immediate danger.

'Nothing,' said Aivar. 'It was late. We go in club, but nobody knows anything. No silver Mercedes. Nothing. Do not like cops. We report to Investigator Rätsepp in his office, and he says to leave it with him. Next day. Next day. Nothing happen. We hear no more. When I ask, he tell me it was not a good lead, that barman was mistaken. We look for Steve again, even though Rätsepp says not to, but we cannot find him. His friend in St Patrick's tell us he return to Australia.'

'So let me get this clear,' said Banks. 'You get a lead to where Rachel went after St Patrick's, probably the last place she was seen alive. You take it to your boss. He tells you to leave it with him. It evaporates.'

'I am sorry?'

'It disappears. Nothing more is done. No follow up.'

'It disappears. Yes. Goes nowhere. No further action. Hr Rätsepp insist.'

'Did you talk to Bill about it?'

'Next day, I try. He is very quiet. Says Rätsepp must be right and barman must be mistaken, and it is not worth following. I do not understand. We are both excited when we talk to Steve. Then Rätsepp call me in his office and tell me I must never question his orders or judgements if I care about my career. I do care then, but not later. I leave after a year. Second day I am at home, two men come and, how do you say . . . they beat me up.'

'How bad?'

'Not so badly I need hospital, but they know how to hurt. Then they tell me if they ever find out I mention Rachel case or club again, they will kill me. I believe them.'

'So you told no one until now?'

'No. I get job in tourist business. Learn better English. Mind my own business. Keep my head down. But I never forget.'

'Did Ursula Mardna know?'

'No. I do not believe Rätsepp tell her.'

Banks felt some relief that his suspicions about Ursula were probably wrong and not everyone on the case was bent or intimidated. But she hadn't known about the lead. Rätsepp hadn't passed it on to her. It stopped with him, and he was Rebane's man.

They passed the execution room with the hole in the floor, where the Russians used to hang people before the Second World War, before the Nazis took over for a few years. Banks had had enough of Patarei by now and suggested they get out of the place. Aivar said they must leave separately, as they came.

'There is just one thing,' Banks said as they shook hands.

'Yes?'

'The silver Mercedes. I don't suppose the barman got the number?'

'Only part.'

'Did you ever find out who owned it?'

Aivar shuffled his feet in the grit. 'Hmm,' he said. 'That was another reason to do as Rätsepp told me.'

'Why is that?'

'I cannot help be curious, so I check. Not so many silver Mercedes. A name comes up.'

'Let me guess,' said Banks. 'Joosep Rebane.'

'No. It was Viktor Rebane. His father,' he said, then he turned and walked off towards the exit.

Krystyna looked a little nervous, as well she might, thought Annie, as she sat in front of the large screen television and watched the VIPER display. With any luck, she was about to identify Robert Tamm as the man who came by Garskill Farm on Wednesday morning over a week ago, the morning that Mihkel Lepikson was murdered. She had already identified Roderick Flinders as the man who had abducted her, tied her up, gagged her and locked her in the basement of his house. Flinders was in custody, and a whole range of charges were being prepared against him. The CPS was having a field day. Annie and Winsome thought they would let him sweat for a while longer before talking to him. All the better to let him contemplate his options, which were getting more limited by the hour.

Of course, Krystyna's identification wouldn't prove that Tamm murdered Mihkel Lepikson, only that he was at Garskill Farm on the morning in question, but taken in concert with the rest of the forensic evidence, including fabrics and the DNA tying him to woods where Bill Quinn was murdered, and the tyre tracks and fingerprints in the glove compartment of the rented Ford Focus tying him to both crime scenes, it would go a long way towards helping convict him. The Glasgow police had found a crossbow in Tamm's cellar, too. So Krystyna was about to bear witness against a hardened hit man.

Luckily VIPER, the Video Identification Parade Electronic Recording, had replaced the old line-ups, where a witness walked in front of a row of people of similar description to the suspect and picked out the guilty one. She didn't have to face that sort of confrontation with Tamm. But she was nervous, nonetheless, especially after her experience with Flinders.

Eventually, it turned out to be a simple matter. He was the fourth individual to be displayed on-screen, and she recognised him immediately. Every little helped. The Glasgow police had located Tamm and picked him up easily enough, and the two officers who delivered him to Eastvale had seemed happy to dump their prisoner and head off for a night on the town on expenses. Annie wished them luck. She knew what a night on the town in Eastvale was like. Glasgow, it wasn't.

Krystyna had returned with Annie to the Harkside cottage on Sunday night after a mandatory stop at the hospital for a quick examination. She was no worse for wear, but a little tearful and contrite. Annie had pampered her with a long bath, pizza, wine and television. Krystyna had even learned a few more words of English, and, to Annie's eye at least, she was putting a bit more meat on her bones with every meal. At Annie's suggestion, Krystyna had actually telephoned her parents in Pyskowice, and there were more tears and talk of reconciliation and going home, or so Annie gathered the from the tone, and from Krystyna's sign language at the end of the conversation. Krystyna seemed more cheerful after the phone call, at any rate, though Annie had a feeling that she wouldn't stay very long in a small town in Silesia. But she did hope that perhaps the next time Krystyna left home, she would do it the right way, with a real job in hand. There might even be something in Eastvale to suit her, if she improved her language skills.

Leaving Krystyna with Winsome in the squad room, Annie took Doug Wilson with her – he needed the experience – and they went into interview room three, where Robert Tamm was sitting as still as a meditating monk, and as expressionless as a stone.

Annie spread her files on the table and leaned back, tapping her pen on the metal surface. 'Well, Robert,' she started. 'Quite a pickle you're in, isn't it?'

Tamm said nothing. Whether he understood her or not, she couldn't tell. She thought 'in a pickle' might be too obscure an expression for a foreigner. 'You're in a lot of trouble,' she said.

Tamm still said nothing. He hadn't asked for a lawyer yet, but they could get a duty solicitor for him quickly enough if he did. He had already been cautioned, and he had indicated that he understood, but he still wasn't saying anything. Clearly he had another plan. Silence. He wasn't the kind to blurt out a confession.

It had been a long day, Annie felt. She and Winsome had done about as much as they could do. She thought they could probably get a conviction on the murders of Bill Quinn and Mihkel Lepikson, especially with the testimony of Gareth Underwood, aka Curly, Krystyna and Roderick Flinders, but they still had nothing to link Tamm to Joosep Rebane. Doug Wilson seemed bored with the lengthening silence already. So much for learning from experience. For that you needed experience of something other than silence.

As for Rachel Hewitt, Annie knew that was not their case, but she also knew that it had become a personal mission for Banks, and she knew what he was like when he got his teeth into something. She wished she were with him in Tallinn, not in a romantic way, but helping on the case. She had seen the trail of damage that Rachel's abduction had left behind – Maureen and Luke Hewitt; Pauline Boyars, the bride that never was. She wondered how Banks was getting on with the Professional Standards woman. Were they still speaking? Was she getting under his feet all the time? Could they possibly be sleeping together? The woman might be married, but she was an icy blonde, after all, and Annie never trusted icy blondes. Not even to be icy.

The case was over bar the formalities now. They had Robert Tamm and Roderick Flinders in custody, and the next few days would be a matter of working with the forensics experts and the CPS to build up a solid case. Flinders was a weak link. He had already talked plenty, and he would probably talk a lot more tomorrow if he thought there was a chance of saving his own skin. A night stewing in the cells would do him good. There were still a few migrant workers from Garskill Farm on the loose, but they would find their ways home, or into the hands of the police, wherever they ended up. Krystyna's friend Ewa had turned up in Liverpool, and Annie had arranged for her to pay a visit to Eastvale sometime over the next few days. Krystyna herself was safe now. Warren Corrigan was dead, and Curly was going straight. He was happy with his deal. He would talk, too, and he knew a lot. Result, then, Annie told herself, as she gestured for Doug Wilson to leave the room with her. Tamm was a dead loss. They'd get no confession from him. She told the officers on duty outside the interview room to take him back to the cells, and she and DC Wilson headed back to the squad room.

Haig and Lombard, the DCs on loan, were long gone, but Winsome and Geraldine Masters were still there, along with Krystyna.

'Come on,' said Annie, dropping her file on the desk. 'It's celebration time. Let's all go and get pissed.' When Krystyna looked puzzled, she said, 'You, too,' and mimed drinking. Krystyna nodded and smiled, and they picked up their coats and filed out to the Queen's Arms.

13

'Viktor Rebane and Toomas Rätsepp grew up together in the fifties in Narva, near the Russian border,' said Erik on the way out to Viimsi on Tuesday morning. Ursula Mardna had arranged a meeting between Banks, Joanna and Viktor Rebane, from which Viktor would walk away as free as he arrived. Joosep, as expected, had disappeared from the radar. Banks was now certain that Ursula knew nothing of the lead that Bill Quinn and Aivar Kukk had passed on to Toomas Rätsepp six years ago, or she wouldn't be helping him so much to uncover the truth. She wasn't in thick with Viktor Rebane; that, as Erik was explaining, was Toomas Rätsepp. Ursula was so angry about what had been done that she swore Rätsepp would go down, despite his friendship with Viktor Rebane, and Banks believed her.

Erik carried on with his potted history. 'It was a very strange time there. Much bomb damage, many Russian immigrants. They came to Tallinn together with their families as young men, and remained friends. When he was old enough, Viktor worked for state industry, and after independence he bought into utilities. Toomas first joined the militia, then he became policeman. At the time Rachel disappeared, Viktor also had a major interest in the nightclub around the corner from St Patrick's. It is said that he never went there, himself, that he was not interested in such pursuits, only in the profits. He had many cars, and his son liked to use the silver Mercedes most of all. Viktor spoiled and indulged him then.'

'And he's powerful enough to get away scot-free.'

'He knows a lot of secrets. But it is not only that. You must understand, Viktor Rebane is really not a bad man. Everyone knows that his son is psycho crazy and feel sorry for Viktor. He has done a lot of good for this country since independence. Much charity work. Many jobs. Remember that. He is a respected citizen. We are close now.'

They had driven from the Metropol and were skirting Kadriorg Park, turning on to the coastal road to Viimsi. Everything had happened so quickly after Ursula Mardna had made the phone call that Banks's head was still spinning. He was sitting in the front of the VW beside Merike, with Erik and Joanna in the back. Joanna had been very terse and offhand with Banks since they had dinner at Mekk on Sunday evening, and he guessed she was wishing she hadn't opened up and told him her personal problems in a moment of weakness. That often happened. You tell someone something that shames you, reveals you, makes you vulnerable, then you close up and wish you'd kept quiet in the first place. It feels almost as if they've got something on you, got a hold over you, the way Joosep Rebane and Warren Corrigan had over Bill Quinn. He wanted to tell her he didn't feel that way, but it wouldn't go down well. Instead, he kept quiet on the subject. If she was still annoyed about trying to solve the Rachel Hewitt case, she was hiding it well, now, and had been as excited as Banks at the latest revelations, and the forthcoming meeting with Viktor Rebane. He felt that she could scent the end, as he could, and the aroma intoxicated her. She might make a homicide detective yet.

Viktor Rebane had agreed to meet the foreign police detectives, who had no power or jurisdiction over him, as a courtesy in a public place of his choice, and they were heading for the restaurant. Apparently he lived in Viimsi, where he had a large modern house in its own grounds, with tennis court and swimming pool.

'So why has he agreed to see us?' Banks asked Erik.

'He is an old man. Sick with cancer. He is tired, and he wants to make amends before he dies. I think he has much on his conscience. He also has assurances from the very top that nothing will come back on him.'

'Even murder?'

'We will see,' said Erik. 'As a journalist, I would give a lot to be at your meeting, but he specified only you and Joanna. We will wait in the car in the parking lot. Perhaps you can help me with a story later, let me interview you? An undisclosed police source?'

'Perhaps,' said Banks. 'If there is a story.'

Merike pulled into a car park off the road, by the shore. 'It's up there.' She pointed ahead to a path by the beach. 'It's called Paat. That means boat. It looks like an upturned boat. Good luck.'

Banks and Joanna walked towards the path. It was another fine day, blue sky striped with milky white cloud, and the sea lapping at the breakwaters. The beach was mostly pebble, with a few sods of grass here and there. Over the other side, to the left, they could see the Tallinn shoreline, and straight ahead was a large island.

The path led them into the restaurant's outside area, where a few sheltered picnic-style benches were set out against the low sea wall. The restaurant itself was nearby, and it did resemble an upturned boat. Banks, however, found his eyes more drawn to the outside area, where an old man in a windcheater sat alone at one of the picnic tables, a mug of tea or coffee steaming in front of him, while two neckless bruisers stood, hands clasped in front of their privates, scanning the grounds. Probably ex-KGB agents, Banks guessed.

When Banks and Joanna approached the table, the bruisers stepped forward and patted them down. They were gentle and discreet enough with Joanna, Banks noticed, but she clearly didn't like it, and he didn't blame her. They were a little rougher with him, but not enough to hurt. When they were satisfied neither had a weapon or a wire, they stood aside, and Banks and Joanna sat opposite Viktor Rebane.

He was a hunched figure, and his chin was tucked into his throat in such a way that he looked permanently on the verge of a particularly noxious burp. His bald head was liver-spotted, as were his lizard-like hands. Frown lines had eaten deep into his brow. He must have been about the same age as Rätsepp, Banks guessed, if they grew up together, but he seemed a good ten years older. The ravages of cancer, no doubt. Or its treatment.

'First, let me not forget my hospitality,' Viktor Rebane said. 'May I offer you both a drink?'

'Why not?' said Banks. 'I'll have beer, please. A. Le Coq if they have it.'

'Excellent choice. And the lady?'

'Just a cappuccino, please,' said Joanna, clearly still smarting from her patting down.

Rebane snapped his fingers and the closest no-neck went off to the bar. As if sensing Joanna's mood, Rebane said, his yellowish eyes twinkling, 'I do apologise about the body search, my dear, but man in my position cannot be too careful. Beautiful woman is often most dangerous weapon.'

'Is that an old Estonian proverb?' said Joanna.

Rebane smiled. 'No. Is old Viktor Rebane proverb. The reason I agree to see you now, so soon,' Rebane continued, 'is I have appointment at hospital this afternoon. I am very tired and sick after chemotherapy, for many days. I am sure you understand.'

'Of course,' said Banks. 'And we're very grateful you took the trouble to talk to us. Perhaps you can help us answer a number of questions?'

'Perhaps. First thing I tell you is I do not know where my

son is, so please do not ask. Joosep and I have not spoken for many years now. He is always difficult child. Wild, unpredictable. Especially after his mother die. He is only ten at the time. He keep very bad company. Perhaps I spoil him. It is fashionable to blame parents, is it not? Do you have a son, Hr Banks?'

'I do,' said Banks. 'He's a musician.'

'Is good. In Estonia we love music. My son is drug-dealer, people-trafficker and gangster. But he is still my son. Do you understand that?'

'I think so,' said Banks.

'How far you go to protect *your* son?'

Banks thought for a moment. 'Probably a long way,' he answered. 'But I might draw the line if he raped and killed women.'

An expression of pain passed across Rebane's face, and immediately Banks felt guilty for being so brutally cruel; it had been unnecessary. No-neck came back with the drinks.

'Joosep tell me the girl die of a drug overdose,' Rebane whispered.

'What girl?'

'The one you are interested in. I am a father. I have daughter, too, with my third wife. She is twenty-one. I am proud of her, and I love her. That is perhaps the real reason I am talking to you. I feel something for the parents of this girl.'

'It's taken you a bloody long time.'

Rebane gave an impatient shake of his head. 'It is easier to forget when nothing reminds you. There are always many other things to think about. I regret most of all the things I did not do, not the things I did. But now . . .' He shook his head slowly. 'Too much has happened. Old wounds have reopened. I am a businessman, Hr Banks. I am not interested in your moral judgements. I have perhaps done many wrong things for my business interests. I have made many enemies. Do you understand?'

'I think so.'

'Six years ago Joosep is my beloved son. Now, he is a stranger to me.'

'Will you tell me what happened six years ago?'

Viktor remained silent for a few moments. Seagulls squealed over a shoal of fish close to shore. 'Joosep come to see me. He is very upset. Most agitated. When I ask him what is wrong, he tell me a girl die of a drug overdose at his party. An English girl. He tell me he is sitting in nightclub. You know which club?'

'I know.'

'He is sitting in nightclub with friends. My nightclub. They are ready to leave, and this beautiful girl comes in. A vision. She has lost her friends. Joosep, he tells me he ask her if she want to go to party, and after he will drive her to her hotel. She says yes, and they go in his car. But at party, girl drinks more and takes drugs, and in morning they find her dead. She has . . . how do you say . . .' He pointed to his throat, what little there was of it to see, 'Choke.'

'Asphyxiated,' said Banks. 'Choked will do. Choked on her own vomit?'

'Yes.'

'So what happened?'

'He is in trouble, and he wants me to help him. Then, on Wednesday morning, Toomas, my old friend, telephones to tell me that Joosep's name, my name, and the nightclub also, have come up in the investigation, and I ask my friend Toomas to stop it, if he can, to make sure it goes no further. It is not too late. Toomas will do that for me. He will help Joosep. And for money, of course. He know I will be very grateful.'

'Of course,' said Banks. 'It's comforting to know that corruption's no different here than anywhere else.'

'Perhaps. I am not so certain. Or you are being ironic, yes? You English.'

'Maybe just a little bit. So Toomas Rätsepp shut down the investigation?'

'He close off that direction. Yes. Is easy because not many people know. Barman from St Patrick pub, of course. But he is easy. Threat of beating and ticket back to Australia. And junior investigator who report his findings to Toomas. Also easy if he want to stay in job, have promotion. Beating, too. English policeman is problem.'

'Bill Quinn,' said Banks.

'Yes. We cannot warn him to stop or threaten him. Is madness to assassinate foreign cop on Estonian soil. We need different solution.'

'And you thought of one.'

'I have trusted colleague pick out pretty girl from club and give her money. You know the rest. Accidental meeting arranged in the hotel bar. Drinks. A sleeping powder. Dinner. Photographs. Easy.'

Joanna charged in now, as Banks had expected she would. This was the part of the story that interested her the most. 'So you're saying that you arranged with the girl to have Bill Quinn seduced, drugged and photographed in a compromising position, then you blackmailed him?'

Rebane nodded, which made him look even more as if he were about to burp. 'It is only way to save my son. I help him out of many difficulties. Back then I always had hope he would change, that he would stop being wild and foolish. But he has gone other direction. I can help him no more. He is lost to me. But you will never find him. Despite everything, he is still my son, and I will not have him locked in prison or mental hospital.'

'And when Bill Quinn's wife died, your blackmail didn't work any more.'

'No,' said Rebane. 'By then Joosep know what I have done, and he has taken photos some years before. He now has business, criminal business, in United Kingdom, and he think it useful to have policeman . . . how you say?'

'In his pocket?' Banks suggested.

Rebane didn't quite seem to understand but grunted his agreement anyway.

Banks said, 'But Bill Quinn was going to tell all after his wife died, wasn't he, so you had to find another way of dealing with him. You sent Robert Tamm.'

Rebane seemed puzzled. 'Robert Tamm? He does not work for me. He work . . .'

'For Joosep?'

'I do not kill Detective Quinn, or order kill. I have nothing to do with murder.'

'Of course not. But your son does, doesn't he? He has already used the blackmail against Quinn over the years to smooth his illegal operations in the UK, and suddenly they're threatened. He finds out that Bill Quinn and an Estonian journalist called Mihkel Lepikson are planning to tell the whole sorry story. So Joosep has them both killed. You might not do it yourself, but you're quite happy to leave him free to murder and maim and rape and ruin as many lives as he wants, aren't you?' said Banks.

Rebane banged his skinny fist on the table. 'He is my son! What would you have me do? I tell you I am not interested in your cheap morality. Take what you are given and be grateful. Like scraps for the dogs. Georg!' One of the no-necks came over. 'Georg. Help me. We will leave now. I am tired.' Viktor Rebane struggled to his feet with Georg's help.

Banks and Joanna remained seated. 'I have one more question,' said Banks.

Rebane stared down at him, still shaking with fury. 'You have great deal of nerve, my friend,' he said through gritted teeth.

'Where is Rachel Hewitt?'

*　　*　　*

During the three hours it took to drive to Võrumaa, Banks sat in the back with Joanna and dozed or gazed out on the scenery, going over the whole case in his mind, especially the end of the meeting at Paat where Viktor Rebane had glared at him for so long he was certain the old man was not going to tell him anything. But Rebane finally whispered a location, then hobbled off with Georg's help.

Erik and Merike sat up front navigating and chatting quietly in Estonian. The radio played quiet jazz.

Perhaps, Banks thought, he had been too hard on Viktor Rebane, but he didn't like gangsters who pretended to be respectable. Maybe Viktor *was* a respectable businessman who had done a lot for his country, but Banks was willing to believe he had done more than a few things that needed sweeping under the carpet, too, and that Toomas Rätsepp had helped him more than once. You don't keep company like the no-necks Viktor was with for no reason. But he was untouchable, and that didn't really matter too much; he was clearly dying. Joosep Rebane was out of sight, perhaps hiding in St Petersburg with his Russian gangster friends, Banks guessed. There would be plenty of police forces watching out for him across Europe, but it was more of a waiting game than a chase or a hunt.

Banks had a suspicion that Joosep would most likely meet a sticky end at the hands of his criminal colleagues once the story came out. Gangsters could be a very moral lot. Murder and mayhem were fine in the service of business. Torture, arson and maiming all had their place in the pursuit of profit, but anything to do with young girls or children was frowned upon. At best, Joosep's colleagues would view him as careless, at worst, as a possible rapist and murderer of an innocent young woman. Either way he would become a liability, if he wasn't one already. The odds were also that Joosep had pissed off enough people before now, and that this would be the last straw.

The countryside rolled by outside the car window, forest and farmland, along with the occasional village and small town. The woods were thick with evergreens, Banks noticed, which must make it beautiful in winter, especially under a blanket of snow. Everyone was quiet, perhaps contemplating the hours ahead, or thinking about the past. He recalled his telephone conversation earlier with a slightly hung over Annie. She seemed pleased with the way things had wrapped up in Eastvale. He hadn't known then, of course, that he would be close to the end of his own investigation in Tallinn.

Viktor Rebane had told Banks that his son had not taken Rachel Hewitt to a party in Tallinn, but to a lake house, which happened to be in an area of small wooded lakes called Võrumaa, in the far south of the country, about a three-hour drive from the nightclub. Joosep often held late night parties there, parties that sometimes went on for two or three days. Cocaine and amphetamines kept people awake, and barbiturates put them to sleep. The lake house belonged entirely to Joosep, Viktor had stressed. Nothing was in his name, and he had never been there. No doubt he had his own secret playgrounds.

Banks couldn't help but wonder whether Rachel had quickly sobered up when she found herself being driven out of the city, far away from everything she knew, unless Joosep had somehow drugged her the way Larisa had drugged Bill Quinn. Rohypnol, or some such thing. Or had she agreed to go? Was it adventure she was seeking? Did she really think it would be fun? By all accounts, Joosep Rebane was a rich, handsome and charming young man, with rock-star charisma and a fancy silver Mercedes. Rachel wasn't a party girl, according to everyone who knew her; she wasn't promiscuous, but she was spontaneous, and she was certainly attracted by wealth and its trappings. Did she believe that Joosep Rebane was the Prince Charming she had been looking for?

Immediately after Viktor and the no-necks had left Paat, Banks had phoned Ursula Mardna, who had pinpointed the location of the lake house for them and said she would arrange for a local CSI team to get over there and start work immediately. If Banks wished, he could set off from Viimsi and meet up with her at the scene.

Merike had a little trouble finding the particular lake once they had left the main highway, and they spent some time driving along unpaved roads through thick forest, stopping to read signs, before they arrived at the end of a long, winding entrance road that led to the simple wooden lake house, with a lawn stretching down to the water's edge. Banks couldn't see any other cottages around, though there were a few outbuildings that clearly belonged to the main house. It seemed the ideal, isolated place for Joosep Rebane's antics.

The path to the house and lake was taped off, and a surly uniformed officer stood on guard. Erik tried to talk to him but got nowhere. Fortunately, Ursula Mardna arrived within half an hour of them and sorted everything out. Erik and Merike were not allowed past the tape, though, only the police, and that infuriated Erik, as he had come so far. He stayed in the car for a while, sulking and smoking with Merike, then they walked as close as they could get. No doubt, Banks thought, he would keep his eyes and ears open for a story, and his mobile phone would have a decent camera. Banks had no problem with the story being told, and he doubted very much that Ursula Mardna would. She was assuming control now, directing the CSIs. If her initial failure in the Rachel case hadn't done her career much harm, finally solving it after all these years could only do it good.

The CSIs were busy inside the house, and outside two of them were digging up areas of the lawn they had decided offered the most potential for buried bodies. Viktor had said Joosep told him he had buried Rachel's body in the garden, but not exactly where. Banks wondered why he hadn't just dumped her in the lake, but dead bodies in the water all float eventually, and perhaps he had worried that there was more chance of someone seeing her, even in such an isolated place as this. Others must live not so far away, and surely ramblers, cyclists or boaters came by occasionally.

Banks and Joanna stood on the deck with Ursula Mardna, watching over the scene. A small motorboat lay moored to the dock at the end of the garden, alongside a rowboat. The opposite shore was about a quarter of a mile away, and as far as Banks could see, there were no lake houses or dwellings of any kind over there. It seemed as if Joosep and his friends had the lake to themselves. Banks could smell the fresh pine and hear the birds singing up in the trees.

There were no signs of recent inhabitation, the Crime Scene Manager told Ursula Mardna; in fact, he said, there were no indications of anyone having being there at all recently. Other than the occasional discussions between CSIs, it was perfectly quiet, much like Banks's own cottage by the beck outside Gratly. The lake house itself was large enough for four bedrooms upstairs and a poolroom in the basement, and the outbuildings were fitted with bunks for extra guests.

The main floor consisted of one large open room incorporating living area, dining table and kitchen. It smelled musty and stale, as if it had been locked up for a long time, and dust motes danced in the rays of sunlight as Banks walked the uncarpeted floor. A few rugs had been thrown here or there, but mostly it was bare boards. There was a wood-burning stove in the living area, which must have been nice and cosy on a winter's night. There were a few battered armchairs, a decent stereo set-up, along with a pile of punk and heavy metal CDs, a collection of hash-pipes, a large flat-screen TV with DVD player and a pile of martial arts movies and Korean bootleg porn. The walls were covered with stylised prints from the Kama Sutra mixed in with cubist and abstract expressionist works.

Banks was happy to go outside again, and when he did, one of the CSIs digging in the garden called out. Banks and Joanna hurried over with Ursula Mardna to join him, as did several of his colleagues, standing around the edge of a three-foot deep pit. Banks could see Erik straining his neck behind the tape, no doubt snapping away with his smartphone camera.

The CSI, a forensic archaeologist, Ursula Mardna explained, carefully brushed away soil from an empty eye socket. The bones had darkened from years underground, where various compounds had leached into the soil. The CSI worked carefully with his brush, and Banks and Joanna watched as the skull slowly came into view. It was going to take a long time, he explained, so there was no point their standing over him. He would call them when he was finished, then would begin the difficult and painstaking process of getting the body from the earth to the mortuary. Only the photographer remained as the archaeologist continued his delicate work.

Banks, Joanna and Ursula Mardna paced the deck as they waited. Someone had a flask of hot coffee, and Banks was grateful for the loan of a plastic cup to drink from, even though it was a warm day, and he would have preferred a cold beer. It was at times like this that Banks also wished he still smoked. When Ursula Mardna brought out a packet of cigarettes and a small tin to contain the ashes, so she wouldn't contaminate the scene, he was tempted to ask her for one, but he controlled the urge.

Everyone seemed vaguely interested in the arrival of the English detectives, especially in Joanna Passero, casting them curious glances every now and then, but nobody paid undue attention to them. Fewer people seemed to speak English here than Banks had encountered in Tallinn. It was early evening, and though it was far from dark, the shadows were lengthening over the water, and the light through the trees was taking on that muted, filtered evening quality.

Eventually, the archaeologist and his assistants called the three of them over. The skeleton Banks looked down on could have been male or female as far as he was concerned, though the pathologist, who also now arrived at the graveside, quickly assured them it was female.

When Banks and Joanna stood at the edge of the shallow grave with Ursula Mardna, Banks knew he had found what he had come for, though he felt no sense of triumph, just a kind of sad relief. It was impossible to see the yellow colour, of course, but fragments of the dress still clung to the darkened bones, as did the white open-toed high-heeled shoes, though they were no longer white, and pieces had disintegrated. There were also the remains of a small handbag, a metal clasp and decayed leather strap. Everything looked as if it might have been tossed on top of the body, and Banks wondered if Rachel had been naked when she was buried.

After all the photographs had been taken, and soil and vegetation samples carefully removed and packaged, one of the CSIs very carefully retrieved the handbag. The fabric had rotted, but some of the contents were still intact: a tube of lipstick, a tattered, mostly rotted leather purse, a plastic hairbrush, keys, some loose coins, mostly Estonian kroon, along with some British pounds, and a Meriton Hotel ballpoint pen. If there had been anything else, it had decomposed over the years, like the flesh.

The pathologist knelt by the body and borrowed the CSI's brush to clear more soil from the neck area. After much umming and ahing, in addition to the use of magnifying glass and a delicate physical examination with gloved fingers, he stood up. Banks heard his knees crack. The man spoke with Ursula Mardna in Estonian. She turned to Banks and said,

'He cannot say for certain, but he thinks she was strangled. There are many small bones broken in the throat.'

'However she died,' Banks said, 'somebody buried her. There'll be an investigation, I assume?'

Ursula Mardna nodded. 'Of course.'

Banks asked whether he could examine the purse, and after a quick glance at Ursula Mardna, who nodded briefly, the CSI handed it to him, after first having him put on a pair of protective gloves. It wasn't because of fingerprints, Banks knew – none would survive after so long – but simply crime scene protocol.

With Joanna Passero by his side, Banks opened the purse carefully. The one thing you could usually depend on surviving most of the elements except fire was plastic, and sure enough, there it was. Or there they were. Tesco, credit and debit cards, Co-op, Boots, Waterstone's, and half a dozen others. All in the name of Rachel Hewitt.

He had found her.

The last thing Banks took out of the purse, stuck in the slot behind her credit card, was a small laminated card inscribed with an image of a man in tails and a top hat helping a voluptuous woman into a coach. Or was he pushing her?

14

Late June sunshine flooded the market square as Banks looked down from his open office window on the shining cobbles, smelling coffee and freshly baked bread, listening to the ghostly harmonies of Erkki-Sven Tüür's *Awakening* from the iPod dock. The gold hands against the blue face of the church clock stood at a quarter past five. A group of walkers dribbled into the square in ones and twos, gathering at the market cross after three or four hours out in the dale, all kitted out with the latest boots, red and orange anoraks, rucksacks and walking sticks, trouser legs tucked into their socks. One of them was clearly the leader, and he carried an Ordnance Survey map in a clear plastic cover around his neck. Already the little wooden platform and tables with umbrellas had been set up on the cobbles outside the Queen's Arms, reminding Banks of his evenings in Tallinn, eating out in the Old Town with Joanna Passero.

It seemed like years since then, but it was only a month and a half. Annie was back at full throttle, as if she had never been away, especially as she had solved Banks's case while he had been off tilting at windmills. She also told Banks with great glee that she had got a letter in very basic English from Krystyna, who was now living in Krakow and working in a traditional Polish restaurant, studying English in her spare time.

Joanna Passero was still at County HQ, about to leave Professional Standards for Criminal Intelligence. Banks thought often about their trip to Tallinn, the city, the people they had met, the discovery by the lake in Võrumaa. They never had got to see the *Danse Macabre*. Another time, perhaps.

As Banks had expected, Joanna's report on Bill Quinn leaked to the press, and there had been a minor furore about policemen and prostitutes. But the brouhaha hadn't lasted long; celebrity phone-hacking had once again taken over most of the media's attention.

Erik Aarma's story, which appeared in late May over two weekly issues of the *Eesti Telegraaf*, did a great deal to restore Bill Quinn's reputation. Erik opened with the murders of Quinn and Mihkel Lepikson, then worked his way through the migrant labour scam, Corrigan's shooting, and all the way back to the disappearance of Rachel Hewitt, making connections with Joosep and Viktor Rebane wherever he could legally do so. Soon the article appeared in translation, sometimes in digest form, in newspapers all over Europe. After all, Rachel's disappearance had been a major story six years ago, and had been kept very much in the public eye since then by her parents' efforts. Though many of the players had to remain anonymous, there could be few readers – in Tallinn, at any rate – who could remain in any doubt to whom Erik was referring when he wrote of a rich and wild young man and his wealthy businessman father.

Viktor Rebane died of lung cancer in Tallinn in the first week of June, just after the article appeared. His son did not appear at his funeral. The following week, a body was pulled out of the Neva river outside St Petersburg with two bullets in the head, and there was little doubt in anyone's mind that it belonged to Joosep Rebane, a conclusion soon borne out by DNA analysis. His criminal masters had clearly taken the moral high ground when they learned that he had been responsible for the death of an innocent young woman. They had no doubt already known he was something of a liability,

Banks thought, and his days had probably been numbered anyway.

Ursula Mardna came out of the whole affair triumphant, her earlier lack of vigilance forgotten, and Toomas Rätsepp was prosecuted for a number of serious offences under Estonian corruption and bribery laws.

Banks returned to his desk and picked up the three sheets of paper he had received in the post that morning, along with a brief covering note from Erik explaining that he had received the letter in response to his article, and Merike had translated it from the Russian. The quiet music, with its drifting harmonies, long notes and high strings, seemed both peaceful and tense at once. Banks sat down, sipped some lukewarm tea and read:

Dear Mr Aarma,

It was with great interest and curiosity that I read your article in a national newspaper recently, and I feel it is my duty to clarify one or two important points for you. Why now, you may ask, after so long? I have no excuses except cowardice and self-interest for not coming forward until now. You say in your article that though certain facts are clear, perhaps nobody will ever know exactly what happened at the lake house in Võrumaa on that July night six years ago. But that is not true. For, you see, I was there.

I worked at a nightclub in the Old Town of Tallinn. It had no name, and we called it simply The Club. I was sharing a flat with another young woman who worked there, a rather naïve Russian-speaking Estonian girl called Larisa, who was not at work on the night I am about to describe.

There was a crowd, or a clique, at The Club, centred around Joosep Rebane, son of Viktor, one of The Club's owners. You refer to both these men in your article, or at least it seems to me from your descriptions that they could be nobody else. Joosep had that 'aura of glamour' you mention, of the movie star or rich playboy, about him. He did not work. He did not have to. He had money. He was intelligent, but not well read or educated. He had charisma, but it was laced with cruelty. He liked to humiliate people, exercise his power over them, and yet people gravitated towards him, especially women. Why? I can't explain. I couldn't then, and I can't now. The excitement? The edge of danger he always seemed to generate?

On weekends, we would often congregate at The Club and then go somewhere else later. The core group was five or six strong, and sometimes others joined up with us later, came from outside the city, even from as far as St Petersburg and Riga. Sometimes Joosep would drive us all down to his lake house in Võrumaa. There we were so isolated we could do anything, and we did.

One night in July six years ago – I do not remember the exact day of the week, or the date, but your article says it happened between Saturday, 22 July and Sunday, 23 July, so I must trust you – a young girl walked into The Club just as we were about to leave. The girl was drunk. She looked lost. Joosep immediately sensed she was vulnerable, and he went to her to ask if he could help. She was just his type, a blonde vision in a short yellow dress, full lips, pale skin. I could not hear all their conversation, but soon he had persuaded her to have a drink, into which I thought later he must have put some Rohypnol, something he had done before, even when the girls were willing.

When we all went outside – there were I think five of us by then – Joosep tried to get the girl into the car. She did not want to come with us at first, but Joosep is very persuasive. The drug had not started working by then. Joosep said we would go to a party at his flat nearby for a while, and then he would drop her off at her hotel. She seemed to like this idea, or at least appeared half-willing, and Joosep bundled her into the back of the car. Then we were off. No party. No hotel. But the lake house. Võrumaa.

I do not remember much about the journey. I think the English girl whimpered a little as she realised we were leaving the city, then she fell silent. I know that Joosep had to practically carry her out of the car when we arrived, and he immediately put her in one of the outbuildings. I have no recollection of him coming back to the main building. It was after four o'clock in the morning by then and starting to get light. We were all somewhat the worse for wear. Time did not matter. We would often sleep for a few hours, then start a party at ten o'clock the following morning, or three in the afternoon, if we felt like it. Sometimes people would turn up unexpectedly, and we would have a party to welcome them. There was always lots of booze and drugs. And sex. That night I believe we smoked one joint, then everybody passed out quite quickly. There was always tomorrow.

It must have been a couple of hours later when I awoke, having heard a sound. Everyone else in the main building seemed to be still crashed out. I went to the window, which was open to the warm night air, and I heard another sound, like a muffled scream, then a gurgling sound and a fist thumping against thick wood, then silence.

Something about the sounds made my skin crawl. I ducked down, so that I could not be seen from outside. Time passed. I do not know how long. The morning light grew stronger. Then Joosep walked out of the outbuilding with a bundle in his arms. I saw the yellow dress, the little handbag hanging from her hand, one white shoe dangling.

He looked around and sniffed the air like a wild animal. I felt fear prickle through me. I thought for certain he would see me or know instinctively that I was there. But he didn't. He looked at the lake, as if contemplating something, then carried on, walking just a few more feet to a spot near where the woods started. There was a spade propped against one of the trees for gardening, and he started digging. The girl lay on the ground beside him. I could not tell whether she was alive or not, but she did not move.

I watched Joosep dig a shallow grave, drop her body into it, and shovel back the earth, tapping down the grass sods on top to make it appear undisturbed. It didn't, but who would care? Who would notice? Soon the turf would knit together again and it would be hidden forever.

He went back into the outbuilding, and I lay down on my mattress again trying to decide what to do. I did not think he had seen me. If he had, I reasoned, he would probably have come and killed me, too. But I could not be certain. Joosep's mind moved in strange ways. All day he kept catching my eye and smiling. He told us that the English girl had run away during the night, and everyone just laughed. Did nobody realise there was nowhere for her to run? When Sasha decided it was time to go back to Tallinn, I asked if he would take me along as I was working at The Club that night. I could not be certain that Joosep believed me, but he let me go.

When we got to Tallinn, I went immediately to my apartment. Larisa was not there. I packed a few clothes and personal things, just one suitcase, and made sure I had my passport. I did not have a car, so I had to hitch-hike. It is not difficult if you are a reasonably attractive young woman. I soon got to Riga, then Vilnius, then Minsk, then . . . But that is where my story ends.

Please do not try to find me. I am sorry for what I did, or did not do. That night has haunted me ever since. There was nothing I could have done to save the English girl,

except perhaps run into the outbuilding and try to stop
Joosep. But no one can make Joosep change his mind once
it is made up, and he is much bigger and stronger than
me. Perhaps I could have told my story sooner to spare
her friends and family the agony of not knowing. I hope
you will understand why I felt I could not do that until I
read your story.

    Juliya K.

Banks folded the sheets, put them back in the envelope and
massaged his temples. 'The Wanderer's Evening Song' was
playing now, and Banks let the strange choral harmonies flow
over him for a few moments. As he did so, his mind went
back to Rachel's funeral in late May, the crowded cremato-
rium, hordes of media outside with their hand-held cameras
and boom microphones, oblivious to everyone's pain and
loss. As the coffin slipped away, Coldplay's 'Fix You' had
played over the music system. It had been Rachel's favourite
song around the time of the hen weekend, her best friend
Pauline said.

Banks went with Annie to the funeral tea afterwards at the
Hewitts' house, where they sipped Harvey's Bristol Cream
and ate little triangular sandwiches with the crusts cut off.
The media were consigned to the pavement beyond the
garden gate, though occasionally an adventurous reporter
managed to sneak closer and press his nose up against the
window behind the lace curtains.

Banks managed to get Maureen Hewitt alone for a few
moments, though her daughter Heather stuck close to her.
The young girl made a ghostly presence, pale-skinned, dressed
wholly in black, and Banks didn't recollect her ever saying a
word. Her expression remained unchanging, too, a sort of
blank grief mixed with anxiety, as if she were always on the
verge of tears, or of jumping up and running away.

Maureen Hewitt thanked Banks for getting to the bottom of the mystery of her daughter's disappearance and assured him that, while she and her husband were devastated that they had not been right about Rachel still being alive, all their lives were much better for the sense of closure that knowing the truth brought. Banks assured Maureen, as best he could, that her daughter's death had been quick and painless, that she had died of a drug overdose on the very night she had disappeared, probably without regaining consciousness. Maureen refused to accept that her daughter would take drugs willingly, and Banks told her that they were probably administered without her knowledge, though he had no real evidence of this at the time. It helped Maureen a little. She said that she and her husband would continue with the foundation and its work for the sake of all the other missing children out there.

Pauline, the would-be bride at the hen weekend, was the only one of Rachel's old friends to turn up. She had clearly had too much to drink, even before she arrived. Her voice soon became too loud, and when she smashed a glass, Mr Hewitt had a quiet word with her. She left in tears. Banks and Annie made their excuses and left shortly afterwards.

Banks looked at the envelope one more time, then he got up, put it in his filing cabinet and walked over to the window again. Juliya's letter and the questions it begged would still haunt him tomorrow, and the day after that. For the moment, though, it was a beautiful late afternoon, the best of the year so far. The tables were fast filling up outside the Queen's Arms, reminding him of the Old Town in Tallinn, and he wanted nothing more than to sit by himself with a cold beer in the cobbled market square and watch the world go by.

ACKNOWLEDGEMENTS

Quite a lot of this book takes place in Tallinn, so first of all, my special thanks to Karen Root, who read the manuscript at an early stage and corrected my Estonian errors. If the Estonian sections ring more true now, it is because of Karen, and if they don't, it is entirely my fault. I would also like to thank my Course Director Krista Mits for sharing her insights into Estonian history and culture, and my students Daniel Vaarik and Anna-Magdaleena Kangro for their wide-ranging conversation on matters Estonian. Also, a big thank you to my students, who all brought something to the experience of writing this book, and were an inspiration: Berit Kaschan, Gunilla Rosengren, Siret Kork, Tana Collins, Kaidi Laur, Adrienn Jankovich and Helen Kalpus. I would also like to thank the Canadian Ambassador to the Baltic States and his wife for the use of their beautiful apartment while I was teaching in Tallinn.

At Hodder & Stoughton, my thanks go to Carolyn Mays, Francesca Best and Katy Rouse in Editorial, and beyond them to Kerry Hood and Jaime Frost in Publicity, and to Lucy Hale and the formidable Hodder production and sales force. Thanks also to Justine Taylor for her thorough copy-editing. At William Morrow, I thank Carolyn Marino and Wendy Lee in Editorial and Laurie Connors in Publicity, along with the Morrow production team and sales reps. At McClelland and Stewart, thanks to Kendra Ward and Ellen Seligman for their editing, Ashley Dunn in Publicity (along with freelance Debby de Groot), and Doug Pepper for the oysters and stout and so much more. Thanks also to the McClelland & Stewart/ Random House sales and productions teams. I would also like to thank my agents Dominick Abel and David Grossman for their continued support. Last but not least, I would like to thank Sheila Halladay for being my first reader, as always, and for making so many useful suggestions at a time when they were probably the last thing I wanted to hear.

PETER ROBINSON
Bad Boy

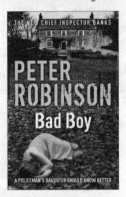

Banks isn't back, and that's the problem.

If DCI Alan Banks had been in his office when his old neighbour came calling, perhaps it would have turned out differently.

Perhaps an innocent man would still be alive.

And perhaps Banks's daughter wouldn't be on the run with a wanted man.

But Banks is on holiday, blissfully unaware of the terrible chain of events set in motion by the discovery of a loaded gun in a young woman's bedroom, and his daughter's involvement with the ultimate bad boy . . .

Out now

HODDER

NAME: Alan Banks.

RANK: Detective Chief Inspector.

DEPARTMENT: Homicide and Major Crimes.

LOCATION: Eastvale, North Yorkshire.

BIRTHDAY: 24th May.

PLACE OF BIRTH: Peterborough, Cambridgeshire.

FATHER: Arthur Banks, sheet metal worker made redundant by Margaret Thatcher.

MOTHER: Ida Banks, retired charlady.

WIFE: Divorced from Sandra, who has now remarried and has another child.

CHILDREN: Brian, a successful rock musician, and Tracy, a postgraduate student.

EDUCATION: Grammar School, two A-Level GCEs; London Polytechnic, Higher National Diploma in Business Studies; various police training courses.

temples. Dark blue eyes. Scar beside right eye. At just over five foot eight and a bit, looks a little short for a policeman. Not especially handsome, but attractive to women. Casual dresser, hates wearing a tie, and if he has to wear one, he will tie it loosely and leave his top shirt button undone.

POLITICS: Not a particularly political creature. Moderate socialist/liberal humanist.

RELIGION: Cautious agnostic.

MUSIC: Fanatical about it. Almost anything – opera, chamber, vocal, orchestral, jazz, rock – but not so fond of country and western, funk, fusion, Gilbert and Sullivan, or hip-hop. Favourite listening spot is his car or his conservatory at night, with a glass of wine in his hand.

FILMS: War films, James Bond, historical epics like *Doctor Zhivago* and *Lawrence of Arabia*, espionage and thrillers. Not much interested in horror, science-fiction, romantic comedies or art cinema, but keeps an open mind. Likes old black and white noir films such as *The Third Man* and *Touch of Evil*, and the old Ealing Comedies.

FAVOURITE ACTOR: Alec Guinness.

FAVOURITE ACTRESS: Julie Christie.

BOOKS: Largely self-taught in the field of literature. Mostly enjoys espionage fiction, writers such as Graham Greene, Eric Ambler, Len Deighton and John le Carré. Not much crime fiction other than Sherlock Holmes. Has far many more books on his 'should read' list than he will ever get around to reading.

HOLIDAYS: Prefers exploring a new city on foot to lounging on a beach in the sun.

ALCOHOL: Enjoys a pint of bitter, especially Theakston's, Tetley's or Black Sheep. Also enjoys Laphroaig single malt whisky occasionally, but mostly drinks red wine, Australian Shiraz being a particular favourite. Rarely drinks to excess, but stress can sometimes push him there. It's more likely to be emotional stress, though, rather than the stress of his job.

LIVES IN: Originally in a semi-detached house in Eastvale, but after his divorce from Sandra, moved to a small cottage in the hamlet of Gratly. The house is isolated at the end of a cul-de-sac, situated by a beck with terraced falls at the edge of the woods.

FEARS: Blindness even more than deafness, despite his love of music. Loss of mobility. Confinement. Spiders.

HUMOUR:

Tends towards the anarchic and satirical, even surreal, and not averse to a bit of slapstick, but equally fond of verbal humour: Peter Sellers, Spike Milligan, W.C. Fields, *Monty Python*, *Fawlty Towers*, *Blackadder*. Not well versed in stand-up or the more contemporary humour.

GENERAL CHARACTER:

Banks is a bit of a maverick in that he likes to get things done his own way, but he doesn't bend the rules to the point of beating suspects or forging evidence against them. He doesn't respond well to authority unless he respects the person who has the job. He's generally a sympathetic person, interested in people and curious about their motives, saddened and angered by murder. His mind is agile, and he is always on the lookout for new experiences – new music, new books, new places. Though at heart a man of reason, he is possessed of a certain amount of intuition and is not afraid to use it. Since his break-up with his wife Sandra, he has had a couple of romantic relationships but has been unable to sustain them and is often baffled by the whole relationship 'thing'. He loves women though, and has many female friends. He doesn't really have a short temper, but he can become very frustrated if he appears to be making no progress in a case, and he can sometimes be abrupt or sarcastic with people.

MOST DEEPLY KEPT SECRET:

That would be telling!

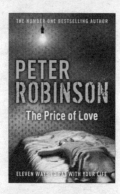

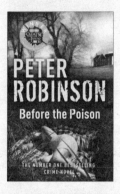

I

Famous Trials: Grace Elizabeth Fox, April 1953,
by Sir Charles Hamilton Morley

Grace Elizabeth Fox rose from her bed and dressed with the aid of her young Attending Officer Mary Swann at 6.30 AM on the morning of 23rd April, 1953. She ate a light breakfast of toast, marmalade and tea, then she busied herself writing letters to her family and friends. After a small brandy to steady her nerves shortly before 8.00 AM, she spent the following hour alone with the Chaplain.

At thirty seconds before 9.00 AM, Mr. Albert Pierrepoint and his assistant entered Grace's cell, and with his usual polite deference and dispatch, Mr. Pierrepoint tied her hands behind her back with a soft calfskin strap and escorted her the short distance to the Execution House directly above. It was a grey, rainy morning, and the stone steps were dark and slick with rain. The small party entered the House, where the Governor, the doctor and two witnesses were already waiting, at 9.00 AM precisely. According to later accounts, Grace comported herself with great dignity throughout, and she never faltered in her steps or uttered a sound, except for a brief shudder and audible inhalation of breath when she first saw the rope.

Once at the gallows, she was placed in position over the chalked 'T' on the trapdoor, and the assistant pinioned her ankles with a leather strap. Mr. Pierrepoint took from his pocket a white cotton hood, which he placed over Grace's head, then he carefully and gently adjusted the leather-sheathed noose around her neck. When all was to his satisfaction, he stepped back, removed the safety pin and pushed the lever away from him in one sharp, swift motion. The trapdoor opened and Grace fell to her death. The whole business, from the cell to the eternal hereafter, took no longer than fifteen seconds.

After a brief examination by the prison doctor, Grace's body was left hanging for the regulation hour, after which time it was removed and washed, then an autopsy was performed. The findings were that she died instantaneously of a 'fracture-dislocation of the spine at C.2 with a 2 inch gap and transverse separation of the spinal cord at the same level'. The pathologist also found 'fractures of both wings of the hyoid and the right wing of the thyroid cartilage'. Grace's larynx was also fractured.

The following day, after Grace's sister Felicity had formally identified the body, a coroner's inquest reported her death: 'Twenty-third April 1953 at H.M. Prison, Leeds: Grace Elizabeth Fox, Female, 40 years, Housewife of Kilnsgate House, Kilnsgarthdale, in the District of Richmond, Yorkshire (North Riding). Cause of Death: Injuries to the central nervous system consequent upon judicial hanging.' The Governor entered in his daily log the simple words, 'The sentence of death on Grace Elizabeth Fox was carried out by means of execution,' and Grace's body was buried within the prison grounds.

October 2010

I had promised myself that when I turned sixty I would go home. Laura thought it was a great idea, but when the day finally came, I was standing at her graveside in the New England rain, crying my eyes out. All the more reason to go, I thought.

'In two hundred yards, bear right.'

I drove straight on.

'In four hundred yards, bear right.'

I continued driving under the canopy of trees, leaves falling and swirling around me. The screen froze, then flickered and dissolved, reforming into new shapes that didn't in the least resemble the landscape I was driving through.

'Please turn around and turn left in three hundred yards.'

I didn't think this could be true. I was sure that my turning lay still about half a mile ahead to the left. It was easy to miss, I had been told, especially if you have never made it before. Satnavs obviously behave strangely in Yorkshire. I decided to leave it on and find out what it said next.

I slowed to a crawl, kept my eyes open, and there it was, a gap in the drystone wall on my left, which resembled a neglected farm track more than anything else, though I could see by the tyre marks that someone else had been that way recently. There was no signpost, and an old wooden farm gate hung open at an angle, broken away from the rusty hinge at the top. The opening was just about wide enough for a small delivery van.

It had turned into a gorgeous day, I thought, as I guided the Volvo through the narrow entrance. The hidden dale opened up to me beyond the overhanging trees like some magical land never seen by human eye before. The car bumped over a cattle grid and splashed through a puddle. It was hard to believe the deluge that had almost washed me off the road between Ripon and Masham, but that's Yorkshire weather for you. If you don't like it, my father used to say, wait ten minutes or drive ten miles.

'Please turn back now,' the satnav said. I switched it off and continued along the lane.

The grass was lush green after the heavy summer rains,

the pale blue sky dotted with fluffy white clouds, the trees resplendent in their muted autumn colours of gold, lemon and russet. They might not be as dramatic as the fall leaves in Vermont, but they have a beauty all of their own, nonetheless. My window was open a few inches, and I could hear the birdsong and smell the wet grass.

I was driving west along the valley bottom, just to the right of Kilnsgarthdale Beck, which was running high, almost busting its banks. The whole dale was probably no more than half a mile wide and two miles long, its bottom a flat swathe of about two hundred yards, along which the beck and the lane ran side by side. Grassy slopes rose gently to a height of about fifty feet or so on either side, a silvery stream trickling down here and there to join the beck, and treelines ran along the top of each side. A few cattle grazed on the slope to my right, which I guessed was attached to a farm out of sight, over the hill. Kilnsgarthdale is a small, secluded dale flanked by woods and drystone walls. You won't see it on any but the most detailed of maps.

I passed a ruined stone barn and the remnants of a drystone wall, which had once marked the boundary of a field on the opposite hillside, but there were no other signs of human habitation until I neared Kilnsgate House.

The house was set about twenty yards back from the lane, on my right, beyond a low drystone garden wall with a green wooden gate in need of painting. I paused and looked through the car window. It was hard to see much more than the chimneys, slate roof and the tops of a couple of upper windows from the lane, because the rest was obscured by trees, and the sloping garden was quite overgrown. I had a curious sensation that the shy, half-hidden house was waiting for me, that it had been waiting for some time. I gave a little shudder, then I turned off the engine

and sat for a moment, breathing in the sweet air and luxuri-
ating in the silence. So this was it, I thought, my journey's
end. Or its beginning.

I know it sounds odd, but I had seen Kilnsgate House only
in photographs up to this point. During the entire purchase
process, I had been involved in a massive work project back
in Los Angeles, and I simply hadn't had the time to jump
on a plane and fly over for a viewing. The whole business
had been handled by the estate agent, Heather Barlow, and
a solicitor, transacted via emails, couriers, phone calls and
wire transfers.

Kilnsgate House was by far the best of many I had viewed
on the Internet, and the price was right. A bargain, in fact.
It had been used as a rental property for some years, and
there was no present occupant. The owner lived abroad and
showed no interest in the place, which was held in trust for
him, or her, by a solicitor in Northallerton. There would be
no problems with onward chains and gazumping, and all
those other odd practices the English go in for when buying
and selling houses. I could move in, Mrs Barlow had assured
me, as soon as I wanted.

She had brought up the issue of isolation, and I saw now
exactly what she meant. This had posed a problem, along
with the size of the house, when it came to renting the place
to tourists. I would be cut off from the world here, she had
said. The nearest neighbours lived more than a mile away on
a farm, over the other side of the hill, beyond the treeline,
and the nearest town, Richmond, was two miles away. I told
her that was fine with me.

I got out of the car, walked through the creaky gate, then
turned and stood by the wall to admire the view of the
opposite daleside. About halfway up stood a stone ruin,

framed by the trees, half buried in the hill. I thought it was perhaps a folly of some kind.

The only other thing that Mrs Barlow had been particularly concerned about was my attitude towards the grand piano. It would be possible to move it out, she said in one of our many telephone conversations, but difficult. There would be no extra charge for it, of course, should I decide to keep it, though she would quite understand if I did want rid of it.

I couldn't believe my luck. I had been about to order an upright piano, or perhaps even a small digital model. Now I had a grand. All I would need, Mrs Barlow went on, surprised and pleased at my acceptance and excitement, was a piano tuner.

Although I was unaware of it at this point, Kilnsgate House also had a history, which would soon come to interest me, perhaps even to obsess me, some might argue. A good estate agent, and Heather Barlow was good, clearly becomes adept in the art of omission.

I was tired after my long journey. I had spent three days in London after my flight from Los Angeles, a confusing period of jetlag punctuated by lunches and dinners with old friends and business acquaintances. I had then bought a new Volvo V50 estate – a good car for northern climes – at a showroom a friend had recommended in Camberwell, and driven down to Bournemouth to spend two days with my mother. She was eighty-seven and still going strong, proud of her son and anxious to show me off to all her neighbours, though none of them had heard of me except through her. She couldn't understand why I was returning to England after so long – it had only gone downhill even more over the years, she insisted – and especially to Yorkshire. She had hardly been able to wait to get out of there, and when my dad, bless his soul, retired in 1988, they had bought a bungalow on the edge of Bournemouth. Sadly, the old man only got to enjoy three years of retirement before succumbing to cancer at sixty-seven, but my mother was still hanging in there, still taking her constitutional on the prom every morning and her medicinal bottle of Guinness every night.

If pressed, I realised that I wouldn't have been able to explain to my mother, or to anyone else, for that matter, why I was returning after so long. I would perhaps have muttered something about coming full circle, though what I was hoping for was more of a fresh start. Perhaps I thought that I could accomplish this time what I hadn't been able to accomplish in my first twenty-five years here, before I went off to America to seek my fortune. The truth was that I hoped, by coming back, that I would discover why I had felt such a deep and nagging need to come back, if that makes any sense.

Now, as I stood before the large house I had bought, suitcase and computer bag in hand, I started to feel the familiar fear that I had overstepped my mark, that gut-wrenching sensation that I was an impostor and would soon be found out. The reality of the house intimidated me. It was much larger than I had imagined, rather like some of the old English-style mansions in Beverly Hills. To enjoy such luxurious excess in southern California had seemed perfectly normal, while back here, in jolly olde England, it seemed an act of encroachment on something that was not, by right of birth, mine. People like me did not live in houses like this.

I grew up in a rough part of Leeds, only fifty or sixty miles away geographically, but a million miles away in every other sense. When I was younger, affluence and privilege had always been more of an affront to me than the source of wonder they seemed to so many Americans, who thought the castles and history and royal family quaint. My family was more of a Royle Family than a 'royal' one. I never forgot that my ancestors were the ones who had to tug their forelocks when the lord of a manor house such as Kilnsgate rode by, nose in the air, and splattered them with mud.

In my youth, I had been an angry young man, if not quite a card-carrying communist, but now I didn't really give a damn. So many years in America had changed me, softened me – central heating, air-conditioning, a beautiful split-level penthouse apartment in Santa Monica, complete with a hardwood floor and a balcony overlooking the Pacific, and a large dose of that 'everyone is created equal and anyone can be president' bullshit.

But the change was only superficial. Some things run far deeper than material comforts. I must admit, as I stood and surveyed my magnificent new home, I could feel the old socialist, working-class values rise and harden into a big chip on my shoulder. Worse, I could feel again that deep-rooted, unnerving sensation that I *didn't deserve* it, that such houses were never intended for the likes of me, that I would wake up in the morning and it would all be gone, and I would be back where I belonged, living in a back-to-back terrace house on a decrepit council estate and working down the pit or, more likely these days, not working at all.

I had once tried to explain all this to Laura in my cups the night I won my one and only Academy Award – that I didn't deserve it, that at any moment the bubble would burst, everyone would realise what a phoney I was, and I would be put back right where I belonged. But she didn't understand. To her American mind, of course, I deserved the Oscar. The Academy wouldn't have given it to me otherwise, would they? So why didn't I just accept the damn thing and enjoy the party like everyone else? Then she laughed and hugged me and called me her beautiful fool.

Kilnsgate House towered over me. It had a typical enough Dales façade, from what I could see as I walked up the path between the trees and the overgrown lawn, a broad symmetrical oblong of limestone with a hint of darker millstone grit here and there, two windows on either side of the front door, the same upstairs, and a slate roof. There was an arched stone porch at the front, with wooden benches on either side, which reminded me of the entrance to an old village church. I guessed that it was a useful area for taking off muddy boots after a day's grouse-shooting or riding with the hunt. There was even an elephant's-foot stand for walking sticks and umbrellas.

Above the lintel was a date stone carved: 'JM 1748', which I took to be the initials of the original owner. The keys were taped under the bench on my right, as Mrs Barlow had promised they would be. She had also said she regretted that she couldn't be there to greet me, as she had an urgent appointment in Greta Bridge, but she promised to call by around six o'clock and see me settled in. That gave me plenty of time to get acclimatised and have a good look around, though I was beginning to regret that I hadn't stopped to pick up some supplies at the Co-op I had passed on my way through Richmond. I didn't want to have to go out again tonight, not now that I was here, but I hadn't eaten since lunchtime, and my stomach was starting to rumble.

It took me a few moments to turn the large key in the deadlock, but I managed, picked up my cases again and walked into the hallway. It was more of a large antechamber or vestibule, by the looks of it, and it took up most of the central part of the front of the house. A small stained-glass square high above the door split the sunlight into blue, red, yellow and purple beams that seemed to shift, kaleidoscope-like, as the trees outside swayed in the breeze and cast shadows with their branches and leaves.

I had seen photographs of the interior, of course, but nothing quite prepares you for the impact of the real thing. Size, for example. Like the exterior, it was so much larger than I had imagined that I felt intimidated at first. In my memory, English houses were small and cramped. But I was standing in a high-ceilinged room large enough for a party, with a broad wooden staircase directly in front of me leading to the upper landing, with railed galleries and doors leading to the bedrooms. I could imagine a host of people in Victorian dress leaning against the polished wooden railings and looking down on some theatrical performance, a Christmas pageant, perhaps, presented below, where I was standing, by unbearably cute children and costumed young ladies demonstrating their accomplishments.

A couple of well-used armchairs stood near the door by an antique sideboard, and a grandfather clock with a swinging brass pendulum ticked away to the left of the staircase. I checked the time against my wristwatch, and it was accurate. The walls were wainscoted to waist height, above which they were covered by flock wallpaper. A chandelier hung from the high ceiling like a fountain frozen in midair. All the wood surfaces shone with recent polishing, and the air smelled of lemon and lavender. Several gilt-framed paintings hung on the walls: Richmond Castle at sunset, two horses at pasture near Middleham, a man, woman and child posing by the front of the house. None of them was especially valuable, I thought, but nor were they the kind of cheap prints people pick up at a flea market. The frames alone were probably worth a fair bit. Who could afford to leave all this behind? Why?

Taking the suitcase that contained my toiletries and what few clothes I had brought with me, I climbed the slightly uneven and creaky wooden stairs to seek out a suitable bedroom.

Two large bedrooms took up the front of the house, one on either side, mirror images across the gallery, and I chose the second one I peeked in. A bright, cheerful room, with cream, rose-patterned wallpaper, it had windows at the front and side, four in all, letting in plenty of sunshine. A selection of sheets and a thick duvet lay folded neatly on a wooden chest at the foot of the bed. The room also had a pine wardrobe, a dressing table and a chair, with enough space left over to hold a tea dance. There were no pictures on the walls, but I would have fun searching around the local markets and antique shops for suitable prints. A second door led from the bedroom to the en suite toilet, washbasin and glassed-in shower unit.

One of the front windows had a small padded seat, from which I could see over the garden trees to the opposite daleside, the beck, the folly and the woods beyond. It seemed a pleasant little nook in which to curl up and read. From the side windows, I had a view back along the dale where I had just driven. I could see that, even though it was only four o'clock, the afternoon shadows were already lengthening. Without even bothering to make the bed, I stretched out on the mattress and felt it adjust and mould to my shape. I rested my head on the pillow – the sort that was thicker at one end than the other, and reminded me of an executioner's block – and closed my eyes. Just for a moment, I could have sworn I heard the piano in the distance. Schubert's third *Impromptu*. It sounded beautiful, ethereal, and I soon drifted off to sleep. The next thing I knew someone was knocking at the front door, and the room was in darkness.

In the best books, the ending often comes as a shock.
Not just because of that one last twist in the tale,
but because you have been so absorbed in their world,
that coming back to the harsh light of reality is a jolt.

If that describes you now, then perhaps you should track down
some new leads, and find new suspense in other worlds.

Join us at www.hodder.co.uk, or follow us on
Twitter @hodderbooks, and you can tap in to a
community of fellow thrill-seekers.

Whether you want to find out more about this book,
or a particular author, watch trailers and interviews, have
the chance to win early limited editions, or simply browse
our expert readers' selection of the very best books,
we think you'll find what you're looking for.

And if you don't, that's the place to tell us what's missing.

We love what we do, and we'd love you to be part of it.

www.hodder.co.uk

@hodderbooks

HodderBooks

HodderBooks

SOCIOLOGY ON THE MENU

An invitation to the study of food and society

Alan Beardsworth and Teresa Keil

Routledge
Taylor & Francis Group

LONDON AND NEW YORK

First published 1997
by Routledge
2 Park Square, Milton Park, Abingdon, Oxon OX14 4RN

Simultaneously published in the USA and Canada
by Routledge
270 Madison Ave, New York NY 10016

Reprinted 2001

Transferred to Digital Printing 2002

Routledge is an imprint of the Taylor & Francis Group, an informa business

© 1997 Alan Beardsworth and Teresa Keil

Typeset in Baskerville by
Pure Tech India Limited, Pondicherry

Printed and bound in Great Britain by
T.J.I. Digital, Padstow, Cornwall

British Library Cataloguing in Publication Data

A catalogue record for this book is available from the British Library

Library of Congress Cataloging in Publication Data

A catalogue record for this book has been requested

ISBN 10: 0-415-11424-1 (hbk)
ISBN 10: 0-415-11425-X (pbk)

ISBN 13: 978-0-415-11424-0 (hbk)
ISBN 13: 978-0-415-11425-7 (pbk)

SOCIOLOGY ON THE MENU

Sociology on the Menu is an accessible introduction to the sociology of food. High-lighting the social and cultural dimensions of the human food system, from production to consumption, it encourages us to consider new ways of thinking about the apparently mundane, everyday act of eating.

This book provides a broad conceptual framework, based on the proposition that the food systems and food consumption patterns of contemporary Western societies are the products of the complex interplay of the social forces of change and innovation on the one hand and, on the other, those which engender stability and continuity. The main areas covered include the origins of human subsistence, the development of the modern food system, food and the family, eating out, diet and health, food risks and food scares, dieting and body image, the meanings of meat, vegetarianism and the role of sweetness in the human diet.

Sociology on the Menu provides a comprehensive overview of the multidisciplinary literature, focusing on key texts and studies to help students identify the main themes. It urges us to reappraise the taken-for-granted and familiar experiences of selecting, preparing and sharing food and to see our own habits and choices, preferences and aversions in their broader cultural context.

Alan Beardsworth is Lecturer in Sociology and **Teresa Keil** is Visiting Fellow, both in the Department of Social Sciences, Loughborough University.

For Helen and Ian

CONTENTS

FIGURES AND TABLES

FIGURES

TABLES

PREFACE

The origins of this book can be traced back to the mid-1980s when we first became aware of the curious fact that food and eating seemed to be topics for enthusiastic discussion for virtually everyone but the sociologist. This realization led us to begin a search for any sociologically relevant material that could satisfy our curiosity. We then went a step further by initiating our own research into the fascinating subject of vegetarianism, a choice of research area which was made in order to give us access to respondents who had critically examined much of our conventional wisdom about the day-to-day realities of eating. Grappling with the problem of explaining our findings helped us to clarify our understanding of what a sociology of food and eating might look like.

Happily, we were not alone in identifying an area of potentially fruitful expansion in sociology. The amount of research and writing in this field began to increase to such an extent that by the early 1990s we felt confident enough to offer an undergraduate course entitled 'Food and Society: Sociological Perspectives'. It is that course which provided the foundations of this book and helped us to identify the themes which we have sought to develop and illustrate.

Many people have provided assistance, both direct and indirect, in the preparation of this text. In particular, we would like to express our appreciation of the interest shown in our work by Alan Bryman, Nick Norgan and Alan Radley, and of the help provided by Frank Parry of the University's Pilkington Library. Special thanks must also go to those colleagues with whom we have worked in the context of a series of food- and nutrition-related projects, namely, Barbara Dobson, Jackie Goode, Cheryl Haslam, Marie Kennedy, Emma Sherratt and Robert Walker. We have benefited enormously from our discussions with them and from their insight and expertise. However, any shortcomings and inadequacies are entirely our own responsibility. The smooth progress of this whole project has also depended heavily on the invaluable secretarial support provided by Ann Smith, and additionally by Christine Mosley.

Alan Beardsworth and Teresa Keil
Loughborough University
October 1995

INTRODUCTION

FOOD AND EATING: A CASE OF SOCIOLOGICAL NEGLECT?

One of the most effective ways of assessing which topics or issues are generally regarded as fundamental to a given discipline is to survey the contents of that discipline's standard introductory textbooks. In such hallowed volumes are enshrined, if only in their most basic form, those principles, theories and doctrines which are deemed essential for all recruits to master. However, scanning the contents pages of the wide range of introductory sociology texts available leads to an inevitable conclusion: alongside the themes which, in various guises, occur again and again (stratification, work and employment, crime and deviance, ethnicity, gender, the family, etc.) you will not come across food and eating as a specifically identified focus of interest. If such issues are addressed at all, they usually appear on the margins of one or more of the central themes.

In one sense, at least, this marginality is not too surprising. Quite clearly, it is feasible for sociologists with imagination and initiative to create an almost endless list of potentially fruitful sub-headings within their discipline (the sociology of housing, the sociology of sport, the sociology of transport, the sociology of tourism – or, more fancifully, why not the sociology of furniture, or the sociology of children's games?). While such lines of intellectual pursuit may yield all kinds of fascinating insights, they are likely to remain relatively specialized interests, coexisting with each other and developing each along its own lines beneath the broad umbrella of sociology. Much the same might be said of the sociology of food and eating. Here we have a specialized area which deserves attention, but which is never likely to be of central importance. This is a perfectly viable position and one that allows interested teachers and researchers to get on with work in this area to the benefit of themselves, their students and their readers. On the other hand, we might argue that attempts to describe and understand the complex interrelations between food and society deserve special attention, deserve elevation to a position equal to that of the major themes of contemporary sociology. This view becomes eminently plausible if one considers

1

just how fundamental a part of human experience eating really is, given the inexorable and relentless demands of the body for nutrients, and given the potent and multifaceted symbolic charges that food can carry. Moreover, enormous amounts of human energy, ingenuity and co-operative effort are devoted to the processes involved in the production, distribution and preparation of food – processes which are absolutely essential to the long-term survival and continuity of any society. What is more, the human food chain, with its myriad interlinked and interacting human and non-human elements, might justifiably be conceived of as the core sub-system of the social system as a whole, the very foundation of human social organization. With these arguments in mind, and given the high level of popular interest in this area, sociology's relative neglect of such issues and their virtual absence from its intellectual heartlands becomes something of a puzzle. However, this is a puzzle to which one might offer some tentative answers.

For example, it may well be that the very much taken-for-granted nature of eating has rendered this activity, and the complex of other activities and relationships which cluster around it, relatively 'invisible' to sociologists. Of course, for eating to be a mundane activity, for food to be an unproblematical aspect of daily life, one crucial condition must be fulfilled: the food supply itself must be secure. This is certainly the case for the vast majority of people in Western societies (and is especially so for the vast majority of sociologists). In circumstances where the food supply is less secure, food-related concerns will usually be a good deal higher on the agenda. In addition, in developed, industrialized societies, the processes of food production and distribution (if not of food preparation and consumption) are usually largely beyond the view and concern of the urban, middle-class individual that is the typical professional sociologist. It is frequently only within the confines of the specialized area of rural sociology that such issues come under sociological scrutiny. Indeed, this effect is mirrored at the domestic end of the human food chain. The purchasing, preparation and presentation of food (and, indeed, the disposal of leftover food and the more menial tasks of the kitchen) are strongly associated with the mundane, unglamourous labour of housework, the traditional domain of women, and hold little intellectual appeal to the male researchers and theorists who have historically dominated the profession.

There is an additional factor which may well have helped to inhibit the development of sociological interest in this area. In a sense, the study and analysis of food-related issues may have been seen as the intellectual property of other professions and other academic disciplines (for example, on the production side, the property of agronomists, economists and geographers, and, on the consumption side, of nutritionists and dietitians). What is more, since the inception of sociology as a recognized discipline, its practitioners have striven to assert its intellectual autonomy and to demonstrate that social processes exist at their own distinctive level and require their own distinctive explanations. This seems to have encouraged sociologists to be somewhat wary of becoming too closely associated with debates about the significance of the physiological bases of human experience and human existence, possibly out of concern about being seen as guilty of reductionism by their colleagues. Thus, activities where the physiological dimension is clearly salient have, to some extent, been seen as outside the proper theoretical preoccupations and research interests of sociologists.

This coyness in relation to food and eating stands in contrast to the long-standing interest in the area shown by some of sociology's neighbouring disciplines. Historians, for example, have shown a good deal of interest in such issues. This is hardly surprising, given the tremendous impact that basic realities relating to the control of and access to food resources can have upon broader social, economic and political events and processes. Similarly, social anthropologists also seem to have been much more willing to incorporate the analysis of matters alimentary into their work. One can perhaps speculate that this fact is, to some extent, due to the nature of the subject matter of the discipline. Social anthropology's major concern in the twentieth century has been the detailed description, documentation and analysis of the workings of relatively small-scale, traditional social systems which have usually been conceptualized in broadly holistic terms. Looking at a traditional society in this holistic fashion virtually demands that some attention be paid to the processes involved in producing, distributing, preparing and consuming food, since these make up a complex of activities which provides the whole framework of life on a daily and a seasonal basis. What is more, in societies where the food supply is somewhat insecure and unpredictable, food-related matters are likely to be much more .salient in the day-to-day concerns of the researcher's subjects.

However, it is perhaps within the discipline of psychology that an interest in food and eating has been particularly well developed. This interest has covered a wide range of topics, including the sensory, cognitive and emotional dimensions of eating, the processes of nutritional socialization and the causes and manifestations of eating disorders. Again, it is possible to speculate about why psychologists have devoted a good deal more of their attention to dietary issues than have sociologists. It may be that the key to this puzzle lies in the nature of the disciplinary range of psychology itself. Those working towards the physiological end of this range are well placed to investigate the physical processes of eating in their immediate sensory and behavioural contexts. On the other hand, those working towards the social end of this range are in a good position to investigate the complex influences of personality, biography and interpersonal relationships. In fact, the interests of the social psychologist may sometimes overlap with those of the sociologist, as, indeed, may those of the social anthropologist and the historian.

A SURGE IN SOCIOLOGICAL INTEREST

Despite what has been argued above, there can be no doubt that recent years have seen a marked increase in the willingness of some sociologists to direct their

3

attention towards this previously neglected set of topics. Evidence for this rising level of engagement comes from a number of sources. Perhaps the most significant indicator is the increasing numbers of books and journal articles produced by sociologists which are either directly or indirectly addressed to food-related issues. While it would certainly be an unwarranted exaggeration to suggest that what had previously been a trickle of material has become a flood, there can be little doubt that the current of publications (to continue the hydraulic metaphor) is now flowing more strongly than ever before.

Other indicators appear to confirm this overall impression. University courses which can be classified under the broad heading of 'Food and Society' are already widely available in the USA and Canada, and have now gained a foothold in the UK. Recent research developments also support this view. Perhaps the most notable is the research initiative entitled 'The Nation's Diet', set up in 1991 by the UK's Economic and Social Research Council. With a budget of £1.4 million, this six-year programme was divided into two phases. In both phases a substantial number of the projects funded were sociological in orientation or contained a significant sociological component. The increasing inclination of sociologists towards research related to the social and cultural dimensions of food and eating is also indicated by their ever more frequent participation in both national and international conferences devoted to nutritional issues. What is more, there is an increasingly wide range of international organizations and associations dedicated wholly or partly to the study of the relationships between nutritional and social processes from a sociological perspective.

Accounting for this surge of sociological interest is undoubtedly as speculative an exercise as attempting to explain previous neglect. However, one factor that is almost certainly of considerable significance is the occurrence in recent years of a shift in the centre of gravity of sociology itself. A discipline once largely concerned with the analysis of the processes of *production* (in terms of their social organization and their consequences for the social, economic and political dynamics of society) is now increasingly turning its attention to the social organization of *consumption*, and to the ideological foundations of consumerism in its many guises. Such a change serves to push food-related issues up the sociological agenda, given the importance of food items in any household's expenditure patterns.

Another important shift in sociology involves the increasing salience of issues relating to the experiences of women, largely as a result of the initiatives taken by writers and theorists informed by feminist perspectives. Since the purchasing, preparation and presentation of food is still regarded, in many senses, as essentially women's work, such activities have been drawn increasingly into the domain of sociological scrutiny. Indeed, this has been closely associated with an enhanced recognition by sociologists of the significance of domestic work and the domestic sphere in general.

Furthermore, sociological concerns are often indirectly (or even directly) linked to the broader political and policy-oriented issues current in the society

4

in which the discipline is practised. In this sense, sociology's increasing interest in food can be seen as, in part, a reflection of the increasing importance of a range of nutritional issues in the various policy arenas. Pressure groups, professional groups and the state itself are engaged in a whole series of debates about dietary standards, food purity and hygiene, production methods and standards, animal welfare, the links between diet and health, and the nutritional adequacy of food intake patterns of certain vulnerable groups such as low-income households, to name but a few key examples. In this connection, it is also worth bearing in mind that environmental issues are now much higher on the agenda in the developed, industrial societies than ever before. Sociologists have realized, some-what belatedly, that this area demands their attention, too. However, environmental concerns almost inevitably entail a consideration of the dynamics of human food chains in all their complexity. The ways in which food is produced and distributed have an enormous impact upon particular ecological systems and upon the environment in general. Conversely, environmental changes (for example, habitat degradation, erosion and various forms of pollution) can have significant implications for food supply and food quality. The increasing willingness of sociologists to focus upon such possibilities has also contributed to a rising awareness of food as a topic.

THE INCORPORATION OF FOOD-RELATED ISSUES INTO SOCIOLOGY

There are, perhaps, two basic routes through which the study of food and eating is being incorporated into the mainstream of sociology. The first of these involves the analysis of food production and consumption (and the elaborate social structures and relationships which underpin these) with the specific aim of illuminating existing sociological preoccupations. Thus, the analysis of patterns of food allocation and consumption has been used very effectively to illustrate the ways in which the underlying dimensions of social differentiation (gender, age and class, for example) manifest themselves in the experiences of everyday life. Similarly, the analysis of the processes of food production and distribution has been used to highlight the workings of capital-intensive, highly rationalized economic systems. The second of these two routes involves the reverse of the first. Instead of food-related social processes being investigated as a means to a particular sociological end, food-based topics can become ends in themselves, that is, specific questions can be asked about how we obtain, share, select, prepare and eat our food, and how we allocate meaning to what we are doing. Once these questions have been posed, well-tried sociological methods, perspectives and theories can be applied in order to attempt to understand what is going on. Of course, these two approaches may happily coexist within one piece of work, since the difference between them is essentially one of emphasis. However, if the sociology of food is to establish itself in the mainstream of the discipline, the second of these two approaches deserves attention, since the social and

5

cultural dimensions of food systems raise many unique and fascinating issues, a selection of which it is the purpose of this book to address.

There can, indeed, be no doubt that the complex of human activities and experiences which relates to producing and consuming food is potentially a source of endlessly tantalizing puzzles for the sociologist. While food intake is an inescapable physiological necessity, eating entails far more than its basic physiological dimensions. Quite clearly, the act of eating lies at the point of intersection of a whole series of intricate physiological, psychological, ecological, economic, political, social and cultural processes. Such intersections present the human and social sciences with some of their most intriguing questions and challenges. However, in order to rise to such challenges, sociologists may need to be prepared to think more flexibly about the traditional boundaries of their discipline. Historically, sociologists have laid considerable stress on the idea of a clear dichotomy between the biological and the social, between 'nature' and 'culture', with the intellectual territory of sociology located firmly on the cultural/social side of this deep divide. In the past, this confident demarcation has proved to be highly fruitful, and capable of stimulating brilliant analyses of the social organization and dynamics of modern societies, centred upon such enduring themes as conflict and integration, change and stability, rationalization and industrialization. However, such a clear-cut demarcation may have contributed to the marginalization of such themes as gender, sexuality, the body, health and illness and, of course, food and eating. For many reasons yet to be documented fully we now seem to be witnessing a softening of this previously strictly enforced boundary and an increasing recognition of its essential permeability. Interactions across this boundary are generating more and more sociological interest, thus opening up novel areas of study and moving previously marginal themes towards the centre of interest and into the mainstream of sociological debate.

THE AIMS OF THIS BOOK

A text such as this one has a number of interrelated aims, and it is helpful for the reader to see these set out at this stage in a reasonably systematic fashion:

1   To highlight for the reader the social and cultural dimensions of the human food system, from production to consumption.
2   To achieve this by providing accounts of key texts and studies which are to be found in the diverse and rather widely dispersed literature which exists in this area.
3   To focus the reader's attention on the main themes which have been addressed in the literature (these themes being reflected in the sequence of chapters which makes up the structure of the book).
4   To draw out the interconnections between these themes and to attempt to set them within a broad conceptual framework, which will be discussed in more

detail in Chapter 3. This framework is based upon the proposition that the food systems and food consumption patterns of contemporary Western societies are the products of the complex interplay of, on the one hand, social forces and processes inducing instability, change and innovation, and, on the other, social forces and mechanisms engendering stability and continuity.

5 To encourage professional social scientists (particularly sociologists) to develop an interest in this area, and, even more importantly, to begin to take up some of the intellectual challenges it presents.
6 To encourage the reader to consider new ways of thinking about the apparently mundane, everyday act of eating, and to see his or her own habits and choices, preferences and aversions in their broader cultural and social contexts.
7 To achieve these admittedly rather grandiose aims by presenting ideas and information in an accessible, although not necessarily undemanding, fashion.
8 Finally, if at all feasible, to entertain and engage the reader with some of the intriguing insights which are on offer.

The approach employed will be a deliberately eclectic one. While sociological sources will provide the bulk of our raw material, the ideas and findings of neighbouring disciplines will also be drawn upon, as and when these can be used in order to support sociological analysis and to extend sociological perspectives. The audience for this book is conceived in similarly broad terms:

1 Students of sociology at all levels, whether in the context of specific food-related courses or in the context of other sociology courses where such topics are relevant.
2 Other social science students, including those studying such diverse disciplines as social policy, psychology, social anthropology and human geography.
3 Students undergoing professional training in the areas of nutrition and dietetics.
4 Students undergoing professional training in the various branches of nursing and medicine.
5 Students undergoing training on food-related vocational courses.
6 Established professionals in areas related to nutrition, health or social policy.
7 The general reader who is attracted to a sociological approach to the contemplation of food and eating.

Quite clearly, with such a diverse readership in mind, the avowed aim of producing a text which is accessible to the non-sociologist but at the same time can provide the stimulus for the sociologically oriented reader to follow up the issues in more depth, is by no means a straightforward one to fulfil.

THE ORGANIZATION OF THIS BOOK

The text is organized into four main parts, each with its distinctive subject matter.

Part I seeks to set the scene by looking briefly at selected aspects of the prehistory and history of human food systems (Chapter 1). Chapter 2 deals with the far-reaching changes in human social organization which have produced a whole series of crucial transformations, culminating in the emergence of the modern food system in all its global complexity. Chapter 3 then goes on to lay down a basic framework for the sociological analysis of the food system and to examine the various sociological perspectives which have been, or might be, employed to carry out such analysis. This chapter also deals with complementary approaches from neighbouring disciplines which have influenced or informed the work of sociologists.

Part II sets out to examine a number of aspects of the social organization of eating. Chapter 4 looks at the processes of social differentiation within the family (for example, by age and gender) that influence the ways in which food is prepared and distributed within the household. The ways in which food consumption patterns can be seen to highlight class differences and reinforce family identity are also considered. Since an increasing proportion of food intake takes place outside the family or household setting, Chapter 5 focuses on the phenomenon of eating out, in its many guises.

Part III attempts to provide an insight into the very broad area of food, health and well-being by focusing on a series of issues which have emerged as important themes in the available literature. Thus, Chapter 6 describes changing conceptions of the linkages between dietary patterns, on the one hand, and health and disease outcomes on the other. Such conceptions, it will be argued, have undergone a fundamental process of rationalization in modern societies. Chapter 7 focuses on the interrelated phenomena of deep-seated chronic food anxieties and acute 'food scares'. Both these phenomena can exert a potent influence on food choices and consumption patterns, and their underlying causes will be analysed. Chapter 8 moves on to consider another characteristic set of anxieties frequently related to food intake. Unease in relation to body image and concern about the acquisition of body fat can reach obsessional levels in certain circumstances, and the cultural and social roots of these effects will be discussed.

Part IV looks at selected examples of patterns of food preferences and, on the other side of the coin, at food prohibitions or avoidances. The subject matter of Chapter 9 is the convoluted and sometimes contradictory symbolism of meat, simultaneously one of the most widely prized components of the human diet and one of the most ambivalent. Meat rejection and meat avoidance figure in Chapter 10, which sets out to describe the origins and multifaceted manifestations of vegetarianism as an increasingly popular dietary option. Chapter 11 takes as its topic the role of sweetness in the human diet, the importance of the production and consumption of sugar for the global food system and the symbolism of confectionery.

In a sense, each of the chapters described here is designed to provide a self-contained introduction to its chosen subject matter. However, the social processes under discussion are themselves frequently shaped by a set of underlying ideological trends and structural transformations in human food systems. As has been indicated above, these trends and structures, which form the framework for the everyday practices of food production and consumption, will be analysed in Chapter 3, along with the various sociological perspectives which can be drawn upon. As a prelude to this, however, Chapters 1 and 2 set out to sketch the background to the emergence of the modern food system, the system which is the basic object of analysis of this book.

Perhaps at this stage the authors can be forgiven for succumbing to the temptation to use a nutritional metaphor in expressing the hope that readers will enjoy selecting from the menu of ideas displayed here and will find that their appetite for more has been whetted!

Part I

THE SOCIAL DIMENSIONS OF THE FOOD SYSTEM

1

THE ORIGINS OF HUMAN SUBSISTENCE

Any attempt to make sense of the contemporary realities of food and eating from a sociological viewpoint must involve some consideration of the past. If we wish to try to understand the food production systems upon which we depend and the food consumption patterns in which we participate, then a familiarity with certain crucial historical themes is essential. Indeed, it is also necessary to push beyond the boundaries of recorded history into the even more speculative and hazy realms of prehistory. The aim of this first chapter is to begin to provide that background. Of course, in this context, such a background cannot be provided in any great detail, since the history and prehistory of food is a vast subject in itself, covering broad sweeps of human activity and experience. Rather, the intention is to draw attention to a number of key ideas which can enhance our comprehension of the foundations of human foodways, foundations which, by their very nature, usually remain unexamined.

Our starting point will be a consideration of the diet of early humans, a contentious and complex question, but one which can lead to insights whose implications are as important now as they were in the early stages of human evolution. The issue of the basic forms of human subsistence will then be raised, along with a discussion of what is arguably one of the most important transitions in human social organization, the shift from an ancient, long-standing dependence on hunting and gathering to food production based on the techniques of agriculture. However, it will be argued that conventional views of this transition may require reconsideration and revision. Finally, we will go on to examine the enormous implications of this transition for human social relations and arrangements, not least of which was the facilitation of the emergence of increasingly complex and large-scale social systems.

THE EARLY HUMAN DIET

Perhaps the most basic nutritional question of all relates to the nature of the 'original' human diet. In other words, we need to ask how our evolutionary history as a species has shaped, or been shaped by, our dietary patterns. Attempting to build up a detailed picture of the foods which our distant forebears ate and the relative importance of the various items which figured in ancestral diets, is a task beset with enormous difficulties. Foodstuffs are, by and large, relatively perishable, and thus traces of them rarely survive over long periods of time to provide the archaeologist with direct evidence about dietary practices and subsistence strategies. Thus, all too often, investigators are compelled to rely upon the indirect evidence provided by more durable artefacts like tools, or upon the animal bones which are assumed to be the remains of ancient meals. However, such evidence can be controversial and subject to conflicting interpretation. As Binford (1992) has pointed out, the fact that animal bones and stone tools are found together in particular caves and rock shelters does not in itself demonstrate that the hominids who occupied those sites were hunters, or were solely responsible for these accumulations, since carnivores like wolves, leopards and hyenas also occupied such sites and also created accumulations of prey animals' bones.

There are, however, alternative ways of addressing these questions, and one of these involves not only looking at evidence about the diet of early hominids, but also comparing human dietary patterns with those of modern non-human primates. This is the approach adopted by Leonard and Robertson (1994), who re-examine a range of nutritional and physiological data relating to humans and their primate relatives. They point out that among primates in general there exists a consistent negative correlation between body size and diet quality. That is, large primates (such as gorillas and orang-utans) depend upon diets which consist of large amounts of bulky, hard-to-digest foods which are relatively low in nutrients per unit of weight (for example, plant parts like leaves, stems and bark). In contrast, smaller primates' diets consist of much higher quality foods, in the sense that such foods are much more densely packed with nutrients and contain far lower proportions of indigestible bulk. Their diets include the reproductive parts of plants, like seeds, nuts, fruits, bulbs and tubers, and a wide range of small animals. The authors give the example of the pygmy marmoset, which tends to focus its feeding behaviour on protein-rich insects and energy-rich plant gums and saps.

The explanation for this relationship between body size and diet quality appears to be related to metabolism, that is, the sum total of the chemical processes which drive and maintain a living body. Smaller animals have higher metabolic costs and energy needs per unit of body weight than larger animals. Although the latter have higher *total* energy needs, they need less per unit of weight, and can, therefore, make a successful living out of consuming large quantities of low-quality but relatively abundant foods. However, what is striking about humans is that they do not fit neatly into this broad overall picture. The authors examine data on the dietary intakes of a number of peoples dependent on foraging (i.e., the exploitation of wild animals and plants) for subsistence. These groups show a far higher level of dietary quality (as measured by a composite index) than would have been expected for primates of their size. They also consume a far higher proportion of animal material (material defined

14

as high-quality in terms of nutrient density) than comparably sized primates (e.g., anthropoid apes). What is more, when the authors looked at data from agricultural societies, where much lower quantities of animal products like meat are consumed, the diet quality is still significantly higher than would have been predicted for primates in general in that size range, since the grains and cereals eaten by these human consumers are much richer in calories than are fibrous leaves and stems.

We are therefore faced with a puzzle, in that humans eat a diet which is of much greater quality than would be predicted by their body size. Indeed, Leonard and Robertson (1994) also demonstrate that this quality is higher than might be expected from humans' resting metabolic rate, a baseline which expresses the amount of energy required for metabolism when the body is at rest. In fact, the authors go on to argue that the key to this puzzle is the size of the human brain. The human brain is, of course, relatively large in relation to body weight compared with other primates, and for that reason its energy demands are proportionately higher. They calculate that humans spend around three to four times more on brain metabolism than do other primates. Thus, in humans 20–25 per cent of the energy expenditure making up the resting metabolic rate goes to the brain, as opposed to an average of 8–9 per cent for our non-human primate relatives. There seems to be a close association between the possession of a large brain with a high energy requirement and the consumption of a high-quality, nutrient-rich diet.

Switching their attention to the archaeological data, Leonard and Robertson (1994) note that early members of our own genus *Homo*, specifically *Homo habilis* and *Homo erectus*, seem to show signs of this characteristically human relationship between brain size, body size and resting metabolic rate. Archaeological evidence also indicates that these species ate higher-quality diets (in that they contained a higher proportion of animal material) than did, for example, the ancient ape-like primates belonging to the genus *Australopithecus*. All this would appear to indicate that in the course of hominid evolution, increasing brain size (with a concomitant increase in the brain's energy demands) would have had to be associated with a shift towards an increasingly nutrient-rich diet. While these authors, quite explicitly, do not argue that somehow dietary factors caused changes in human brain evolution, they do seem to demonstrate that a move towards a higher-quality diet would have been a necessary condition for sustaining an evolutionary trend towards a larger and more powerful brain.

If we accept the arguments of these two biologists, we are led to a striking conclusion: the very basis of our human distinctiveness, our large and uniquely sophisticated brain, appears to demand that we maintain a high-quality, energy-rich diet. This appears to be confirmed by the fact that the human digestive tract is relatively short compared to most other primates, indicating its adaptation to high-energy, easy-to-digest foods. All these factors add up to what are, in effect, the nutritional 'facts of life' for human beings, facts rooted in our evolutionary past and our actual physiology. However, to state this is not to argue for a form

15

of biological determinism. Our humanness imposes certain nutritional imperatives upon us, making us ominivores with a need for a high-quality diet, but these imperatives do not determine human nutritional endeavours and choices, rather they set a framework within which they are played out. Within that framework there is the scope for enormous variation, since human ingenuity is capable of generating an apparently infinite variety of solutions within an impressive range of cultural and ecological settings.

HUNTING AND GATHERING

However, varied as these solutions may be, attuned as they are to the mix of opportunities and constraints presented by their own unique circumstances, they can be placed into more general categories. Quite clearly, if we wish to consider the earliest forms of human subsistence, then we will need to focus our attention upon that broad category of activities that are often referred to as 'foraging'. In this sense, the term is used to describe the exploitation for food of plants and animals over which the user has little or no control (in other words, organisms which can be seen as 'wild'). When the organisms in question are animals that have sufficient agility and alertness to require active pursuit or stalking, the term 'hunting' is used. When the organisms consumed are plants, or animals with little or no mobility, the term 'gathering' is conventionally applied. (Trapping can be seen as an intermediate category, since certain forms of it permit the capture of active animals without the need for pursuit.) The combination of hunting and gathering has provided our species with its sustenance for most of its evolutionary history.

It is intriguing to note, however, that from the early days of scientific debate concerning ancestral patterns of human subsistence, far more stress has been placed upon the hunting component of the hunter/gatherer lifestyle than on the gathering component. Hunting has conventionally been seen as having exerted a potent formative influence upon human social and physiological evolution. Perhaps the clearest and most explicit academic expressions of the role of hunting in the development of human social, cultural and physical characteristics can be found in papers which emerged from a highly influential symposium entitled 'Man the Hunter', held at the University of Chicago in 1966. Thus, Washburn and Lancaster (1968) argue that human hunting (an activity almost entirely the preserve of males) represents a form of subsistence and a way of life that has provided the common factors which have dominated human evolution for over 99 per cent of its course. They point to key physiological and social adaptations which they see as closely associated with hunting: the development of a large brain, the use of tools and weapons which demand high levels of skill in their production and use, a sexual division of labour with females concentrating on food gathering and child rearing while being supplied with meat by males, and the development of complex forms of communication and co-operation between males to facilitate hunting success. From this list, it is

16

apparent that this view of hunting sees it as the root of human features as diverse as skill in the creation of artefacts, the male-dominated family and the emergence of that most sophisticated of communication devices, language.

This hunting-centred view is presented even more emphatically by Laughlin, who goes as far as to assert that, 'Hunting is the master behaviour pattern of the human species' (Laughlin 1968: 304). He maintains that the fact that the human species achieved worldwide distribution while dependent on hunting for subsistence demonstrates the universality of this particular adaptation. What is more, he also suggests that an impressive range of human physical attributes arises directly from our hunting past. These include muscular strength and a high load-carrying capacity, sustained endurance at running speed, a high level of agility and manual dexterity, excellent colour vision, good hearing and a remarkably tough and durable outer skin. These features provide a degree of physiological flexibility sufficient to enable humans to colonize habitats far more diverse than those available to any other comparable animal. When these features are combined with a high-capacity memory, superior learning ability, the use of tools and language, and the development of complex forms of co-operation (these features also being seen as emerging out of the demands of a hunting way of life), the recipe for human success as a species appears to be complete. Indeed, so compelling is this view of human development that it has strongly influenced popular views of human origins and human nature.

THE EMERGENCE OF AGRICULTURE

However, while what has been termed the 'Hunting Hypothesis' does provide us with a number of fascinating possibilities concerning the links between human subsistence strategies and dietary patterns on the one hand, and human evolution on the other, it does exhibit some significant limitations. We will return to these limitations later in this chapter, although before doing this it is necessary to confront a fundamental conundrum which has been puzzling scholars for several generations: if the hunting and gathering approach to subsistence is such a successful one, and if it is so closely integrated with human evolutionary developments, why does there eventually occur a radical shift towards a very different form of subsistence? This novel approach to providing food involves deliberately and systematically *producing* food, rather than capturing food animals or gathering food plants which exist independently of human activities and interventions.

The timing of this shift is, in geological terms, comparatively recent. The end of the Pleistocene, some 14,000 years ago, saw the retreat of the glacial ice in the northern hemisphere, accompanied by dramatic climate changes. Tundra and grasslands were, in many areas, replaced by forests, and humans were compelled to adapt their hunting and gathering patterns accordingly. Foraging strategies appear to have become more diversified, since vast herds of large herbivorous mammals inhabiting wide, open plains were no longer available to the same extent in the northern temperate zones to provide human hunters with an

17

abundant food supply. Shortly after these far-reaching environmental changes occurred, the emergence of agriculture began, spanning a period dating from between 9,000 and 12,000 years ago. As Hole (1992) points out, the shift to agriculture appears to have begun in the warmer latitudes and spread later to temperate regions. The process was dependent upon the domestication of a range of plant species, domestication itself being conventionally viewed as the replacement of the pressures of natural selection with artificial selection carried out by human beings. Artificial selection is seen as enabling humans to modify food plants in ways which make them more productive (in terms of yield per unit of land area), which make them more palatable, easier to harvest, store or process, and even aesthetically more pleasing.

The emergence of agriculture can be dated to approximately 10,000 years ago in southwest Asia (Palestine) and approximately 8,000 years ago in Central and South America. However, as Hole (1992) notes, although agriculture took hold in several other locations, the dating of these events is less certain. Nevertheless, it is clear that by 4,000 years ago all the basic agricultural techniques, such as ploughing and irrigation, had been developed. At each location in which agriculture was established, it was based upon a characteristic mix of domest-icated plants which Hole documents in some detail. For example, the so-called 'fertile crescent' of southwest Asia is associated with wheat, barley, various legumes, grapes, melons, dates and almonds, while the area around the northern Mediterranean is characterized by olives, grapes, figs and cereals. Tropical West Africa embraced such crops as yams and oil-palm, whereas the eastern sub-Saharan zone is associated with millet and sorghum. The complex of domest-icated plants originating in Southeast Asia includes such species as taro, yam, breadfruit, sago-palm, coconut and banana, although Hole notes that the origins of the current staple food of much of Asia, rice, are poorly understood. The region that is now Central America gave rise to such major domesticated species as maize, beans, squash and tomatoes. White potatoes originated in the Andean mountains of South America, and the Amazon basin saw the domestication of manioc and sweet potatoes. Of course, in the intervening millenniums, many of these crops have spread throughout the world, to become staples in areas far removed from their region of origin.

Hand in hand with the domestication of plant species went the domestication of animals. Domesticated animals, of course, did more than provide readily available sources of food products like meat, and non-food products like hides, hair and bone that might otherwise have been obtained from wild animals. Certain species also provided a source of muscle power far in excess of that achievable by human beings, muscle power which could be harnessed directly to agricultural activities (e.g., ploughing) and which could also be used for trans-portation purposes. The domestication of animals has had an enormous impact on human foodways, dietary patterns and social organization, yet our under-standing of exactly how this process occurred is largely based upon supposition (Reed 1984: 2). Nevertheless, it is possible to identify certain key attributes

18

which, in effect, render a given species suitable for domestication (Clutton-Brock 1987: 15–16). These include the ability of the young to survive removal from the mother and to adapt to a novel diet and environment, plus the possession of a set of behavioural patterns which facilitate the animal's incorporation into human society. Specifically, this requires a social animal, whose behaviour is based upon a dominance hierarchy, which will adopt a submissive role *vis-à-vis* its human companions. In addition, the species must be able to adapt to confinement and must be capable of breeding freely under such constrained conditions. All these features require an innate gregariousness on the part of the animal in question, as well as a relatively placid temperament that will tolerate human proximity and human interventions without exhibiting excessive signs of stress.

Domestication in mammals, for example, is usually accompanied by a number of characteristic physiological changes (Clutton-Brock 1987: 22–4). In the early stages of the process, there is often a reduction in body size as compared with the wild ancestor (although this may be reversed later). In addition, domestic mammals tend to carry a higher burden of fat beneath the skin and distributed through muscle tissue. Perhaps most strikingly, the brain becomes much smaller in relation to body size, and sense organs are also reduced. What is more, in the skull, the facial region and the jaws may become much shorter and more compressed, which may in effect involve the retention of juvenile characteristics.

Animal domestication occurred in a number of locations around the world (Clutton-Brock 1992). In western Asia, around 9,000 years ago, there is archaeological evidence for the domestication of sheep and goats, although they appear to have been domesticated later than the dog, whose domestication is usually estimated at approximately 12,000 years ago. Domestic cattle and pigs appear to originate in western Asia roughly 8,000 years ago (although in the case of the pig, its progenitor, the wild boar, is so widespread there may have been several separate centres of domestication). The domestic horse originated in central Asia 6,000 years ago, about the same time that the donkey (descended from the wild ass) appeared in Arabia and North Africa. The domestic chicken (descended from the jungle fowl) can be traced to southern Asia approximately 4,000 years ago. The New World has contributed such species as the llama and the alpaca (domesticated in South America, roughly 7,000 years ago) and, more importantly in a global sense, the turkey (North America, 1,500 years ago). As we have already noted, the causes of the shift to agriculture, based on the domestication of key species of plants and animals, remain a puzzle. As might be expected, however, there has been much speculation about these causes. For example, Hole (1992) argues that a series of interconnected changes in global temperatures, sea levels and the distributions of plants and animals generated a range of human responses, one of which was a move towards agriculture and direct food production. This author suggests that, in a sense, the ecological and social limits of the hunting and gathering lifestyle had been reached. This idea is echoed by Van der Merwe (1992), who argues that archaeological evidence suggests that

19

agriculture may have developed in response to situations in which the rates of food extraction by hunter-gatherers had begun to exceed the carrying capacity of the environments in which they were active.

However difficult it may be to identify the actual causes of these transformations in the ways in human beings obtained their food, there can be no mistaking the enormous and far-reaching consequences of these changes. Indeed, these consequences have proved so momentous that the shift from foraging to food production is often referred to as the agricultural or neolithic 'revolution', despite the fact that this was a revolution which took some thousands of years to run its course. Perhaps the most obvious consequence was a dramatic increase in the impact upon the natural environment of human subsistence-related activities. Of course, hunter-gatherers can have a significant impact upon the habitats in which they live. In intensely foraged areas, the whole balance of flora and fauna may be modified by human activities. In addition, hunters may use fire as a means of driving prey towards ambush or as a way of generating new plant growth to attract quarry species into the group's territory. The habitual burning of vegetation can produce extensive environmental changes if repeated over long periods of time. However, once agriculture takes hold, the rate and extent of environmental impact increases rapidly. Early agriculture took place on a shifting basis, involving, as Hole (1992: 374) puts it, 'a cycle of use, abuse, abandonment and re-use'. The clearance of forests (by burning and felling) and the ploughing of relatively unstable or fragile soils could result in severe erosion and the wholesale degradation of the landscape. Such effects would also be exacerbated by the cumulative impact of heavy grazing and browsing by domesticated herbivores. In regions of settled agricultural activity, the progressive depletion of the surrounding habitat would be an ever-present hazard.

So extensive has been the impact of agriculture upon the natural world that in the regions of the globe in which it has been practised for several millenniums, it is now difficult to identify many areas which can in any sense be seen as 'natural' in the sense of being completely untouched by human intervention and manipulation. Indeed, the whole thrust of this great revolution has been to replace the diversity of natural ecological systems with a much narrower range of plants and animals linked to human beings through the nexus of domestication.

As well as transforming the interactions between humans and the natural world, this agricultural revolution was inevitably associated with fundamental changes in the organization of human social relationships. Relatively settled agriculture facilitated the building up of stocks of food (in the form, for example, of relatively durable grains, or livestock 'on the hoof'). Such stocks, quite clearly, might be built up as an insurance against future shortages or famines, but in social terms they could represent very much more than that. The power over others that flows from the control of food stocks means that the whole concept of *ownership* becomes crucial in such societies. Stocks of wealth in the form of stored food surpluses could be used, within an appropriate system of barter and exchange, to command the labour, obedience or political allegiance of others.

20

Gifts of food or the use of food animals in religious sacrificial rites could also be employed to gain status and enhance political influence. In short, the initiation of a system of agricultural production greatly facilitates the extension and elaboration of patterns of social differentiation and inequality. Privileged groups or elites could now emerge and be supported by the sustained efforts of their subordinates. There is clear archaeological evidence that such elite groups typically enjoyed higher nutritional standards than those lower in the social order. For example, in the Sumerian civilization in Mesopotamia, detailed records of the food rations allocated to the various strata in that society indicate that the highest groups enjoyed a rich and varied diet, while the diet of the lower orders was heavily dependent on a single staple, barley (Gordon 1987: 28). For such subordinates, subsistence-related activities became ever more unlike those of hunters and gatherers.

There is a good deal of evidence to suggest that hunters and gatherers, on average, need to spend only relatively short periods of time actually engaged in catching or searching for food items in order to meet their nutritional needs (Sahlins 1974: 14–27). What is more, the nutritional standards of early human hunter-gatherers in the Paleolithic appear to have been good, even compared with modern Western standards (Gordon 1987: 30), given the typically diversi-fied and balanced nature of their diets. The relatively low levels of effort, and the abundance of leisure time, has led Sahlins (1974: 1–39) to refer to the hunting gathering lifestyle as 'the original affluent society'. In contrast, however, farmers find themselves committed to much more onerous, protracted and physically demanding inputs of labour, inputs which may be determined not only by their own subsistence needs, but by the need to generate food surpluses to support the debts and obligations they may owe to individuals who control more resources or wield more power than themselves. Indeed, it is tempting to assert that the actual concept of 'work' is one that could only have come into existence after the advent of agriculture.

Demographic changes were also associated with the spread of agricultural systems. The population densities of hunter-gatherers, depending upon the habitat, may be in the order of one person per square mile. In contrast, the densities of some early farming populations may have exceeded the level of sixty persons per square mile (Hartley 1972). These higher population densities, in turn, created the conditions for increases in overall population levels. Indeed, in certain circumstances population densities would eventually reach unpreced-ented values. This occurred through the creation of a novel form of human settlement, the city, a complex physical and social structure drawing its food resources from a wide agricultural hinterland (Sjoberg 1960). Thus, between 6,000 and 5,000 years ago there occurred in Mesopotamia, for example, what Roaf (1990) has termed an 'urban explosion'.

The shift towards agriculture was, therefore, clearly associated with a series of social and cultural transformations whose long-term implications were to prove enormous. However, the impact upon human nutritional and health standards was, in fact, often deleterious (Gordon 1987: 30) (although privileged strata may have been protected from such effects to some extent). As has already been noted, agricultural diets are in general much more narrowly based than those of hunter-gatherers, often with a much greater emphasis on the consumption of carbohydrates and with lower intakes of protein. Hole (1992: 378) suggests that relatively poor dietary standards led to higher levels of diseases related to nutritional deficiencies and also of infectious and parasitic diseases, which could spread more readily in the insanitary conditions pertaining in more densely populated, sedentary societies. He also argues that dietary changes may have led to an increased incidence of dental caries.

Van der Merve (1992: 372) presents a striking case study which demonstrates dramatically some of the negative effects of the nutritional changes associated with agriculture. The people of the lower Ilinois Valley (of what is now the central USA) around the year AD 600 were still largely dependent for food upon wild plants and animals (although they obtained some maize by trading with neighbouring agriculturalists). However, by AD 1200 their society had undergone a radical transformation. By this time they had become maize growers in their own right, and their population was concentrated in large villages. However, these changes were accompanied by an increase in weaning deaths among infants and a slowing down in skeletal development, so that maturity was not reached until age 25. In addition, the incidence of the bone disease porotic hyperostosis (caused by iron-deficiency anaemia) had increased to such an extent that it was affecting over half the population. In fact, as the author points out, the increases in population levels associated with agriculture were not the result of improved life expectancy (which remained about the same as for hunter-gatherers) and were apparently accompanied by a heightened incidence of nutritional stress.

What is more, a dependence on agriculture could have other serious disadvantages. Thus, while a settled, food production approach to subsistence could facilitate attempts to even out short-term fluctuations in food supply (i.e., through food storage), more long-term fluctuations, produced by such factors as drought, climatic change and resource depletion, could potentially generate chronic food shortages (Gordon 1987: 30). In the most severe instances such shortages could become full-scale famines. In contrast, hunter-gatherers were much less exposed to chronic food shortages and famines. The diversity of their diets made them less reliant on any one food item, and therefore a failure in the availability of any given food source was not as likely to prove catastrophic. In addition, the geographical mobility associated with foraging lifestyles would have meant that hunter-gatherers were much more capable of moving quickly away from areas of food shortage into areas where food resources were more abundant. The development of agricultural systems also appears to have increased the scale and heightened the intensity of another of the major scourges of humankind, warfare (Harris 1978: 35). With permanent settlements and the ownership of land, crops and livestock comes a much stronger sense of the occupation of an exclusive territory which must be defended from the incursions of others or, indeed, expanded at the expense of others.

Given some of the unwelcome effects of a shift towards agriculture, it is perhaps hardly surprising that we find evidence of hunter-gatherers actively resisting making the switch away from the foraging approach to subsistence (Van der Merve 1992: 370). Sahlins (1974: 27) provides the contemporary example of the Hadza people of Africa, foragers inhabiting a region of abundant wild food supplies, who, until recently, successfully resisted taking up agriculture despite being surrounded by cultivators. Given what we know about the spread of agriculture (for example, from southern Europe into northern Europe), it is tempting to speculate that an emphasis on farming did not replace the exclusive reliance on foraging because the former represented a more appealing and secure lifestyle (which it almost certainly did not). Rather, it may well have been that, once established, agriculturalists, as a result of their greater numbers and more intensive approach to warfare, could readily displace foragers from territory that was suitable for agricultural exploitation and settlement.

HUMAN SUBSISTENCE RECONSIDERED

In the previous section we examined a view of the origins and development of the basic forms of human subsistence which consists of a number of key elements, for example, the idea that the hunting component of the hunting and gathering lifestyle has had a particularly powerful influence on human physical and social evolution, and the notion that environmental changes and pressures eventually led human beings to respond by shifting their subsistence activities towards agriculture. This broad view carries considerable authority and appears to provide a coherent and plausible perspective on the prehistory of human food systems. However, as a perspective, it has its limitations and its critics, and these demand our consideration before we move on to the next stage of the discussion.

The first point which needs to be addressed relates to the conventional view that hunting represents an extremely ancient approach to human subsistence. While it has frequently been assumed that the animal remains associated with early hominid species demonstrate a reliance upon hunting as a food source, this view has frequently been questioned. Reviewing a broad spectrum of evidence, Gordon (1987) suggests that for early hominids, the acquisition of animal protein through scavenging may have been more likely than through actual hunting. It is only in the middle and upper Pleistocene that the clearest evidence exists for sophisticated hunting strategies and for the successful killing of large numbers of game animals. Thus, the claim put forward by advocates of the 'Hunting Hypothesis', that hunting dominated the subsistence activities of the various hominid species for 99 per cent of human prehistory (Washburn and Lancaster 1968: 293; Laughlin 1968: 304) needs to be viewed with some caution. The picture is further complicated if we consider the hunting-gathering cultures of modern humans which have survived to the present day, or at least survived long enough to become the objects of systematic study by anthropologists. While some of these cultures did rely very heavily on meat and other animal products for subsistence (the Innuit of the high Arctic are usually cited as prime example; see Damas 1972), in general food gathering was probably the predominant activity. In most foraging societies, the hunting of game animals, which is the preserve of men, is a sporadic and often unpredictable activity, yielding highly variable returns according not only to the methods employed but to uncontrollable fluctuations in such factors as the weather and the behaviour of quarry species. On the other hand, the activity of gathering (and this includes 'gathering' immobile or slow-moving small animals as well as plant foods), generally the preserve of women, tends to provide the bulk of resources for everyday subsistence. Thus, the meat of game animals, although the single most highly prized category of food in such societies, does not usually constitute the principal source of nutrients.

A particularly interesting reinterpretation of the development of human subsistence patterns is offered by Foley (1988), who invites us to consider the possibility that evolutionary changes have occurred in our species since its first appearance, particularly relating to the ways in which we obtain our food. Examining data concerning the Cro-Magnon populations of the Upper Paleolithic period in Europe (the earliest anatomically modern humans), he notes two striking features. Firstly, the stature and 'robusticity' of these people was much greater than that of later populations. Secondly, the degree of sexual dimorphism (e.g., in terms of the larger size of adult males compared to adult females) was also more pronounced than that found in later populations. Foley puts forward the proposition that the powerful stature of these males was an adaptation which facilitated the hunting of the big game animals that were abundant during this period in this area and may also have been related to competition between males, where size and strength would have conferred clear advantages. The exploitation of abundant big game would then have enabled these males to support dependent females and their offspring.

However, as we have already noted, far-reaching environmental changes were afoot at the end of the Pleistocene (about 10,000 years ago). Foley (1988) points out that at this time there is a reduction in overall body size and a reduction in the degree of sexual dimorphism. He argues that these anatomical changes in humans were associated with the changed subsistence patterns which accompanied the disappearance of the vast herds of big game animals upon which the Upper Paleolithic peoples had depended. A more 'gracile' and less 'robust' anatomy, and reduced differences between male and female, may have reflected the fact that the foraging strategies of the sexes now became much more similar, and indeed, in a sense, more balanced and egalitarian. It is at this point in his argument that he introduces his most interesting contention. The Upper Paleolithic hunters who exploited the rich reserves of game in the late Pleistocene, he suggests, were very different from more recent hunter-gatherers, in that they had more complex social structures, a far heavier dependence on hunting and even a

24

different, more robust, physical appearance. This leads him to argue that 'modern' (i.e., post-Pleistocene) hunting and gathering are not, in any sense, ancestral to agriculture. Rather, the hunter-gatherer lifestyle, examples of which have survived to the present day, was itself an adaptation to post-Pleistocene conditions and involved diversification of foraging strategies and a much increased significance for the gathering activities of women. Thus, recent hunter-gatherer lifestyles on the one hand, and agriculture on the other, are seen as parallel adaptations to the same set of environmental changes.

While such views are, by their very nature, somewhat speculative, they do help to shed some light upon otherwise puzzling facts. For example, it is intriguing that humans appear to have exploited intensively certain plant species for long periods before those species began to show signs of actual domestication (Gordon 1987: 26). Moreover, despite the conventional use of the term 'revolution' to describe the switch to agriculture, this term is more appropriately applied to the eventual consequences of this change than to the timescales involved, which were often protracted. Indeed, many agriculturalists retained an involvement in foraging, particularly hunting, and such activities remained a significant component of their day to day activities (see e.g., Rosman and Rubel 1989; Sponsel 1989).

There is an additional aspect of the debate about the prehistory of human subsistence patterns which also needs to be approached with some caution. Much of the literature appears to be based upon the view that the process of domestication, upon which the development of agriculture inevitably depended, was a process which was quite deliberately and consciously initiated and carried through by human beings. This view of domestication and the emergence of agriculture is, of course, in line with our common-sense ideas about the ambitions and abilities of humans to exercise control over the natural world and to shape it according to human priorities. From this perspective, domestication would be seen as the result of the active selection of particular strains of plants and animals in terms of the desirable characteristics they exhibit. The processes of reproduction are then manipulated and regulated to ensure that these desirable characteristics are passed on to subsequent generations of the domesticated species.

While this might be a reasonably plausible description of the theoretically and scientifically driven forms of plant and animal breeding which have been developed in recent centuries, serious doubt has been cast upon the idea that domestication could actually have been *initiated* in this calculating manner. One of the most detailed challenges to the conventional view is presented by Rindos (1984). In fact, Rindos does not seek to deny that people act consciously and that these actions are oriented towards goals. However, he argues that in the context of plant domestication, for example, people could never have intentionally domesticated a crop, thereby deliberately 'inventing' agriculture. This is because the biological and evolutionary processes involved in domestication cannot be accounted for in solely cultural terms. The long-term effects of deliberate environmental manipulations and attempts at selective breeding are highly unpredictable, and domestication-related changes can only occur within the genetic parameters of the species in question. Thus, human intentions can only play a limited role in the whole process. This is perhaps best illustrated by the existence of weeds. These plants have evolved alongside 'desirable' plants as part of the whole process of the development of agriculture. They are, in a sense, domesticated plants, but they are not wanted by farmers, who expend considerable effort in ultimately unsuccessful attempts to eliminate them.

Thus, Rindos is suspicious of the argument that agriculture developed as a deliberate response to specific environmental stresses in given historical situations. Rather, he argues that domestication arose out of an *interactive* process between plants and humans. Indeed, it would make just as much (or just as little) sense to say these plants 'chose' humans to protect and disseminate them as to say early agriculturalists 'chose' to domesticate them. In fact, Rindos suspects that crops evolved through a natural process, with humans acting as a largely unintentional selective force, the process itself conferring some evolutionary advantages on both the people and plants involved. Thus, Rindos reminds us, although we use the idiom of intention as a kind of literary convention, it is, in effect, a metaphor and not a description of reality. Agriculture, then, according to Rindos, represents a form of co-evolution between humans and certain plant species and is, in effect, a highly developed form of symbiosis. The term 'symbiosis', meaning a situation in which at least two different species interact to their mutual benefit, is also used by Reed (1984) to describe agriculture and domestication. However, he also adds the concept of the 'secondary energy trap'. In a symbiotic relationship, each symbiant represents a reserve of energy other symbionts may be able to draw upon (and thus a way of storing energy outside their own bodies). Agriculture, therefore, represents a complex system of mutual secondary energy traps for the species involved, with plants and animals drawing upon stored human energy for protection and dissemination, and humans drawing upon stored plant energy for food and stored animal energy for food and motive power.

Once we begin to think of agriculturally based food systems in these terms, our whole view of human subsistence necessarily undergoes an important shift. Domestication and agriculture come to be seen as something more than innovations created initially by the intentional application of human ingenuity. The impressive selective advantages which accrue to domesticated plants and animals through their association with humans become much more visible. Domesticated species have, by and large, achieved spectacular increases in their populations (or the sheer volume of 'biomass' which they make up) and in their geographical ranges and the environments they occupy. This has been achieved, in some instances, by species which, prior to domestication, may well have been on the verge of disappearance. For example, the Aurochs, which is now actually extinct in its wild form, is the direct ancestor of domestic cattle, and this animal is now one of the most numerous and widely distributed large mammals on earth.

Furthermore, the impact of these changes on human beings may now be seen from a rather different perspective. Human population densities and overall numbers saw increases far beyond what could have been sustained by foraging lifestyles, although these increases were sometimes associated with an actual deterioration in nutritional standards. Extensive changes in culture and patterns of social relations also associated with the development of agricultural systems, and the move towards an emphasis on food production, saw human communities become increasingly sedentary and spacially restricted, their members (at least in the lower strata) committed to the physically demanding seasonal inputs of agricultural labour.

In seeing the human food system that emerged after the introduction of agriculture as a complex form of symbiosis, we begin to recognize the ways in which the biological and reproductive potential of a complex of domesticated plants and animals came to be organized and articulated through the unique adaptabilities of human intelligence and human culture. If, following the advice of Rindos (1984), we are cautious about using the idea that early farmers 'intended' to domesticate plants and animals, and 'intended' to create agriculture, then we ought also to be cautious about using terms like 'exploitation'. In an agricultural system, who is exploiting whom? Conventionally, we accept the idea that humans are the exploiters, although we base this notion upon the fact that we are at the top of the agricultural food chain (we eat the other members, but they do not eat us). But it would be equally logical to assert that the other members of these systems exploit humans (for dissemination, protection and nurture). In a very real sense, *Homo sapiens* in an agricultural system is also a domesticated animal, subject to the increasing demands and the unforgiving disciplines attached to our species' role in the complicated networks of symbiotic relationships. The human species must exhibit, in these circumstances, such domesticated characteristics as an acceptance of restricted mobility and a tolerance of crowding and close proximity with humans and non-humans.

There can be no doubt that the symbiotic complex that we call agriculture has come to dominate the land surface of large areas of the earth and, indeed, is continuing to extend this domination. At this stage in our argument, doubt must now be cast upon the notion that humans are actually in control of this process. Despite Western culture's deep-seated inclination to emphasize the idea of human control and manipulation of the natural world, it is extremely unlikely that generation upon generation of agriculturalists were really able to foresee in any detail the longer-term outcomes of their activities. This point is reinforced when we take into account the unpredictable nature of climatic and environmental fluctuations and the immensely complex genetic and environmental processes involved in the evolution of domesticated species, and of the diseases, pests and parasites which infest and colonize agricultural systems. Thus, although human agricultural activities are themselves goal-oriented and driven by more or less explicitly recognized intentions, their long-term outcomes may be quite unintentional, and often unforeseeable.

27

THE EMERGENCE OF THE STATE

It has already been argued that agriculture created the conditions in which increasing levels of population density and degrees of complexity in social organization became possible. These changes were eventually to give rise to forms of social organization which created, for the first time, many of the features of economic, cultural, political and religious life which we now take virtually for granted. In other words, conditions were formed in which the emergence of states was possible. The creation of states was to see a fundamental change away from the situation of human social groupings comprising relatively small mobile bands or relatively small sedentary villages. Where such units maintain their autonomy, levels of individual freedom and control over the pace and nature of daily and seasonal activities is relatively high and access to natural resources is relatively open (although it may be subject to competition). However, increasing social complexity appears to bring in its wake increasing social inequality. Highly privileged political, military and intellectual elites become increasingly distant in outlook and lifestyle from the strata beneath them, made up of castes or classes whose autonomy is severely limited by the power and authority of those they serve. We might legitimately ask how such highly structured relationships of dominance and subordination could come about. This is, clearly, a large question and has absorbed the efforts of generations of scholars of many different persuasions. However, of particular interest from our point of view are the ideas of Harris (1978: 67–82), who puts forward the proposition that the control and redistribution of food resources may have been vital factors in this process.

Harris's specific concern is the issue of how a 'pristine' state can emerge, a pristine state being one which arises spontaneously, not as a result of the influences or effects of other states which have a prior existence. In fact, it is Harris's view that the pristine state can be seen as a consequence of attempts to intensify agricultural production (i.e., to increase agricultural output) in order to provide short-term relief of the pressures generated by a rising population. This contention is hardly a remarkable one, but what is interesting about Harris's analysis is his description of the mechanism through which this intensification may come about. He refers to the phenomenon that social anthropologists term the 'big man' (1978: 70–1). These big men are typically renowned and respected war leaders, but in pre-state societies loyalty can only be maintained if the leader can keep up a constant flow of rewards to his followers. Food, of course, is one of the principal forms such rewards can take. What is more, in order to enhance further their prestige, these ambitious individuals may exhort and cajole their followers and relatives into increasing food output so that a spectacular feast can be held. This feast provides not only an abundance of food for his followers and their dependents, but also enhances the standing in the community of the leader himself and, by implication, that of all his supporters. Thus, we have what Harris terms 'redistributor war chiefs' (1978: 73–6), who

28

have the ability to accumulate large food stocks and then to expend these stocks in such a way as to entrench and extend their own power. Harris actually calls these individuals 'food managers' (1978: 71), given their crucial position at the centre of a web of food production and distribution. It is then but a short step for the chief-manager role to evolve into that of a hereditary ruler with coercive powers, the 'great provider' (1978: 71) who can build up substantial reserves of storable foodstuffs on the basis of his position. As populations become larger and denser, food redistribution systems become larger and more elaborate, and the more powerful becomes the individual at the centre. In effect, the chief becomes a monarch, and what were voluntary contributions become obligatory taxes and tithes.

Thus, a crucially significant reversal takes place. Whereas the chief is dependent on the generosity and allegiance of his followers, the subjects of a monarch come to be seen as dependent on his (or, more rarely, her) generosity and dispensations. Indeed, even access to land and other natural resources comes to be defined in terms of such royal dispensation. The subjects themselves also become increasingly differentiated. Around the monarch there builds up an increasingly elaborate hierarchy of functionaries (military personnel, priests, administrators, artists and craft specialists) all supported and fed from the reserves controlled by the monarchy itself. Members of this network experience a lifestyle and enjoy privileges which set them apart from the strata of agricultural drudges below them. The embryo state is given further impetus towards even greater elaboration by the process that Harris terms 'impaction' (Harris 1978: 78). This effect occurs when fertile land upon which the state relies is in limited supply, being bounded by relatively or largely infertile areas. This means that it is not feasible for outlying groups in the population to escape from demographic pressures and central control by moving outwards. The system is turned in on itself, and the processes of intensification are given further impetus. Harris cites the civilizations which developed in areas of high fertility surrounded by zones of much lower agricultural value, for example, the Nile delta in Egypt, the flood plain of the Tigris and the Euphrates in Mesopotamia, the flood plain of the Indus in what is now Pakistan, and the margins of the Yellow River basin in China.

Once this process of impacted intensification takes off, it appears to engender a self-reinforcing cycle of further intensification through increasing levels of taxation, tribute extraction, labour conscription and food production integration. In addition, relationships with neighbouring societies in terms of warfare, conquest, trade, or all three, also intensify. However, once pristine states have become established, secondary states may begin to emerge. These may develop among peoples seeking to resist conquest by a pristine state that has moved into an expansionist phase or, indeed, among peoples who seek to plunder the riches of a pristine state which is vulnerable to external attack.

Harris (1978) makes it perfectly clear that he regards the formation of a pristine state as an essentially unconscious process, not as an outcome of deliberate planning, manipulation or conspiracy. Over many generations, imperceptible shifts in the balances of power relating to the control and redistribution of resources in general, and food resources in particular, eventually produced social institutions and relationships whose forms and directions could not have been foreseen by those involved. In this sense, we can see a close parallel with our earlier discussion of the changes which led to the establishment of symbiotic links between humans and domesticated species and the emergence of agriculture (an emergence which was a necessary condition for the later emergence of the state itself). These changes, in an important sense, can also be seen as the unforeseen and unintended consequences of incremental adjustments and adaptations in the ways in which humans went about the task of satisfying their nutritional needs.

OVERVIEW

In this brief sketch of the origins of human subsistence patterns attention has been drawn to several crucial insights. Perhaps the most striking of these is the idea that the extraordinarily high energy demands of the brain, arguably the very seat of our human distinctiveness, require us to consume a 'high-quality', energy-rich diet. Our basic physiology simply does not allow us the option of grazing or browsing directly upon the enormous quantities of structural plant material (stems, leaves, bark, etc.) which blanket vast areas of the earth's surface. For most of the history of our species (and of our closely related species) humans have relied upon harvesting wild animals and plants in order to obtain the dietary quality and variety that we need. The development of relationships of domestication with certain key animal and plant species brought about far-reaching changes, not only in human subsistence patterns but also in human social organization. However, the causes and the dynamics of domestication and the move to food production remain obscure, even mysterious. We simply cannot assume that domestication and agriculture were, in the first instances, conscious human inventions or deliberately adopted strategies aimed at coping with reproductive or environmental pressures. These changes may indeed have provided adaptive advantages for all the species that were to become part of the human food system, but that does not prove that humans intended to obtain these advantages any more than it proves that cattle and rice plants, for example, 'intended' to obtain them. As we have seen, when dealing with relationships of symbiosis (of which the human food system is a particularly complex example), references to the intentions of the species involved are essentially metaphorical rather than literal.

With the establishment and development of the first pristine states, all the features that we would recognize as fundamental to agricultural production were in place. These included an extensive range of domesticated plants and animals, the use of the plough, the construction of irrigation systems, the use of natural fertilizers and the use of fallowing to allow land to regain fertility after cropping.

What is more, trading in relatively non-perishable foods (for example, grains) became feasible with the production of food surpluses, and such foods, in turn, were to become the currency of tribute and taxation. The motive power for these agricultural systems came primarily from muscles, animal and human, although renewable sources of inanimate power (wind and water) also played a part.

On the basis of these forms of agricultural production, societies ranging from the limited world of the small village to the dazzling power and complexity of the ancient civilizations could be constructed. We have already referred to the intensification of food systems, but this was an intensification that occurred within the limits set by available technologies and forms of social organization. However, eventually these limits were to be overcome and new waves of much more rapid intensification and integration were set in train, waves which were to lead to what we now conceptualize as the modern food system.

2

THE MAKING OF THE MODERN
FOOD SYSTEM

CONTRASTING TRADITIONAL AND MODERN FOOD SYSTEMS

A visit to any supermarket, with its elaborate displays of food from all parts of the world, is a readily available demonstration of the choice and variety available to the modern consumer. The supermarket itself may be considered one of the most successful outcomes of the development of modern systems of food production and distribution, indicating the extent of control over quality and the reliability of supplies. It might be tempting to consider such quality and reliability as unequivocal evidence of progress. However, in trying to understand the developments and beliefs which underpin the modern food system, we are faced with a fascinating paradox. In the past, certainly in the West, ascendancy over the natural world was taken for granted, yet it was not always possible to use that ascendancy to provide constant and reliable supplies of food. However, in modern society, where food supplies are virtually guaranteed, there are now serious doubts about the extent and moral acceptability of our control over the natural environment. In parallel with the technological, engineering and scientific changes which have established control over food production and distribution, serious debate has emerged about the unanticipated consequences of such changes, together with challenges to the allegedly overconfident exploitation of natural resources. Thus, in giving an account of the development of the modern food system, it is important to include some discussion of several issues: the character of the food system itself; the processes which made it possible; the operation of the system; current debates about the system. These issues are the focus of this chapter and all are relevant to understanding the making of the modern food system as we know it today.

The use of the term 'food system' may conjure up an idea of a formally organized set of links between food production, distribution and consumption which is arranged according to some well-thought-out plan or scheme. The issues discussed in Chapter 1 and the studies covered in the following pages will make it clear that such a model is inappropriate and unworkable. However, if we are careful not to assume that there is some underlying plan which informs its organization, the term food system can be a convenient way of drawing attention to the particular character of the complex of interdependent interrelationships associated with the production and distribution of food which have developed to meet the nutritional needs of human populations. (In Chapter 3 we will examine specific examples of the kinds of model which social scientists have devised to provide descriptions of such systems.)

In trying to understand the making of the modern food system, it is necessary to be aware of both continuity and change in the social processes which shape the ways in which food is produced, distributed and consumed. Chapter 1 has identified the physiological need for variety in food, the constant interaction between humans and their environment and the importance of the social and political control of food production and distribution. If we were to choose to emphasize continuity, it could be argued that the modern system is merely the most recent attempt of human societies to come to terms with these perennial problems of providing food, and that the only distinguishing characteristic is the scale of the endeavour. However, it has also been argued that the modern food system is, in many respects, radically different from what has gone before. It is this assertion which we explore and which provides the starting point for the discussion in this chapter.

An emphasis on change and discontinuities draws attention to the main contrasts between the food systems of traditional and modern societies. These are set out in Table 2.1. For ease of discussion, a distinction has been

Table 2.1 Contrasts between traditional and modern food systems

Activity	Traditional systems	Modern systems
Production	Small-scale/limited	Large-scale/highly specialized/industrialized
	Locally based for all but luxury goods	De-localized/global
	High proportion of population involved in agriculture	Majority of population have no links with food production
Distribution	Within local boundaries	International/global
	Exchange governed by kinship and other social networks	Access governed by money and markets
Consumption	Swings between plenty and want dependent on harvests and seasons	Food always available at a price/independent of seasons
	Choice limited and dependent on availability and status	Choice available to all who can pay
	Nutritional inequalities within societies	Nutritional inequalities between and within societies
Beliefs	Humans at the top of the food chain/exploitation of the environment necessary	Debate between those who believe in human domination of the environment and those who challenge such a model

made between the processes of production, distribution and consumption, even though in practice it is not always easy to separate them. In addition, it has been necessary to emphasize the similarities between traditional societies in order to bring out the contrasts with modern societies which are to be discussed. For example, although there is a wide variety of traditional systems, each associated with a particular organization of the interaction between humans and their environment, it is possible to identify some shared characteristics. For a start, traditional food systems are characterized by patterns of local, relatively small-scale production. In addition, the division of labour associated with food production involves a relatively high proportion of the population. Further, both distribution and consumption are linked to established social relationships, in particular, those of status and kinship. Gifts of food are often exchanged between relatives rather than being sold in the market, and social position determines the amount and type of food received. Importantly, choice is often limited for all consumers, whatever their status, and is constrained by the seasonal and local availability of food supplies. As a consequence, swings between times of plenty and those of want, particularly from season to season, are taken for granted. Also, there is little evidence of sharp differences in beliefs about dietary practices, possibly because food supplies are relatively uncertain and unreliable. There is one characteristic, that of nutritional inequalities, which appears in relation to both traditional and modern food systems. However, it can be argued that such inequalities are structured and organized in different ways and are underpinned by quite different assumptions about who may have access to food and the conditions in which it can be acquired.

At the risk of oversimplifying complex processes, the modern food system may be considered to have five key characteristics which differentiate it from those of traditional societies. Firstly, there is a highly specialized, industrial system of food production. This is large in scale, yet involves relatively small numbers of the working population. Indeed, it could be argued that most of the food production for modern societies goes on virtually concealed, not necessarily deliberately, from the mass of consumers. Secondly, distribution is through the commercial market; whatever our status, as long as we have the money, food is readily accessible. Thirdly, as the example which opened this chapter indicates, a visit to any supermarket demonstrates the opportunities for consumption and emphasizes choice and variety, and this is largely true for smaller food outlets as well. Fourthly, since the markets for buying and selling food are international, even global, shortages are rare. However, that is not to say that shortages do not occur in particular places for particular groups, only that these arise from social and political constraints rather than from the issues related to the availability of food. This latter point links with the final characteristic of the modern food system: constant debates about the sustainability of the system itself and the choices to be made about its future development.

34

THE EMERGENCE OF THE MODERN FOOD SYSTEM

The documentation of the transformation from the traditional to the modern food system has attracted the efforts of social historians, economists and nutritionists using a variety of approaches (Mennell, Murcott and Van Otterloo 1992). They have sometimes focused on one particular feature in explaining the changes observed, such as technology or transport, for example, or have attempted to analyse the entire process. Whatever the focus of any particular contribution to the literature, it is important to bear in mind several points which provide the context for all discussions. The first is that, in comparison with the period of time for which we have evidence of human social organization, writers who focus on the shaping of the modern food system are usually considering relatively recent developments, beginning approximately in the eighteenth and gathering momentum in the nineteenth century. The second point to bear in mind is that, although many writers document changes, they do not necessarily offer explanations of what happened, and, where they do, such explanations are often the focus of disputes about the validity of the evidence. Thirdly, even where writers concentrate on one particular aspect of change, it is important for the reader to recognize the interrelationship between factors of supply, distribution and demand. Each may have been stimulated by the other and, indeed, by yet other social and economic changes which at first sight do not seem to be linked in any way with food. These accounts and debates in the literature are valuable for giving an indication of the complexity of the processes which contributed to the shape of the modern world and provide a context for the sociological analysis in later chapters.

The process of urbanization in the ancient world had already broken the direct links between food production and consumers and had provided the necessary stimulus for developments in food production. However, it was the process of industrialization which altered the scale of urbanization, created an unprecedented demand for food supplies and distanced urban populations yet further from the sources of their food. Britain, as the first industrial nation, is one of the best-documented examples of the ways in which such changes took place and provides an ideal case study of the processes which contributed to the development of the modern food system. The precise turning point for industrial 'take-off' is still a matter of debate (Rostow 1990; Hudson 1992), but there is no doubt that industrialization 'created machines, factories and vast suffocating cities' (Tannahill 1973: 257). Oddy (1990) argues that this rapid urbanization in the eighteenth century was a major contributor to the commercialization of food markets, since urban living, with its pattern of waged work and separation from the agricultural base, prevented greater populations than ever before from being self-sufficient in food. As these urban centres grew, the food demands of such concentrations of population could not be met from local resources, however efficiently organized. This precipitated the rapid growth of trade over longer distances in produce such as livestock and vegetables. For example,

London as a metropolitan market drew on national and not just local or regional sources for its food supplies. The markets at Smithfield for meat, at Covent Garden for fruit and vegetables and at Billingsgate for fish were renowned for the quantity and range of the produce they handled on a daily basis in response to the demand of the growing metropolis (Burnett 1989).

Such a rapid increase in demand created pressures to produce more, giving all those involved in agriculture an incentive to introduce new techniques and to change the scale of food production. For example, horticulture expanded in areas adjacent to the expanding conurbations (Scola 1992). Deliberate and systematic selective breeding of livestock spread rapidly from the middle of the eighteenth century as well as systematic seed selection for increased arable output and the widespread use of specialized agricultural equipment. Possibly one of the most significant changes was the move to the use of chemical rather than natural fertilizers (Sykes 1981). Increased yields and improved stock gave landlords a better return on their investments. Land rents were raised, putting pressure on farmers to change the pattern of land use to make it even more productive. One of the by-products of this transformation was to change the appearance of the landscape from open fields to fenced and hedged farms (Turner 1985).

A key element which ensured that these newly expanded food supplies reached their markets was the parallel expansion of methods of transport (Bagwell 1974). Traditional drove roads, along which animals were herded to market, often over long distances, were augmented by turnpike roads and canals in the later eighteenth century. These enabled agricultural produce to be moved in bulk, where speed mattered less than cheap and reliable delivery. From the middle of the nineteenth century the capacity of internal transport was further augmented by a railway system which was rapid, reliable and flexible in bringing food supplies to distribution centres and markets. By the end of the nineteenth century railways were even able to provide specialized facilities for handling foods such as fresh milk and chilled or frozen meat. At the same time, the rapid transport of fish from trawler catches in the North Sea and the Atlantic was possible. In the case of Britain, this was said to have established one of the most popular meals of the working classes, fish and chips (Walton 1992).

Specialized facilities for handling food resulted from scientific and technological advances in preservation. Traditional preservation methods, such as salting, pickling and drying, continued in use alongside the greater use of sugar as well as chemical additives (Roberts 1989; Muller 1991). As we shall see in Chapter 11, until the late eighteenth century, sugar had been a luxury confined to the use of the rich, but mass-production made it available for use in a very wide range of food processing (Mintz 1985). The metallurgical development of cheap sheet steel, covered with a veneer of tin, made canning an economic process with minimal health risks, whilst refrigeration and other types of temperature control extended the opportunities to abolish seasonal supply problems (Roberts 1989; David 1994). New foodstuffs were literally invented by food

36

scientists (margarine, for example), or manufactured (condensed milk, block chocolate and cornflakes). The life of some foods, such as milk, was extended by pasteurization. Because of improvements in temperature control in transport by sea, bananas became available in Europe for the first time in the 1890s.

By the beginning of the nineteenth century, Britain was a net importer of food and the contribution of overseas supplies to the British larder became of ever greater importance, particularly from the last quarter of the nineteenth century. In the twentieth century, such was the reliance on these overseas food supplies that Britain continued to import food even during two world wars when transport by sea was both dangerous and uncertain. The diminished quantities of these supplies led to wartime food rationing (Burnett 1989).

As a particularly powerful and affluent nation by the standards of the time, Britain was able to draw upon food supplies on a worldwide basis: grain from the Midwestern USA; dairy products from Denmark and Holland; beef from Argentina; lamb from Australia; tea from the Indian sub-continent; coffee from Brazil; cocoa from West Africa; sugar from the West Indies. All this was made possible by emerging international agricultural specialization combined with improved transport over long distances. By 1850, an international economy had been established which had transformed the landscapes and the organization of agriculture in the participating countries (Foreman-Peck 1993). Many of these, for example the tea gardens, the sheep pastures and the cattle ranges, remain and are part of the current global food system. (However, it is important to note that not all prospered and some led to ecological disaster, for example, the 'dust bowl' created in part of the American Midwest by attempts to grow grain.) Trade was often two-way. Countries of the British Empire, together with a number of nations with close economic ties to Britain, such as Argentina, Chile and Uruguay, paid for imports of capital and of manufactured goods from Britain by the export of food (Cain and Hopkins 1993; Saul 1960). Indeed, Tannahill (1973: 257) suggests that 'the quest for empire was partly quest for overseas markets'. Studies of trade in specific foods (Hobhouse 1985; Mintz 1985; Solokov 1991; Visser 1986) have drawn attention to the ways in which such trade has shaped international relations.

Governments were not neutral in the development of the international economy. In Britain, there were parliamentary debates about the most advantageous policies to pursue in relation to trade with particular consequences for food, the most important debate being that focused on the relative merits of 'free trade' versus 'protection'. The publication in 1774 of Adam Smith's *The Wealth of Nations* anticipated by two years the Boston Tea Party, which signalled the determination of the American colonists to have 'no taxation without representation'. Indirect taxes on food levied by the British government have been cited amongst the causes of the American War of Independence (Langford 1989). Once the Americans had secured their victory, British governments moved with hesitating steps towards free trade and the removal of taxes on food and drink. The main opposition came from agricultural interests which wished to retain protection for the cultivation of wheat. The failure of the potato crop in Ireland in 1845, with its terrible consequences of starvation for large numbers of the rural population, convinced the British government of the wisdom of seeking the cheapest food prices on world markets by removing all import taxes on food (Salaman 1985: 289–316).

Governments had always been concerned to maintain standards in the food market, and weights, measures and qualities had long been the subject of legislation and intervention (Ministry of Agriculture, Fisheries and Food 1989). However, intervention in cases of food adulteration, which was alleged to have become much more common in the nineteenth century because of increased demand and unsupervised production, proved difficult. The development of scientific analysis, particularly in chemistry, made it possible to have reliable tests for impurities. In Britain, the prevention of food adulteration was part of the public health movement which culminated in the appointment of medical officers of health after 1848. Legislation specifically concerned with food and drugs followed once the scientific tests were acceptable to the legislature. In Britain the first law to protect consumers from adulterated food took effect in 1875 (Burnett 1989).

During this time there were concurrent developments in the distribution and retailing of food. Consumers in rural society usually had direct contacts with their suppliers at local markets or by regular contact with the dairy or the bakery. Once towns grew beyond a population of a few hundred families the establishment of regular shops became the norm, a process that accelerated with the urbanization which accompanied industrialization. As supplies to shops became both more regular and reliable, consumers lost contact with processes of production. The number of shops and their range of products increased rapidly with the expansion of retail trade in food. For example, the late nineteenth century was the time when greengrocers, confectioners and other specialist outlets came into separate existence (Fraser 1981).

These changes occurred in advanced economies during the nineteenth century. Large-scale production had begun during the eighteenth century with the establishment of larger breweries, such as Guiness in Dublin and Barclay's in London. A similar willingness to invest in technologies on a large scale to meet the demands of the growing market for manufactured foods gave rise to companies making a wide range of products, from custard powder to margarine. In Britain, from the middle of the nineteenth century, the use of brand names became an advantage in reaching consumers through advertising. The national market, by the end of the nineteenth century, covered a wide range of branded food products in most lines of grocery and confectionery (Roberts 1989).

At the same time as brands replaced locally produced foods or wholly new items became available, retailing itself underwent major changes. The reasons for this were not only a consequence of production methods or the supplies of products from overseas, but also the need to reach the greater numbers and variety of consumers in urban centres. Such consumers included those who wanted value for money and guaranteed quality. In responding to such consumers in the working class, first in the field in Britain was the retail co-operative movement which had its successful origins in Rochdale in 1844. Within twenty years most towns had a co-operative society. Co-operative customers had a widening range of demands and the Co-operative Wholesale Society, established in 1864, had its own factories and, in due course, even its own tea gardens in the Indian sub-continent. Competition for these predominantly working-class customers led to the rapid development after 1870 of various retailing chains, for example, Lipton and Griegs. By the end of the century, there were shops glorying in their overseas connections, with names such as Home and Colonial and International (Matthias 1967).The chains of grocers were matched by chains of butchers. The Dewhurst company, for example, owned its own cattle ranches in Uruguay and imported meat, frozen, chilled and canned, from its plant in Montevideo. Interestingly, the middle and upper classes remained the customers of privately owned and independent shops (Adburgham 1989; Davis, D. 1966).

The mass market in Britain, the United States and in Europe created the conditions for international companies to emerge. Examples originating in the United States include the meat packing firms of Armour and Swift, the Heinz company and General Foods. In Switzerland, Nestlé, which began by selling condensed milk, was established. However, the response to the mass market was not one of uninterrupted expansion. The economic problems of the years between the beginning of the First World War and the middle of the 1950s limited or prevented many developments as large-scale unemployment diminished demand. Where prosperity continued even during the Depression of the 1930s, some retail chains continued to grow. The expansion of retail chains into supermarkets came with the prosperity, particularly related to higher incomes, of the late 1950s onwards. In organizational terms the self-service supermarket became the hallmark of the most successful retail traders. This self-service element depended on sophisticated packaging of all kinds of foods and appropriate marketing skills to persuade customers to buy. Large numbers of urban consumers moved from older style shops to self-service stores. Experiences in the United States encouraged some retailers in Britain to create supermarkets and hypermarkets which offered a wide range of products, not only foodstuffs, for sale. Amongst the first were the French owned Carrefour and the American ASDA company. Soon British firms, such as Sainsbury, joined in the provision of newer-style shopping facilities (Williams 1994).The style relied not only upon most customers using cars but also upon their ownership of refrigerators. By the 1970s domestic freezers became a prerequisite when deep frozen foods were available for home storage. The middle of the 1980s saw the wider availability of microwave ovens giving scope for the expansion of sales of ready-prepared frozen or chilled dishes. Alongside these developments there occurred an increase in the numbers of those employed to prepare food outside the home (Gabriel 1988). All these processes combined to abolish the constraints of seasonal supply and made available to the general population foods which had

39

previously only been available to the wealthy. This also permitted the expression of dietary preferences catered for by specialist, independently owned, shops.

This record of the triumph of technology and the organizaton of food production and distribution should not lead us to imagine there were no differences between consumers. Considerable inequalities remained, particularly in the nineteenth century (Tannahill 1973). Such divisions in society were reflected in differences between the diets of the rich and the poor. The poor, particularly the industrial poor living in housing with low standards of sanitation and lacking pure water, subsisted on a relatively narrow range of foods, for example, bread, tea, potatoes and a little meat (Tannahill 1973: 287). The rich had access to a wider variety and, by the later nineteenth century, were beginning to demand consistent quality and stable prices. In the middle were greater numbers of people earning higher incomes as industrialization proceeded. These artisans and middle-class consumers had an increasing choice and variety of food. They also had access to the newspapers, magazines, cookery books and guides to household organization and cuisine. Perhaps the most famous example is Mrs Beeton's book on household management, first published in 1868, which remained in demand, with revisions, for more than a century. Ironically, the scientific revolution and its application to the manufacture of new foods sometimes worsened rather than improved the diet of the poor, for example, the cheaper brands of condensed milk (which were made with skimmed rather than whole milk and which contained a high proportion of sugar as a preservative) lacked fats and vitamins A and D, and may, in fact, have increased the incidence of rickets (Tannahill 1973: 332). There are parallel arguments about the use of white bread, with its lack of wheatgerm, rather than brown bread (Tannahill 1973: 333).

INTERNATIONAL INEQUALITIES

In the accounts which are focused on the development of the modern food system in the West, there is an emphasis on changes which can be interpreted as progress: the triumph over the difficulties of improving the scale and quality of production; the technological achievements in both preservation and the food distribution network; the extension of consumer choice free from seasonal constraints. However, considered from a global rather than a Western standpoint, a different picture emerges, one which draws attention to the variable consequences of such changes for those not in the 'First World'. For example, Pelto and Pelto (1985) argue that the transformation of world dietary patterns may be characterized using the concept of 'delocalization' in relation to food production and distribution. By delocalization they refer to the processes in which food varieties, methods of production and patterns of consumption are 'disseminated throughout the world in an intensifying and ever-increasing network of socio-economic and political interdependency' (Pelto and Pelto 1985: 309). They acknowledge that the process of delocalization makes it possible for an increased proportion of the daily diet to be drawn from distant places and that it arrives through commercial channels. However, they also draw attention to the fact that the same process of delocalization has quite different consequences in industrialized societies compared with those which are less industrialized.

In industrialized societies, delocalization is associated with an increase in the diversity of foods available and an increase in the quantity of food imports. Initially, access to such foods may have been for those in privileged positions only, but in the twentieth century they become widely available to most of the population, with the exception of the very poorest. In contrast, delocalization has the opposite effect in less industrialized countries. Where people have been traditionally dependent on locally produced supplies and have distributed food outside the commercial network, the delocalization process draws them into the farming of non-traditional plant and animal varieties, into commercial production of cash crops and new kinds of food-processing on an industrial scale, and into migration from rural to urban settings. In consequence, there is not only a deterioration in food diversity locally but also a loss of control over distribution. In other words, these traditional societies are not in the process of 'catching up' with the West but are caught up in a global system which provides food choice and variety for industrialized societies at the expense of economically marginal peoples.

Bennett (1987) takes this argument even further and suggests that the subordination of underdeveloped soceieities' economies to the production of food and other commodities for the West can be identified as 'The Hunger Machine'. Drawing upon a considerable range of evidence from the Third World in the 1980s, Bennett argues that famines are, in fact, relatively rare and account for only a fraction of hunger-related deaths. It is poverty, and its associated inability to afford an adequate diet (what Bennett terms 'normal' hunger) which kills children in their first year or undermines the health of those who survive into adulthood. In seeking to explain such a state of affairs, Bennett argues it is important to look beyond conventional Western explanations, such as localized food shortages, overpopulation or droughts, and to consider the 'institutions, policies and ideologies which serve to widen the gap between rich and poor' (Bennett 1987: 13). These create the distinctions between the powerful North (that is, industrialized societies) and the subordinate South (that is, non-industrialized societies). Bennett's analysis draws attention to the impact of the pursuit of profits through cash crops which are exported, to the burden of Third World debt and to the use of food as a weapon in the political struggles between colonizers and the colonized. These are the dramatic consequences of the disappearance of the traditional food systems of the Third World which, Bennett argues, were rational, relatively well-balanced adaptations to the local environment.

The differences between the North and the South are not the only inequalities which can be understood in terms of a political analysis of the global food

41

system. It has been suggested that 'The world re-discovered hunger in the mid-1980s' (Warnock 1987: ix), not only in the Third World but also in the cities of the West. Warnock draws attention to the contradictions in the policies of governments, such as those of the United States and the European Union, which either pay farmers not to produce or allow food 'mountains' to accumulate, whilst at the same time some groups in these societies go hungry. All the evidence suggests that there is no shortage of food on a worldwide basis, that food supplies have been increasing and that reserves of several staples, for example, grain, are high. The question then becomes that of why hunger persists in a world of plenty.

For Warnock, the question of who is undernourished and why, draws attention to issues which challenge Western complacency and optimism and are uncomfortable to contemplate from the perspective of the secure middle and upper classes. For example, 'free' trade in food does not necessarily benefit all countries equally and the model of the 'developing' country which suffers temporarily in the transition to fully developed status conceals the structure of political domination from which it is difficult to escape. Even the so-called 'Green Revolution', entailing the use of scientific knowledge to improve Third World agriculture, benefits the elites of the Third World and the general population of the North, to which foods are exported, more than the underdeveloped countries as a whole. These writers make the reader aware that the modern food system is not a neutral organization of food production and distribution but a political system which benefits some nations more than others. The solution to the problems of world hunger and the inequalities within specific societies are, they argue, political. 'The elimination of poverty and hunger comes at a high price' (Warnock 1987: 297). This price includes challenges to the hierarchical structure and lack of democratic control in the institutions of government, including those linked with the production and distribution of food.

REFASHIONING NATURE

The literature outlined in this chapter presents us with contradictory accounts of the making of the modern food system. It first provides a perspective of growth, expansion and rapid change, all of which appeared to be leading to increases in choice and quantity of food for all, and to a food system which has a responsive and sophisticated articulation between production, distribution and consumption. More recently, the note is more cautious, emphasizing the inequalities, particularly in the distribution of food, and indicating that no society, whether of the North or of the South, is exempt from sharp differences in access to food resources and that the modern food system has variable consequences which depend on political power. From the first perspective the future is bright; any problems can be viewed as temporary and resolvable with the application of the knowledge currently and potentially available. From the second perspective, the picture is of food supplies as precarious, or potentially so, and of a food system which cannot be sustained without continued exploitation of some Third World food producers.

One way of accommodating such contradictory analyses is offered by Goodman and Redclift (1991). Focusing on food supply, they argue that the development of the modern food system and its current operation can be seen as the outcome of a series of changes which they sum up as Western societies' attempt at 'refashioning nature'. Their argument is complex and recognizes the importance of taking into account all kinds of changes, not necessarily all closely connected with food in the first instance, and of drawing upon the materials provided by the literatures on agricultural development, technology, food policy and diet. Their argument is designed to encourage the reader to consider the ideological and economic framework within which the food supply is located. The processes of change they identify are, they argue, part of a process which changed not only how we think and behave towards food but also how we see the world and our own place in relation to nature.

Using such a framework of interconnected structures, it is not always easy to disentangle causes and effects. However, Goodman and Redclift group the changes under several major strands. The first identifies the social processes associated with the household which have accompanied the increasing commoditization of food, which they summarize as 'food into freezers; women into factories' (Goodman and Redclift 1991: 1). They focus on British experience during the twentieth century and note the coincidence of the diversification of household consumption with the movement of more women into paid employment. They also note the production of consumer goods for the home, for example, cookers, refrigerators and other 'white goods', which, in turn, is linked with a switch towards a greater emphasis on processed food products. However, these processes have not been taken to their extremes: neither women's work nor food are fully commoditized. The 'naturalness' of food and the work of women in their homes remain valued. None the less, it can be seen that the modern food system represents a new construction of social and economic divisions in the public domain of paid employment and the private domain of the household. Women's increasing involvement in the labour market has inevitable implications for the gendered division of labour in the home and particularly for the gendered division of labour in relation to food work (purchasing, preparation and presentation).

A further strand in the changes which have contributed to the modern food system is the transformation of food production itself. The modern food system requires reliable and stable supplies of food and conditions of social stability in which to bring about increases in production. These have been achieved by what Goodman and Redclift term a 'social contract' (Goodman and Redclift 1991: xiv) between farmers and government in the West which facilitated the integration of agriculture and industrial activities, increasing the investment in, and scale of, farming. Such processes, they argue, reduced resistance to the implications of refashioning nature on the farm. The industrialization of farming, along with the drive to control nature in controlling agricultural output, began with farm mechanization and the use of agri-chemicals and is continuing currently with the use of revolutionary advances in plant and animal genetics. The latter are being developed for commercial gain by private corporations which are in competition with each other and are thus 'refashioning nature according to the logic of the market place' (Goodman and Redclift, 1991: xvi).

Here there is the recognition that not all will benefit from such processes and that there are contradictions as well as evidence of progress in the modern food system. The South appears to have benefited from cheap food policies designed to accelerate industrialization whilst, at the same time, having its peasant agriculture and self-provisioning weakened and a dependence on imported food established. In other words, the South is caught up in the contradictions of the modern food system. The West itself is also becoming aware of the costs of this system, for example, the loss of sustainability and the destructive effects of some modern agriculture. Alternative models for refashioning nature have emerged, providing a counter-culture opposed to the scale of industrialized agriculture and to its established practices. Opposition focuses on production processes (for example, protests about the use of pesticides and factory farming) as well as· on the quality of food (for example, concerns about the use of food additives and a perceived loss of 'naturalness'). The entire analysis indicates that the concept of 'refashioning nature' may be the central one for interpreting the processes which have produced the modern food system. However, the evidence indicates also that this refashioning is an extremely difficult task and that control of the process is precarious and controversial.

The issue of control also emerges as a key feature of the argument of Tansey and Worsley (1995) who focus on the development of the modern food system since the Second World War. Although the book is intended to be a guide to the entire food system, discussion concentrates on 'the rich, industrialized world where the global food system is being developed and promoted' (Tansey and Worsley 1995: 1). For these authors, the notion of a food system implies links between three different processes: the biological (including the production of food); the economic and political (in particular, the power and control exerted over the components of the food system); the social and cultural (especially those factors which shape the ways in which people select and use food). The links are not always necessarily easy to examine and the authors identify part of their task as drawing the reader's attention to events and developments which can have unanticipated consequences for the range of food available as well as its quality and quantity. Indeed, the book is aimed at alerting 'ordinary citizens', as well as students and professionals, to the balance of power between consumer and producer and to the ways in which this might relate to the practicalities of food safety and its availability for various social groups.

The authors provide a wide range of material from official and other surveys to inform the reader about the biological and ecological basis of food production, the structures and processes associated with what they term the 'key actors', such as farmers, distributors and consumers. They emphasize the ways in which science, technology, information and management, as well as the legal framework, can be used to control the production and distribution of food. They argue that the outcome of such interrelationships in the food system is a triumph, in that more people than ever are being fed and, in the industrialized and some developing countries, famine and scarcity no longer occur. However, the system also provides challenges in that some countries still experience malnutrition, or even famine, and long-term sustainability on a worldwide basis is in doubt. The authors identify six major changes that are likely to have an impact on the food system: increasing longevity (with its consequent strain on the ecosystem); increasing urbanization (which will extend the food chain); globalization of the food market (with large companies controlling a larger share and being independent of national boundaries); increasing technological (including biotechnological) change; changes in attitudes and values (consequent upon any shifts in power); and the decline in the traditional 'housekeeping' role of women as they participate more in the labour market and convenience foods are readily available. The authors conclude that if we wish to avoid the development of a system shaped only by the workings of the commercial market, then it is necessary to have clear food policy goals. The authors make clear their own preference for a food system which has the characteristics of being sustainable, secure, safe, sufficient, nutritious and equitable, and aimed at achieving 'a well-fed future for all' (Tansey and Worsley 1995: 232).

OVERVIEW

In this chapter we have sought to map the major contrasts between the traditional and modern food systems, with particular emphasis placed upon the dramatically increased scale and the extensive delocalization of the productive process. Using Britain as our case study, we have employed an historical perspective to outline the key developments in the emergence of the modern food system, with particular reference to the way that industrialization has transformed the nature of agricultural production and ensured the security of food supplies in the developed countries through the application of sophisticated scientific and technological knowledge.

However, at an international level, we have noted the way in which the globalized modern food system provides benefits for some countries by imposing costs on others, with the disadvantaged South seen as subordinated to the privileged North. The evolution of the modern food system, it has been argued, is also closely associated not only with industrialization itself but with far-reaching changes in the nature of the labour market and the division of labour within the household. Such structural changes appear, themselves, to be linked to some of the most deep-seated features of Western culture, particularly in relation to

45

the right and ability of human beings to refashion and exploit the natural world. However, currently we are experiencing controversy and reappraisal in relation to these deeply rooted ideas in the form of the environmentalist challenges to established ideas.

3

SOCIOLOGICAL PERSPECTIVES
ON FOOD AND EATING

In the previous chapter we examined the complex set of transformations which gave rise to the modern food system, a system whose characteristic features distinguish it from earlier modes of producing and distributing food in crucial ways. In a sense, the main object of analysis of this book is the modern food system itself, in terms of its multiplicity of aspects, dimensions and relationships. What is more, just as this system emerged out of far-reaching changes, the system itself is subject to continuing change. Thus, we will also be required to try to make sense of these changes, in terms of their causes and their directions. However, alongside change there is also continuity and stability in certain aspects of the system, and the bases of these features also demand attention and explanation.

THE CONCEPT OF THE HUMAN FOOD SYSTEM

Up to this point we have used the concept of the human food system in a general rather than a specific sense. At this stage it is worthwhile attempting to make more explicit its particular features, linkages and relationships. Of course, at its most basic, the modern human food system can be conceptualized as an immensely complicated set of biological relationships between human beings and symbiotically linked domesticated plants and animals, not forgetting the myriads of micro-organisms upon which the system depends and the hosts of pests and parasites which colonize it at all its tropic levels (see e.g., Jeffers 1980). However, for the purposes of this book, the primary focus is not on the biological but on the social and cultural dimensions of the system. As a starting-point we can take the basic scheme put forward by Goody (1982: 37). In Goody's view, providing and transforming food can be conceptualized in terms of five main processes, each process representing a distinct phase and taking place in a characteristic location, as shown in Table 3.1.

Thus the process of 'growing' food (including the rearing of animals) equals the 'production' phase, and is located on farms. The processes of allocating and storing food are identified as the 'distribution' phase, located in, for example, granaries and markets. Cooking, the preparation phase, takes place in the

Table 3.1 The features of the food system

Processes	Phases	Locus
Growing	Production	Farm
Allocating/storing	Distribution	Market/granary
Cooking	Preparation	Kitchen
Eating	Consumption	Table
Clearing up	Disposal	Scullery

Source: Adapted from Goody (1982)

kitchen, and eating, the consumption phase, takes place at the table. The fifth process, clearing up (which, Goody rightly points out, is often overlooked) represents the disposal phase, located in what he rather quaintly refers to as the 'scullery'. In fact, Goody's scheme is rather rudimentary, and clearly omits many of the crucial linkages in the modern food system. Yet it does draw our

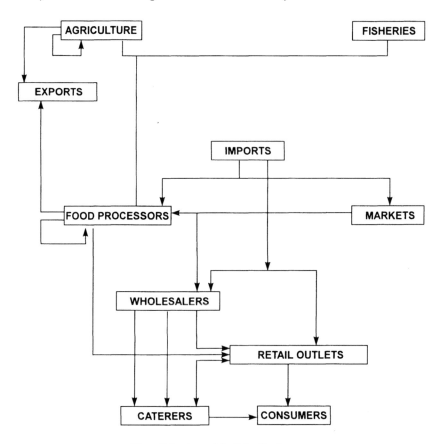

Figure 3.1 A model of the food system
Source: Adapted from Freckleton, Gurr, Richardson, Rolls and Walker (1989)

48

attention to all the basic processes involved, and it does allow us to begin to conceptualize how we might formulate sociological questions about each of the five phases which make up the system's underlying sequence.

A much more elaborate model of the contemporary food system is offered by Freckleton, Gurr, Richardson, Rolls and Walker (1989), who employ the biological term 'food chain' to refer to their scheme, although the scheme itself is an explicit description of the human, social framework of the system.

As can be seen from Figure 3.1, these authors detail the inputs into the system provided by agriculture (and by fisheries, which still exploit stocks of undomesticated animals) and include the fact that in any 'local' system there are outflows (exports) and inflows (imports). The central role played by food processors is referred to, that is, manufacturing organizations who obtain 'raw' food items from the primary producers (usually through specialist markets) and transform them into marketable products. The model also highlights the role played by wholesalers, who supply products from food processors, or items from specialist markets, to food retailers or to caterers of various kinds, who supply their products direct to the consumer. (For a model describing the food system in terms of factors affecting supply and demand potential see Pierce 1990: 7.)

Examining the multiplicity of flows and linkages in this model, it becomes evident that sociologists (and indeed social scientists in general) can pose a host of fascinating questions about the ways in which each of the components is organized, the ways in which the linkages between the components are actually articulated and the ways in which the system is monitored and regulated (usually by the state). However, even though the whole system is, in principle, susceptible to sociological analysis, there has been a notable tendency to concentrate attention on the consumption end. In effect, in the expanding literature on the sociology of food and eating the practices, preferences, choices, concerns and prejudices of consumers appear to have been allocated priority, although, of course, the beliefs and actions of the food consumer are located by sociologists within broader cultural, ideological and structural frameworks. The production, processing and distribution elements of the system have received, relatively speaking, a good deal less attention. In a sense, this is a curious state of affairs, given that, historically, mainstream sociology has always placed a strong emphasis on the analysis of the processes of production and on the idea that work and work roles play a crucial part in creating individual identity and in locating the individual in the wider social order. It is only comparatively recently that there has been something of a swing away from this production-centred approach towards a greater concern with the dynamics of consumption (Bocock 1993).

In a way, the sociology of food and eating has anticipated this trend, and the contents of this book, of necessity, reflect these priorities. However, there is literature, albeit somewhat fragmentary, on the productive processes of the system, both in domestic and commercial settings, and this literature will be drawn upon to provide context and background. Given the relatively recent arrival of food and eating as objects of analysis within sociology, there are still significant gaps in our knowledge of the human food system. The topics in this book have explicitly been chosen to provide the reader with an introduction to those areas where substantial sociological insights are available.

FROM THE NUTRITIONAL TO THE CULTURAL

In biological and behavioural terms humans can be classed as *omnivores* since they obtain their required nutrients from both animal and plant sources, and do not exhibit the kinds of physiological specializations which identify the dedicated herbivore or the confirmed carnivore. Nutrients can be defined as those chemical components of foods which contribute to one or more of the following vital bodily processes:

1 the production of energy;
2 the growth and repair of body tissue;
3 the regulation and control of energy production and tissue generation.

There are five basic groups of nutrients which we require to fulfil the above functions:

- *carbohydrates* which are primarily sources of energy;
- *fats* which are also, among other things, important energy sources;
- *proteins* which are the sources of the amino acids required for tissue growth, but which can also play a role in the other two functions listed above;
- *minerals* which are inorganic substances which contribute towards tissue growth (e.g., in bones and teeth) and the regulation of bodily processes;
- *vitamins* which constitute a very broad group of substances which function to facilitate the reactions required for the body's nutritional chemistry.

In a sense, water might also be classed as a nutrient, in that this essential compound plays many roles in the human body, e.g., in the breakdown of food into its constituent nutrients (through hydrolysis) and in the transport of those nutrients in the blood. (For introductory discussions of human nutrition, see e.g., Brownsell, Griffith and Jones 1989; Birch, Cameron and Spencer 1986. For a useful reference work see Anderson 1993.)

What is particularly striking about human beings, in nutritional terms, is the sheer diversity of the sources from which they can, and do, obtain the nutrients required to keep the body in existence and to fuel its day-to-day activities. Any attempt to list the whole range of plant and animal products that currently contribute to, or have in the past contributed to, the human diet would be a task of such enormity that it certainly cannot be attempted here. What is the case, however, is that this truly impressive nutritional versatility, probably unequalled by any other omnivore, has been a vital factor in the evolutionary success of our species. *Homo sapiens* has successfully colonized virtually every available habitat type and, along with our domesticated symbionts, we have established effective dominance over a high proportion of the land surface of the earth. None of this would have been feasible for a species with specialized feeding requirements.

However, being an omnivore does involve certain risks in addition to conveying the advantages associated with flexibility and versatility. Investigating and sampling new substances may lead to the discovery of valuable new food resources, and the present diversity of human eating patterns is the result of trial and error exercised over countless generations. But, inevitably, trial and error, as well as providing positive outcomes, can also lead to bad experiences, for example as a result of encountering unpalatable or even dangerously toxic or contaminated items. Thus, we are forced to confront what has been termed the 'omnivore's paradox', the tension between *neophilia*, the drive to seek out novel food items, and *neophobia*, the fear that novel items may be harmful (Rozin 1976; Fischler 1980). Thus, omnivores must successfully balance curiosity and caution, and this is as true for humans as for any other omnivorous animal. This tension is one of several deep-seated conflicts at the very foundation of human eating patterns, conflicts to which we will return in due course.

Of course, for humans, eating is not simply an activity aimed at obtaining required nutrients. There is clearly much more to it than that. This becomes all too obvious when we consider the fact that all cultures are highly selective in what they actually define as food, that is, as items acceptable for human consumption. In fact, Falk (1991) argues that one of the most fundamental distinctions made by human beings is that between *edible* and *inedible*, closely related to more abstract binary oppositions such as *us* and *them, same* and *other, inside* and *outside, good* and *bad, culture* and *nature*. Something edible is something which may be safely taken into the body. However, the cultural sense of inedibility/edibility is not simply a function of some wisdom of the body based upon metabolic processes and nutritional efficiency (Falk 1991: 55). Indeed, any given culture will typically reject as unacceptable a whole range of potentially nutritious items or substances while often including other items of dubious nutritional value, and even items with toxic or irritant properties. For example, the mainstream culinary cultures of the United States and the United Kingdom rule out horses, goats and dogs from the range of mammalian species suitable for inclusion in the human diet, whereas in other cultural contexts all these species have been, or are now, eaten with relish. (Religious beliefs may also play a role in the exclusion of certain items from the diet, obvious examples being the avoidance of pork prescribed by Judaism and Islam, and the avoidance of beef prescribed by Hinduism. We will return to such avoidances in a later chapter.) Conversely, Anglo-American cuisine incorporates large quantities of nutritionally suspect substances like refined sugar, and substances which are actually valued for their irritant properties, like pepper and mustard.

Indeed, when we eat, we are not merely consuming nutrients, we are also consuming gustatory (i.e., taste-related) experiences and, in a very real sense, we are also 'consuming' *meanings* and *symbols*. Every aliment in any given human diet carries a symbolic charge along with its bundle of nutrients. Thus, our view of a particular food item is shaped as much by what that item means to us as by how it tastes or by its ability to satisfy the body's nutritional needs (although, of course, the latter two features may get themselves incorporated into the aliment's charge of meanings). In fact, the symbolic dimensions of the foods we eat are of such central importance to us that in extreme instances we might even envisage starving rather than eat technically eatable substances that our culture defines as prohibited. Perhaps the most dramatic example of this is the near universal taboo on the consumption of human flesh. Instances of the violation of this taboo, e.g., in extreme situations of food deprivation, are regarded with a mixture of abhorrence and morbid curiosity.

Thus, it is no exaggeration to say that when humans eat, they eat with the mind as much as with the mouth. Indeed, the symbolic potential of food and eating is virtually limitless, and food items and food consumption events can be imbued with meanings of great significance and surpassing subtlety, according to the occasion and the context. Particular foods and food combinations, in particular cultures, can be associated with festivity and celebration, with piety, religious observance and sacred ritual, and with the rites of passage which mark crucial status transitions in the life cycle. What is more, gifts of food can be employed as rewards or as demonstrations of affection or approval. In Western cultures confectionery has a particular role to play in this context. Closely connected with this idea of the association between food and reward, is the association between certain foods and hedonism. Some foods may carry powerful meanings which go beyond the actual gustatory satisfaction they offer, being charged with overtones of luxury and self-indulgence. However, it is at this point that the darker side of food symbolism may come to the fore. Luxury and self-indulgence may generate guilt as well as pleasure. Thus, foods such as chocolate may develop ambivalent symbolic charges related to pleasure but also to anxieties concerning the health-related implications of their consumption. Indeed, in a more extreme sense, in specific cultural and historical contexts, particular food items may come to bear a potent negative symbolic charge, carrying meanings associated with the dangers of disease, immorality or ritual pollution. Of course, the reverse is also the case, in so far as other food items may develop associations with health, moral rectitude and spiritual purity. (Some of these issues will be explored further in later chapters.)

Food exchanges between individuals can be used to symbolize their mutual interdependence and reciprocity, whereas the routine provision of food for another, without reciprocity, can express one's dominance over a subordinate. In a domestic context, the preparation and serving of food for a family can express care and concern although, more subtly, the discharging of the responsibility to prepare food for others may also be seen as an expression of the server's effective subordination to the household's provider or 'breadwinner'. Indeed, in more general terms, food represents a powerful symbolic resource for the expression of patterns of social differentiation. If we consider the underlying dimensions of social differentiation which sociologists seek to analyse and under-

52

stand (class, gender, age and ethnicity), it is clear that food can, and frequently does, play a crucial role in symbolizing and demonstrating social distinctions. Thus, specific foods become associated with a high social class location, with high status or with socially superior aesthetic tastes. Conversely, other foods may symbolize a low social class position, low status or the condition of poverty (economic or aesthetic). There is also no doubt that in many cultures (including modern Western settings) some foods can carry a distinctively masculine or feminine charge. Frequently, this gender charge is centred upon conceptions of strength, with 'strong' foods symbolizing masculinity and the needs of men, and 'weak' foods seen as appropriate to feminine needs and inclinations. Conceptions of this sort may also be implicated in age-related food symbolism. Strong, adult foods are often seen as unsuitable for young children. Similarly, particular foods or food combinations come to be seen as especially well-suited to children's needs and tastes, and these can take on an 'infantile' identity or association. At the opposite end of the age scale, a similar process may occur, with some foods being seen as especially appropriate for the elderly. These associations may also be linked with conceptualizations concerning differences in the appropriate diets of the healthy and the infirm. Of course, the role of food and food preparation conventions in symbolizing ethnic differences is also significant, given the fact that these conventions are such central features of cultural distinctiveness, and can retain their potency among minority groups for several generations after their physical separation from the parent culture.

In the chapters that follow, the theme of food symbolism will occur again and again, and many of the aspects of such symbolism mentioned above will be discussed in more detail in the context of actual empirical studies in which they occur as salient features. However, significant as the idea is that food can be used to *express* social differentiation, it is important not to lose sight of the fact that the food options and choices of specific categories or groups also *reflect* the inequalities inherent in such differentiation. The diet of the poor reflects the economic disadvantages with which they have to cope; the diet of children reflects (to some extent) their subordinate position *vis-à-vis* the adults who wield authority over them.

FOOD, IDENTITY AND SOCIALIZATION

So powerful is the symbolic potential of food that Fischler (1988) argues that it is absolutely central to our sense of identity. However, it is not only true that the eating patterns of a given group assert its collective identity, its position in a wider hierarchy, its organization, etc.. Fischler also points out that food is central to *individual identity*. The crucial process here is that of 'incorporation', the act which involves food crossing the barrier between the 'outside' world and the 'inside' world of the body. But the process, as Fischler points out, is not only conceived as a physiological one. We do not simply think in terms of the incorporation of chemical nutrients into the physical fabric of the body, but also in terms of our beliefs and our collective representations. For example, a widespread feature of human culture is the idea that the absorption of a given food, particularly when occurring repeatedly, can have the effect of transferring certain symbolic properties of that food into the very being of the eater. Fischler cites as a positive example the idea that red meat, with its high blood content, confers strength. (Later in the book we will examine beliefs which are very different from this view.) As a negative example, he cites the belief among French eaters that consuming turnips induces 'spinelessness' or, literally, 'turnip blood' (Fischler 1988: 279–80). Thus, for Fischler, the German aphorism *man ist was man isst* (you are what you eat) has both biological and symbolic dimensions. What is more, not only are the properties of food seen as being incorporated into the eater, but, by a symmetrical process, the very absorption of given foods is seen as incorporating the eater into a culinary system and into the group which practises it.

Both in terms of the formation of individual identity and the transmission of culture from generation to generation, the process of socialization is of central importance, that is, the process through which we internalize the norms and values of society, and learn now to perform the social roles in which we find ourselves. Socialization begins in infancy through the primary agencies of the family and the school, but is not confined to childhood, and represents a continuous process throughout the life cycle, with many other agencies taking a hand. What is more, socialization is not merely a passive process. The individual is also active in socializing himself or herself, and we should beware of accepting an 'oversocialized' view of the human individual, since there is always leeway for a degree of choice, deviance or innovation, and there may be conflicting pressures from different agencies. The socialization of an individual into the foodways of the culture into which he or she has been born effectively begins at weaning. At this stage the infant is encouraged to sample what is, at first, a relatively narrow range of solid foods. This range is progressively widened as the child is introduced to more of the food items and preparations regarded as suitable for the young. Crucially, at these early stages, the child will be taught, and will learn by experience, how to distinguish between foods and non-foods. Young children typically place a variety of objects in the mouth in order to use its elaborate sensory apparatus to investigate their physical properties. Children may also attempt to eat substances which are not actually eatable, and to drink liquids which are not actually potable. Even a small sample of parents could provide an interesting inventory of such substances, ranging from relatively harmless ones like garden soil, to highly toxic ones like domestic bleach.

Thus, a crucial feature of nutritional socialization involves learning how to reduce the risk of introducing hazardous substances into the body, although such hazards may be symbolic as well as physiological. Thus, equally importantly from a sociological point of view, the child must learn how to recognize *food* from among a plethora of potentially edible items with which he or she may be surrounded. As we have already noted, in all cultures, whatever the form of subsistence upon which they are based, humans exploit for food only a relatively small proportion of the available plant and animal species around them. However, in Western society, for example, young children, while unsupervised, may sample such perfectly eatable items as earthworms or pet food, and find them good. The horrified reactions of parents, siblings or peers, nevertheless, may soon convince them that such delicacies are, most emphatically, not appropriate for human consumption. In other words, a central part of learning to be human involves learning what humans, as opposed to non-humans, eat.

A whole range of strategies and verbal devices may be employed by parents to exert control over the child's eating patterns and to encourage, cajole or coerce him or her into the consumption of what is seen as a suitable diet (Widdowson 1981). These strategies may include the offer of rewards if the child consumes what the parents regard as desirable foods and the threat or application of punishments if such foods are persistently refused. Indeed, these threats may be accompanied by the invocation of supernatural agencies who are portrayed as ready to intervene to reinforce parental authority in the face of an offspring's persistent nutritional defiance. A particularly graphic example of such a device is provided by Widdowson, who describes the character of the Crust Man, a figure in Newfoundland folklore. Portrayed as taking the form of a large, ugly man, he was said to patrol the community ensuring that children ate their bread crusts. Those who refused to do so were likely to be carried off in the night by this awesome being!

As the individual's nutritional socialization proceeds, in Western cultures an ever-widening range of agencies, including advertisers, the mass media in general, various professional groups, state institutions and ideological or religious movements, can come to play a role. The individual goes on to learn not only how to distinguish foods from non-foods (fit only for animals or foreigners), but how to recognize appropriate preparation techniques, appropriate combinations of food items, and the conventions which govern where and when one eats, and with whom. Furthermore, socialization involves the familiarization of the individual with the food categorization system of his or her culture. Thus, Jelliffe (1967) describes a range of general categories which underlie the food classification schemes of most cultures. These categories are: *cultural superfoods*, the main staples of the society in question; *prestige foods*, whose consumption is limited to special occasions or to high-status groups; *body-image* foods, which are seen as directly promoting health and bodily well-being; *sympathetic magic* foods, which are believed to have desirable properties which can be acquired by those who eat them; and, finally, *physiologic group* foods, which are seen as suitable for specific categories of individuals defined, for example, in terms of gender, age and bodily condition related to health, pregnancy, etc. (For a discussion of this, and other food classification schemes, see Fieldhouse 1986: 45–54.)

As such conventions and categories are mastered, the satisfaction of the body's nutritional requirements is given its shape as a complex *social* activity, as opposed to a mere set of internally driven behavioural responses to the need for nutrients.

In this way, as Mennell (1985: 20–1) points out, the physiological and psychological phenomenon of *hunger* is transformed into the sociological phenomenon of *appetite*. However, appetite, preferences and food symbolism are not necessarily static entities, fixed once and for all in the mind of the individual by the socialization process. Individuals may undergo significant changes in their socially formulated appetites or may experience important transformations in the meanings which they attach to specific food items or, indeed, to the whole process of eating. Thus, in a sense, an individual can be seen as having what can be termed a 'nutritional career'. This career is closely related to the life cycle, as the individual moves through childhood, adulthood and old age, and his or her nutritional practices and preferences change according to changing bodily needs and cultural expectations. In addition, individuals may deliberately initiate changes in their dietary patterns, for a whole range of reasons which they may or may not be capable of comprehending and articulating.

Indeed, modern Western societies can be seen as providing particularly suitable conditions for nutritional careers which commonly include substantial changes. While the nutritional culture of such societies may be characterized by relative stability, continuity and conservatism in some areas of diet (e.g., in relation to cultural superfoods), there is typically a willingness, often an eagerness, to promote and accept change in other areas (say, in relation to body-image foods and physiologic group foods). Indeed, in highly developed, affluent societies the appetite for gustatory and nutritional novelty is actively encouraged (often by commercial interests) and food-related 'sensation-seeking' activities are seen as a normal and accepted part of society's nutritional practices. What is more, in such settings, many agencies (including the state, professional bodies and pressure groups) may deliberately seek to modify the public's food consumption patterns either generally or in relation to particular target groups in the population. Thus, individuals may be undergoing sporadic episodes of resocialization in respect of food choices, practices and beliefs. Such a state of flux has far-reaching implications for many of the topics discussed in this book, and the theme of change will recur frequently in subsequent chapters.

THEORIZING THE FOOD SYSTEM

The question now arises as to what theoretical resources have been brought to bear by sociologists in order to analyse food systems in terms of their symbolic properties and in terms of the intricate webs of social relationships and social processes which articulate them. In this section we wish to offer a broad overview of the various approaches which have been employed. Of course, any scheme for classifying these approaches should be seen simply as an heuristic device. It can only be offered as a summarizing framework to give the reader a sense of the broad picture, a sense of the main theoretical lines which have been pursued by sociologists in the area of food and eating, and can make no claim to be an authoritative description of reality *per se*. What is more, it is important to bear in mind a point made by Goody (1982: 8) concerning the very nature of sociological theories themselves. He draws a clear contrast between theoretical innovations in the natural sciences, which may well produce revolutionary paradigm shifts (Kuhn 1964), and theoretical innovations in sociology (and its sister discipline, social anthropology). In sociology, such innovations are not the cues for the total reorientation of the discipline's research activities and intellectual efforts. Rather, they indicate shifts of emphasis between possibilities which are always present in the act of sociological analysis. Such possibilities may be conceived of in terms of binary oppositions, for example: a focus on the subjective world of the social actor versus a holistic focus on social structure; a focus on qualitative versus quantitative methods; a focus on synchronic versus diachronic analysis; a focus on surface structure versus a focus on deep structure, and so on. All this implies that changes in sociological theory are, in effect, 'repetitive', involving cycles of changing emphasis in relation to the underlying, recurring themes of the discipline. Thus, when we examine a specific area of sociological analysis and research like food and eating we might logically expect it to reflect the changing fashionability of the approaches. Furthermore, particular studies will also reflect these changes, although we should not be surprised to discover that such studies may actually be quite difficult to classify according to any broad scheme, given that they may involve the hybridization of two or more approaches.

Goody's (1982) own classificatory scheme identifies three main approaches: the *functional*, the *structural* and the *cultural*. Having discussed these three, he then goes on to examine approaches which introduce historical and comparative data, although he does not actually provide these approaches with their own distinctive label. Writing somewhat later, Mennell, Murcott and Van Otterloo (1992) put forward a very similar scheme, suggesting that the three main headings under which studies of food and eating can be conveniently classified are *functionalism, structuralism* and *developmentalism* (although the authors do point out that many studies in this area have been empiricist in style or largely policy-oriented, and hence difficult to classify in terms of theoretical approach). Combining these two schemes would provide us with a four-category classification of approaches: functional, structural, cultural and developmental (the latter heading actually being implicit in Goody's own discussion). However, the cultural will be omitted as a separate heading, as Goody's argument does not actually establish the need for this as a category in itself, since it is a concept so fundamental to the other three approaches. We can now examine each of these in turn, analysing its underlying logic and the kinds of questions it poses, and looking at representative examples of its use.

I The functionalist approach

Functionalist perspectives have exercised a powerful formative influence on sociology and on its sister discipline social anthropology. Functionalism is based upon an analogy between a society and an organic system, like a living body. Just as a body is seen as made up of a set of specialized organs, each playing its own unique and indispensable role in the maintenance and continuity of the living system, society is seen as made up of a set of features and institutions which make their own contribution to the cohesion and continuity of the social system. Thus, society is seen in holistic terms and as having emergent properties which spring from the complex interrelationships and interdependency of its component parts. Functionalist analysis consists essentially of examining particular institutions with a view to describing their functional significance. For example, the institution of marriage might be analysed in order to understand its contribution to the long-term viability and continuity of a given social formation. Functionalist theory makes an important distinction between the *manifest* function of some feature (i.e., the function explicitly recognized by members of the society in question) and that feature's *latent* function (i.e., a function that a feature may fulfil, but which may not be recognized or admitted by society's members). Functionalist theory also recognizes that a social system may exhibit *dysfunctional* features which disrupt that system and lead to states which are analogous to pathology in a living body, i.e., to 'social pathology'. Some of the leading figures in sociology have made contributions of central importance to the development of functionalist perspectives, for example, Davis (1966), Durkheim (1984), Merton (1957) and Parsons (1951).

However, the whole funtionalist approach has attracted a barrage of criticism. It has been accused, for example, of being an essentially static view of human social organization, overemphasizing stability and integration, and poorly equipped to explain the presence of conflict and change in social systems. What is more, the approach has also been criticized for failing to account causally for the origins of particular institutions or features in society, assuming that describing a particular institution's alleged role or effects is, in itself, an adequate explanation for its presence. Perhaps even more problematic is the assumption that we can specify the functional needs of a social system in the same way that we might specify the physiological needs of a living body. Given that social systems have the ability to undergo far-reaching structural changes, the notion of a set of immutable and unavoidable functional needs is somewhat implausible.

As a result of such criticisms, functionalism is now out of fashion within the discipline of sociology, although certain aspects of the critique may have been overstated (for example, functionalist perspectives are not totally incapable of coming to terms with conflict and change in a social system). However, functionalist interpretations remain at the core of much sociological analysis, albeit in an implicit form.

It is possible to conceive of a range of questions which could be asked about food and eating from a broadly functionalist perspective. For example:

- How are the food production, distribution and consumption subsystems organized and how do they contribute to the continuity of the social system as a functioning whole? (In posing such questions, the organic analogy upon which functionalism is based is very much to the fore, in that society might be viewed as analogous to an enormous superorganism, feeding itself and distributing nutrients around its 'body'.)

- What are the social (i.e., non-nutritional) functions of patterns of food allocation and consumption? For example, how do allocation and consumption conventions act to express and reinforce the social relationships upon which the stability of the whole system is supposed to depend? One expression of such an issue might be the idea that food-related practices may reinforce gender divisions, such divisions being seen as functional for the system in that they could be regarded as forming the basis of the conventional nuclear family, the institution which organizes reproduction and primary socialization.

- Can we identify, in food systems, dysfunctional features, alongside the kinds of latent functions discussed above? How do such dysfunctional elements arise? What are their consequences for the social system as a whole? (In this connection, for example, we might analyse eating patterns which appear adversely to affect the health of the population, or the mechanisms which generate disruptive food-related anxieties and scares.)

Significantly, perhaps, those studies which can most clearly be identified as adopting a functionalist approach to food and eating are to be found within social anthropology. More specifically, they are to be found within the British school of social anthropology, a branch of the discipline which, in its formative years, was dedicated to the functionalist, holistic analysis of traditional social systems. Thus, one of the founders of this school, Bronislaw Malinowski, provided a highly detailed ethnographic account of food production and allocation systems in the Trobriand Islands, and of the complex patterns of belief and social reciprocity which articulated these systems (Malinowski 1935). One of Malinowski's own students, Audrey Richards, set out to analyse, from a functionalist perspective, the ways in which the production, the preparation and particularly the consumption of food among the Bantu were linked to the life cycle, to group structures and to the social linkages which constituted them (Richards 1932). In a later study of the Bemba (Richards 1939), she attempted to place the nutritional culture of a traditional people into its broader economic setting. A recurring theme in Richard's study was the symbolic significance of food and of nutritional practices, a symbolism which served to express, for example, vital ties of kinship, obligation and reciprocity.

The functional significance of food and foodways was also highlighted by social anthropologists writing more general monographs on traditional peoples. For example, in his discussion of the Andaman Islanders, Radcliffe-Brown (1922) had sought to demonstrate the way in which food-related rituals and taboos were used, not only to impress upon the young the social value of food but also as devices for dramatizing the collective sentiments of the community, hence facilitating the individual's socialization. What is more, the co-operative production of food, and its sharing within the community, were activities which served to emphasize a sense of mutual obligation and interdependence, and hence to reinforce the integration of Andaman society (Radcliffe-Brown 1922: 270–1). In what is undoubtedly one of the classic texts of the British school of social anthropology, Evans-Pritchard (1967) set out to document the political and ecological dimensions of Nuer society. He described in detail the relationship between kinship systems and spatial organization, and demonstrated the extent to which the food system of this pastoralist people was based upon, in his memorable phrase, a form of 'symbiosis with cattle'. In a sense, in a study like Evans-Pritchard's, the functional linkages in a food system are far more visible than in a modern system, where such linkages do not have the same immediate proximity to everyday life. However, for the Nuer, the realities and exigencies of food production, and the seasonal migrations they entail, are integral features of every individual's experience.

The studies discussed above were carried out several decades ago under the aegis of a theoretical approach which has more recently been relegated to the margins of sociology. However, functionalist ideas have proved quite resilient, either as explicit neo-functionalist arguments or as an implicit set of assumptions. As we will see later in this book, functionalist or quasi-functionalist perspectives lie behind some of the questions which we continue to ask about the non-nutritional role of food in society and in everyday life. These questions may not be framed in terms of what might be called 'grand theory' functionalism, but they do attest to the continuing significance of this organic analogy, albeit in a partially concealed form.

II The structuralist approach

Structuralist analyses of social phenomena differ from the functionalist approach in a particularly important respect. Whereas functionalism seeks to theorize the ways in which the various components of the system interrelate with each other to form a coherent whole, structuralism claims to look below these 'surface' linkages into the 'deep structures' which are alleged to underpin them. Thus, structuralism claims to analyse the very structure of human thought, even of the mind itself (Goody 1982: 17). Of greatest interest to the present discussion is the structuralism of the French anthropologist Lévi-Strauss (1963, 1966a, 1970). Lévi-Strauss, unlike the functionalists, is not primarily concerned with producing holistic descriptions of particular traditional societies. Rather, he sets out to examine a wide range of anthropological material and ethnographic data (notably in relation to myth) on the assumption that the examination of these surface features can lead to the recognition of universal, underlying patterns. These patterns are the deep structures, structures which represent the unvarying foundations of the enormous diversity of surface cultural forms which we can observe. There is assumed to be an affinity between the deep structures of the human mind and the deep structures of human society. Just as functionalism is based upon an analogy between society and a living organism, so structuralism also rests on an analogy. In this instance, the analogy is a linguistic one, with cultural surface features seen as generated in the same way that everyday speech is seen as produced by an underlying system of rules (Saussure 1960).

Thus, the questions posed about food and eating from a structuralist perspective have a different emphasis as compared with those posed from a functionalist viewpoint. Rather than focusing upon the practicalities and the social processes involved in producing, allocating and consuming food, the structuralist gaze is directed towards the rules and conventions that govern the ways in which food items are classified, prepared and combined with each other. The assumption is that these surface rules of cuisine are themselves manifestations of deeper, underlying structures. These rules are almost like a language which, if we can decipher it, will tell us much about the organization of the human mind and human society.

Lévi-Strauss uses this analogy directly by referring to the constituent elements of cuisine as 'gustemes', deriving this term from the linguistic concept of the phoneme. His argument is that such gustemes can be analysed in terms of certain binary oppositions. These are endogenous/exogenous (local versus exotic), central/peripheral (staple versus garnish or accompaniment) and marked/not marked (strong flavour versus bland flavour). He actually sets out to analyse the differences between English and French cuisine using this scheme, suggesting that in English cooking the endogenous/exogenous and central/peripheral distinctions are highly pertinent, whereas the marked/not marked opposition is not. In contrast, in French cuisine, the endogenous/exogenous and central/peripheral oppositions are not so pertinent, whereas the marked/not marked opposition is emphasized (Lévi-Strauss 1963).

However, certainly the best known and most widely quoted example of Lévi-Strauss's structuralist approach to cuisine is his analysis of the transformations involved in the actual cooking of food. Cooking is seen as a crucial operation, given that Lévi-Strauss argues that a universal feature of human thought involves linking the distinction between raw ingredients and cooked food with the fundamental distinction between nature and culture (Lévi-Strauss 1966b). Thus, in the sphere of eating, cooking is what transforms nature (raw ingredients) into culture (acceptable food for humans).

Lévi-Strauss formulates these ideas in terms of his so-called 'culinary triangle' (Figure 3.2), which lays out in diagrammatic form the transitions between nature and culture which are associated with food.

Thus, raw food, at the apex of the triangle, becomes cooked food through a cultural transformation. However, cooked food may be reclaimed by nature through the natural transformation of rotting. Of course, raw (fresh) food can itself be transformed from one natural state into another natural state through the process of rotting, as the triangle indicates. Lévi-Strauss takes the position that the transformational operations of cooking can be seen as a kind of

61

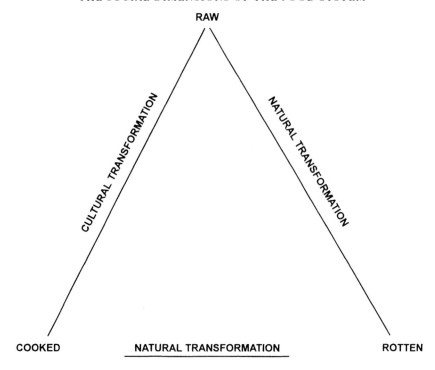

Figure 3.2 The culinary triangle
Source: Adapted from Lévi-Strauss (1966b)

language, in the same way that he regards marriage regulations and kinship systems as a kind of language for establishing and regulating linkages and communication between social groups in traditional societies (Goody 1982: 21).

Developing the basic culinary triangle, Lévi-Strauss then puts forward a more elaborate triangle of recipes, arguing, for example, that roasting is a cooking technique which is closer to the 'raw' apex (since it is seen by him as producing relatively little change in meat, for example). On the other hand, he sees smoking as a technique as closer to culture, since it transforms meat into a durable commodity. He asserts that boiling, which is mediated by water, produces results which are closer to the 'rotten' corner of the basic triangle. As Lévi-Strauss elaborates his arguments, the justifications for his assertions appear to become ever more idiosyncratic and even fanciful. This has led some authors to raise doubts about the actual analytical and heuristic usefulness of such a scheme. For example, Mennell (1985: 9) points out that when Lévi-Strauss attempts to explain the foodways of European societies, his celebrated triangles are of comparatively little use and, in effect, he falls back on common-sense arguments. What is more, Goody (1982: 31) suggests that there is a certain circularity in arguing that by analysing surface structures (like culinary practices) we can deduce the deep structures of the mind or of society, and that these deep structures are what 'generate' the surface effects we observe.

Another social anthropologist, Mary Douglas, also has close links with the structuralist approach to food and eating, but in an important sense her concerns are less arcane and less obscure than those of Lévi-Strauss, and more clearly rooted in a less exotic, more familiar everyday world. She bases her analysis on the structuralist idea that food can be treated as a code, and the messages that it encodes are messages about social events and about social relations like 'hierarchy, inclusion and exclusion, boundaries and transactions across boundaries' (Douglas 1975: 61). Douglas employs the scheme devised by Halliday (1961) who puts forward a framework of categories for the description of eating. The uppermost category is the daily menu, below this is the meal, below this is the course, below this the helping and at the base of the structure is the mouthful, which he regards as the equivalent of the gastronomic morpheme. He then goes on to show how these categories can be elaborated in terms of primary and secondary structures so that a complete description of all the elements of a daily menu could be produced using a grammatical format. In fact, Halliday's purpose in offering such a scheme was to cast light on the problems of grammatical categorization, but Douglas takes up the basic idea and applies it to the analysis of the eating patterns of her own family. In so doing, she is able to provide a fascinating insight into the way in which the same structure appears to underly most meals in English cuisine, and the ways in which this structure repeats itself over a whole range of meal occasions, from the most mundane to the most festive. (In a later chapter we will examine Douglas's analysis of family meal structures and their broader social significance in much more detail.) Certainly, the strength of Douglas's use of structuralist perspectives is that she never loses sight of the fact that, while food may be seen as a metaphor, a symbol or a vehicle of communication, it is, above all, a life-giving substance, and a meal is a physical as well as a social event (Douglas 1984).

In any discussion of the structuralist approach to food and eating reference must also be made to the work of the French author, Roland Barthes. Barthes (1979) firmly locates himself within the structuralist framework, as his terminology clearly testifies. For him, an item of food constitutes an item of information. All foods are seen as signs in a system of communication. Thus, in theory, the conceptual units for describing food can be used to construct 'syntaxes' (or 'menus') and 'styles' (or 'diets') in a semantic rather than an empirical fashion. Hence, it becomes possible to ask to what these food significations refer. Looking at food advertising as an example, Barthes identifies one theme in which specific foods are used to signify continuity with tradition and the past. A second major theme embodies the distinction between masculinity and femininity, and involves an element of sublimated sexuality. A third theme revolves around the concept of health, in the rather specific sense of 'conditioning' the body via appropriate foods with associations like 'energy', 'alertness' or 'relaxation' (Barthes 1979: 171). For Barthes, in the developed countries there has emerged a nutritional consciousness which is 'mythically directed' towards adapting human beings to the modern world, and at the same time an increasingly diverse range of behaviours is expressed through food (for example, work, sport, effort, leisure and celebration). Mennell (1985) is critical of Barthes' lack of any systematic historical perspective and of his tendency to draw upon the resources of his own common-sense views of historical knowledge. However, despite these criticisms, the food-related themes Barthes identifies are striking ones (and will recur at various points in this book), even though he cannot actually deliver a fully elaborated 'grammar of food'.

As a perspective, structuralism has been subjected to numerous critical attacks and reappraisals. While this is not the place to discuss this critique in any detail, some of the criticisms which have been levelled at the application of these ideas to food-related issues do need to be reiterated and made explicit at this point. Certainly, by focusing attention on the idea of food as communication, structuralism effectively rules out the analysis of the crucial interconnections which articulate the human food system as a whole. The links between food production and consumption and the wider economic order tend to fade from view, as does the consideration of the significance of the hierarchical organization of human societies and any potential influences of biological or climatological factors (Goody 1982: 28–9). What is more, the structuralist analysis of foodways and food consumption patterns has had little to say about the origins of such patterns, that is, about the specific social and historical conditions which give rise to them. However, despite these shortcomings, the structuralist approach, with its use of a linguistic metaphor, has succeeded in highlighting some key themes. These themes, as we will see, continue to inform the sociological analysis of food and eating. This is despite the fact that structuralism (like functionalism), in its various guises and phases, has now largely passed into unfashionability, and also that the grandiose promise of unlocking the underlying grammar of food has remained largely unfulfilled.

Perhaps the most telling criticism of the structuralist analysis of food is highlighted by Mennell (1985: 13–14). He refers to the point made by Elias (1978a) that structuralism is based upon an assumption fundamental to Western thought, namely, the idea that underlying the surface changes of the everyday world there are deep-seated relationships which are themselves unchanging. The tendency to allocate overriding significance to such hypothetical underlying entities is referred to by Elias as 'process-reduction'. In fact, Mennell implies, this process-reduction assumption seriously undermines attempts to get to grips with the nature and origins of the significant changes under way in human food systems. It is for this reason that he lays such emphasis on what he terms the 'developmental' approach, in which the analysis of change is placed centre stage.

III   The developmental approach

The developmental approach to which Mennell (1985) refers directly, and to which Goody (1982: 33–7) refers in a more indirect fashion, does not really represent an explicit perspective and a coherent body of theory in the same sense as functionalism and structuralism do. Rather, it is something of a residual category into which can be placed a range of approaches which exhibit some common features and preoccupations. The most fundamental of these common features is the assumption that any worthwhile attempt to understand contemporary cultural forms or patterns of social relations must take into account the ways in which these are related to past forms. Thus, social change becomes a primary focus, in terms of its directions, its processes and its origins. Once change is given primacy in this fashion, the presence of conflicts and contradictions in social systems may also become a much more important strand in sociological analysis.

Mennell's own principal contribution to the sociology of food, a comparative study of eating and taste in England and France (Mennell 1985), fits very neatly into the developmental category. This study draws its theoretical underpinnings from the work of Elias (1978b, 1982), whose broad developmental theory ranged from the processes of state formation to the formation of individual personality and conduct. One of the central contentions of Elias's work was the view that an extensive and protracted civilizing process has been at work in Western societies for several centuries. One of the notable effects of this process has been a progressive shift from the exercise of external constraints upon individuals towards the development of internalized constraints which, in effect, individuals exercise upon themselves. This switch from external to internal constraints affects many areas of social life, including eating. It leads to what Mennell (1985: 20–39) terms the 'civilizing of appetite', a concept which has considerable explanatory power in relation to nutrition-related phenomena as diverse as anorexia nervosa and vegetarianism. In fact, Mennell's work represents an ambitious attempt to apply Elias's figurational or sociogenic approach to understanding the contrasts and similarities of two developing systems of cuisine. How 'figurations', or sets of social, cultural, economic or political arrangements, change over time in the context of the ebb and flow of competing ideas and interests is the key question. Mennell's study is arguably one of the best and most fully worked out examples of the developmental approach, and his ideas will be examined in more depth in Chapter 4.

Goody, too, can be located unequivocally in the developmentalist camp. His major study of food and eating (Goody 1982) focuses much of its attention on the cuisine and foodways of two ethnic groups in northern Ghana. However, Goody's book is not simply a narrowly conceived anthropological monograph. He makes a concerted attempt to analyse the changes going on in the groups he studies in terms of the development of what is, in effect, an increasingly globalized food system. Thus, he argues, for example, that the African peoples he studied have not given up their traditional cuisine. However, just as they now employ the English language in areas like politics, religion and education (as a result of the impact of colonialism), they also use English cooking techniques and conventions in certain formal contexts (Goody 1982: 184). Significant changes in a particular set of foodways are shown to be the result of processes of change which are literally occurring on a global scale. Thus, an important part of Goody's analysis is an examination of the development of what he terms 'industrial food', with all the complexities of processing, preservation (through techniques like canning and freezing), mechanized distribution and large-scale retailing. Indeed, the global perspective which forms a background to Goody's analysis provides the central theme of the fascinating study by Mintz of the crucial role of sugar in the nutritional practices and preferences of the Western industrial working class. Mintz (1985) sets out to demonstrate how dramatic rises in sugar consumption were linked to political and economic processes acting at a global level. Mintz's convincing and comprehensive analysis will be discussed further in Chapter 11.

A particularly significant contribution to the sociological and social anthropological analysis of food and eating has been made by Harris (1986). Harris's approach, which he describes as a form of cultural materialism, is not easy to classify under the three broad headings, although Mennell, Murcott and Van Otterloo (1992) opt to locate him under the developmental umbrella, if only because his stance is assertively anti-structuralist. Harris is highly critical of the notion that the symbolic dimensions of food and eating are the overriding ones and that these dimensions can be analysed independently of the nutritional, ecological and economic realities of human life. Harris's own study consists of a series of essays in which he looks at a number of food prohibitions or taboos which appear to have an essentially symbolic, moral or religious basis (e.g., the prohibition on beef associated with Hinduism, the prohibition on pork associated with Judaism and Islam). He sets out to demonstrate that such ideas, and the nutritional practices derived from them, may well have a strong practical logic behind them, a logic which springs out of a society's attempts to adapt to its physical environment and exploit available resources effectively. Mennell and his co-authors see this line of thinking as consistent with the developmental approach, in so far as Harris is seeking to describe the specific conditions and processes which have given rise to a particular feature of a food system or a nutritional culture. However, it is probably fair to say that Harris's form of explanation also has marked affinities with the functionalist approach discussed earlier. We will return to examine some of Harris's distinctive ideas in more detail in Chapter 9.

Mennell, Murcott and Van Otterloo (1992) place the work of the French sociologist Claude Fischler in the structuralist category, while noting that his position is decidedly critical of the limitations of structuralism and shows significant linkages with the developmental approach. Certainly, from the point of view of the present book, it is the developmental aspects of Fischler's concerns that are of particular interest. A crucial thesis put forward by Fischler is the idea that the traditional rules, norms and meanings which structure human food intake (which he labels collectively as the rules of 'gastronomy', the word being used in its literal sense) are increasingly being subjected to 'disaggregation'

(Fischler 1980: 947). This disaggregation involves a breakdown of these long-established rules, and this crisis in gastronomy leads to a state that Fischler terms 'gastro-anomy' (a concept closely linked with Durkheim's concept of anomie). Fischler suggests that this situation arises out of a proliferation of contradictory and inconsistent pressures acting upon the contemporary food consumer (e.g., from the food industry, advertising and the state). What is more, the uncertainties and anxieties created by gastro-anomy and the expansion of agro-industry and industrialized food production are seen as generating disturbances in those processes through which culinary culture helps to create and sustain the individual's very identity (Fischler 1988: 288–90). Fischler's acute and sometimes disturbing analysis will be spelled out in more detail in Chapter 7, when we will examine the interrelated phenomena of food risks, food anxieties and food scares.

The picture of the cultural dimensions of the modern food system painted by Fischler, is, in some senses, a decidedly pessimistic one. However, he does point out that there are likely to be individual and collective attempts to restore order to eating practices and food meanings. Thus, individuals may adopt dietary regimes (weight-loss diets, vegetarianism, etc.) in an attempt to restore some 'normative logic' into their eating (Fischler 1988: 290–1). This idea leads on to the work of the present authors, whose theoretical orientation can also be located beneath the broad umbrella of the developmental approach. The starting point of this analysis is the concept of the aliment, that is, any basic item recognized as edible within a given nutritional culture. The term 'aliment' is employed in preference to the term 'gusteme' which is used by Lévi-Strauss, since it is a more general notion and does not carry the structuralist implications of the gusteme concept (Beardsworth and Keil 1992a: 287–9). Hence, the *alimentary totality* of a society is made up of the whole range of aliments available during a particular time period. At this point the central concept of the 'menu' can be introduced. This term is used in a more abstract and general sense than its employment in everyday speech. It refers to those sets of principles which guide the selection of aliments from the available totality. Clearly, these menu principles can take a multiplicity of forms, and a range of examples can serve to illustrate the possibilities. Thus, *traditional menus* draw their recommendations and rules of food choice and combination from customary practice. Such customary practices, and their supporting beliefs, are built up over many generations and derive their authority and their legitimacy from their long-established status. The prescriptions and prohibitions of traditional menus have a taken-for-granted nature for those socialized into their acceptance, so taken for granted that the rules appear natural and immutable. Violations of these rules are likely to induce consternation, contempt or disgust, as are the rules of other cultures, which, if encountered, may be seen as barbarous or perverse.

In contrast, *rational menus* involve selection criteria which are designed explicitly to achieve some specified goal. These goals may include weight loss, weight gain, improvement of physical or mental performance, the avoidance of particular diseases or the generalized promotion of good health. Such rational menus are commonly based upon scientific or quasi-scientific principles and often involve the elements of deliberate measurement and calculation. Closely related to rational menus, we might identify *convenience menus*, where the overriding goal is the minimization of the time and effort required for acquiring, preparing and presenting food. Another sub-type of the rational menu group is represented by *economy menus* where the prime consideration is to keep food costs within a strict budget. In a similar vein, a whole group of *hedonistic menus* can be identified, based on the goal of maximizing gustatory pleasure. In contrast to these types of menu, a group that can be termed *moral menus* can be identified, where the predominant food selection criteria are derived from ethical considerations (related, for example, to political or ecological issues, or to issues relating to animal welfare or animal rights).

In any given society, we might expect to observe a degree of *menu differentiation*, that is, different categories of individuals within the population (defined in terms of gender, age, class, caste, etc.) would be expected or compelled to make characteristically different choices from the aliments made available within a given menu. The developmental thrust of this whole scheme becomes clear when we note that in traditional societies, characterized by relatively low rates of social change, there may be, in effect, one traditional master menu, which coincides with the boundaries of the alimentary totality. In contrast, in modern and modernizing societies, with more rapid rates of social change, the exercise of choice between a whole range of contrasting and competing menu principles becomes increasingly possible. Thus, individuals will find it ever more feasible to construct their own personal *diets* by making more or less deliberate choices between alternative menus, possibly adjusting their menu choices to suit their mood, economic circumstances or the setting in which the eating event is taking place. This situation can be described as one of *menu pluralism*, that is, a situation in which many alternative schemes to structure food choice and eating patterns are on offer. This pluralism is, in an important sense, a product of the very processes which have combined to create the modern food system with its globalization of food supply, its industrialization of production and distribution. As we have seen, Fischler sees these processes as leading to a breakdown in the rules of gastronomy and a rise in gastro-anomy, with all its negative conse-quences. He does, however, hold out the possibility that these effects are being countered. Indeed, it may well be that the uncertainties of gastro-anomy are but symptoms of the strains involved in the emergence of a new, more open, flexible and pluralistic nutritional order (Beardsworth and Keil 1992b). These issues will re-emerge several times later in this book, particularly in Chapters 7, 9 and 10.

This vision of menu pluralism can be seen as having some connections with the concept of postmodernity which has gained considerable ground in sociology and other related disciplines within the last decade or so. As it has come to be used in sociology, this term refers to a phase in the development of capitalism where, it is argued, the location of individuals in the social order, and the formation of personal identity, are less and less a matter of class position and work roles. Instead, an ever-increasing emphasis is placed upon consumption patterns as ways of demonstrating an individual's position and expressing personality and individuality (Bocock 1993: 77–9). Thus, it is clear that, within a setting of menu pluralism, the dietary choices made by each person within the context of an increasing variety of menu principles on offer become ever more important devices for establishing a sense of personal identity and for expressing personal distinctiveness. However, we need to exercise some caution in applying the broad concept of the ideology of consumerism (whether in its 'mass-consumption' or its 'postmodern' form) to the activity of eating. For example, Baudrillard (1988) takes up the idea that 'wants' are unlimited, an idea deeply rooted in modern Western thought. He argues, in effect, that there are no limits to consumption, since in modern and postmodern societies consumption is essentially the consumption of signs and symbols. It does not literally involve 'devouring' and absorbing the objects themselves. In effect, we consume with the mind, and the mind is potentially insatiable. This argument may sound convincing for goods and services like cars, video machines, audio equipment, domestic appliances, clothes, holidays, entertainment, etc. However, it is only partially applicable to food items. While we have already argued very strongly that the symbolic dimensions of food and eating are crucial for the sociologist, the fact remains, of course, that when an individual eats, he or she consumes not only the symbolic ingredients of that item but also its physical components and nutrients. These nutrients can and do produce actual physiological satiety (through ingestion and absorption) in a way that other commodities cannot. Hence, there are always physical limits on the socially constructed demands of appetite. Even if a particular food item (oysters, for example) were seen as conferring high social status and a strong sense of self worth, an individual could eat these only in limited quantities and with limited frequency before the body itself exercised the sanctions of nausea or even physical expulsion. Thus, while it may be important to understand the changes taking place in the broader areas of consumption and consumerist ideology, we must always bear in mind the unique features of eating.

OVERVIEW

In this chapter we have begun to consider food and eating at a number of different levels: initially at the system level, as a complex framework of productive and distributional relationships, and subsequently at the cultural level, as a highly elaborate corpus of ideas, symbols and meanings. The personal level has also been introduced, as issues concerning nutritional socialization and the significance of food symbolism for personal identity have been raised.

As has already been emphasized, any attempt to provide a tidy classification of sociological approaches to food and eating is bound to lead to a somewhat arbitrary outcome. However, the exercise is worthwhile, if only because it highlights certain conclusions which are worth bearing in mind. While we have, so far, placed a deserved emphasis on the symbolic dimensions of food and eating, the relative lack of success of the structuralist approach in delivering convincing explanations of food-related practices and beliefs in purely symbolic terms should give pause for thought. We clearly also need to consider the linkages and interrelationships between the various components of food systems, and the ways in which these are articulated by actual social and economic relationships. What is more, we must also consider the connections between the food system and other subsystems of society (e.g., domestic, political, medical, hierarchical, etc.). However, a static view of these connections is not sufficient in itself. The emphasis given in this chapter to developmental approaches reflects the importance of trying to describe and explain the ways in which the features of the food systems of contemporary Western societies are themselves the products of long-term processes of social change. Of course, current processes of change, as well as those which occurred in the past, also demand our attention. The present stage of development of the sociology of food and eating means that there are still many gaps in our understanding. The chapters that follow have been designed to provide the reader with an overview of those areas where substantial bodies of knowledge do exist.

While the focus of this chapter, and indeed of the whole book, is upon sociological perspectives, this does not imply that the contributions of related disciplines will be ignored. We have already drawn upon the ideas of sociology's sister discipline of social anthropology, and in subsequent chapters findings and insights from outside sociology will be borrowed quite explicitly where these can be put to a sociological purpose. The work of psychologists, nutritional anthropologists and economic and social historians can be mined to enrich the sociological analysis of food-related issues. Feminist perspectives in various forms have also made significant contributions to the development of our understanding of certain key questions in the area of food and eating, and such perspectives will figure prominently in Chapter 8 and will also put in an appearance in Chapters 5, 9 and 10. The whole gamut of methods will be encountered: the exploitation of historical sources and secondary data, surveys, semi-structured interviews and participant observation. In short, most of the familiar weapons in the armoury of the social scientist will appear, plus, on occasions, specialized techniques like the dietary diary.

Each topic is of intrinsic interest in itself, but our hope is that the whole will prove to be more than sum of its parts. As we proceed through diverse subject matter and varied sources, the intention will be to draw out the underlying foundations of continuity and the significant currents of change which coexist in contemporary food systems.

Part II

THE SOCIAL ORGANIZATION OF EATING

4

FOOD, FAMILY AND COMMUNITY

In this chapter, the emphasis is upon the significance of food and eating within the private sphere of the family. Of course, adopting such a perspective does not imply that the private sphere is some kind of hermetically sealed microcosm that can be examined in isolation. The domestic world of the family is inextricably linked to the structures of the wider social system, and this is no less true of eating than of any other aspect of family life. In a sense, the sociological analysis of the family is pervaded by two apparently opposing themes. On the one hand, the family is seen in essentially positive terms, as an intimate, supportive institution. It is seen, at one level, as contributing to the continuity and stability of society as a whole, and at another level as providing the individual with a secure refuge from a demanding world. On the other hand, the family has been viewed in more sinister terms, as a locus of conflict, oppression and even overt violence, with the power differences between men and women, and parents and children, seen as particularly important. Both of these views will be reflected in the material discussed in this chapter, although we might sensibly regard them as two sides of the same coin, rather than mutually exclusive claims to absolute truth. Whatever the viewpoint adopted, however, there can be no doubting the family's continuing importance as a unit of consumption and the powerful formative influences it continues to assert over its members.

Before our discussion proceeds, a simple but basic terminological point is worth making. The terms 'family' and 'household' are not synonymous. The nuclear family (parents and children) may or may not make up a household (which is a group of people sharing accommodation and, to varying degrees, pooling their resources). The intact nuclear family is only one type of household, and is characteristic of a particular stage of the life cycle. There are, of course, many other types of household, and nuclear families may be part of wider extended family systems. These rather obvious distinctions do have important implications for the issues raised in this chapter, as we examine the ways in which food can be used to mark and forge links across family boundaries, the ways in which food is implicated in differentiation within families and between families, and the long-term processes of change in domestic foodways which appear to be under way.

MARKING THE BOUNDARIES OF THE FAMILY

In the section dealing with structuralist approaches in Chapter 3 we have already encountered the work of Mary Douglas, who has suggested that food-ways can be seen as a kind of language encoding patterns of social relations, particularly those connected with social boundaries and with processes of inclusion and exclusion (Douglas 1975). We can now look at Douglas's ideas in rather more detail. In order to examine this food language and its messages she adopts the somewhat unusual methodological strategy of analysing the food-related ideas, categories and practices in use in her own home. Her first point is to argue that there is a crucial distinction between *drinks* and *meals*. Meals are sequenced through the day and their elements are linked together in pre-determined combinations and successions of courses. Drinks, on the other hand, are not so highly organized. Douglas then goes on to describe the key features of meals as consumed within her own family:

- Meals require a table with a seating order, and entail the restriction of movement. Thus, a meal 'frames the gathering' and effectively rules out certain simultaneous activities.
- Meals incorporate significant contrasts like hot/cold, bland/spiced and liquid (or semi-liquid)/solid.
- Meals incorporate a broad range of nutrient sources (cereals, vegetables, animal proteins and fats, etc.).

(Douglas 1975: 65–6)

Douglas also observes that these meals have a characteristic 'tripartite' structure, consisting of one 'stressed' or main element accompanied by two 'un-stressed' or supporting elements. She describes this structure with the simple algebraic expression $A + 2B$. What is more, she sees meals as arranged in a hierarchy according to their importance and symbolic significance. For her family, at the bottom of this hierarchy is the routine weekday lunch, with just one course. This single course (A) itself exhibits the tripartite structure $a + 2b$. Further up the hierarchy is the Sunday lunch, consisting of two substantial courses (main and dessert). Such a meal is described as $2A$, with each A having the $a + 2b$ structure. At the top of the hierarchy for her family come celebratory meals (Christmas, birthdays, etc.). Here the whole meal can be described as $A + 2B$, with a main course and two supporting courses. Each of the three courses is, as usual, structured in terms of $a + 2b$.

In effect, Douglas is arguing that this repeating $A + 2B$ pattern means that every meal carries within it something of the structure and meaning of all other meals. What is more, participation in this repetitive, structured sequence of meals is one of the key ways of expressing and experiencing family membership. The sharing of meals is drawing the boundaries of the family's symbolic and emotional existence, and only certain very specific categories of non-family are permitted to cross these boundaries. In contrast, drinks can be shared much more widely. As Douglas herself puts it:

74

Drinks are for strangers, acquaintances, workmen and family. Meals are for family, close friends, honoured guests.

(Douglas 1975: 66)

Of course, Douglas's analysis does have its limitations. It refers to the practices of just one upper-middle-class English family and so we must be very cautious about attempting to generalize its arguments. A study based on participant observation of four English industrial working-class families (Nicod 1980) found that the four families in question each had rather different ways of drawing the boundaries of the family unit in nutritional terms. Looking at three staple food items (potato, bread and biscuit), the relationship between intimacy and the foods shared varied considerably from family to family. These findings suggest that while families do draw boundaries with food; there is considerable leeway for each to establish its own ways of expressing inclusion and exclusion. More-over, as Lalonde (1992) points out, Douglas's structuralist analysis, by its very nature, is concerned primarily with describing the structure of the meal-as-object. However, he reminds us that it is not simply the meal's *structure* which expresses its symbolic significance. The meal-as-event (as he calls it) is a lived experience which draws its meanings from a complex array of sensory and cognitive factors, factors which a structuralist account tends to neglect.

Of course, while food consumption patterns can be seen as highlighting the boundaries of the nuclear family, food and eating can also act as linkages between the nuclear family and the extended family and, indeed, between the nuclear family and the wider community. The use of food to articulate such linkages is neatly demonstrated by an intensive study of two Italian-American families in an industrial suburb of Philadelphia (Theopano and Curtis 1991). Through the use of participant observation techniques the researchers were able to uncover the ways in which elements of Italian and American cuisine were combined in this close-knit community, which they referred to by the pseud-onym 'Maryton'. Their findings make it very clear that women bear the main responsibility for sustaining domestic and social life and maintaining social networks. This is borne out by the fact that, although over 80 per cent of the women observed were in full- or part-time employment, they essentially held 'jobs' rather than pursued 'careers', and their main preoccupations were still marriage, maternity and domestic responsibilities. The authors set out to show the ways in which the bonds of family and community are expressed through food exchange by focusing attention on two particular women, whom they refer to as 'Marcella' and 'Anne'.

Marcella's social life revolves around an extensive network of relatives and friends. She exchanges food and hospitality with, for example, her two sisters and her brother (and his wife), with her three daughters and with certain intimate friends. The authors describe a series of exchange events, including a buffet dinner for thirty people, the invitation of her daughter's fiancé to dinner, the shared preparation of dishes with her sisters and, on Easter Sunday, the serving of breakfast to daughters, grandson, daughter's fiancé and the serving of dinner to nine people. Anne's social network is described as more limited than Marcella's, with a strong emphasis on ties with her two sisters, her two sons (one married) and her one daughter. She is also a close friend of Marcella. Examples of food exchanges documented include participating in a celebratory meal at her cousin's home, taking dinner at her daughter-in-law's home, eating out (dinner) with Marcella and inviting twelve people to her own home for Sunday dinner, including her son and his family, two friends (Marcella and Andrea) and her daughter's boyfriend (plus the two participating and observing researchers, with one spouse and one child).

The authors describe the various forms of exchange which are being employed in such settings:

- the exchange of hospitality (inviting guests and being invited);
- the sharing of non-mealtime eating (snacks, etc.);
- the exchange of raw foodstuffs or cooked dishes (e.g., desserts);
- payment for services with food, often in the form of the 'specialities' of the giver;
- co-operative provisioning and preparation of family dinners, celebratory meals, etc.

The reciprocity involved in these exchanges varies according to whether the relationship is symmetrical (between social equals and members of the same generation) or asymmetrical (where there are differences in status or generation) and according to the relationship's level of intimacy. It is also affected by the nature of the occasion, i.e., whether it is a 'recurrent' event (festivals, birthdays, etc.) or a 'milestone' event (weddings, graduations, etc.). According to the combination of these factors, the expectation may be for immediate reciprocity, long-term reciprocity or there may actually be no expectation of reciprocity at all (see Figure 4.1).

The sheer volume of food exchange taking place in such close-knit communities is illustrated by the fact that, in the course of the two-month period of

CATEGORY OF RELATIONSHIP	CATEGORY OF OCCASION	
	Recurrent	Milestone
High intimacy		
symmetrical	immediate	immediate
asymmetrical	no expectation	long duration
Low intimacy		
symmetrical	immediate	long duration
asymmetrical	immediate	no expectation

High intimacy = immediate/extended family, friendship network (frequent contact)
Low intimacy = workmates, friendship network (infrequent contact)

Figure 4.1 Expectations for reciprocity
Source: Adapted from Theopano and Curtis (1991)

observation, guests were present at food events on more than 100 occasions in Marcella's household. Over the same period, Anne participated in sixteen food exchanges and had guests for thirty food events. All this took place within a system of cuisine that was far from rigid, since what the authors term 'menu negotiation' produced variation from family to family and from year to year. Thus, even in a community with a relatively distinctive cultural identity, reciprocity based on food exchange does not necessarily rely entirely upon the persistence of a conservative, ethnically marked cuisine. Even in the face of change and variability food exchange can play a crucial articulating role. As the authors themselves put it:

> Through the food system, women express and maintain their social positions in the community... Exchanging food in Maryton is a token of social bonding and integral to all social interaction.
>
> (Theopano and Curtis 1991: 171)

FOOD AND DIFFERENTIATION WITHIN THE FAMILY

The quotation which rounded off the preceding section emphasizes the positive aspects of women's relationships to food provision and food exchange in domestic settings. There is, however, a more pessimistic view of such relationships, which suggests that gender differentiation within the family in respect of food preparation responsibilities and food consumption patterns can work to the disadvantage of women. Indeed, it has been argued that in traditional societies there may exist significant nutritional inequalities related to gender (and to age). An example of such inequality is provided by a study of the foodways of the traditional peasant family in rural France by Delphy (1979). Men, the author points out, customarily held a privileged position in relation to scarce food resources, this applying particularly to male heads of households. Thus, butcher's meat, a relatively rare item on this traditional menu, was largely reserved for men or, if it was shared, men were allocated the choice cuts. Indeed, traditional peasant culture characterized adult men as 'needing' such meat in a direct, physiological sense. In contrast women (plus the young and the elderly) were not seen as having this need in the same way. What is more, men were typically seen as requiring larger quantities of food than women, and one of the ways in which this idea was justified was in terms of differences in energy expenditure. However, as Delphy demonstrates, this notion did not rest on realistic calculations of energy expended in different types of work but was, rather, related to the gendered nature of particular tasks. Thus, carrying water (a task for women) was defined as 'light work', whereas carrying manure (a task for men) was classed as 'heavy work'. Interestingly, such attitudes were also applied to alcohol consumption. Red wine was seen as making men strong, whereas a woman who drank this beverage in quantity would be regarded with contempt (hence the saying, *femme de vin, femme de rien*).

These inequalities were woven into the very fabric of the rural culture. Thus, the young were socialized into internalizing a whole range of food prohibitions and deprivations, such socialization being backed up by a range of repressive measures and sanctions. Indeed, it was a widespread cultural assumption that a chronic feeling of hunger was normal for children and adolescents. Similarly, women were socialized into accepting the idea that they should consume only meagre portions of the dishes they prepared, and into accepting that they had a duty to provide the best food for others. Delphy contends that differentiation of this sort may have produced significant nutritional deficiencies (especially of protein) in the diets of the elderly and the very young, with consequent implications for general health. The impact on adult women may have been compounded by the added burdens of pregnancy, and heightened rates of infant and maternal mortality in rural areas appeared to support this contention (Delphy 1979: 223).

The picture painted by Delphy is a bleak one, although she emphasizes that the conditions she is analysing are specific to a particular historical period and a specific cultural and economic setting. However, the question inevitably arises as to whether such inequalities might be observed in more contemporary settings. Some significant insights into this issue are provided by a comprehensive study of food and families carried out in the north of England (Charles and Kerr 1988; Kerr and Charles 1986). The research project in question was based upon a survey involving 200 women with pre-school children, and employed semi-structured interviews and entailed the completion of detailed food and drink diaries for a two-week period. The study's aim was to examine a range of issues relating to food practices, but most importantly to examine nutritional differentiation within the family based on gender and age. As might be expected in this type of household (most were intact nuclear families with both parents, and all had young children) the women had the main responsibility for buying, preparing and serving food. Indeed, after the arrival of their first child, many had given up work to devote their time to domestic tasks, and cooking skills, for example, were seen as crucial by these respondents.

A central finding of Charles and Kerr's study is the importance of the concept of the 'proper meal'. The proper meal, based upon freshly cooked meat supported by potatoes and vegetables, was construed as fundamental to the identity of the family and to its well-being. Indeed, the authors argue, the provision of proper meals (in their everyday or more elaborate festive forms) was viewed by respondents as a key indicator of a 'proper family'. This underlying symbolic significance of the proper meal (readily described in terms of Douglas's $A + 2B$ formula) appeared to hold across social class divisions in the sample. Significantly, in terms of our earlier discussion of Delphy's arguments, Charles and Kerr's respondents reported that men's tastes and preferences took priority over those of women and children. The provision of proper meals, in line with the relatively conservative tastes of the husband, was seen by wives as a way of showing affection, and as a device for retaining the husband as a breadwinner and keeping him working. Thus, these wives were portraying themselves as food servers, 'refuelling' an active male breadwinner (even though many of the men were in occupations which did not demand high levels of physical exertion) to whom they were subordinate and on whom they were economically dependent. The authors conclude that such women are, in effect, in a position of responsibility without authority in relation to food, given their husbands' economic dominance and priority of preference. What is more, they conclude that the men in these households actually did eat what the authors define as 'high-status' foods more frequently than women (and children) and they also consumed alcohol more frequently. They argue that these differences reflect the essentially patriarchal structure of the nuclear family, and their findings appear to support the view that the gender- and age-based nutritional inequalities characteristic of many traditional rural settings may find echoes in the contemporary urban milieu.

In Table 4.1 some of their most interesting results are laid out. The data shown consist of the average frequency of consumption of selected food items over the two-week period covered by the dietary diaries. The researchers did not actually ask to have recorded the quantities of food consumed, only frequencies,

Table 4.1   Average frequency of consumption of selected items over a two-week period

Item	Women	Men	Children
High-status meat	4.5	4.9	3.1
Medium-status meat	6.8	9.0	5.3
Low-status meat	5.1	6.8	5.2
Whole fish	1.7	1.9	0.9
Low-status fish	1.6	1.5	1.7
Eggs	4.4	5.1	3.5
Cheese	5.6	5.8	3.8
Green leafy vegetables (cooked)	2.9	2.8	2.1
Other vegetables (cooked)	7.9	8.2	6.8
Fresh fruit	5.9	5.2	7.3
Potatoes (boiled/roast)	6.4	6.6	6.3
Chips	7.0	7.0	7.0
Bread	19.0	21.6	17.4
Breakfast cereal	5.2	5.3	10.4
Cakes	6.7	7.3	4.9
Biscuits	8.0	6.4	11.3
Puddings	7.0	7.0	9.3
Sweets	3.5	2.6	8.1
Soft drinks	2.7	2.0	22.5
Baked beans, etc.	1.9	2.0	2.9
Milk	6.0	6.3	21.5
Tea/coffee	58.0	54.3	13.4
Alcohol	2.7	4.4	0.2

Source: Adapted from Charles and Kerr (1988)

hence these results may somewhat understate differences, as men are claimed to consume larger portions.

One immediately striking finding is that men do indeed eat meat more often than do women and children. This applies to 'high-status' meat (which the authors define as red meat in joints, chops, etc.), 'medium-status' meat (white meat like chicken) and 'low-status' meat (e.g., processed products like sausages and hamburgers). What is more, children eat medium- and low-status meat more frequently than high-status meat and adults eat medium-status food like cheese and eggs more often than do children. Children eat fresh fruit (which the authors classify as a low-status food) more often than do adults, and women and children eat biscuits (low status) more frequently than do men. Not surprisingly, children are reported as consuming sweets and soft drinks far more frequently than adults, and the same also applies to milk. The various differences visible in this table are taken by the authors to be reflections of the status and power hierarchy within the patriarchal nuclear family, with men at the top, women in the middle and children at the bottom.

While this conclusion may be basically plausible, we should note a number of reservations. For example, the women frequently reported that they found it difficult to get children to eat 'proper meals', hence children's consumption of 'low-status' foods may actually be a reflection of their own tastes. What is more, children's more frequent consumption of such items as fresh fruit and milk, which the authors do not see as high-status items, would conventionally be construed as conferring a nutritional advantage. The male/female differences in meat consumption also appear somewhat marginal, and may be partly accounted for by the reported practice of giving men leftover cold meat in sandwiches. Further, the whole picture is complicated by the decidedly ambivalent attitudes to food reported by the study's women respondents. Concern with slimness and body image was frequently mentioned, coupled with attempts to restrict food intake (no less than 34 per cent of respondents were actually dieting at the time of the study). The authors note that for many women:

> the questions on dieting seemed to release a flood of dissatisfaction and guilt, not only with their bodies and their weight but with their whole social situation.
>
> (Charles and Kerr 1988: 143)

Charles and Kerr suggest that, in a sense, for women food is 'the enemy'. This concern with the desire to restrict food intake in the face of a readily available supply is a very different predicament from the potential threat of malnutrition for women described by Delphy. (We will return to these complex and contentious issues in Chapter 8.)

A later study carried out in Manchester (Warde and Hetherington 1994) based upon questionnaires returned by 323 households, produced results broadly similar to those of Charles and Kerr, but with some important differences. The gender division of labour in respect of food-related tasks comes out

Table 4.2   Persons last doing specific food-related tasks in households
              containing a couple

Task	Man (%)	Woman (%)	Other (%)	Shared (%)	N
Cake baking	5	61	31	4	243
Jam making	6	63	28	3	68
Cooking meals	11	79	5	5	271
Bread making	9	57	27	7	89
Preparing packed lunches	13	64	20	3	234
Main shopping	14	54	2	30	272
Doing the dishes	23	46	20	10	274
Take-away meals	42	21	26	10	242
Beer or wine making	64	12	11	14	94
Cooked barbecue	59	9	22	11	153

Source: Adapted from Warde and Hetherington (1994)

clearly in Warde and Hetherington's findings, which document which person or persons last performed specific tasks (see Table 4.2).

As might be expected, women predominate in the key activity of preparing meals, whereas men predominate in more marginal areas of foodwork like collecting take-away meals, beer or wine making and barbecue cooking. Significantly, however, in 30 per cent of households containing a couple, main shopping was a shared activity. What is more, Warde and Hetherington's results highlight a limitation of Charles and Kerr's study which has been pointed out by a number of commentators (Beardsworth and Keil 1990; Prout 1991). Because Charles and Kerr deliberately chose to look at households with at least one pre-school child, the focus is very much upon one particular stage of the life course. On the other hand, the households in Warde and Hetherington's study were rather more 'mature', and 81 per cent of the women in the sample were in paid employment, compared to 40 per cent in Charles and Kerr's study. Warde and Hetherington note that the woman's being in full-time employment was the most important factor in inducing men to cook family meals. Thus, they argue, Charles and Kerr's findings cannot necessarily be generalized as applicable to all adult men, since the very nature of their study design tended to exclude those men (with wives in full-time employment) who were most likely to be involved in food preparation (Warde and Hetherington 1994: 765). What is more, a class factor appeared to be at work here. For example, in households where the woman was in a salaried occupation or self-employed, the man was more likely to have cooked the last family meal. In contrast, in households where both partners were working class, there were no cases where the man had cooked the last meal. (These issues of social class will be discussed in more detail later in this chapter.)

The wider international applicability of the conclusions drawn by Charles and Kerr and Warde and Hetherington in relation to families in England is indicated by the fact that similar studies in the USA (DeVault 1991) and Sweden (Ekström 1991) appear to have produced broadly similar findings. DeVault's study was based upon interviews in thirty households located within the city or suburbs of Chicago, selected to ensure ethnic and social diversity. She interviewed the individual who bore the main responsibility for what she terms 'feeding work' within the family. Unsurprisingly, the overwhelming majority of these were women, 50 per cent of whom also worked outside the home. What emerges very clearly from the interview material is the primary role which women continue to play in the planning, provision and preparation of meals, and the extent to which this role is perceived as an onerous one. Fascinatingly, she notes that a concept analogous to Charles and Kerr's notion of the proper meal also exists here (although the nature and content of such meals, as we might expect, shows significant cultural variations). In effect, DeVault argues, women's work of feeding the family, of creating and staging the family-meal-as-event, can be seen as counteracting the centrifugal forces which push apart the activities of the individual family members, each with his or her own schedules, commitments, interests and priorities. In this sense, she maintains feeding literally *produces* 'family'. However, this work of socially constructing the family through feeding is largely invisible, so much so that women respondents often appeared to experience some difficulty in explaining their taken-for-granted deference to their husband's tastes and preferences. In fact, DeVault sees women's apparent autonomy in the organization and execution of domestic routines as masking the fact that they are essentially making choices to please and accommodate others, and suggests that these responsibilities effectively contribute to their oppression.

Ekström's analysis of food provision and cooking in Sweden provides a useful quantitative insight into the extent to which these tasks continue to be associated with women in contemporary urban settings. Her study was based on a simple random sample of 348 families with children, and employed the usual data-gathering devices (a questionnaire and a food diary, supplemented by qualitative interviews with selected respondents) The results of the study are presented under four headings (Ekström 1991: 151):

- planning meals;
- shopping for food;
- the preparation of breakfast;
- the preparation of dinner.

The results for the 292 families in the sample where both parents were present are clear cut, as can be seen in Table 4.3.

In relation to the activity of planning, the categories 'mother alone' and 'both, mother most part' clearly predominate. It is very rare for fathers to take much responsibility in this area. There appears to be underparticipation in the activity of shopping, although the modal category is the joint one, in which mothers take main responsibility. The provision of breakfast shows some interesting diversity, fathers clearly taking responsibility more frequently. In a significant number of

Table 4.3   The division of labour in two-parent families

Agent(s)	Planning %	Shopping %	Breakfast %	Dinner %
Mother alone	44	16	34	59
Father alone	1	1	13	2
Both, mother most part	34	49	0	0
Both, father most part	2	6	0	0
Adults	8	16	24	29
Adults and child	10	9	5	5
Child/children	0	0	1	0
Each individual	–	–	14	0
Others	1	2	8	5
Total (N = 292)	100	99	99	100

Source: Adapted from Ekström (1991)

households (24 per cent) breakfast is the generalized responsibility of all the adults in the household and in 14 per cent individuals cater for themselves. For the main meal of the day (dinner) 59 per cent of households rely entirely on the mother, with individual fathers figuring very rarely. However, interestingly, in 29 per cent of cases responsibility for this meal is shared among all the adults in the household. What is more, a familiar picture emerges from Ekströms's qualitative interviews, with women placing a strong emphasis on pleasing their husband and providing a good service in relation to food preparation and presentation, an emphasis which they see as a feature of a mutual but unconscious contract between couples based on the explicit or implicit subordination of women.

Perhaps one of the neatest demonstrations of this process of subordination through the imposition of culinary and nutritional responsibilities on women is provided by Murcott's influential analysis of the significance of the 'cooked dinner' in a community in South Wales (Murcott 1982). Murcott's research consisted of unstructured tape-recorded interviews with thirty-seven expectant mothers between the ages of 16 and 40, and her aim was to document what she terms 'folk models' and the 'properties of domestic eating' (Murcott 1982: 678). The finding which dominates her results is the central importance of the 'cooked dinner' for her respondents. This dish was seen as the centrepiece, indeed, the defining feature, of a 'proper meal', and its provision on a regular basis (say three to four times a week) was seen as vital for the health and welfare of family members, and therefore as one of a woman's most crucial obligations. The features of the cooked dinner, as an expression of the traditional menu of British culinary culture, can readily be specified in detail:

- Its focal point, or stressed element, must consist of the flesh of a warm-blooded animal (beef, lamb, pork, chicken, turkey at Christmas). Ideally, the meat should be fresh not frozen.
- The preferred method of cooking this meat is roasting or grilling.
- Potatoes must be served (boiled, mashed or roasted).

- Vegetables must be served. If there is only one vegetable, ideally this should be green). Again, these should be fresh.
- The components of the dish must be arranged in neat piles on a single plate.
- The components must be moistened and co-ordinated with gravy, but not submerged or disguised by it.
- Portions must be large.
- The dish must be eaten with knife and fork.

Such dishes clearly take a highly conventionalized form, offering little scope for innovation, and were seen by respondents as geared to their husband's tastes and perceived nutritional needs. In other words, it is the husband's preferences which dictate the choices made within this rigid culinary framework. What is more, the elaborate nature of this dish requires the attention of the cook over relatively long periods of time, in terms of preparing as well as actually cooking the ingredients. The fresh ingredients themselves demand regular shopping and cannot be bought in advance and stored for long periods. The cooking techniques and skills employed are those passed on from mother to daughter over several generations, emphasizing the continuity of women's domestic obligations. On the basis of these features, Murcott argues that the cooked dinner has important social (as opposed to purely nutritional) functions. In effect, the provision of a cooked dinner for her family demonstrates that a wife has been spending her time in an activity appropriate to her status and gender. The extended time commitment and the protracted labour involved can be seen as devices for tying the wife into the domestic setting, enforcing and expressing her femininity and her domesticity. Thus, the cooked dinner is seen as exerting a form of control (Murcott 1983: 88) as well as constituting a symbol of the inequality which segregates the gender roles of wife and husband.

There is a good deal of evidence to suggest that, in some family settings, the failure of a wife to fulfil her husband's expectations concerning the carrying out of domestic tasks may lead to violent retaliation. Ellis (1983) draws upon her own research into violent families (and that of other authors like Dobash and Dobash (1980)) to demonstrate that physical attacks by husbands on their wives are frequently triggered by some aspect of a husband's dissatisfaction with his wife's culinary performance. Ellis cites the expectation in British working-class households that a wife should have a hot meal ready for her husband as soon as he returns from work. Case material examples are cited where failure to provide this meal provoked an attack. In even more extreme instances, violent men might expect a meal to be provided at any time when they arrived in the household (even if this were unexpectedly in the early hours of the morning after a drinking bout). Physical force (or the direct threat of it) might then be used to compel the wife's compliance. Similarly, when men's expectations concerning the quality of cooked meals or the range of food choice were not fulfilled, violence might well be the result. It is Ellis's contention that the tendency to see such phenomena as indicating that violence can be provoked by 'trivial'

incidents is somewhat misguided. The fundamental significance of food preparation and serving obligations for female gender roles means that non-compliance
may be regarded as a particularly serious dereliction of female 'duty'. In
certain households, actual physical assaults, of varying levels of seriousness,
may be the habitual response, although Ellis sees this food-related violence as
simply the most explicit manifestation of a more general pattern of patriarchal
domination.

Significantly, the study of divorce and remarriage carried out by Burgoyne
and Clarke (1983) with forty remarried couples in Sheffield found that tensions
in marriage frequently centred upon food and mealtimes. For example, the
Sunday dinner, supposedly a focus of family integration and harmony, could
become the occasion for the more or less overt expression of intra-familial
conflicts and interpersonal jealousies. What is more, where women were perceived by their spouse as having failed in their wifely duties with respect to the
provision of meals, the authors came across evidence of violent responses by
husbands similar to the incidents described by Ellis (Burgoyne and Clarke 1983:
154–5). However, the authors also provide some fascinating evidence concerning the responses of divorced fathers who were allocated custody of their
children. In some cases, such men (who were somewhat over-represented in
this study) went to considerable lengths to maintain conventional eating patterns
in order to sustain a sense of domestic security and continuity for their children,
even to the extent of taking on the preparation of Sunday dinners (Burgoyne and
Clarke 1983: 157–8). In describing the process of finding a replacement partner,
respondents noted the difficulties that could be involved in establishing new and
mutually acceptable domestic arrangements with respect to food preparation
and mealtimes, describing in some detail the problems of adapting and accommodating to each other's established habits and preferences. Certainly, the
emphasis placed on food by these respondents demonstrates a number of
important points. Not only are food and food-related domestic arrangements
central features of family functioning, they may also play a crucial role in family
breakdown. What is more, attempts by divorced individuals to reconstitute the
family through remarriage may be dependent on the successful re-establishment
of a domestic food provision routine acceptable to the various parties concerned.
Food may, therefore, play a role in the continuity, the breakdown and the
reconstitution of the nuclear family.

The evidence we have been discussing appears to paint a fairly consistent
picture. Within the family women are seen as essentially subordinate to men and
are required to assume responsibility for preparing and serving food while
actually exercising relatively little control over the underlying patterns of provisioning and food selection, in which areas men's tastes and preferences are the
authoritative ones. Such perspectives lead McIntosh and Zey (1989) to adopt a
highly critical approach towards earlier views of women's relationships to food
and the family which suggested that women wield considerable power in this
area. For example, it has long been assumed that women act as 'gatekeepers',

controlling the flow of goods (food in particular) into the household and controlling the channels through which food reaches the table. However, McIntosh and Zey cite a range of studies (e.g., Burt and Hertzler 1978) which support the contention that, within families, the father's tastes take precedence. They also demonstrate that this precedence is usually linked to the husband's economic predominance within the household; the higher his earnings, in general, the greater his power (McIntosh and Zey 1989: 323). Raising doubts about the gatekeeper model which, as the authors point out, has long been relied upon by nutritionists and those concerned with nutritional policy, has a number of implications beyond purely sociological ones. For example, targeting nutritional education information at women in order to engineer what are seen as health-promoting dietary changes within families could be largely ineffectual in the light of what may be women's relative powerlessness in this area.

The studies which we have examined in this section are predominantly guided by feminist perspectives on the complex interactions between food, gender and domestic life. Two basic themes run through such perspectives: firstly, the idea that women's food-related roles in effect *express* and *reflect* their subordination and, secondly, the idea that the food-related obligations and duties imposed upon women actually serve to *enforce* their subordination. This enforcement is seen as being achieved through the fact that responsibility for domestic 'feeding work' is deeply embedded within the core of the whole concept of femininity, through the socialization of women into the acceptance of such obligations as natural and through the sanctioning of women who fail or refuse to fulfil these obligations. When the processes we have been examining are formulated in this way, the affinity between such views and functionalist forms of explanation becomes apparent, in that one of the 'functions' of gendered feeding work is seen as the maintenance of patriarchal family configurations.

The consistency of the results of the various studies across national and cultural boundaries is striking (although, in fairness, it should be noted that this may be due in part to some of the shared theoretical perspectives and expectations of the researchers). There is, however, one important limitation common to most of these studies which should be recognized. With the exceptions of Burgoyne and Clarke (1983) and Warde and Hetherington (1994), they rely almost exclusively upon adult female respondents. Men's ideas, viewpoints and accounts are rarely, if ever, heard at first hand, and where they do figure they are often reported at second hand by women. The same can also be said of children's accounts and preferences. Whether the picture which emerges would have been significantly different if men's and children's ideas had been given equal weight is an open question, and one which could be resolved only by suitably designed empirical research. Of course, the emphasis on women's accounts is not determined solely by theoretical and ideological factors; it also emerges out of practical considerations. The empirical studies from which our insights are derived by and large focus their attention on the individual in the household who bears the main responsibility for feeding work.

86

This understandable methodological strategy necessarily generates predominantly female response groups.

FOOD AND DIFFERENTIATION BY SOCIAL CLASS

Having considered the ways in which food-related differentiation operates within families, attention can now be turned to differences and inequalities which separate individuals, families and households along the broader lines of social class. We do not need to look too far back into Europe's historical past, for example, to find instances where class-based nutritional inequalities were literally a matter of life and death. Disastrous famines (often resulting from crop failures) continued to occur in Europe well into the eighteenth century (Mennell 1985: 24–7). An individual's risk of dying of starvation or of experiencing protracted hunger and damaging malnutrition was very much a function of his or her position in the economic and social hierarchy. As late as the latter part of the nineteenth century, the poor in England, for example, subsisted on a chronically inadequate diet, as classic studies of poverty like that of Rowntree (1901) clearly demonstrate. The consequences of such deprivations included endemic deficiency diseases like rickets, high urban infant mortality rates and poor levels of physical development in those who survived to maturity (Burnett 1989: 61). Clearly, in developed Western societies at least, the economic inequalities of social class no longer generate nutritional inequalities in such extreme forms, although they may now have subtler and less dramatic manifestations. Of greater relevance and interest for the contemporary sociologist are the cultural, economic and ideological differences between social class groupings in relation to food, and the ways in which these differences produce characteristic patterns of food preference and facilitate or constrain food choice.

A useful starting-point for the discussion of such differences can be found in the work of Bourdieu (1984). Bourdieu sets out to analyse the ways in which upper- and lower-class tastes are generated and reproduced in relation to the realities of social class in contemporary France, although his analysis is not confined to food, covering areas as diverse as art, literature, cinema, dress, interior decoration and hairstyles. Bourdieu stresses the competitive dimension of taste, seeking to demonstrate the ways in which conceptions of taste, and actual consumption practices, are used to create and sustain distinctions between social classes and to maintain the elevated status of those groups at the upper levels of the class hierarchy. However, Bourdieu sees eating and drinking as one of the few areas where working-class ideas challenge what he terms the 'new ethic of sobriety and slimness' (Bourdieu 1984: 179). The tastes in food of high-status individuals like professionals and senior executives tend towards 'the light, the refined and the delicate', which serves to set them apart from popular, working-class tastes for the 'heavy, the fat and the coarse' (Bourdieu 1984: 185). The middle and upper classes, largely freed from economic constraints on food consumption, actually come to lay increasing stress upon slimness and refined eating, and become increasingly censorious of coarseness and fatness. Middle-class groups like teachers, rich in what Bourdieu terms 'cultural capital' if not in economic capital, are seen as maintaining distinctiveness by cultivating tastes for exotic and foreign foods. In contrast, members of the working class put a greater emphasis on indulgence, spend a higher proportion of their income on food, and consume larger quantities of bread, and fat-rich foods like pork, milk and cheese.

Bourdieu sees these differences in dietary preference as also related to differences in each class's perception of the body and of the effects of food on the body. Of central significance in this respect is the working-class emphasis on the importance of the strength of the male body, hence an emphasis on cheap and nutritious food to build and fuel such a physique. This stands in sharp contrast to what Bourdieu regards as the professional classes' emphasis on tasty, health-promoting, light and non-fattening foods. These ideas are closely bound up with working-class conceptions of masculinity in relation to the actual act of eating. Men are seen as larger, needing more food and as eating in gulps and mouthfuls, and hence foods which require picking and nibbling (e.g., fish) are seen as unmanly, as essentially feminine and suited to the needs and inclinations of women (Bourdieu 1984: 190–2).

Of course, differences in eating patterns related to social class are not static, they change over time. Such changes may be driven by cultural processes, as higher social groupings develop new tastes and preferences in order to maintain their distinctiveness from the strata below them, but they are also a function of fundamental political and economic changes. A useful case study of class-based nutritional change is provided by Nelson (1993), who examines long-term trends in British diet over the period 1860 to 1980. Nelson bases his analysis on household data drawn from budget surveys. While he acknowledges the limitations of such data, he is able to outline the broad features of the changes in class differentials which have been under way. For example, he demonstrates that in the latter part of the nineteenth century the dietary differences between the highest and the lowest strata in Britain were extreme ones, with the poorest in the population living barely above subsistence level on a meagre diet of bread, potatoes and limited amounts of fats (usually butter or dripping), and small amounts of meat (usually pork or bacon). These low-income diets were low in energy, protein, fat, calcium and vitamins A and C, but high in carbohydrate and fibre. In contrast, the diets of families in the middle and upper ranges of the class structure contained more eggs, fish, meat, sugar and fat and were richer in calcium and vitamins (Nelson 1993: 103–4).

However, the twentieth century has seen a series of significant shifts in this overall picture. Government food policies during the First World War produced some temporary narrowing of class differentials in nutrition, and during the 1920s and the 1930s there was a gradual narrowing of differences. However, the most dramatic changes occurred during the Second World War, when government rationing policies, which were introduced in response to food shortages, effectively lowered the intake of many food items among upper-income groups and increased the intakes of lower-income groups, producing striking convergences. What is more, after the Second World War and the end of rationing, this narrowing of class differentials was maintained, due largely to rising real incomes and to the state's welfare policies. Indeed, not only were narrowed differentials maintained but, in the case of certain foodstuffs, there was actually an inversion of the previous relationship, with items once consumed in greater quantities by higher-income groups now being consumed at higher rates by lower-income groups and vice versa.

These changes can be illustrated by looking at specific examples. In the case of bread, flour and grains, consumption of this group of foodstuffs has been in chronic decline in lower-income families throughout the twentieth century (except for a brief rise during the years of the First World War). In higher-income groups consumption actually rose, but then began to decline in the 1930s. In 1980 the high-income group in Nelson's data consumed approximately 2 lb per person per week, and the low-income group approximately 2.5 lb. The figures for 1900 were approximately 3.3 lb and 5.6 lb, respectively. In 1860, middle-class families consumed mainly white bread, whereas lower income groups ate mainly brown or wholemeal. However, due to innovations in milling, by 1900 cheap white bread had become a working-class staple. Since 1970, the amounts of brown and wholemeal bread consumed have once more increased, but with an inverted class relationship. In 1980 the highest of Nelson's income groups ate 6.85 oz per person per week, compared with 4.25 oz per person in the lowest group (Nelson 1993: 105–6).

Meat and meat products show a dramatic convergence pattern. In 1900 the high-income group as defined by Nelson consumed an estimated 54 oz of meat and meat products per person per week, as compared to a figure of 20 oz for the low-income group. But by the early 1940s these two figures were virtually identical at around 25–6 oz per week. After the Second World War both increased, but hardly diverged, to give 1980 figures of roughly 42 oz (high-income group) and 38 ounces (low-income group) per person per week. Fish and eggs show the same convergence of inequalities in consumption, to the point where an inversion occurred for both foodstuffs in the 1960s and 1970s, with consumption in the low-income group overtaking that in the high-income groups. Convergence from a position of inequality of consumption also occurred in the 1940s in the case of fats and of sugar, syrup, treacle and jam. By the 1960s low-income group consumption of sugar, syrup, treacle and jam actually exceeded that of the high-income group, and by the 1970s the low-income group had overtaken the high-income group in fat consumption. These shifts are clearly reflected in Nelson's data for overall average per capita energy intake. In 1900 the energy intake for the high-income group is estimated by Nelson to have been around 2,750 kilocalories per person per day, substantially higher than the low-income group at around 1,650 kilocalories. Virtual convergence was achieved in the 1940s, and the 1980 data show both groups at just over

2,000 kilocalories, with the low-income group's figure actually marginally the higher of the two. Thus, the evidence presented by Nelson (which also covers nutrients like vitamins and minerals) appears to suggest that gross nutritional inequalities between classes in developed economies like the UK have been largely removed, although some especially vulnerable groups or individuals may still experience nutritional deprivation.

However, while overall convergence can be demonstrated in terms of broad estimates of nutrient intake, the question inevitably arises as to whether there remain significant ideological and cultural differences between classes in relation to food, as Bourdieu's analysis would predict. To throw some light upon this issue we can turn to the work carried out by Calnan and Cant (1990), which consisted of an exploratory qualitative study based upon households made up of married couples or couples living as married, with at least one partner in paid employment. Their response group consisted of twenty-one households which can be termed 'middle class' (drawn from what the authors refer to as social classes I & II) and sixteen households which can be termed 'working class' (drawn from what the authors refer to as social classes IV and V). Households were sampled on the basis of a community survey carried out in a local district in southeast England. The study does indicate that there are a number of underlying similarities between middle-class and working-class families with respect to food and eating. For example, the two groups appeared to have similar shopping patterns and, in both classes, women were primarily respons- ible for food shopping and cooking. What is more, it was largely upon wives that the responsibility for 'healthy eating' appeared to fall, although the authors note that women in both class groups faced considerable difficulties in introducing 'healthier' foods into the household, due to resistance from other family mem- bers (Calnan and Cant 1990: 59).

However, some significant differences between the two groups did emerge. For example, in connection with views concerning healthy eating, far more middle-class than working-class women had purchased 'healthy diet' items, such as margarine high in polyunsaturated fats, wholemeal bread and semi- skimmed or skimmed milk, in the week before the interview. What is more, when respondents were encouraged to discuss the issue of the link between diet and health, working-class women tended to refer to the specific health problems of particular members of their family. On the other hand, middle- class women were more likely to refer to a more generalized form of health knowledge consisting of ideas drawn from sources like books and the medical press. Interestingly, however, concern with weight loss, dieting and calorie counting was mentioned more frequently by working-class than middle-class women.

As might be expected when comparing two groups in significantly different positions in the socioeconomic hierarchy, there are clear contrasts in food- related spending patterns. For example, the middle-class families spent a mark- edly lower proportion of their disposable income on food (an average of 20 per cent) than did working-class families. The latter spent, on average, 30 per cent of their disposable income on food, a disposable income which was itself on average only about 60 per cent of the middle-class figure. While all the work-ing-class women reported careful budgeting of food expenditure (with some flexibility for treats or money shortages), this was not the case for the middle-class women. In general, they did not work on the basis of a fixed food budget, and felt that if they overspent they could readily have access to further funds. Interestingly, however, although working-class women appeared to be more price conscious, neither group was particularly enthusiastic about the practice of 'shopping around' to take advantage of bargain food prices, as this was seen as excessively time-consuming. Not surprisingly, the price consciousness and strict budgets of working-class women meant that they put a greater emphasis on cost as a factor affecting food choice than did the middle-class respondents, who tended to stress food quality as the main selection criterion. Some striking differences emerged when respondents were asked what foods they would like to purchase but could not actually afford. Working-class women tended to mention 'high-status' meat (red meat in the form of joints, steak, etc.), whereas middle-class women were more likely to mention what they regarded as luxury items, including exotic foods and elaborate prepared dishes.

There also appeared to be an important difference between the two groups in relation to the processes of food choice and food-related decision-making. Calnan and Cant's results suggest that the middle-class husbands were much more directly involved in food selection and food purchasing decisions than were the husbands in the working-class group. In the middle-class families this was more likely to be a joint process, whereas in working-class families the husband's influence was more indirect, it being more or less tacitly assumed that the wife was responsible for buying food and preparing meals which suited her partner's tastes. Attitudes to cooking also exhibited a significant class-related difference, despite the fact that in both groups it was seen as essentially women's work, with men usually involved in cooking only in specific circumstances (e.g., at the weekend or when the wife was ill), rather than taking it on as a routine responsibility. In fact, working-class women were much more likely to express the view that cooking was an important skill for a woman to possess. Among the middle-class women this view was much more rarely expressed, even by respondents who rated themselves as good cooks.

Calnan and Cant's study (1990), despite its admittedly small scale and its essentially qualitative nature, does strongly suggest that in urban communities in contemporary developed societies class continues to exert an important influ-ence upon patterns of eating and upon nutritional beliefs and practices. The proportion of income spent on food, the financial management of food expend-iture, attitudes to 'healthy eating' options, the nature of household decision-making and views on women's feeding work skills are all apparently sensitive to variations in social class. Broadly speaking, the working-class families in the sample seem to have remained closer to what might be regarded as 'traditional' or relatively long-standing ideas concerning the linkages between food, health, status and gender.

Consideration of class-based differences in nutritional attitudes and practices inevitably raises a further question. How do those at the bottom of the socio-economic hierarchy of contemporary society fare? What are the effects on these beliefs and practices when choices and possibilities are tightly constrained by poverty? A number of studies, British and American, are available to provide us with some direct empirical evidence on the implications of low income for food choices and eating patterns. For example, Charles and Kerr, whose major study of food and families has already been discussed above, in the course of their main survey, came across seventeen families who were living on state benefit and whose incomes were, by contemporary British standards, very low. The authors subjected this sub-sample to detailed scrutiny and published these results in a separate paper (Charles and Kerr 1986a). Of these seventeen low-income house-holds (all of which contained at least one pre-school child, given the design of the main study), ten were headed by a female single parent, six were made up of women living with an unemployed male partner and one was headed by a woman whose husband was in prison at the time of the interview. On average, these families were spending approximately one-third of all the income coming into the household on food (a figure marginally higher than the 30 per cent estimate made by Calnan and Cant (1990) for the food expenditure of their working-class response group). Although, in a sense, food expenditure was seen as a protected, priority area, with economies being made first in such areas of expenditure as heating and clothing, respondents reported reductions in the consumption of items such as fresh fruit, take-away meals, milk and desserts.

However, the area of economy and reduced consumption which was most frequently mentioned, and which appeared to generate most concern for these women, was meat. This was a specific form of meat: the joints, steaks and chops which qualify as the centre-piece of a 'proper meal'. Alternatives like mince, liver and belly pork had been taken up, but these were seen as less desirable substitutes. Like the rest of the sample, these low-income respondents subscribed strongly to what appears to be one of the cornerstones of the dominant British food ideology, the idea that the 'proper meal' represents the foundation of sound nutrition for the family. Hence, a strong sense of deprivation was reported by respondents who could not provide 'proper meals' on the regular basis they deemed necessary. Significantly, however, where a male partner was present in the household, there was a much higher frequency of proper meals (or 'cooked dinners' in Murcott's terminology). This was the case, even though it might well mean that as a result less money was available for food items like fresh fruit, milk and cereals. Charles and Kerr report that women saw the presence of a man as creating a 'proper family', and hence the need for 'proper meals'. In fact, the authors argue, in nutritional terms, women tended to privilege men at their own and their children's expense (Charles and Kerr 1986a: 245). Overall, because of their low income, these families found it extremely difficult to maintain adherence to the dominant food ideology's insistence on the proper meal. In a very real sense, they found themselves in a position where 'they could not live up to the social and cultural standards which are an accepted part of family life within British Society' (Charles and Kerr 1986a: 427). Thus, it becomes clear that the food-related penalties of living on a low income in contemporary developed economies are as much a question of social and cultural deprivations as nutritional ones.

Quite clearly, the insights offered by Charles and Kerr are based upon a relatively small group of low-income respondents who happened to come to the researchers' attention in the course of a larger-scale, more general study. However, information concerning the food-related ideas and choices of low-income families is also available from such studies as that conducted by Dobson, Beardsworth, Keil and Walker (1994), which take such issues as the main focus of attention. Dobson and her co-workers carried out a qualitative analysis of the nutritional practices and ideas of a group of forty-eight low-income families, using a combination of individual interviews, expenditure diaries, food consumption diaries and, where feasible, combined family interviews. Their response group was made up of a mix of families with children. Some were families which had just begun to receive state benefits (income support). Some were families who were long-term recipients of such benefits (that is, had been in receipt of income support for more than twelve months) and others were low-income families who were not receiving such benefits. The study itself was carried out in a large industrial city in the British Midlands.

One of the study's main findings was that the families who had been living on state benefit for longer periods had effectively adapted their expenditure patterns and lifestyles to their restricted circumstances, and were less likely to experience financial crises than new benefit recipients. What is more, food expenditure proved to be one of the few areas where many of these families had any elasticity or flexibility in their budget. In some weeks their already minimal expenditure on food would be reduced in order to meet a pressing bill or some unanticipated expense. Coping with financial adversity was achieved through extremely strict budgeting, which was carried out largely by women, who also were mainly responsible for food shopping and preparation in all these families (as one might expect). What is more, these women adopted a number of strategies to deal with the problem of their limited resources. For example, the researchers noted that the less money a family had to spend on food, the more frequent was food shopping. Thus, in extreme cases, food shopping was carried out on a daily basis, on the principle that, if more than one day's supply of food was in the house, the extra was likely to be eaten, creating a shortage on subsequent days. Food shopping patterns were also heavily biased towards local discount stores, as opposed to the more desirable large supermarkets with their wider range of more prestigious food products. In addition, many women reported using the strategy of doing the food shopping alone, in order to keep strict control of expenditure and to avoid arguments over what should be bought and impulse purchases by other family members. Processed and frozen food products were often bought, as these were calculated to be cheaper overall than preparing dishes from fresh ingredients.

Also strategically significant was the maintenance of relatively conservative eating patterns. The logic behind this stance was a simple but compelling one: women often would not risk trying to introduce unfamiliar foods or dishes into their family's diet (either for health reasons or as an economy measure), since if the novel item was rejected, this would involve a substantial element of wastage which could seriously disrupt an extremely tight food budget. Interestingly, DeVault's Chicago study also noted this reluctance on the part of poor families to experiment with unfamiliar food items. This arose out of a fear that the results would be unpalatable and hence lead to unacceptable wastage, although in this instance reference was being made to dubious bargain items of suspect quality (DeVault 1991: 178–9). Coupled with this nutritional conservatism was a form of enforced commensality that many families adopted, since they could not afford to cater for the differing tastes and divergent needs of individual family members. Having the whole family eat the same meal at the same time was an important economy measure in itself.

The relatively conservative approach to eating indicated above, however, has wider implications than its function as a means of avoiding waste. It was clear from the interview material presented by Dobson and her colleagues that for these families it was of paramount importance to maintain conventional eating patterns as far as possible. By and large, they were not willing to introduce far-reaching changes into their diets in a radical attempt to obtain sufficient nutrients at a drastically reduced cost. As we have argued elsewhere (Beardsworth and Keil 1993b) even though it is feasible to derive all one's nutritional requirements from an extremely simple, low-cost diet, to subsist on such a diet would involve being, in effect, a kind of nutritional deviant, a violator of basic Western cultural assumptions about the contents and combinations that go to make up orthodox meals. For these low-income families, the effort expended in order to maintain conventional eating patterns was worthwhile, in so far as it helped them to maintain a sense that they were still in touch with the main-stream of consumer culture. This desire manifested itself most clearly in relation to children. For example, although they could rarely if ever afford to provide food for others outside the family (e.g., by inviting guests), many mothers sought to avoid their children's becoming isolated from their peers by being unable to accept and reciprocate invitations to eat at friends' homes. Thus, special planning and savings would be undertaken so that invited friends could be offered a conventional array of snack foods and branded products. In one particularly poignant case, a mother described how she usually poured low-cost cola into a Coca-Cola bottle before serving this to her son's friends, to avoid his being teased by his brand-conscious young guests. In a similar vein, mothers regarded it as important that their children should be able to take conventional snacks and packed lunches to school, in order to avoid the public stigma of poverty.

The food-related deprivations suffered by these families were primarily those associated with a lack of access to preferred, higher-status foods. What is more, particular strains were imposed upon women, whose task it was to cope and to adapt, and to try to protect other family members from the consequences of economic privation. For women, food shopping became a tiring and demoralizing chore, and large amounts of time were spent seeking competitively priced items. The very act of food shopping appeared to serve as a constant reminder of their poverty, of the desired items they could not afford. Shopping, one of the key leisure activities of consumer culture, could not be enjoyed but only endured. Similarly, many women reported that the constant worry over food budgeting and economizing actually meant that they derived little pleasure from eating. For the family as a whole, having to eat together could be a source of tension and a reminder that the household did not have the resources to provide the individual choice and flexibility that are seen as becoming the norm in more affluent households. However, in a sense, these families are examples of relatively successful adaptations to the constraints of feeding a household on a very restricted budget, and it was not uncommon for respondents to express some pride in their ability successfully to manage the feeding of the family in such circumstances. Indeed Sharman (1991: 180) notes a similar pride in feeding and nurturing the family in deprived conditions in her study of low-income households in a large city in the northeastern United States, based upon the analysis of life histories.

The above discussion of the impact of low income on food consumption and nutritional practice is essentially based on data derived from families located in urban households. There is a temptation to assume that low-income families in rural settings, families with close connections to the processes of food production, might be in a relatively advantageous position, possibly benefiting from direct access to agricultural produce of various kinds. However, as an image of the position of agricultural workers and their families in a modern, developed society, this may be a somewhat misleading picture. Indeed, Newby (1983) demonstrates that in certain circumstances such families may actually be at a disadvantage compared with their urban counterparts. Newby's study is based upon participant observation carried out while living with a farmworker's family in Suffolk, in eastern England. What Newby is able to show is that farmworkers employed by large commercialized food production units are just as effectively alienated from the fruits of their labour as is the typical factory worker. This family had no privileged access to produce and its situation was very far from anything like self-sufficiency. Despite the fact that the family did grow some vegetables and kept two goats for milking, its actual eating patterns were essentially the same as those of an equivalent low-income urban family. There was the same repetitive and conservative pattern of food consumption, the same obligatory commensality, the same gender division of labour and the same assumption that adult men require larger portions (an assumption more obviously appropriate in this setting, given the nature of farmworkers' energy expenditure). In other words, there was nothing distinctly rural about this diet (Newby 1983: 33).

However, what was distinctly rural about this family's predicament was the cost penalty it bore in relation to food purchasing. The nearest shops were in a town 2 miles away and since the family could not afford to run a car, these had to be reached by bicycle, apart from a monthly 'stocking-up' visit, when bus transport was used. Food prices in this small town were significantly higher than those in large supermarkets. However, the nearest of these was in Ipswich, and reaching it by bus involved so time-consuming and expensive a journey that the family was unable to take advantage of the lower prices. The family was thus aware of a puzzling contradiction. Although their 'breadwinner' was deeply involved on a day-to-day basis in the production of food, the family actually paid considerably more for their food than did the urban dweller, who lived far removed from the toils and vicissitudes of agriculture. In fact, Newby's respondents admitted that they were baffled by this contradiction, which the author explains with reference to the fact that they could see only the two ends of the commercial food chain at first hand (initial production and eventual retailing of processed and packaged food items). What they could not see, and therefore could not comprehend, was the monolithic and increasingly vertically integrated structure of modern agri-business. As we have already noted when considering the making of the modern food system, the manufacturing, distribution and retailing of food have been increasingly concentrated into the hands of a relatively small number of very large firms. Since the aggregate added value of these processes greatly exceeds that generated by production itself, these firms have achieved a high level of dominance in a marketplace which emphasizes diversity of choice, convenience and attractive packaging. In such a marketplace, low-income families, rural as well as urban, find themselves marginalized, often clinging tenuously to the mainstream of nutritional culture.

OVERVIEW

With the diverse material discussed in this chapter we have sought to demonstrate the complex ways in which nutritional activities and family life interact. Thus, while eating patterns reflect family processes, at the same time, family relationships and family boundaries are expressed and reinforced by the day-to-day routines of provisioning, preparation and consumption. Similarly, the division of labour with respect to feeding work reflects gender inequalities and male dominance within the family. At the same time, the obligations imposed upon, and by and large accepted by, women to take primary responsibility for such work have been seen as serving to perpetuate their effective subordination, a subordination which has been characterized by some of the writers whose work we have considered as having fundamentally oppressive or even violent undertones.

Clearly, food choices and eating patterns are influenced by broader social class inequalities, with those at the lower end of the socioeconomic hierarchy struggling with financial deprivations and experiencing severely restricted access to the wide range of food items and dietary options on offer to the rest of the population. However, as we have seen from the ideas of writers like Bourdieu, nutritional differences between social classes are not only reflections or manifestations of their economic and cultural inequalities. Such differences, in the form of refined tastes and cultivated preferences, become vehicles for maintaining the distinctions between the layers of the social hierarchy. What is more, these distinctions are reproduced from generation to generation as the processes of nutritional socialization shape the individual's exposure to and experience of the dishes, food items and food ideologies characteristic of his or her location in the wider social order.

Some of the limitations of the studies discussed in this chapter have already been mentioned, for example, the strong tendency on the part of investigators to rely heavily (and often exclusively) on the evidence provided by women respondents when attempting to build up a picture of food-related beliefs and activities within the family setting. In many instances, this tendency reflects an explicit intention to give priority to women's views and women's experiences, on the grounds that in the past these have been all too often neglected by social scientists. Furthermore, since it is a consistently observed fact of life that women bear most of the responsibility for feeding work in the domestic sphere, in terms of economy of effort it clearly makes sense for the researcher to use women as informants. Yet there is a distinct possibility that significant bias can be introduced in this fashion, when conclusions are drawn and generalizations put forward concerning the dynamics of an entire household on the basis of the accounts of just one of its members. The accounts of husbands or partners, and of younger and older children, must become the focus of increased research attention if our view of food and the family is to become a more rounded and complete one.

When sociological attention is being focused on eating in the private domain (as opposed to eating out in the public domain), there is a widespread assumption that this essentially involves examining the dynamics of the nuclear family, conventionally composed of parents and their children. The bulk of the research carried out in this area is founded on this assumption, and this in turn is reflected in the contents of this chapter. However, this basic assumption is one whose relevance to future research in this area needs to be subjected to critical questioning. The nuclear family represents specific phases in the life cycle of any given individual. Admittedly, these phases are of crucial importance (for example, he or she will be undergoing primary socialization and also may be responsible for the primary socialization of his or her offspring). However, many other household types exist. For example, households containing a single person, households made up of an adult couple (married or not, different sex or same sex), households made up of a nuclear family plus other relatives, households made up of extended kinship groups and households made up of groups of individuals not related by kinship at all. In fact, there are numerous possible

97

combinations, and each combination is likely to exhibit a variety of food selection, preparation and consumption patterns which may cut across conventional assumptions concerning gender differentiation and class differentiation, for example. Thus, in households consisting of an adult couple, both of whom are in full-time employment, might we expect traditional assumptions concerning the gendered nature of feeding work to be less binding and less closely adhered to? In households consisting of unrelated adults (students, for example) we might ask how shopping, cooking and eating are organized – whether collectively or individually – and how such groups negotiate their feeding arrangements and their household division of labour.

It also needs to be recognized that the distribution of household types has been changing consistently in recent decades. Thus, in the UK in 1979, 31 per cent of all households consisted of the classic nuclear family, that is, a married couple with dependent children (Thomas, Goddard, Hickman and Hunter 1994: 21). Overall, in that year, 49 per cent of the total population of the UK lived in such households. However, by 1992, such households had declined to 24 per cent of the total, and contained only 40 per cent of the population. In contrast, single-person households over the same period rose from 23 per cent (containing 9 per cent of the population) to 27 per cent (containing 11 per cent of the population). Other household types also showing increases over this period are those containing a lone parent with dependent children and those containing couples with no children. The picture is a similar one in the USA. Between 1980 and 1992 the proportion of households made up of married couples with children under 18 declined from 31 per cent to 26 per cent, to a point where they contained just 41 per cent of the total population (a figure virtually identical to that in the UK). Over the same time period, the number of households made up of lone women with children under 18 went up by 29 per cent, and those consisting of lone men with children under 18 rose by 108 per cent. Single male households rose by 41 per cent, and single female households by 29 per cent (U.S. Bureau of the Census 1993). These far-reaching shifts in household composition seem to represent underlying trends which are likely to persist. The implication must be that if we wish to develop a more complete sociological insight into domestic nutritional activities, the whole spectrum of household types will need the attention of researchers.

Even within the nuclear family household itself changes are clearly under way. The increasing involvement of women in the labour market has resulted in a steady increase in the demand for, and the supply of, convenience foods. The use of such products, the components of what we have already termed the 'convenience menu', has the potential to produce fundamental alterations in the nature of feeding work within the family, especially when linked to innovations in food manufacturing and food preparation (the increasing domestic use of microwave ovens being an obvious example of the latter). Such possible changes include a shift towards a more co-operative and less gender-differentiated mode of allocating feeding work, and towards much more personalized patterns of eating, where individual family members increasingly make their own idiosyncratic food choices and time their eating to co-ordinate with their own personal schedules and priorities. If such possibilities really do represent the future development of eating within the domestic sphere, then the eclipse of more traditional notions of commensality and the symbolic significance of proper meals could be seen as holding the promise of lightening what has been seen as the oppressive burden of feeding responsibilities borne by women. What is more, such changes would also imply the gradual breakdown of the allegedly conservative influence of the dominance of the husband's tastes within the setting of the family. This, in turn, would imply an enhancement of the permeability of the boundary between the family and the outside world, which would render it increasingly susceptible to the influences of such agencies as advertisers, health educators and food propagandists of various kinds.

Of course, the above discussion is, of necessity, a somewhat speculative one. Future developments will depend upon the outcome of the complex interplay of two opposing sets of forces. On the one hand, there is the braking effect of customary food ideologies and long-established nutritional practices which can command habitual, almost taken-for-granted obedience. On the other hand, there are the change-inducing effects of underlying demographic, economic and cultural trends. Describing and explaining this interplay, and monitoring its outcomes, will represent a major task for sociologists working in this area over the next few decades.

5

EATING OUT

> The restaurant is the tank in the warfare of cookery because it has always been a major instrument for smashing old eating habits. Take-away food is the guerrilla of cooking.
>
> (Zeldin 1983: 147).

Such dramatic assertions raise expectations that the analysis of some, if not all, kinds of eating out will present major contrasts with the patterns of eating at home considered in the previous chapter. For the most part, studies of the household emphasize the important contribution of patterns of food preparation and serving in maintaining traditions, particularly stability of food choice, in setting reassuring boundaries between members of the household and others, and providing a means of social communication and identity and a constant reaffirmation of the existing divisions of labour and power hierarchies within the family. However, before it is possible to make any assessments as to whether eating away from home is different from eating at home, and the extent to which Zeldin's assertions are justified, it is necessary to consider information about a series of relevant issues. For example, it is important to clarify what is meant by 'eating out', how and why opportunities for eating away from home emerged, became established, were organized and staffed and, perhaps the most intriguing issue, what we know of how such opportunities are used, perceived and experienced by consumers.

From the point of view of the late twentieth century, it is easy to imagine all the activities which might take us away from home, and which might entail our being compelled or choosing to find something to eat. We could consume anything ranging from a snack to a full meal, and it could be eaten with friends or family in their homes. However, even if we did not have any social contacts, we could still eat. In most situations in our society, access to a wide range of food would be readily available, providing, of course, that we were able to afford it. It is the kind of food made available for money, from commercial outlets such as shops, take-aways, fast-food and other restaurants, that has been identified as a twentieth-century 'revolution' in our eating habits (Gabriel 1988: 7). The identification of these commercial food outlets also draws our attention to the fact that the food sold is eaten in public rather than in private and that it is likely to be eaten alongside, but not with, strangers.

Comparisons with the past suggest that there are differences of degree as well as of kind in the balance between public and private eating. It would not be possible to argue that there was no market for food outside the home before modern times, but it was a relatively undeveloped market and most food would have been provided within a framework of social obligation rather than as a commercial transaction. In all the social anthropological and historical accounts of traditional societies there is strong emphasis on the importance of hospitality. Such hospitality would be extended to travellers (many societies had particularly strong culturally defined obligations to welcome strangers). Neighbours too, often identified in terms of lineage and kinship, would be invited to share food, often on the occasions of feasts. Some of the meals recorded in the anthropological literature were spectacularly generous, involving the preparation of foods which took time and were scarce and therefore valuable. One of the most dramatic and well-recorded examples is the 'potlatch' held by American Indians who lived along the northwestern Pacific coast from Oregon to Southern Alaska. The potlatch host not only provided a feast for other members of the group but also gifts of food and other goods which were distributed to the visitors when the feast was over. Indeed, gifts and feasts were often closely interconnected and indicated the ways in which the welcome to neighbour and stranger was embedded in a framework of social relationships. The potlatch was a regular occurrence and, without any formal or explicit calculation, there would be an approximately equal balance of gifts and feasts between those involved. In other words, the feast locked members of the society into a pattern of reciprocal obligations. Social anthropologists have identified the latent and manifest functions of such obligations, amongst them the sharing of current food surpluses (particularly of perishable foods) and the provision of a virtual guarantee that they, in turn, would benefit from feasts with others when their own supplies were short (Farb and Armelagos 1980: 176–90). The network of social relationships within which such feasts were set brought many social and economic benefits, but ruled out as totally inappropriate any calculation or payment at the time when they occurred. Of course, the importance of food as a means of expressing social solidarity continues to be recognized in modern societies. 'Sharing food is held to signify "togetherness", an equivalence among a group that defines and reaffirms insiders as socially similar' (Mennell, Murcott and Van Otterloo 1992: 115). The bond created by eating and drinking together operates in a wide range of social contexts. There are formal dinners, even feasts, to mark political agreements and, linking private lives with the transition to new social statuses, there are wedding 'breakfasts' and celebrations which involve food for birthdays and other occasions of symbolic significance. As in traditional societies, there is no explicit calculation of cost or notion of payment, but there is a recognition of reciprocal obligation.

EATING WITH OTHERS: THE DEVELOPMENT OF TABLE MANNERS

The evidence of the continued importance of kinship connections when away from home suggests that the first experience of eating away from home was likely to have been as the guest of others in their homes. Visser (1993) turns her attention to the 'rituals of dinner' and focuses on how we eat and why we eat as we do. She argues that, given all the effort of acquiring food, eating it should be the easiest part but we 'cloak the proceedings with a system of rules about places and times to eat, specific equipment, decoration, sequence, limitations of movement, bodily propriety' which are not a biological necessity but a 'carefully cultured phenomenon' (Visser 1993: ix). Paying particular attention to the European and American tradition, she analyses current and historical material to consider why rules were established and how rules are taught. She draws attention to the ways in which table manners force us into ever stricter control of our bodies and the implements for serving and eating food, and illustrates the process by discussing all the stages associated with eating out at the invitation of others in their home. Visser's underlying theme is to argue that such controls are necessary because eating together, and sharing such a valuable resource as food, is potentially dangerous. Violence could erupt at any time and table manners are social agreements devised to defuse such a possibility. Just as weapons are not brought to meals in traditional societies, modern societies have rules about cutting and the style and placement of knives which reassure us, at however deep a level, that we are in safe company. However, at the same time, it is recognized that table etiquette relies on both training and knowledge so that table manners may be used to serve a class system and to reinforce snobbery. Visser acknowledges and documents the fact that the presentation of food and associated table manners change, and gives as an example the shift, which began in the eighteenth century and was virtually completed by the end of the nineteenth, the change from service *à la française* to service *à la russe*. The social consequences of this shift were considerable. Service *à la française* was a meal pattern which involved two servings of a large range of food (before and after the 'remove'). Such display was a feast for the eyes of guests as well as nourishment, and good manners demanded that they helped themselves and others (by directing servants) to any of the dishes on display. She suggests that this pattern, where the guest must be active in choosing, remains in buffet meals and in airline food (Visser 1993: 197). Service *à la russe* was a meal pattern which involved a succession of dishes with lots of courses. Guests are helpless and passive and are always served. In contrast with the earlier pattern of selection, the same food is offered to all. There is less display of food and more emphasis on the equipment for service – platters, place settings and table decorations. Visser's account makes it quite clear that each pattern had important consequences for the behaviour of hosts and guests.

The direction of such changes was examined by Elias (1978a), one of the first to attempt to analyse the social significance of something as 'everyday' as table manners. Elias sees the history of manners as part of the 'civilizing process'. Central to the study is the identification of modes of behaviour considered typical of Western 'civilized' man in the twentieth century. If such a person could be transported to the past, say to the fourteenth century, it is certain that he would recognize the prevailing behaviour as quite different and more unrestrained than our own. He might find it repulsive or attractive, but would definitely notice a difference. Elias sets out to investigate what changed and how the change occured or, in Elias's terms, how Western Europe became 'civilized'. Elias makes a specific study of the transformation of behaviour in relation to manners through the study of texts (beginning with that of Erasmus in the fifteenth century, which was dedicated to the son of a prince) written for the instruction of high-born boys on 'outward bodily propriety'. The guidelines are highly specific: for example, do not stare at others and take care over dress. Readers are also advised to wipe their noses, to use clean knives for food, not to make belching or other noises, not to slurp food, to consider others, and so on. Facial expressions are argued to be the expression of the inner person and should be controlled to indicate appropriate attitudes. Changes in the focus of such texts indicate 'gradual civilization' through changes in feelings of shame and delicacy as society demands and prohibits different manners. There is a move from unrestrained and spontaneous behaviour towards socially instilled displeasure and fear. We become increasingly self-conscious and less impulsive, always concerned about how we appear to others. Elias argues that these changes reflect broader changes in the links between society and the individual, together with a process of distancing between adults, and between adults and children. In psychological terms, Elias argues that these changes indicate the formation of the superego. Explanations of the historical changes which encouraged the development of such civility towards others, and the civilizing process itself, are, Elias argues, associated with state formation and centralization as well as with the state's monopolization of force which began in the fourteenth century and continues into the twentieth.

The important lesson to be learned from these writers for the analysis of eating out is that the changes they describe continue to the present day to influence our table manners and behaviour with others. We learn to handle cutlery and other equipment, together with ways of being considerate to others, which vary according to whether we are hosts or guests. We have moved from the situation where food is not a topic of conversation because we eat food appropriate to status and respectability to a context where food is always a topic of conversation as we seek to select that which displays taste, respectability, knowledge and a 'search for marginal differentiation' (Mennell, Murcott and Van Otterloo 1992: 4). We learn to control the way we sit, talk and eat at table. In addition, just as in the times described by Elias and Visser, if we are uncertain about how to conduct ourselves, we can consult books on social etiquette.

THE BEGINNINGS OF COMMERCIAL PROVISION OF EATING FACILITIES

In the context of well-established patterns of mutual obligation which persist even in the most modern societies, the question arises as to why it was necessary for a market in the provision of food to arise. Part of the answer appears to lie in the process of modernization itself, in particular, the gradual breakdown of the importance of kinship and social obligations based on status ascription, combined with the process of urbanization. When individuals and groups, no longer tied to their local regions, were free to travel throughout large geographical areas or to be away from their homes in an urbanized context and when there was, as a consequence, no longer any guarantee of being able to link with kin, we see the beginnings of eating out on a commercial rather than a reciprocal basis. There are examples from widely different societies and historical periods. The Romans, for example, had a highly developed system for selling food and drink on a commercial basis in their cities. There were also hostelries along the roads of the empire to provide food and lodging for any traveller who could afford the charges. In another imperial setting, China, the earliest records show there were inns providing both food and accommodation for travellers, often officials on imperial business, as well as stalls selling food to those who worked away from home in the larger towns and cities. There are even records, from the T'ang dynasty which reigned over the Chinese empire from AD 618 to 907, of the existence of restaurants offering meals as part of the enjoyment of leisure rather than as mere necessity (Farb and Armelagos 1980: 232). The records also show that in many societies there were food sellers of every sort, who set up on the occasions of markets and fairs or wherever large numbers of people gathered. All these are 'modern' in the sense that they catered for all who could pay (and operated in a cash economy) rather than for those who had some call on the resources of their kin, however distant, when away from home. For most people, however they did not form a major part of the experience of eating.

Apart from the sales of food at markets and fairs and the sale of ale at inns, commercial eating out in Europe developed relatively slowly. Until the end of the feudal period, a high proportion of the population was tied to the land and had no opportunity to travel. Travel for the sake of it was rare and those who did travel, often on official business of one kind or another, were able to claim hospitality from the kin of their masters at their manors, or they stayed at inns. Other travellers, such as pilgrims, were provided for by the religious houses on the routes to shrines and other centres of worship. It is interesting to note that although there was a Christian duty to be charitable, such charity was aimed at the poor, so that staying at religious houses was not necessarily at no cost. Pilgrims were supposed to be self-supporting and to make contributions for their keep. Except for members of the nobility, who might be offered more privacy, both food and accommodation at these religious houses were very simple and offered little choice. With minor variations, all shared the food available that season or from store. Merchants and others who needed to move from place to place often stayed at religious houses too, and some houses, located in important centres of pilgrimage or trade, eventually separated the care of travellers from their day-to-day activities by establishing inns run on commercial lines. Indeed, Medlik (1961) goes so far as to argue that the dissolution of the monasteries in England in 1539 set in train changes which encouraged more rapid development in the range and quality of provision, in that it was part of the break-up of the feudal system and encouraged movement to the towns.

With the breakdown of feudalism and the growth of towns, many more were free to travel either locally or over large distances. Such changes precipitated the development of existing provision and the establishment of new types. Whilst the grandest travellers still looked to their kin to house and feed them on their journeys, those without such contacts would stay with local households willing to take lodgers overnight, or in inns. In both cases, travellers would share whatever food and accommodation were available. Inns and lodging houses increased in number and size as demand rose. However, it was in the cities that entirely new opportunities for eating away from home for pleasure, as much as necessity, developed. One of the earlier examples which is relatively well-documented is the establishment of the coffee house in the seventeenth century. Coffee had been introduced to Europe in the early seventeenth century but took some time to become popular. However, according to Visser, 'The birth of cafés in the late seventeenth century in Europe was one of the prerequisites for the growth of modern city life' (Visser 1993: 123). Their contribution, she argues, was in providing a non-hierarchical, or even anti-hierarchical, location for meeting and discussion where those present could not be 'placed' in a social sense. In both Paris and London special coffee shops opened near theatres as places for conversation (Leclant 1979). However, they developed in each society in rather different ways. In France, the café continued as one of the most popular locations for food and drink and continued to be open to all, whereas in England the coffee house became associated with work as well as leisure, a place where men could drink coffee, read newspapers (at that time too expensive for individual purchase) and transact some kinds of business. For example, Lloyds coffee house was where insurers met, particularly those involved in marine insurance, and the organization of Lloyds 'names' remains to the present day. In England, particular coffee houses became so exclusive that they eventually became gentlemen's clubs. The term 'café' was also used and, to some extent, paralleled the development in France as a place open to all levels of society. However, there were exceptions, for example, very grand establishments such as the Café Royal were frequented by the very rich and, at the other end of the social scale, cafés attracted the working classes (and became more likely to serve tea than coffee). Interestingly, the term 'coffee house' was used by the temperance movement in the second half of the nineteenth century for the eating places provided for the working classes as an alternative to public houses where alcohol was sold (Harrison 1971). Possibly because they tried to 'improve' as well as feed their customers, they were not very successful and did not last much beyond the 1890s. However, the new style coffee houses did something which public houses of the time rarely did: provide a wide range of food, from full meals to what we would now call snacks. Girouard (1984) argues that, as a consequence, they reinforced the pattern of eating out amongst the working class and contributed to the success of cafés, which were 'straightforward, unambitious and useful' and did not try to improve their customers. He also argues that they precipitated change in public houses which, in the face of such competition, were forced to provide food as well as drink. Some, like their twentieth-century counterparts, even started to serve coffee (Girouard 1984: 205–6).

The provision of commercial facilities for eating out accelerated during the nineteenth century. Freeman (1989) provides a vivid historical account of the Victorians and their food. She describes the food sold at markets and at fairs and by street-sellers. For example, in London, street-sellers sold food to take home or eat on the spot: hot eels, pea soup, fried fish, pickled whelks, nuts, apples, cakes, potatoes, roast chestnuts and, later, ice-cream. Cows were kept in St James's Park and milked to order. Fresh food in season, for example, fruit, was brought in from the countryside. However, more formal eating out did not develop to any great extent until well into Victoria's reign, largely because

> [since] eating out was looked on as a matter of necessity rather than pleasure, most establishments were utility rather than luxurious, and fashionable restaurants in the modern sense did not exist – fashionable dining being a matter of eating in (in the sense of in private houses) rather than out.
>
> (Freeman 1989: 179)

In addition, opportunities for eating out were radically different for men compared with women. Middle- and upper-class men could dine at their clubs, which were the nearest equivalent to restaurants, or at a handful of relatively high-class taverns. Freeman (1989) gives examples of one at Greenwich which specialized in serving fish and one in the City which was so famous for its turtle soup that customers could visit the basement and view the live turtles before eating. Taverns were noisy places, where waiters called out what was on offer and shouted the orders to the kitchen. It was not acceptable for ladies of standing to visit such places; the only public places where they could dine respectably were at inns and hotels, and even then they probably followed the custom, which earlier had been the rule for both sexes, of taking their meals in private rooms. For the growing middle classes working in the cities, the cheapest eating places were initially the coffee houses, which were perceived as 'worthy and conservative' (Freeman 1989: 273) eating places for those whose work kept them from home. Coffee houses offered some of the earliest 'take-aways' in that people at work could send out to a local coffee shop for food to be delivered to them. The development of railways and linked suburban housing meant that commuters were able to travel considerable distances to work. The distance travelled, and the time workers spent away from home, gave yet further impetus to the development of places to eat lunch at all social levels and all prices.

Change and expansion also came with the development of the tourist as well as the commuter trade. Larger and smarter hotels were built, often associated with and near railway stations. Simmons (1984), in his study of the development of the Victorian hotel, argues that the new London hotels built in the 1850s and later were quite different from the inns of earlier periods for several reasons. Firstly, they offered choice and a fixed tariff of prices. Even more importantly for their subsequent development, they offered opportunities for respectable women to dine in public and be seen in the public parts of the hotel (in ways which had always been available to men) rather than in the 'purdah of private-sitting rooms' (Simmons 1984: 10). Indeed, he comments that 'Hitherto the whole world of inns and hotels, still more of eating-rooms, in London had been a man's world' (Simmons 1984: 9). Interestingly, these new hotels, in London and elsewhere, checked rather than encouraged the development of independent restaurants, because guests were expected to eat in the hotel as well as to stay there. Particular hotels became associated with famous chefs (for example, Escoffier and the Savoy hotel) and reinforced them as centres for prestigious eating out. Such hotels also prevented the development of the type of hotel already common in the rest of Europe, offering just rooms or rooms with breakfast only. It was argued that, since the English insisted on elaborate cooked breakfasts, hotels must employ kitchens and staff and these could only be profitable if they were used to prepare other meals, too (Simmons 1984: 20).

Mennell, Murcott and Van Otterloo (1992: 81–3) argue that the restaurant as a social institution was, to some degree, a product of the French Revolution. Eating places open to the public existed in Paris before the Revolution. However, the social upheaval and its consequences for the collapse of the French aristocracy increased the availability of skilled professional cooks, who had formerly worked only for specific aristocratic houses. They opened dining rooms where they continued to prepare food to the highest standards (*haute cuisine*), this time for those who could pay. At its most elaborate, these chefs produced food of a range and quality which would have been impossible in private homes without a great deal of money to spend on ingredients and a large kitchen staff. However, Aron (1975) documents the development of a range of restaurants to suit all levels of expenditure. The restaurants which gave the middle and upper classes some insight into the quality and style of aristocratic dining are viewed by Mennell (1985) as part of a process of the democratization of luxury and an attack on privilege, with the restaurateur as someone who made accessible to the lower orders secrets from superior classes. Since 'Britain forgot how to cook at the time of the Enclosures and the Industrial Revolution' (Driver 1980: 170), it was French cuisine which set the standard all over the Western world, though Driver (1983: 89) adds the rider that the preference might have been as much for its expense and exclusiveness as for its taste. The social groups who were willing to pay for *haute cuisine*, Driver argues, were also the people who bought various guides to good food when eating out.

Driver emphasizes that styles of public eating vary and restaurants flourish for a range of reasons. 'In France, the public restaurant was a by-product of the Revolution; in mid twentieth-century Britain, of imperial decline' (Driver 1980: 178). Driver writes about the rise of immigrant cuisines as the 'collision of food worlds' (1980: 73) and suggests that they can be considered as either a triumph or a tragedy: as a triumph because they offered cooks and eaters access to many major culinary civilizations (Chinese, Indian and Middle Eastern, and later Italian), and as a tragedy because of the contempt which could be shown between 'native and newcomer'. Driver makes the comment that interest in these new cuisines did not initially arise from foreign travel (it is sometimes argued that many British people abroad insist on traditional foods), but from the opportunity to eat cheaply in ethnic restaurants (which also offer informality and extended opening hours). Such ethnic restaurants, together with other types which also offer informal modes of dining (for example, vegetarian), can provide a 'tentacle of taste, extended laterally to global foodways that lie outside the British tradition' (Driver 1980: 176).

Mennell (1985) argues that these changes carried with them a shift in the balance of power in favour of chefs and against the paying customer. Some chefs achieved fame and fortune not only through their restaurants but through their writing on cooking and cuisine. Often these books became regarded as the classic statements on French cookery and guides for subsequent training of new chefs. Examples are Careme and Escoffier in nineteenth-century France and Soyer, whose career was mostly spent in England but who was French-trained. Mennell also argues that these chefs shaped the menus and practice of the twentieth century, which rested on a wide range of ingredients, a large kitchen with a high degree of specialization and a standard of presentation which would be virtually impossible for the amateur cook. In due course, there were reactions to the dominance of this model of the restaurant, for example, the enthusiasm for country recipes and provincial styles of presentation. In the twentieth century, perhaps the most spectacular challenge came from *nouvelle cuisine*, associated with the name of Paul Bocuse. The emphasis on fresh ingredients (determined by what was available at market that day), the minimum of cooking and awareness of health considerations, made for meals which could not be planned in advance or produced on a large scale. Significantly, the practitioners of *nouvelle cuisine* were mostly chef-proprietors who created dishes in a highly individualistic manner. Wood (1991) describes the development of the *nouvelle cuisine* restaurant in terms of the 'shock of the new' and argues that this cuisine is a type of cooking of increased refinement, where the 'producer' continues to dominate. However, the fact that there are barriers to routinizing and incorporating *nouvelle cuisine* suggests that it is not the last word in the refinement of taste. For Wood, *nouvelle cuisine*:

is a social construct rather than a culinary one, reflecting the narrow concerns of, and changes within, the middle-class. Nouvelle cuisine is the fish and chips, hamburger, pizza and pancake of the middle-classes. It may become an integral part of the culinary scene but it will always be on the periphery of 'serious' food and eating, remaining far more interesting for its sociological, rather than gastronomic, significance.

(Wood 1991: 337)

The nineteenth century is associated with the development of one of the most popular street foods: fish and chips. Walton (1992) provides a detailed account of the trade's economic, social and political relevance. Walton acknowledges that little is known of the origins of the fish and chips, which became established in the form we know today before the end of the last century. Ironically, Walton concludes that this 'great and quintessentially British institution' (Walton 1992: 1) probably arose from ethnic diversity, when Jewish migrants to the East End of London fried the fish left over from fresh fish vending, for sale in the street to eat immediately or take home. Walton also argues that fish and chips, whether eaten in the street or taken home, was initially and continues to be, for the most part, food for the working classes. Buying fish and chips to eat out was always seen as rather 'common'; it had little appeal to the middle classes because of the smells, dubious hygiene and rough behaviour said to be associated with it. Walton also suggests that this may be part of the reason why the industry was neglected by historians. He shows that the growth of fish and chip retail outlets, particularly as they emerged from their down-market, backstreet origins to respectable locations with improved hygiene and strict controls on their operations, stimulated considerable capital investment. Such expansion introduced sophisticated technology and became an important component of the national fish trade and the demand for potatoes. There is also evidence to suggest that fish and chips was an important element in the regular diet of a large proportion of working-class families and that there was a constant debate amongst those concerned with the nutritional standards of the poor as to whether the dish was a healthy contribution to working-class diets, or part of secondary poverty induced by incompetent use of limited resources. The supporters of fish and chips, who included some medical practitioners, argued that the dish offered good food value at low cost. As part of the food eaten at home, it was one of the earliest convenience foods for working wives: easily accessible, highly palatable and time-saving. In addition, the food did not demand investment in expensive domestic technology. Not all working-class people considered it respectable to eat fish and chips in the street from newspaper, although the dish was a popular street food for people coming out of cinemas and public houses. In the 1940s researchers for the Mass Observation organization noted that sales of fish and chips fluctuated with the closing times of pubs (Mass Observation 1987).

Walton (1992) also draws attention to the social functions of the fish and chip shops. They were centres of gossip and sociability and, in contrast to many of their higher-status equivalents, welcomed women and children. In the interwar period, when many shops were refurbished, they were associated with warmth and comfort. They were also associated with courting, particularly for adolescents, where calling for fish and chips marked the end of an evening out. The lack of general appeal to the middle classes is highlighted by accounts of the exception: Harry Ramsden's. Harry Ramsden built his fish and chip 'palace' in the Yorkshire countryside in the 1930s, complete with seating for 200 in a restaurant which was carpeted and lit by chandeliers. He succeed in attracting large numbers of the middle classes who could afford to travel to his restaurant by car. However, his success rested on having the custom of both the 'upmarket' trade and the regular daily orders from the local mill workers. As incomes rose, other restaurants, for example those in department stores, hoped to attract the skilled working classes to their stores and to the experience of eating out in restaurants. To complaints from the independent fish fryers, who resented the competition, the stores' restaurants began to do this by including the ever popular fish and chips on their menus. Fish and chips also became available in works canteens.

Studies from the United States argue that there the development of commercial facilities for eating away from home was similar but more rapid than in the UK. The essentially rural character of much of the country meant that commercial developments were concentrated in the cities and on the coast. For example, Pillsbury (1990: 13) asserts that 'Most colonial Americans never dined in a restaurant even once'. Their experience of eating away from home would have been at non-commercial social gatherings or in the homes of others at weddings and funerals. Travel for pleasure was rare and was seen as the prerogative of the very rich; travel for business would involve staying at taverns, inns or boarding houses where facilities were basic and there was little or no choice of food or accommodation. There were restaurants (specializing in selling food for consumption on the premises) at the beginning of the nineteenth century and it was these, together with the coffee houses already established in the larger cities, which expanded to meet the demands of the 'mercantile age'. For Pillsbury, it was the industrial revolution of the late nineteenth century that brought about 'a new set of operational assumptions and parameters' (1990: 33) to meet the demands of the growing urban centres with their 'unparalleled need to feed the multi-shift factory workers at all times of the day and night' (1990: 37). The boarding houses and taverns, with their fixed times of eating, were insufficiently flexible and the need was met by street vendors and then by 'diners' (wagons where patrons could sit whilst eating) which became more and more sophisticated in their design and provisions. From the 1870s onwards, demand was met by 'new restaurants for a factory age' (Pillsbury 1990: 48) which included lunchrooms, cafeterias and diners, often supplied with quality foodstuffs by the fast and efficient railways.

It was at this time that the hamburger became part of the basic menu offered (with the first reference to a 'hamburger steak' as early as 1834, although the first hamburger sandwich was recorded much later in 1916). The first quarter of the twentieth century saw the rapid growth of all kinds of catering and the establishment of chains, both regional and national, and the development of franchising. Eating away from home from choice during leisure time became popular amongst the middle and working classes at this period, particularly when car ownership became more widespread. The 'drive-in' concept was developed in the 1920s and along with all catering outlets in residential neighbourhoods (where they were associated with pleasure rather than work). 'These new stores targeted the discretionary food dollar, not the work dollar. They represented pleasure not a necessary evil' (Pillsbury 1990: 77). Pillsbury attempts to make sense of a situation where the choice of eating out facilities was so great that 'chaos rules our palate' (1990: 3) by drawing a distinction between body food (to fuel the body) and soul food (to serve the inner person). Each is a matter of time, money and intent and, in the late twentieth century, it is possible to have the choice. 'The restaurant is simply a place where, for a fee, one may dine away from home; a modest concept which has taken on literally thousands of expressions in the world around us' (Pillsbury 1990: 225). In sum, he sees the restaurant as a mirror of its society. This echoes the concluding comments of Farb and Armelagos (1980: 266), who noted that, in responding to the new rituals of eating based on automobiles, television, technology and efficiency (which cut across previous religious affiliations, ethnic loyalties and class allegiances), we make choices which are cultural statements, and that our eating patterns are reflections of contemporary social formations.

Levenstein (1988) identifies a special factor in the expansion of commercial facilities for eating out in the United States: the prohibition on the public sale of alcohol in 1920. This destroyed the ascendancy of French cuisine in the highest-status restaurants (because it was virtually impossible to cook many of the dishes without wine or to enjoy them without an accompanying wine). It also undermined such restaurants economically, in that many of them had relied on the profits from their alcohol sales to subsidize the provision of high-quality food. However, the catering industry expanded at other levels, providing for the growing numbers of men and women of the middle classes who worked and ate a midday meal away from home. The new lunchrooms, tearooms and self-service cafeterias provided low-cost food served quickly. They also offered respectable places for women workers and shoppers to eat, something which had not been available in the era of the dominance of restaurants and hotels. Women's food preferences for light snacks and salads also shaped the menus offered to workers, whilst American rather than French cuisine featured in the restaurants more geared to the leisure trade. Levenstein (1988: 192) argues that these changes had a considerable impact on the pattern of employment in that 'most food preparation could be accomplished by unskilled, barely trained, cheap, male labor'.

The period of dramatic expansion, particularly of chains and franchise outlets, is documented by Carlioro (1994) in tracing the 'odyssey' of eating out over the seventy-five years up to 1994. Whilst many of the chains whose histories he

111

describes are great business success stories and have become household names, Carlioro also identifies the risks and uncertainties of the commercial sector of catering provision. Following the financial and organizational strategies of earlier successes does not necessarily guarantee further success. There is evidence of both spectacular failures and a continued enthusiasm on the part of new entrepreneurs for trying to meet the demands of a public whose willingness to spend cannot always be evaluated – entrepreneurs who may be faced with unexpected costs such as health care for their employees (Carlioro 1994: 190). Although, as Carlioro points out, in spite of economic depression, world wars and the unpredictability of the dining public, the history of the restaurant industry in America is one of resilience and expansion.

'BEHIND THE SCENES': EMPLOYMENT IN THE CATERING INDUSTRY

In his study, Walton (1992) also addressed the issue of the fish and chip shop as a small business. The pattern varied over time, but Walton argues that owners were usually located at the margin of the lower middle and upper working classes, recruited from skilled and supervisory labour. The shop was sometimes a supplementary source of income where one or more wage earners worked outside the home. Typically, the shop was a small family business rather than part of a chain. Husband and wife often worked together with heavy dependence on child labour. In contrast to some of their more modern competitors, they remained small-scale, labour-intensive operations.

Clearly, the provision of food for those at work or at leisure makes work, and there has been a series of attempts to analyse the work of those 'behind the scenes' (Mennell, Murcott and Van Otterloo 1992: 85). The literature available varies according to the work undertaken. For example, cooks and chefs as a group are under-researched although there is a range of literature about cooking and waiting occupations. Such literature varies in its focus from analyses of tensions within the kitchen from a management perspective (Whyte 1948) to the study of catering as an example of routine, semi-skilled work (Gabriel 1988). In addition, Wood (1992) reviews this and other literature in his study of the 'hospitality industry' of hotel and catering work. In contrast, and more recently, Adkins (1995) has discussed the special character of service work, particularly its gendered organization. There is also literature about food workers, particularly waiters, as part of the illegal economy (Mars 1982). All agree that many jobs in catering are stressful and poorly paid, with little training and low expectations amongst workers, and often with high turnover of staff. There is often little mutual understanding between cook, waiter and customer, which Driver (1980: 153–5) puts down to the complacency of large commercial organizations which claim that they rarely receive complaints. Even the highest-status personnel, chefs and cooks, have a long training with relatively poor pay and see themselves as artists unappreciated by their patrons (Mennell, Murcott and Van Otterloo 1992).

Gabriel's (1988) study is an attempt to make up for some of the gaps in our knowledge about working lives in catering. The preface states that 10 per cent of British workers are catering employees and are part of the service sector, which accounts for 62 per cent of all jobs. Yet the area has been described as the 'stepchild of economic research' (Gabriel 1988: 6). He argues that the expansion in catering jobs reflects changes in eating and drinking habits over the past twenty to thirty years in terms of what is eaten and where and how it is prepared. The central features of change are the growth of consumer interest in take-away meals, fast food, health food, ethnic restaurants, cafés, wine bars, and *haute cuisine* restaurants. In the past it has been acknowledged that these enterprises are, by their nature, labour-intensive. However, the trend is towards the industrialization of service and the substitution of labour by machinery and technology. Such changes have come through the availability of frozen foods and routinized production so that cooks become 'material handlers' and waiters become 'interface workers'. With fascinating prescience, Gabriel even writes (1988: 4) of the 'McDonaldization of the Economy' but does not pursue the social consequences of such a process.

Gabriel's own field research covers a range of situations in which food is prepared: a traditional mass catering unit in a hospital, the modern frozen food unit in a community centre, a fast food chain, a traditional fish and chip restaurant, a kebab house and a gentlemen's club, using interviews to reveal the diversities and similarities of the working lives which are described. The chapter headings ('Home cooking for thousands', 'The cooking factory', 'The fun food machine', 'Craft cooking for gentlemen', 'The small independent restaurant or café: the price of independence') touch on the analysis of gendered work in the service sector, but the chief focus is indicated by the title of the concluding chapter, 'Conclusions: keeping the lid on', which emphasizes the similarities, not differences, between these workers and other workers. In the context of economic depression and fear of unemployment, these workers are argued to be trapped in jobs with poor pay, variable job satisfaction (with the cooks and private dining room workers having highest and the others very little) and little economic power as workers. These themes are echoed and developed by Wood (1992) in his account of work in hotels and catering. Drawing upon a considerable literature about the hospitality industry, he confirms the lack of empirical data but argues that there is sufficient in what exists to support the general agreement about the low level of rewards for work which is often both insecure and carried out in unpleasant conditions. Wood discusses the problems of high levels of labour turnover, the frequent lack of collective organization in regard to pay and conditions, de-skilling and the demand for flexibility from the work-force, and the lack of appreciation from the customer for services provided. In his concluding observations, Wood (1992: 163–5) considers the possibility of a future where the exploitative relationships of work in hotels and catering will produce a hospitality industry in which most employees will work for a brief time only, as one phase in their movement towards a career in some other part of the economy.

Mars (1982) includes hotel workers amongst his potential 'cheats at work' in that they operate in a work setting which provides them with motives and opportunities for 'fiddling'. His analysis of 'covert reward systems' covers four job categories (designated 'hawks', 'donkeys', 'wolves' or 'vultures'), each with structural characteristics in common and broadly similar opportunities to rob, cheat, short-change and 'fiddle' in transactions with customers, employers, subordinates and the state. Waiters are placed amongst the vultures, in that they need the support of a group but act on their own 'at the feast'. They are linked to the common base, depending on support and information from colleagues, but still being competitive and acting in isolation. The waiter gets formal rewards (basic pay) with informal rewards ('free' meals, accommodation, tips) and potentially illegal 'alternative' rewards in the 'black economy', through access, for example, to pilfered food and opportunities to short-change customers.

Adkins (1995) raises more directly the links between the public and the private domains and the special character of service work. She focuses on the gendering of the contemporary labour market, in particular the processes through which power relations between men and women in employment are constituted, specifically in paid work in the service sector associated with leisure. The nature of service work is discussed and, in particular, how and in what way service work differs from other forms of wage-labour relations. Adkins argues that, unlike other kinds of work, service work cannot be understood in terms of economic rationality alone. She agrees that the imperatives of management are economic rationalization and standardization. However, some autonomy must be allowed to the service provider to ensure that the specific requirements or situations of customers can be accommodated. Such autonomy is not *ad hoc* but has the important social function of the maintenance of 'normal conditions' (Adkins 1995: 6), since service work is not just fixed outcomes and rigid controls but also the (re)production of the social structure. The processes of mediation and normalizing are central to understanding the dynamics of service work, including employment relations. Where there is spatial and temporal proximity between production and consumption, services for customers/clients/guests have to be delivered in the same place and at the same time as produced. In other words, Adkins argues, in service work the quality of the social interaction between the provider and the consumer of the service becomes part of the product. As a consequence, the cultural expectations of consumers regarding service provision have particular significance in structuring the form of service delivery, and hence employment relations, because consumers are buying a particular kind of social experience. Thus, the social composition of 'front-line/high-contact' workers becomes part of what is sold. Race, age, gender all become relevant in recruitment and employers intervene in areas of dress, speech, behaviour and training. In other words, it is recognized that service employment may involve carrying out what Adkins identifies as 'emotion work' in relation to customers. Even though it is difficult to get accurate data because service workers are often working in non-standard kinds of employment (for

114

example, part-time, casual or temporary), estimates support the view that front-line consumer service work is typically carried out by women. In 1991, 81 per cent of all employed women worked in service occupations and in 1990 70 per cent of the total hotel and catering work-force was female.

Adkins's field work was undertaken to explore the gendered dynamics of service employment in the context of a leisure park and amongst hotel and catering managers. Data were collected on the gendered structure of employment, the construction of work relations and the significance of sexuality. The analysis suggests that these service workers, particularly the women, were operating in a more complex framework than other workers (Adkins 1995: 144). Far from existing outside the domain of employment, both family and sexual relations played a significant role in structuring gendered work relations within the labour market. In the case of management in hotel and catering, work relations (or relations of production) within the occupation were shown frequently to be organized by the patriarchal relations of the family. For example, husband and wife were hired as a 'team', yet the husband directly controlled the wife's occupational work, to the benefit of employers, even though the wife had no wage-labour agreement or contract. The wives worked under the marriage contract in a family mode of production, organized in a patriarchal way. In the leisure park, there was patriarchal structuring of waged-labour. To get a job, most women (regardless of occupation) were required to fulfil conditions which related to the production of an 'attractive' female work-force, which included expecting and dealing with forms of 'sexual objectification from men customers and men co-workers' (Adkins 1995: 145). It is emphasized that only women had to carry out such 'sexual work' in order to have the opportunity to exchange labour in the marketplace. 'Men and women were constituted as different kinds of workers within these workplaces, even when they were located in the same jobs' (Adkins1995: 147). To be workers, women had to be 'attractive' and carry out forms of sexualized work, whereas men did not have to do this. Women not only had to take orders, serve food and drinks and clear tables, they also had to provide what Adkins sees as 'sexual services' for men, both customers and co-workers (for example, by smiling, looking flattered, entering into jokes, etc.). It is acknowledged that such interaction was not always unpleasant. However there were cases of dismissal where women had resisted conventional asumptions about their behaviour. Adkins' analysis challenges and invites a reinterpretation of a range of studies of restaurant work and of the selection and training of workers in various types of food outlets.

CONTEMPORARY PATTERNS OF EATING OUT

The USA is often used as an indicator of what is likely to become the pattern in the UK. McCarthy and Strauss (1992) report on a survey about the 'Tastes of America 1992'. After a drop in 1990, the amount spent per week on eating out continued to increase. However, although spending was up, the frequency of dining out had declined. 'Customers often see eating out as a treat – and, as the survey shows, they expect the service they receive to live up to that perception' (McCarthy and Strauss 1992: 25). For example, 70 per cent were reported as eating at 'full service' restaurants to celebrate a special occasion. The survey polled 4,000 households and 2,502 responded. Almost all (98 per cent) had eaten out during the previous month. Typically, households ate out 9.42 times a week with adult males eating out 4.68 times a week on average, compared with 3.76 for an adult female and 4.16 for 'child/teen'. Married couples with two incomes and at least one child spent most per household, with singles under 30 spending the most per capita. Healthy eating, such as ordering salads, was often offset by also ordering french fries, although the evidence indicates an increase in orders for grilled rather than fried chicken.

Although not directly comparable with the American material, a useful over-view of the pattern of eating out in the UK is provided by Payne and Payne (1993). Since the authors are writing for the business community, they are concerned to highlight the features of the market, consumer attitudes and the prospects for the 1990s. They emphasize the growth of the market, calculating that the consumer catering market (excluding institutional catering but including drinks consumed with meals) was worth £16.6 billions in 1992, an increase of 69 per cent on the figure for 1986. Even taking into consideration the recession, they argue that the long-term trend is for real spending on eating out to increase (and for it to increase as a proportion of consumer spending overall). Compared with 109,471 in 1980, they identify 124,900 catering businesses in the UK in 1990. The great majority of these businesses (120,168) operated in the consumer catering sector and the number of actual outlets was around double that figure. Public houses were the most common type, with around 70,000 outlets (two-thirds of them serving snacks and meals at the bar and 40 per cent having a restaurant). Change has occurred with franchising increasing in importance and a nationwide network of outlets being built up by catering chains. In addition, in-store restaurants have changed as shopping centres grow in number and with them food courts, offering a range of food from a number of counters.

Payne and Payne (1993) draw upon the National Food Survey to show that in 1990 the average number of meals taken outside the home totalled 195 per person, of which 100 were consumed at lunchtime. People with higher incomes, and Londoners, were the most likely to eat out. They also report on the Economist Intelligence Unit survey of consumer attitudes to and patterns of eating out of a sample of 1,000 people aged 16 and over (see Table 5.1)

A detailed analysis of the results showed that: people aged 55 and over and those in the 'DE' socioeconomic groups were considerably less likely than others to have eaten out in the previous 12 months. Pubs, hotels and fish and chip shops showed a broad-based popularity; other 'English' restaurants, Indian restaurants, French restaurants and roadside diners showed a strong male bias; ethnic restaurants were preferred by those in the younger age groups, while pizza houses, French restaurants and vegetarian restaurants displayed a strong

Table 5.1 Types of restaurant meals eaten during the
last twelve months (1991)

Type of outlet	Respondents (all adults) (%)
Pub	60
Hotel	31
Chinese	29
Roadside diner	28
Pizza	24
Indian	24
Fish and chip restaurant	23
Steakhouse	21
Other 'English' restaurant	16
American style	16
Italian	16
Wine bar	8
French	7
Greek	7
Vegetarian	4
Other	6
None of these/don't know	13

Source: Adapted from Payne and Payne (1993: iii)

upmarket bias. Regional results varied greatly but Londoners were far less likely to have eaten in a pub and considerably more likely to have eaten in ethnic restaurants (Payne and Payne 1993: iii).

Respondents were also asked their main reasons for choosing a restaurant. In descending order of importance they were quality of food, value for money, range of menu, attentiveness of service, overall atmosphere, the welcoming of families, availability of parking and convenience of location. The first two factors were considerably more important than any other. For an ordinary meal most people aimed to spend less than £10 per head, for a special meal they would spend between £10 and £40.

On the basis of their study, Payne and Payne predict that there will be the further spread of systems catering (i.e., chains with a standardized menu and format), food courts and themed restaurants. Two significant factors – convenience and health – will also continue to be influential, with convenience expressed in terms of the growth in home delivery (and intense competition between suppliers) and the health influence reflected 'in an increased offering of salads, low fat food, vegetarian meals and, perhaps, fresh and healthy ingredients' (Payne and Payne 1993: iv). They also predict that ethnic food will become more popular, with more ethnic restaurants and an increase in non-ethnic restaurants offering some of the most popular ethnic dishes. Writing about Britain, Jones (1985) also predicts intense competition amongst fast food companies, with a small number of large operators continuing to dominate the sector. Farb and Armelagos (1980: 197) argue that, on the one hand, national cuisines are basically conservative and that successful developments (for example, the expansion of fast food outlets with limited menus which give the assurance of familiarity) support this view. On the other hand, they also recognize that new foods are constantly being added and suggest that national cuisines can be flexible in exploiting novel cultural and environmental resources.

SOCIOLOGICAL ANALYSES OF CONTEMPORARY EATING OUT

Wood (1992) draws attention to the fact that, typically, sociological concern has been on 'domestic dining' rather than on dining out, even though dining out is experienced and enjoyed by all except the poorest members of society. Drawing upon a range of studies, Wood estimates that there are about 231,750 'commercial catering outlets' in Britain (including hotels, restaurants, public houses, commercial travel catering, major fast food chains, cafés and take-aways, and club, leisure and entertainment catering). In addition, there are 72,610 outlets in non-commercial catering (including staff canteens, health care catering, education and public service catering). He alerts readers to the fact that the term 'eating out' can be misleading in that a substantial proportion (about two-thirds) of the meals served in the cafés and take-aways, which represent 18 per cent of meals served in the commercial sector, are consumed on a take-away basis and may well be eaten at home. He also draws attention to the fact that dining out as an ancillary activity (for example, food eaten when out shopping) may have a different symbolic significance from that of dining out as a leisure activity in itself. Wood identifies these issues as part of an agenda for sociological research. He also advocates the further exploration of the family and gender dimensions of food choice as experienced in the public domain.

Mazurkiewicz (1983) had already identified the relevance of gender and argued that not all food outlets are equally accessible to men and women, although more research is need to document these differences in detail. She focuses on women's access to and use of the facilities and services in the commercial sector of the hotel and catering industry in the context of reports concerned with the failure of this sector to cater for female customers, particularly female business travellers. In contrast to those who see the problem as one of inadequate marketing, Mazurkiewicz makes the case that there are social barriers to women's use of hotel and eating out facilities. Women's defined location in the private sphere of the home, their prescribed roles and expected behaviour patterns, and male domination and control of women in the public areas of life, combine to generate social barriers which exclude unaccompanied women from public places. These patterns are reinforced by the managerial strategies of hotels and public houses which respond to female customers in terms of such stereotypes.

Finkelstein (1989) offers an analysis of dining out as 'a sociology of modern manners'. The focus is on the 'ordinary'. Dining out, she argues, is very popular and it has been estimated that by the close of the twentieth century two-thirds of all meals in the United States will be purchased and consumed outside the home. Finkelstein's study is an attempt to examine dining out for the presuppositions and concealed values it contains. The starting-point is the popularity of restaurants and the ways in which their use might reflect changing family patterns and, in particular, changes in the functions of the nuclear family. However, it is not possible to argue that restaurants are used because they save time during the working week, because restaurants are actually busier at weekends. Nor can it be argued to be a question of physiological pleasure from consumption because there is sometimes distress from overindulgence and also a willingness to eat junk foods when out. So there is a need to explain why people derive such pleasure from eating in the public domain. Clearly this is more complex than mere eating and represents a range of meaningful activity. Finkelstein suggests several possibilities: pleasure in the sense of occasion; an opportunity to demonstrate our knowledge of how to behave; participation in a form of entertainment and spectacle through visual images and imagined atmosphere. In sum, these are all aspects of 'bourgeois sensibility' of self – the opinions of others, the appearance of wealth and being in control. Dining out may be viewed as the convergence of the private and the personal with the public and social. There are even different restaurants for different moods (for example, McDonald's for family unity, a bistro for romance) as well as 'waves of style' in fashions of dining out (Finkelstein 1989: 3).

However, Finkelstein argues against the popular view that dining out is an expression of individuality, choice, spontaneity and that we select restaurants for food and price in ways which demonstrate our discrimination and what we value and desire. On the contrary, dining out has the capacity to transform emotions into commodities which are made available to the individual as if they were consumer items. The styles of interaction encouraged in the restaurant produce an 'uncivilized sociality'; the restaurant makes dining out a mannered exercise, disciplined by customs in a framework of prefigured actions. We act in imitation of others, in accord with images, in response to fashions, out of habit, without need or thought for self-scrutiny. Far from being in control, we are relieved of the responsibility of shaping our relationships with others. For Finkelstein (1989: 8), this provides an extension of Elias's analysis, in that, for her, civility refers to exchanges between individuals who are equally self-conscious and attentive to each other, who avoid power differentials, and do not mediate exchanges through status and prestige. Civility is not unthinking obedience to habit and custom but intentional exchange (even if it is sometimes difficult, conflictual, raucous). It is reflected in the degree of engagement required of those who interact. It follows that if people are being used to serve self-interest, then there cannot be civility. For example, the business lunch is not the setting for civilized exchange, even if the hidden agenda is known; it is merely a pretence of cordiality.

Finkelstein comes to the thought-provoking conclusion that restaurants have structural characteristics which make the social exchange there inherently uncivilized. There is artifice and pretence, diners are under close surveillance from waiters, they are guided through the menu so that the waiter is between food and eater, wine waiters subdue the diners and establish boundaries and hierarchies and assure diner discomfort. The restaurant owner greets and guides in ways which enhance control. Dining out is mediated through money and engenders callous and calculative orientations. Finkelstein is aware that this is not the way diners perceive the dining out experience. They may well view it as a pleasure, highly convenient and entertaining, with social formulae which make it easier to act without thinking. However, she wants us to be aware that the underlying processes she describes are linked to the rise of modern bourgeois culture and the 'democratization of luxury' argued by Mennell (1985). Dining out gives license to take pleasure where there is no sense of accountability or personal history, since it takes place amongst strangers. It is democratic and open to all with money, so remote from the everyday that it permits the confident presentation of self. The restaurant is part of the entertainment industry in Westernized societies and is concerned with the marketing of emotions, desires, states of mind. Finkelstein (1989) identifies a paradox: as with all leisure activities in modern society, dining out weakens participation in the social area even as it appears to increase such participation. By offering social formulae for relationships with others, it prevents the development of what Finkelstein (1989: 5) terms 'the examined life' expressed as a civilized awareness of others.

From a somewhat different theoretical starting point, Ritzer (1993) analyses what is perhaps the most characteristic type of eating out in the second half of the twentieth century: 'fast food', which can be either eaten in a restaurant or taken away. There are many outlets and chains currently, each competing to become a household name. Ritzer (1993: 30) gives an account of the first fast food restaurant opened by the two McDonald brothers in 1937 in Pasadena, California. Their established restaurant had experienced high demand at specific times (for example, workers' lunchtimes) and they responded with a circumscribed menu (burgers) and were able to serve large numbers at high speed and low price. The assembly line procedures, with food preparation and serving made into simple repetitive tasks, combined with a specialized division of labour for each stage, have been recognized as constituting the first 'fast food factory'. In 1954 the brothers moved and followed the same pattern in San Bernardino, California. They continued to prosper but were merely a local sensation until visited by Ray Kroc, an enthusiast for scientific management. It was he who suggested the idea of franchising which led, eventually, to expansion world-wide. The particular franchise package used retained centralized control, maintained conformity throughout the system and gave the company a return on all sales. Such rationalization of the fast food business through uniformity in production, a standardized menu and systematic staff training provided customers with a guarantee of a familiar setting and the same quality of food prepared in the same way wherever they ate at McDonalds. The demand in the USA and internationally for such eating out seems insatiable and, as Ritzer says, 'the rest is history'. He argues that developments in fast food were possible because of the processes of formal rationality already in place, such as scientific management, assembly-line work, the mass-production of cars and homes and the development of centres for shopping, parts of which became 'amusement parks for food', where both the setting and the food on offer were guaranteed to be familiar and unchanging. In addition, families, particularly those with children, could eat without anxieties about cutlery, tableware and the disapproval of other customers. Interestingly, in terms of Elias's notions of civility, this is an example of 'uncivilized' behaviour. However, Ritzer also makes us aware that such efficiency, predictability and control extends to control over the customer. Fast food is served so that the customer is encouraged to leave and make room for the next person. There is little choice and the food served has been criticized by nutritionists for being high in calories, fat, salt and sugar.

Ritzer goes on to argue that rationalization (or what he terms 'McDonaldization') is not only characteristic of fast food but also of society in general and is becoming an all-embracing feature of life. He makes a case for education, commerce, industry and medicine all being influenced by the push towards higher profits and lower costs. Such pressures can only be countered by individual subversion or by circumstances in which post-Fordism has lead to greater diversity of provision and hence more choice. Ritzer makes it plain that he wishes to encourage such responses. For example, he mentions the importance of eating seasonally and, along with others (for example Driver 1980), advocates 'slow' rather than 'fast' food (Ritzer 1993: 184).

OVERVIEW

The foregoing discussion has indicated some of the ways in which eating occasions are situated in a complex social space. Eating events can clearly be seen to be located at points upon a number of dimensions. For example, we might identify a dimension which has eating events shaped by personal social obligations and relationships at one end and, at the other, eating events articulated by a commercial nexus between a consumer and a service provider. We can also recognize a dimension which ranges from informal eating situations only loosely constrained by culture and convention to formalized, highly structured eating events. Finally, this chapter and the previous chapter have indicated that, in an important sense, there is also a continuum linking domestic food events at one end and public food events at the other, and that there is not necessarily a simple dichotomy between 'eating in' and 'eating out'.

The studies discussed in this chapter indicate the changes which have occurred and the continuities which have remained. The commercialization of eating out was a consequence of the breakdown of traditional social relationships, particularly those of feudalism, and the growth of towns and cities. Such changes, which accelerated after the industrial revolution and the separation of home from work, had far-reaching consequences for the organization of both employment and domestic life. Economic resources and socioeconomic position continue to exert a powerful influence upon patterns of dining out. However, despite the somewhat pessimistic assumptions of authors like Finkelstein and Ritzer, at whatever level one eats out there has been a significant expansion in the range of choice. Depending on the context and cuisine chosen, eating out may be either similar or radically different from eating at home. The very diversity of contemporary opportunities for eating out challenges conventional ideas about resistance to change being at its strongest in relation to what we eat.

Part III

FOOD, HEALTH AND WELL-BEING

6

CHANGING CONCEPTIONS OF DIET AND HEALTH

The linkage between diet and health is an inescapable fact of life. However, in some senses this linkage can be a complex and subtle one, and clear causal pathways may be very difficult to establish, whether by time-honoured intuitive techniques or by the sophisticated, systematic methods of modern science. Thus, while this link is widely recognized in human culture, there are seemingly endless variations in the ways in which it is conceptualized and in the ways in which such conceptualizations are translated into actual beliefs and practices. However, as a starting-point it is useful to see conceptualizations of the relationship between diet and health as having two opposed aspects: positive and negative. The positive aspect is based upon the idea that certain food items, combinations of food items or diets can produce beneficial health outcomes. These beneficial outcomes may be viewed, by those who accept such ideas, as generalized and unspecific. That is, certain dietary choices are seen as maintaining, or actually enhancing, an individual's resistance to disease or as promoting the efficiency or durability of the body. However, such ideas can be much more specific. For example, particular dietary options or particular foodstuffs may be seen as capable of preventing a particular disease. Similarly, certain food items, or a given dietary regime, may be seen as suitable for treating a disease or for managing a disease and relieving its symptoms.

Many of the negative aspects of the linkage between diet and health are self-evident. Most obviously, a grossly inadequate food intake will lead to weight loss and eventually to death (either through starvation or the onset of a related disease). However, nutrient deficiencies which fall short of the absolute deprivation of starvation can result from low food intake, an unbalanced diet or poor assimilation. Thus, dietary protein deficiency in infants after weaning can result in the disease known as kwashiorkor. A deficiency of vitamin D can cause rickets, a disease which mainly affects children and is characterized by the softening of developing bone (resulting in bow legs). The disease scurvy results from a lack of vitamin C, and produces anaemia, spongy gums, and, in infants, is associated with malformations of bones and teeth. Furthermore, inevitably, food intake can act as a channel for the introduction of harmful agents into the body. These may be toxins (whether organic or inorganic, naturally occurring or synthetic) or any of a vast array of disease-inducing organisms. What is more, in many cultures such agents may be conceptualized in ways which modern Western rationality would regard as supernatural or mystical.

The purpose of this chapter is to focus attention upon such cultural constructions of the connections, or supposed connections, between what an individual eats and that individual's state of health. Of course, such ideas, particularly in the context of Western societies, are not static. They change, sometimes radically, over time. Thus, this dynamic perspective is essential, as we look firstly at examples of traditional forms of belief and practice in relation to diet and health and then at the gradual rise to dominance in Western culture of more systematic and rationalized perspectives. The dominance of such perspectives, however, is by no means complete, as will become evident when contemporary common-sense ideas and 'alternative' dietary ideologies are examined.

TRADITIONAL PERSPECTIVES ON THE LINKS BETWEEN DIET AND HEALTH

Traditional forms of understanding and practice clearly cover an impressive array of activities, including hunting, fishing, agriculture, the manufacture of tools, weapons and other artefacts, healing, divination, and so on. Such traditional forms of understanding, often termed 'folk knowledge' or 'pre-scientific knowledge', are usually based upon the accumulation of often highly detailed empirical information. Accumulation typically takes place over many generations, as concepts and techniques are refined through a repetitive, if somewhat haphazard, process of trial and error. Change in such knowledge is usually slow, although the patient exercise of everyday curiosity plus the occasional fortuitous insight or discovery can lead to effective and sophisticated ways of controlling and manipulating the world. However, it should be borne in mind that traditional knowledge frequently incorporates conceptualizations of cause and effect which modern scientific perspectives would see as essentially irrational, assuming causal mechanisms which would not stand up to rigorous examination. The term 'magic' is conventionally used to refer to such ideas, usually somewhat dismissively and disparagingly. Nevertheless, in traditional societies magical techniques and their associated rituals are employed in many areas of everyday life, particularly where there is uncertainty and unpredictability. What is more, accumulated empirical knowledge and magical formulations of cause and effect become enmeshed with one another, the one difficult to distinguish from the other in any absolute sense, forming a single holistic system of thought. Thus, while the hard lessons of trial and error may eventually be incorporated into practice, where there is ambiguity and ambivalence 'supernatural' forms of explanation have a flexibility which allows them to adapt and survive apparent refutation. We can now turn to actual examples of such traditional ideas in the area of food and health.

Perhaps the most widespread of these traditional conceptualizations of the ways in which diet and health interact are those which are based upon classification according to a hot–cold dimension. In this sense, hot and cold do not refer to the actual physical temperature of the food, but to a more elusive (and in rational terms possibly a more illusory) property of food. In addition, herbs, beverages, medicines, illnesses and even people may be classified in this way in many such belief systems. As Manderson (1987) points out, hot–cold concepts can be found in cultures in Latin America, Asia and Africa. These ideas also appear to have an affinity with ancient traditions of humoral medicine that have existed in Europe, in the Islamic world and in China and India. However, ethnographic evidence indicates that such belief systems are often very variable and are characterized by inconsistencies and disagreements (Manderson 1987: 329). In other words, they exhibit the typical flexibility and elasticity of traditional modes of thought. In certain circumstances, as we will see, these properties enable hot–cold conceptions to survive, and adapt to, the impact of modernization.

Malaya provides an example of a society whose people's beliefs place a strong emphasis on the link between diet and health. In that country, hot–cold categorization remains an important feature of folk medicinal systems and of the practices of the folk healers who are the custodians of these systems. Manderson provides us with a general description of Malay hot–cold ideas, indicating the way in which these are sometimes related to a concept of balance. Thus, food classified as hot may be taken to alleviate 'chilling', but consuming hot foods to excess may result in such unwelcome complaints as rashes, fevers and constipation. These complaints can be relieved by the consumption of foods classified as cold (and such foods are also seen as beneficial for the young, whose bodies by their very nature, are hot). However, an excess of cold foods is seen as leading to weakness and lethargy, and to arthritis and rheumatism in the aged. In Malay communities, some illnesses are also classified as hot or cold. For example, measles, smallpox and chickenpox are hot infections and the patient should avoid hot foods until after recovery. Conversely, chills, arthritis, rheumatism and neuralgia are cold ailments and their symptoms can be relieved by reducing the consumption of cold foods and increasing the consumption of hot foods and medicines (Manderson 1987: 330). In some cultural groups, individuals may be seen as varying in terms of hot and cold (for example, the old may be seen as colder than the young, and men as hotter than women), and there may even be a personal dimension (what is hot for one individual being cool or neutral for another). Even within Malaya there is considerable variation in these beliefs, and hot–cold is often seen more in terms of a subtle continuum than as a simple binary opposition. However, broadly speaking, foods which are spicy or which are higher in fats, calories or protein (e.g., animal products) are located towards the hot end of the continuum, and foods higher in water content (fruits, vegetables, etc.) towards the cold end.

A more detailed ethnographic account is provided by Wilson's participant observation study carried out in a fishing village on the east coast of the Malay

Peninsula. In fact, this study detected a considerable amount of variation in individuals' opinions concerning exactly how particular items should be classified. However, there was broad agreement that such foods as chicken, beef, goat, eggs, manioc, yeast, chilli peppers and spices are hot, and that fruits and vegetables are cold. Rice and fish, the two basic ingredients of Malay cuisine, were regarded as neutral (Wilson 1981: 391). What is more, certain foods were seen as having direct health implications over and above the hot–cold dimension. For example, rice was seen as endowed with an innate vital force which generates strength-giving, curative powers, and there was no condition for which it was regarded as a forbidden food. Garlic was seen as good for the relief of stomach ache, ginger as relieving fatigue, and young coconuts were said to be good for general health. Conversely, some foods could present health hazards. Papaya was said to give small children worms, and prawn paste could give rise to headaches (Wilson 1981: 394–5). Food substances might also be used externally by these villagers for medicinal purposes, for example, in the form of poultices to treat headache, toothache, boils, chills, fever and dizziness. Thrush in a newborn infant was treated by placing the cut end of a young coconut, covered with powdered medicinal leaves, on the infant's stomach. By and large, these can be regarded as essentially magical treatments, although Wilson does admit that in some instances the plant substances employed may have active pharmacological properties.

In fact, these Malay villagers recognize a whole range of diseases which could be seen as having a magical or supernatural causation, and response to such ailments frequently involves food prescriptions or proscriptions. Thus 'seduan', an upper respiratory disease, was believed to be caused by an evil spirit and, if neglected, as likely to lead to serious damage. Treatment entailed the use of incantations and root medicines and the avoidance of soy sauce, groundnuts, duck, prawns and most kinds of fish. In addition, ailments which were not seen as having supernatural causes might also require the avoidance of certain foods. Thus, 'medu', a condition involving breathing difficulties and pain throughout the body, was seen as caused by constipation, and such cold foods as okra, eggplant, pumpkin and papaya were regarded as harmful for sufferers.

As well as employing self-diagnosis and self-treatment, Malays consult both traditional healers and doctors trained in modern medicine, according to the nature of the illness concerned. Western medicines are incorporated into the traditional conceptual scheme, in so far as such substances (whether in liquid or solid form) are classified as hot, and thus eating hot foods while taking them is prohibited. In fact, certain foods like eggs may become *bisa* (toxic) when taking Western medicines like pills. The flexibility and adaptability of hot–cold beliefs in Malay culture is further illustrated by the fact that novel food items, introduced as a result of the modernization of some aspects of Malay society, have been absorbed into the system. These include bread, flour, refined sugar, ice-cream, soft drinks and foreign fruits and vegetables which have been assimilated into the categories used for local produce. While Wilson suggests that traditional food prohibitions may, in certain circumstances, adversely affect the nutrient intakes of women subject to the high physiological demands of reproduction, she recognizes the extent to which these ideas form a coherent, integrated and reassuring body of belief and practice. In fact, as Manderson (1987: 330) notes, the power of such ideas resides in their ability to provide plausible and intelligible explanations for (and accessible responses to) otherwise incomprehensible processes of affliction and recovery.

Some valuable insights into the cognitive foundations of hot–cold classification systems are provided by Messer (1987). Focusing her attention on hot–cold beliefs in indigenous Mesoamerican thought, she notes the essential syncretism between European versions of the 'humoral' medical framework (introduced by the Spanish) and the deeply rooted concepts based on a hot–cold continuum found, for example, in Aztec and Mayan culture. In fact, Aztec hot–cold beliefs were not limited to such areas as food, health and medicine. Indeed, this basic duality appears to have been seen as encompassing the entire cosmos and was applied to plants, animals, minerals, stars and supernatural beings. Among the Aztecs, in food terms, dark-coloured substances, piquant flavours and sweet fruits were regarded as hot, whereas wild animals, sour fruits and thick-skinned fruits were regarded as cold. The Mitla Zapotec people (like the Aztec, indigenous to Mexico) classify foods according to digestibility. 'Hard to digest' foods are classified as hot or cold according to whether the individual regards his or her body to be hot or cold at the time of eating (Messer 1987: 341–2). Thus, care must be taken, since a hot–cold imbalance may cause illness or aggravate an existing condition.

What Messer attempts is a general description of the underlying logic of such hot–cold classifications. Taking the classification of herbs as an example, she suggests that three types of attribute may be taken into consideration by those operating hot–cold ideas. The first of these types she terms 'perceptible' attributes (those which can be seen, tasted, etc.). These perceptible attributes may be intrinsic (e.g., red colouring is often associated with hot) or extrinsic (e.g., plants which require sunny conditions may be regarded as hot). Secondly, 'functional' attributes may be referred to, again split between intrinsic and extrinsic. As an example of an intrinsic functional attribute, Messer cites the belief that certain herbs may act to 'cook' uncooked foods in the stomach, and are therefore hot. An example of an extrinsic functional attribute is the idea that a given herb is hot because it can be applied externally to treat a 'cold' headache. Finally, 'affective' attributes operate in terms of good and bad. Hot herbs may be regarded as bad if they produce an excess of hot over cold in the eater and thereby result in illness. Messer suggests that children learn these principles through a gradual process of socialization, although the vagueness and essential flexibility of the system allows for competing and sometimes flatly contradictory classifications to be arrived at by different individuals apparently operating the same classificatory criteria.

It is Messer's contention that the hot–cold duality may represent an opposition which is as primordial and as universal as the fundamental opposition between male and female. Such an opposition, being 'good to think' (Messer 1987: 344), is therefore good for classification. Hot–cold beliefs, deeply embedded in the epistemological foundations of many traditional cultures, can provide a potent conceptual framework for articulating the complex linkages between diet and health. While the linkages and mechanisms proposed by such ideas may seem eccentric or implausible according to the criteria of Western scientific, medical and nutritional discourses, they do provide their adherents with a framework of everyday understanding and practical action. Indeed, built up over many centuries and elaborated by dedicated specialists, such beliefs may evolve into highly complex systems of thought. Perhaps one of the most highly developed of these systems, in which food items can be construed as having important medicinal properties, is represented by Chinese traditional medicine (see, e.g., Read 1982).

RATIONALIZATION AND MODERN VIEWS OF DIET AND HEALTH

The process of rationalization represents a powerful driving force in modern societies, placing strong emphasis on measurement, calculation, prediction and systematic organization. The analysis of this process has been one of sociology's central and most enduring themes, a theme which has already been confronted at least twice in this book (in Chapter 2 in relation to the emergence of the modern food system and in Chapter 5 in relation to Ritzer's (1993) 'McDonald-ization' thesis). However, the principles of rational calculability have been extended beyond the spheres of food production, distribution and marketing, and have been applied to diet itself. Turner (1982: 255) draws a parallel between earlier religious asceticism and modern medical regimens, both of which seek to discipline the body by the imposition of rules, and both of which commonly use diet as a focus for such discipline. Turner points out that the development of formal rationality and its application to an ever-widening range of human activities is a process which in turn generates a broad spectrum of specialist professional groups, whose specific collective interests are closely bound up with the process itself. What is more, the rationalization of diet, and the production of rational scientific conceptions of the links between diet and health, required the creation of a new metaphor for the body. That metaphor emerged as the Cartesian concept of the body as machine, a machine whose functioning, inputs and outputs could all be subjected to precise measurements and quantification (Turner 1982: 258–9).

In order to illustrate the emergence of rational medical views of diet and health, Turner examines the career and ideas of George Cheyne, an influential Scottish physician born in 1671 or 1673 in Aberdeenshire. Having studied medicine at Edinburgh University under Archibald Pitcairne, a proponent of the application of mathematics to medicine, by the 1720s Cheyne had become a highly successful medical practitioner in London, with many individuals from England's aristocracy and political and literary elites among his patients. He also published a series of books on his medical ideas and treatments, which were translated into several European languages. In a very real sense, Cheyne's approach to the issue of the link between diet and health was directly connected to his experience of a crisis in his own health. As a result of a prodigious appetite for food and drink, Cheyne's weight rose to a grotesque 448 lb. He experienced considerable difficulty in walking and, understandably, lapsed into a state of deep depression. However, after a period of experimentation, Cheyne devised a treatment scheme for himself based upon a diet of milk and vegetables, regular exercise on horseback, strictly limited alcohol intake and regular periods of sleep. This self-imposed discipline proved highly successful, in that his weight was significantly reduced and he survived to the age of 70.

Cheyne's therapeutic system was based upon a specific and explicitly rationalistic view of the nature of the human body. This was conceptualized by Cheyne as a hydraulic machine, a complicated interlocking system made up of pumps, pipes and canals around which circulated a vital liquor. This machine could only function satisfactorily with the correct inputs of foods and liquids, and the qualities and quantities of these foods and liquids were seen as crucial for proper digestion. In turn, proper digestion and evacuation, and suitable levels of exercise, were seen as the foundations of good health, the role of medical practitioners being conceived as essentially a secondary, facilitating one. In fact, what the body machine required was the careful monitoring of its inputs and outputs, an approach which Cheyne termed 'Diaetetick Management'. In his view, threats to the smooth functioning of the body machine came from a number of sources. First among these were dietary changes in the eighteenth century which had particularly affected the more affluent sections of English society. The expansion of trade had brought numerous rich and exotic foods and wines within reach of the upper strata, and it was overindulgence in such delicacies, coupled with an inactive lifestyle, that was seen by Cheyne as the root cause of most of the illnesses which afflicted his privileged clients. Of particular concern for Cheyne was the consumption by the rich of strong wines and potent spirits, which had the lethal potential to dry up the body machine's vital juices. However, he also laid considerable emphasis on wider environmental factors. Not least of these was another of the consequences of economic success and the advance of civilization, the increasing levels of overcrowding in expanding urban areas like London. Insanitary conditions and poor air quality could create a reservoir of diseases which could threaten the most affluent as well as the most impoverished.

Given the central importance of digestion to Cheyne's views on health and illness, it is not surprising that, as part of his system of Diaetetick Management, he set out to classify foods according to their 'digestibility'. White flesh and dry, fibrous and mild-tasting foods were deemed easy to digest, whereas red flesh and

Table 6.1 Cheyne's classification of foods according
to digestibility

Easy to digest	*Less easy to digest*
Spring vegetables	Pears
Asparagus	Apples
Strawberries	Peaches
	Nectarines
Poultry	Cows
Hares	Horse
Sheep	Asses
Kids	
Rabbets (sic)	
Whiting	Salmon
Perch	Eel
Trout	Turbot
Haddock	Carp
Pullet	Duck
Turkey	Geese
Pheasant	Woodcock
	Snipe
Veal	Red deer
Lamb	Fallow deer

Source: Adapted from Turner (1982)

fatty and strong-tasting or spicy foods were deemed hard to digest. Turner (1982: 263) provides a schematic representation of Cheyne's classification based upon these principles, as is shown in Table 6.1.

Furthermore, Cheyne favoured 'natural' foods, uncomplicated by exotic preparation techniques and ingredients, which could inflame 'unnatural' appetites. Cheyne's approach led him to devise a whole series of dietary regimens, each one appropriate to a given age group and lifestyle.

Many of Cheyne's ideas may seem eccentric to the modern reader, and the classification scheme laid out in Table 6.1 has an appealing quaintness about it, appearing to have a closer affinity with traditional beliefs about food than with current dietary ideas. Yet, on the other hand, other features of Cheyne's perspectives appear strikingly familiar, from his hydraulic metaphor of the body to his insistence on the importance of 'natural', minimally processed plain foods, moderation in alcohol consumption and regular exercise. His warnings concerning the negative effects of overcrowded, urban living also strike a familiar note. In fact, his ideas are prototypically modern, emphasizing as they do the rational, instrumental use of dietary regimens to enhance health and avoid disease. There is a clear linkage between Cheyne's conception of the nutritionally disciplined, healthy body and the ideas of Elias on the internalization of restraint which we encountered in Chapter 5.

As we have seen, Cheyne's system was aimed specifically at 'a class of people that was professional, sedentary, urban and engaged in mental activity' (Turner 1982: 265). This was essentially a discipline for the elite, overindulged body, in many ways irrelevant to the demands imposed upon the labouring body, a body all too often on the verge of malnutrition, or even starvation, in the eighteenth century. However, by the late nineteenth and early twentieth century this rational gaze was to be turned upon the problem of managing and modifying the diets of the lower strata of society. Turner's analysis of the grounds for this shift in focus rests upon the argument that a number of major issues came together to concentrate the concerns of the elite upon the health and dietary standards of the masses. Such issues included the fear that the insanitary and overcrowded conditions of the working class could always pose an indirect threat to the middle and upper classes through the spread of contagious diseases, and there was also an unwillingness to bear the burden of taxation involved in maintaining an extensive system of relief for the destitute and malnourished. But, underlying such concerns, Turner identifies deeper anxieties among the elite concerning the state of the working classes. Not only could an undisciplined work-force be seen as a threat to the stability of a civilized capitalist state, but also unhealthy and undernourished working classes could present a threat to society's very continuity and long-term survival. Thus, Turner argues that the findings of Rowntree's influential study of urban poverty (Rowntree 1901), pointing out the significant undernourishment of the bulk of the industrial population who carried out the heaviest manual labour, are symptomatic of a rising awareness that the nutritional status of the working classes is, in some senses, the responsibility of the state.

In fact, from the latter part of the nineteenth century onwards, the government of the United Kingdom was increasingly to involve itself in attempts to monitor, regulate and improve the dietary standards of the mass of the population. This increasingly interventionist stance on the part of the state went hand in hand with the development of an ever more sophisticated and rationalistic intellectual apparatus whose theories and methods could be applied to measuring the extent of these problems and devising suitable responses and solutions. Thus, scientific and statistical disciplines like demography, dietetics and biology could be harnessed to the attempt to apply a form of social engineering to the British diet (Turner 1982: 267).

Yet it is, perhaps, a tragic irony that the most powerful single impetus which drove the British government towards ever more ambitious attempts to improve the population's health by improving its dietary standards was in response to the demands of modern mass warfare. In fact, at least one historian has suggested that the disclosures of social reformers like Rowntree concerning the poor state of nutrition of lower sections of the working classes initially had relatively little impact on the thinking of those in power (Burnett 1989: 243). The piece of information which appears to have attracted the attention of the government was a finding by the Director General of the Army Medical Service during the

Boer War in which the United Kingdom was engaged towards the end of the nineteenth century. No less than 38 per cent of the men who volunteered for military service were rejected on grounds of ill health, including heart disease, defective vision, defective hearing and decayed teeth (Burnett 1989: 243). The concern generated by this finding caused the government to set up the Inter-departmental Committee on Physical Deterioration and, in 1906, to pass an Act of Parliament providing free school meals for deprived children. The govern-ment also began to provide grants for infant welfare centres, set up to advise mothers on child-rearing practices. However, it was to be the food crises created by the First World War which were to push the state gradually towards a more interventionist stance. Initially, the government was reluctant to intervene in food markets, but by 1916 food supplies had been severely disrupted by the German submarine campaign. In 1916 the Ministry of Food was established, and a Committee of the Royal Society was asked to draw up minimum food requirements for the population. Measures introduced included, in 1917, a subsidy for bread and the fixing of milk prices. Early in 1918, rationing for key foodstuffs like meat and butter was introduced. Burnett, in assessing the success of the government's food measures, points out that Britain was far better fed than her enemies, with average intakes remaining over 3,300 kilocalories per day (Burnett 1989: 249). However, that there remained an enormous legacy of the consequences of earlier poor nutritional standards in Britain is indicated by the fact that of 2,500,000 men medically examined in 1917–18 as a prelude to conscription, 41 per cent were graded as C3 and unfit for military service (Burnett: 1989: 254). Such findings meant that national nutritional and health standards, and the state's responsibility for these, were becoming an increasingly important political issue in the United Kingdom (Tannahill 1988: 334).

The interwar years saw a general rise in dietary standards in Britain, although on the basis of 1933 data it has been estimated that some 30 per cent of the population were still technically 'undernourished', according to standards laid down by the British Medical Association for a basic minimum diet devoid of obvious deficiencies (Burnett 1989: 271). On the basis of data gathered in 1936–7 it was calculated that over 17 per cent of the population, nearly eight million people, were spending less on food than the minimum necessary total set by the BMA. However, state interest in such results was rising, and an increasing amount of work on nutritional standards and related health issues was being carried out by such agencies as the Medical Research Council, the Food Investigation Board and local Medical Officers of Health. It is Burnett's conten-tion that by 1939 the government had begun to acknowledge that nutritional policy would have to form an integral part of any system of health services, and that professional dieticians, armed with ever more sophisticated nutritional knowledge, were pressing for the state to take on an enhanced role in this area.

It was, however, the outbreak of the Second World War which pushed the British government into far-reaching intervention. Food price controls and a detailed system of food rationing were rapidly introduced and effectively im-

CHANGING CONCEPTIONS OF DIET AND HEALTH

plemented in response to the threats to Britain's food supply posed by the hostilities, threats all the more serious given the United Kingdom's continued reliance on food imports. Improving levels of knowledge concerning nutritional needs allowed rationing to be placed on a much more precise scientific basis. In addition, the nutritionist, Professor J. C. Drummond, in his role as Chief Scientific Adviser to the Ministry of Food, was able to use his position of power and influence to see that food controls were used to raise overall dietary standards, especially those of the poorest sections of the population (Burnett 1989: 290). Schemes were introduced to provide additional proteins, vitamins and minerals to vulnerable groups like pre-school children and pregnant and nursing mothers. On the other hand, for the general population, animal proteins and fats, for example, were strictly rationed, whereas carbohydrate-rich foods like bread and potatoes were freely available at controlled prices. Government measures, including the provision of communal eating facilities in factory and school canteens, did eventually produce actual improvements in nutritional standards in Britain over the war period. Thus, Burnett notes that by 1944, the pre-war average intake of 3,000 kilocalories per head per day had risen to 3,010 and total protein intake had risen by 6 per cent above its pre-war level. What is more, there were also improvements in the intake of minerals like calcium and iron and also of riboflavin, vitamin B and vitamin C. Overall, these improvements appear to have played a significant role in a fall in infant mortality and a rise in the birth rate in Britain over the war years. In stark contrast, over the same period Germany saw a decline in the birth rate and a rise in infant mortality.

Burnett's analysis demonstrates just how successful was the British government's attempt to regulate the food system and to protect the nutritional welfare of the population, despite the demands placed upon the state by the conduct of warfare on a global scale. While much of the bureaucratic apparatus of regulation was eventually to be dismantled (although it was some years after the end of the Second World War that the last food rationing measures were abolished), the ideological apparatus of intervention, once created, proved to be more enduring. However, in the intervening decades, the logic of intervention has undergone a number of very significant changes. For example, once direct state control could no longer be justified on the grounds of national emergency, more subtle forms of indirect intervention gradually came into play. In the post-war period an increasing emphasis has been placed upon the individual's responsibility to protect his or her own health through adopting the eating patterns and dietary choices congruent with current scientific orthodoxies concerning the links between diet and health. Hence, regulation and rationing have, in the longer term, been replaced by education and exhortation. What is more, dietary threats to health have been fundamentally reconceptualized. Food deprivation and serious nutritional deficiencies, historically two of the most widespread threats to human well-being, have been banished to the margins of public concern in most modern, developed societies. Currently, concern has become focused squarely upon the nutritional problems associated with affluence and over indulgence.

By 1983 professional and official consensus concerning the most pressing issues relating to diet and health had developed to a sufficient degree to permit the publication of specific dietary targets for the UK population. In that year the National Advisory Committee on Nutrition Education (NACNE) under the aegis of the Health Education Council, put forward proposals for a set of explicit nutritional guidelines. The Committee was particularly concerned with the effects on health, not only of actual obesity, but also of relatively mild levels of overweight, especially in relation to such ailments as coronary heart disease, high blood pressure, diabetes mellitus and gall bladder disease. Lack of exercise was cited as a contributory factor to the diseases associated with being over-weight, and recommendations concerning slimming diets and the control of food intake were also made (National Advisory Committee on Nutrition Education 1983: 10–14). The targets set by the Committee were detailed and explicitly quantified. They included recommended reductions in fat intake, in saturated fatty acid intake, in sucrose intake, in salt intake and in alcohol consumption, plus a rise in the intake of dietary fibre (see Figure 6.1).

---

i.   Fat intake should be reduced to an average 30% of total energy intake.

ii.   Saturated fatty acid intake should be reduced to an average 10% of total energy intake.

iii.   Average sucrose intakes should be reduced to 20 kg per head per year.

iv.   Salt intake should fall on average by 3g per head per day.

v.   Alcohol intake should decline to 4% of the total energy intake.

vi.   Protein intake should not be altered, but a higher proportion of vegetable proteins is appropriate.

vii.   Fibre intake should increase on average from 20g per head per day to 30g per head per day.

Figure 6.1 Selected long-term dietary aims for the UK population proposed by the National Commitee on Nutrition Education (NACNE)
Source: Adapted from National Advisoty Committee on Nutrition Education (1983)

The Committee went on to discuss a whole series of measures that would be involved in achieving such targets. These included not only education-based attempts to encourage individuals to modify their own diet, but also the selective breeding of leaner food animals, the reduction of fat content in meat products and the labelling of food products with energy, sugar and fat content.

Some eight years later, an independent, multidisciplinary committee noted that obesity in Britain was, in fact, increasing (Jacobson, Smith and Whitehead 1991: 44). The report reiterated the kinds of dietary targets that had been set by the Committee on Medical Aspects of Food Policy (COMA) which, in turn, were closely related to those proposed by NACNE (Jacobson, Smith and Whitehead 1991: 249). COMA's advice at that stage included a reduction of the amount of energy from total fats to 35 per cent or less of energy intake, reductions in sugar and salt consumption, and the replacement of fatty and sugary foods with cereals and starchy foods. The need to increase levels of exercise was also stressed, particularly in relation to what was seen as the role of exercise in the prevention of coronary heart disease and the maintenance of general health. *The Health of the Nation* white paper also recommended the setting up of the Nutrition Task Force, and this recommendation was carried out in 1992. Two years later the Nutrition Task Force itself published a detailed action plan to achieve the targets which had been set out (Department of Health 1994). The components of this action plan included proposals for schematic dietary models for conveying information to the public (e.g., in the form of plates or pyramids), liaison with the advertising industry in the promotion of approved dietary patterns, and extending the role of the educational system in disseminating official conceptions of healthy diets. The action plan also included proposals to recruit the support of the catering industry in achieving nutritional targets (e.g., hospital and school caterers, restaurants and fast food outlets). Indeed, the production, manufacturing and retailing sectors of the food industry were also to be drawn into the process, particularly in terms of undertaking an industry-wide 'fat audit' to examine the possibilities for reducing fat content across the whole product range. This whole strategy, it was suggested, should be supported by enhanced training for health professionals, nutritionists and dieticians, and by improved research into the relationship between nutritional factors and clinical outcomes.

This ambitious and far-reaching programme of nutritional intervention and persuasion provides a graphic demonstration of the extent to which the state has taken on a central role in shaping national dietary patterns with a view to improving overall health standards. However, what is arguably the most distinctive aspect of this process is the striking family resemblance between eighteenth-century conceptions of diet and health and the medically and scientifically informed targets and guidelines which form the basis of current thinking. The dietary prescriptions and proscriptions are decidedly similar, as are the emphases on the deleterious effects of excessive weight and low levels of physical exercise. However, as we have seen, Cheyne's criticisms, admonitions and treatments were aimed at high-status and relatively sedentary elite groups, and in his day had little relevance to the broader population. The emergence of the modern food system, and fundamental changes in work organization and activity levels, have been construed as requiring the degree of dietary restraint and control on the part of the whole population that was formerly seen as appropriate only to the privileged and overindulgent few. The mantle of George Cheyne, successful nutritional and medical moral entrepreneur, has been assumed by an expanding army of professionals, bureaucrats and politicians, who increasingly claim ownership of what can be regarded as nutritional wisdom and acceptable dietary practice. However, whereas Cheyne was a physician, in direct contact with his patients and tailoring his therapeutic recommendations to what he perceived to be their specific needs, the current role of the state is an essentially impersonal one. Quantified nutritional objectives have been established for the entire population, yet the translation of such objectives into dietary choices and practices at the individual level remains problematic. For example, while it may make sense to recommend that no more than 35 per cent of energy should be derived from fats as a long-term aim for the population as a whole, such a recommendation is of little relevance to the day-to-day decisions of the individual consumer, who is not equipped to monitor food intake in this quantified fashion. There are clearly limits to the application of rational, systematic conceptualization of the links between diet and health to the mundane routines of everyday life.

Further dimensions are added to our understanding of the modern rationalization of diet by Levenstein's account of the evolution of nutritional theory and nutritional policy in the USA. In the last two decades of the nineteenth century, for example, an ambitious attempt was made to rationalize the eating patterns of the poor in order to improve their nutritional standards while actually reducing the amount spent on food. A Boston businessman, Edward Atkinson, taking up recent developments in scientific knowledge concerning the nature of human nutritional requirements propounded by the chemist Wilbur Atwater, put forward the argument that those on low incomes could achieve greater 'nutritional efficiency' by avoiding the consumption of expensive food items selected merely on the basis of taste or prestige. Instead, he argued, they should consume cheaper items (e.g., less expensive cuts of meat) which, though less prestigious, nevertheless provided an equivalent input of nutrients for the body (Levenstein 1988: 45–8). In co-operation with a nutritionist and a chemist (both women) Atkinson was instrumental in setting up public kitchens to demonstrate to the working classes the benefits of selecting foods on the grounds of nutrient content and value for money, and of preparing these foods in a fuel-saving, slow-cooking oven of his own invention. However, despite some initial success in Boston and New York, the quaintly named 'New England Kitchen' culinary regime had little impact on the eating patterns of the American working classes, which was probably just as well, given its heavy emphasis on the consumption of animal fat, and its serious vitamin deficiencies, the significance of which was not understood at the time (Levenstein 1988: 57–8).

In fact, the proponents of the New England Kitchen concept were soon to shift their attention towards the middle and upper classes, on the assumption that good nutritional practices, once entrenched in the upper reaches of society, would eventually 'trickle down' to the lower orders. At the same time, 'home economics' and 'domestic science' were undergoing a process of professionalization, involving their inclusion in programmes at the University of Wisconsin in 1895 and subsequently at the University of Illinois. What is more, the teaching of these subjects in schools shifted away from an exclusive emphasis on cooking skills towards the physiology and chemistry of food and eating. Thus, by the early twentieth century large numbers of young American women who had graduated from the public school system had absorbed at the least the rudiments of the rational scientific view of human nutrition (Levenstein 1988: 79–80). It is Levenstein's contention that American middle-class women were able to use these ideas to rationalize and simplify domestic cuisine in order to reduce the burden of food-related work in a situation in which domestic servants were becoming increasingly difficult to acquire and retain.

As in Britain, but to a lesser extent, the First World War acted as a catalyst which stimulated government intervention in the food system of the United States. Food prices, already on an upward trend, rose sharply in 1916, partly due to the demands of the Allies actually involved in the war, and there were foot riots in some eastern cities (Levenstein 1988: 109). With America's entry into the war imminent, the Food Administration was set up (headed by Herbert Hoover). Its task was to seek to regulate the food supply and to encourage Americans to reduce food wastage and to cut down on their consumption of meat, white wheat flour, sugar and butter, substituting more readily available items like beans, pulses, cornmeal, oats, lard and vegetable oil. Levenstein notes the similarity between these ideas of substitution and those of the nutritionists who had already sought to rationalize the diets of the poor. The Food Administration harnessed the ideas of the home economists and embraced the scientific approach to nutrition as a means of putting the American diet on a war footing. While it seems clear that these exhortations had little effect on the mass of the American population (for example, beef consumption actually rose in 1917 to above pre-war levels) the more affluent classes did appear to have reduced their food consumption. What is more, in the interests of sound nutrition and the avoidance of waste, the War Department, in 1916, issued a new manual for army cooks based upon the new nutritional principles, and dieticians were recruited to oversee food provision in army hospitals. In this way, Levenstein argues, through the experience of military service, large numbers of American men were exposed to rationalized and simplified diets (Levenstein 1988: 145–6).

However, in the decades after the First World War, discoveries in the new science of nutrition led to an increasing emphasis on the role of vitamins and minerals in the diet. These innovations in nutritional knowledge were enthusiastically taken up by large food processing firms eager to promote their products using the latest scientific ideas, aiming at a public ever more susceptible to rationalized conceptions of food quality and suitability (Levenstein 1988: 152–3). The impact of the Second World War also appears to have been a significant one. Levenstein points out that dieticians played an even greater part in the rationalization of the feeding of the armed forces than in the First World War. The Institute of Medicine's Food and Nutrition Board created generous dietary standards for the population, and food shortages, while never as severe as had been expected, were managed through direct state intervention in the form of rationing and price controls. The standards set down by the Food and Nutrition

Board were first established in 1941, and took the form of Recommended Dietary Allowances (RDAs), these being defined as the level of intake of essential nutrients adequate to meet the nutritional needs of healthy individuals, as currently understood. The first edition of these standards was published in 1943, and by 1989 the publication had reached its tenth edition, these regular revisions reflecting the constant elaboration and extension of scientific nutritional knowledge in the intervening decades. Drawing upon a truly impressive range of scientific research, the tenth edition lays down detailed, updated recommendations concerning energy intake, protein allowances, and the intake of such vitamins as K, C, B_6 and B_{12}. It also covers changes in the RDAs for such minerals as calcium, magnesium, iron, zinc and selenium, and changes in scientific views on estimated safe and adequate intakes of such substances as copper, manganese and molybdenum. The central role played by the RDA concept in the scientific and medical rationalization of nutritional ideas and practices is demonstrated by an extract from the tenth edition itself:

> Over the years, RDAs have become widely known and applied. They are typically used for planning and procuring food supplies for population subgroups, for interpreting food consumption records of individuals and populations, for establishing standards for food assistance programs, for evaluating the adequacy of food supplies in meeting national nutritional needs, for designing nutrition education programs, and for developing new products in industry.
>
> (National Research Council 1989: 8)

In addition to the RDAs, the Food and Nutrition Board has also set out a series of dietary guidelines or targets for the American population. These are broadly comparable to those which have been laid down for the population of the UK and reflect similar scientific and medical views concerning the links between diet and health, and the prevention of specific illnesses. These targets (expressed in terms of individual diets) include the reduction of total fat intake to 30 per cent or less of total calories consumed, the daily consumption of five or more servings of fruit and vegetables, the moderation of protein intake levels, the balancing of food intake with physical activity level, the limiting of sodium intake and the maintenance of adequate calcium consumption (see Figure 6.2 and compare Figure 6.1).

As well as setting these targets, the Food and Nutrition Board provides a highly detailed set of recommendations about how they might be attained in everyday settings by real individuals making real food choices. The advice provided ranges from the selection of low-fat meat to the use of lemon juice and salt-free seasonings to reduce sodium consumption (Thomas 1991: 84–109).

As has been suggested earlier in this chapter, there can be no doubt that the rationalization of conceptions of diet and health has been associated with the professionalization of nutritional science and dietetics. Riska (1993), in outlining

i.	Reduce total fat intake to 30% or less of calories. Reduce saturated fatty acid intake to less than 10% of calories and the intake of cholesterol to less than 300 mg daily.
ii.	Eat five or more daily servings of a combination of vegetables and fruits. Also, more daily servings of a combination of breads, cereals and legumes. Increase carbohydrate intake to more than 55% of total energy.
iii.	Maintain protein intake at moderate levels.
iv.	Balance food intake and physical activity to maintain appropriate body weight.
v.	Limit alcohol consumption to the equivalent of less than one ounce of pure alcohol per day.
vi.	Maintain adequate calcium intake.
vii.	Avoid taking dietary supplements in excess of the RDAs in any one day.
viii.	Maintain an optimal intake of fluoride.

Figure 6.2   Dietary guidelines for North Americans from age 2
Source: Adapted from Thomas (1991)

this process of professionalization in the USA, shows how women largely succeeded in capturing this area for their own. She points out the central role played by women in the health reform movement in the latter part of the nineteenth century, with its strong emphasis on hygiene and a nutritious diet. At the same time, middle-class women in America were increasingly infiltrating the sciences and the professions, although they were mainly channelled into 'female' areas like home economics and domestic science, and women physicians were concerned primarily with the care of women and children. This form of professional separatism, Riska argues, led to the development of separate institutions, and the American Dietetic Association founded in 1917 was dominated by women. However, from the Second World War onwards, nutritional science as an area of study has been largely male dominated (see e.g., Copping 1985). On the other hand, women have retained their dominance in the dietetics profession, which has been incorporated into the health care system. The professionalization of dietetics was enhanced when in 1969 the American Dietetic Association instituted the credential 'registered dietician', and this licence is currently held by approximately 60,000 practitioners (Riska 1993: 175). The processes of social closure and collective upward mobility promoted by professionalization have also been enhanced by a drive towards increased specialization within dietetics itself. However, the profession as a whole remains one of relatively low status and remuneration, largely subordinate within the health care system to a medical establishment which is still male-dominated. Indeed, Riska highlights a fundamental dilemma for dieticians. In stressing the medical importance of diet, that is, in 'medicalizing' food choice and nutritional practice, dieticians reinforce their own claims to professional status. At the same time, however, this strategy seems to guarantee continuing subordination to the medical profession, which jealously guards its exclusive title to medical diagnosis and treatment.

In this section we have seen how the rationalization, and indeed the medicalization, of diet was initially a process aimed at a relatively inactive and 'overfed' elite. Eventually, however, the political and social establishment in both Britain and America chose to concern itself more and more with the nutritional standards of the poor and the underprivileged. In both countries, reformers, nutritional moral entrepreneurs and the state itself, employing the increasingly sophisticated knowledge made available by a rapidly developing science of nutrition, sought to lay down adequate nutritional standards and to intervene in the dietary affairs of groups perceived as disadvantaged and nutritionally vulnerable. Such intervention took many forms, from attempts at exhortation and education to rationing, subsidies and the provision of free foods and supplements. In recent decades, a distinct shift of emphasis has become obvious, as concern has switched away from a preoccupation with nutritional deficiencies to a preoccupation with the implications of the overconsumption of certain nutrients and food items. Thus, contemporary official guidelines and targets are not so much aimed at bringing standards up to specified levels as at encouraging the reduction of the intake of specific nutrients to below what are seen as desirable upper limits. Thus, in a sense, the controls on food intake that characterized George Cheyne's recipes for the dietary chastening of the privileged have been generalized for whole populations, for whom overindulgence rather than deprivation is seen as the main problem.

Of course, the whole process of rationalization has been facilitated by key professions, not only medical practitioners and physicians, but also scientists, nutritionists and dieticians. In a sociological sense, it is perhaps not surprising that dietetics as an occupation has developed as an essentially feminine profession, which can be seen as an extension of customary assumptions about women's domestic duties, obligations and competences into the public domain.

CONTEMPORARY COMMON-SENSE IDEAS AND ALTERNATIVE IDEOLOGIES

There can be little doubt that rationalized and medicalized models of the links between diet and health have come to exert enormous influence over public perceptions. However, although public awareness of official dietary guidelines is increasing, such awareness is sometimes confused and lacking in clarity, for example, in relation to fat, a group of nutrients which has certainly figured particularly prominently in current nutritional messages (Thomas 1991: 48–9). Indeed, guidelines and targets expressed in scientific and quantitative terms may be extremely difficult for members of the public to interpret, and even more difficult to translate into informed choices and everyday decisions at the supermarket or in the kitchen. In effect, rationalized views of diet may lack some of the intuitive comprehensibility of more traditional ideas, and thus it is hardly

142

surprising that common-sense notions survive and continue to shape nutritional ideologies and practices in modern Western societies. These notions come in many guises and range from claims that excessive sugar consumption causes diabetes, that red meat causes aggressiveness and that eating fried food causes acne, to beliefs in the medicinal properties of substances like honey and garlic. Some of these ideas do appear to find some support from current medical and scientific knowledge, whereas others are inconsistent with, or actually contradict, orthodox scientific views (Rinzler 1991). Happily, there exist several sociological studies which can provide us with direct insights into the contents and logic of such common-sense ideas and their relationship in everyday life to more rationalized and systematic forms of knowledge.

Inevitably, there is likely to be a good deal of variation from individual to individual and from household to household in exposure to and reliance upon rationalized conceptions of diet as opposed to 'folk' or lay conceptions. Pill (1983) set out to examine working-class mothers' views on food and health by studying a sample of forty-one women from South Wales, all aged between 30 and 35, living with their husband and at least one primary-school-age child. In fact, Pill uncovered a clear distinction between what she termed the 'lifestyle' group and the 'fatalist' group. The former tended to see illness as caused by environmental and lifestyle factors. Thus, by implication, health and resistance to disease could be enhanced by making the correct lifestyle choices. On the other hand, the fatalists tended to see illness as caused by factors over which the individual had little or no control, and resistance to disease as an unchangeable personal characteristic, determined largely by heredity. Not surprisingly, these two groups held sharply contrasting views on the relationship between diet and health. Members of the lifestyle group were much more likely to mention foods that they avoided for health reasons (e.g., foods with a high sugar content) and foods they deliberately selected for health reasons (e.g., wholemeal bread). These mothers also appeared to be attempting to plan and control their family's diet explicitly in order to improve its members resistance to disease. In contrast, the fatalist mothers were much less likely to mention specific health-oriented avoidances and selections. While both groups emphasized the value of fresh food, the fatalists stressed taste as the main advantage whereas the lifestyle mothers tended to mention the importance of vitamin content and the perceived health dangers of processed foods. However, the defining characteristic of the fatalist mothers' view on food and health was the emphasis they placed upon the traditional 'cooked dinner' as the epitome of good food and the source of nutritional well-being. The customary combination of roast meat, gravy, potatoes and vegetables clearly retained a powerful symbolic significance for this group of respondents (Pill 1983: 122–4).

It is a plausible hypothesis that adherence to the concept of the 'cooked dinner' as a basis for good health is related to respondents' age. It would seem likely that older respondents would be more attached to long-established common-sense views of diet and health than would their younger counterparts.

143

Some supporting evidence for this contention is to be found in a study of fifty-eight three-generation families carried out in a Scottish city (Blaxter and Paterson 1983). Amongst the two generations of working-class women studied, the authors did indeed uncover a powerfully nostalgic attachment on the part of the older women to the 'good' food of the past. For them 'goodness' was equated with simple and natural foods, prepared in basic, uncomplicated ways (boiling or baking, for example). Meat and vegetables were seen as essentials, and slow cooking (boiling meat and vegetables together) was seen as a process which could, in effect, distil the very essence of goodness (Blaxter and Paterson 1983: 97). The very opposite of 'good' food was food which has been manufactured or processed, food which replaced 'proper' meals: snacks, sweets and biscuits. Indeed, almost any food item, except fruit, eaten outside the context of the proper meal, was classed as 'rubbish' in health terms. In contrast, the younger generation of women was actually less likely than the older to mention food when asked, for example, about how children's health could be protected. Fewer mentioned the proper meal as the basis of healthy eating, and those who did were noticeably less enthusiastic than their elders.

The importance of such symbolic considerations in common-sense conceptions of diet and health is demonstrated even more clearly by a study which included an analysis of French mothers' views concerning children's health and nutritional needs (Fischler 1986). The study was based upon semi-structured interviews with a sample of 161 mothers with children aged from 4 to 14, drawn from six socioeconomic categories and various regions of France. Fischler concludes that, for these mothers, the feeding of children is, in fact, a highly 'medicalized' issue. In the course of interviews, respondents were at pains to exhibit their knowledge of the technical terminology of nutritional science and, indeed, a rudimentary familiarity with the basics of rationalized concepts of health and nutrition was perceived by these interviewees as an indispensable requirement for the responsible and competent mother (Fischler 1986: 948). However, Fischler, despite the fact that he finds the medicalization of lay discourses on diet and health unsurprising, goes on to pose a crucial question: 'Just what do these mothers know about the science of nutrition, and just what are the contents of their own ideas?' In fact, what Fischler uncovers is a series of themes, but these are sometimes not quite what they seem. For example, the desire to limit children's sugar intake appeared to be as much about preventing the child from subverting the parent's dietary authority by 'nibbling', as about preventing tooth decay. Starches were seen by many as implicated in obesity (Fischler 1986: 953) and therefore to be limited in children's diets, and fats invoked a good deal of disapproval, but for reasons little connected with nutritional science.

Yet, the most striking aspect of these mothers' views on children's nutritional needs is the concept that was mentioned more frequently than any other: the notion of 'balance'. The idea of a balanced diet was clearly gleaned from professional discourses on nutrition, but many of the respondents' nutritional

144

ideas showed significant discrepancies in relation to current medical views. As suggested above, starch was given largely negative connotations (a contradiction of contemporary medical evaluations) and ideas relating to fat and fat intake did not necessarily coincide with the current medical orthodoxy. In fact, Fischler claims, the concept of dietary balance, although often discussed by respondents in nutritional terms, is a pre-scientific as well as a scientific concept. The idea of achieving an 'equilibrium' in terms of food intake is a feature of many forms of traditional medicine, and has an ancient pedigree. What is more, balance is an open-ended, self-justifying concept, and can mean quite different things to different respondents. In common-sense thought, it goes beyond merely techni-cal considerations. As Fischler puts it:

> However, for the greater number of respondents, a true dietetic balance seemed to result from equilibria of another nature, i.e., as it were, of a moral order. Balance, in more than one way, could indeed be viewed as an almost ethical requirement. What must be balanced, the interviewees believed, was pleasure and health, gratification and duty, appetite and reason.
>
> (Fischler 1986: 961)

Thus, the need for balance in contemporary common-sense thought is seen as deeply rooted in traditional ideas and as expressing the fusion of what Fischler sees as 'modern' and 'archaic' symbolic demands. Evidence for the universal appeal of this concept of balance is provided by a study carried out in a context very different from that discussed by Fischler. In the course of a long-term analysis of African-American folk beliefs concerning health and illness, Snow (1993) notes a recurring theme of balance and moderation in food intake as a means of preventing ill health. Snow's respondents also laid stress on the idea that not only could overindulgence and eating the 'wrong' foods induce illness, but that even 'good' foods could be hazardous if eaten in the 'wrong' context. For example, foods suitable for fit adults might be too 'strong' for children, invalids and the elderly. What is more, good foods might pose a threat to health if eaten in the wrong combinations. The author came across respondents living in Michigan who reiterated traditional beliefs from the South, such as the idea that eating fish and drinking milk at the same meal is dangerous, and that one should never consume whisky and watermelon together for fear of a potentially fatal toxic reaction (Snow 1993: 78). What is more, there is also evidence for the survival of beliefs concerning sorcery and witchcraft in relation to food, with one respondent describing the way in which magically doctored food could pose a very real hazard to the intended victim (Snow 1993: 79). However, certainly the central theme running through these beliefs is the idea that diet influences health through the effects that it has on the blood. The basis of good health is seen as 'good blood' (Snow 1993: 95–113). A balanced food intake is viewed as crucial, in that certain foods are seen as having the effect of changing the actual composition of the blood, making it too 'thick', too 'thin' or too 'acid'. Thus, it is vital for the individual always to be aware that one's dietary choices will have a direct impact upon the blood and hence upon one's state of health.

Folk beliefs of this kind can often form a backdrop to the mundane routines of everyday life and act as a set of taken-for-granted assumptions about the relationship between food intake and bodily well-being. As such, they may require deliberate probing by the social scientist to bring them to light and to render them intelligible. On the other hand, lay or non-medical perspectives on the links between diet and health can also develop into much more elaborate and explicit conceptualizations, which are not simply the vestiges of a folk tradition but which enter into the public domain and attract public attention in their own right. Perhaps the best example of such conceptualizations are the ideas behind what are widely known as 'health foods'. From the point of view of the sociologist, one of the problems involved in explaining such ideas is their very diversity. However, a study by Kandel and Pelto (1980) of what they term the 'health food movement' in the USA provides a clear and convincing analysis of the underlying features which underpin the surface variations in the contents of these beliefs. Kandel and Pelto carried out their study in the Boston area and at a rural university centre, using a battery of techniques including survey methods, 24-hour recall diet histories and participant observation.

On the basis of their results, the authors conclude that the beliefs and practices they studied had two significant aspects. The first of these is what they term 'social revitalization', a process through which a cult or movement provides its followers with the means radically to restructure their cultural affiliations and ideological postures in order to lead a more satisfying way of life. The ideologies of these revitalization cults may include metaphysical as well as dietary tenets (Kandel and Pelto 1980: 337). Secondly, these beliefs may constitute what the authors call an 'alternative health maintenance system', a system which is seen by its adherents as a viable alternative to modern medicine, which may be characterized as fragmented and unable to adopt a holistic approach to the individual, and preoccupied with the treatment of disease rather than its prevention. The alternative view of health maintenance sees food choice as one of the most direct and practical ways an individual can influence his or her health standing. In fact, the authors identify three recurring themes which run through the dietary ideologies of these alternative systems. The *vitamin motif* often uses a terminology similar to that employed in the technical discourses of nutritionists, but participants may believe certain nutrients are required in very large amounts (e.g. massive supplementary doses of certain vitamins or minerals daily). The *organic motif* places a high value on what are seen as the health-giving properties of 'organic' or 'natural' foods, which have been subjected to a minimum of human interference and processing. Stress is laid upon what are perceived as the harmful effects ascribed to 'synthetic' foods, whose production may involve, for example, artificial fertilizers, additives, colourings and preservatives. Finally, the *mystical motif* represents food selection according to the symbolic rather than the nutritional properties of foods. For example, 'life

146

energy' may be seen as inherent in raw vegetable foods, or foods may be selected explicitly to achieve a mystical balance, as in the balancing of positive and negative forces (*yin* and *yang*) in the macrobiotic dietary system.

The authors go on to describe the complex social networks which make up the broad health food movement, with their different cults and their different levels of participation, including the largely independent followers, the peripheral social members and the committed full 'joiners' (Kandel and Pelto 1980: 339). In addition to these fluid categories of membership, there are many styles of leadership and many channels of communication (ranging from books, articles and television to face-to-face channels like lecture tours and word of mouth spread through friendship networks, health food outlets, etc.).

The clear implication of the arguments put forward by Kandel and Pelto is that the potent symbolism inherent in the very idea of health foods represents a challenge to more orthodox modes of conceptualizing human health, and, indeed, the relationship between the 'cultural' and the 'natural'. This notion is taken up and developed by Atkinson (1980), who points out that health food use often takes place in the context of broader 'alternative' and unorthodox movements and ideologies (particularly alternative views of science and medicine). In the health sphere, such ideologies may include acupuncture, herbalism, faith healing, popularized forms of psychotherapy, and so on. These forms of belief frequently depend upon challenges to conventional divisions like mind/body and human/non human. A crucial feature of such thinking is the ubiquitous emphasis on 'naturalness' also noted by Kandel and Pelto. Modern life is seen as antithetical to 'balance', and modern foods are seen as overprocessed, contaminated and nutrient-deficient. In contrast, health foods offer naturalness, and explicitly appeal to tradition and folk wisdom. The emphasis laid upon avoiding foods which have undergone elaborate transformations and manufacturing represents a desire to benefit from the perceived virtues of 'pure' food. By implication, pure and natural foods offer a counterbalance to what are seen as the destructive, stressful and unhealthy features of modern lifestyles. Atkinson argues quite explicitly that such ideas are closely related to pre-scientific modes of thought, and summarizes the symbolic significance of health foods in the following terms:

> They convey the message that ills are created by the particular characteristics of modern living, specifically by virtue of a fracture between the realms of Nature and Culture. Hence health foods provide a concrete resolution of this separation. Therein lies their symbolic power.
>
> (Atkinson 1980: 87)

However, despite the fact that health foods promise benefits by putting the consumer back into contact with a more 'natural' way of life, there can be a subtle irony at work here. For example, in an earlier paper Atkinson provides a fascinating account of the way in which certain features of the folk medicine of rural Vermont were taken up and propounded in the 1960s by a medical practitioner, D. C. Jarvis (Atkinson 1979). Jarvis was concerned to promote the alleged health-giving properties of a traditional blend of honey and vinegar. Despite a negative reaction in several medical journals and an investigation by the Food and Drugs Administration, both Jarvis's books, and the commercial version of this preparation (under the brand name 'Honegar'), sold well. In effect, Atkinson demonstrates how folk beliefs can be rediscovered and packaged for sale to a public eager to benefit from customary wisdom. What is more, commercial appropriation of concepts of 'naturalness' and 'tradition' in relation to foodstuffs, and their health implications, can take place on a large scale. Thus, health foods themselves are increasingly mass-produced while still being marketed on the basis of an appeal to naturalness. What is more, in the marketing of a much broader range of foods (and, particularly in the UK, beverages like beer) manufacturers and retailers increasingly use the rhetoric of tradition and of rural life to enhance the appeal of their merchandise (Atkinson 1983: 15–16). Attached to food products, such terms as 'farmhouse', 'granary', old-fashioned', 'dairy', 'heritage', 'natural' and 'traditional', all serve to evoke a connection with what is seen as an older and less synthetic way of life. Yet, the irony is that elements of common-sense beliefs concerning food and health have been taken over and recycled in the pursuit of profitability by a highly rationalized and industrialized commercial food production and distribution system.

In fact, Belasco (1993) makes the bold claim that, from the 1960s onwards in the USA, the health food movement, as a form of radical consumerism, represented a kind of 'counter-cuisine'. He sees the challenge that it presented to the orthodox food system, dominated by the great food producing, processing and retailing corporations, as central to the broader challenge mounted by the 'counter-culture' to some of American society's most basic assumptions and institutions. Yet, what had begun as a challenge to the commercial food system turned out to be a golden marketing opportunity. Through a process of 'nutrification' (Belasco 1993: 218) food manufacturers could add back the nutrients lost through processing and charge a premium for the new product. Yet, despite this process of incorporation and attempts by the food industry to contradict the claims of the 'counter-cuisine', Belasco contends that it has had a significant impact on American attitudes to food and health.

OVERVIEW

As we have sought to demonstrate in this chapter, the intimate and intricate connections between one's eating patterns and one's state of health are an enduring focus of human concern. Modern societies have witnessed a fundamental and far-reaching transformation in the ways in which these concerns are conceptualized. Traditional beliefs, while rich in detail and highly ingenious and imaginative in the causal mechanisms they postulate, are essentially straightforward in their underlying logical structure. They offer plausible ways of explaining events and experiences relating to health and illness which might

148

otherwise be perceived as driven by arbitrary and capricious forces, largely beyond the reach of human intervention. What is more, these explanations can be readily understood by any competent adult because of the nature of their basic structure. Although specialist healers (individuals perceived as gifted with special powers and insights) may be consulted, by and large the patient will be conversant with the reasoning behind the treatments being used. The manipulation of diet represents a response to illness (or the threat of potential illness) which is clearly within the realm of the individual's own control. Whatever else they offer, traditional conceptions of diet and health can provide a reassuring sense that the individual has access to remedies which are, in both a practical and an intellectual sense, readily within his or her own reach.

However, the rationalization and medicalization of diet and health issues has brought about a significant change in this connection. There can be no doubt that, in a technical sense, modern scientific formulations of the physiological mechanisms which articulate the links between diet and health, offer great explanatory power and theoretical sophistication. But, by their very nature, such formulations have become the intellectual property of specialized and highly trained professionals: medical practitioners and researchers, physiologists, nutritionists and dieticians. As such, they are not readily within the reach of the average member of the public, whose grasp of them will be at best partial and selective and at worst confused. Yet the rationalization of diet has seen professional groups, and the state itself, progressively claim ever more authority over nutritional knowledge and over dietary choices, in so far as these affect both short- and long-term health outcomes. Recommendations concerning the restraint of the appetite for certain foodstuffs, originally relevant only to the eating habits of a privileged minority, have now been generalized to entire populations in societies like the USA. and the UK.

Yet the public's response to the nutritional pronouncements of the 'authorities' (in the widest sense of that term) has often been uneven and inconsistent. Common-sense conceptions clearly continue to play a central role in the public's views on diet and health. What is more, as we have seen, 'alternative' frameworks of explanation, in the form of what might loosely be termed the 'health food movement', have emerged and established themselves as offering versions of the 'rational menu' which, within a climate of menu pluralism, can attempt to compete with or complement orthodox perspectives. Certainly, a good measure of the appeal of the health food approach is related to a characteristic it shares with traditional modes of belief: its promise to provide individuals with a sense that they can influence their own health for the better by means of choices and practices which they feel they personally can control and comprehend.

149

7

FOOD RISKS, ANXIETIES AND SCARES

The risks and anxieties associated with eating in modern Western societies need to be placed both in economic and historical context. Quite clearly, for large numbers of people in the contemporary world the overriding anxiety relating to food emerges out of a concern that now or in the future one simply will not be able to get enough food to remain healthy and active or, for that matter, alive. Similarly, even in Europe, we do not need to reach very far back into history to come across situations in which food shortages affected the lives of millions of individuals. The Second World War, for example, saw widespread food shortages in continental Europe, although they were often unevenly distributed in geographical and social terms. Indeed, in some instances, large numbers starved, or were starved, to death. As we have already seen, low nutritional standards and inadequate food intake were common in the lower orders of British society in the nineteenth century. Indeed, Mennell (1985: 27) argues that centuries of recurrent famine have left their mark upon the European mind, with such themes as starvation and cannibalism woven into the very fabric of European folklore.

Risks other than shortage have long threatened the food consumer. The contamination of food with naturally occurring micro-organisms and toxins has always posed threats to human health, all the more disturbing when the underlying mechanisms were not understood. Perhaps one of the most chilling and bizarre manifestations of such contamination is the illness known as ergotism. Ergot is a fungal disease which affects cereals, the grain becoming infested with the spore-bearing bodies of the fungus. Rye is particularly susceptible to this fungus, and if the grain is badly affected cooking may not neutralize the toxic effects, rendering bread baked with the affected flour highly dangerous. The symptoms of ergotism include either burning pains and gangrene in the limbs, or itching skin and convulsions, hence the names 'Holy Fire' or 'St Anthony's Fire' given to the disease. An outbreak in the Rhine valley in AD 857 is thought to have caused literally thousands of deaths (Tannahill 1988: 101). The disease occurred all over Europe throughout the Middle Ages, causing intense suffering, insanity and death. Its actual cause was not discovered until 1670, when a French country physician, a Dr Thuillier, after years of patient study of the

150

affliction, deduced its connection with the rye bread which was the staple of rural peasant families (Carefoot and Sprott 1969: 19–21). However, it was not until 1853 that the fungus parasite itself was identified and its connection with disease finally proven.

Yet, if in the past the presence of natural contaminants and infections could pose a threat to the food consumer's well-being and peace of mind, so too could the presence of deliberately introduced substances in food placed there for fraudulent purposes. As Burnett (1989: 86) reminds us, food adulteration has a long history, but the increasing industrialization and urbanization of society meant that from the late eighteenth century onwards food adulteration became increasingly feasible, profitable and widespread. The work of the chemist Frederick Accum, published in 1820, revealed the diversity and the seriousness of the abuses taking place, including the use of copper to colour pickles green, the use of sulphuric acid to 'age' beer, the use of verdigris to give a green bloom to dried hedgerow leaves passed off as tea, and the use of red lead to colour the rind of cheese. Such adulterations were not only an assault on the consumer's purse, but on his or her long term health. Later in the nineteenth century a voluminous treatise running to nearly 900 pages (Hassall 1876) detailed the adulteration, often with hazardous substances, of a wide range of everyday foodstuffs, including tea, coffee, cocoa, sugar, honey, bread, flour, milk, butter, cheese, lard, potted meat, preserves, mustard, vinegar and spices.

Currently, of course, the kinds of food hazard discussed above no longer appear to menace the consumer in quite such a direct way. Life-threatening food shortage or starvation are pressing concerns for few, if any, individuals in most modern societies. Advances in medicine and the biological sciences have provided the means to comprehend and avoid the deleterious effects of microbial contamination. In relation to deliberate adulteration, the state has increasingly taken upon itself the task of creating a legislative framework to ensure the purity of food (Paulus 1974). Indeed, there now exist substantial bodies of legislation in countries like the UK and the USA governing such aspects of food processing as additives, contaminants, packaging, labelling and hygiene (Jukes 1993). Yet, perhaps ironically, despite these undoubted advances in food safety, food-related anxieties persist, sometimes in a decidedly disturbing form. It may even be the case that once many of the traditionally most threatening food risks have retreated into the background, other, subtler anxieties, perhaps previously masked and relatively low in visibility, have become more prominent and have thereby gained more public attention. The aim of this chapter is to analyse such anxieties and to attempt to uncover some of the mechanisms which generate and sustain them. In order to achieve this aim, we will first need to consider the fact that the very act of eating can be charged with ambivalence, and then go on to examine customary modes of coping with the anxieties such ambivalence may produce. It will then be argued that these customary modes of managing food-related anxieties may be breaking down, a breakdown which has given rise to both acute and chronic effects on consumers' food choices and attitudes. Whether new modes of sustaining food confidence and alleviating anxiety are, in fact, emerging is a question which will also be addressed.

THE DIMENSIONS OF FOOD AMBIVALENCE AND THEIR ASSOCIATED ANXIETIES

In Chapter 3 we encountered the concept of the omnivore's paradox. This paradox, it will be recalled, emerges out of the fact that all omnivores (and this includes, of course, the human omnivore) experience the opposing pulls of *neophilia* (the inclination to sample novel food items) and *neophobia* (caution when confronted with novel items, based on the possibility that they may be harmful). All omnivores must find ways of coping with this paradoxical juxtaposition of attraction and repulsion. Thus, for the omnivore, eating is a profoundly ambivalent activity, as is the individual's relationship to food itself. However, for the human omnivore, eating with the mind as much as with the mouth, immersed in the symbolic nuances of food, this ambivalence has many more dimensions than the basic tension between neophilia and neophobia. In a study of vegetarianism, the present authors identified three additional paradoxes which can be seen as generating ambivalence for the food consumer (Beardsworth and Keil 1992a), and these can be used as examples in order to develop the argument. Each of the three paradoxes consists of an opposition between a positively valued and a negatively valued feature of food (see Table 7.1).

Table 7.1 The paradoxical nature of food

Positive	Negative
1. Food provides gustatory pleasure, satiety, etc.	Food can produce gustatory displeasure, dyspepsia, nausea, vomiting.
2. Food is required for vigour, energy and health.	Food can introduce illness or disease.
3. Food is required for the continuation of life.	Food entails the death of the organisms consumed.

Source: Adapted from Beardsworth and Keil (1992a)

Paradox 1 (what might be termed the pleasure/displeasure paradox) refers to the fact that while food can provide gustatory gratification and a welcome sense of fullness and satisfaction, it can also produce sensations and reactions ranging from mildly unpleasant to severely distressing. The anxieties associated with these negative possibilities are largely self-evident. For example, there is the fear of encountering unpalatable flavours or textures, as well as the fear of experiencing digestive distress, in the form of sensations of 'bloatedness' or nausea. Concerns about such unwelcome effects are likely to be particularly prominent when the individual encounters a novel food item, and such concerns represent an important component of neophobia. Indeed, disgust when encountering novel food items may, in certain circumstances, represent an important safeguard against biological hazards, even though its origins may be largely cultural (Fischler 1988: 282–4). In addition to these anxieties about effects which may be felt by the eater himself or herself, there may be fears about potential effects of food intake which may be disapproved of by others (for example, short-term effects like flatulence and belching, and long-term effects like weight gain, regarded as cosmetically undesirable).

Paradox 2 (the health/illness paradox) is based upon the fact that, while food is the source of physical energy and can be conceived of as the foundation of vitality and health, it is also recognized as having the potential to introduce disease-inducing substances or organisms into the body. As has been argued in the previous chapter, the issue of the ways in which the connections between diet and health are conceptualized is a complex one. However, it is clear that this paradox can give rise to anxieties about acute effects (e.g., rapidly acting toxins and infections) and chronic effects (e.g., slow-acting toxins, disease-causing agents or long-term nutrient deficiencies).

Paradox 3 (the life/death paradox) emerges out of the fact that, while the consumption of food is absolutely essential for the maintenance of life, the act of eating usually entails the death and dissolution of other organisms. There are, of course, some qualified exceptions to this general rule. Fruits can be consumed without the destruction of the donor plant, and cereals are derived from plants that in any case have an annual life cycle. Nevertheless, fruits, seeds and vegetables are living organisms. There are also some animal secretions which can be used for food without necessarily entailing the killing of the donor animal itself. Two significant examples are milk and honey. Some pastoralist peoples also use blood from their livestock as a source of nutrients, opening a blood vessel to draw off the required quantity, thus obviating the need to slaughter the animal. However, although the use of such animal products does not directly involve the taking of life, it is usually based upon a regime of husbandry of which this is an integral part. For example, aged or unproductive dairy cows are slaughtered and eaten, as are the male offspring of dairy herds.

Typically, the consumption of plants and plant products gives rise to little or no concern, since plants are generally not regarded as sentient organisms. Animals, however, are an altogether different matter, and paradox 3 may generate a whole range of anxieties related to ethical concerns about inflicting suffering and death upon food animals. This is not to argue that all animals are likely to stimulate the same level of ethical interest, since there is clearly a distinct 'hierarchy of sympathy'. Invertebrates of all kinds are obviously very near the bottom of this hierarchy, with 'cold-blooded' vertebrates a step up the ladder. At the top of the hierarchy are 'warm-blooded' vertebrates, particularly large mammals, with their perceived proximity to the human species.

TRADITIONAL MODES OF COPING WITH FOOD AMBIVALENCE AND ANXIETY

Coping with or managing the anxieties generated by the kinds of food paradox discussed in the previous section is not a process which goes on merely at the individual level. Rather, solutions and coping strategies must emerge and be sustained at the cultural level, and thus be available as ready-made social constructs upon which the individual can rely to make sense of his or her experiences and to produce a feeling of ease and confidence. In traditional societies with relatively low rates of social change, long-established customs, beliefs and rituals provided a taken-for-granted frame of reference within which food-related anxieties could be submerged or neutralized. It is, of course, difficult to sustain hard and fast generalizations concerning the nature of traditional societies given the fact that they have exhibited such tremendous variety in culture and institutional forms. However, it is possible to identify a number of common features of premodern social systems which contributed to the process of anxiety neutralization.

A prime factor in the neutralization of paradox 1 (pleasure/displeasure) anxieties is undoubtedly the long-term stability of what we have termed the 'alimentary totality' of traditional societies, that is, the sum total of all the items defined as food suitable for humans. Changes in the alimentary totality are rare and gradual, with the result that familiarity with staple foods breeds in individuals a largely unquestioning confidence that they understand the implications and conditions which cluster around the consumption of a particular item. What is more, long-established rules of cuisine also work to sustain a sense of familiarity and confidence. Rozin and Rozin (1981) note that many traditional cuisines, that is, bodies of rules and recipes governing the preparation of food, have at their foundations distinctive 'flavour principles'. Such flavour principles actually consist of specific combinations of flavouring elements which provide each cuisine system with its own characteristic gustatory identity. The authors point out that the principles operated by major 'cuisine groups' like those found in India, China and Mexico, have remained relatively stable over long periods of time. Thus, in traditional societies, not only does the sum total of food items remain relatively unchanging, but so do the modes of cooking, combining and flavouring these items. Indeed, Rozin (1976) argues that established flavour principles can also mitigate the effects of neophobia. Unfamiliar or novel food items can be rendered less threatening by being suffused with familiar flavours, flavours which the author suggests can reduce the 'tensions of ingestion' which are necessarily inherent in omnivorous eating patterns (Rozin 1976: 66–7). In fact, the entire traditional culinary culture, based upon a set of flavour principles, can operate to sustain confidence and reassurance. Taken-for-granted rules concerning the structure and timing of meals, the appropriateness of given foods in relation to the gender, age and rank of the individual, and the division of labour in respect of food production and preparation, all serve to maintain an overarching framework of familiarity.

Digestive distress produced by overeating, which is also one of the anxieties associated with paradox 1, may be of somewhat different significance in traditional societies. For all but the most privileged, opportunities for overindulgence are likely to be rare, with food shortage being a more likely possibility. Chronic insecurity in the food supply can give rise to a characteristic oscillation between fasting and feasting, with occasional gorging (often associated with particular rituals or observances) providing a periodic release from fears of food deprivation and starvation (Mennell 1985: 23). Anxiety concerning the experience of embarrassment due to the effects of eating and digesting (also related to paradox 1) is likely to be much less salient in traditional societies. For example, medieval Europeans seem to have been largely uninhibited about the physiological processes of digestion, and the sounds and odours they can produce (Elias 1978a: 129–43). Embarrassment in relation to these effects seems to be a product of the civilizing of appetite discussed in Chapter 5. Indeed, in some traditional cultures, manifestations which would be seen by modern Westerners as dreadful lapses in good manners may be required expressions of politeness. For example, Grimble (1952: 35–6) noted that, among the people of the Gilbert Islands in the Western Pacific, a guest who had been provided with food was expected to belch loudly after eating to show his or her appreciation.

In Chapter 6 we have already come across some of the ways in which beliefs and practices in traditional societies can act to neutralize paradox 2 (health/illness) anxieties. We have noted the way in which the combination of tried and tested empirical knowledge and flexible magical beliefs can cope well with threatening aspects of daily life. In relation to food and illness, such a combination can provide intelligible and plausible explanations for disease. In addition, however, traditional cultures provide ways of responding to such misfortunes. Afflicted individuals have, within their realm of common-sense knowledge, criteria for the selection or avoidance of specific foods or food combinations, as well as remedies which are within their own grasp and under their own control. The very fact that traditional knowledge and ethnomedical practices evolve slowly, without frequent or obvious disjunctures in their continuity, provides them with the power to reassure. Their taken-for-granted nature is, perhaps, the best guarantee of the suppression or masking of paradox 2 anxieties. To a degree, this guarantee can operate independently of the actual technical efficiency of the particular avoidances, dietary regimes and treatments that a given traditional culture prescribes. Given the flexibility of common-sense knowledge and magical beliefs, apparent failures can be accommodated or explained away without their presenting a damning challenge to the whole system. Thus, the very resilience of these ideas, along with their apparent immutability, is a powerful factor behind the maintenance of a sense of confidence in the face of the threat of ingesting harmful as well as nutritious substances in the course of day-to-day eating.

As we have already noted, most animal-derived foods (although not all) directly entail the killing of the donor animal, although the extent to which this fact gives rise to ethical concern on the part of the human consumer is likely to vary markedly from species to species. Thus, the probability of the emergence of anxieties related to paradox 3 will itself vary according to the species being eaten. As a broad generalization, warm-blooded animals seem to elicit most concern, especially mammals. Indeed, the larger the mammal the more intense is likely to be the moral unease associated with dining upon it. However, inside paradox 3 is yet another paradox, for the flesh of large mammals, in Western culture at least, is traditionally accorded high status and credited with great potency. This is demonstrated, for example, in its role as the focal or 'stressed' element in the 'cooked dinner' or 'proper meal' which is such an important feature of British culinary culture. (The multiple significances of meat will be dealt with in detail in Chapters 9 and 10.) Within the cultures of many traditional societies are to be found deeply rooted beliefs and customs which serve to legitimize the use of animals for food and to allay any qualms the individual might entertain concerning the morality of eating meat.

Such beliefs and customs are particularly clear and explicit in cultures which derive a significant proportion of their protein resources from the hunting of large game animals. These ideas can take many forms, including ritual apologies to the slain animal and the notion that the purpose of the prey animal's existence is to provide for the needs of the hunters and their dependants. For example, in the past the Akoa pygmies of West Africa would chant a formal incantation of apology to each elephant they killed, absolving the hunter of blame for the animal's death and exhorting the creature's spirit not to return and take revenge upon them. The Mbuti pygmies of the same region also carried out elaborate rites over the body of a freshly killed elephant to appease its affronted spirit (Coon 1976: 140–4). A rather different approach to the explicit rituals of the Akoa and the Mbuti is found in the culture of the Chipewyan, a people of the boreal forests of Canada. In Chipewyan thought, animals are seen as exhibiting features which locate them both in the realm of the natural and of the supernatural, mystically renewing themselves to become rejuvenated each spring. Such beings, reason the Chipewyan, can only be killed with their own consent, voluntarily giving themselves up to the hunter they deem worthy of their sacrifice (Sharp 1988: 187). Indeed, the Chipewyan believe that respect must be shown for game animals at all times, since offending or insulting them could lead them to withdraw their consent to be preyed upon, with disastrous consequences for a people traditionally dependent on the resources of the wilderness for their subsistence. The Bushman hunters of the African Kalahari desert protect themselves from moral qualms by emphasizing the 'otherness' of the animals upon which they prey, rather than seeing them as surrogate humans (Guenther 1988: 198–9). Thus, although these people express affection, respect and aesthetic appreciation in connection with their quarry animals, they see them as sufficiently distinct and distant from themselves to render them legitimate sources of food.

If the hunting of wild mammals presents ethical problems, so too does the slaughter of domesticated mammals. Among pastoralist and agricultural peoples the belief is often found that humans have been granted permission by a creator or supreme being to exploit and subjugate the natural world for their own benefit. Within this context, the use of domesticated animals for food is seen as a divinely licensed practice. This idea is, for example, deeply rooted in Judaism, Christianity and Islam, and in each of these three religions it is seen as based upon the consent given by God to Noah to consume flesh. However, within Judaism, privileges such as this are hedged around with a complex set of food prohibitions, including detailed specifications of those animals which are 'clean' and therefore can be eaten, and those which are 'unclean' and therefore forbidden. A taboo is also placed upon the consumption of an animal's blood, since this is regarded as the medium which contains its vitality (Lowenberg, Todhunter, Wilson, Savage and Lubowski 1974: 207). Thus, slaughter must be carried out in a ritually prescribed fashion, to ensure that all the blood is drained from the animal so that its spirit can flow into the earth (Farb and Amelagos 1980: 23–4). Islam, too, specifies animals which are clean and unclean, and forbids, for example, the consumption of animals that die by strangulation or are beaten to death (Lowenberg, Todhunter, Wilson, Savage and Lubowski 1974: 216).

Even in the context of religions which explicitly forbid the killing of animals, customary practices and beliefs can emerge which legitimize such killing or purge the agent of any culpability. For example, although practising Buddhists are prohibited by their religious beliefs from slaughtering animals or even witnessing slaughter, they are permitted to consume meat as long as they did not participate directly in the taking of the animal's life (Harris 1986: 23–4). In fact, blame may be transferred down the social hierarchy or to pariah groups which specialize in slaughter (Simoons 1961: 11–12). In Buddhist Thailand, villagers usually sell pigs to Chinese dealers to be slaughtered and sold. Similarly, Thai villagers, for whom fish is an important addition to their rice-based diet, argue that they do not actually kill the fish, but merely remove them from the water (Lowenberg, Todhunter, Wilson, Savage and Lubowski 1974: 226). Despite the apparently rigid ban on the killing of cattle in India, Harris (1986: 60–1) points out that Hindu farmers can circumvent this prohibition in a fashion which obviates any sense of guilt. They simply sell surplus animals to Muslim traders, and the resulting meat is consumed by Muslims, Christians and even lower-caste Hindus. This conscience-easing accommodation is supported by the common practice of referring to such meat euphemistically as 'mutton'.

THE EROSION OF TRADITIONAL MODES OF MANAGING AMBIVALENCE AND ANXIETY

In the above section we have examined examples of the ways in which the kinds of anxieties associated with the three paradoxes detailed in Table 7.1 have been managed within the settings of traditional cultures, ranging from hunting-gathering peoples to long-established civilizations like those of the Middle East and India. However, a whole series of factors has been working to erode these reassuring beliefs and practices along with the high level of nutritional confidence (in relation to our three paradoxes) that comes with participation in a world-view which provides effective protection from anxiety and guilt. In broad terms, the factors associated with this erosion are linked to more general processes behind the emergence of the modern food system that were outlined in Chapter 2. The intensification and industrialization of food production and processing, and the globalization of food supply, have led to a veritable explosion in food choice. Coupled with rising affluence and purchasing power in Western economies, this has meant that food consumption patterns have been freed from many of the traditional constraints of locality and season, constraints which would once have generated a framework of familiarity and a sense of cyclical participation in the annual rhythms of agriculture. Indeed, the industrialization of the food system means that food production and processing increasingly take place beyond the view of the average food consumer, involving techniques that he or she is only vaguely aware of or simply does not understand. Thus, many of the food items routinely purchased may be perceived as having unknown features or unknown ingredients, with a consequent loss of the consumer's confidence. This effect is reinforced by the fact that modern food manufacturing techniques, including the use of synthesized substances and flavourings, can imitate or conceal 'natural' textures or tastes, leaving the consumer effectively unable to trust the sensory messages given off by any given food product as a reliable guide to its actual nature (Fischler 1988: 289).

Many of the cultural features of late capitalist societies also appear to contribute to the erosion of the traditional bases of nutritional confidence. The whole ideology of consumerism, driven by an emphasis on a ceaseless search for novel consumption experiences, is essentially antithetical to the maintenance of long-term stability in eating patterns. This hunger for novelty is, in turn, fostered and extended by the mass media, most obviously through explicit advertising and less obviously through the assumptions built into the content of the messages which are conveyed to the various audiences being targeted. Coupled with the globalization of the food supply and the expansion of the alimentary totality of each developed society, virtually open-ended wants can become a salient factor in the affluent consumer's views on food. However, it is not simply that a somewhat bewildering level of choice emerges in relation to food items as such. Even underlying flavour principles, which once served mainly to mark the identity of a particular cuisine and thereby could help sustain confidence and familiarity, have now been effectively uncoupled from the regions and cultures which gave birth to them. In effect, flavour principles themselves have become commodities, options on a kind of meta-menu which consumers with sufficient resources can select from at will. The result is that the long-standing features of the consumer's own native set of flavour combinations become submerged in the sheer variety of principles on offer, with the consequence that they may tend to lose the authority which once made them so reassuring.

If traditional flavour principles can be seen to be losing their central place in the experience of eating, then the changes in the actual patterns of eating that have already been discussed in earlier chapters can also play a role in the erosion of food confidence. Given the changing role of women in the labour market, the modern household (or indeed, the 'postmodern' household) has been characterized as one where the multiple and often conflicting activities and priorities of its members mean that the familiar patterns of commensality, with their confidence-enhancing rituals and habits, have begun to break down. A greater reliance on pre-prepared convenience foods, for example, has led to a situation in which the family meal is far less significant as an occasion for expressing time-honoured assumptions about age, gender and status which serve to locate each individual within the taken-for-granted order of everyday social life (Gofton 1990: 92).

In the previous section, it was suggested that religious beliefs can play a part in the alleviation of food-related anxieties, particularly those pertaining to the moral concerns arising out of the killing of animals for food. However, with the extensive secularization of contemporary Western society, the theological and philosophical supports for the use of animals as food sources have themselves been weakened. More generally, accompanying the broad processes of secularization has been the extensive and impressive development of the scientific world-view, which has transformed the ways in which humans seek to understand and explain the natural world. As we saw in Chapter 6, despite the fact that common-sense ideas and 'alternative' views on food manage to persist, it is the professionally accredited voice of the nutritionist, the dietician, the physician, the microbiologist, the toxicologist and the physiologist which speak with the greatest authority on matters nutritional. Yet, professional scientific discourses on diet are by no means necessarily reassuring ones in relation to our three paradoxes. By its very nature, scientific knowledge is always provisional, subject to controversy, challenge, refutation and replacement. In this sense, it is very unlike common-sense knowledge and traditional empirical/magical thinking, whose elastic and slowly evolving nature makes them appear both homely and proverbial. Scientific knowledge can be subject to disturbing and bewildering changes of revolutionary significance, and its ideas are often largely inaccessible, except in the broadest terms, to those outside a specific discipline. Thus, scientific discourses on food and nutrition do not necessarily produce reassurance and confidence in the public mind.

Indeed, the possibility exists that such discourses may also actively generate public anxiety. This possibility arises out of the fact that science continually and inevitably raises what are, in effect, 'trans-scientific' questions. Weinberg (1972) defines trans-scientific questions as those which scientists can pose quite rationally and reasonably on the basis of widely held views within a given discipline, but to which science itself cannot actually provide satisfactory or unambiguous responses. Questions which appear to require no more than a recourse to suitable facts or data to settle them once and for all can turn out to be highly intractable, with little prospect of clear solutions in the medium or even the long term. There can be a whole range of reasons behind such intractability. For example, there may be compelling ethical barriers which prevent the necessary experimentation on human subjects. Cause and effect linkages may be extremely difficult to detect if they are embedded in a complex matrix of interacting variables which are difficult or impossible to control. Some effects may be long-term or delayed and may need decades of study to detect, and others may be so complex as to require enormous resources for thorough investigation. In fact, Tracey (1977) argues that some aspects of human nutritional needs and requirements have these trans-scientific dimensions. Indeed, it has been suggested that many of the current issues relating to links between diet and health do appear to exhibit trans-scientific aspects, which may mean that scientists may not be able to provide clear-cut answers to seemingly straightforward questions (Beardsworth 1990). Two striking examples of such questions are whether the consumption of beef from cattle infected with bovine spongiform encephalopathy (BSE) can produce an analogous disease in humans, and the nature of any long-term effects of chronic exposure to pesticide residues in food. Both these questions can be posed in such a way as to alert public attention to possible risks, but both raise extremely complex scientific issues and have generated considerable professional debate and controversy. However, the doubt and uncertainty surrounding such questions in scientific circles, and the controversies they create, may not be well understood by the general public.

Indeed, many members of the public at large lack the basic mathematical skills and insights to assess the practical significance of risks to their health which are pointed out by scientists but are expressed in quantitative or statistical terms. As a result, many individuals may experience exaggerated levels of anxiety and even demand guarantees of freedom from risk which would be virtually impossible to implement (Paulos 1988). It is, perhaps, rather ironic that scientific pronouncements and warnings may act to stimulate food-related anxiety at precisely the time when greatly expanded scientific knowledge has produced significant advances in food hygiene and food safety generally.

SOME CONSEQUENCES OF THE EROSION OF FOOD CONFIDENCE

The thrust of the argument being put forward here is that many of the structural and ideological features of modern food systems have the effect of raising the visibility of the paradoxical nature of food and eating. The resulting anxieties and sense of insecurity about food are characterized by Fischler (1988: 288–90) as, in effect, a significant 'disturbance of modern identity'. In fact, as was noted in Chapter 3, Fischler goes so far as to argue that modern societies are witnessing a crisis in gastronomy which involves the breakdown of regulating and reassuring rules, producing a state of *gastro-anomy* (Fischler 1980: 947–48). It is Fischler's contention that modern individuals, less than ever integrated into supportive networks of family and community, increasingly have to make their nutritional decisions in a kind of cultural vacuum, unrestrained by the limitations of season and locality. This nutritional normlessness is, in itself, an anxiety-generating feature of modern society. It clearly goes hand in hand with the erosion of the traditional modes of anxiety management that we have already been discussing. These interlinked phenomena clearly interact with each other, compounding their negative effects upon the confidence and the peace of mind of the contemporary food consumer.

Warde (1991) summarizes this situation by highlighting the three principal competing forces at play in the modern food system, all of which can be seen as pulling in conflicting directions. The first of these forces is made up of the professional nutritional discourse and the official health-oriented dietary advice which were discussed in the previous chapter. The second consists of the customary practices and beliefs which survive in modern societies from traditional culinary culture (which contain the protective elements outlined above). The third force Warde identifies as the taste for novelty, which is a characteristic of the consumption patterns of modern societies in general (and, in a sense, might be seen as an exaggerated manifestation of nutritional neophilia). Each of these three forces is seen as exercising its own potent influence over public attitudes and practices, and the contradictions between them are seen as giving rise to what Warde rather dramatically calls 'a mire of uncertainty' (Warde 1991: 9).

The overall consequence of these gastro-anomic effects and conflicting forces at the cultural level of the food system, exacerbated by the erosion of traditional modes of sustaining confidence, has been a general rise in food-related anxieties in the context of all three of our paradoxes. For example, in relation to paradox 1 (pleasure/displeasure) Mennell (1992) seeks to show how in England from the early nineteenth century onwards both professional medical practitioners and members of the public became increasingly obsessed with the uncomfortable or embarrassing aspects of eating and digestion. The practice of attempting to classify foods according to their perceived ability to generate unwelcome effects, like 'indigestion', constipation and flatulence, became increasingly widespread and led to such potentially harmful effects as the increased use of laxatives and the exclusion of an ever-widening range of items from anxious individuals' diets (Mennell 1992: 7–8). In more general terms, it may also be the case that intensified paradox 1 anxieties may be one of the contributing factors behind the modern preoccupation with body fat, body shape and the restriction of food intake through dieting (which issues will be discussed in some detail in the next chapter). These modern concerns with body fat have, of course, both medical and cosmetic dimensions.

Tensions and anxieties related to paradox 2 (health/illness) also seem to have intensified in the modern setting. Indeed, one of the unintended consequences of official nutritional and health education campaigns may have been a rise in public nervousness over health and food issues, which would have to be set alongside the beneficial outcomes such campaigns may be capable of generating. Interestingly, however, there is some evidence that the public's perceptions of food-related health risks may be significantly different from those of professional experts. For example, a study carried out in Sweden suggests that lay opinion actually reverses the rank order of risks as assessed by experts. Thus, experts tended to place dietary fat, sugar and salt high on their list of food hazards, followed by food poisoning, natural poisons, residues and additives. Conversely, consumers appeared to regard poisons as the greatest risk, with concern expressed in relation to such substances as mercury and heavy metals. Then came pesticides, bacteria and mould poisons, with fat, sugar and salt well down the rank order (Sellerberg 1991: 197). A similar finding has been reported from the USA (Schafer, Schafer, Bultena and Hoiberg 1993). A study based on a random sample of 630 adults indicated that respondents perceived the highest food-related risks as coming from chemicals and the lowest risks from bacterial contamination (although, to place this finding in context, respondents rated concerns about food safety lower than concerns about such issues as cost and taste). However, a study of adult Texans which investigated public knowledge concerning the specific risks associated with undercooked meat products (McIntosh, Acuff, Christensen and Hale 1994) found that of the 46 per cent of respondents who identified a risk, the majority of these (52 per cent) cited food poisoning as the most likely hazard. Indeed, the cross-cultural study by Jussaume and Judson (1992), examining public perceptions of food safety in the USA and Japan, indicates that food safety concerns are becoming globalized in modern societies. With particular reference to pesticide residues and additives, the researchers found analagous levels of concern in the US and Japanese samples, with particular anxiety in households in which children under the age of 18 were present (Jussaume and Judson 1992: 246).

A rise in ethical concerns relating to food seems to suggest an intensification of anxieties in connection with paradox 3. Most obviously, these concerns manifest themselves in the context of heightened interest in issues of animal welfare and animal rights. However, they can also find more indirect expression in the attention increasingly being paid by consumers in modern, developed societies to the environmental implications of intensive food production techniques and to the ethical dilemmas raised by the extreme inequalities in nutritional standards which are present in the global food system. These issues will re-emerge as important themes in Chapters 9 and 10.

THE PHENOMENON OF THE FOOD SCARE

The effects that we have been discussing so far are, in a sense, broad and somewhat diffuse ones, representing gradual shifts at the cultural and ideological levels of the food system. On the other hand, it may well be possible to identify phenomena which are related to the changes in nutritional confidence outlined above, but which manifest themselves in a much more dramatic fashion. One such phenomenon is the so-called 'food scare', an acute outbreak of collective nutritional anxiety which can seize hold of public awareness and can give rise to significant short- and long-term consequences. The typical food scare seems to exhibit a fairly consistent pattern, which for the purposes of presentation can be conveniently presented as consisting of a sequence of steps:

1   An initial 'equilibrium' state exists in which the public are largely unaware of or are unconcerned about, a potential food risk factor.
2   The public are initially sensitized to a novel potential food risk factor.
3   Public concern builds up as the risk factor becomes a focus of interest and concern within the various arenas of public debate.
4   Public response to the novel risk factor begins, often consisting of the avoidance of the suspect food item. (This response may be an 'exaggerated' one, apparently not in proportion to the 'actual' risk.)
5   Public concern gradually fades as attention switches away from the issue in question and a new 'equilibrium' state establishes itself. However, chronic low-level anxiety may persist, and can give rise to a resurgence of the issue at a later date.

In recent years a series of such food scares has occurred in Britain (Mitchell and Greatorex 1990). The scares themselves have been centred upon a diverse range of perceived hazards, including the presence of the dangerous organism listeria in pâté, cook-chill foods and soft cheeses, the presence of salmonella in eggs and the risks posed to human health by the outbreak of bovine spongiform encephalopathy (BSE) in British cattle. Alarm has also been generated by revelations concerning the contamination of bottled spring water with benzene, and by acts of 'food terrorism', where food products have been deliberately contaminated with poisonous substances or foreign bodies, usually as a means of blackmailing large retail food companies. From a sociological point of view, there are two major questions to be addressed here. Firstly, 'How do we explain the sudden and dramatic nature of these surges of public concern?' Secondly, 'Why do nutritional issues seem prone to this kind of effect?'

In relation to the first of these questions, both Gofton (1990) and Beardsworth (1990) have suggested that the concept of the 'moral panic' may be a relevant one (although reservations about the application of this concept to food scares have been expressed by Miller and Reilly (1995: 328–9), who point out that the concept originally implied the focusing of public and official concern on specific marginal or deviant groups who could be characterized as posing a threat to social order). The term itself is to be found in the work of Cohen (1971, 1973) who set out to analyse society's reactions to a series of incidents involving violent public disorder in a number of English coastal resorts in the 1960s. His argument is that the sensationalized coverage of these events by the mass media had two effects. Firstly, it sensitized the public at large to what was perceived as a novel and threatening form of deviance. Secondly, it may even have acted to sharpen and solidify the collective identities of the two rival youth factions involved in the clashes, providing the stimulus for subsequent repeat perform-ances. Cohen uses the term 'moral panic' to describe the rapid surge of public concern which commonly accompanies intensive mass media coverage of such phenomena. The workings of this effect have also been analysed by Hall, Critcher, Jefferson, Clarke and Roberts (1978), who examine the emergence of the 'mugging' scare which occurred in Britain in the 1970s. Although no specific crime of 'mugging' exists in law, for example, the authors argue that the term itself was imported from the USA by British newspaper and television journal-ists. The mugging concept was then used as a category into which a whole range of violent street crimes could be reclassified. Thus combined, these crimes could then be presented to the public as a frightening new phenomenon which demanded action from the authorities. In response to rising public concern, the police and judiciary reacted by increasing the severity of penalties for street violence. Examples of such severe penalties were highly newsworthy and were widely reported in the media, as were the pronouncements of senior police officers, judges and members of the establishment. Such reports themselves added more fuel to the public's collective anxiety, and expressions of such anxiety were frequently featured in press reports. In fact, Hall and his co-authors maintain, this intensive media coverage created the impression of a serious crime wave, although it is by no means clear that violent street crime was actually increasing rapidly at this time.

The mechanism which creates these relatively intense but short-lived 'panics' can be seen as a kind of 'news spiral' consisting of a positive feedback loop. Figure 7.1 provides a simplified diagrammatic representation of the workings of this feedback effect.

The stages in this simplified model are virtually self-explanatory. Initially, a novel issue or phenomenon emerges into the public sphere through reporting in the mass media. Next, the public become sensitized to this issue through their exposure to such coverage. Subsequently, the public are likely to react to the issue to which they have been sensitized. Of course, such reactions may be difficult to predict, as mass media audiences are not simply passive recipients of media messages, but actively select and interpret. Audiences' reactions are themselves newsworthy, although not all audience members' voices have an equal probability of being heard, with those in authority and those claiming 'expert' status likely to receive greater attention. The reporting of audience reactions itself increases public awareness of the issue and increases the level of sensitization, thereby closing the feedback loop and allowing a spiralling level of anxiety to build up. This mechanism does appear to be capable of generating acute surges in collective anxiety, and in recent years in the UK such surges have characterized a wide range of issues, including soccer hooliganism, child abuse, dog attacks on humans, and various forms of criminal behaviour and drug abuse.

Of course, the anxiety 'amplification' produced by this feedback effect is bound to be a self-limiting process, and public and media interest in a topic

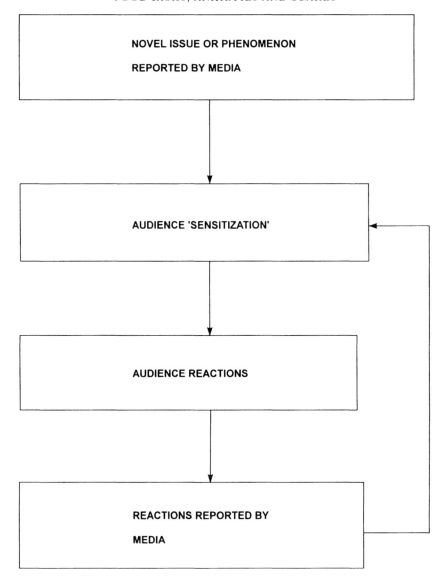

Figure 7.1 A simplified model of the news spiral

will eventually start to decline as that topic goes 'stale' in news terms. This effect is clearly documented by Miller and Reilly (1995: 320–2), who present data showing peaks in the frequencies of items in the British press relating to salmonella and BSE between 1988 and 1994. In effect, public attention can be seen as a kind of scarce resource for which the media have to compete

(Hilgartner and Bosk 1988). The development of a particular topic as a problem or scare will be affected by what Hilgartner and Bosk see as the limited carrying capacity of the public arenas within which issues can be debated and played out by rival authorities, opinions and interest groups. Eventually, a kind of saturation will occur in connection with a given topic, and the media's need to maintain a sense of novelty and dramatic interest will mean a switch to competing issues in order once again to command public attention. However, even though such scares are of limited duration, they may well produce enduring effects. Official policies may be changed, new legislation may be introduced and long-term alterations in the public's activities and attitudes may be produced. What is more, months or even years after a scare episode, an issue may re-emerge and, given the right conditions, generate further surges of acute anxiety.

We have already noted several examples of food scares which seem to have been characterized by this moral panic effect (although, given that the term 'moral panic' was originally coined to describe reactions to social deviance, in the food context the more neutral term 'news spiral' may be rather more appropriate). Nevertheless, such scares, augmented by powerful news spirals, can and do have both short- and long-term effects on consumer choices and food habits. For example, the scare concerning the dangers of salmonella contamination in eggs caused a dramatic and sudden fall in egg consumption in the UK, with the result that large numbers of laying birds were slaughtered and many egg producers were forced out of business. The scare concerning BSE among British cattle caused some local authorities to remove beef products from their school meals menus and moves were made in some European countries to ban the importing of British beef. The scare itself has arguably accelerated the long-term decline in beef consumption in the UK. The revelation of benzene contamination in a well-known brand of mineral water necessitated a temporary withdrawal of the product and the resulting media coverage and public concern is likely to have produced a significant decline in that product's previously dominant market share.

Thus, in the acute phase of a food scare, consumers are likely to respond by switching away from the affected products or brands. Of course, in a market in which there is an abundance of choice, there are likely to be numerous sub-stitutes for suspect products and therefore switching will be relatively easy, involving little or no deprivation for the consumer. This fact in itself is likely to exaggerate the effects of food scares on consumer behaviour. Once the acute phase of the scare is over, there are several possibilities. Demand may stabilize at a lower level, go into chronic decline or recover to the levels which pre-dated the news spiral, depending upon such factors as the appeal of available substitutes and the intensity and durability of the public concern generated. The impact of food scares upon the food industry of a modern economy is, therefore, likely to be somewhat unpredictable. What is more, this impact will vary from sector to sector of the industry. For retailers, product switching by consumers will be relatively easy to accommodate, as purchasing and stocking policies can be modified quickly. Food manufacturers and processors, heavily committed in capital terms to particular products or product areas, may find rapid adaptation difficult. At the level of the agricultural foundations of the food system, food producers may find rapid responses to changes in consumer demand generated by acute scares virtually impossible, given that significant shifts in patterns of production may take years or even decades to accomplish.

Although news spirals touching upon a whole range of issues can be seen as regularly occurring features of the cultural landscape of modern societies, there are several factors which might render food-related topics particularly prone to this effect. Certainly, questions raised about threats to human health are likely to be newsworthy, virtually guaranteed to gain public attention. Threats to health posed by food are likely to be especially newsworthy, since such threats activate those deep-seated anxieties associated with what we have already argued is one of the fundamental paradoxes associated with food: its ability to provide vital nourishment alongside its ability to introduce disease into the body which it feeds. Given that we have proposed that customary ways of submerging or coping with this paradox have been eroded, the cultural ground is fertile for the food scare to take root. Furthermore, as we have seen, the trans-scientific nature of many food and health issues fuels uncertainty and heightens anxiety. Constant debate and dispute between experts, which are essential to the conduct of the natural sciences as professional discourses (Gilbert and Mulkay 1984), when reported through the mass media, can convey to the public a sense of confusion, indecision and even incompetence in the face of what are seen as serious threats to well-being. Indeed, the coverage of such disputes and controversies is often a crucial component of the food scare news spiral. We must add to these factors the recognition that scientific, technological and organizational innovations in food production, processing, storage and transportation have been so successful as to raise public expectations concerning food quality and food safety to unprecedented levels. These high expectations themselves make a direct contribution to the public's susceptibility to food scares.

Significant levels of public anxiety in relation to food, occasionally manifesting themselves as acute scares, indicate how firmly issues relating to the overall acceptability of food have now taken on a prominent place in the arenas of public debate. While it was the case in the UK, for example, that after the Second World War and until a few years ago, decisions pertinent to issues like food quality and food safety were taken within a relatively closed and elitist 'policy community', this is no longer so (Smith 1991). Increasingly in Britain, food-related issues have become politicized, and the original, officially-based policy community can no longer exclude other voices and opinions. Indeed, those agencies which once constituted the closed policy community (both governmental and commercial) may be viewed by the mass media and the public as excessively secretive and potentially untrustworthy (Miller and Reilly 1995: 316– 18). Currently, many competing groups seek to influence the public's ideas and to shape food policy. What we now have is an 'issue network' (Smith 1991: 236), with food firmly established on the political agenda and food controversies far more visible to the public at large.

THE RECONSTRUCTION OF FOOD CONFIDENCE

This chapter has been primarily concerned with the idea that traditional modes of shielding the individual from underlying food anxieties have been eroded, leading to a rise in both chronic and acute manifestations of nutritional unease. However, from a sociological point of view, it is important to consider the question of whether a culture is likely, in the longer run, to permit a set of anxiety-provoking dilemmas to remain excessively visible or effectively unresolved. As Sellerberg (1991: 193) observes, humans *need* to trust in the food they eat. Like any other animals, they have to eat to live yet, unlike other animals, they can and do reflect upon the darker symbolic significances of the food items they consume, and they can at times confront in a conscious fashion the risks and hazards that eating can entail. Yet such reflection and confrontation cannot possibly be undertaken at every meal, or with every mouthful. The result would be a kind of nutritional paralysis or alimentary dithering which would be a constant source of distress. As Sellerberg found from her own study of food trust and mistrust, and as we would expect, most people, most of the time, are not experiencing a constant sense of turmoil about the food they eat. Sellerberg tries to identify what she terms 'strategies of confidence' (Sellerberg 1991: 196) which individuals employ to reassure themselves in the face of confusing advice, alarms and reports. Such strategies include emphasizing the choice of foods which are regarded as 'natural' and avoiding those perceived as 'unnatural', and deliberately developing a repertoire of trusted foods and then excluding all others from the diet.

Yet Sellerberg's strategies of confidence are seen as essentially personal and individual. On the other hand, Fischler (1988) advances the proposition that at the social and cultural level there may be forces working to re-establish some kind of equilibrium in the face of modern insecurity and uncertainty in relation to food. As an illustration of this he refers to the increasing demand for what he terms the 're-identification' of foods (Fischler 1988: 290). This re-identification involves ever more detailed labelling of food products with elaborate listings of ingredients, and formalized guarantees of purity and quality, often sponsored by official bodies. Similarly, expanding forms of what Fischler calls 'food sectarianism' are also seen as capable of playing a role in this overall process. For example, in the previous chapter we considered the significance of the health food movement in this context, and in Chapter 10 one of the many aspects of vegetarianism that will be discussed will relate to its anxiety-relieving features. In fact, Fischler argues, the aim of such diverse processes is to attempt to re-introduce a sense of order into everyday eating, to provide it with an intelligible normative logic and a coherent framework.

Indeed, it may well be that the state of gastro-anomy which Fischler (1988) describes is an essentially transitional one, a feature of the strains involved in the breakdown of a more traditional set of foodways and the emergence of a new, more pluralistic nutritional order (Beardsworth and Keil 1992b). This menu pluralism, which we have already suggested is an important emergent feature of contemporary Western food systems, can be seen as providing the setting within which the existence of a multiplicity of menu principles, flavour principles and systems of cuisine is seen as quite normal and essentially unproblematic. Thus, sampling different principles and cuisines, switching from one to the other as mood, context and conscience dictate, can become normal. Traditional, stable and established foodways may be less and less important for the maintenance of nutritional confidence, as long as there exists a relatively stable overall framework within which the choices, whims, fashions and fads of a pluralistic approach to eating can be played out.

There is, perhaps, a certain irony in suggesting that the commercial dynamics of the modern food system are capable of providing such a framework, since capitalism itself has been seen as containing inherently anomic features. Yet there are clearly identifiable aspects of the commercial food system which do act to generate consumer confidence and to counterbalance gastro-anomic forces. One striking example that we have already come across is the commercialization of certain features of the health food movement. The mass-production and mass marketing of health food products and the commercial appropriation of rhetorical devices like 'tradition', 'naturalness', 'wholesomeness', make available to an ever wider public ranges of products which have reassurance as one of their principal ingredients. Broadening the argument to consider the whole field of food marketing, the larger food producers and manufacturers, in particular, make great efforts to establish and maintain high levels of brand loyalty to their products. Such efforts can be extremely costly, in terms of advertising expenditure alone, but clearly can be effective in maintaining or improving market share and profitability. Yet brand loyalty can also provide a form of benefit for the consumer, in that recognized brands provide a sense of familiarity and reassurance in terms of the quality and safety of the products to which they are attached. What is more, capitalist food organizations which own widely recognized and respected brands will make strenuous efforts to protect such commercially valuable assets and to avoid damage to a brand's reputation. Food brands, in fact, provide some of the symbolically most potent and instantly recognizable icons of Western consumer culture. Established brands can thus assume the taken-for-granted acceptability once reserved for the most basic staple foods.

A particular dimension of this brand loyalty effect is related to the phenomenon, discussed in Chapter 5, which Ritzer (1993) terms 'McDonaldization'. The extensive rationalization of fast food catering epitomized by the McDonald's organization is quite clearly geared to control, efficiency and profitability. However, this relentless rationalization of the product range and the methods of handling, preparing and serving the food items on offer also produces an additional crucial feature: predictability. As we have already noted, wherever the outlet, the consumer can feel confident that the food product purchased will be predictably familiar in terms of portion size, texture, taste and ingredients. In the context of the increasing globalization of culture and increasing levels of both social and geographical mobility, standardized branded food items for consumption inside or outside the home provide sources of nutritional confidence which transcend class, cultural and sometimes even national boundaries.

The commercial food system offers products which assuage not just the anxieties generated by our first two paradoxes, but also ease those moral qualms which emerge out of the third paradox. Worries regarding the possible suffering imposed upon food animals in the course of rearing, transportation and slaughter can be tempered by the consumption of food products which offer guarantees or assurances concerning the conditions and treatment to which domesticated animals have been subjected. There is, in the UK, for example, an established market for so-called 'free range' eggs and 'free range' poultry (chickens and turkeys). Some consumers are clearly willing to pay a significant premium for such products, which are not the results of highly intensified 'battery' farming characterized by very high densities of birds in extremely restricted conditions, but purport to be derived from livestock enjoying more 'natural' living conditions. Thus, in certain circumstances, humane production techniques become important saleable features of animal-based food products, with the potential for providing extra peace of mind for the consumer and extra profits for the producer. This principle can also operate in a broader sense, since, as we have already seen, wider moral and ecological anxieties may also be associated with the third paradox. Products advertised as being 'ecologically friendly' also offer the dual benefits of consumer reassurance and premium prices. One example of this effect relates to widespread concerns about the large numbers of dolphins killed annually by becoming entangled in tuna nets. Canned tuna carrying a printed guarantee that it has been produced using techniques and equipment which avoid such undesirable consequences, offers a form of reassurance which can be lifted directly off the supermarket shelf.

Anxiety-reducing or confidence-generating food products can be turned out at all levels of the commercial food system. They may be the stock-in-trade of small, specialized producers, and retailed through specialized outlets and co-operatives catering for highly specific minority tastes and requirements. On the other hand, such items increasingly figure in the product ranges of the giant national and multinational food processing and food retailing corporations, as they move towards the kind of niche marketing necessary to exploit the increasingly pluralistic diversification of tastes, priorities and menu principles.

Of course, it is also the case that a whole range of official agencies and professional bodies is engaged in attempts to influence the public's dietary practices and to shape the public's nutritional beliefs and priorities. By implication, this also represents a form of confidence maintenance, in this context confidence in the officially or professionally sponsored view of what constitutes safe, healthy or ethically acceptable food. Yet these official sources of reassurance are likely to be somewhat ambivalent ones. The guidelines on healthy eating, upon which the state's dietary targets are based, are themselves founded upon the shifting sands of scientific opinion. Even when an orthodoxy has been established which is intelligible to the public at large (for example, in connection with the links between diet and heart disease), that orthodoxy is always open to challenge and is always susceptible to being undermined by the publicity given to evidence which does not fit the prevailing view. There also appear to be circumstances in which official reassurances concerning the safety of specific suspect food items have the opposite effect to that intended. For example, at the height of the BSE scare in the UK, statements by government ministers and by senior medical officers were juxtaposed by the mass media with dire warnings from controversial dissenters from the official line. The official statements were themselves highly newsworthy and effectively added further fuel to an already vigorous news spiral. Once issues of food safety, for example, have escaped the control of a closed, oligarchical policy community and truly entered into the public domain, the official voice becomes only one voice among many, each presenting its own competing account. What is more, the state's ability to sustain confidence and generate reassurance may be further compromised in the UK setting, for example, where the Ministry of Agriculture, Fisheries and Food, one of the main government agencies in this area, is widely perceived, rightly or wrongly, to accord higher priority to the interests of food producers than to the interests of food consumers.

OVERVIEW

The underlying paradox beneath all the issues and debates which have been discussed in this chapter is one which has already been touched upon in several contexts: the fact that food anxieties persist (and even intensify) in modern food systems, despite the advances made in such systems which have improved the reliability and safety of the food supply. As we have seen, this effect is due in part to the fact that those features of traditional cultures and traditional food systems which could sustain nutritional confidence have been eroded or diluted by the processes of modernization. What is more, the very success of modern food systems in delivering to the consumer an abundance of varied, high-quality foodstuffs has in itself led to a cycle of constantly rising expectations on the part of the public. With immediate and obvious threats to nutritional well-being fading into the background, the consumer is able to occupy himself or herself with more arcane and subtle threats and misgivings relating to food. An anticipation of continually rising standards is established, and members of the public become less and less tolerant of real or supposed food hazards, although the priorities accorded to such hazards may be very different from those calculated by scientists, who may perceive a rather different hierarchy of risks.

Yet there are clearly conflicting forces at work here. On the one hand, we have examined those forces and tendencies which appear to be undermining confidence and generating anxiety. On the other, we have also analysed in some detail the social mechanisms which may be capable of rebuilding and sustaining confidence and assuaging anxiety. It is tempting to speculate which of these two opposing sets of forces is likely to prevail. Should we predict a slide into ever deepening gastro-anomy, or should we anticipate the emergence of a new, stabilized nutritional order? The probability is that neither extreme case is a particularly likely one. Rather, the two tendencies will continue to coexist and interact with each other. If a new form of equilibrium is emerging, it is an equilibrium which is going to remain vulnerable to disturbance.

Perhaps the most plausible scenario is one characterized by periods of calm, during which chronic anxieties remain relatively dormant. However, such periods are likely to be punctuated by episodes of acute anxiety, produced either by the surfacing of underlying worries or by the introduction of novel scares which tap those deep-seated misgivings inherent in our three paradoxes. Indeed, it is possible to envisage potential food scares waiting in the wings for their day in the public eye. For example, the irradiation of food items in order to reduce microbiological contamination, slow down deterioration and extend shelf life, is already technically feasible. Similarly, the use of the hormone bovine somato-tropin (BST) to increase the milk yields (and therefore the profitability) of dairy cows is also a technically feasible option. However, at the time of writing neither of these measures has been fully implemented in the UK, despite their obvious advantages for producers and distributors. This reluctance to sanction the introduction of these types of new high-profile food technologies is almost certainly born of a recognition of the public's enhanced sensitivity to such potentially emotive and anxiety-generating innovations. Such are the implications of a cultural climate in which volatile public reactions to nutritional issues remain an ever-present possibility.

8

DIETING, FAT AND BODY IMAGE

Many sections of this book may be read as something of a celebration of the conquest of food shortage, of the growth in the security of supplies and of the varieties of food available. It is true that there are issues about access to food by the very poor but, for the majority, food resources are readily available. As a consequence, it may seem rather surprising to be introducing debates about the control of eating by dieting amongst some of the most prosperous groups in society and drawing attention to attempts to explain why some eating disorders, notably those which involve reducing food intake, are so severe that they threaten the life of the individuals concerned. However, these are some of the issues to be addressed if we want to understand current patterns of dieting and the powerful fear of fat which is expressed in popular literature about food, health and body shape in modern western societies.

Although there are many established ways in which these issues may be considered, addressing them also involves the sociologist in a relatively novel activity, one which has been absent from mainstream sociology until relatively recently: the analysis of the ways in which our bodies are socially constructed and experienced in modern society. Featherstone, Hepworth and Turner (1991: vii) argue that the sociology of the body is a way of focusing on 'one of the crucial instances of the complex interrelationships of nature, culture and society'. However, it was neglected as an area of study for a range of reasons, in particular because the early sociologists concentrated on questions concerning society, social change and social relations as a denial of the 'natural' as an explication of the social (Turner 1991: 8). Of course, these interests remain in current sociology, expressed in the continued interest in the social relations of production and the use of occupation as a key to understanding individual social position, but they are no longer considered to be the only ways of understanding social organization and social relationships. The new emphasis is on how people present themselves and appear to others. For example, Cash (1990: 52) argues that 'Physical appearance is often the most readily available information about a person and conveys basic information about that person – most obviously, for example, the person's gender, race, approximate age, and possibly even socio-economic status or occupation'. The interest in and development of the sociology of the body can be viewed, according to Turner (1991) as the consequence of several broad social changes. These include the growth of consumer culture in the post-war period, the development of postmodern themes in the arts, the feminist movement and changes in the demographic structure of industrial societies. For example, he argues that the 'erosion of competitive capitalism based on a disciplined labour force and heavy industrial production for a world market' (Turner 1991: 19) has been associated with the growth of the service sector and the development of new lifestyles which emphasize consumption and leisure. Associated with these is 'commercial and consumerist interest in the body' and its representation in art and advertisements together with an emphasis on 'keeping fit, the body beautiful and the postpone-ment of ageing by sport' (Turner 1991: 19). Feminist criticism of the sub-ordinate position of women in society has created a much greater sensitivity to issues of gender, sexuality and biology. The body as a focus of medical control and intervention also becomes important where improvements in standards of living and medicine have increased life expectancy and changed the age dis-tribution to one which is historically unique in that there is a growing proportion of the elderly and the control of disease and of ageing itself are of increasing concern.

An awareness of the reasons why the sociology of the body has become the focus of interest does not necessarily inform us about the specific issues which should be on the sociological agenda. For these we need to consider current writing about dieting, fat and body image, where it is possible to identify at least four major puzzles of interest to the sociologist. The first is the knowledge that, as food supplies become both more secure and more plentiful, a substantial proportion of the population is on a diet with the aim of achieving weight loss and so are trying to avoid eating the range and variety of foods now available. The second is the awareness that, as the average body weight increases in the general population, the preferred (perhaps even the 'ideal') body image as shown in the media and entertainment industry and as demanded by commercial and industrial organizations emphasizes the slim, the slender and the underweight. The third is the fact that the second half of the twentieth century is associated with a rise in eating 'disorders', that is, problems which arise from weight loss which is so extreme as to endanger health and even life (anorexia nervosa) or from a pattern of unrestrained eating (bulimia nervosa) which again threatens the health of the sufferer. The fourth puzzle is highlighted by the data which show that most, if not all, of those involved in dieting and suffering from eating disorders are women, that is, the people who are normally responsible, or will as adults become responsible, for the selection, preparation and serving of food. As Brown and Jasper (1993) argue so cogently, if we are to contribute anything to the analysis of such issues we should find answers to these questions: 'Why weight?' 'Why women?' and 'Why now?'

Anyone interested in these issues has a wide range of sources of information to consider. Much of the writing about dieting, fat and body image appears in popular magazines and other media output. Where these issues emerge in the academic literature, they are discussed by nutritionists, medical researchers, psychologists and also, more recently, by feminists and sociologists. Amongst the multitude of discussions on topics such as body image, dieting and eating disorders, contrasts are often drawn between those who focus on individual experience and those who focus on social constraints. However, it is equally important to be aware of two other contrasting approaches: firstly, those where the underlying purpose is intervention, for example, to help individuals to be slimmer, recover from an eating disorder, adjust to lack of success in dieting. In such writing, the problem may be identified as individual or social in origin; however, the 'solution' is offered at the individual level. The second (and rarer) approach is where the underlying purpose is an analysis of the contemporary cult of slimness, the social pressures to 'shape up' to perceived expectations or the social conditions for the occurrence of eating disorders. Even where these studies give detailed accounts of particular individuals, the analysis remains at the level of the social and does not attempt to offer individual solutions. Although this latter approach may seem unsympathetic to individual sufferers, it may offer useful clues for sociological answers to the questions we have identified.

WHY NOW? THE MAKING OF THE CONTEMPORARY CULT OF SLIMNESS

In her analysis of sociocultural determinants of body image, which she defines as 'the way people perceive themselves and, equally important, the way they think others see them' (Fallon 1990: 80), Fallon emphasizes that the concept of beauty has never been static. She traces Western cultural ideals through time with particular reference to body shape and weight. Drawing upon art as an indicator of the ideals of male and female beauty, she argues that from the fifteenth to the eighteenth centuries fat was considered both erotic and fashionable and the 'beautiful woman was portrayed as a plump matron with full, nurturant breasts' (Fallon 1990: 85). By the nineteenth century there were two contrasting models of the female ideal. They shared small waists (with an 18-inch circumference where possible) but were different in that one was 'a fragile lady who was admired for her moral values, social status, and beauty' and the other was 'a bigger, bustier, hippier, heavy-legged woman found among the lower classes, and actresses and prostitutes' (Fallon 1990: 85). Both these ideals were modified in the twentieth century, initially towards an ideal body that was 'almost boylike' (Fallon 1990: 87). Fallon argues that the rise of the mass media, particularly film, probably contributed to the imposition of more general standards of beauty and fashion in the West. Since the media often focused on high-status groups, it was these groups' standards which became widespread. In the

USA the 1950s saw the glorification of large-breasted women in films and magazines, followed by the return to an emphasis on slimness in the 1960s. Similarly, in Britain in the 1960s a young woman nicknamed 'Twiggy' and weighing only 97 lbs, became one of the most famous fashion models of her generation. Fallon draws attention to data from studies of the winners of the Miss America contest between the years 1959 and 1978 indicating a decline in average weight related to height (that is, successful contestants increased in height and declined in weight over the period) and to a similar trend among the women featured in the centrefolds of Playboy magazine between 1960 and 1978 (Fallon 1990: 89–90). Fallon also reports on studies of the changes in the commercial images of women, from nineteenth-century curvaceousness to the 1980s' 'more muscular, healthy ideal of the female body' (Fallon 1990: 91). She reiterates the point made by other authors that such shapes are neither average nor 'natural' and can only be achieved by those who have the time, the money and the appropriate lifestyle.

Summarizing a wide range of research, Fallon shows that attractiveness is important for the positive evaluation of adults and that slimness is a component of attractiveness. However, many people, particularly women, are dissatisfied with their own weight and shape, with most women preferring to be lighter than their current weight. For example, a study discussed by Fallon (1990) reports that:

> College students judged their current figures to be significantly heavier than their ideal figure. In contrast, male college students (as a group) feel themselves to be close to their ideal in weight. Both men and women in their 40s and 50s share similar dissatisfaction with body shape; both judge their ideal to be significantly thinner than their current shape.
>
> (Fallon 1990: 93)

For those of us who take for granted the desirability of being slim, Fallon's work is an important reminder that ideals of beauty are variable and that the emphasis on slimness is a very recent characteristic and, even today, occurs only in modern western societies. There are other illustrations of the processes Fallon describes. For example, in the medieval period it was said: 'Eating made one handsome. A thin wife brought disgrace to a peasant. But of a plump wife it was said that 'a man will love her and not begrudge the food she eats' (quoted by Mennell 1987: 147). The notion that eating made people handsome was not confined to women, nor to those who worked on the land; there are many portraits of the rich, both men and women, who are shown in 'magnificent amplitude'. This emphasis on the importance of size remained an important theme at least until the end of the nineteenth century. Similarly, in modern non-Westernized societies, the ideal woman is much larger than in the West. For example, Buchanan writes of Tanzania that 'men expect their wives to gain weight once they are married: "If she doesn't get fat, people will think I'm not taking good care of her!" men often say' (Buchanan 1993: 36). In the light of

176

such evidence, it is clear that the task is to identify what it is about modern Western societies which is different from Western societies in the past and non-Western societies of today.

These studies raise an important question: 'If standards of attractiveness and ideals of beauty are highly variable, why is the mid- and late-twentieth century associated with an ideal of slimness?' Fallon suggests that the 'curvy look, associated with motherhood, may have lost much of its value in a world striving for zero population growth' (Fallon 1990: 88). For Mennell (1985) the key lies in changed historical circumstances and, in particular, the increasing security of food supplies. As we have already seen in earlier chapters, he argues that, in the premodern period, fluctuations between fasting and feasting, want and plenty, were taken for granted. Even when supplies increased, the fear of food scarcity remained because of the lack of coordination between the location of needs and supplies of produce. The change towards greater security of supplies was a consequence of other changes, for example, the development of trade and a more specialized division of labour in the context of the development of the nation-state. Mennell (1985) maintains that changes in the regulation of appetite in the quantitative sense paralleled the civilizing process and the development of manners. He distinguishes between hunger and appetite and sees appetite as controlled by the 'appestat'. With the appestat set too high, we eat too much food; with it set too low, we eat too little. The setting of the appestat is influenced, even controlled, by both individual and social factors. For example, in Western society the move is towards greater self-control over appetite, a change encouraged by the growing medical opinion, based on rational medical knowledge, that moderation is healthier than excess and that gluttony was coarse. Over time, these processes have culminated in the twentieth-century fear of fatness. This began with the elite and then moved downwards and was associated with the growing confidence in food supplies and the unlikelihood of dearth. Indeed, Mennell (1987) goes so far as to argue that the fear of fat, and certainly the eating disorders of anorexia nervosa and obesity, are problems of prosperous Western societies. His case is supported by the incidence of anorexia nervosa which is thought to have first occurred amongst high-status families. However, the more general approval of self-control over appetite is now part of the message of all magazines going to every social level where slimness is equated with health and sexual attractiveness.

The issue of control is argued by Turner (1991) to be of particular importance in what he terms the production of 'disciplined' bodies. Featherstone (1991) in the same volume draws attention to the contemporary emphasis on general 'body maintenance' which sometimes culminates in an obsession with the procedures for presenting oneself as youthful, healthy and beautiful, almost regardless of biological age. People are willing to spend large sums of money and to invest time and effort in order to overcome any perceived defects or to improve their appearance. Slimness is part of the demonstration to others of individual success, with fat becoming associated with lack of control ('letting oneself go') and thus with moral failing. This preoccupation with fat, diet and slenderness is viewed by Bordo as 'one of the most powerful "normalizing" strategies of our century, ensuring the production of self-monitoring and self-disciplining "docile bodies"' (Bordo 1990: 85). She points out that this creates a situation in which the individual becomes habituated to self-improvement and self-transformation. For historical reasons, she suggests, women are subjected to this form of control to a greater extent than are men, and the idea that women's divergence from these norms is somehow 'pathological' is a powerful device for the reproduction of conventional gender relations. Such a position leads to a closer consideration of other writers' ideas about the links between gender and a concern with body weight and shape.

WHY WOMEN? THE IMPORTANCE OF GENDER

Meadow and Weiss (1992) write as psychologists who work with women suffering from eating disorders. They argue that their work, together with all that they have read in the popular literature and observed 'in the culture', leads them to the view that food and eating are 'a metaphor for what is required for survival as a woman in today's society' (Meadow and Weiss 1992: ix). They contrast the contemporary situation with the 1950s and 1960s, when eating disorders were rare and almost unheard of, and magazines showed food as a natural part of life with none of the 'romantic, mysterious and forbidden connotations that it has today' (Meadow and Weiss 1992: 60). At that time, the ideal figure was voluptuous. However, it must not be assumed that it was easy to achieve. Women struggled to achieve it in the same way as they try to attain today's ideal of the thin and sinewy body. They argue that women 'have always defined themselves in terms of an external ideal' which 'simply reflects the norms of the times' (Meadow and Weiss 1992: 96). The authors are in no doubt that the norms are set by men and that women tend to be evaluated on the basis of their physical appearance as an indicator of their value in the marriage market. Traditionally, the great majority of women would have been financially as well as emotionally dependent on men, and would have been able to embrace the qualities of caretaking and nurturing as an integral part of the 'female psyche', leading them to place particular value on sexual and social relationships.

However, the current preoccupation with thinness for women has its origins in a series of social changes: the new youth culture of the 1960s with its emphasis on the natural, youthful look; the demands for equality from the women's movement and the move towards a more androgynous body image; reliable contraception; greater access to career opportunities in the labour market where a 'motherly image' would be positively disadvantageous; the fitness movement and ideas about the ways in which exercise could change the look of the body. In sum, 'Through her perfect body, she announces that she can have it all: look like a woman and succeed like a man' (Meadow and Weiss 1992: 99). The preoccupation with thinness is so powerful that 'Fat oppression, the fear and hatred of fat people, remains one of the few "acceptable" prejudices still held by otherwise progressive persons' (Meadow and Weiss 1992: 133).

Meadow and Weiss argue that the tension between the demands of personal relationships and those of the marketplace place women in a situation where there is conflict between the desire for dependence and the need for self-expression, a conflict which manifests itself through food. They argue that the link between food and love begins at birth, and that food can become a source of love, comfort, warmth and security, particularly in a society where high divorce rates offer no guarantees of permanent partners and providers and where women are encouraged to maintain their independence. However, although food offers the advantages of asking nothing from you other than that you enjoy it, and is an area of life where one can put one's own needs ahead of others, it also presents problems in that 'food is a destructive lover, a double-edged sword. At the same time that it offers immediate gratification and comfort, it insidiously builds up a layer of fat that society states is guaranteed to make one unlovable' (Meadow and Weiss 1992: 125). The authors conclude that there is a direct link between eating disorders and the powerful emphasis on slimness as the basis of female beauty. For the authors, the solution to the problem of eating disorders is to challenge the rules by recognizing that it is impossible to attain bodily perfection and that slimness does not automatically deliver love and happiness.

Charles and Kerr (1986b) point out that most empirical studies of women and food focus on women who have some kind of eating disorder and that there is virtually no research exploring women's 'normal' relationship with food. Drawing upon their own sociological research based on interviews with 200 women, research which was discussed in detail in Chapter 4, they argue that virtually all women have a relationship with food which is problematic and that individual responses lie on a continuum with eating disorders at one extreme. Women are caught up in a contradiction: they must be both the guardians of their families' health and see that they are properly fed, whilst at the same time they must be attractive for their husbands by being slim and fashionably dressed. It is slimness which is equated with sexual attractiveness in our society and it is also legitimized by the medical profession as being healthy, yet these views do not fit with the ideologies of maternity and maternal care. There is clearly a tension inherent in being both slim and going through pregnancies and in feeding others and yet remaining slender. A further tension is caused by the fact that sweet foods are used to reward and comfort. It is no surprise that the women in the sample were dissatisfied with their present weight and not happy with their body image. Only twenty-three (11.5 per cent) of the women in the sample claimed never to have dieted nor to have had worries about their weight. Dissatisfaction was reinforced by the negative comments of men, particularly their partners. Except when pregnant, it was virtually impossible to be relaxed about food. Since the women in the sample were no longer in employment, there were tensions because they were constantly in the presence of food, acknowledging it as a source of comfort, yet wanting to avoid eating it. All wished to be a few pounds lighter and

179

successful dieting was reported to give a feeling of well-being, achievement and control, yet it was extremely difficult to manage. Charles and Kerr (1986b) also present the argument that this situation of tension is the consequence of women's position of relative powerlessness in capitalist society, where control is exerted over women by ideologies which define female beauty in terms of unnatural slimness to which, by definition, most women's bodies do not approximate. At its most serious, the body and food are regarded as hated enemies. For example, some women even start smoking in an attempt to suppress appetite or to avoid eating. Charles and Kerr emphasize that these are not the problems of those with identifiable eating disorders; these problems are the product of women's structural position and are a function of their marginal and powerless situation in society.

Cline (1990) draws upon qualitative interviews with women in England and in North America, together with her own experiences in relation to food, to argue a similar case: that women's relationship to food rests on contradictions. However, she goes further and argues that food is yet one more focus for the battle between men and women. The writing is vivid and direct: 'Women's bodies have always been a screen onto which different values, such as receptive sexiness or fecundity, have been projected by men' (Cline 1990: 164). Thus, the ideal might vary over time (for example from rounded to 'razor thinness') but the models are always defined by men, and women strive to achieve each in order to obtain men's approval. When the ideal is to achieve extreme slimness, then women take seriously the latest diet and fear the possibility of getting fat. All this makes food a source of danger for women. In common with Charles and Kerr, Cline emphasizes the widespread character of these concerns and argues that eating disorders have to be seen in this context. As the Western cultural ideal weight continues to decline, all women's eating habits become destabilized, raising the possibility of higher levels of clinical disorders. The author sees it as a tragedy that 'there is hardly a woman in the West between adolescence and old age who does not desire to alter something about her shape or size' (Cline 1990: 187). If they do not achieve the changed shape or weight loss, then women feel themselves to be failures. This is also a tragedy in that women, Cline asserts, are challenging their own biology, a biology which may be geared to maintaining a certain fat level and which may resist attempts to achieve a permanent reduction in that level.

One of the most famous contributions to the general debate about the cult of slimness is *Fat is a Feminist Issue* (Orbach 1988). Originally intended to be a self-help guide to compulsive eaters, the book has subsequently been interpreted as having a more general relevance. Orbach locates the preference for being thin in the structure and organization of patriarchal society of late capitalism where middle-class female socialization offers contradictory expectations: an egalitarian emphasis on educational and work opportunities existing alongside an emphasis on traditional female sexual identity in motherhood. The outcome is confusion, insecurity, low self-esteem and negative body images which are expressed in ambivalence about eating and ambiguities about women's aspirations. The solution offered by Orbach is for women to abandon dieting and to allocate priority to their own interests and their own life. Once fat is no longer a central concern, weight will no longer be a problem, in that a more 'natural' (and lower?) body weight will be achieved. Examples are given from her own and others' experiences. Orbach writes as a 'feminist therapist' with a commitment to help women who suffer from compulsive eating to reduce both their anxieties and their weight. Diamond (1985) contends, however, that it is inappropriate for feminists to engage in discussions about weight and body image, in that involvement in such discussion takes for granted, instead of challenging, the thin/fat opposition and, in particular, the privileging of thin over fat. In Diamond's view, feminists should be concerned to develop, collectively, new arrays of identities and alternative body images.

A collection of contributions from academics and from those involved in therapy and in community education edited by Brown and Jasper (1993) reports on feminist approaches which present challenges to the conventional pressures on women to police their own bodies through habitual dieting. There are women, they argue, who are prepared to accept their bodies as they are and to reject the treadmill of constant nutritional self-denial. The editors indicate their preference for avoiding terms such as 'eating disorders', 'anorexia', and 'bulimia' because they are terms which originated in psychiatric literature and are associated with a medical or disease model, a model which they wish to criticize. However, in the end, they retain the use of such terms because they are everyday terms which are readily comprehensible to a wide readership. Interestingly, whilst they recognize that words like 'obese' and 'overweight' imply deviation from some objective standard, the editors recommend reclaiming the word *fat* by shedding its pejorative overtones and using it simple to refer to a particular body type.

Brown and Jasper's answer to the questions 'Why weight?' 'Why women?' and 'Why now?' is similar to those identified above, in that they see the ideal of the slim body as a product of industrialization, the increasing participation of women in the labour force and the impact of feminism with its pressure for increased social equality.

RECENT TRENDS IN BODY WEIGHT

Alongside feminist analyses of the significance of slimness in the context of the control of women in a patriarchal framework, there does, of course, exist a medical model of the significance of body weight. In contemporary medical discourse slimness is often equated with health and a range of diseases and disorders has been directly linked to obesity. For example, the US Food and Nutrition Board of the Institute of Medicine (Thomas 1991: 102–3) began its discussions on dietary recommendations by noting that body weight and body mass index are increasing in the USA and other Westernized societies and also noted that excess weight is associated with an increased risk of several health disorders, including certain types of diabetes, hypertension and coronary heart disease. The Board also note that, in the USA, disadvantaged groups are more likely than the general population to suffer from diseases associated with obesity. Although some feminists might deplore an argument which equates fatness with pathology, seeing it as part of an oppressive patriarchal ideology, we nevertheless need to confront the question of how weight varies in the populations of countries like the USA and the UK, and whether the patterns are currently undergoing change. Ironically, as the evidence about the links between weight level and health builds up, there is also evidence that an increasing proportion of the population falls into the category of being medically defined as obese. The government-initiated *Health Survey for England 1991* (Office of Population Censuses and Surveys – Social Survey Division 1993: x) summarizes the situation as follows: 'There is a considerable amount of epidemiological evidence that obesity is related to ill health and results in increased risks of a number of diseases including hypertension and CVD [cardiovascular disease].' The report employs the standard measure known as body mass index (BMI), calculated by dividing the weight of the individual in kilograms by the square of his or her height in metres. The BMI, a continuous variable, can be divided into a series of categories and the ones used in the report are those used by the Royal College of Physicians (See Table 8.1).

Table 8.1 Body mass index categories

Level of BMI Index	Description
20 or less	Underweight
over 20 to 25	Desirable
over 25 to 30	Overweight
over 30	Obese

Source: Adapted from Office of Population, Censuses and Surveys 1993

   The 1991 data indicated that mean BMI for men was 25.6 and for women 25.4. However, 53 per cent of men and 44 per cent of women were shown to have a BMI of over 25 and, indeed, 13 per cent of men and 16 per cent of women fell into the category over 30 and therefore were defined as obese. The report also identified significant increases in mean BMI for men and women in the 16–64 age group over the previous decade (for men an increase from 24.3 to 25.5 and for women an increase from 24.0 to 25.2). The report also compares the situation in 1991 with that which pertained in 1986/7 and notes a striking increase in the proportion of adults aged 16–64 with a BMI of over 30. For men the figure rose from 7 per cent to 13 per cent and for women from 13 per cent to 15 per cent (OPCS 1993: x).

   The association between BMI and such variables as age, social class and education is also discussed. BMI tends to increase with age up to 65 but then tails off. Men in non-manual social class categories tend to have a higher BMI than those in manual categories although, interestingly, the reverse is the case for women, with those in non-manual groups tending to have a lower BMI than those in manual groups (OPCS 1993: x).

These figures suggest yet another paradox within the realm of food and eating. If we accept the contention that Western society places a heavy emphasis on the slender body as a cultural ideal, these data suggest that the average woman (and, indeed, the average man) is actually moving further away from this ideal, and for an increasingly large number this ideal is completely out of reach. This ideal and the divergence from it creates the conditions for the development of a thriving slimming industry. It is an industry with a guaranteed clientele in those who strive for slimness but may actually see their goal constantly retreating before them. This is illustrated dramatically by the estimates given by Meadow and Weiss (1992) in their discussion of the scale of the slimming market in the USA. Over 60 per cent of women are said to be dieting at some point in a year and that number may be increasing. The authors present calculations to show that more than $10 billion a year are spent on 'diet drugs, diet meals, diet books, exercise tapes, weight-loss classes, and fat farms' (Meadow and Weiss 1992: 25). Within this overall figure, they estimate that $800 million are spent on frozen diet dinners and another $200 million on diet pills. There are no directly comparable firgures for the UK. However, there is evidence to suggest that the UK slimming product market is also big business. For example, the market for all types of reduced-calorie foods was estimated at £1.5 billion in 1994 (Economist Intelligence Unit 1994: 48). Within this figure, the market for slimming foods (defined as including meal replacements, very low-calorie diets and appetite suppressants) was valued at more than £69 million. In the previous three years, meal replacements were the fastest-growing sector of the slimming foods market with the market in very low-calorie diets declining and the market in appetitie suppressants remaining a relatively low but stable sector of the market. The authors refer to medical research which indicates that up to 24 per cent of women and 37 per cent of men are 'overweight'. Even so, it is women who are more likely to be involved in slimming. As the association of slimness with health (rather than with responsiveness to social pressures to be slim) becomes established, the authors argue that a more 'unisex image' is likely to develop, with men and women associating slimming with movement towards a more healthy lifestyle. If this happens, the writers argue, the market in slimming foods is likely to change and there may be a blurring of the lines between foods which are marketed as slimming and those which are marketed as being associated with more general healthy eating (Economist Intelligence Unit 1994: 52). There is nothing to suggest that such foods will not also be marketed aggressively in an effort to continue to profit from the manufacture and sale of special foods.

EATING DISORDERS

The paradoxical nature of the situation in which there simultaneously exists a cultural ideal of slimness and a rising trend towards obesity, as we have already noted, is one which potentially creates a certain tension for many individuals in their relationship to food. It is clear that a significant proportion of the population of societies like the UK and USA experience a chronic state of concern about their weight and that conventionally this is seen as a concern which affects women more frequently than men. However, in certain circumstances, disturbances related to eating and weight can be so severe that they are clinically defined as serious eating disorders, which can be very debilitating and, indeed, even life-threatening to the sufferer.

Any discussion of such eating disorders is likely to rely heavily upon studies of those specifically involved in the analysis, treatment and management of anorexia nervosa. This particular disorder has certainly attracted the major share of attention in this area. Amongst such studies is the work of Bruch (1978) who was one of the first to draw attention to the increase in the number of cases amongst young women and to the contradictions and paradoxes associated with the disease. Although focused on a set of case studies from her own therapeutic practice, Bruch sets her analysis in the context of cultural and, indeed, physiological responses to food and uses this context to highlight the underlying and often unrecognized logic of her patients' anorexic behaviour. Bruch's interpretation of her case studies is that these young women from upper-middle- and upper-class homes use their anorexia, consciously or otherwise, to draw attention to themselves, possibly in an exhibitionistic fashion, in order to make sure that others care for them. In a sense, she suggests, their behaviour attracts a degree of awe and even admiration from people for whom self-starvation is a course of action which they would never countenance for themselves. She goes on to argue that the disease gives the girls power through the control of their eating. In contrast to those who argue that women are passive recipients of cultural expectations, Bruch uses her case material to argue that the sufferer is an active participant, rejecting food that is offered and available and becoming resentful of attempts to restore 'normal weight', because this process of starving 'in some strange way... fulfils their urgent desire to be special and outstanding' (1978: 20–1).

Bruch's book is entitled *The Golden Cage*, a title derived from an image used by one of her patients to explain her feeling both of being unworthy of all the privileges and benefits offered by her family and of at the same time being constrained and deprived of freedom of action. The question thus arises as to what kind of home relationships could produce feelings of this kind, so powerful that the outcome was a health-threatening condition. Bruch indicates that many of her patients had in common small family size with a predominance of daughters (two-thirds of the families had daughters only), and older parents. The impression of the harmonious home and the initially compliant behaviour from the child may conceal complex relationships of high expectations and parental lack of awareness concerning the extent to which the child is being controlled and restricted. Bruch argues that their inability to let go and permit the child to develop independently may contribute to and sustain the illness. Her

184

case material seemed to indicate that the illness often manifested itself at a point where the young women were confronted by some new experience, such as going to a new school or to college, where they no longer had the support of the family and where they were anxious about having to cope with relationships outside the family and to perform on the basis of their own merits. In other words, they seemed to be afraid of becoming teenagers with all the independence and femininity implied. In extreme cases, Bruch argues, the patients' weight loss enabled them to return to childhood. Bruch even goes as far as to suggest, perhaps very contentiously, that this behaviour may be interpreted as a means of avoiding the end of 'a secret dream of growing up to be a boy' (Bruch 1978: 69). In addition, dieting could provide an area of control and accomplishment and, paradoxically, patients could even experience a sense of satisfaction in relation to their own self-imposed ill-health. Within this framework, treatment involves the family as well as the specific sufferer and is considered successful when the young women involved both are able to gain sufficient weight so that their health is not endangered and to be recognized within the family as an individual with independent needs. Interestingly, Bruch is one of the few writers on this topic who see the possibility of a decline in the incidence of anorexia nervosa. She notes the way in which, when she first had sufferers referred to her, each of her patients would emphasize her uniqueness. In recent years, not only do patients know of other sufferers but they have also read a great deal about the illness (including Bruch's own contributions to the literature), so Bruch speculates that, if anorexia nervosa becomes sufficiently common, it will, in a sense, become 'commonplace'. Thus, sufferers would no longer gain the same sense of satisfaction at being special through achieving something that others cannot achieve.

One of the most comprehensive reviews of the literature on the characteristics of those suffering from eating disorders is that of Hsu (1990), which was written specifically to provide a summary of current knowledge on the eating disorders of anorexia nervosa and bulimia nervosa. The focus is on attempts to define and identify the disorders in a clinical sense and also to provide information about empirical findings, although there is more information about anorexia nervosa than about bulimia nervosa. Like other writers, he notes that the first use of the term 'anorexia nervosa' (from the Greek term for 'loss of appetite') was relatively recent, even though the condition had been recognized earlier as an illness which occurred infrequently. The term was used first in 1874 by the medical practitioner Sir William Gull to identify the eating problems of some of his young, female patients. The term has remained and is used widely in non-medical contexts, even though Hsu argues that it may, in fact, be a misnomer, since the evidence suggests that many patients have not 'lost' their appetites and often, in fact, wish to eat but are afraid to do so. Many studies show that patients identified as suffering from anorexia nervosa exhibit similar characteristics. However, the boundary between this disorder and 'normal' dieting is recognized as a blurred one and Hsu (1990) raises the question of whether anorexia nervosa is, in fact, an extreme form of the widespread phenomenon of dieting but a form which has run out of control. Having recognized what he sees as a 'behavioural continuum' between dieting and anorexia nervosa, Hsu takes the view that the crucial task is to identify those factors which might push the individual towards the anorexic end of this continuum. Thus, he identifies the central feature of the anorexia nervosa sufferer as a severe distortion of attitudes towards weight, eating and fatness. Hsu notes that the resultant fear of fatness actually intensifies as the individual loses weight, though for sufferers from bulimia nervosa the fear is accompanied by powerful urges to overeat or 'binge' and then to shed the unwanted food through vomiting or the use of laxatives. Since Hsu's task is largely informed by a wish to provide information which could form the basis for the treatment of disorders, he is primarily concerned to analyse the available data in such a way as to reveal crucial interactions between the cultural, psychological and biological processes involved. The survey of empirical investigations of these which Hsu provides is an attempt to examine data on such interactions.

Hsu begins by summarizing the data recorded about sufferers from eating disorders and indicates that those most commonly affected consistently exhibit certain features: they are young (often adolescent), white, female (the ratio of female to male is ten to one), and drawn from families located in the middle or upper social classes. They are also likely to already have been involved in attempts to control weight. Reviewing the clinical data from the available American and British studies, Hsu notes that most cases are presented to the medical practitioner when the sufferer is in her late teens. The case notes which Hsu reviews indicate that approximately 25 per cent of anorexics and about 40 per cent of bulimics were recorded as overweight before the onset of their illness and thus he concludes that attempts to control weight are the initiating phase of both these illnesses, though once there has been some weight loss, the two disorders diverge (Hsu 1990: 14). The anorexic person pursues thinness in spite of escalating weight loss; the bulimic person establishes a pattern of fasting, bingeing and purging with two-thirds using vomiting to control their weight. In ways which are similar to accounts of those who have been forced on to starvation diets because of external factors such as war or imprisonment, sufferers from eating disorders also begin to show an increased preoccupation with food and eating and an obsessive interest in recipes and cooking.

At the very point when family, friends and medical advisers are deeply concerned about the pattern of rapid weight loss, the sufferers themselves often deny that they are ill. Some even claim that they feel special or unique because of their thinness and experience despair and panic if they begin to gain weight. Some, indeed, claimed explicitly that their thinness demonstrated their autonomy. However, few were able to explain their fear of fatness. Those suffering from bulimia nervosa also feared fatness but were less able to control their food intake. Various situations or experiences could trigger binges. There are considerable problems involved in obtaining accurate information about the events which may have precipitated these eating disorders. However, the material

186

provided by patients includes a range of possibilities which seem to emphasize the significance of social relationships and potentially stressful events in adolescence. Such events included feelings of being too fat, being teased about size, the occurrence of interpersonal conflicts, separation from the family, personal illness or failure and family crises. In relation to the latter, Hsu draws attention to the importance of recognizing that, in certain circumstances, the illness might prove useful to the family by, for example, stabilizing its relationships by focusing collective concern on the person who is ill.

Anxieties about weight appear to be accentuated amongst higher socio-economic groups where thinness is sought after yet where there is ample food available. The high-status young women described in the case material were particularly aware of the importance of a favourable evaluation from others for the maintenance of their self-esteem. In addition, many of the young women in these groups aspired to combine professional careers with motherhood, that is, non-traditional aspirations informed by new models of women's potential. For some, these tensions about social identity could lead to eating disorders. Indeed, as Hsu asserts, 'Thus it would appear that the feminist movement has so far brought mixed blessings for women' (Hsu 1990: 86).

The range and detail handled by Hsu in his analysis is impressive. However, he is not able to come to any precise conclusions about the causes of eating disorders and sees treatment of them as involving a largely pragmatic selection from a wide range of possible therapeutic responses. None the less, Hsu's account involves more than mere summary. He makes an important argument that, if eating disturbances occur on a behavioural continuum, then the prevalence of eating disorders will increase or decline in proportion to dieting behaviour in the population. Associated with this is his observation that, although eating disorders appear to be linked with dieting behaviour, not everybody who diets moves along the continuum towards an eating disorder. This means that an interesting research issue would be an attempt to identify those influences which moderate eating patterns as well as those which precipitate disordered eating patterns.

Whilst Hsu acknowledges the significance of sociocultural factors, it is not his primary concern to analyse these in detail. However, for other authors such factors provide their central interest. For example, Brumberg (1988) focuses on the cultural context of eating disorders, in particular, anorexia nervosa. In common with other writers, she recognizes that anorexics frequently belong to prosperous families in an affluent social world: 'In other words, the anorexic population has a highly specific social address' (Brumberg 1988: 13). Brumberg sees anorexia nervosa as the outcome of the 'psychopathology' of middle-class life which, for some, generates tensions between a preoccupation with looks, dating rituals and pressures to succeed in both the private and the public domains. In more general terms, she suggests that the idealization of the thin and weak female body is a symptom of the female subordination which is characteristic of capitalism and patriarchy.

MacSween (1993) takes previous studies as her starting-point with the aim of providing a perspective on anorexia nervosa which is both feminist and sociological. She notes the ways in which anorexia nervosa has recently moved from being a relatively unknown psychiatric illness to a position where the term has been incorporated into the popular vocabulary and is increasingly used to label any woman in the public eye who is perceived as underweight. Anorexia nervosa is seen by MacSween as of particular interest for feminists and for sociologists in that its apparent increasing incidence has taken place among middle-class women at precisely the time when feminism is challenging female subordination. MacSween argues that most discussions recognize these issues and make reference to them but few actually attempt to provide a satisfactory sociological analysis. Her own analysis is based upon an examination of anorexic meanings and practices as revealed by interview material from one bulimic and eight anorexic women, together with the results of a postal questionnaire completed by women who had experienced or were experiencing this disorder. MacSween wishes to avoid what she terms an 'added on' sociological perspective which simply argues that, while there are 'social pressures' on young women, it is some shortcoming in the sufferer prior to the onset of anorexia nervosa which explains why one woman rather than another becomes anorexic. On the contrary, she asserts that 'in the anorexic symptom women try to synthesize contradictory elements in their social position through the creation of an "anorexic body"' (MacSween 1993: 2).

In discussing the rejection of such social causation by writers who emphasize the importance of individual psychology in the onset of anorexia nervosa, MacSween (1993) argues that it is important not to assume that social pressures constrain all individuals in similar ways and to recognize that circumstances do not determine behaviour but rather set the framework within which a range of behaviours can occur. In this author's terms, anorexia nervosa is one particular response to the contradictions and pressures experienced by women in a patriarchal and capitalist setting. Anorexia nervosa is one response to the contradictions inherent in female identity as constructed in a patriarchal capitalist system which, in effect, survived the onslaught of feminism and continued into the post-feminist era. A further barrier to a fuller understanding of the social construction of conditions like anorexia nervosa and how they are experienced is the emphasis of many writers on therapy and treatment. Psychological analysis, in particular, appears to be based on the assumption that the cause of anorexia nervosa is to be found at the individual level and therefore it should be treated at the individual level. In MacSween's view psychological analysis overemphasizes the idea that the causation of anorexia nervosa can be understood at the individual and interpersonal level and, therefore, puts too much faith in the effectiveness of treatment at the individual level. From this point of view, the emphasis on therapy, with its model of the 'natural', 'whole' person which can be reclaimed through successful treatment, gets in the way of a thorough going analysis of the roots of the problem. According to MacSween, the social construction of bodies in bourgeois society involves gender defined in terms of an opposition between masculine as active and feminine as passive. The problem for women in modern society is to reconcile the contradictory demands of being both active and passive, both assertive and responsive. It is MacSween's contention that this struggle can be manifested at the level of the body, through the production of the classic symptoms of anorexia nervosa.

The strength of MacSween's position as a feminist sociologist is that it encourages us to be aware of the cultural and structural setting which can give rise to such apparently bizarre phenomena as eating disorders. There is, of course, the strong implication in this view that, while an individual 'cure' for an individual case of, for example, anorexia nervosa might be achieved through skilful and dedicated therapy, the underlying conditions and contradictions remain. Not surprisingly, from her sociological perspective, MacSween takes the view that only a transformation guided by feminist principles of the structural conditions which sustain the subordination of women can have any long-term effect on the incidence of eating disorders of the kind we have been discussing in this chapter.

OVERVIEW

There can be little doubt that concern with body image, body fat and dieting is so pervasive within contemporary popular consciousness that it represents one of the more distinctive cultural obsessions of our age. We are faced with an apparent paradox: in the context of an abundant food supply many Western consumers (particularly women) become preoccupied with the desire to restrict food intake. However, in a sense, this apparent paradox is dispelled when we recognize that in a situation where food is not abundant and the food supply is not reliable the restriction of food intake to control body weight is, for the most part, an irrelevance. In this sense, the highly productive nature of the modern food system itself generates the motivation to control the quantity of nutrients absorbed. In fact, we have noted the existence of a more clear-cut paradox: the observation that, at precisely the time when our cultural preference for the slim body has been intensifying, actual body weights and levels of obesity in the population (as measured, for example, by mean BMI) have been rising. The response of commercial interests within a capitalist system has been to focus these anxieties by the provision of special diets, foods and relevant information and to capitalize on them to enhance profits.

The feminist contribution to the whole debate concerning body image and dieting has been a considerable one. It has encouraged social scientists to pay due attention to the patriarchal and capitalist context of the social construction of the feminine body. Similarly, feminist analyses have made a valuable contribution to the enhancement of our understanding of eating disorders by requiring that they be extracted from the narrow confines of a purely clinical setting and placed within a broader context of gender politics. As we have seen, the already complex debate concerning the causation of eating disorders has itself been complicated by a division between those who are primarily concerned to offer treatment at an individual level, and those whose main concern is to offer a sociological analysis which may emphasize structural constraints and contradictions which could only be resolved through collective action or far-reaching social transformations.

Quite clearly, this chapter, in attempting to provide a review of the literature on dieting, body image and eating disorders, inevitably reflects that literature's preoccupation with the predicament of women. However, we must bear in mind the distinct possibility that concern about weight and even the incidence of eating disorders may actually be rising amongst men. To date, this issue has received comparatively little attention from social scientists. If it should prove to be that case that issues of body weight and disordered eating become entangled with masculinity as well as femininity, then currently widely accepted explanatory frameworks, particularly those based on feminist perspectives, would need extensive reappraisal and revision.

Part IV

PATTERNS OF PREFERENCE AND AVOIDANCE

9

THE MYSTERIOUS MEANINGS
OF MEAT

Meat, in its many forms, represents what is probably the most universally valued of foods across the broad spectrum of human cultures. For an omnivorous species like ourselves, it can be construed as a food of particularly high nutritional value, especially as a source of protein. However, this whole book is, of course, based upon the premise that human food consumption is not only a question of satisfying nutritional needs. Certainly, it could be argued that there is much more to meat eating than the ingestion of a conveniently packaged range of important nutrients. For example, meat is arguably one of the most ambivalent of food items in terms of the three paradoxes discussed in Chapter 7. In gustatory terms, in health terms and in moral terms, meat carries particularly potent connotations, both positive and negative.

This chapter is concerned with the fundamental questions of why humans eat meat, and why they endow it with such significance. Are these effects largely a function of its physiological and nutritional relevance to the human diet or is its symbolic potential the more important source of its widespread appeal? We will consider these questions by examining the work of a range of social scientists whose views are sometimes in conflict, but who all acknowledge the singular salience of this particular food. However, initially we will need to consider briefly, by way of background, the nutritional import of meat in the human diet before examining the argument that our appetite for meat is, at root, a physiologically driven imperative which finds expression in many ways and in many guises. The symbolic dimensions of meat will be introduced by reconsidering examples of the taboos and prohibitions which exist, or have existed, in more traditional cultures. This will then lead us to an examination of the complex and often highly ambiguous symbolism associated with meat in contemporary Western culture. Finally, we will assess the view that the underlying meanings of meat in Western thought are undergoing far-reaching changes, associated with broader shifts in ideas about the relationship between humans and the natural world.

MEAT IN THE HUMAN DIET

In order to understand the role of meat in the human diet, a necessary first step is to attempt to clarify just what is meant by this term. In fact, in English the word 'meat' has a very broad meaning and can, indeed, signify literally anything that is edible. However, in its narrower sense, the word has come to denote the flesh of animals in general. Even more narrowly, in everyday parlance, the word 'meat' can be used quite specifically to refer to the flesh of mammals. What is more, the term 'meat' is usually assumed to refer to lean skeletal muscle tissues, that is, muscle tissue attached to the skeleton directly, and thus excluding the muscular tissues of such organs as the heart and the tongue. Indeed, in contemporary British culinary culture these organs are classified as 'offal' and usually regarded as cheap, low-status and not particularly palatable food items. Nevertheless, in the UK food manufacturers and retailers are permitted by law to label quite a wide range of offal as 'meat' on their product packaging. As well as heart and tongue, this category includes kidney, liver and pancreas, but excludes brain tissue and parts of the alimentary canal and reproductive system. It is clear, then, that the word 'meat' is something of a semantic minefield, with its multiple meanings and convoluted connotations. In this chapter we will be using the term in the broader sense of animal flesh in general, as well as in the narrower sense of lean muscle tissue (usually, but not necessarily, derived from a mammal).

Lean meat (i.e., lean muscle tissue) is composed of approximately 70 per cent water and 20 per cent protein before cooking, plus variable amounts of fat, connective tissue, vitamins and minerals. The amount of fat in muscle tissue depends upon a range of factors related to genetics, feeding and activity levels. Wild mammals, for example, have significantly less fat inside their muscle tissues than do domesticated mammals. The actual structure of meat is complex. It is composed of muscle blocks made up of bundles of elongated cells capable of contraction and relaxation to produce movement in limbs and organs. Muscles are bound together with connective tissue containing the proteins elastin and collagen (which yields gelatin on boiling) and are served by an elaborate network of blood vessels and nerves. Well-used muscles are made up of thicker fibres and contain more connective tissues than less-used muscles and therefore produce tougher meat. Meat intended for human consumption is usually cooked in order to neutralize potentially harmful organisms it may contain and to tenderize it. Tougher meat is often subjected to 'moist' cooking methods like boiling and stewing, since these are more effective in breaking down connective tissue than 'dry' methods like grilling and roasting. Hanging meat after slaughter is also a common practice, as this allows rigor mortis to wear off and facilitates the tenderizing effect brought on by complex chemical changes in the tissues themselves.

The nutritional significance of meat for humans is related to our specific needs for certain amino acids. The proteins which are indispensable constituents of the human body (as they are of all living things) are made up of chains of amino acid molecules. Some of the amino acids which make up human proteins can be made by the body itself, and do not need to be supplied in a ready-made form in the diet. However, other amino acids cannot be synthesized by the human body and have to be obtained directly by breaking down proteins that have been ingested. These are termed *essential* amino acids, in the sense that they are essential components of any nutritionally adequate diet. There are eight of these essential amino acids for adults, and ten for children. Quite clearly, dietary proteins whose components most closely match human essential amino acid requirements will be of particular nutritional value. In fact, the closest match is provided by egg protein, and this is often used as a kind of standard against which other proteins can be compared. Proteins which are rich in essential amino acids are conventionally termed 'high biological value' proteins (Brownsell, Griffith and Jones 1989: 40), and as well as eggs include a wide range of meat, fish and other animal products. Those which are deficient in one or more of the essential amino acids are termed 'low biological value' proteins. All plant proteins fall into this category, since no plant proteins contain all the essential amino acids. Of course, the full inventory of essential amino acids can be obtained by consuming a suitable combination of plant-derived foods. However, what is distinctive about animal-derived proteins like meat is that they contain all the essential amino acids in one readily assimilable package. In addition, animal products also provide the crucial vitamin B_{12}, which is not found in vegetable food items. Liver is the richest source of this vitamin, although it is also present in meat, milk, eggs and fish. A deficiency of vitamin B_{12} causes the disease pernicious anaemia, which is associated with such symptoms as spinal cord lesions, weakness, numbness of the arms and legs, and diarrhoea. This disease is usually the result of the body's failure to absorb vitamin B_{12}, but pernicious anaemia among vegans, arising from the total exclusion of animal products from the diet, has been observed (Gaman and Sherrington 1981: 96). Thus, the use of dietary supplements containing synthesized B_{12} is a sensible precaution for anyone following a strictly vegan dietary regime.

As a rough rule of thumb, it has been suggested that the typical adult requires approximately one gram of protein per kilogram of body weight per day, whereas children, with the added demands of growth, require approximately two grams per kilogram of bodyweight per day. Protein requirements rise during pregnancy and lactation, and during illness and convalescence. Various attempts have been made to calculate the sources of protein in the average British diet, and from these we can obtain some idea of the significance of meat in this respect. Thus, Gaman and Sherrington (1981: 80–1) estimate that meat in all forms contributes around 31 per cent of protein intake. Fish contributes approximately 4 per cent (being eaten much less frequently), milk 18 per cent, cheese 5 per cent and eggs 5 per cent. Significant contributions from non-animal products include bread and flour (19 per cent) and other cereal foods, such as rice, pasta and breakfast cereals (7 per cent). Later estimates offered by Brownsell, Griffith and Jones (1989: 45) provide a broadly comparable picture, with meat making a 30 per cent contribution to the protein component of the British diet, fish 4 per cent, milk 18 per cent, eggs 5 per cent and bread 20 per cent. While these figures are only broad approximations, they do indicate the centrality of meat as a protein source, and the overall preponderance of animal products in this respect.

Meat has long held a dominant position in the typical American diet, a dominance which has its origins in the early days of European settlement and the abundance of game species (Thomas 1991: 42). Levenstein (1988: 4–5) also links the centrality of meat in American diets to the long-term influence of British culinary culture, in which meat has traditionally been accorded pride of place. Thus, for example, nineteenth-century American cuisine involved the consumption of large quantities of pork, plus lesser amounts of lamb and poultry. Beef, however, was pre-eminent in terms of the status accorded to it and the symbolic value placed upon it. On the other hand, as Levenstein points out, the early New Englanders held fruit and vegetables in relatively low esteem, consuming them in comparatively small quantities. Indeed until the mid-nineteenth century constipation seems to have been regarded as a widespread national affliction among Americans, due to the large quantities of meat and starch consumed, compared to the modest intake of fruit and vegetables (Levenstein 1988: 5).

However, although meat has historically played a central role in British and American diets, the actual patterns of meat consumption are by no means static. In fact, in the course of the twentieth century a number of significant trends have emerged. For example, if we consider meat consumption patterns in the

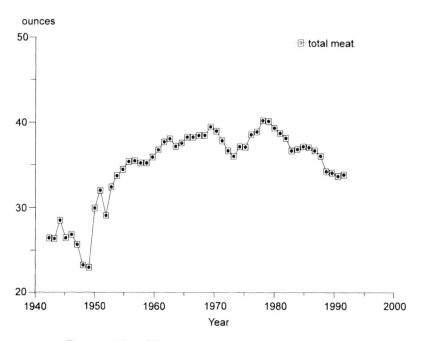

Figure 9.1   Total UK meat consumption (oz per person per week)
Source: Ministry of Agriculture, Fisheries and Food (1991, 1994)

UK from the Second World War onwards, we can detect not only changes in overall consumption but also noteworthy shifts in the consumption of specific types of meat and meat products. Figure 9.1 shows the total consumption of meat and meat products in the United Kingdom from 1940 until 1993, expressed in ounces per person per week. This graph has some very clear features. Meat consumption was relatively low during the Second World War as a result of meat rationing, although it dropped even lower during the late 1940s as a result of post-war austerity measures. However, from the early 1950s onwards meat consumption began to rise consistently in response to increased affluence resulting from rising real incomes. After a temporary dip in the 1970s, the figures peaked at 40.27 oz per head in 1979, and then went into decline in the 1980s. Within these broad overall trends, different pictures emerge for different types of meat. Figure 9.2 provides details of consumption trends for beef and veal, mutton and lamb, and poultry, also for the years 1940 to 1993 in oz per person per week. Figure 9.3 shows the same data for pork, bacon and ham, and sausages.

Thus, for example, the consumption of beef and veal, relatively low in the 1940s, rose in the mid-1950s and peaked in 1957 at 10.54 oz per person per week. It then appears to have gone into a rather erratic decline, down to a figure of 4.68 oz by 1993. Mutton and lamb seem to have followed a similar pattern, with consumption peaking at 7.16 ozs in 1956 and declining to 2.33 by 1993. Pork consumption, low in the 1940s, peaked in 1982. Bacon and ham peaked in

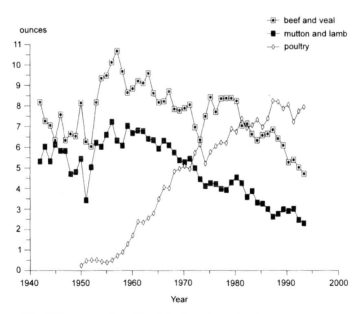

Figure 9.2 UK consumption of beef, lamb and poultry (oz per person per week)
Source: Ministry of Agriculture, Fisheries and Food (1991, 1994)

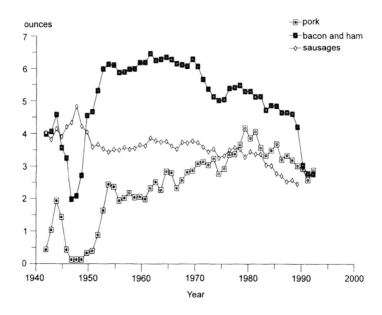

Figure 9.3 UK consumption of sausages and pork products (oz per person per week)
Source: Ministry of Agriculture, Fisheries and Food (1991, 1994)

1962 and then also declined. Sausages showed their highest level of consumption as early as 1948 and then their popularity began to diminish steadily and consistently. In stark contrast, the data for the consumption of poultry (in the UK this category is made up largely of chicken) exhibits the opposite of the trends we have so far been discussing. From very low levels in the early 1950s (well under 1 oz per person per week on average) consumption climbed steadily to peak at no less than 8.14 oz in 1987. In 1993, poultry was the most popular category of meat in the UK by a wide margin. This trend towards poultry is due in large part to the dramatic drop in its price relative to other meats, a fall which is a result of the progressive intensification of poultry production techniques in a drive to reduce costs and improve profitability. The data indicate a clear pattern, which involves a switch away from meat derived from mammals to meat derived from birds and, broadly speaking, from red meat towards white meat.

A broadly similar picture emerges for the USA when we examine data relating to the quantities of various types of meat available to the public. Such data are not, in themselves, directly comparable to the survey based per capita consumption statistics in Figures 9.1, 9.2, and 9.3, since they are actually attempting to estimate the disappearance of food into both wholesale and retail markets. This is achieved on an annual basis by subtracting exports, year end inventories and non-food uses from production, start of year inventories and imports. Of course, the availability levels will be higher than actual consumption

Table 9.1   Quantities of meat available for consumption in the
US food supply (lb per capita per annum)

Type of meat	1909–13	1929–33	1944–8	1970–4	1975–9	1987
Beef	53.2	38.2	48.2	83.9	87.8	73.4
Veal	6.3	5.9	9.8	2.0	2.8	1.5
Pork	60.9	63.6	63.9	62.1	55.8	59.2
Lamb & mutton	6.2	5.8	5.4	2.6	1.5	1.3
Chicken	14.9	14.4	19.3	40.5	44.8	62.7
Turkey	1.1	1.6	3.1	8.6	9.1	15.1
Total	142.6	129.5	149.7	199.7	201.8	213.2

Source: Adapted from Thomas (1991: 44–5)

levels, due to wastage in distribution and processing, and in the home (Thomas 1991: 42). Table 9.1 shows the quantities of various types of meat available for consumption in the USA, covering the period 1909 to 1987.

The data for beef show a significant dip in the period 1929–33 and then a dramatic rise to the levels of 1970–4 and 1975–9. This latter period, however, seems to represent a peak, and the figure calculated for the year 1987 shows a significant fall. Veal availability peaks much earlier, in the period 1944–8, and lamb and mutton decline steadily throughout the entire period covered. Interestingly, pork availability seems to remain remarkably stable. In contrast, the availability of chicken rises dramatically, to a level in 1987 which is approximately four times that of 1909–13. The rise of turkey is even more spectacular, to a level in 1987 which is nearly fourteen times higher than the 1909–13 figure. Thus, once again, we observe the stagnation or decline of red meat and a clear trend towards white meat.

However, the trends in meat consumption in countries like the UK and the USA clearly need to be placed in a wider global context. Such a global context is provided by Grigg (1993) who uses the Food Balance Sheets produced by the Food and Agriculture Organization (FAO) as a source of comparative data. For each member country over eighty food items are listed along with the weight available for consumption each year. Items are also converted, for example, into calories per capita per day and grams of protein per capita per day. The data are arrived at by starting with national agricultural production statistics and adding imports and the quantities withdrawn from storage, and then deducting exports, industrial usage and crops retained on the farm. Finally, 10 per cent is deducted to allow for wastage between the production and retailing stages. Although, as we have already noted, actual consumption is lower than availability and, in addition, these statistics can be criticized on several counts, they do provide at least some basis for international comparisons. Perhaps the most useful comparative measure is that which converts food items into calories per capita per day. On this basis, for the years 1986–8, in worldwide terms animal-derived foods provided only 15.7 per cent of per capita calories daily. In fact, meat itself provided only 7.0 per cent of per capita daily calories on a global basis. This figure masks a significant difference between developed and developing countries, however. In the former, on average, individuals derive 30.8 per cent of their daily calories from animal products and 13.1 per cent from meat specifically. In developing countries these figures are only 8.9 per cent and 4.3 per cent respectively (Grigg 1993: 67). Indeed, there appears to be a consistent positive correlation between Gross Domestic Product per capita and livestock-derived calories per capita consumed daily. In short, in worldwide terms, meat eating is clearly associated with wealth. Indeed, the extent of the inequalities in meat consumption becomes even clearer when the data are broken down on a regional basis, as shown in Table 9.2.

Table 9.2 Available meat supply by region expressed as calories per capita per day (1986–88)

Region	All meat	Bovine meat[1]	Sheep meat[2]	Pig meat	Poultry meat	Other meat
Western Europe	476	121	22	269	56	8
Australasia	593	189	168	143	89	4
North America	641	259	1	247	131	3
Eastern Europe & USSR	359	171	13	132	40	3
Latin America	210	113	5	48	42	2
Near East	95	34	42	–	18	1
Far East	30	7	4	12	6	1
Africa	32	23	9	–	–	–
Developed	436	161	15	190	66	4
Developing	100	21	7	60	11	1
World	182	55	9	92	24	2

Note:
1 Cattle and buffalo
2 Includes goat meat
Source: Adapted from Grigg (1993)

There are clearly considerable regional variations in the patterns of meat consumption. For example, the availability of beef-derived calories is particularly high in North America and Australasia, and the same is true for poultry meat. The availability of pig-meat calories is even higher in Western Europe than in North America, and sheep meat is far more common in Australasia than in any other region. Yet the most striking features of Table 9.2 relate to the differences between developed and developing countries, with on average 436 calories per person per day available from meat in the former, and only 100 calories in the latter. Comparing regional inequalities provides even more striking results. The Far East and Africa show only 30 and 32 calories respectively available from meat daily, just about one-twentieth of the level of availability in North America.

Despite the limitations inherent in the statistics Grigg employs, his results clearly demonstrate the extent to which levels of meat consumption vary between the richer and poorer regions. In general, as wealth rises, meat consumption also tends to rise, indicating the extent to which the desirability of this food item is translated into actual demand. Moreover, it should be noted that the comparative data we have considered, given that they are per capita averages, conceal the extensive inequalities which often exist between individuals within a given society or culture, related to status, gender and age, for example. Thus, when we consider the role of meat in the human diet, we must always bear in mind that, while for some individuals this role may be highly significant, for others it may be minimal, and that this state of affairs is as likely to be due to economic constraint as to cultural dictate or personal preference.

THE IDEA OF 'MEAT HUNGER'

In the above section we have noted the nutritional significance of meat in the human diet, in the setting of particular societies like the UK and the USA as well as in a global context. In addition, important changes in meat consumption patterns have been pointed out. Before possible explanations for such changes can be considered in further detail, it is necessary to pose a very fundamental question: 'Why, in fact, do humans go to all the trouble of eating meat?' After all, in its wild form it is often difficult to pursue and hard to catch (Farb and Armelagos 1980: 44). In its domesticated form it is decidedly expensive to obtain. For example, animal protein produced in modern intensive agricultural systems by feeding grain to livestock involves the input of large quantities of vegetable protein. For every kilogram of poultry-meat protein, a chicken needs to be fed 5.9 kilograms of grain protein. For every kilogram of pork protein a pig must be fed 7.7 kilograms of grain protein. Grain-fed beef produced in feedlots is even more demanding, requiring 22 kilograms of grain protein per kilogram of beef protein (Allaby 1977: 20). Thus, in terms of yield per unit of land, livestock products apparently cannot compare in efficiency with vegetable products. Indeed, it has been estimated that every calorie of animal foodstuff produced requires the input of five to eight primary calories (Borgstrom 1972: 31). However, it should be noted that in less intensive agricultural systems, animal husbandry may be a much more obviously efficient use of resources. For example, domesticated food animals can be fed on vegetable by-products and food wastes inappropriate for direct human consumption. Also, areas unsuitable for arable farming (e.g., low-fertility uplands, semi-arid or arid zones) can be used for food production by stocking with grazing or browsing ruminants which can consume high-cellulose plant foods with which the human digestive system cannot cope (Blaxter 1986: 55).

Perhaps the most obvious answer to the question of why humans eat meat (despite the fact that, as already noted, its production can appear inefficient compared to that of vegetable-based foods) relates to the fact that it represents a compact and palatable package rich in nutrients. Some social scientists accept this view as their starting-point for explaining patterns of meat consumption, arguing that the complex symbolic significances which cultures ascribe to meat are, in effect, manifestations or reflections of this underlying nutritional attraction. In contrast, others have argued that the symbolic dimensions of meat, the potent meanings it bears within a given cultural context, provide the principal reasons for its consumption, with nutritional considerations taking second place. Of course, these two views are not, in practice, mutually exclusive, although they do represent an important difference in emphasis, a difference which can lead to very different conclusions. In this chapter we will examine both these views, beginning with what is perhaps the intuitively more obvious one: the idea that humans are drawn to the nutritious properties of meat, and that this is a basic inclination of primary significance.

This idea finds its most direct expression in the work of Harris (1986), who explicitly entitles one of his chapters 'Meat hunger'. Harris bases his argument for the universal appeal of meat for humans on the idea that, although we are not true carnivores, meat provides an especially appropriate source of nutrients for our species. He refers specifically to the profile of essential amino acids which meat contains and to its provision of the vitamin B_{12}, which features were discussed in some detail above, as well as to its provision of essential minerals like iron, zinc, copper and iodine. Indeed, the contention is put forward that the evolutionary background of the human species is at the root of this match between meat and our most basic nutritional needs. The inability of the human digestive system to deal with bulky and fibrous plant tissues rich in cellulose and lignin is seen as associated with our preference for high-energy, high-protein and low-bulk foods, of which animal products represent one of the most desirable categories (Harris 1986: 36–7).

It will be recalled that in Chapter 1 we came across the argument that the human need for a high-quality, high-energy diet is related to the unusually high metabolic demands of the human brain, which typically takes up 20–5 per cent of the energy expended at the resting metabolic rate. Thus, in Harris's terms, meat consumption could be seen as part of a broader set of nutritional needs related to low bulk and high quality. What is more, as Harris (1986: 29–31) and Farb and Armelagos (1980: 43) point out, with the exception of larger species like the gorilla, our close primate relatives are by no means exclusively vegetarian. For example, baboons, although largely dependent upon vegetable foods, will eat insects, reptiles, birds and small mammals. Both baboons and chimpanzees will also engage in the co-operative hunting of small primates and the young of small grazing animals like gazelles. On these grounds, it would appear that the incorporation of meat into the diet as a significant, if not necessarily dominant, component is a common feature of the order of mammals to which our own species belongs. It is in this evolutionary context that authors like Harris, and Farb and Armelagos, locate their argument for an inbuilt meat hunger related to the intrinsic nutritional needs of humans. This position is closely related to the somewhat contentious viewpoint discussed in Chapter 1 which allocates central significance to hunting, not only as the basic mode of subsistence of early humans but also as the key driving force behind the initial development of human co-operative capacities and human culture.

In order to support his contention that meat represents an intrinsically pre-ferred element in the human diet, Harris points out the esteem in which meat is held, not only in Western cultures but also in a wide range of traditional societies. He provides ethnographic evidence relating to traditional cultures where meat is accorded significantly higher status and desirability than plant foods, and points out that the languages of traditional peoples may contain explicit concepts of 'meat hunger', that is, a hunger which is construed as focused specifically upon animal flesh, and one which can be satisfied by no other foodstuff. For examples of the use of such a concept he cites the Canela of Amazonia and the Semai people of Malaysia (Harris 1986: 26–7). Indeed, he argues that meat is so highly valued that there usually exist elaborate rules which govern the way in which the carcass of a game animal or slaughtered domesticated beast is divided up and the parts then distributed through the community. Such rules appear to ensure access to this prized food by a wide range of individuals and also establish and maintain obligations of reciprocity which guarantee future supplies of meat when one's own hunting or husbandry is less productive. (See Coon 1976: 201–4 for exam-ples of meat sharing rules among such hunting peoples as the Tigarans, the Ona, the Birhors and the Mbuti.) As Farb and Armelagos (1980: 48) point out, using the Inuit as an example, such is the value placed on meat in hunting-gathering cultures that the consistently successful hunter is accorded a unique degree of prestige. In contrast, the providers of gathered (e.g., plant) foods are accorded far less prestige, this differential being closely associated, as we might expect, with gender. Indeed, the intense desire for meat, Harris argues, can lead to disputes and quarrels when the supply is reduced and reciprocity gives way to jealousy and resentment. He cites the case of the Yanomamo of Amazonia, whose communities may split and separate as a direct result of the tensions generated by meat shortages which begin to occur when the group's hunters have seriously depleted the stock of game in the immediate locality (Harris 1986: 28).

Such evidence, then, is taken as demonstrating the unique status of meat, placing in its true nutritional and cultural contexts the considerable amount of effort and ingenuity humans expend in order to obtain this particular source of nutrients. Yet, even if we accept, at least in broad principle, Harris's view that there is a powerful physiological factor behind meat eating by humans, this position does not necessarily lead to clear-cut conclusions about the role of meat in the diet of members of affluent, industralized societies. In such societies, a foodstuff traditionally hard to obtain and often in relatively short supply, be-comes abundant and accessible. In such circumstances, its nutritional and symbolic significances may undergo fundamental changes.

MEAT TABOOS AND PROHIBITIONS IN TRADITIONAL CULTURES

However, having examined the argument for human 'meat hunger', we need to confront an apparently awkward question: 'If humans have an innate taste for meat, why is this prized food item the object of complicated taboos and prohibitions in many traditional societies and in some of the world's major religions?' Perhaps the best documented and most detailed study of the diverse customs of meat avoidance found around the world is provided by Simoons (1961). In effect, the study is based upon the premise that flesh foods are far more likely to be the subjects of powerful prohibitions supported by punitive sanctions than are vegetable-based foods (Simoons 1961: 108). Such prohibitions, therefore, demand description and explanation, and Simoons examines the patterns of acceptance and avoidance relating to six types of meat: pork, beef, chicken, horse flesh, camel flesh and dog flesh.

In relation to pork, Simoons notes that the pig is a very significant source of meat for a substantial proportion of the world's population. Pork was a favoured food among the Greeks and the Romans, and the pig was introduced as a domesticated animal into Africa south of the Sahara from the fifteenth century onwards. Pig keeping is widespread in South East Asia, in Polynesia and Micronesia, and is particularly important in China, where pork is a highly valued food. Yet, despite the importance of the pig as a domesticated animal, its use for food is totally rejected by adherents to two of the world's major religions, Judaism and Islam, whose doctrines define the animal as unclean and unfit for human consumption. (As we noted in Chapter 7, this rejection of pork is part of wider sets of prohibitions relating to flesh foods contained in the teachings of these two related religions.) What is more, Hindus also regard the pig as unclean, and in India these animals are raised and eaten mainly by aboriginal peoples.

Domesticated cattle, in all their various breeds and forms, constitute the single most numerous large herbivore on earth. Their flesh is consumed with relish in Europe, North and South America, Africa and Australasia, and consumption has also begun to rise in areas like China and Japan, where traditionally it was relatively low. Yet, apparently paradoxically, Hinduism, the major religion of India, a country estimated to contain a fifth of the world's cattle, prohibits the consumption of beef. This prohibition appears to be related to the status of the cow as a sacred animal and to the fact that vegetarianism and the avoidance of flesh foods is associated with the higher ranks of the Indian caste system.

While the prohibitions which relate to the consumption of pork and beef are well known to most Westerners, far less well known in the West are the widespread taboos which exist around the world relating to the eating of chicken and eggs (Simoons 1961: 65). In fact, Simoons describes the rejection of the flesh of domestic fowl by such peoples as the Vedda of Ceylon (Sri Lanka) and provides numerous examples of beliefs which hold that the consumption of chicken or eggs can be positively dangerous (e.g., the belief among the rural Annamese that chicken is toxic for pregnant women). What is more, there is a widespread dislike of chicken among Hindus, which seems to be related to vegetarian preferences and to the belief that because of its eating habits, the chicken is unclean. Similarly, Buddhist beliefs are largely antithetical to the consumption of chicken, again possibly related to distaste for the bird's feeding habits. Thus, in Tibet, chickens are seen as 'sinful' and 'unclean' since they eat worms (Simoons 1961: 70).

In contrast to his discussion of prohibitions which run counter to Western dietary practices, Simoons also describes avoidances and taboos which the average Western consumer would find entirely in line with his or her own nutritional culture. For example, horse flesh is a prohibited food in a wide range of societies and cultural settings, including Europe, where the influence of Christianity gradually eliminated the practice of eating horse, which had strong associations with pagan beliefs (Simoons 1961: 83–4). The teachings of Islam are somewhat ambivalent on the acceptability of horse flesh, and in Hindu India only a few untouchable groups eat horse meat. Camel flesh is widely consumed in the Muslim world, but is a prohibited food among many non-Muslim peoples of the Middle East. Camel meat is also widely avoided in the Far East, and in Mongolia camel milk is drunk but the flesh is rejected as a food item.

Faced with the wide range of prohibitions on flesh foods, of which the above are only illustrative examples, the challenge of explaining their origins and significance is a decidedly daunting one. This is particularly so when neighbour-ing cultures contain quite different forms of avoidances and taboos. In fact, Simoons offers a number of explanations, each of which is tailored to the taboo in question. By and large, his explanations rest upon the premise that such prohibitions are primarily based upon the symbolic significance of the foods or animals in question, and that the avoidance of particular flesh foods can often be a powerful expressive act in itself. For example, in discussing the range of explanations which has been put forward to explain the Hindu rejection of beef, he gives particular prominence to the view that this rejection had its roots in rivalry between Brahmans and Buddhists. Indeed, one argument maintains that Brahmans gave up cattle sacrifice and beef eating in order to improve their moral and political credibility in the face of Buddhist criticisms of these prac-tices. What is more, Simoons suggests that such a move could have been facilitated by the long established sacred character of cattle in Indian culture (Simoons 1961: 61–3). This line of reasoning concerning the expressive signifi-cance of meat rejection is closely related to the view that the rejection of a certain animal as a source of food may be a way of showing disapproval of, or contempt for, those peoples or cultures with which that animal is associated. Thus, for example, the taboo on pork characteristic of Judaism and Islam has been characterized as having its early roots in the pastoralist's disdain for the way of life of the settled agriculturalist. Given that the conditions needed for successful pig rearing can only be achieved by settled farmers, and that pigs are quite unsuited to a nomadic, pastoralist way of life, they came to symbolize, as an animal and a food source, the very antithesis of nomadic culture.

In effect, what is being suggested is that the rejection of a particular flesh food can be a powerful cultural device to reinforce and emphasize a particular group's collective identity, as can the acceptance of a given flesh food. Thus, the acceptability of camel flesh to Muslims may be countered by the rejection of camel flesh by non-Muslim groups wishing to resist Muslim cultural influences (Simoons 1961: 121). Indeed, the prophet who initiates a new religion or cult may lay down a whole series of dietary regulations and avoidances to enable the faithful clearly to distinguish themselves from non-believers. As we have already noted, such symbolic avoidances can be associated with carefully specified rituals concerning the slaughtering of animals and the preparation of flesh foods for human consumption. Flesh not prepared according to the prescribed rituals is likely to be seen as dangerous or polluting. The rejection of such flesh is in itself a clear expression of the individual's continuing commitment to the religion or system of belief in question.

As well as the flesh avoidances which are integral to some of the world's major religions, magical beliefs leading to the avoidance of the flesh of particular animals also appear to be very widespread. Indeed, Simoons provides a wide range of examples of such beliefs, which often take the form of the idea that eating a given animal will magically produce specific undesirable or dangerous effects. One instance of this is the avoidance of venison by warriors and young men among the Dyak of Northwest Borneo, for fear that they would become timid like deer (Simoons 1961: 117). Where totemic beliefs are present in a culture, individuals may be required to honour and protect their totemic animal and forbidden to kill and eat it under threat of dire supernatural sanctions. It has even been suggested by structuralists like Mary Douglas that animals which present taxonomic contradictions within a given culture will be rejected as food sources because of their disturbing symbolic import (Douglas 1966: 54–6).

The argument that meat taboos, generally speaking, have their origins in the diverse symbolic significances and cultural meanings attached to this particular form of food can, as we have seen, be countered with a much more pragmatic view of such prohibitions. In essence, the pragmatic perspective argues that meat prohibitions frequently have a real practical utility and that this utility is the fundamental reason for their existence, any symbolic or expressive attributes being merely reflections or reinforcements. One of the best-known versions of this pragmatic view is the idea that certain forms of meat prohibition have important hygienic aspects. For example, animals which act as scavengers and consume waste products may be seen as sources of health hazards, a view which has often been cited to explain pork avoidance in Judaism and Islam. A similar argument suggests that pork may be avoided in warmer climates because of its supposed susceptibility to rapid decay and spoiling. Perhaps the most sophisticated of these hygienic arguments relates to the disease trichinosis. This serious illness produces nausea, diarrhoea, fever and swelling of the muscles, and is caused by eating undercooked pig muscle tissue infested with the larvae of the parasitic nematode worm *trichinella spiralis*. However, both Harris (1986) and Simoons (1961) are sceptical concerning such arguments, pointing out, for example, that it is only comparatively recently that the aetiology of trichinosis has been fully understood, and that other serious diseases like tapeworm infestation can be contracted from other forms of undercooked meat. Furthermore, since the delay between the ingestion of the larvae and the onset of symptoms is a relatively long one, it is unlikely that traditional cultures could have established the causal link and made it the basis of a prohibition. In fact, hygiene-based explanations may be little more than modern rationalizations of much more ancient and deep-seated taboos and prejudices (Simoons 1961: 16).

A much more convincing example of the attempt to explain meat taboos in pragmatic terms is provided by Harris's analysis of the Hindu prohibition on beef consumption. Harris confronts the apparent irrationality inherent in the fact that India has the largest cattle population of any country on earth (a significant proportion of this population being sick, barren or dry) along with a very large population of humans, many of whom are desperately short of dietary protein. In these circumstances, a taboo on beef eating seems the height of folly, a curious religious observance which wastes precious resources and condemns many to malnutrition. However, Harris seeks to demonstrate that the prohibition on beef consumption may actually have crucial practical advantages, protecting and enhancing the living standards of some of the poorest sections of Indian society. The whole argument hinges upon the nature of the humpbacked Zebu breeds of cattle which are found in India. These breeds are capable of providing the motive power for ploughing, even in extreme conditions of heat and drought, and can survive on very meagre rations of feed and fodder, often consisting of little more than such items as stalks, chaff, leaves and waste left over from human food consumption (Harris 1986: 56). Harris points out that such animals are, in fact, far more cost-efficient than tractors for ploughing purposes, given that most Indian farming units are very small and taking into account the very high initial investment that mechanization demands. Indeed, cows provide the Indian peasant with several valuable products: oxen for ploughing, milk (a precious source of fats and protein even if available only in small amounts) and dung (a clean and effective fuel for cooking in an environment where wood is scarce). In short, Harris argues that the prohibition on killing cows effectively enhances the long-term viability of Indian agriculture. It encourages farmers to resist the temptation to eat temporarily useless animals during periods of food shortage and climatic stress. If they were to succumb to this temptation, their ability to resume the cycle of agricultural production when conditions improved would be seriously compromised, and many of the poorest farmers would be driven off the land and into an even more marginal existence in already overcrowded cities.

As further evidence of what he sees as the underlying pragmatism of Indian attitudes to cattle, Harris cites a number of practices, some of which have already been referred to in Chapter 7. For example, surplus animals are sold off to Muslim traders, and many of these animals are actually destined for slaughter and consumption. Cows which die of natural causes or neglect become available as food to carrion-eating castes, who consume the edible parts and recycle the rest of the carcass. What is more, the sex ratios within the cattle population vary significantly from region to region in India, according to local agricultural requirements and practices. Harris suggests that such differences can only be produced by farmers' favouring calves of the preferred sex and neglecting calves of the non-preferred sex, thereby producing significant differences in mortality rates (Harris 1986: 59–60).

Harris also seeks to find a similarly pragmatic explanation for the avoidance of pork inherent in the teachings of Judaism and Islam. For example, he is highly critical of the view put forward by Douglas (1966) that this pork taboo emerges out of the idea that the pig represents a kind of taxonomic anomaly in terms of the dietary laws of the Old Testament, which require that in order to be acceptable to eat an animal must both chew the cud and be cloven-hoofed. Since the pig only fulfils one of these conditions but not the other (it does not chew the cud), Douglas maintains that it came to be seen as a dangerous abomination and therefore as unclean, unfit for human consumption. Harris (1986) rejects what he sees as the circularity of this kind of structuralist argument, looking instead for a more mundane and practical basis for this prohibition. In effect, his explanation is an ecological one. The deforestation of the Middle East and the degradation of farmland into desert progressively removed the conditions in which pig husbandry could be practised economically. Pigs require shade, water, mud for wallowing and a relatively high-quality diet which in many ways overlaps with that of humans. All these features would militate against their use as food animals in arid conditions. On the other hand, cloven-hoofed, cud-chewing ruminants like cattle, sheep and goats can survive even in near-desert conditions and can subsist on high-bulk, fibrous plant foods like leaves and stems that humans simply cannot digest. Thus, in agricultural and ecological terms, the ruminants were clearly a better option than the pig in the arid Middle East. This inescapable fact of life represents, for Harris, the basis of pork rejection in these cultures.

There can be no doubting the ingenuity and the plausibility of arguments like those of Harris. The value of such arguments is that they remind us that no food system can possibly maintain its continuity in the long term other than within the parameters set by economic, climatic and ecological realities. Yet, within the framework provided by those parameters there is often enormous scope for humans to exploit the multilayered symbolic potential of food for a whole range of expressive and cultural purposes. This is certainly the case when we consider the logic behind meat prohibitions of various types. Such prohibitions certainly carry potent symbolic charges. They are loaded with meanings, some explicit, some more implicit, but they may also carry some direct or indirect pragmatic advantage, at least for some of the parties who subscribe to the taboo. Any attempt to assess the relative weightings of symbolic and practical factors is fraught with difficulty, particularly as the two are inevitably closely, often inextricably, intertwined with each other. Even more difficult is the attempt to allocate priority to one or other. Do pragmatic choices and strategies give rise to prohibitions, which are then enshrined in the symbolic vocabularies of ritual, custom and religion? Or do attempts to create meaning, order and legitimacy at the symbolic level give rise to prohibitions which later have retrospective pragmatic rationalizations attached to them? In the case of meat prohibitions these are unresolved, perhaps unresolvable, questions. This lack of resolution means that we must keep both possibilities in mind when analyzing the role of meat in any nutritional culture.

MEAT SYMBOLISM IN CONTEMPORARY WESTERN CULTURE

Of course, meat prohibitions are not limited to traditional cultures, but also exist in modern Western societies and can exert a significant influence on dietary patterns. For example, while the flesh of wild mammals and birds currently furnishes only a very small proportion of the protein component of Western diets, some species are still hunted for recreational purposes and as seasonally available sources of food. However, in general, only a very narrow range of fish, bird and mammal species is defined (legally and culturally) as 'game', although the actual list does vary somewhat from society to society (North American hunters, for example, regard the grey squirrel as an edible quarry species, whereas in Britain the same animal is regarded either as an inedible pest or as an attractive decorative feature of park or garden, depending on one's point of view). Thus, in effect, all wild species outside the definition 'game' are prohibited flesh for the average Westerner, and eating them would be virtually inconceivable. This taboo upon the eating of wild species is so ingrained in Western culture as to be totally taken for granted by the average individual. Yet it stands in sharp contrast to the dietary practices of our not-too-distant forebears, who were happy to feast upon a veritable menagerie of wild creatures should their status and the occasion permit. For example, the menus of courtly feasts provide ample evidence of the variety of species that were prepared and served, often in highly elaborate dishes. Explaining this near universal Western taboo is by no means easy. It has been suggested that the taboo on eating the flesh of predatory, meat-eating birds and mammals arises out of the idea that, in symbolic terms, they are too 'strong' for human consumption, and we will return this notion below. The prohibition on eating other wild species, which might otherwise be regarded as palatable and nutritious, may be largely the result of the changing orientation of increasingly industrialized and urbanized cultures to the natural environment, and this is also an issue to which we return later in the chapter.

Western meat taboos quite obviously do not apply only to wild animals but also to certain domesticated species. The most notable of these prohibited species is the horse which, despite the fact that it has been used as a food animal in many cultures, has long been taboo in Europe. In ancient Greece and Rome, as in Christian Europe, horse flesh was regarded with aversion, only eaten in times of starvation or desperate need. Despite the efforts of nineteenth-century advocates of the hygienic and dietary advantages of horse flesh like the

Frenchman Geoffroy de Saint-Hilaire to encourage its use, the prohibition on horseflesh remains as powerful as ever for most Westerners (Toussaint-Samat 1992: 98). Similarly, the dog, also a prized source of flesh in a variety of cultures ranging from Polynesia to China, is a taboo species in the West, where the idea of consuming dog flesh would generally be regarded with horror. Indeed, in contemporary Western culture both these animals would be construed as 'pets', although the horse, given its size, is not suited to quite the same level of domestic integration within a human household as a dog. The notion of eating a pet seems self-evidently abhorrent, since such animals can be seen as entering into a social relationship with their human owners. They are given names, credited with personalities and granted quasi-human status in certain limited respects. Anthropomorphism of this kind would thus appear to render the eating of pets, in symbolic terms, almost the equivalent of cannibalism, the focus of the most potent flesh taboo of all.

However, just as he seeks to demonstrate that meat prohibitions in traditional societies may have pragmatic foundations, Harris also suggests that prohibitions on eating horses and dogs may also have sound practical bases, rather than being merely the manifestations of emotional attachment to pets. Indeed, he points out that in New Guinea people frequently become emotionally attached to their pigs, and treat them as pets, but still slaughter and eat them (Harris 1986: 176). Horses, given the nature of their digestive system, are not particularly efficient converters of feed into flesh, and thus rearing them for food does not make economic sense when more efficient species are available. The horse is far more useful for transportation and, particularly more recently, as an aid to recreation. Similarly, dogs in a Western setting make little economic sense as food animals, yet can provide valuable services, notably companionship and security (the latter being particularly pertinent in areas of high crime or for vulnerable individuals or households). In short, domestic animals that are more use alive than dead are likely to be the focus of an eating prohibition, according to Harris.

Yet, despite the force of Harris's arguments, the symbolic potency of meat in contemporary thought is self-evident. How, then, can meat be seen as fitting into the broad framework of meaning which underpins Western culinary and nutritional culture? One attempt to provide such a framework takes the form of a hierarchy of status and potency (Twigg 1979). Twigg locates red meat near the top of this potency hierarchy, with white meat and fish below it, other animal products like eggs and cheese below these and vegetable foods lowest of all. What her scheme represents is her conception of the conventional rankings of animal and plants foods in terms of power, status and desirability (see Figure 9.4)

The feature which places red meat in such a high position, she argues, is its high blood content, the same feature which gives it its characteristic colour. It is the compelling and ambivalent symbolic charge of blood which gives red meat its power and its appeal. Blood is seen as bearing the special essence of the person or the animal, and is associated with virility, strength, aggression and

TOO STRONG: (TABOO) *DOMINANT CULTURE BOUNDARY*	Uncastrated animals Carnivorous animals Raw meat
STRONG: POWERFUL/BLOOD LESS POWERFUL/NON-BLOOD *VEGETARIAN BOUNDARY*	Red meat Chicken Fish
LESS STRONG: *VEGAN BOUNDARY*	Eggs Dairy products
TOO WEAK	Fruit Cereals Root vegetables Leaf vegetables

Figure 9.4   The conventional hierarchy of food status and potency
Source: Adapted from Twigg (1979: 18)

sexuality (Twigg 1979: 17). Yet, at the same time, it is a dangerous and potentially polluting substance. Eating red meat is seen, in a sense, as the ingesting of the very nature of the animal itself, its strength and its aggression. However, in Western culture, there is an element of ambivalence present. There is danger involved in the ingestion of too much power. Thus, as Figure 9.4 indicates, there is a cultural boundary near the top of the food hierarchy, and above that boundary are items which are defined as too potent for humans to eat. Raw meat is seen as too obviously charged with the power of blood; it is therefore taboo and has to undergo deliberately induced transformations (cooking, smoking, curing, etc.) to wrest it from the realm of nature and bring it into the realm of culture, where it can be safely consumed. Similarly, the flesh of animals which are themselves flesh eaters is seen as too powerful for human consumption, even when cooked, and is taboo in Western culture. Even the flesh of uncastrated male domesticated animals like bulls and boars is seen as too strong, as tainted with an excess of virility which renders it unpalatable in a conceptual if not a gustatory sense.

However, below red meat comes white meat like poultry. This is 'bloodless' and therefore seen as less powerful, as is fish, which comes immediately below it in the hierarchy. Both these 'bloodless' forms of flesh, when prepared by boiling or poaching, are seen as suitable for those perceived as having a delicate digestion (e.g., invalids and children). Eggs and dairy products, although of animal origin, are even further from the blood-rich summit of the hierarchy

211

and therefore even less potent. Finally, vegetable foods at the bottom of the hierarchy are commonly regarded as too weak to provide adequate nutrition in themselves, or to furnish the stressed or central element of a conventional meal. (As we will see in the next chapter, vegetarian ideology may actually seek to invert this overall scheme.)

We have already noted in Chapter 5 the central significance of the 'cooked dinner' (Murcott 1982) or the 'proper meal' (Charles and Kerr 1988) in twentieth-century British culinary culture. In such meals, which are conventionally seen by many women as the very foundation of the family's nutritional well-being, meat is the central feature. Its presence, preferably in roasted form is, in effect, the defining element, and all the other elements (which are mainly of vegetable origin) are subordinated to it and are seen as playing an essentially supportive role in the careful composition which appears upon the plate. Given Twigg's hierarchy, red meat can be regarded as the most desirable and the most prestigious form of this dominant element. What is more, the above authors argue that women explicitly relate the importance of the proper meal, arranged around its definitive core of meat, to the tastes and needs of adult men (in the studies in question, usually the respondent's husband). In this sense, then, meat-based meals are seen as associated with masculinity and with the demands which men make upon women on the basis of what is conceptualized as a dominant and nutritionally privileged position. Indeed, the idea that women's purchasing and preparation of red meat is influenced by their husband's perceived views is given some indirect empirical support by a study of intentions to consume beef carried out in the USA. Zey and McIntosh (1992) interviewed by telephone a sample of 400 women in the state of Texas. Their findings suggest that women's intentions to consume beef are not so much influenced by their own attitudes (e.g., concerning its health implications and gustatory features) as by what they believe to be the attitudes and beliefs of their spouse and, to a lesser extent, of their friends. These findings were largely supported by a similar study by Sapp and Harrod (1989), which was carried out after Zey and McIntosh's field work was completed.

However, perhaps the most radical and far-reaching analysis of the association between meat and masculinity in Western culture is put forward by Adams (1990). Her starting-point is the crucial association in patriarchal societies between meat eating and male power. Not only is meat eating seen as an essentially masculine activity, but the consumption of meat is also seen as strongly associated with virility and male physical strength. She mentions, for example, the importance placed upon feeding beef to American soldiers during the Second World War (Adams 1990: 32). Thus, if meat eating is to be symbolically equated with male dominance, men must maintain a privileged access to meat, even though, as Adams points out, women's protein needs may be higher than men's during the crucial periods of pregnancy and lactation. However, she does admit that in times of affluence, gender-related differences in meat consumption may be much less significant than in times of shortage.

Furthermore, class-based differences in meat consumption, she suggests, may be of greater magnitude than the differences between men and women in the same class location.

If meat is effectively a symbol of male dominance, then vegetables, defined as 'women's foods', are seen as inherently less desirable and less potent, as second-class foods fit only for second-class citizens. Adams notes that the word 'meat' has the connotation of 'essence' or 'most important feature' (as in the 'meat of the argument'). On the other hand, 'vegetable' suggests monotony, dullness and inactivity, and the verb 'to vegetate' implies leading a passive, inactive existence. Thus, there emerges a kind of symmetrical symbolism between meat and vegetables, masculine and feminine: men are active and consume foods imbued with power (the power of active animals), and women are passive, and consume foods derived from 'inactive', 'immobile' forms of life (plants) (Adams 1990: 36–7). What is more, the responsibility imposed upon women for the cooking of meat for consumption by men is seen as a further expression of patriarchal power and female subordination. On the other hand, men who refrain from meat eating may be regarded as repudiating or undermining conventional conceptions of masculinity.

The whole argument, however, is taken a crucial step further by Adams, who draws a direct analogy between the oppression of women by men and the oppression of animals by (male) meat eaters. Even more disturbingly, an analogy is also drawn between the killing and dismemberment of women and the slaughter and butchering of animals in the process of converting them into meat (Adams 1990: 45–61). She notes how in everyday speech the equation of the female body with meat involves processes of objectification and fragmentation which facilitate the occurrence of sexual violence towards women-as-objects (Adams 1990: 47). In this sense, she implies, the association between meat consumption and male power reaches its most extreme and potentially most dangerous form of expression.

As we will see in the next chapter, which focuses upon vegetarianism, Adams' exploration of the darker regions of meat symbolism in Western culture also entails a powerful polemic in favour of fundamental changes in Western foodways and the values and ethics which underpin them. Indeed, the argument has been advanced that, in relation to meat eating, such changes may already be under way.

THE MEANING OF MEAT: THE BEGINNINGS OF CHANGE?

If we take the patterns of meat consumption in the UK as our case study, there appear to be a number of clear trends which demand explanation. It will be recalled, for example, that total meat consumption in the UK peaked in 1979, and has since been declining steadily (see Figure 9.1). Even more strikingly, the consumption of red meats has declined quite sharply. As we have seen, the peak year for beef and veal consumption in the post-war period was 1957, and by 1993 consumption had fallen to well under half the peak level. The peak year for mutton and lamb was 1956, and by 1993 British consumers were eating under one-third of the peak level (see Figure 9.2). While significant increases in the consumption of poultry have meant that overall meat consumption has not shown such dramatic falls, it is very clear that there has been a fundamental shift in the demand for red meat. Once wartime and post-war shortages and rationing were over, the amounts of red meat eaten in Britain rose, in line with what would be predicted on the basis of the well-established correlation between levels of affluence and levels of meat consumption. The fact that in Britain the link between rising living standards and rising demand for meat appears to have broken down presents us with a genuine puzzle, particularly in relation to red meat. If we accept the argument that red meat is at the pinnacle of the Western status hierarchy of foods, that it carries a heavy symbolic charge of power, strength, prestige and virility, why does it seem to be falling from favour? What is more, although this phenomenon is particularly marked in Britain, it appears also to be affecting other European countries to some extent. Data produced by the European Commission indicate that, in the European Community, beef and veal's share of total meat consumption fell from 38 per cent in 1961 to 25 per cent in 1991 (Bansback 1993: 2). What is more, between the years 1981 and 1991 per capita consumption of beef and veal declined in eight out of the twelve nations which then made up the community, by amounts ranging from 3 per cent in the Netherlands to 33 per cent in the Irish Republic (Bansback 1993: 3).

Some empirical evidence concerning the reasons for reduced meat consumption in Britain is provided by Woodward (1988). Woodward's study was based upon a sample of 584 respondents drawn from three cities in the north of England. The findings indicated that, overall, around a third of the respondents who were meat eaters (87 per cent of the total sample) felt that they were now eating less meat than they had in the past. This proportion of meat reducers was fairly consistent across social class groups (Woodward 1988: 102). When questioned concerning their motives for reduced meat eating, 51 per cent indicated health reasons, 46 per cent referred to cost, 22 per cent referred to the increased availability of acceptable alternatives and 19 per cent indicated that it was a question of taste. Misgivings concerning production methods were indicated by 16 per cent, and 12 per cent and 11 per cent respectively voiced misgivings about the use of growth hormones and antibiotics. Issues relating to animal welfare were highlighted by 12 per cent of the meat reducing respondents (Woodward 1988: 103). These results seem to support the contention that the decision to reduce meat consumption is an essentially instrumental and pragmatic one, dictated largely by economic considerations and by some consumers' acceptance of health education messages which have consistently encouraged the reduction of red meat intake in particular. This interpretation receives further support from attitude survey data published in the United Kingdom.

Questioned in 1986, only 66 per cent of respondents classified beef, pork and lamb as 'good for people', and 3 per cent actually characterized them specifically as 'bad for people'. A follow-up survey in 1989 found that the proportion classifying these three meats as 'good for people' had fallen to 57 per cent, and the proportion classifying them as specifically 'bad' had risen to 6 per cent (Jowell, Witherspoon and Brook 1990: 148). The authors also report that health concerns were commonly cited by respondents as reasons for eating less beef, pork and lamb (Jowell, Witherspoon and Brook 1990: 156).

However, we must also consider the possibility that trends in meat consumption in Britain, particularly the observed decline in the eating of red meat, are not driven purely by pragmatic factors. Is it also possible that the very meaning of meat is changing, and changing in line with much more fundamental shifts in the very foundations of British culture? This proposition is at the centre of the analysis of the significance of meat as a 'natural symbol' which is put forward by Fiddes (1991). The starting-point of his argument is the claim that 'meat's pre-eminence in our food system derives primarily from its tangibly representing to us the principle of human power over nature' (Fiddes 1991: 225–6). The human need to dominate the natural world and to control the environment is seen as deeply rooted in human history and prehistory, in terms of a desire to mitigate the threats posed by unpredictable natural processes and to maximize security (especially of the food supply). This means that animal flesh, in Fiddes' view, is prized so highly as food, not in spite of the exploitation of animals which it entails but precisely because of that exploitation. Despite the fact that individuals may experience unease, meat eating is approved and encouraged at the cultural level because it effectively demonstrates and symbolizes power over nature. Indeed, as we noted in Chapter 7, individual anxieties connected with such exploitation can be accommodated within a suitably protective cultural framework. It is Fiddes' contention that the significance of meat, both in terms of the quantities consumed and the symbolic charge it carried, began to increase markedly from the seventeenth-century onwards. This was precisely the period in which the rationalist scientific world-view was placing greater and greater emphasis on the human domination of nature. In such circumstances, where such dominance can be construed as a moral as well as a practical imperative, meat eating could be seen as an even more compelling expression of overriding human authority in relation to the natural order.

However, Fiddes maintains that this long-established orthodoxy, celebrating and legitimizing the extension of human power, is in decline, and that powerful ideological currents are now flowing in the opposite direction (Fiddes 1991: 116). The human domination of nature is now seen by many as having gone too far, with the threat of dire ecological consequences. There has emerged a whole range of environmentalist movements and factions dedicated to slowing, or even reversing, this process. Indeed, as Thomas (1983) has pointed out, misgivings concerning the anthropocentric world-view, which saw nature as ripe for human exploitation, were present in embryonic form on the English cultural scene by the late seventeenth century. Such ideas, Fiddes argues, have now assumed a much more prominent position and are leading to a more generalized acceptance of the view that the relationship of humans to the natural world should be one of sensitivity and stewardship rather than unrestrained power. It is in this context that the meaning of meat (and that of red meat in particular) is seen as undergoing an important transformation. Its consumption is no longer seen as a reassuring and assertive expression of human dominance, but as a potentially disturbing reminder of a more 'barbarous' and insensitive past. Thus, we become more squeamish in relation to meat and meat products, requiring them to be prepared and presented to us in a disguised and sanitized form. There is a parallel here between Fiddes's argument and that advanced by Elias (1978a: 120–2), even though the two authors actually operate with rather different conceptualizations of civilization and the civilizing process. In fact, Elias contends that the civilizing process itself entails, among other things, the cultivation of increasingly delicate sensibilities, which in turn generate what he terms an advancing 'threshold of repugnance' (1978a: 120). As an example of this advancing threshold he cites the gradual decline of the practice of carving whole animals (or large sections of animals) within sight of those who were to dine upon them, as diners became progressively less willing directly to contemplate the actual origins of their meal.

Thus, for Fiddes, increasing squeamishness, the decline of red meat consumption, the ever more widespread acceptance of the view that red meat is 'unhealthy', the rise of environmentalist movements and the increasing salience of animal rights issues are all interlinked phenomena. They are each, in their own way, manifestations of far-reaching changes in an entire world-view. Indeed, he goes as far as to suggest that eventually meat eating may come to be seen in the same light as smoking and drug addition: as an anti-social and damaging practice attracting general disapproval. Thus, 'the turbulently declining reputation of meat ... may be a harbinger of the evolution of new values' (Fiddes 1991: 233).

OVERVIEW

In this chapter we have encountered what appear to be, at first sight, two fundamentally opposed views of the role of meat in the human diet. On the one hand, meat's appeal for its human consumers is seen as rooted in its nutritional properties, particularly in its ability to provide a comprehensive range of nutrients. On the other hand, meat's significance is said to reside in its symbolic charge, in the complex meanings relating to power, status, strength and gender which it can be used to convey. Clearly, stated in this stark and uncompromising way, this opposition is a false one. Meat is quite capable of delivering both a nutritional reward and a symbolic message simultaneously. Thus, sociological and other analyses of the role of meat will, in effect, vary largely in terms of the emphasis they place on these two aspects of the issue.

However, this does not prevent some authors from quite deliberately and openly overstating their case, for example, in relation to the priority of symbolism over nutrition, in order to press home what they regard as an important and otherwise neglected point (Fiddes 1991: ix). In truth, the nutritional and symbolic properties of meat are inextricably interlinked, the one, metaphorically at least, feeding off the other.

When we consider the changes in the patterns in meat consumption which have been taking place (in the UK and in other advanced Western societies), we are faced with a range of possible explanations. For example, the shift away from red meat might be explained in economic terms, with rising affluence producing an initial increase, and then a decline as an ever wider choice of substitutes and alternatives becomes available. There may also be an instrumental or pragmatic factor at work, as individuals become sensitized to current health education messages and make what they regard as rational choices to improve health or to avoid disease. Finally, as Fiddes claims, this particular trend may be an indication that Western culture's whole conceptualization of its relationship to the natural world is undergoing changes which will transform the entire human food system. Of course, it may well be that only a culture in which the food supply is secure and which can provide good nutritional standards and an extensive range of food choices for the majority of its members could ever afford to develop the kinds of sensibilities which might ultimately transform the meaning of meat from delicacy to anathema. However, at this point we may need to exercise a degree of caution concerning Fiddes's overall argument. Powerful as the imagery and symbolism of red meat may be, we should, perhaps, be wary of loading too much significance onto trends in its consumption as indicators of broader changes in ecological awareness and environmental sensitivity. After all, other forms of consumption which might have an equal or greater claim to symbolize the human domination of nature, continue to be embraced with undiminished enthusiasm.

Speculating about future trends in the consumption of this most ambivalent of foodstuffs, with its heavy symbolic baggage of contradictory and sometimes disturbing connotations, poses considerable difficulties. It might seem reasonable to assume that current trends away from red meat will continue, and that some other Western countries may even begin to follow the trend evident in the UK, with an overall decline in total per capita meat consumption. If this were to happen, the implications for the agricultural, processing and distribution sectors of the food system would be considerable. The deep-seated, 10,000-year-old symbiosis between humans, domesticated plants and domesticated animals would be transformed as the animal participants in this convoluted web of interrelations were progressively removed from the system. Whether such a transformation is actually feasible, given the close interweaving of the relationships that make up the system, is a matter for debate. What is certain is that the unravelling of these relationships would have social, economic and ecological consequences which might be quite unforeseen.

10

THE VEGETARIAN OPTION

The speculations which concluded the previous chapter concerning the long-term consequences of a possible decline in meat eating generally, or in the consumption of particular types of meat, lead inevitably to our next major topic: vegetarianism. For, if meat eating is replete with symbolism, then the deliberate rejection of meat as a foodstuff must also carry a compelling symbolism of its own. However, as we also noted in the previous chapter (Table 9.1), in many developing countries meat consumption appears to be very low indeed, particularly in the Far East and Africa. Indeed, even when we take into account the whole range of animal products consumed by humans (including offal, fats, milk products, eggs and fish) the number of calories consumed per capita per day from all livestock products in Africa is 111 and in the Far East 151. This compares with 1,255 in Western Europe and 1206 in North America (Grigg 1993: 69). Given that within these averages there is a wide range of individual variation, it becomes clear that large numbers of people in the developing world are effectively vegetarian. This vegetarianism, however, is generally not a matter of choice, and the individuals concerned would usually consume more animal products had they the means to do so.

The real challenge for the social scientist, in fact, is the explanation not of involuntary but of voluntary vegetarianism. In other words, the pertinent question is: 'What are the conditions in which vegetarianism can emerge as a viable and attractive option and what cultural forces and individual motivations encourage its adoption?' Any attempt to answer such questions, however, is complicated by the fact that vegetarianism itself is by no means a clear-cut concept and, indeed, the term itself is of relatively recent origin. Individuals who define themselves as 'vegetarian' may have widely differing dietary patterns. Perhaps the most straightforward way of coming to terms with this variation is to conceptualize it in terms of a simple linear scale relating to the strictness of the exclusions involved. At the left-hand, or least strict, end of the scale will be those self-defined vegetarians who may consume eggs, dairy products, fish (or shellfish) and even meat (especially white meat) on rare occasions. Moving to the right, we find those who exclude all meat and fish, but still consume eggs and dairy products. Further to the right are those who exclude one or other of these latter

218

categories and individuals who consume only rennet-free cheese, for example. Further still to the right we arrive at the boundary of veganism, which requires abstention from all animal products. However, even veganism is scaled according to strictness. There may be controversy among vegans about whether honey should be consumed and whether non-food animal-derived products should be used (for example, leather shoes and certain drugs). At the extreme right of the scale is the fruitarian, who will consume only vegetable products which do not entail killing the donor plant.

Quite clearly, then, vegetarianism is a complex set of interrelated foodways, and in this chapter we look briefly at its historical background as well as at current trends, at the arguments which have been advanced to support it and at the insights into its contemporary manifestations which can be derived from recent empirical studies by social scientists.

THE HISTORICAL AND CULTURAL BACKGROUND

In Chapter 1 we looked in some detail at the origins of human subsistence patterns and noted how the versatility of the human hunter-gatherer, exploiting perhaps the widest range of food sources of any single species, can be regarded as one of the most important factors behind the evolutionary success of the human species and its progressive colonization of an enormous diversity of terrestrial habitats. Of course, survival in demanding conditions necessarily entails making the most of the available food resources, with diversity providing invaluable insurance against the shortages of particular food items which are bound to occur due to natural fluctuations. In these circumstances, it seems highly unlikely that humans would have chosen quite deliberately to exclude a whole class of nutrient sources (i.e., animal products generally, or meat specifically); such voluntary abstention would simply have been too risky for an omnivore to adopt. Of course, this is not to suggest that from the early stages of the development of culture humans did not practice particular avoidances or recognize particular taboos in relation to specific food items. Yet, the decision completely to forego the consumption of all forms of meat, for example, is one which could only have been taken in the context of access to an assured food supply which could provide the required nutritional inputs. This in turn implies that voluntary meat rejection is probably most likely to have occurred first in the context of settled agricultural societies, among individuals or groups in a nutritionally privileged and secure position. Such a rejection would almost certainly have carried a powerful symbolic message, possibly one of dissent from prevailing cultural assumptions.

What little we know about meat rejection in the early stages of the evolution of civilization appears to be consistent with this proposition. For example, the Greek philosopher and mathematician Pythagoras (born in approximately 580 BC) propounded the doctrine that the soul was immortal and could migrate into other living creatures. Thus, the killing and eating of any living creature could be construed as murder, since the transmigration of souls implied a kindred and common fate for all animals. The teachings of Pythagoras seem to be a fusion of ideas derived from Egypt, Babylon and possibly even from Hinduism and Zoroastrianism (Spencer 1993: 59), and imposed upon his immediate followers a strict vegetarianism. Although the actual details of Pythagoras' life are very sparse, he and his inner circle of devotees appeared to have subsisted on a diet of bread, honey, cereals, fruits and some vegetables (Spencer 1993: 46). In a sense, this meatless diet, and the doctrine upon which it was based, can be recognized as, in part, a reaction against the emphasis placed by Greek culture on the consumption of large amounts of meat and the linking of such gorging with Herculean strength and athletic prowess (Spencer 1993: 38). What is more, Pythagorean teaching also embodied what would now be construed as environmentalist elements, and Pythagoras' opposition to some of the mainstream elements of his society's *status quo* is indicated by the fact that his devotees were essentially outsiders, deliberately seeking solitude and separation (Dombrowski 1985: 50).

Among the intellectual elite of the Hellenistic era and of the Roman world, certain key figures stand out for their vegetarianism, developing and extending the arguments advanced in previous centuries. The Roman Seneca argued for vegetarianism on moral grounds, although the fact that this stance probably led him to become politically suspect meant that his public advocacy was relatively muted (Dombrowski 1985: 81). The poet Ovid's advocacy of vegetarianism was also morally based, his position on the sufferings of animals being traceable back to the earlier arguments of the Pythagoreans. The Greek biographer and philosopher Plutarch (born around AD 46) wrote a treatise specifically on the issue of meat eating and the moral and philosophical grounds for abstention from this practice. Interestingly, Plutarch argued emphatically that meat eating was a grossly unnatural act for human beings. He sought to demonstrate this proposition by suggesting that those who wished to eat meat should try killing the animal themselves, unaided by any tools or weapons, as carnivorous animals do, and then consume the flesh raw (Dombrowski 1985: 93). The average human's inability, or unwillingness, to perform such directly carnivorous acts was taken as an indication of the inappropriateness of meat in the human diet. The only other philosopher of the ancient world that we know to have devoted an entire work to the debates surrounding vegetarianism was Porphyry, who was born in Tyre in AD 232. His great treatise, divided into four books, is remarkable in so far as it examines in great detail not only the arguments in favour of vegetarianism, but also the arguments, both philosophical and popular, against vegetarianism, in order to refute them. However, as Spencer (1993: 107) points out, Porphyry died in AD 306, just a few years before Christianity was recognized as the official religion of the Roman world in AD 313 by Emperor Constantine. The Christian doctrine of human supremacy in relation to the natural world became the dominant one, and the Pythagorean tradition of which Porphyry was, in a sense, the heir, with its rejection of the killing of animals for food, was to be effectively suppressed for many centuries to come.

In the Greek and Roman worlds vegetarianism among the elite and the learned was, in effect, a kind of critique of orthodox moral and cultural assumptions. In contrast, in India, vegetarianism developed as a set of ideas and dietary strictures which eventually came to be located at the very core of religious and ethical beliefs. Hinduism's central doctrine of the transmigration of the soul through a perpetual cycle of death and rebirth, holds the promise of release from this cycle only through progressive purification until the soul itself can be reunited with Brahman (or Brahma), the divine life force of the universe from which all being originates and to which it ultimately returns. This doctrine, which embodies the notion of the sacredness of the cow, as we noted in Chapter 9, effectively entails vegetarianism, given the presence of a soul in all living things. What is more, the principle of karma dictates that the act of killing itself will be punished in one's next reincarnation by demotion down the scale of life forms (which has devil at the bottom and cow just one place below human). These Hindu doctrines, of which vegetarianism is an integral part, are very ancient, their origins dating back to teachings which existed in written form as early as 800 BC (Spencer 1993: 77).

Buddhism, founded by the nobleman Gautama Siddhartha, who is believed to have been born around 566 BC in northern India, also embraces the doctrine of transmigration. Nirvana, the final release from the cycle of reincarnation and the attainment of absolute blessedness, is only to be achieved through the extinction of all desires and earthly preoccupations. Gautama (known as Buddha or the enlightened one) preached compassion to all living creatures and the avoidance of violence. However, the incorporation of explicit vegetarianism into Buddhist doctrine appears to have come rather later and is laid out most clearly in a text translated into Chinese in AD 430 (Spencer 1993: 84). Buddhism was to spread widely outside India (for example, into China, Tibet and Japan). By way of contrast, Jainism, also founded in the sub-continent (by Mahavira, born in 599 BC), with its requirement of total non-violence and strict vegetarianism, has remained largely restricted to western India.

While an impulsion towards vegetarianism or abstention from flesh foods is inherent in Hinduism, Buddhism and Jainism, this is certainly not the case in Judaism and Christianity. In fact, the elaborate list of clean and unclean creatures to be found in Leviticus and Deuteronomy implies that the orthodox will indeed consume the flesh of those creatures whom God has decreed fitting. What is more, given the influence of Mosaic dietary laws on Christian beliefs, and the doctrine that God has granted humans dominion over the natural world, vegetarianism and Christianity appear somewhat at odds with one another. Thus, Spencer (1993: 127) points out that in the early Christian Church it was only possible totally to renounce meat eating as an aid to achieving a higher degree of asceticism and spirituality. Indeed, the rejection of meat eating came to be associated with radical heresies which challenged the authority of the Catholic Church. Two notable sects which included vegetarianism in their heresies were the Bogomils, who emerged in Bulgaria in the tenth century, and the Cathars, who flourished first in northern Italy and later in France from the eleventh century to the fourteenth century. Paradoxically, perhaps, the centrality of meat in the Christian's diet was confirmed by ecclesiastical rules which required abstention from this prized food on specific days or in the context of specific religious festivals (Montanari 1994: 78). These temporary abstentions could act as clear demonstrations of penitential self-denial.

However, by the time of the Renaissance the ideas of the classical thinkers had once again become influential. Criticisms of the cruelties inflicted upon animals by humans appeared in the works of the Dutch scholar Erasmus and the English statesman Sir Thomas More (Spencer 1993: 185–6), as well as in those of the French humanist Michel de Montaigne (Barkas 1975: 75–6). The man who is perhaps the leading figure of the Renaissance, retrospectively viewed as its very embodiment, Leonardo da Vinci, was a dedicated vegetarian. However, it has been argued that there is a deep and unresolved contradiction between Leonardo's vegetarianism and compassion for animals on the one hand, and his enthusiastic involvement in the arts of war and the design of weapons on the other (Barkas 1975: 72).

In 1558, at the age of 83, an Italian nobleman, Luigi Cornaro, published the first of a series of essays extolling the hygienic and health-giving properties of a meatless diet. Barkas (1975: 73–5) regards Cornaro (who lived to be 100 years old) as the first modern exponent of the idea of vegetarianism as a device for promoting health and longevity. In the next century an Englishman, Thomas Tryon, wrote a series of books, including *The Way to Health*, in which he argued vehemently against flesh eating on both moral and health grounds, and passionately argued the virtues of a vegetarian diet. However, Tryon and other advocates of vegetarianism around this time (who included the physician George Cheyne, whom we encountered in Chapter 6), were relatively isolated voices in a general climate within which meat eating was becoming more popular, and in which Henry More could claim in 1653 that cattle and sheep had only been granted life to keep their flesh fresh until it was needed for human consumption (Spencer 1993: 213). However, Spencer argues, with the rise of humanism and increasing questioning of the Christian world-view, vegetarianism was able to win over an increasing number of high-profile converts, one of the most eminent and controversial of whom was the poet Shelley, as well as the co-founder of Methodism, John Wesley, and the prison reformer John Howard.

Perhaps the single most important event in the development of vegetarianism as a coherent movement as well as a set of ideas and arguments, took place on 30 September 1847, at Northwood Villa, Ramsgate, Kent. From this meeting emerged the Vegetarian Society, and the term 'vegetarian' was officially adopted. (Although, for convenience, we have used the term vegetarian so far in this chapter to refer to meatless diets in general, the word did not achieve currency until the 1840s, and previously such terms as 'Pythagoreans' and 'vegetable regimen' had been used to refer to vegetarians and vegetarianism respectively.) With the founding of the Vegetarian Society, a wide range of individuals practising meatless diets, for whatever reasons, now had a focus for their beliefs and a forum for debate (Barkas 1975: 85). As a direct result of the founding of the British Vegetarian Society, an American Vegetarian Convention assembled in New York in 1850, and in 1867 the German Vegetarian Society was founded, maintaining close links with the British and American movements (Spencer 1993: 274). What is more, the international visibility of vegetarianism was further advanced by its espousal by such pre-eminent literary figures as Tolstoy and George Bernard Shaw (although the latter was always careful to point out that his vegetarianism was related to health and economic issues, not to a rejection in principle of the killing of animals). For Spencer, however, it is no coincidence that a coherent vegetarian movement emerged first in England, in the nineteenth century. Urbanization itself brought together vegetarians and concentrated them, while at the same time separating and insulating them from the harsher realities of rural life. Moreover, throughout the nineteenth century and into the twentieth vegetarianism maintained its long-standing links with radicalism and dissent, developing in association with such kindred movements as socialism, animal welfare and pacifism (Spencer 1993: 294).

ESTIMATING THE EXTENT OF CONTEMPORARY VEGETARIANISM

In our discussion of the historical roots of vegetarianism it is difficult to avoid the conclusion that this particular set of dietary beliefs and practices has character-istically been an option selected by exceptional or unusual individuals. In a sense, the decision to reject the consumption of meat could be seen as a stance which accentuated and dramatized that individual's distinctiveness, even super-iority, in a moral or intellectual sense, in relation to the rest of humankind. However, this association between vegetarianism and the exceptional individual (the intellectual, the artist, the philosopher, the visionary) has, in recent decades, undergone some significant changes. In some Western societies, vegetarianism appears to have broadened its appeal beyond relatively small circles of devotees, to a point where its adherents would no longer be counted in handfuls but in millions. Quite clearly, such a striking change in the popularity of a once obscure and arcane dietary option demands an attempt at explanation, and later in this chapter we will review the kinds of explanations which have been advanced. However, if we are asserting that vegetarianism has now become a 'mass' phenomenon, we do need to have some idea about the numbers involved and the percentage of the population of a country like the UK, for example, that can be regarded as vegetarian. There are considerable difficulties involved in finding answers to such questions. As we have already seen, vegetarianism is by no means a straightforward concept, and it has many varieties which shade into one another. The researcher inevitably faces the problem of whether to generate a set of objective definitions of varieties of vegetarianism, and work in terms of these or, alternatively, to work with the subjective self-definitions of respondents, which may be somewhat variable and even positively idiosyncratic.

In fact, the data available for countries like the UK and the USA are sparse and rather fragmentary. Perhaps the most consistent set of results for the UK comes from a series of surveys carried out for the Realeat Company between 1984 and 1993 by Gallup (Realeat Survey Office 1993). Over this decade the proportion of respondents reporting themselves as vegetarian or vegan rose steadily, from 2.1 per cent in 1984 to 4.3 per cent in 1993. Over the same period, the proportion of respondents reporting avoidance of red meat rose from 1.9 per cent to 6.5 per cent, and the proportion reporting reduced overall meat consumption rose from 30 per cent to 40 per cent. The next survey in this series was carried out in 1995, using a similar methodology of a sample of 4,237 interviewees aged 16 and over, stratified by region and town size (Realeat Survey Office 1995). This yielded an estimate of 4.5 per cent as the proportion of vegetarians in the adult population. Interestingly, the results also appear to suggest that overall some 12 per cent of the adult population might be regarded as non-meat-eaters (i.e., as vegetarian, vegan, or as no longer eating red or white meat). The 1995 survey results also appear to indicate that those respondents moving away from meat consumption tended to stress health concerns when questioned about their motivations. The significance of gender also emerges clearly in these data, with women (at 5.8 per cent) showing twice the rate of vegetarianism as men. The influence of age as a contributory factor is indicated by the fact that the highest proportion of vegetarians in the 1995 survey was found in the category which covered women aged 16 to 24, the figure being 12.4 per cent. Indeed, the survey found that no less than 25 per cent of its young female respondents in this age group reported abstinence from meat consumption. The survey also highlighted a distinctive social class gradient in vegetarianism, with the highest rates being indicated by respondents in the 'AB' category (6.2 per cent).

A slightly different picture emerges from a single survey carried out for the Vegetarian Society by researchers from the University of Bradford (Vegetarian Society 1991). The study was based upon a quota sample (designed in terms of age, sex, socioeconomic group and region) consisting of 942 adults (aged over 18) and 2,651 young people aged between 11 and 18 years. Among the 11–18 year olds, 8 per cent of the respondents claimed to be vegetarian, the figure for the sample as a whole being 7 per cent. Among the adults in the sample, women indicated a significantly higher rate of vegetarianism than men (10 per cent as compared to 4 per cent). Interestingly, however, the study did not reveal the kind of class gradient in adherence to vegetarian dietary patterns suggested by the Realeat surveys. In fact, the highest rates of vegetarianism were reported by respondents in the 'C1' and 'C2' categories. What is more, although the Realeat surveys identified health issues as the prime motivations behind a switch to vegetarianism, the Bradford data suggest that, among adults, concerns relating to the treatment of food animals rank equally with concerns about human

224

health. Indeed, in the 11–18 age group, concern about the treatment of domesticated food animals outranks concern with health as the prime motivation
behind a switch to vegetarianism.

Although there are some noticeable differences between the findings produced by these two sources, it does seem reasonable, on the basis of these
results, to estimate the proportion of self-defined vegetarians in the UK population (excluding young children) at between 4 per cent and 7 per cent, and to
conclude that this proportion is rising steadily. Indeed, an indirect indication of
the increasing popularity of vegetarianism in Britain is provided by the membership statistics of the Vegetarian Society itself, which more than doubled from
1980 to 1995 (from approximately 7,500 to 18,550). Of course, such an increase
cannot be taken as direct evidence of the rise of vegetarianism (as we will see
later in this chapter, research indicates that there is a significant difference
between 'joiners' and 'non-joiners' among vegetarians). However, what this
increase does highlight is the enhanced visibility of vegetarianism and the
complex issues which surround it.

There have been various attempts to estimate the number of vegetarians in
the USA. Citing the ASPCA as their source, Delahoyde and Desperich (1994:
135) offer a figure of approximately 15 million. Stahler (1994) cites a 1977–8 US
Department of Agriculture nation-wide food consumption survey in which 1.2
per cent of the 37,135 respondents reported themselves vegetarian, and suggests
that more recent estimates have ranged between 3 per cent and 7 per cent.
More interestingly, however, Stahler describes the results obtained from a
question on animal products in the diet which was included in a Roper poll
carried out in 1994. This poll was based upon home interviews with 1,978
respondents aged 18 and over, the sample being designed to be representative of
the adult population of the continental USA. The question posed did not rely
upon the self-definitions of interviewees, but asked them to indicate which
animal products they *never* ate, the list they were offered being made up of the
following categories: meat, poultry, fish/seafood, dairy products, eggs, honey.
On the basis of the results obtained, Stahler (1994: 6–9) argues that there is a 95
per cent probability that the proportion of vegetarians/vegans in the US population falls in the interval 0.3 per cent to 1 per cent. This, of course, is a much
lower figure than that typically obtained when a more straightforward self-
definition approach is used. Such findings provide some empirical support for
the proposition that many individuals may regard themselves as vegetarian while
still consuming (if only occasionally) animal products other than dairy products
and eggs.

We have already noted that vegetarianism and veganism cover a broad
spectrum of dietary choices and avoidances. Thus we must always bear in
mind the fact that an individual's actual eating patterns and his or her conceptualization of those eating patterns as a dietary stance or lifestyle may not
always fit neatly with each other. In sociological terms, the conceptualizations
must be as worthy of attention and analysis as the observed or reported patterns.

225

Thus, in effect, self-defined vegetarianism and veganism are the principal objects of analysis in this chapter.

MOTIVES AND RHETORIC

The data we have considered are, admittedly, relatively sparse, but they do appear to indicate that in Western societies like the UK and the USA, self-defined vegetarians can be numbered in millions. Accounting for the emergence of vegetarianism as a large-scale phenomenon is a process which must operate on at least two levels. Firstly, we must consider the issue of the motives behind individual decisions to adopt some form of vegetarianism. Secondly, we must attempt to describe the broader social and cultural processes or conditions which can facilitate such a shift towards meat avoidance or the avoidance of animal products in general. In this section we will examine the kinds of motives which adherents of vegetarianism describe. However, in such a context, it is not necessarily easy to distinguish between the considerations which may impel an individual to make a particular choice and the arguments that individual may employ retrospectively to justify that choice or, indeed, to encourage others to make the same choice. In a sense, then, the themes discussed here refer both to motivations and to what Maurer (1995: 146–7) refers to as the 'rhetorical idioms' which can be employed in the advocacy of vegetarianism. Of course, the thematic headings used below, in some instances, overlap one with another and it should be borne in mind that they are not being offered as mutually exclusive categories.

The moral theme

We have already seen how a moral concern in relation to any animal suffering entailed in obtaining meat was a central feature in the thinking of those classical philosophers who advocated vegetarianism. This same moral concern featured strongly in the arguments of later advocates, and has been developed and discussed in considerable detail by a number of contemporary philosophers. Singer (1976), for example, presents an ethical argument for vegetarianism on the basis of a rejection of 'speciesism', a form of discrimination against non-human creatures which he sees as paralleling racism and sexism in the context of human relationships. The capacity of animals to experience suffering and enjoyment implies that they have interests that should not be violated and that they are not simply Cartesian automata, oblivious to pain and beyond the boundary of moral consideration. Thus, the fundamental utilitarian principle of the minimizing of suffering is seen as demanding the adoption of a vegetarian diet. Other philosophers, like Midgley (1983), also reject the view, deeply embedded in the religious and philosophical traditions of Western thought, that animals can legitimately be excluded from moral consideration and can, therefore, be freely exploited as food sources and for other purposes. Indeed,

226

Midgley explicitly argues that the boundaries of moral consideration have, historically, been advancing continually, and that we must recognize that they can now breach the species barrier to embrace certain non-human creatures.

However, reservations about the problems involved in attempting to use utilitarian concepts to discuss animal rights (as suggested by Singer 1976) lead other philosophers to adopt alternative lines of reasoning to provide a moral basis for vegetarianism. For example, Regan (1984) argues that, even if we accept that animals cannot be moral agents, certain categories of animals can be regarded as moral patients and as therefore having inherent value which demands our respect. This respect principle effectively rules out their use for food. Similar arguments are used by Clark (1984), who lays considerable emphasis on the idea that humans, by their very nature as intelligent beings, bear a special responsibility of stewardship towards the creatures with whom they form a complex community of living things, such stewardship entailing the rejection of the exploitation of animals that is involved in meat eating.

What, in effect, the detailed and sometimes convoluted discourses developed by philosophers like these represent are attempts to elaborate and make explicit deep-seated anxieties and misgivings concerning the use of animals for food (anxieties which were set in a broader context in Chapter 7).

The food production theme

This theme is based upon the premise (discussed in the previous chapter) that the production of meat represents an unjustifiably extravagant use of natural resources. It is argued that the production of vegetable crops for direct human consumption avoids the energy losses involved in feeding livestock with products (like grains) which are suitable for meeting human nutritional needs. This kind of argument has both ecological and moral implications. In ecological terms, meat production is seen as a process which places an unnecessarily heavy load on the natural environment, which is exploited both extensively and intensively in order to maintain or increase the output of animal proteins. Particular attention has been focused on the destruction or degradation of natural habitats, like tropical rainforests, in order to extend the areas available for cattle ranching, and on the long-term environmental effects of overgrazing and overstocking, especially in arid or semi-arid areas. In this way, the concerns of the vegetarian become linked with those of the environmentalist, and vegetarianism is presented as a set of dietary options which involve food production patterns which have a lower environmental impact than modern farming methods and are ultimately more sustainable.

The moral dimension of the food production theme is not related to animal rights and interests (as in the first theme) but to the interests of humans. The argument here is that clear global inequalities in nutritional status are due, at least in part, to the diversion of resources towards the production of meat for the benefit of consumers in the most affluent economies. In this connection, vegetarianism is conceptualized as a way of reducing what is perceived as the distorting effects of meat production on the global food system, freeing crucial resources for the production of vegetable foods. Such increased production, it is then envisaged, could be used to alleviate hunger and malnutrition in those areas where food shortages are endemic.

The religious/spiritual theme

The religious or spiritual element in vegetarian ideologies is very ancient, and can be traced back, as we have seen, to doctrines relating to the transmigration of souls found in ancient Greek thought and in such major religions as Hinduism and Buddhism. In medieval thought, abstention from flesh foods was often associated with spirituality, purity and asceticism, since such foods were seen as embodying all that was carnal, worldly and corruptible. Meat was also associated with animal passions, and its avoidance was seen as enhancing the individual's control of his or her appetites and sexuality. Twigg (1979) maintains that in the context of contemporary vegetarianism similar ideas have persisted, but in a somewhat modified form, entailing what she terms a 'this-worldly form of mysticism' (Twigg 1979: 26). Concern is not for the wellbeing of some disembodied soul or spirit, but for the 'spiritual body' itself, the body as 'an immortal, youthful temple of the spirit' (Twigg 1979: 27). Such beliefs entail a kind of revulsion for the carnal and the physical, for the processes of digestion and elimination. The adoption of a vegetarian diet and the rejection of meat are characterized as key features of the quest for an ageless and uncorrupted body.

The 'New Order' theme

As well as discussing the spiritual element in contemporary vegetarianism, Twigg also seeks to demonstrate how vegetarian ideologies can embody a critique of what is regarded as the conventional social order, and a vision of a new, alternative mode of patterning social relationships. Thus, for example, vegetarian dishes commonly violate the highly structured form of conventional meals and are presented in a mixed, undifferentiated form. This repudiation of the structure of conventional eating can be seen as symbolic of a repudiation of wider patterns of hierarchy and power, in which the symbolism of meat carries such a positive potency. Nature itself, Twigg argues, is redefined and reconceptualized as a realm characterized not by conflict, competition and suffering, but by harmony and beneficence. This harmonized model of nature is then used as a yardstick against which to measure the deficiencies of contemporary human society, which is seen as having lost touch with the natural, becoming distorted and artificial (Twigg 1979: 22). The vegetarian diet, as a more 'natural' mode of eating, is seen as a device for restoring contact with harmonious nature. Even more ambitiously, however, vegetarian beliefs may entail a quest for a 'New Moral Order' (Twigg 1979: 29), and a vegetarian diet becomes a manifestation

228

of a commitment to reform and social change. Indeed, a particularly radical example of such thinking can be found in the feminist arguments advanced by Adams (1990), for whom the practice of vegetarianism is advocated as a challenge to the male power symbolized by meat and as a means, ultimately, of achieving what she terms the 'destabilizing of patriarchal consumption' (Adams 1990: 186–90).

The health/physiological theme

Issues of health in vegetarian ideologies are closely related to concepts of disease-prevention. Non-vegetarian diets are seen, in effect, as pathogenic. The primary feature of this view is the idea that meat itself is hazardous as a foodstuff, replete with substances or agents, both naturally occurring and artificial, which pose threats to human health. The second, less specific, feature of this view is the idea that modern diets are inherently unhealthy in so far as they rely upon food items which are deficient in crucial nutritional properties as a result of excessive processing and refining. Additionally, such food items are seen as possibly contaminated with a whole range of synthesized additives whose purpose is commercial rather than nutritional, and which also pose potential health threats. In contrast, vegetarian diets, by eliminating meat products, avoid the hazards associated with them. What is more, the emphasis commonly laid upon the consumption of fresh fruits and vegetable products, subjected to minimal amounts of processing, is seen as a means of restoring the diet to a form more closely matching human nutritional needs and of avoiding the ingestion of dangerous substances. (There are clear parallels here with the health food beliefs discussed in Chapter 6.)

The conceptualization of meat as a hazardous food item may, in fact, be taken a stage further. A recurring theme in vegetarian discourse is the view that meat is not a 'natural' component of the human diet at all. It is argued that human physiology (e.g., dental and digestive) is quite unsuited to a carnivorous diet, and that meat eating, by implication, is likely to be deleterious rather than beneficial in health terms.

The aesthetic/gustatory theme

Revulsion in relation to the appearance, tactile properties and taste of meat also figures prominently in vegetarian concerns. Meat may be characterized as an object of disgust rather than as an object of appetite and gustatory enjoyment. The conventional positive symbolism of meat (particularly red meat), with its connotations of virility, strength and power, is rejected – and in its place a highly negative and pejorative symbolism occurs consisting of notions of violence, death and decay. In contrast, vegetable foods are described in highly positive language, not only in terms of their gustatory properties, but also as being charged with life, as opposed to the death associated with meat (Twigg 1979). What is more, underlying concepts of purity (vegetable foods) and contamination (flesh foods) form a highly emotive refrain in vegetarian beliefs.

The themes discussed above can in no sense claim to be exhaustive, although they do describe the main components of contemporary vegetarian ideologies. In fact, Maurer (1995) suggests that there is a deeper underlying rhetorical structure underpinning these themes. Drawing upon the work of Ibarra and Kitsuse (1993), she is able to identify two basic rhetorical idioms which are used to support the claims inherent in vegetarian discourse. The first of these idioms is that of 'entitlement', which emphasizes freedom, justice, choice and liberation, and which, in vegetarian rhetoric, can be applied to selected animal species as well as to humans. The second idiom is that of 'endangerment'. Here the emphasis is on health and the physical welfare of the body, and in vegetarian discourse the consumption of meat is construed as an irremediably 'endangering' activity.

Inevitably, of course, a whole range of much more personal or idiosyncratic motivations and justifications may figure in the experiences of particular individuals. For example, the adoption of vegetarianism may reflect a desire to conform with the expectations of those whom the individual concerned respects. Conversely, vegetarianism may be used as a means of demonstrating distance from individuals or groups towards whom there is a sense of antagonism or resentment. Or, perhaps more straightforwardly, a move towards vegetarianism may reflect simple curiosity and an attraction towards novelty. What is more, the motivations which an individual experiences or the justifications which he or she employs frequently combine and interact with one another. Although some individuals may identify a single dominant motive, others may be unwilling or unable to do so. Such variations will be discussed further when we consider a number of empirical studies of vegetarian beliefs, attitudes and practices.

The thematic strands of contemporary vegetarianism are not without their contradictions and tensions, however. Perhaps ultimately the most contentious of these themes is the moral one. Certainly, the argument that comprehensive moral considerations should be extended across the barrier between humans and other species inevitably involves both ethical and practical conundrums, which have been explored by such philosophers as Townsend (1979) and Frey (1983). Particular problems may arise when the argument shifts from a concern with animal welfare to a concern with animal rights. Whether animals can have rights, which animals should have rights and how those rights could be respected and protected, are issues which pose awkward questions for reflective vegetarians. In direct practical terms, for example, vegetarianism which entails the consumption of dairy products generates questions about the treatment of dairy cows and their fate when aged and unproductive, and about the disposal of unwanted male offspring. Indeed, in Western economies, the ready availability of reasonably priced cow's milk is bound up with the meat production industry. Similar problems are posed by the use of eggs in vegetarian diets, particularly the disposal of unproductive birds and unwanted males. Depending on their level of ethical sensitivity, some vegetarians may choose to ignore, or at least to set aside, such questions, whereas others may seek solutions. However, even veganism, with its more or less strict avoidance of animal products, does not provide a complete solution. The vast majority of the food items eaten by vegans are the products of farming, and farming itself inevitably entails the initial destruction of pristine ecological systems and their original plant and animal inhabitants. What is more, such processes as pest control, ploughing and harvesting inevitably involve the destruction of large numbers of small invertebrate and vertebrate animals, which have to be ruled outside the boundaries of moral consideration if food production is to continue. In this sense, the pursuit of what might be termed a 'blameless menu' looks to be a daunting task for the vegetarian and even the vegan.

Similarly, other pro-vegetarian arguments related to food production may present certain problems. The contention that the direct consumption of vegetable products by humans is a more efficient use of natural resources than using agricultural produce to feed livestock is not quite as straightforward as it appears. Vast areas of the earth's surface occupied by humans are quite unsuited to the growing of arable crops and can only be exploited by using browsing and grazing domesticated herbivores. In fact, the argument applies largely to the agricultural sectors of the developed economies, where intensively produced crops are fed to intensively reared food animals, and is, therefore, by no means universally applicable. What is more, we should be cautious about accepting the view that vegetarianism, were it to become the dominant dietary pattern in the developed economies, would automatically increase food availability in the Third World countries. As it stands, the argument does not address crucial problems of distribution. These problems refer not only to the practicalities involved in the transportation, storage and allocation of foodstuffs, but also to questions concerning the distribution of wealth and income. Those who suffer malnutrition and starvation tend to be those people who lack the resources to produce, or the purchasing power to buy, the food that they need. Such structural inequalities, and their political, economic and cultural roots are at least as significant as any notion of a global pool of foodstuffs that would be increased by vegetarian consumption patterns.

The spiritual dimensions of contemporary vegetarian ideologies also contain inherent tensions, for example, between a deep-seated asceticism on the one hand, and an emphasis on the care and cultivation of the body on the other. Even the vegetarian espousal of 'nature' and the 'natural' is fraught with difficulty, as the more brutal and ruthless manifestations of the interactions between individuals of the same or different species are masked with images of harmony and unity. Similarly, the radical or reformist dimensions of vegetarian thought may be said to suffer from a tension between, on the one hand, a stress on individual well-being and personal development and, on the other, a view of vegetarianism as a collective phenomenon, as a movement with broader political and moral aims.

However, despite such tensions, the underlying themes discussed above, in various forms, figure strongly in the pro-vegetarian literature (e.g., Amato and Partridge 1989) and in the thinking of practising vegetarians and vegans.

EMPIRICAL STUDIES OF CONTEMPORARY VEGETARIANSIM

Although there is an ever-lengthening list of books and articles advocating vegetarianism or providing advice and guidance for practising or aspiring vegetarians, there are comparatively few studies in this area carried out from a social scientific stand-point. In this section we will examine examples of such studies in order to gain some direct empirical insight into the everyday realities of vegetarian belief and practice.

Research published in the 1970s (Dwyer, Mayer, Dowd, Kandel and Mayer 1974) provided detailed information on the attitudes and dietary patterns of 100 young American adults who had converted to vegetarianism after maturity. Using a battery of interviews, questionnaires and dietary histories, the authors explore a range of issues, including reason for dietary change, attitudes to diet and health, abstinence patterns and religious, ecological and ethical views. The most frequently cited reason for conversion to vegetarianism was related to health, followed by ethical concerns. Spiritual or 'metaphysical' concerns were ranked next, followed by ecological issues, ranked equally with gustatory or aesthetic preferences linked to a distaste for meat. The authors make an important distinction between what they term 'joiners' (who had affiliated themselves to wider movements like macrobiotics, health foods and yoga) and 'loners' who were not affiliated in this way. They also distinguish between circumscribed avoidances (that is, where the diet excluded only quite a small range of items) and far-reaching avoidances (where the diet entailed the exclusion of a wide range of items). Some significant differences appeared to emerge on the basis of these distinctions. For example, the 'loners' with circumscribed avoidances tended to isolate their dietary patterns from other aspects of their daily lives, and many had gone to considerable lengths to devise a personal dietary system, often in the light of advice from health professionals. In contrast, the joiners with far-reaching avoidances tended to exhibit attitudes and practices similar to those found in extremist factions of sects or cults. These included rigidly observed abstinences, the performance of rituals and a sense of mission impelling them to seek to convert others (Dwyer, Mayer, Dowd, Kandel and Mayer 1974: 534).

A later study (Freeland-Graves, Greninger and Young 1986) attempts a direct comparison between vegetarians and non-vegetarians. The researchers studied a response group consisting of 150 vegetarians and 150 non-vegetarians living in Austin, Texas. The non-vegetarian group was created by matching each vegetarian respondent with a non-vegetarian respondent of the same sex and a similar age. While there were many overall similarities between the two groups, there were some interesting contrasts. Only 26 per cent of vegetarians were practising

232

followers of traditional religions, as opposed to 59 per cent of non-vegetarians, and vegetarians' involvement in more exotic sects and non-Western religions was relatively low, leading the authors to suggest that the link between vegetarianism and 'cultism' is in decline. What is more, the vegetarians in the study showed a higher tendency to join clubs and organizations, went out more frequently with friends and entertained friends at home more frequently than did the non-vegetarians. There was evidence to indicate that vegetarians, and especially vegans, tended to form supportive networks of family and friends who were also vegetarian. In fact, 44 per cent of the vegetarian respondents reported that other family members also practised vegetarianism. Coupled with the fact that vegetarians tended to live in larger households (especially vegans), the findings suggest that collective social support may be an important component of the maintenance of vegetarian dietary practices for this particular set of respondents.

Strikingly, however, parental influence did not appear to have been a strong factor influencing the decision to become vegetarian. The authors argue that the choice of a vegetarian lifestyle may often involve the deliberate rejection of the meat-based dietary practices of parents. Indirect evidence for this proposition comes from the study's finding that, on average, vegetarians lived at greater distances from their parents and visited them less frequently than did non-vegetarians. It is perhaps ironic, then, that the majority of the vegetarian respondents (indeed, all the vegans) anticipated that their own children would remain vegetarian in adulthood, that is, would conform to parental expectations (Freeland-Graves, Greninger and Young 1986: 910).

Further information concerning the ideas and practices of American vegetarians is provided by Amato and Partridge (1989). Although their work is primarily concerned with making a case for vegetarianism and with providing guidance and support for existing or would-be vegetarians, the authors did engage in the collection of some pertinent data. Respondents were recruited by placing notices in the newsletters of vegetarian organizations, and 209 responses were received. A further sixty-one individuals were sent detailed questionnaires for completion. The authors accept that their response group, being essentially self-selected, cannot be regarded as in any sense statistically representative of all vegetarians in the USA; indeed, they admit, for example, that it is biased towards those holding professional or managerial positions in the occupational structure. Nevertheless, the authors argue that the group is sufficiently broadly based to provide valuable insights into the motives and experiences of vegetarians. The motivations of this group leaned heavily towards concerns about animal suffering or animal rights (mentioned by 67 per cent) and health concerns (which were mentioned by 38 per cent). Spiritual or religious factors were mentioned by 17 per cent of respondents, and aesthetic factors or dislike of meat by 12 per cent (Amato and Partridge 1989: 34). In fact, 43 per cent of respondents stressed a single reason for becoming vegetarian, whereas the remaining 57 per cent gave multiple reasons. The single-reason respondents were mainly those motivated by animal rights issues. What is more, motivations tended to change over time,

233

with, for example, individuals who originally made the change for reasons based on self-interest (such as health concerns) gradually becoming aware of the ethical dimensions of vegetarianism. The authors also provide insights into the dynamics of the conversion process, describing how the decision may be influenced by friends, relatives, vegetarian literature or mass media coverage of the issues. They also give graphic accounts of instances where the individual's conversion was prompted by some dramatic and often distressing experience, for example, the witnessing of animal slaughter (Amato and Partridge 1989: 74–6). Less extreme instances may involve a sense of repulsion or disgust when the individual suddenly makes a previously unadmitted or suppressed connection between flesh food and the animal from which it came, particularly if that is an animal which would otherwise be accorded affection or regard.

The impact of the individual's conversion to vegetarianism upon his or her personal relationships is also analysed by Amato and Partridge. Parental reaction to the conversion of a son or daughter was reported by many respondents to be a very negative one. While this negative reaction was sometimes related to parents' concerns about the health and dietary implications of vegetarianism, it also appeared to emerge out of a sense that the rejection of the parents' eating patterns implied a rejection of the parents themselves and of their values and priorities. Conversely, however, some parents were approving and supportive. Most significantly, perhaps, the authors argue that the conversion to vegetarianism of a family member can lead to major changes in family relationships, which may be strengthened or, at the other extreme, may break down completely (Amato and Partridge 1989: 181–2). What is more, the stresses and strains which can be introduced into the family setting may be present in other forms in other settings. Workplace relationships, eating out and socializing with non-vegetarian friends may all become potential sources of tension or embarrassment with which the practising vegetarian has to learn to cope.

There are striking parallels between the findings presented by Amato and Partridge and a qualitative study of vegetarians, their motives and experiences carried out in the UK (Beardsworth and Keil 1992a). The UK study was based upon interviews with seventy-six respondents, recruited on a 'snowball' sample basis in the East Midlands region. The interviews themselves were open-ended and discursive in nature, in order to provide respondents with an opportunity to present their own accounts and experiences in their own terms as far as possible. All interviews were taped and fully transcribed, generating several hundred thousand words of transcript material, which was then analysed by being sorted into a series of emergent thematic categories. The response group generated showed a higher level of average educational attainment than the general population, and this is reflected in the fact that twenty-three out of the seventy-six respondents were in professional or managerial occupations. There was a roughly equal balance between the sexes, although the age distribution showed a marked clustering in the ranges 26–30 years and 31–5 years, and the majority of the respondents were without dependent children.

The motivations for conversion to vegetarianism (all but one of the respondents were converts; just one had been brought up vegan) were classified as moral, health-related, gustatory and ecological. A total of forty-three respondents maintained that, for them, moral motivations were primary; health-related motivations were reported as primary by thirteen respondents. Priority was allocated to gustatory factors by nine respondents, and only one indicated ecological concerns were paramount. However, from respondents' accounts it was clear that although primary motives could be readily identified in most cases, motives were interwoven and tended to support each other. What is more, the balance of motivations could change over time, with the emphasis shifting significantly. There were examples of individuals who had set out with primarily health-related concerns and who had subsequently moved towards a preoccupation with animal rights; there were also examples of individuals who had undergone the reverse of this process.

The actual conversion to vegetarianism also proved to be a decidedly variable experience. For example, some respondents described a protracted process of conversion, during which vague concerns and misgivings, which might reach back even as far as childhood, gradually came into focus and eventually prompted the progressive initiation of dietary changes. In contrast, some respondents reported undergoing a dramatic 'conversion experience' (Beardsworth and Keil 1992a: 257), which literally shocked them into an abrupt switch into vegetarianism. Such experiences could involve acute sensations of revulsion while eating meat (in which it is suddenly perceived as 'dead flesh', for example), being confronted with the sight of the remnants of slaughtered animals or even viewing a particularly powerful and disturbing television programme.

The implications of a move into vegetarianism for the individual's social and personal relationships drawn out by Amato and Partridge (1989) also came to the fore in the UK study. Significant contrasts emerged, for example, between situations where relatives (e.g., parents, siblings, in-laws) were reasonably approving and supportive of the convert and situations involving more or less severe disapproval. In the latter case, serious tensions could emerge, leading to the attenuation or even breakdown of the relationships in question.

The study also sought to analyse the powerful ideological currents present in vegetarian beliefs and priorities. Interestingly, for this group of respondents, at least, what might be termed the 'anti-meat theme' appeared to be more potent than the 'pro-vegetarian theme' (Beardsworth and Keil 1992a: 272–6). That is, anti-meat sentiments related to moral outrage, repulsion, disgust or to a sense of meat as wasteful of economic resources or as a food unsuitable or even dangerous for humans, seemed to dominate respondents' nutritional conceptualizations. Indeed, the vocabulary employed in expressing these ideas was often extreme and disturbing, conjuring up images of blood, slaughter and dismemberment. In contrast, respondents' discussions of the virtues of vegetarian dietary regimes were much more muted and less emphatic. In addition, the study also uncovered examples of respondents who were all too aware of the moral tensions involved in the vegetarian's use of dairy products or even of non-food products like leather. Vegan respondents tended to be critical of vegetarians in this respect, while often themselves acknowledging the difficulties involved in following a strictly vegan regime and the virtual impossibility of a totally harmless diet (Beardsworth and Keil 1992a: 282–3).

EXPLAINING THE RISE OF VEGETARIANISM

If we accept the contention that vegetarianism now represents an increasingly significant dietary option in countries like the UK and the USA, we are faced with the problem of trying to explain the rise in popularity of a dietary regime which was previously followed only by a tiny minority. In this chapter we have already examined the rhetoric of vegetarian ideologies, a rhetoric which permits the individual to think through his or her own priorities and concerns and to arrive at a decision as to whether or not to embrace vegetarian preferences and prohibitions. Of course, this is not to suggest that such a decision is necessarily a purely rational one, as a whole range of emotional and, indeed, gustatory factors may also be involved. Nevertheless, such rhetorical resources allow the decision to be formulated and, if necessary, described and justified to others.

However, merely citing such rhetorical themes does not in itself constitute a viable attempt to explain the rise of vegetarianism. What is required, in addition, is some grasp of the changes (sociological, cultural and economic) which have created the conditions in which vegetarian ideologies can thrive and can attract increasing numbers of adherents. In Chapter 9, the argument put forward by Fiddes (1991) to account for long-term falls in the consumption of red meat was described in some detail. It will be recalled that Fiddes maintains that the trend away from red meat is the result of an underlying cultural shift in that particular food item's symbolic significance. Whereas the production and consumption of red meat have traditionally acted as powerful expressions of the human ability to dominate and exploit the natural world, our collective perceptions of our relationship to that world have recently undergone a transformation. We no longer confidently celebrate our ascendancy over nature through a kind of triumphalist consumption of the flesh of large and powerful creatures. Rather, says Fiddes (1991: 219–23), an ideology of care and responsibility is replacing the doctrines of exploitation. In such a cultural climate, the adoption of a vegetarian diet and the avoidance of all meat can be construed as an expression of environmental concern and sensitivity, and thus perceived as having a clear logic behind it, a logic in tune with increasingly widely held values. In this sense, the contemporary increase in the popularity of vegetarianism is conceived of as but one component in a complex package of recent developments, which include the mounting salience of ecological and conservation issues, the emergence of environmentalist movements and the rise of 'green' politics and ethics. The implication of this view is that vegetarianism as a dietary option has, effectively, become more appealing because of its fit with deeper cultural trends.

The argument put forward by Fiddes that the reduction or avoidance of meat consumption, or the adoption of vegetarianism, are features of an underlying cultural shift is consistent with the concept of the 'civilizing of appetite' employed by Mennell (1985). This concept, which we have already encountered, refers to the process by which the celebration of gluttony and the indulgence of 'gargantuan' appetites characteristic of medieval culture, was progressively replaced by an emphasis on the refinement of taste and the exercise of self-restraint in relation to food consumption. Mennell (1985: 38–9) actually suggests that this cultural fixation on self-control in relation to appetite may well be implicated in eating disorders like *anorexia nervosa*, which formed a major theme in Chapter 8. However, it is also quite possible that it forms a component of vegetarian ideology. The symbolism of meat, as we have seen, is replete with the imagery of physical strength, animal nature, passion and power. All of these features are antithetical to notions of self-restraint and refinement. The vegetarian appetite, then, might be characterized as one strongly influenced by this civilizing process. Even where an affinity for 'nature' and the 'natural' is expressed, this is, as Twigg (1979) has pointed out, based on a conceptualization of nature which has been harmonized and sanitized, indeed, in a sense, civilized. The concept of an underlying civilizing process originates, of course, in the work of Elias. This author himself suggests that the advance of the civilizing process may also entail an advance in what he terms the 'threshold of repugnance' (Elias 1978a: 120). The culture of refinement and restraint means that individuals are less and less willing to confront the potentially disturbing and distasteful aspects of the production and processing of animal-derived foods. As a result, such features of the food system are increasingly concealed from public view. However, vegetarianism may represent an attempt to repudiate these features, at least partially, and veganism an attempt to repudiate them totally.

There also exists the distinct possibility that recent cultural and ideological changes which have begun to affect the balance of power in the realm of sexual politics may also have contributed to the emergence of a climate more congenial for vegetarianism. The arguments put forward by Adams (1990) concerning the complex symbolic and metaphorical associations between meat eating and male power over women (which were discussed in Chapter 9) lead her to exhort women to adopt a vegetarian diet as part of a challenge to male dominance. In fact, she sees vegetarianism, not only as historically associated with feminism but as a virtual obligation for the truly committed feminist. References to feminist values and priorities do not appear to figure significantly in the findings of the limited number of empirical studies of vegetarianism which are available, although this may be due in part to the original design and concerns of the studies in question. Certainly, the fact that what data we have suggest that rates of vegetarianism tend to be higher among women than among men, and especially among women in younger age groups, may provide some indirect support for the contention that the recent rise in the salience of feminist ideas could be a contributory factor in the increased popularity of this particular dietary option.

On the other hand, the empirical material does provide much more direct evidence that changing views of the links between diet and health have influenced the level and incidence of vegetarianism. Health concerns consistently appear in the accounts of vegetarian respondents, and some accord them overall priority. Health education messages and dietary guidelines promoted by government agencies, stressing the need to increase intakes of dietary fibre and fresh fruit and vegetables, can also be seen as contributing to a general climate more sympathetic to vegetarianism. In addition, given the continuing significance of common-sense conceptions of the connections between diet and health (see Chapter 6), vegetarianism may increasingly be seen as a strategy for the individual to exercise a degree of personal control over his or her health outcomes and physical well-being.

In a sense, this line of thought brings us back to the arguments developed in Chapter 7 concerning the ways in which the potential anxieties created by the underlying paradoxes of food and eating can be coped with or managed. Thus, vegetarianism may be one of the more significant emergent cultural devices for dealing, for example, with health-related food anxieties. Within the framework of vegetarian belief, the exclusion of meat from the diet is, in effect, the exclusion of a health-threatening substance. These threats to health are seen as arising from meat's supposed unsuitability for the human digestive system, its fat content, its proneness to bacterial infestation or its contamination by artificial additives and residues. Additionally, and even more obviously, vegetarianism can provide some sort of solution to the anxieties and the sense of guilt which may be generated by the killing of animals for food. As was suggested in Chapter 7, as traditional modes of coping with such concerns go into decline, their place is likely to be taken by alternative practices, conceptualizations and rhetorical devices. Thus, vegetarianism (and, perhaps to an even greater extent, veganism) is both a practice and a discourse well suited to the needs of the contemporary anxious eater. It is certainly significant that, in the transcript material reported in Beardsworth and Keil (1992a: 287), vegetarian respondents repeatedly stressed the idea that their dietary stance was, in part, an attempt to regain what they explicitly referred to as 'peace of mind'.

While it is perfectly feasible to itemize the kinds of factors which can be seen as making some contribution to the widening popularity of vegetarianism, it is far more difficult to try to rank them in order of importance. Indeed, any attempt to weight the relative contribution of any given factor is bound to be complicated by the possibility that these ideas may interact with each other in complex ways. Evidence for these interactions at the personal level is provided by the empirical studies discussed above, which show how respondents' own accounts interweave the various motivations they describe, and often portray them as supporting and confirming each other. At the social level, given the variety of themes and causes that can be accommodated beneath the vegetarian umbrella, it is open to question as to whether vegetarianism itself can be conceptualized as a reasonably coherent movement. Certainly, the findings in

238

the empirical literature which point out an important distinction between 'join-ers' and 'loners' suggest that the adoption of vegetarianism does not necessarily entail a sense that the individual should become involved in collective attempts to promote its values or to convert others to its dietary practices. Yet, the distinct possibility exists that the emergence of vegetarianism as a dietary option with a following counted in millions may well be one manifestation of a broad spectrum of underlying cultural shifts and reassessments.

In fact, if we seek to assess the position of vegetarianism in the modern food system, it becomes apparent that this system actually facilitates a vegetarian regimen. The sheer range of vegetable-based foodstuffs now available to the affluent Western consumer, a range largely free from the restrictions of season and locality, makes feasible the creation of a vegetarian cuisine characterized by variety and novelty. Variety and enjoyment are features of food which many vegetarian respondents emphasize (Beardsworth and Keil 1992a). In contrast, adhering to a vegetarian diet in the context of a more localized and seasonal food supply would be an altogether less appealing prospect. For example, a vegetarian diet based solely on the produce of traditional northern European temperate agriculture could prove somewhat monotonous and restrictive.

If we accept the contention that the ideological levels of the food systems of Western societies are increasingly characterized by menu pluralism, there are clear implications for our understanding of contemporary vegetarianism. In a menu-pluralistic setting, the availability of a variety of menu principles (rational, moral, hedonistic, etc.), provides the individual with a good deal of flexibility (within certain social and economic constraints, of course) when it comes to the construction of his or her own personal dietary regimen. In such a climate, the adoption of vegetarianism is increasingly likely to be seen as just one more diet and lifestyle choice from among the many options on offer, and less likely to be construed as a form of dietary deviance or non-conformity. While this may actually render vegetarianism rather less attractive to those seeking ways of demonstrating difference or expressing protest, it will enhance its attractiveness to a wider range of potential converts.

This conclusion presents us with an interesting paradox, however. The rheto-ric of vegetarianism tends to place considerable emphasis on the idea of a challenge to conventional foodways. Such a challenge, as we have seen, may be couched in ethical terms, in nutritional terms, in terms of concepts of 'nature' and the 'natural', and so on. Yet it can be argued (Beardsworth and Keil 1993a) that this challenge to the conventional food system is, in practice, in the process of being re-incorporated into it. For a capitalist, market-based food system, vegetarian tastes and requirements present novel marketing and profit-making opportunities. Thus, specialized products and services aimed at vegetarian con-sumers are created to respond to the demands of a significant new minority niche. These developments are explicitly recognized by many respondents who have been vegetarian for some decades, as they comment on the improvements they have experienced in the availability of vegetarian dietary items, restaurants, etc. (Beardsworth and Keil 1992a). As vegetarianism is absorbed into the capitalist food system and converted into one more routinely available dietary option, its threshold of entry will effectively be lowered. In this way, the current following is likely to be maintained, or even significantly extended, as potential recruits are offered a progressively more straightforward process of conversion.

OVERVIEW

In this chapter we have traced the path which has led vegetarianism from its position as a long-established, but in a sense deviant, nutritional regimen to a position of being an increasingly popular dietary option among an array of other options on offer. The analysis of the shifting cultural, social and economic conditions behind this transformation might push us towards the conclusion that, in some senses at least, contemporary concerns, priorities and anxieties may be evolving in ways which are bringing them more and more into line with the preoccupations of vegetarianism. For these reasons, what was once a quint-essential nutritional heresy is now becoming a kind of nutritional orthodoxy, with a substantial and expanding nucleus of adherents and a larger periphery of sympathizers and potential converts. This process is aided by the commercial dynamics of a food industry willing, indeed eager, to cater for novel forms of demand.

Predicting the future of vegetarianism in Western societies like the UK and the USA might seem to be a simple matter of extrapolating from existing trends. On this basis, it might even be anticipated that vegetarianism, at varying levels of strictness, would eventually become the dominant dietary pattern, with meat eating confined to a deviant and furtive minority. However, the data upon which we might base our views of overall trends in vegetarianism are currently far too fragmentary to generate much predictive confidence. What is more, these fragmentary data suggest that trends in meat consumption and meat avoidance are somewhat variable, even between the nations of Europe, for example. Even if clear trends could be established, their ultimate directions would still be shrouded in mystery. Could we expect vegetarianism to continue its inroads into conventional foodways on a steady basis? Would it, on the other hand, reach a kind of plateau, a level of penetration beyond which it could not extend? On the other hand, would it eventually begin to contract, losing ground to other priorities and nutritional ideologies as the cultural and economic frameworks of food production and consumption undergo changes as yet unforeseen? Or should the future of vegetarian cuisine simply be seen as one more culinary option which individuals can employ as and when they feel inclined?

While such questions are, for the time being, unanswerable, there is a pressing need for more empirical research in this area. More extensive and comprehensive survey data are needed to provide a clearer idea of the underlying trends. Survey work based on a comparative approach is also required to provide a clearer indication of the important contrasts which appear to exist between different, albeit neighbouring, societies. Additionally, as a complement to such data, more qualitative material is required, derived from small-scale, intensive studies, in order to enhance our insight into the subjective dimensions of vegetarianism. In particular, vegetarian biographies require attention, in order to reveal the ways in which motivations and accounts vary over time, as well as the patterns of conversion, adjustment and lapsing which commonly occur. Only through such work will we achieve the insights necessary to place the contemporary vegetarian phenomenon in its sociological and historical context.

11

SUGAR AND CONFECTIONERY
Sweetness in the human diet

James (1990) writes of the Baka of the Cameroons who, once a honey comb is located in the topmost branches of the rainforest canopy, spend time and effort in order to obtain it. 'They will quite literally go to enormous heights and put their lives at risk to obtain the honey' (James 1990: 632). She also draws our attention to a television advertisement in our own society which portrays a man undertaking a series of dangerous and acrobatic feats to deliver a box of chocolates to the woman he admires. What have these accounts in common? They are, argues James, just two examples of the extent to which sweet foods are valued. In each culture the source of sweetness may vary, as will the kinds of food, but the preference for sweet tastes remains a constant. There are many discussions about the biological basis and physiological functions of this prefer-ence for sweetness. However, for sociologists it raises questions about the social organization of the production, distribution and consumption of such highly valued foods and about the part which sweet foods play in society.

Any superficial account of the increase in the accessibility and consumption of such foods as sweets, confectionery and chocolate gives an impression that here is yet another success story involving human ingenuity in processing natural raw materials and, in relatively recent human history, the application of sophisticated technology to produce and distribute quantities of sweet foods on a scale unknown in previous historical periods. However, it is also relevant to recognize that, whichever aspect of the story of sweetness is considered, there are also contradictions and conflicts and a more complex account to be given. There are many examples, amongst the most revealing about social processes and relation-ships, of the consumer's ambivalence about a food which is, at the same time, both desirable and 'bad', and of the human as well as the economic price to be paid for the increase in the production of such sweet foods as sugar.

THE PHYSIOLOGICAL BASIS FOR THE PREFERENCE FOR SWEETNESS

Cultural analyses of food preference emphasize the fact that, of all the poten-tially edible foods available, human beings select relatively few and that these choices are shaped by social experiences, each society building up a set of food resources appropriate to its physical and social environment. By way of contrast, the preference for sweetness is said to be innate. It is assumed to be linked to the fact that sweetness is the characteristic taste of many attractive energy sources, such as fruits (Rozin 1982: 228). Although we do not have a complete understanding of the biological function of the human preference for sweetness (Booth, Connor and Marie 1987: 156), there is agreement that 'Sweetness is the most neurally distinct of gustatory qualities' (Scott and Giza 1987: 28). The sensory receptors for detecting the chemicals associated with sugars appear to have emerged very early in primate evolution and to have persisted in modern primates including humans (Beidler 1982: 5). Human infants have been shown to prefer sweet solutions immediately after birth. As children grow up and become adult, the specific sweet foods chosen, together with their quantity and quality, are constrained by social and economic factors. Beauchamp and Cowart (1987: 136) review the available data on the development of sweet perception and draw the following conclusions. Newborn babies and young children demonstrate an avid taste for sweetness, which seems to be largely independent of the degree of early exposure to sweet tastes. However, the nature of dietary exposure to sweet tastes that the child experiences does appear to shape the expectations and the degree of acceptability of particular sweet foods. Strikingly, however, the taste for sweetness appears to decline with maturity, with adults judging lower levels of sweetness to be most pleasant as compared with the levels preferred by children.

This preference for sweetness is argued to be so powerful that, according to Rozin (1982: 228-9), it is in sharp contrast to many other foods in that it provides an example of one of the most straightforward links between biology, individual and culture. He suggests that there exists a relatively straightforward progression between the biological fact of the innate human liking for sweetness and the development of behaviour patterns designed to seek out sweet foods in the environment. Once such items are discovered, Rozin argues, they are readily incorporated into culture and, more specifically, into cuisine. Once incorporated, their presence provides the opportunity for further exposure to sweet tastes, thereby reinforcing their role in the human diet. Rozin sees these steps to the incorporation of sweet foods into culture as far simpler and more direct than the much more complex processes which may be involved in learning other flavour principles which are not so closely tied to any discernible physiologically innate taste preferences.

THE HISTORY OF SUGAR

Most of the historical studies of sweet foods (examples are Abbot 1990; Deerr 1949, 1950; Lees 1983; Mintz 1985; Toussaint-Samat 1992) tend to focus on the discovery and deliberate cultivation of plants, such as cane and beet, which produce sugar, with most attention on the development of sugar cane. However, these authors also give some insight into other sources of sweet foods. For example, Deerr (1949, 1950) in a two-volume history of sugar begins by indicating the importance of honey and fruits as sweet foods for 'primitive man' and reproduces a rock painting of neolithic honey gathering (Deerr 1949: 5). Sources such as honey and fruits have remained important but may have received less attention because they have never been the focus of the same level of sociopolitical intervention in their production and distribution as sugar cane and beet.

Although the large-scale consumption of sugar is relatively recent in Europe, there is evidence that sugar produced from cane on a commercial basis was widely available in India and China from ancient times. The cane is said to have originated in the south Pacific region and been transferred, first to India and later to China, into those areas where it was possible to find the right conditions for its growth: rich, moist soil for planting and great heat and ventilation for ripening (Toussaint-Samat 1992: 552–63). The ancestors of the Buddha were said to have come from 'the land of sugar', or Bengal, and Toussaint-Samat records a reference to a banquet in 1200 BC 'with tables laid with sweet things, syrup, canes to chew' (Toussaint-Samat 1992: 552). This fact, together with evidence of sugar prepared on a commercial basis for food preparation in China, is of particular interest in that it supports the notion that sugar was available in these societies as part of the general cuisine. This contrasts with evidence from other geographical areas and historical periods in Europe and the Middle East (for example in ancient Egypt and later amongst the Greeks and Romans) which suggests that sugar was only available in very small quantities and that its use was restricted to medicinal purposes. The Persians were said to have discovered the reed 'that gives honey without the aid of bees' (Toussaint-Samat 1992: 552) when they invaded the Indus valley, and it was they who first established the routes which brought sugar to Europe as part of the spice trade. In medieval Europe the crystallized sap of sugar cane was initially called 'Indian salt'. Its use gradually spread as it established itself as an exotic luxury food or medicinal substance available only to the wealthy. The large sums of money exchanged in the operation of the spice trade accounted for much of the prosperity of ports such as Venice during this period. However, sugar prices rose even higher as this precious commodity was distributed inland from the ports. Indeed, Toussaint-Samat illustrates the value placed on this substance by citing a thirteenth-century example from Burgundy in France, where sugar changed hands on the basis of its weight in silver (Toussaint-Samat 1992: 554).

The voyages of exploration of Christopher Columbus and others constituted the turning-point for sugar production and initiated its transformation from a medicine and a luxury into a more widely available and ultimately cheap food. These explorers discovered, in the 'New World' of the Americas, land that provided the particular conditions in which sugar cane would grow. Entire continents were claimed in the names of European sovereigns. For the first time, European societies such as Spain, Portugal, France, and later England and the Netherlands (in the East Indies), had access to sources of sugar over which they had political control. The plantations which were established continued the traditional, labour-intensive ways of growing cane, although the scale of production expanded. The main developments were in processing and it became the pattern to export unrefined sugar from the colonies for capital-intensive refinement in the European countries which controlled the plantations. Lees (1983) provides an account of the scientific (particularly chemical) and technological developments which made possible the wide range of sweets, chocolate and other confectionery, as well as refined sugar itself, which have been available to the British consumer since the middle of the nineteenth century. After an uncertain start and variable success, the Caribbean islands had become the world's leading producers and suppliers of sugar by the eighteenth century (Abbot 1990: 11), with production and trade expanding at a pace which accelerated in the nineteenth century, along with constant improvements in the reliability and predictability of supplies.

It is interesting to note that sugar cane production became so well established and the initial concerns about the security of supplies so diminished that there was little interest in exploiting knowledge of the high sugar content of a type of beet grown in Italy which had been documented as early as 1575 (Toussaint-Samat 1992: 560). That waited until the nineteenth century when countries such as France, when at war, could no longer be confident about supplies from their colonies. Compared with sugar cane, beet had the advantage that it could be planted as part of crop rotations and could be processed directly into refined sugar in on-site factories. These characteristics made sugar beet a highly profitable commodity and it was so successful that production continued when the political reasons for its development no longer obtained. Ironically, successful production of beet sugar in Europe contributed to uncertainty in the market overall. The proportions of cane and beet sugar have varied over time but cane sugar has remained at over half of the total supply (Abbot 1990: 12). By the 1970s the combination of sugar cane and beet production outstripped the demand for sugar as a foodstuff and experiments began for using sugar in other ways, for example, as a raw material for the production of fuel.

Any history of sugar which emphasizes the development of increasingly efficient production and the growth in consumption may give the impression that the history of sugar is merely one of the commercial and industrial adjustment between supply and demand. However, there is another story, that of the exploitative social relations involved in the use of sugar cane by Europeans who might not be able to grow the cane in their own temperate climate but who wielded power over both the peoples and the processes involved in sugar production in their colonies overseas. As Toussaint-Samat puts it dramatically: 'So many tears were shed for sugar that by rights it ought to have lost its sweetness' (Toussaint-Samat 1992: 560). According to Mintz (1985), an understanding of the history of sugar demands an analysis of power relationships between the 'Old' and the 'New' worlds.

The beginning of Mintz's account is familiar. As we have seen, the early status of sugar was as an expensive medicine, sold along with spices in apothecaries or pharmacies. It was regarded as beneficial but powerful, so that it was important not to eat it inappropriately (i.e., when not sick) or to excess. The production of sugar from cane grown in tropical or sub-tropical conditions in the Nile valley and some parts of the Mediterranean was highly labour-intensive, which explains the expense. However, Mintz argues that Columbus's second voyage to the New World in the late fifteenth century would transform the scale of sugar production when the explorer recognized the West Indies as offering the ideal conditions for growing sugar cane. However, in the newly established plantations the processing of the cane remained labour-intensive. It is in the provision of forced labour for the sugar plantations that power relations are revealed. Since a large proportion of the indigenous population of the West Indies had been taken to work the gold mines in South America, labour had to be imported. Since the aim was also to keep the cost of working the plantations as low as possible, already established links with the coastal peoples of West Africa were brought into play, as these peoples could provide slaves drawn from the African interior. The first of these were transported to the West Indies in 1505.

Other countries soon entered the competition for control over the New World, and the control of sugar became a political and military, as well as an economic, struggle. The first slaves reached an English colony in the West Indies in 1619 and, from then onwards, the English became the major and most successful players in the struggle. The sugar trade can be regarded as part of an economic investment where production and demand expanded together. The slaves themselves were rarely considered as human. They were treated as commodities in the two 'triangular trades' which hinged on sugar cane growing. The first of these trades involved the export of British finished goods to Africa, the transportation of slaves from Africa to the West Indies and the shipping of sugar from the West Indies to England. The other trade involved the export of New England rum to Africa, the transportation of slaves from Africa to the West Indies and the shipping of molasses from the West Indies to New England. These trading patterns were highly profitable activities from their beginnings, bringing at least three benefits to the home economy: firstly, returns on the initial investment; secondly, the export of machinery, cloth and even instruments of constraint and torture to plantations; thirdly, the import of a low-cost food for the labouring classes. The entire system of production was supported by the political and military strength of the British Empire, which shaped the asymmetrical power relationships between the home economy and the colonies. In such a context, it is easy to explain Britain's initial reluctance to abolish slavery and the fact that, even when West Indian slaves were given their freedom, their role continued to be limited to that of labourers in the sugar industry. Indeed, it was the government's deliberate policy to deny them the opportunity of becoming as rich as their previous masters from the production and export of sugar. Ironically, however, the exploitative conditions and relationships which characterized sugar production in the West Indies provided what can only be described as a bonanza of sweetness for the working classes in Britain.

Mintz (1985) argues that the pattern of consumption in Britain showed two characteristics: 'intensification' and 'extensification'. By intensification he means that the lower classes emulated the upper classes in the use of sugar, for example, in having elaborate wedding cakes which, until the availability of cheap sugar in the nineteenth century, had been unachievable luxuries even for the middle classes. By extensification, Mintz means that new ways of using sugar were developed, aimed at all social levels. Such products included condensed milk, chocolate, sherbert, sweets and biscuits, which meant that, increasingly, sugar was 'pumped into every crevice in the diet' (Mintz 1985: 188). The link between high levels of production and high levels of consumption in Britain is emphasized by contrast with the situation in France. The French too had colonially based sugar plantations but never exploited them to the same extent. As a consequence, sugar remained only a limited part of French cuisine and contemporary sugar consumption in France is only about one-tenth of that in Britain.

TRENDS IN SUGAR PRODUCTION AND CONSUMPTION

Focusing on the twentieth century in particular, Abbot (1990: 17–29) presents data on world sugar production and consumption. In discussing production he describes the ways in which the desire for self-sufficiency had the consequence of increasing the numbers of countries producing sugar. He calculates that by 1990 there were more than 120 sugar-producing countries. Production seems to follow a cycle which runs for between six and nine years and which is linked to fluctuations in demand and consequent prices on world markets. None the less, the pattern after a major expansion in the 1960s has been 'of alternating peaks followed by troughs with each peak higher than the last' (Abbot 1990: 17). The developing countries appear to be the major contributors to this overall rise in production (Abbott 1990: 17–20).

The figures for sugar consumption are also documented by Abbot. They show that the world consumption of sugar has increased almost fourfold in the first fifty years of the twentieth century, despite wide fluctuations in world prices. Abbot's detailed data are for the years 1972 to 1986 inclusive and document separately the consumption in what he defines as the 'developed', 'developing' and 'centrally planned' economies. The greatest increase in consumption was in the developing countries, whose share of world consumption rose from 34 per cent to approximately 45 per cent. However, there was a decrease in the total annual consumption in the developed countries, possibly because consumers in richer countries have become more calorie-conscious. However, the developed countries still consume the highest per capita quantities of sugar, for example, per capita consumption in Europe and North America is roughly twice the world average figure. In addition, there is evidence to suggest that any decline in sugar consumption in Western economies is not necessarily a decline in the overall demand for sweetness. A whole range of alternative sweeteners has been developed and the production and consumption of these is largely located in the developed world.

More refined data concerning per capita sugar consumption trends in the UK are available from the *Household and Food Consumption Expenditure Survey* which we have already encountered in Chapter 9 (Ministry of Agriculture, Fisheries and Food 1991). The data published here cover approximately five decades and document a steady rise in per capita sugar consumption from a level of 8.41 oz per person per week in 1942 to a peak of 18.49 oz per person per week in 1963. After this peak, a decline set in and by 1990 the level of consumption had fallen below the 1942 figure, having dropped to 6.04 oz per week. In parallel, certain other high-sugar foods also show this pattern of peak and decline, for example, preserves (including jams, honey and syrups) were consumed at the rate of 4.93 oz per person per week in 1942 and peaked in 1950 at 6.30 oz. Consumption of these foods then began to diminish consistently so that by 1990 only 1.69 oz per person per week were being consumed. Other sweet foods like cakes and pastries show a similar pattern of decline, although the consumption of biscuits, which peaked at 5.84 oz per person per week in 1958 has not fallen so markedly, the value in 1990 being still as high as 5.26 oz per person per week (Ministry of Agriculture, Fisheries and Food 1991: 96). However, the same source shows that within these figures there are wide variations by social class. For example, at the beginning of the period studied, the rationing of sugar resulted in very little difference in consumption levels by households in different income groups. However, over time, consumption in income groups 'A' and 'B' fell to below the average and that of groups 'D', 'E' and pensioners rose above it. Indeed, by 1990, pensioner households were consuming 82 per cent more sugar and preserves than the average, whereas group 'A' households were consuming 30 per cent less than the average (Ministry of Agriculture, Fisheries and Food 1991: 46).

In contemporary societies, the taste for sweetness can be satisfied by the consumption, not only of refined sugar, preserves, cakes and biscuits but also by the consumption of a very wide range of confectionery. Indeed, the demand for confectionery in the developed economies appears to be high and this is particularly true of the UK. For example, figures provided by James (1990: 668–9) indicate that the UK confectionery market in 1988 was worth £3,285 million, more than bread (£2,375 million) and cereals (£650 million). She adds that a 1990 survey indicated that about 95 per cent of the population ate chocolate confectionery at least once a day, with an average of 9.2 oz of confectionery being eaten per person per week in 1988. This is much higher than most other European countries, with only West Germany matching the British capacity for consuming confectionery (James 1990: 637). Sugar confectionery (that is, non-chocolate confectionery including boiled sweets, chewing-gum, liquorice and mints) is eaten vast in quantities in countries like the UK, whose consumption of such high-sugar items rose from 286,000 tonnes in 1987 to 302,000 tonnes in 1991 (Market Research Great Britain 1992: 83–101).

THE SYMBOLISM OF SWEETNESS

The data we have examined above demonstrate clearly the sheer scale of consumption of sweet foods in contemporary societies such as the UK. In one sense, this might be seen simply as a reflection of an innate human craving for sweetness which is indulged more and more frequently as sweet foods become increasingly available. However, in sociological terms, such an observation can only ever be a partial explanation. Just as we have had to consider the geopolitical background to historical increases in sugar production, we must also consider the cultural and symbolic context in which sweetness is consumed. For example, in spite of the cheapness and ready availability of sugar and other sweeteners in the Western world, Western cuisines rarely, if ever, contain sweet main courses. Since there is no nutritional reason why a main course could not be sweet, we are compelled to consider what kind of cultural or symbolic charges sweetness may carry which define this particular taste experience as one which is appropriate in some contexts and not in others.

The high intake of sugar in the British diet provides the main focus of the study by James (1990). She addresses the issue of why, in spite of what she terms the 'body technocrats' who warn us about the dangers of overindulgence, sugar and confectionery continue to play such a prominent part in our everyday eating. For James, the key lies in the place of confectionery in our system of food classification. In a sense, confectionery is regarded as both food and non-food. As such, it can take on meanings relevant to either identity and sometimes may even be assigned qualities which go beyond the properties of 'ordinary' food. She gives the example of Kendal Mint Cake, which is not in fact a cake but a mint-flavoured sugar bar, which has come to be regarded as an essential component of any mountaineer's survival kit (James 1990: 674). Culturally, confectionery itself is never regarded as part of a conventional meal, given its 'in-between' status as food and non-food. However, the flexibility created by this duality allows confectionery to take on a wide variety of social meanings. There are many examples: confectionery as a gift for mediating and repairing relationships between individuals; confectionery eaten on ritual occasions such as birthdays, Christmas and Easter. In addition, expensively packaged chocolates, presented as an extravagant gift within a framework of sentimentality and romanticism are seen as a particularly suitable gift for women (Barthel 1989). In other words, confectionery constitutes a kind of generalized symbolic currency acceptable to all. For most of us, to use 'ordinary' foods which do not have this dual status (for example, vegetables or cuts of meat) would seem inappropriate and even eccentric. However, there is also an element of ambivalence here, in that the pleasurable nature of chocolate and confectionery can become associated with self-indulgence and guilt. In contrast, 'goodness' and 'virtue' can become associated with 'dull' food. James illustrates this argument by pointing out the way in which parents may sometimes encourage children to eat 'dull/virtuous' foods by rewarding them with limited amounts of 'pleasurable/bad' foods like sweets and chocolate. In fact, she concludes that the symbolic significance of confectionery in the British diet is so powerful that it provides a serious challenge to attempts by officials and professionals to bring about an overall reduction in intake. As this author puts it: 'An apple a day may keep the doctor away but it does little to promote social relationships. That is the role of sweets, as a root symbol for all that is "naughty but nice" in the world of food' (James 1990: 685).

This moral ambivalence associated with sugar and confectionery is explored by Rozin (1987), who speculates about the relationship between sweetness, sensuality and sin. Rozin points out that, although refined sugar is one of the few chemically pure substances that are regularly consumed, and is an important source of gustatory pleasure, it has nevertheless become associated with 'sin' and 'danger'. He seeks to explain this association in a number of ways. The first of these explanations is based upon sugar's links with other self-indulgent substances, such as coffee, tea and sweetened alcohol. The second explanation relates to the set of 'Puritan values', which he sees as prevalent in the USA in particular, which suggests that anything that is extremely pleasurable must be bad. In some cases, he argues, this has reached the extreme that only the consumption of sugar-free food that is non-fattening and non-toxic can permit the consumer to occupy the moral high ground (Rozin 1987: 100). The third reason is that sugar is linked with obesity and, in a society where obesity is believed to be a moral failing, this may also contribute to the notion that sugar consumption is sinful. Rozin also speculates that the strength of feeling about sugar may be explained by the operation of powerful traditional beliefs, for example, that we are what we eat (so that by consuming sugar we become sinful) or that some foods, either on moral or health grounds, can simply 'taste too good to be good for you' (Rozin 1987: 101). Interestingly, in connection with the point made by James about the use of sweet things as a reward for eating 'dull' foods, Rozin argues that the outcome of such a strategy is somewhat unpredictable. In some instances, individuals rewarded with sweetness in this way come to develop an enhanced liking for the 'dull' food, whereas other individuals may experience a reduction in their liking for the food in question (Rozin 1987: 108). Thus, although the human taste for sweetness appears to be innate, the role of sweetness in particular dietary contexts can be complex and variable.

The increase in sugar consumption is also the focus for the analysis by Fischler (1987). As consumption increased, so reservations about the use of sugar began to appear, becoming, according to Fischler (1987: 86–7), ever stronger as the 'vulgarisation' of sugar occurred. It was almost as though sugar became more dangerous as it became more accessible to the lower classes. In a review of the literature on contemporary attitudes to sweetness, Fischler identifies what he terms 'saccarophobia' and illustrates this by citing studies which relate sugar consumption to a range of individual and social problems, including criminal behaviour, depression and divorce as well as diabetes, obesity and hyperactivity in children (Fischler 1987: 87–9). For Fischler, such condemnation has its origins in modern society's ambivalence about the social management of pleasure. Sweetness is, on the one hand, both gratifying and it makes for emotional security yet, on the other, it generates a sense of danger and feelings of undeserved gratification. This ambivalence is handled by socialized and ritualized consumption, which (in parallel with potential pleasures such as alcohol and sex) is more acceptable than individual, solitary use. To be socially acceptable, the consumption of sweet foods requires a clear social context and legitimization. If this is the case, Fischler argues, sweets and chocolates can only be given to children under supervision and if they behave well. There is some support for this contention from James (1982), who writes about the special category of children's sweets which are bought and eaten away from the supervision of adults. Such sweets are often considered 'rubbish' by adults and are eaten in ways which disobey adult rules, for example, they are not wrapped but are handled directly and they may be removed from the mouth and passed on to other children. In a sense, these violations of adult rules can be interpreted as a child's way of defining self and a rejection of the adult control which, Fischler argues, is so important for adults to exercise in this context.

The ambivalence of sugar and sweetness within culinary culture and within our gustatory experience is recognized by those responsible for marketing sweet food products. Whereas some of these products may make a direct and explicit appeal to our taste for sweetness (whether as nourishing snacks or as luxurious indulgences), other sweetened foods may be marketed in a more indirect way. For example, some products which tend to have a relatively high content of added sugar are not marketed explicitly in terms of their sweetness in order to avoid connotations of being highly calorific or unhealthy (Schutz and Judge 1987). Indeed, these authors also point out that in marketing foods for weight-conscious consumers, manufacturers may attempt to break the association between sweetness and high calorific content and may also distinguish between 'natural' sweetness and sweetness produced 'artificially' by the use of added sugar or synthetic sweeteners. In effect, food manufacturers and distributors are responding to the market opportunities generated by the powerful human preference for sweetness, sometimes through explicit appeals to our cravings and sometimes through the less publicized inclusion of sweetness in a wide range of everyday foods.

The fact that sweetness, particularly in the form of refined sugar, is so readily available and penetrates our culinary culture so pervasively raises an interesting question. What are the implications for individuals who, for health or social reasons, find themselves denied what most of us have come to regard as taken for granted, ready access to sugar and sweetness? Perhaps one of the most dramatic examples of the experience of sugar deprivation is the study by Posner (1983) which investigates the social dynamics of the management of the diabetic diet. Such a diet requires the avoidance of sugar no matter what foods it may be incorporated into (for example, sweets, jelly, ice-cream, biscuits, cake and chocolate). However, although the removal of such 'bad' foods from the diet might conventionally be construed as a move to a healthier pattern of eating, Posner makes the point that the consumption of such items is so deeply engrained in cultural terms that many diabetics may be reluctant wholly to give them up. Thus, in order for the diabetic to continue to be as 'normal' as possible and to have access to these symbolically significant items, a whole range of diabetic versions of sweet foods has been developed. In a sense, then, the consumption of synthetic sweetness permits the diabetic to attempt to hold on to the conventions and taste sensations of the sweetness culture.

Other kinds of consumer may also find it difficult to participate in the sweetness culture, but for very different reasons. This emerges strikingly in the study of low-income families carried out by Dobson and her colleagues which was discussed in Chapter 4 (Dobson, Beardsworth, Keil and Walker 1994). The study uncovered instances where mothers had gone to considerable lengths to manage a very tight family food budget in such a way that their children were still able to take chocolate bars or other sweet snacks to school. Superficially, this may appear to be an almost perverse use of very limited resources, particularly as food expenditure was one of the areas that these families had to control very rigorously. However, in sociological terms, the inclusion of such marginal or nutritionally dubious items in the family budget is not as puzzling as it might first appear. Given the cultural and symbolic power of these items, their significance is clearly much more than a merely nutritional one. Their consumption could allow an otherwise deprived child to retain a sense that he or she was still able to participate in the mainstream of consumer culture with its cornucopia of distinctively branded and heavily advertised products. What is more, such a child could also avoid any loss of face in the eyes of his or her peers that might arise from an inability to consume as others consume.

OVERVIEW

The consumption of sweet foods provides yet another example of the fascinating intersection of the biological, the psychological and the sociological dimensions of human activity. What appears to be an innate human preference has provided the foundation for the development of an enormous international apparatus for producing, manufacturing and distributing sweetness. Certainly, the special conditions required for the production of refined sugar (particularly from sugar cane) have meant that from the very beginning this has been an essentially de-localized crop which has been particularly susceptible to political control and manipulation. Consequently, sugar has been, historically, a particularly significant commodity within the emerging system of world trade. In this context it has also been associated with the extension of colonial domination and the exploitation of slave labour.

The pervasiveness of sweetness (based mainly on sucrose) is perhaps one of the most distinctive features of Western culinary culture. Yet, as we have seen, such sweetness is charged with ambivalence. Sweet foods are seen, on the one hand as delicious and attractive, and on the other as self-indulgent and potentially harmful. This good/bad duality is nowhere more apparent than in the case of chocolate and confectionery. Yet, in sociological terms, the ambivalence of those two items is of particular interest because they are seen both as foods and non-foods, and exist on the margin between the nutritious and the harmfully indulgent. But it is for this very reason that these products can be used as currency in patterns of gift giving which express a great variety of social relationships. Since they are in one sense non-foods and 'luxuries', they can be given by one individual to another without the implication that the recipient is in any way deprived or in need of the support of gifts of 'real' food. However, since, in another sense, they are also foods, they can be consumed by the recipient and will provide a degree of gustatory pleasure. The fact that such gifts are consumable may also be relevant since they do not accumulate and can be used to express relationships from the most permanent to the most ephemeral. It seems clear, therefore, that sweet foods in the multiplicity of manifestations in which they are available in Western society will continue to play a significant if controversial role in contemporary nutritional culture despite, or perhaps even because of, their symbolically paradoxical character.

EPILOGUE

In the course of the previous eleven chapters we have threaded our way through a maze of issues, studies and sources all related, directly or obliquely, to the search for a better understanding of the social and cultural dynamics of food and eating. At this point it is time to take stock, in order to attempt to provide some sort of overall appreciation of just what it is that emerges from this broad spread of material, and in order to begin to speculate about the possibilities for the future.

Of course, the core aim of this book, around which all the other aims laid out in the introduction revolve, is to introduce the reader to the main themes in the literature and to provide a reasonably full account of the ways in which these themes have been dealt with by the authors who have sought to address them. Inevitably, however, we have not necessarily been able to do full justice to the detailed arguments contained in our chosen sources, largely because we have been primarily concerned to extract the specifically sociological implications of the material. Furthermore, there are, inevitably, significant gaps in the existing literature, gaps produced by a lack of theoretical formulation, empirical research, or both. Thus, in a sense, the themes upon which this book is based are shaped as much by what *is not* available as by what *is* available in terms of knowledge. Drawing out the connections between the themes and the ways in which they are interwoven with each other is clearly important. Yet, the understandable desire to see some explicit, all-embracing framework within which these interconnections can be formalized in an integrated fashion is one which, at this stage in our knowledge, is likely to be only partially fulfilled. The very diversity of the material we have encountered is at the same time the source of its richness and a barrier to the creation of a single, authoritative synthesis.

Nevertheless, a brief recapitulation of the main themes we have encountered can serve to highlight deeper, underlying refrains which have expressed themselves repeatedly in the foregoing pages. The arguments discussed in Part I concerning the origins of human patterns of food production and consumption were, of necessity, somewhat speculative ones, given the difficulties of producing reliable data on the prehistory and early history of our species. In examining the emergence of the modern food system, however, we were on somewhat firmer ground, with a much clearer and more highly developed historical perspective to hand. Certainly, two major transformations can be seen as of central importance to any understanding of human foodways: the emergence of domestication and agriculture, beginning up to 10,000 years ago, and the intensification, industrialization and globalization of food production, which began much more recently and which has proceeded so rapidly.

In Part II we examined food preparation and consumption in two contrasting settings: the private domain of the household and the public domain of the inn, restaurant or fast food outlet. Here again, the emphasis was on change. While the household setting may well continue to reflect relatively long-standing assumptions concerning age and gender differentiation, we noted that the distribution of household types is changing and that the social organization of eating within these various types is unlikely to remain static in the near future. Meanwhile, eating out, the consumption of food in the public domain, continues to expand and to form an increasingly important component of the experience of eating in contemporary Western society. In Part III the insistent refrain of change was also present, as we considered the ways in which conceptions of the links between diet and health have been strongly influenced by the processes of rationalization which are such central features of modern societies. Yet, running parallel with the increasing emphasis on the rational regulation of diet to promote the maintenance of health, we noted other, more sinister developments: the emergence of food-related anxieties, the periodic occurrence of major food scares, and Western culture's increasing 'fat phobia', plus an emphasis on the restriction of food intake in order to control weight, an emphasis which in extreme cases can take the form of a clinically recognized eating disorder. Finally, in Part IV, attention was directed towards two classes of food items (animal products and products characterized by high levels of sweetness) which are both, in some senses, problematical. It has been argued that humans may have some kind of 'innate' taste for both classes of foods, and yet both are loaded with powerful cultural and symbolic connotations which have potent negative as well as positive aspects.

Of course, the refrain of change is the one which reappears most frequently. Indeed, as was indicated in the Introduction, this refrain provides the central thread linking together the diverse contributions that make up the subject matter of this book. Changes in food production, food consumption and, indeed, in food symbolism, have all been linked to broader processes of change involving industrialization, rationalization, globalization, labour market restructuring, long-term modifications in gender roles and gender expectations, and far-reaching ideological and cultural shifts in the ways in which we view our relationships with other humans and with the natural world.

Yet, if the refrain of change is one whose importance was anticipated from the start, a second refrain emerged during the course of the writing of this book whose significance was not initially so clearly recognized: the refrain of ambivalence. For example, in Chapter 4 the essential ambivalence of women's

255

general responsibility for carrying out the preparation and presentation of food in the domestic setting emerged clearly. On the one hand, the successful completion of such tasks might conventionally be seen as an expression of the caring and nurturing aspects of feminine gender roles. However, on the other hand, the imposition of these responsibilities, which may well be perceived as unwelcome and onerous, might be construed as a component of the cultural apparatus which serves to perpetuate the subordination and control of women within a patriarchal context. The refrain of ambivalence is even more salient in relation to the questions of diet and health linkages which were raised in Chapter 6, in the sense that rational/medical models of healthy diet may be at odds with many individuals' gustatory habits and preferences. Thus, the following of what is prescribed as a healthy diet may come to involve a burdensome element of self-denial and self-discipline. A similar form of ambivalence concerning food intake figured significantly in Chapter 8. For many individuals, particularly women, food is seen both as a source of pleasure, gratification, reward or compensation and as an enemy, a threat to one's ability to achieve and maintain a desired weight or body shape.

Indeed, in Chapter 7 the concept of ambivalence took centre stage, as the fundamental paradoxes inherent in the very act of eating were subjected to detailed analysis. The fact that eating potentially provides both pleasure and discomfort, is both a source of sustenance and of danger, both maintains life and entails its destruction, generates deep-seated anxieties which, we have argued, require effective forms of masking and management. In this connection the ambivalence of meat as a source of nutrients was given particular attention (in Chapter 9), given its conflicting connotations of strength, power, vigour and masculinity on the one hand, and of suffering, death and decay on the other. Of course, the moral ambivalences that can be linked to the consumption of meat are not limited to concerns about the animals eaten but, as we saw in Chapter 10, may also extend to issues relating to global inequalities in nutritional standards and to the impact on the environment of what are seen as destructive or non-sustainable forms of animal husbandry. Even the human taste for sweetness, perhaps superficially to be viewed as a source of unalloyed pleasure, turns out to have ambivalent implications in the modern context of sucrose superabundance: sugar itself comes to be viewed as both desirable and dangerous, as a treat and a sinful indulgence, as a food and a nutritionally vacuous non-food.

Pondering on these two recurrent refrains of change and ambivalence leads almost inevitably to speculations about possible future trends in the context of the food system and of eating patterns. For example, are we likely to witness a continuing expansion in the range of choice of food items, dishes, flavour principles and menus available in contemporary Western societies, all located within an increasingly pluralistic framework within which variety and flexibility become the dominant values? Are we to anticipate the continuing expansion of the practice of eating out and will this necessarily be accompanied by a decline in long-established patterns of domestic eating and commensality? Does this, in turn, imply the continuing increase of the use of convenience foods in the domestic setting and will this lead to a decline in the culinary skills required for more 'traditional' forms of food preparation? Should we also anticipate fundamental changes in the gendered nature of foodwork as women's participation in the labour market changes and as the distributions of household types and life cycle patterns shift significantly? Can we expect to see the continuation of official attempts to set dietary targets and to promote current rational/medical conceptions of healthy diets? Are such attempts likely to result in the establishment of a clear consensus and to continuing modifications of national dietary practices? Pursuing an alternative line of thought, we might ask whether the ethical dimensions of food and eating are set to rise in importance. Will there be a trend towards increasingly 'humane' diets, based upon foods produced in ways seen as minimizing animal suffering? Are vegetarianism and veganism established on a consistent upward trend or will they reach a plateau or go into decline in terms of numbers of adherents? Along similar lines, should we expect to see the emergence of 'ecologically sensitive' dietary patterns?

Of course, any attempt to make actual predictions would be foolhardy, which is why the preceeding paragraph is composed of questions rather than statements. However, beneath all these questions there is, perhaps, a deeper underlying question. Are we about to witness (or indeed, are we now witnessing) the emergence of what might loosely be termed a 'postmodern' food system and 'postmodern' eating patterns? Can we say that the monolith of the modern food system, with its emphasis on large-scale, intensive production and standardized manufacturing, on mass marketing and retailing, is in the process of giving ground to a more diversified and fragmented situation in which idiosyncratic, even 'playful', combinations of aesthetic, ethical, culinary and gustatory preferences can be assembled by individual consumers or groups of consumers? Or, are the foundations of the modern food system so deeply entrenched, and now so indispensable, that they must continue to underpin what are merely superficial fads and fashions?

The very fact that this book, in attempting to provide the reader with an overview of what we currently know about the social and cultural aspects of food and eating, leads us towards these types of questions is, in itself, highly significant. It provides a clear indication that a sociology of food is feasible, either through the application of established sociological concepts and perspectives or through the posing of novel questions about such biological and social processes. We are participating in the beginning of an important and distinctive sociological project which offers a wealth of opportunities for theoretical development and empirical research. Such opportunities include, for example, the design and implementation of effective longitudinal studies in order to document evolving trends in the domestic organization of eating and in domestic foodwork arrangements (particularly in respect of their gendered nature). Such a longitudinal approach would also be a valuable device for monitoring significant changes in patterns of food preference and avoidance, and for investigating the motivations behind them or the accounts, agendas and explanations provided by those whose diets exhibited such changes. Data generated in this way could potentially allow us to gain clearer insights into the ways in which such factors as health concerns, ideas of preferred body shape, ethical preoccupations and the drive for gustatory pleasure and novelty interact with each other and shift in terms of their relative weightings. Such an approach could be effectively complemented by studies focused more specifically on issues of food and identity. This particular focus would serve to extend our understanding of the ways in which such factors as class, ethnicity and gender shape our tastes while framing and constraining our experiences of eating.

In addition, there is enormous scope for the further development of the sociological analysis of the supply side of contemporary food systems. Supply side processes and institutions have not really attracted a great deal of attention from sociologists so far, and this fact is reflected in the structure and content of this book. Food production, processing, distribution and retailing are all areas of human activity which are worthy of a sustained effort to add a sociological perspective to complement those already offered by such disciplines as economics, agronomy, geography and history. Thus, the sociological gaze might be focused upon the multiplicity of occupations which make up the labour force of the food system – the farmer, the abattoir worker, the supermarket manager, the chef, the food technologist, the food co-operative organizer are just a few examples. At a quite different level, the globalization of the food supply has begun to generate food branding and marketing strategies which transcend local cultural differences, a process which is driven by the activities and interests of multinational corporations which contain extensive food producing, manufacturing or retailing divisions. These strategies, and the organizational and commercial ideologies which underpin them, also deserve the scrutiny of the sociologist.

The political dimensions of the food system also represent a fertile area for further sociological enquiry. The constantly evolving role of the state, and its various agencies, in the creation and elaboration of frameworks of regulation for the food industry is a topic of crucial interest. Similarly, the state's continuing attempts to set dietary targets for the general population and to achieve health improvements through the modification of eating patterns raise questions of direct sociological significance. Of course, the state is not the only player in this particular political arena, and the sociologist will also need to pay attention to the parts played by a plethora of commercial interests, pressure groups and professional bodies, each with its own goals and priorities.

Finally, there remains the challenge of extending and refining the theoretical apparatus through which we can apprehend and explain the cultural and symbolic levels of the food system. In a very real sense, these dimensions cross cut all aspects of this system, but equally they form an object of analysis in their own right. Describing the complex and changeable nuances of meaning in the realm of food symbolism promises a fascinating prospect for future sociological endeavour. This is particularly true in situations in which the availability of food, in abundance and in great variety, has become a taken-for-granted fact of life. In such settings the enjoyment of food may come to consist more and more of the consumption of images, representations and ideas of food, subtly crafted and 'fed' to us through advertisements, sumptuously illustrated cookbooks, newspaper features and a seemingly endless stream of television cookery programmes. We may need to ask whether, in such circumstances, we are quite literally eating ideas, experiencing gustatory pleasure directly with the mind, without the need for the participation of the mouth and the stomach!

The above paragraphs are intended to provide a guide to future possibilities, not an exhaustive list of topics for investigation or a definitive programme of research. Yet it is our hope that, in writing this book, we have provided, not only an insight into the present state of knowledge in the sociology of food but the stimulus to go further, to pose new and more searching questions. For the professional social scientist, we may have succeeded in encouraging him or her to make a direct contribution to this expanding area of scholarship. Equally importantly, we would like to think that we may have helped a much wider readership to begin to think critically about the apparently mundane and unremarkable act of eating and all that it entails. For when we do begin to think in this fashion, we find that on the intellectual menu there are insights, surprises, puzzles and paradoxes that all of us can savour.

BIBLIOGRAPHY

Abbot, G.C. (1990) *Sugar*, London: Routledge.

Adams, C.J. (1990) *The Sexual Politics of Meat: A Feminist-Vegetarian Critical Theory*, Cambridge: Polity Press.

Adburgham, A. (1989) *Shops and Shopping 1800–1914*, London: Barrie & Jenkins.

Adkins, L. (1995) *Gendered Work: Sexuality, Family and the Labour Market*, Buckingham: Open University Press.

Allaby, M. (1977) *World Food Resources, Actual and Potential*, London: Applied Science Publishers.

Amato, P.R. and Partridge, S.A. (1989) *The New Vegetarians: Promoting Health and Protecting Life*, New York: Plenum Press.

Anderson, K.N. (1993) *The International Dictionary of Food and Nutrition*, New York: Wiley.

Aron, J.P. (1975) *The Art of Eating in France: Manners and Menus in the Nineteenth Century*, London: Peter Owen.

Atkinson, P. (1979) 'From honey to vinegar: Lévi-Strauss in Vermont', in P. Morley and R. Wallis (eds) *Culture and Curing: Anthropological Perspectives on Traditional Medical Beliefs and Practices*, Pittsburgh, Pa.: University of Pittsburgh Press.

Atkinson, P. (1980) 'The symbolic significance of health foods', in M. Turner (ed.), *Nutrition and Lifestyles*, London: Applied Science Publishers.

Atkinson, P. (1983) 'Eating virtue', in A. Murcott (ed.) *The Sociology of Food and Eating*, Aldershot: Gower.

Bagwell, P. (1974) *The Transport Revolution from 1770*, London: Batsford.

Bansback, B. (1993) 'Meat demand economics', in *Meat Consumption in the European Community*, Luxembourg: Office for Official Publications of the European Communities.

Barkas, J. (1975) *The Vegetable Passion: A History of the Vegetarian State of Mind*, London: Routledge & Kegan Paul.

Barker, L.M. (1982) *The Psychobiology of Human Food Selection*, Chichester: Ellis Horwood.

Barthel, D. (1989) 'Modernism and marketism: the chocolate box revisited', *Theory, Culture and Society* 6: 429–38.

Barthes, R. (1979) 'Toward a psycho-sociology of contemporary food consumption', in R. Forster and O. Ranum (eds) *Food and Drink in History*, Baltimore, Md.: The Johns Hopkins University Press.

Baudrillard, J. (1988) *Selected Writings*, Cambridge: Polity Press.

Beardsworth, A.D. (1990) 'Trans-science and moral panics: understanding food scares', *British Food Journal* 92, 5: 11–6.

Beardsworth, A.D. and Keil, E.T. (1990) 'Putting the menu on the agenda', *Sociology* 24, 1: 139–51.

Beardsworth, A.D. and Keil, E.T. (1992a) 'The vegetarian option: varieties, conversions, motives and careers', *The Sociological Review* 40, 2: 253–93.

260

Beardsworth, A.D. and Keil, E.T. (1992b) 'Foodways in flux: from gastro-anomy to menu pluralism?', *British Food Journal* 94, 7: 20–5.

Beardsworth, A.D. and Keil, E.T. (1993a) 'Contemporary vegetarianism in the U.K.: challenge and incorporation?', *Appetite* 20: 229–34.

Beardsworth, A.D. and Keil, E.T. (1993b) 'Hungry for knowledge? The sociology of food and eating', *Sociology Review* (November). 11–5.

Beauchamp, G.K. and Cowart, B.J. (1987) 'Development of sweet taste', in J. Dobbing (ed.) *Sweetness: International Life Sciences Institute Symposium*, London: Springer-Verlag.

Beidler, L.M. (1982) 'Biological basis of food selection', in L.M. Barker (ed.) *The Psychobiology of Human Food Selection*, Chichester: Ellis Horwood.

Belasco, W.J. (1993) *Appetite for Change: How the Counterculture took on the Food Industry*, Ithaca, N.Y.: Cornell University Press.

Bennett, J. (1987) *The Hunger Machine: the Politics of Food*, Cambridge: Polity Press.

Binford, L.R. (1992) 'Subsistence – a key to the past', in S. Jones, R. Martin and D. Philbeam (eds) *The Cambridge Encyclopedia of Human Evolution*, Cambridge: Cambridge University Press.

Birch, G.G., Cameron, A.G. and Spencer, M. (1986) *Food Science*, Oxford: Pergamon Press.

Blaxter M. and Paterson E. (1983) 'The goodness is out of it: the meaning of food to two generations', in A. Murcott (ed.) *The Sociology of Food and Eating*, Aldershot: Gower.

Blaxter, K. (1986) *People, Food and Resources*, Cambridge: Cambridge University Press.

Bocock, R. (1993) *Consumption*, London: Routledge.

Booth, D.A., Conner, M.T. and Marie, S. (1987) 'Sweetness and food selection: measurement of sweeteners' effects on acceptance', in J. Dobbing (ed.) *Sweetness: International Life Sciences Institute Symposium*, London: Springer-Verlag.

Bordo, S. (1990) 'Reading the slender body', in M. Jacobus (ed.) *Body/Politics*, New York: Routledge.

Borgstrom, G. (1972) *The Hungry Planet: The Modern World at the Edge of Famine*, New York: Collier.

Bourdieu, P. (1979) 'Toward a psycho-sociology of contemporary food consumption', in R. Forster and O. Ranum (eds) *Food and Drink in History*, Baltimore, Md.: The Johns Hopkins University Press.

Bourdieu, P. (1984) *Distinction: A Social Critique of the Judgement of Taste*, London: Routledge & Kegan Paul.

Brown, C. and Jasper, K. (eds) (1993) *Consuming Passions: Feminist Approaches to Weight Preoccupation and Eating Disorders*, Toronto: Second Story Press.

Brownsell, V.L., Griffith, C.J. and Jones, E. (1989) *Applied Science for Food Studies*, Harlow: Longman.

Bruch, H. (1978) *The Golden Cage: The Enigma of Anorexia Nervosa*, London: Open Books.

Brumberg, J.J. (1988) *Fasting Girls: The Emergence of Anorexia Nervosa as a Modern Disease*, Cambridge, Mass.: Harvard University Press.

Buchanan, K.S. (1993) 'Creating beauty in blackness', in C. Brown and K. Jasper (eds) *Consuming Passions: Feminist Approaches to Weight Preoccupation and Eating Disorders*, Toronto: Second Story Press.

Burgoyne, J. and Clarke, D. (1983) 'You are what you eat: food and family reconstitution', in A. Murcott (ed.) *The Sociology of Food and Eating*, Aldershot: Gower.

Burnett, J. (1989) *Plenty and Want: A Social History of Food in England from 1815 to the present day*, third edition, London: Routledge.

Burt, J.V. and Hertzler, A.V. (1978) 'Parental influence on child's food preference', *Journal of Nutrition Education* 10: 123–34.

Cain, P.J. and Hopkins, A.G. (1993) *British Imperialism*, London: Longmans.

Calnan, M. and Cant, S. (1990) 'The social organization of food consumption. A comparison of middle class and working class households', *International Journal of Sociology and Social Policy* 10, 2: 53–79.

Carefoot, G.L. and Sprott, E.R. (1969) *Famine on the Wind: Plant Diseases and Human History*, London: Angus & Robertson.

Carlioro, B. (1994) '75 years: the odyssey of eating out', *Nation's Restaurant News* January: 11ff.

Cash, T.F. (1990) 'The psychology of physical appearance: aesthetics, attributes, and images', in T. Cash and T. Prusinsky (eds) *Body Images: Development, Deviance and Change*, New York: Guilford Press.

Cash, T.F. and Prusinsky, T. (eds) (1990) *Body Images: Development, Deviance and Change*, New York: Guilford Press.

Charles, N. and Kerr, M. (1986a) 'Eating properly, the family and state benefit', *Sociology* 20, 3: 412–29.

Charles, N. and Kerr, M. (1986b) 'Food for feminist thought', *Sociological Review* 34, 3: 537–72.

Charles, N. and Kerr, M. (1988) *Women, Food and Families*, Manchester: Manchester University Press.

Clark, S.R.L. (1984) *The Moral Status of Animals*, London: Oxford University Press.

Cline, S. (1990) *Just Desserts*, London: Andre Deutsch.

Clutton-Brock, J. (1987) *A Natural History of Domesticated Mammals*, Cambridge: Cambridge University Press/British Museum (Natural History).

Clutton-Brock, J. (1992) 'Domestication of animals', in S. Jones, R. Martin and D. Philbeam (eds) *The Cambridge Encyclopedia of Human Evolution*, Cambridge: Cambridge University Press.

Cohen, S. (1971) 'Mods, rockers and the rest: community reactions to juvenile delinquency', in W.G. Carson and P. Wiles (eds) *Crime and Delinquency in Britain*, London: Martin Robertson.

Cohen, S. (1973) *Folk Devils and Moral Panics: The Creation of the Mods and Rockers*, London: Paladin.

Coon, C.S. (1976) *The Hunting Peoples*, Harmondsworth: Penguin.

Copping, A.M. (1985) 'The founding fathers of the Nutrition Society', in D. Oddy and D. Miller (eds) *Diet and Health in Modern Britain*, London: Croom Helm.

Damas, D. (1972) 'The Copper Eskimo', in M.G. Bicchieri (ed.) *Hunters and Gatherers Today*, Prospect Heights, Ill.: Waveland Press.

David, E. (ed. J. Norman) (1994) *Harvest of the Cold Months: The Social History of Ice and Ices*, London: Michael Joseph.

Davis, D. (1966) *A History of Shopping*, London: Routledge & Kegan Paul.

Davis, K. (1966) *Human Society*, New York: Macmillan.

Deerr, N. (1949) *The History of Sugar: Volume One*, London: Chapman Hall.

Deerr, N. (1950) *The History of Sugar: Volume Two*, London: Chapman Hall.

Delahoyde, M. and Desperich, S.C. (1994) 'Creating meat-eaters: The child as advertising target', *Journal of Popular Culture* 28, 1: 135–49.

Delphy, C. (1979) 'Sharing the same table: consumption and the family' in C. Harris (ed.) *The Sociology of the Family*, Sociological Review Monograph Number 28.

Department of Health (1994) *Eat Well! An Action Plan from the Nutrition Task Force to Achieve the Health of the Nation Targets on Diet and Nutrition*, Heywood: BAPS, Health Publications Unit.

DeVault, M.L. (1991) *Feeding the Family: The Social Organization of Caring as Gendered Work*, Chicago: The University of Chicago Press.

Diamond, N. (1985) 'Thin is the feminist issue', *Feminist Review* 19, Spring: 45–67.

Dobash, R.E. and Dobash, R. (1980) *Violence Against Wives*, London: Open Books.

Dobbing, J. (ed.) (1987) *Sweetness: International Life Sciences Institute Symposium*, London: Springer-Verlag.

Dobson, B., Beardsworth, A.D., Keil, E.T. and Walker, R. (1994) *Diet, Choice and Poverty: Social, Cultural and Nutritional Aspects of Food Consumption among Low-Income Families*, London: Family Policy Studies Centre/Joseph Rowntree Foundation.

Dombrowski, D.A. (1985) *Vegetarianism: The Philosophy behind the Ethical Diet*, Wellingborough: Thorsons.

Douglas, M. (1966) *Purity and Danger: An Analysis of Concepts of Pollution and Taboo*, London: Allen & Unwin.

Douglas, M. (1975) 'Deciphering a meal', *Daedalus* 101, 1: 61–81.

Douglas, M. (1984) 'Standard social uses of food: introduction', in M. Douglas (ed.) *Food in the Social Order: Studies of Food and Festivities in Three American Communities*, New York: Russell Sage Foundation.

Driver, C. (1983) *The British at Table 1940–1980*, London: Chatto & Windus.

Durkheim, E. (1984) *The Division of Labour in Society*, Basingstoke: Macmillan.

Dwyer, J.T., Mayer, L.D.V.H., Dowd, K., Kandel R.F. and Mayer, J. (1974) 'The new vegetarians: the natural high?', *Journal of the American Dietetic Association* 65, November: 529–36.

Economist Intelligence Unit (1994) 'Slimming foods', *Retail Business* No.432: 48–58.

Ekström, M. (1991) 'Class and gender in the kitchen', in E.L. Fürst, R. Prättälä, M. Ekström, L. Holm, and U. Kjaernes (eds) *Palatable Worlds: Sociocultural Food Studies*, Oslo: Solum Forlag.

Elias, N. (1978a) *The Civilizing Process, Volume I: The History of Manners*. Oxford: Basil Blackwell.

Elias, N. (1978b) *What is Sociology?* London: Hutchinson.

Elias, N. (1982) *The Civilizing Process, Volume II: State Formation and Civilization*, Oxford: Basil Blackwell.

Ellis, R. (1983) 'The way to a man's heart: food in the violent home', in A. Murcott (ed.) *The Sociology of Food and Eating*, Aldershot: Gower.

Evans-Pritchard, E.E. (1967) *The Nuer: A Description of the Modes of Livelihood and Political Institutions of a Nilotic People*, Oxford: Clarendon Press.

Falk, P. (1991) 'The sweetness of forbidden fruit: towards an anthropology of taste', in E.L. Fürst, R. Prättälä, M. Ekström, L. Holm and U. Kjaernes (eds) *Palatable Worlds: Sociocultural Food Studies*, Oslo: Solum Forlag.

Fallon, A. (1990) 'Culture in the mirror: sociocultural determinants of body image', in T. Cash and T. Prusinsky (eds) *Body Images: Development, Deviance and Change*, New York: Guilford Press.

Farb, P. and Armelagos, G. (1980) *Consuming Passions: The Anthropology of Eating*, Boston, Mass.: Houghton Mifflin.

Featherstone, M. (1991) 'The body in consumer culture', in M. Featherstone, M. Hepworth and B.Turner (eds) *The Body: Social Processes and Cultural Theory*, London: Sage.

Featherstone, M., Hepworth, M. and Turner, B. (eds) (1991) *The Body: Social Process and Cultural Theory*, London: Sage.

Fiddes, N. (1991) *Meat: A Natural Symbol*, London: Routledge.

Fieldhouse, P. (1986) *Food and Nutrition: Customs and Culture*, London: Croom Helm.

Finkelstein, J. (1989) *Dining Out: A Sociology of Modern Manners*, Cambridge: Polity Press.

Fischler, C. (1980) 'Food habits, social change and the nature/culture dilemma', *Social Science Information* 19, 6: 937–53.

Fischler, C. (1986) 'Learned versus "spontaneous" dietetics: French mothers' views of what children should eat', *Social Science Information* 25, 4: 945–65.

Fischler, C. (1987) 'Attitudes towards sugar and sweetness in historical and social perspective', in J. Dobbing (ed.) *Sweetness: International Life Sciences Institute Symposium*, London: Springer-Verlag.

Fischler, C. (1988) 'Food, self and identity', *Social Science Information* 27, 2: 275–92.

Foley, R. (1988) 'Hominids, humans and hunter-gatherers: an evolutionary perspective', in T. Ingold, D. Riches and J. Woodburn (eds) *Hunters and Gatherers 1: History, Evolution and Social Change*, Oxford: Berg.

Foreman-Peck, J. (1993) *A History of the World Economy*, Hemel Hampstead: Harvester.

263

Fraser, W.H. (1981) *The Coming of the Mass Market 1850–1914*, London: Macmillan.

Freckleton, A.M., Gurr, M.I., Richardson, D.P., Rolls, B.A. and Walker, A.F. (1989) 'Public perception and understanding', in C.R.W. Spedding (ed.) *The Human Food Chain*, London: Elsevier Applied Science.

Freeland-Graves, J.H., Greninger, S.A. and Young, R.K. (1986) 'A demographic and social profile of age-and sex-matched vegetarians and nonvegetarians', *Journal of The American Dietetic Association* 86: 907–13.

Freeman, S. (1989) *Mutton and Oysters: The Victorians and Their Food*, London: Victor Gallancz Ltd.

Frey, R.G. (1983) *Rights, Killing and Suffering: Moral Vegetarianism and Applied Ethics*, Oxford: Blackwell.

Gabriel, Y. (1988) *Working Lives in Catering*, London: Routledge & Kegan Paul.

Gaman, P.M. and Sherrington, K.B. (1981) *The Science of Food: An Introduction to Food Science, Nutrition and Microbiology*, second edition, Oxford: Pergamon Press.

Garfinkel, P.E. and Garner, D.M. (1982) *Anorexia Nervosa: A Multidimensional Perspective*, New York: Brunner/Mazel.

Gilbert, G.N. and Mulkay, M. (1984) *Opening Pandora's Box: A Sociological Analysis of Scientists' Discourse*, Cambridge: Cambridge University Press.

Girouard, M. (1984) *Victorian Pubs*, New Haven, Conn. and London: Yale University Press.

Gofton, L. (1990) 'Food fears and time famines: some aspects of choosing and using food', *British Nutrition Foundation Bulletin* 15, 1: 78–95.

Goodman, D. and Redclift, M. (1991) *Refashioning Nature: Food, Ecology and Culture*, London: Routledge.

Goody, J. (1982) *Cooking, Cuisine and Class: A Study in Comparative Sociology*, Cambridge: Cambridge University Press.

Gordon, K.D. (1987) 'Evolutionary perspectives on human diet', in F.E. Johnston (ed.) *Nutritional Anthropology*, New York: Alan R. Liss.

Grigg, D. (1993) 'The role of livestock products in world food consumption', *Scottish Geographical Magazine* 109, 2: 66–74.

Grimble, A. (1952) *A Pattern of Islands*, London: John Murray.

Guenther, M. (1988) 'Animals in Bushman thought, myth and art', in T. Ingold, D. Riches, and J. Woodburn (eds) *Hunters and Gatherers 2: Property, Power and Ideology*, Oxford: Berg.

Hall, S., Critcher, C., Jefferson, T., Clarke, J. and Roberts, B. (1978) *Policing the Crisis: Mugging, the State and Law and Order*, London: Macmillan.

Halliday, M.A.K. (1961) 'Categories of the theory of grammar', *World Journal of the Linguistic Circle of New York* 17: 241–91.

Harris, M. (1978) *Cannibals and Kings: The Origins of Cultures*, London: Collins.

Harris, M. (1986) *Good to Eat: Riddles of Food and Culture*, London: Allen & Unwin.

Harrison, B. (1971) *Drink and the Victorians*, London: Faber & Faber.

Hartley, S.F. (1972) *Population: Quantity vs Quality*, New Jersey: Prentice Hall.

Hassall, A.H. (1876) *Food: Its Adulterations, and the Methods for Their Detection*, London: Longman, Green & Co.

Hilgartner, S. and Bosk, C.L. (1988) 'The rise and fall of social problems: a public arenas model', *American Journal of Sociology* 94, 1: 53–78.

Hobhouse, H. (1985) *Seeds of Change: Five Plants that Transformed Mankind*, London: Sidgwick & Jackson.

Hole, F. (1992) 'Origins of agriculture', in S. Jones, R. Martin and D. Philbeam (eds) *The Cambridge Encyclopedia of Human Evolution*, Cambridge: Cambridge University Press.

Hsu, L.K.G. (1990) *Eating Disorders*, New York: Guilford Press.

Hudson, P. (1992) *The Industrial Revolution*, London: Edward Arnold.

Ibarra, P.R. and Kitsuse, J.I. (1993) 'Vernacular constituents of moral discourse: an interactionist proposal for the study of social problems', in G. Muller and J. A Holstein (eds) *Constructionist Controversies: Issues in Social Problems Theory*, New York: Aldine de Gruyter.

Jacobson, B., Smith, A. and Whitehead, M. (eds) (1991) *The Nation's Health: A Strategy for the 1990s*, London: King's Fund Centre.

James, A. (1982) 'Confections, concoctions and conceptions', in B. Waites, T. Bennett and G. Martin (eds) *Popular Culture: Past and Present*, London: Croom Helm/Open University Press.

James, A. (1990) 'The good, the bad and the delicious: the role of confectionery in British society', *Sociological Review* 33, 4: 666–88.

Jeffers, J.N.R. (1980), 'Ecological concepts and their relevance to human nutrition', in K. Blaxter (ed.) *Food Chains and Human Nutrition*, Barking: Applied Science Publishers.

Jelliffe, D.B. (1967) 'Parallel food classification in developing and industrialized countries', *American Journal of Clinical Nutrition* 20: 279–81.

Jones, P. (1985) 'Fast food operations in Britain', *Services Industries Journal* 5, 1: 55–63.

Jowell, R., Witherspoon, S. and Brook, L. (eds) (1990) *British Social Attitudes: 7th Report*, Aldershot: Gower.

Jukes, D.J. (1993) *Food Legislation of the U.K.: A Concise Guide*, third edition, Oxford: Butterworth Heinemann.

Jussaume, R.A. and Judson, D.H. (1992) 'Public perceptions about food safety in the United States and Japan', *Rural Sociology* 57, 2: 235–49.

Kandel, R.F. and Pelto, G.H. (1980) 'The health food movement: social revitalization or alternative health maintenance system?', in N.W. Jerome, R.F. Kandel and G.H. Pelto (eds) *Nutritional Anthropology: Contemporary Approaches to Diet and Culture*, New York: Redgrave.

Kerr, M. and Charles, N. (1986) 'Servers and providers: the distribution of food within the family', *The Sociological Review* 34, 1: 115–57.

Kuhn, T. (1964) *The Structure of Scientific Revolutions*, Chicago, Ill.: The University of Chicago Press.

Lalonde, M.P. (1992) 'Deciphering a meal again, or the anthropology of taste', *Social Science Information* 31, 1: 69–86.

Langford, P. (1989) *A Polite and Commercial People: England 1727–1783*, Oxford: Oxford University Press.

Laughlin, W.S. (1968) 'Hunting: an integrating biobehaviour system and its evolutionary importance', in R.B. Lee and I. Evore (eds) *Man the Hunter*, New York: Aldine Publishing.

Leclant, J. (1979) 'Coffee and cafés in Paris, 1644–1693', in R. Forster and O, Ranum (eds) *Food and Drink in History*, Baltimore, Md.: The Johns Hopkins University Press.

Lees, R. (1983) 'The sweet history of Britain', *New Scientist* 100: 873–7.

Leonard, W.R. and Robertson, M.L. (1994) 'Evolutionary perspectives on human nutrition: the influence of brain and body size on diet and metabolism', *American Journal of Human Biology*, 6: 77–88.

Levenstein, H. (1988) *Revolution at The Table: The Transformation of the American Diet*, New York: Oxford University Press.

Lévi-Strauss, C. (1963) *Structural Anthropology*, New York: Basic Books.

Lévi-Strauss, C. (1966a) *The Savage Mind*, London: Weidenfeld & Nicolson.

Lévi-Strauss, C. (1966b) 'The culinary triangle', *Partisan Review* 33: 586–95.

Lévi-Strauss, C. (1970) *The Raw and the Cooked*, London: Jonathan Cape.

Lowenberg, M.E., Todhunter, E.N., Wilson, E.D., Savage, J.R. and Lubowski, J.L. (1974) *Food and Man*, second edition, New York: John Wiley & Sons.

McCarthy, B. and Straus, K. (1992) 'Tastes of America 1992. Who in America eats out? Why do they? And what are they eating?', *Restaurants and Institutions* 102, Pt 29, December, 24–44.

McIntosh, W.A. and Zey, M. (1989) 'Women as gatekeepers of food consumption: a sociological critique', *Food and Foodways* 3, 4: 317–32.

McIntosh, W.A., Acuff, G.R., Christensen, L.B. and Hale, D. (1994) 'Public perceptions of food safety', *The Social Science Journal* 31, 3: 285–92.

MacSween, M. (1993) *Anorexic Bodies: A Feminist and Sociological Perspective on Anorexia Nervosa*, London: Routledge.

Malinowski, B. (1935) *Coral Gardens and their Magic*, New York: American Book Company.

Manderson, L. (1987) 'Hot–cold food and medical theories: overview and introduction', *Social Science and Medicine*, 25, 4: 329–30.

Market Research Great Britain (1992) *Market Focus Food: Sugar Confectionery*, London: Euromonitor.

Mars, G. (1982) *Cheats at Work: An Anthropology of Workplace Crime*, London: George Allen & Unwin.

Mass Observation (1987) *The Pub and the People*, London: Century Hutchinson Ltd.

Matthias, P. (1967) *Retailing Revolution*, London: Longmans.

Maurer, D. (1995) 'Meat as a social problem: rhetorical strategies in the contemporary vegetarian literature', in D. Maurer and S. Sobel (eds) *Eating Agendas: Food and Nutrition as Social Problems*, New York: Aldine de Gruyter.

Mazurkiewicz, R. (1983) 'Gender and social consumption', *Services Industries Journal* 3, 1: 49–62.

Meadow, R.M. and Weiss, L. (1992) *Women's Conflicts about Eating and Sexuality: The Relationship between Food and Sex*, New York: The Haworth Press.

Medlik, S. (1961) *The British Hotel and Catering Industry: An Economic and Statistical Survey*, London: Sir Isaac Pitman & Sons Ltd.

Mennell, S. (1985) *All Manners of Food: Eating and Taste in England and France from the Middle Ages to the Present*, Oxford: Blackwell.

Mennell, S. (1991) 'On the civilizing of appetite', in M. Featherstone, M. Hepworth and B. Turner (eds) *The Body: Social Process and Cultural Theory*, London: Sage.

Mennell, S. (1992) 'Indigestion 1800–1950: aspects of English taste and anxiety', paper presented to the inaugural meeting of the British Sociological Association Sociology of Food Study Group, BSA annual conference, University of Kent.

Mennell, S., Murcott, A. and Van Otterloo, A.H. (1992) *The Sociology of Food: Eating, Diet and Culture*, London: Sage.

Merton, R.K. (1957) *Social Theory and Social Structure*, New York: The Free Press.

Messer, E. (1987) 'The hot and cold in Mesoamerican indigenous and hispanicized thought', *Social Science and Medicine* 25, 4: 339–46.

Midgley, M. (1983) *Animals and Why They Matter*, Harmondsworth: Penguin.

Miller, D. and Reilly, J. (1995) 'Making an issue of food safety: the media, pressure groups, and the public sphere', in D. Maurer and J. Sobal (eds) *Eating Agendas: Food and Nutrition as Social Problems*, New York: Aldine de Gruyter.

Ministry of Agriculture, Fisheries and Food (1989) *Loaves and Fishes: An Illustrated History of the Ministry of Agriculture, Fisheries and Food*, London: HMSO.

Ministry of Agriculture, Fisheries and Food (1991) *Household Food Consumption and Expenditure 1990, with a Study of Trends over the Period 1940–1990*, London: HMSO.

Ministry of Agriculture, Fisheries and Food (1994) *National Food Survey 1993*, London: HMSO.

Mintz, S.W. (1985) *Sweetness and Power: The Place of Sugar in Modern History*, New York: Viking.

Mitchell, V.W. and Greatorex, M. (1990) 'Consumer perceived risk in the UK food market', *British Food Journal* 92, 2: 16–22.

Montanari, M. (1994) *The Culture of Food*, Oxford: Blackwell.

Muller, H.G. (1991) 'Industrial food preservation in the nineteenth and twentieth centuries', in C. Wilson (ed.) *Waste Not, Want Not: Food Preservation from Early Times to the Present Day*, Edinburgh: Edinburgh University Press.

Murcott, A. (1982) 'On the social significance of the "cooked dinner" in South Wales', *Social Science Information* 21, 4/5: 677–96.

Murcott, A. (1983) ' "It's a pleasure to cook for him": food, mealtimes and gender in some South Wales households', in E. Gamarnikow, E. Morgan, J. Purvis and D. Taylorson, (eds) *The Public and the Private*, London: Heinemann.

National Advisory Committee on Nutrition Education (1983) *A Discussion Paper on Proposals for Nutritional Guidelines for Health Education in Britain*, London: The Health Education Council.

National Research Council (1989) *Recommended Dietary Allowances*, tenth edition, Washington, D.C.: National Academy Press.

Nelson, M. (1993) 'Social-class trends in British diet, 1860–1980', in C. Geissler and D.J. Oddy (eds) *Food, Diet and Economic Change Past and Present*, Leicester: Leicester University Press.

Newby, H. (1983) 'Living from hand to mouth: the farmworker, food and agribusiness', in A. Murcott (ed.) *The Sociology of Food and Eating*, Aldershot: Gower.

Nicod, M. (1980) 'Gastronomically speaking: food studied as a medium of communication', in M.Turner (ed.) *Nutrition and Lifestyles*, London: Applied Science Publishers.

Oddy, D.J. (1990) 'Food, drink and nutrition', in F.M.L. Thompson (ed.) *The Cambridge History of Britain 1750 – 1950 Vol. 2 People and their Environment*, Cambridge: Cambridge University Press

Office of Population Censuses and Surveys – Social Survey Division (1993) *Health Survey for England 1991*, London: HMSO.

Orbach, S. (1988) *Fat is a Feminist Issue*, London: Hamlyn.

Parsons, T. (1951) *The Social System*, London: Routledge & Kegan Paul.

Paulos, J.A. (1988) *Innumeracy: Mathematical Illiteracy and its Consequences*, London: Viking.

Paulus, I.L.E. (1974) *The Search for Pure Food: A Sociology of Legislation in Britain*, London: Martin Robertson.

Payne, M. and Payne, B. (1993) *Eating Out in the UK: Market Structure, Consumer Attitudes and Prospects for the 1990s*, Economist Intelligence Unit Special Report No. 2169, London: Economist Intelligence Unit Ltd.

Pelto, G.H. and Pelto, P.J. (1985) 'Diet and delocalization: dietary changes since 1970', in R. Rotberg and T.K. Rabb (eds) *Hunger and History*, Cambridge: Cambridge University Press.

Pierce, J.T. (1990) *The Food Resource*, Harlow: Longman Scientific and Technical.

Pill, R. (1983) 'An apple a day... some reflections on working class mothers' views on food and health', in A. Murcott (ed.) *The Sociology of Food and Eating*, Aldershot: Gower.

Pillsbury, R. (1990) *From Boarding House to Bistro: The American Restaurant Then and Now*, Boston, Mass.: Unwin Hyman.

Posner, T. (1983) 'The sweet things in life: aspects of the management of diabetic diet', in A. Murcott (ed.) *The Sociology of Food and Eating*, Aldershot: Gower.

Prout, A. (1991) 'Review of Women, Food and Families', *The Sociological Review* 39, 2: 403–5.

Radcliffe-Brown, A.R. (1922) *The Andaman Islanders*, Cambridge: Cambridge University Press.

Read, B.E. (1982) *Chinese Materia Medica: Insect Drugs, Dragon and Snake Drugs, Fish Drugs*, Taipei, Republic of China: Southern Materials Center.

Realeat Survey Office (1993) *The Realeat Survey 1984–1993. Changing Attitudes to Meat Consumption*, 2 Trevelyn Gardens, London.

Realeat Survey Office (1995) *The Realeat Survey 1984–1995. Changing Attitudes to Meat Consumption*, 2 Trevelyn Gardens, London.

Reed, C.A. (1984) 'The beginnings of animal domestication', in I.L. Mason (ed.) *Evolution of Domesticated Animals*, London: Longman.

Regan, T. (1984) *The Case for Animal Rights*, London: Routledge.

Richards, A. (1932) *Hunger and Work in a Savage Tribe: A Functional Study of Nutrition among the Southern Bantu*, London: Routledge.

Richards, A. (1939) *Land, Labour and Diet in Northern Rhodesia*, Oxford: Oxford University Press.

Rindos, D. (1984) *The Origins of Agriculture: An Evolutionary Perspective*, Orlando, Fl.: Academic Press.

Rinzler, C.A. (1991) *Feed a Cold, Starve a Fever: A Dictionary of Medical Folklore*, New York: Facts on File.

Riska, E. (1993) 'The gendered character of professions in the field of nutrition' in U. Kjaernes, L. Holm, M. Ekström, E.L. Fürst and R. Prättälä (eds) *Regulating Markets, Regulating People: on Food and Nutrition Policy*, Oslo: Novus Vorlag.

Ritzer, G. (1993) *The McDonaldization of Society*, Newbury Park, Calif.: Pine Forge Press.

Roaf, M. (1990) *Cultural Atlas of Mesopotamia and the Ancient Near East*, Oxford: Equinox.

Roberts, G.K. (1989) 'Food' in C. Chant (ed.) *Science, Technology and Everyday Life*, London: Routledge/Open University.

Rosman, A. and Rubel, P.G. (1989) 'Stalking the wild pig: hunting and horticulture in Papua New Guinea', in S. Kent (ed.) *Farmers as Hunters: The Implications of Sedentism*, Cambridge: Cambridge University Press.

Rostow, W.W. (1990) *The Stages of Economic Growth*, third edition, Cambridge: Cambridge University Press.

Rotberg, R. and Rabb, T.K. (1985) *Hunger and History: The Impact of Changing Food Production and Consumption Patterns on Society*, Cambridge: Cambridge University Press.

Rowntree, B.S. (1901) *Poverty: A Study of Town Life*, London: Macmillan.

Rozin, E. and Rozin, P. (1981) 'Some surprisingly unique characteristics of human food preferences', in A. Fenton and T.M. Owen (eds) *Food in Perspective: Proceedings of the Third International Conference on Ethnological Food Research, Cardiff, Wales, 1977*, Edinburgh: John Donald.

Rozin, P. (1976) 'The selection of food by rats, humans and other animals' in J.S. Rosenblatt, R.A. Hinde, E. Shaw and C. Beer (eds) *Advances in the Study of Behaviour*, Vol. 6, London/New York: Academic Books.

Rozin, P. (1982) 'Human food selection: the interaction of biology, culture, and individual experience', in L.M. Barker (ed.) *The Psychobiology of Human Food Selection*, Chichester: Ellis Horwood.

Rozin, P. (1987) 'Sweetness, sensuality, sin, safety, and socialization: some speculations', in J. Dobbing (ed.) *Sweetness: International Life Sciences Institute Symposium*, London: Springer-Verlag.

Sahlins, M. (1974) *Stone Age Economics*, London: Tavistock Publications.

Salaman, R. (1985) *The History and Social Influence of the Potato*, Cambridge: Cambridge University Press.

Sapp, S.G. and Harrod, W.J. (1989) 'Social acceptability and intentions to eat beef: an expansion of the Fishbein–Ajzen model using reference group theory', *Rural Sociology* 54, 3: 420–38

Saul, S.B. (1960) *Studies in British Overseas Trade*, Liverpool: Liverpool University Press.

Saussure, F. de (1960) *Course in General Linguistics*, London: Owen.

Schafer, E., Schafer, R.B., Bultena, G.L. and Hoiberg, E. (1993) 'Safety of the US food supply: consumer concerns and behaviour', *Journal of Consumer Studies and Home Economics* 17: 137–44.

Schutz, H.G. and Judge, D.S. (1987) 'Sweetness in marketing', in J. Dobbing (ed.) *Sweetness: International Life Sciences Institute Symposium*, London: Springer-Verlag.

Scola, R. (1992) *Feeding the Victorian City: The Food Supply of Manchester 1770–1870*, Manchester: Manchester University Press.

Scott, T.R. and Giza, B.K. (1987) 'Neurophysiological aspects of sweetness', in J. Dobbing (ed.) *Sweetness: International Life Sciences Institute Symposium*, London: Springer-Verlag.

268

Sellerberg, A.M. (1991) 'In food we trust? Vitally necessary confidence and unfamiliar ways of attaining it', in E.L. Fürst, R. Prättälä, M. Ekström, L. Holm and U. Kjaernes (eds) *Palatable Worlds: Sociocultural Food Studies*, Oslo: Solum Forlag.

Sharman, A. (1991) 'From generation to generation: resources, experience and orientation in the dietary patterns of selected urban American households', in A. Sharman, J. Theopano, K. Curtis, and E. Messer, (eds) *Diet and Domestic Life in Society*, Philadelphia, Pa.: Temple University Press.

Sharp, H.S. (1988) 'Dry meat and gender: the absence of Chipewyan ritual for the regulation of hunting and animal numbers' in T. Ingold, D.Riches and J. Woodburn (eds) *Hunters and Gatherers 2: Property, Power and Ideology*, Oxford: Berg.

Simmons, J. (1984) *The Victorian Hotel: The Sixth H.J. Dyos Memorial Lecture*, Leicester: University of Leicester, Victorian Studies Centre.

Simoons, F.J. (1961) *Eat Not This Flesh: Food Avoidances in the Old World*, Madison, Wisc.: University of Wisconsin Press.

Singer, P. (1976) *Animal Liberation*, London: Jonathan Cape.

Sjoberg, G. (1960) *The Preindustrial City*, New York: The Free Press.

Smith, M.J. (1991) 'From policy community to issue network: salmonella in eggs and the new politics of food', *Public Administration* 69, Summer: 235–55.

Snow, L.F. (1993) *Walkin' over Medicine*, Boulder, Colo.: Westview Press.

Solokov, R. (1991) *Why We Eat What We Eat: How The Encounter between the New World and the Old Changed the Way Everyone on the Planet Eats*, New York: Summit Books.

Spencer, C. (1993) *The Heretic's Feast: A History of Vegetarianism*, London: Fourth Estate.

Sponsel, L.E. (1989) 'Farming and foraging: a necessary complementarity in Amazonia?', in S. Kent (ed.) *Farmers as Hunters: The Implications of Sedentism*, Cambridge: Cambridge University Press.

Stahler, C. (1994) 'How many vegetarians are there?', *Vegetarian Journal* July/August: 6–9.

Sykes, J. D. (1981) 'Agricultural science', in G.E. Mingay (ed.) *The Victorian Countryside*, London: Routledge & Kegan Paul.

Tannahill, R. (1973) *Food in History*, first edition, London: Eyre Methuen.

Tannahill, R. (1988) *Food in History*, revised edition, Harmondsworth: Penguin.

Tansey, G. and Worsley, T. (1995) *The Food System: A Guide*, London: Earthscan Publications Limited.

Theopano, J. and Curtis, K. (1991) 'Sisters, mothers and daughters: food exchange and reciprocity in an Italian-American community', in A. Sharman, J. Theopano, K. Curtis, and E. Messer (eds) *Diet and Domestic Life in Society*, Philadelphia, Pa.: Temple Press.

Thomas, K. (1983) *Man and the Natural World: Changing Attitudes in England 1500–1800*, London: Allen Lane.

Thomas, M., Goddard, E., Hickman, M. and Hunter, P. (1994) *General Household Survey 1992*, London: HMSO.

Thomas, P.R. (ed.) (1991) *Improving America's Diet and Health, From Recommendations to Action: A Report of the Committee on Dietary Guidlines Implementation, Food and Nutrition Board, Institute of Medicine*, Washington, D.C.: National Academy Press.

Toussaint-Samat, M. (1992) *A History of Food*, Oxford: Blackwell.

Townsend, A. (1979) 'Radical vegetarians', *Australian Journal of Philosophy* 57, 1: 85–93.

Tracey, M.V. (1977) 'Human nutrition', in R. Duncan and M. Weston-Smith (eds) *The Encyclopaedia of Ignorance: Life Sciences and Earth Sciences*, Oxford: Pergamon Press.

Turner, B. (1982) 'The government of the body: medical regimens and the rationalization of diet', *The British Journal of Sociology* 33, 2: 254–69.

Turner, B.S. (1991) 'Recent developments in the theory of the body', in M. Featherstone, M. Hepworth and B. Turner (eds) *The Body: Social Processes and Cultural Theory*, London: Sage.

Turner, M. (1985) *Enclosures in Britain 1750–1830*, London: Macmillan.

Twigg, J. (1979) 'Food for thought: purity and vegetarianism', *Religion* 9, Spring: 13–35.

U.S. Bureau of the Census (1993) *Statistical Abstract of the United States*, Washington, D.C.: U.S. Government Printing Office.

Vegetarian Society, The (1991) *The 1991 Food Survey: Trends in Vegetarianism Amongst Adults and Young People*, Altrincham: The Vegetarian Society of the United Kingdom Limited.

Van der Merve, M.J. (1992) 'Reconstructing prehistoric diet', in S. Jones, R. Martin and D. Philbeam (eds) *The Cambridge Encyclopedia of Human Evolution*, Cambridge: Cambridge University Press.

Visser, M. (1986) *Much Depends on Dinner*, Harmondsworth: Penguin.

Visser, M. (1993) *The Rituals of Dinner: The Origins, Evolution, Eccentricities, and Meaning of Table Manners*, Harmondsworth: Penguin.

Waites, B., Bennett, T. and Martin, G. (eds) (1982) *Popular Culture: Past and Present*, London: Croom Helm/Open University Press.

Walton, J.K. (1992) *Fish and Chips and the British Working Class, 1870–1940*, Leicester: Leicester University Press.

Warde, A. (1991) 'Guacamole, stottie cake and thick double cream: elements of a theory of modern taste', paper presented to the British Association for the Advancement of Science annual conference, Polytechnic Southwest.

Warde, A. and Hetherington, K. (1994) 'English households and routine food practices: a research note', *The Sociological Review* 42, 4: 758–78.

Warnock, J.W. (1987) *The Politics of Hunger: The Global Food System*, New York: Methuen.

Washburn, W.L. and Lancaster, C.S. (1968) 'The evolution of hunting', in R.B. Lee and I. Devore (eds) *Man the Hunter*, New York: Aldine Publishing.

Weinberg, A.M. (1972) 'Science and trans-science', *Minerva* 10, 2: 209–22.

Whyte, W.F. (1948) *Human Relations in the Restaurant Industry*, New York: McGraw Hill.

Widdowson, J.D.A. (1981) 'Food and traditional verbal modes in the social control of children', in A. Fenton and T.M. Owen (eds) *Food in Perspective*, Edinburgh: John Donald.

Williams, B. (1994) *The Best Butter in the World: A History of Sainsbury's*, London: Ebury Press.

Wilson, C.S. (1981) 'Food in a medical system: prescriptions and proscriptions in health and illness among Malays', in A. Fenton and T.M. Owen (eds) *Food in Perspective*, Edinburgh: John Donald.

Wilson, C.A. (ed.) (1989) *Waste Not Want Not: Food Preservation from Early Times to the Present Day*, Edinburgh: Edinburgh University Press.

Wood, R. (1992) 'Dining out in the urban context', *British Food Journal* 94, 9: 3–5.

Wood, R.C. (1991) 'The shock of the new: a sociology of nouvelle cuisine', *Journal of Consumer Studies and Home Economics* 15, 4: 327–38.

Wood, R.C. (1992) *Working in Hotels and Catering*, London: Routledge.

Woodward, J. (1988) 'Consumer attitudes towards meat and meat products', *British Food Journal* 90, 3: 101–4.

Zeldin, T. (1983) Listener article, 15 April 1982, quoted in C. Driver, *The British at Table*, London: Chatto & Windus.

Zey, M. and McIntosh, W.A. (1992) 'Predicting intent to consume beef: normative versus attitudinal influences', *Rural Sociology* 57, 2: 250–65.

AUTHOR INDEX

SUBJECT INDEX

275